Colleen #302

After various careers from cocktail waitress to kibbutz worker, Lesley Lokko trained as an architect but always dreamed of being a writer. Several novels later, Lesley now splits her time between Johannesburg, Accra and London. Find out more at www.lesleylokko.com

By Lesley Lokko

Sundowners
Saffron Skies
Bitter Chocolate
Rich Girl, Poor Girl
One Secret Summer
A Private Affair
An Absolute Deception

An Absolute Deception

Lesley Lokko

An Orion paperback

First published in Great Britain in 2012
by Orion
This paperback edition published in 2013
by Orion Books,
an imprint of The Orion Publishing Group Ltd,
Orion House, 5 Upper St Martin's Lane
London WC2H 9EA

An Hachette UK company

3 5 7 9 10 8 6 4 2

A CIP catalogue record for this book
is available from the British Library.

ISBN 978-1-4091-0247-2

Typeset at The Spartan Press Ltd,
Lymington, Hants

Printed and bound in Great Britain
by Clays Ltd, St Ives plc

The Orion Publishing Group's policy is to use papers
that are natural, renewable and recyclable products and
made from wood grown in sustainable forests. The logging
and manufacturing processes are expected to conform to
the environmental regulations of the country of origin.

www.orionbooks.co.uk

For Tash. I miss you, girl.

Acknowledgements

A very large part of this novel is about a country, Namibia, which I first visited in 1992. I met scores of wonderful, interesting people then who shaped this novel in some way, most of whom have disappeared into the mists of time. I'd like to thank Glynn Huaraka for taking me there in the first place; Klaus and Anita Brandt, for their long-standing friendship and Anita for so kindly chasing down the oshiWambo translations; my darling friend Dieter Brandt for our great conversations, laughter and enduring love; Bridget Pickering for her friendship and her suggestions in this novel and elsewhere; Adrian and Janet Hallam for keeping the link and my dearest friend Iain Low, whose support, friendship (and patience!) this year has been so gratefully received. I'm also particularly grateful to the lovely Dr Heidrun Sarges for her insights into post-war Berlin; to Jutta Berns-Mumbi, Dr Bernd Schroers, Lorenz Wyss and Stephen Ata, for their kind help with the many German translations, and to Annette Sommer for her help with the Norwegian translations and fact-checking. I would also like to thank Tara O'Connor and Chiluba Mumbi for their help in understanding and visualising Kitwe, 'Centre of the Universe'. As ever, this book was written between Johannesburg and Edinburgh and I'd like to thank everyone in both places (far too many to list!) for their support, insights and laughter during its making, but especially Morag, 'Charlie', Bernd and John for making Edinburgh feel so much like home. The Kates (Mills *and* Shaw), Susan Lamb, Jade Chandler and Gaby Young are, increasingly and always, wonderful, and I consider myself blessed to have such a fantastic team behind me. I also read widely whilst writing this novel and no account of Namibia is complete without reference to *The Kaiser's Holocaust* by David Olusoga and Casper W. Erichsen (Faber & Faber, London, 2010), which gave me more insight and empathy than I can say.

Although this *isn't* the novel that's about her (that's the next one), one of my closest friends, Natasha Olympio, died suddenly whilst I was writing it – it's a loss I feel every single day. Each sadness supposedly teaches us something. I don't know if that's true. I do know that in thinking about her, one phrase does come to mind: *carpe diem*. Seize the day. Thank you to *everyone* for helping all of us who knew her get through those very hard days.

While all deception requires secrecy,
all secrecy is not meant to deceive.

Sissela Bok, Swedish philosopher

PART ONE

Prologue

Pointe Milou, St Barts, French West Indies, 2009

Seen from a distance, their voluminous black dresses rucked up around their hips, the local women had the profile of wading birds as they bobbed up and down on the wet sand, kicking their legs in the spray as the tide yawned endlessly in and out. They were collecting the pale, pearly pink shells to make necklaces that the foreigners who lived in the villas on the island sometimes came to buy. Far above them and unseen, a tall, silver-haired woman with the graceful bearing of a dancer walked unsteadily down the path that led to the sea, arms outstretched in a childish balancing act, as though she were preparing for flight. The long white train of her sheer cotton kaftan billowed out behind her; a few strands of hair blew across her face, momentarily obscuring sun, sand and sea.

The woman paused for a moment and turned, looking back at the hill behind her. It was nearly seven a.m. The sun had been up for an hour. Up there, perched on the top of the hill, looking out across the bay towards the emerald, hump-backed islands of Frégate and Toc Vers, her guests would slowly be stirring. In the kitchen, Hélène, oblivious to everything that had gone on during the night, would have already begun preparing the gorgeous buffet breakfast for which Scheherazade, her villa on St Barts, was renowned. An invitation to spend a Christmas or usher in the New Year with Anneliese Zander de Saint Phalle was something to be cherished, sought after. In the thirty-odd years she'd owned Scheherazade, she hadn't missed a single winter, not once. Until now. She closed her eyes briefly, then continued resolutely on her way.

At last she reached the end of the path. Her feet sank into the warm, soft sand. She lifted a hand to shade her eyes and looked out across the tough, glittering skin of the sea. The air was warm and balmy, not yet hot. Back in London, in the tall, five-storey townhouse in St John's Wood that had been home for almost the same length of time, another damp, cold winter's night would be drawing in. She could just see Mrs Betts, her house-keeper, moving around the vast open space of the first floor where she entertained guests and friends, switching on lamps, plumping the odd pillow, checking on her collection of rare and beautiful orchids in the silver planters that Callan had given her for one birthday or another, over the years. Another winter's evening, no different this year from any other. Except this one *was* different.

She kicked off her sandals, letting her bare soles slide and burrow into the pale, silky sand. She left the sandals there – they were from her S/S 09 collection, flat, a very slight wooden stacked heel with a simple leather T-bar disappearing discreetly into the sole. She looked down at the label. *AdSP. Anneliese de Saint Phalle.* A strip of chocolate brown linen with white letter-ing. Helvetica font, very plain, except for the 'd', in a flowery, cursive italic. It was a nice detail. Bruno had come up with it in 1967, the year they'd launched her label together. It was a tribute to his unerring sense of style that they'd never changed it. A*d*SP. It was her trademark, her signature, her *sign*. Every so often, she changed colours – grey on white; navy blue and lime green; oatmeal and plum – but never the basic style. There was no need. *Get the basics right and the rest will follow.* She could no longer remember where she'd first heard it but the simple philosophy had served her brilliantly in almost everything she did. It had won her legions of well-dressed, supremely confident and wealthy-in-their-own-right women who followed her col-lections with the slavish devotion of groupies. Her clientele.

Her showroom in London was booked out months ahead of her new collections. Her private viewings, scheduled almost a year in advance, were as sought after as her invitations to

Mustique. And their new line, *A+*, her much-anticipated foray into the mass market, had done better than anyone expected. For a brief, fleeting second, the corners of her mouth tugged upwards. Wasn't it only last month that she'd had to reschedule one of her regular customers to accommodate a last-minute request from the White House? She could still hear his voice. Director of Communications. The White House. On the line from Washington. A smooth voice, like polished silk, cascading water, whisky over ice. The First Lady would very much like to visit AdSP's London store ahead of her upcoming trip to Japan. *It would be her husband's first*, he said, smooth, unctuous. *Mrs Obama thought AdSP's latest collection would go down particularly well in Osaka, given the parallels between spare Japanese modernism and the clean structural lines of AdSP's latest collection.* He'd obviously done his homework. In spite of herself, Anneliese was impressed. But she didn't like being rushed, and she positively hated the impromptu. She'd turned the request down. Bruno had looked at her as though she were mad. 'Are you crazy?' he'd shouted as soon as she hung up the phone.

'Crazy? No. I don't need Michelle Obama's stamp of approval.'

'This isn't about approval, *mein Schatz*. You call them back *right now* and say "yes".'

Now it was her turn to look at him as though he were mad. 'So what's it about, then?' she shot back. 'Money? Power? I don't need either. You know that.'

He'd looked at her in that maddeningly cryptic way of his, raising his eyebrows. 'It's about influence, my darling,' he said, suddenly calm. '*Much* more interesting than power. You know that better than anyone. Call them back.'

A week later, Michelle Obama flew in from Washington to see her. She could not have been more charming. They had afternoon tea together in the studio. Models were brought in, fabrics and cut discussed, measurements taken by her assistants, but it was the conversation between them that was the real surprise. Anneliese had never met anyone like her. They covered everything from the recent oil spill off Florida's coast to the Huguenot lace-makers of Lille. Sitting opposite the tall, supremely confident woman whose long legs were elegantly crossed at the knee, Anneliese's memory gave one of those violent kicks that she'd spent the past forty years suppressing. For one brief, mad moment she'd allowed herself to consider the possibility – but she stopped herself just in time.

She reached the water's edge. It curled and lapped around her bare toes, drawing her in with its slack warmth. In spite of the dark fist of pain that had closed itself around her heart, she turned around to look up at the green-fringed land, bathed in such beauty – the splendid, gently swaying giant coco-de-mer palms; the glittering light blue sky, still tinged with night; the horizontal white slash of concrete that was the roof of Scheherazade, nestled discreetly amongst the trees. Impossible to think that only a few hours earlier she'd been sitting at her dressing table, brushing the neat, silver-blonde cap of hair that was as much her trademark as her elegant, understated clothes, preparing herself for another successful New Year's Eve party at her island home. That was last night. Before.

The water was up to her knees now. She looked down and the fabric of her kaftan swirled around her in great, looping drifts. The sand was soft and clean, as weightless as the water. Air and water were the same element; she waded further in, up to her chest, then sank further still. She drifted in the pale, turquoise transparency, a medium that required no effort, bore no resistance. She floated, turning eyelids of dancing sunlight up to the sky. A peacock-shaded sea. Far down the beach, away from the pristine strips of white sand which were reserved for the very wealthy who wintered here, the local women were picking up the last of the shells and heading back up the path to the small township where most of them lived. They were the workers on the island – the maids, cooks, gardeners and drivers whose job it was to ensure the smooth running of the palaces to which the rich and famous like her escaped.

The tide was coming in; she could feel its muscular, insistent tug swirling beneath the surface. In a few minutes she'd be out beyond the first shelf of sand to where the water ran deep and blue. Beyond that, beyond the rocky outcrop that marked the edge of the headland, the water turned black. Something caught hold of her, a sudden swirl of water that took the edge of her kaftan and pulled it downwards, pulling her with it. She did not fight; she submerged herself and was submerged in turn, water filling her eyes and nose, rushing over her ears. Two or three seconds, then she was pushed upwards, breaking free. She took in a mouthful of air but before she could properly exhale, the current took hold of her again. Down, down . . . a sideways thrust . . . back up and then just as quickly down again. A giant hand, pushing and pulling, shoving and twisting, tossing her about, a plaything . . . rag doll in her sodden white dress. She bobbed for a second on the surface and then it caught her, more roughly this time. There was a last glimpse of the island and its canopy of thick, lush trees and then the water closed in. It happened so fast that she barely had time to think. No question now of changing her mind. For the second time in her life – all sixty-four years of it – it was too late. The words came floating back up to her through the foggy mists of time and memory. *Ondeku lyuulukwa.* I will miss you. The language she'd never forgotten.

1

HANNELORE
Bodenhausen, Okahau, South-West Africa, 1948

'Hannelore! Hannelore!' The shout was taken up by the rag-gedy, pot-bellied servants' children who lived in the single row of shacks at the edge of the farm, down there by the bore-hole where animals sometimes came to drink. In their mouths her name took on another consonant – *Hannah-lorah! Hannah-lorah!* Their repeated shouts became a jeer. *Hannah-lorah! Hannah-lorah!* Hannelore put her hands over her ears, blocking out the sound. It was Ella, her nanny, calling her. 'Hannelore! Come now! Come . . . where are you? Your mama is calling you.' No, she's not, Hannelore thought to herself mutinously. *You're* calling me. She lay on her back on the damp, smooth earth floor, looking up into the roof. She liked the way the beams made the pattern of a spider's web as they fanned out-wards from the peaked centre. She began to count them. One, two, three, four—

'Hannelore! What are you doing there?' The wooden door burst open. Ella was standing in the doorway, her large, soft body framed in light. Her hands were on her hips as she surveyed her charge. 'Naughty, *naughty* girl . . . your dress will be dirty and then your mama will be annoyed with me. What's wrong with you?'

'What's wrong with you! What's wrong with you!' Outside the door, the children took up the shout joyfully. They spoke no English; the words were repeated phonetically; they rolled them uncomprehendingly around in their mouths. Amongst each other and with Hannelore they spoke only oshiWambo,

9

the language of the land. Ella did not speak oshiWambo. She spoke only Afrikaans, which Hildebrand, Hannelore's mother, loathed. '*Das ist keine Sprache*,' she said, her lovely, red-painted mouth turning down on itself in disdain. 'That isn't a language. It's a disease.' She spoke it reluctantly to Ella – she had no choice – but in the family, between the three of them, they spoke only *hochdeutsch*, High German. The language of Schiller and Heine, not the bastardised, vulgar-sounding *platte* German of their neighbours. On this point both Hannelore's parents were united. There would be no slipping, no relaxing of the rules. There were *standards* to be upheld, particularly in this god-forsaken half-forgotten corner of Africa which, as far as Ludwig von Riedesal was concerned, would be for ever German. *Not* South African, most emphatically not, no matter what the League of Nations had decided. To have lost the First World War was a bitter enough blow but to have lost their prized African colonies as well was almost too much to bear. As soon as the League declared the end of German rule, those bastards to the south simply marched in, bringing that dreadful tongue, Afrikaans, with them, imposing it everywhere. Well, Hildebrand von Riedesal said firmly, the South Africans could do what they liked with road signs and the like but they weren't going to tell her what and how she should speak in her own home, on her own farm, *on her own land*. Language, the five-year-old Hannelore was beginning to grasp, was more than simply a collection of sounds.

Suddenly she was hauled roughly to her feet. Her dress was indeed dirty; red dust streaks ran from her back all the way down to the hem. Ella's hand came down, whacking off the dust, catching her bare legs and bottom in the process. The children who were standing wide-eyed at the door giggled as one. Her cheeks reddening, Hannelore was frog-marched out the door and back up the short grassy incline that led to the back of the house. She hated being shown up like that, especially in front of *them*.

*

Later that afternoon when the sun in the garden had burned the already-scorched grass to a crisp, she sat in the bath in a pool of tepid brown water, watching flies buzz themselves to death against the windowpanes. The house was quiet; from somewhere came the soft tinkle of the piano, caught on the breeze. Her mother was playing. She played every afternoon, all year long. In the winter when the grasses around the farm were yellow and blonde and the air was so cold and dry it crackled, her mother would don one of her stylish fur jackets and a pair of kid leather gloves and sit at the piano in the draughty room, and play. Mozart, Stravinsky, Bach and, her father's favourite, Beethoven. Germans, mostly, with the odd Austrian thrown in. Besides, as Ludwig was fond of saying, Austrians really were Germans. Once or twice a year, when there were visitors to the farm and the rooms were made beautiful with long candles that dripped thick, creamy ribbons of wax onto the floor, she would play for others, sitting in that majestically upright way of hers, her fingers moving expressively over the keys. Those were evenings to remember and cherish. The whole house would have been scrubbed from top to bottom, inside out, swept, polished, dusted and swept again. Bed sheets were boiled and hung out to dry, flapping gustily in the wind; the kitchen and dining room were thick with the scent of baking and making. On the long wooden tables big, floury loaves of German *Schwarzbrot* were set to cool. If it was summer and Christmas approached, there were plates of gingerbread biscuits and tiny round cakes that melted in your mouth. Christmas in Okahau was very different from the Christmases she'd heard her mother and father talk about back home.

Home. Hannelore often puzzled over that word. Home seemed to be *not* where they were, but in some mythical, magical place across the sea, across the whole of the vast continent of Africa, deserts, jungles, rivers and all. Somewhere in the shadow of the Schwarzwald, close to the town of Lörrach in Baden-Württemberg, was the von Riedesal zu Lörrach – to use their full aristocratic name – ancestral home. Hannelore had only seen pictures of it. She had never been to Europe. When she was four, a year or so earlier, her mother left the farm to go to Europe by ship to have the baby brother she had been waiting almost a year for. She left on a Thursday afternoon, with Papa, leaving a tearful Hannelore behind with Ella. It would take Mama and Papa almost the whole day to drive to Swakopmund, on the coast, where Mama would board the ship for Europe. Two weeks of sailing around the bulge of West Africa, then straight north towards the Canary Islands, Spain, Portugal, France, slipping in through the English Channel until she reached Hamburg. Together Hannelore and Papa traced her journey on the large globe that sat in the library. From there it would be another long train journey south through Germany and the Schwarzwald until she reached Lörrach. After the baby was born, she would wait another two months and then make the journey back to Okahau in return.

As soon as she was gone, Hannelore began to count the days to their return with a nervous joy that sometimes made her sick. Everything was ready for the baby boy on whom Papa's happiness seemed to depend. She was too young to understand why a male child was so important but anything that made Papa happy made her happy too.

But Mama's return wasn't what she had planned – or indeed what *anyone* had planned. She came back alone. The baby was dead. He'd died in the small hours of one of those inky black nights off the coast of Senegal where the wind drops to a whisper and the stars are so bright you could read by them – or so she overheard Mama say to Papa one day. She'd just come out with it. '*Die Sterne . . . so hell, Ludi, so hell. Du kannst es dir gar nicht vorstellen. Nie. Warum sind sie so hell?*' Why are the stars so bright? A funny sort of question. She was given to questions like that, Hannelore saw, questions where no answer was expected, or given. Papa just stroked her hand or her hair, whichever was closest, and left the room. They never mentioned the baby by the name they'd all chosen before Mama left. Sebastian Christian von Riedesal zu Lörrach. He was always just 'he'. *He died. He cried. He. He. He.* Sebastian. Sebastian Christian. Like the farm children, she too rolled the words lovingly around in her mouth, like marbles. But only to herself, never to Mama. And certainly never to Papa.

Bodenhausen was their vast, sprawling farm, running from the tip of the low hills at one end of the horizon all the way to the hills at the other. In summer the grasses were green-tinged, the result of the night-time dew. In winter they were white-blonde, like Mama's hair. It rained perhaps once or twice a year, summer storms that came out of nowhere: silvery, flickering tongues of lightning and a low, thunderous rumbling that preceded the rain. There was just one road that led away from the farm, a reddish scar in the landscape that turned to smooth black just before the turning to the next farm, some twenty kilometres away. The government had tarred it, though no one quite knew why. The land was still and silent; animals lived in it as though they were inside a house. You never knew when a small burrow would open up in front of you and one of the slow, deadly rock vipers that slithered over the grass as though it were water would slink out. Or when a twitch in the elephant grasses meant an antelope was nearby. Or a kudu, a blackbuck, an impala, a gazelle. She knew the names of every animal, insect, reptile and bird to be found on the farm. That was Papa's doing; those were the lessons he taught her. The great outdoors was his domain.

The farmstead was neatly divided into a series of zones where the various people who lived and worked on it were housed. First, of course, there was the beautiful farmhouse, reserved for the family. Built out of the pale stone that came from the quarry over the hill, it had a deep veranda all along the north-facing side that protected the rooms from the fierce African sun in summer, but whose roof was high enough to allow the same sun to penetrate in winter, when the rooms were cold. A clever design, copied from the British. Papa explained it to her. He showed her how the sun moved around the earth at different times, how what would be in shadow here – pointing with his finger to the spot on the globe that marked where they were – would be in full sunlight in winter. She nodded vigorously, even if she couldn't quite grasp how it worked. The house had two wings – one reserved for family, the other for guests. Not that they had many guests, mind you. Südwest Afrika was a long way away from those nearest and dearest to them.

Nevertheless, Mama kept the place spotless. In addition to Ella, who was only allowed in the house during the day, there was Witbooi who washed and scrubbed the floors twice a week, Getrude who did most of the cooking; Nadine who chopped and washed up and Bettina who did the laundry. Those were their German names, the ones Mama had given them. They had other names, too, in their own languages, which meant things like 'God has done well' or 'Born when the moon is rising', or even 'She will bring rain'. Hannelore liked those names much more than the boring German ones. The house was full of people, in the daytime at least. There were more servants than masters, she'd overheard Ella say once and she wasn't laughing when she said it either. The five house-servants were all Coloureds, of mixed-race descent. They lived with their families in a row of white-washed cottages a little distance from the house, screened from it by a row of magnificent blue-gums that whispered gently in the wind.

Further away from them, in a low dip in the landscape and hidden from view of the house, was a cluster of small houses made of a mixture of dung and brick where the black farm workers lived. She didn't know them all by name. Peter, Toivo, Samuel, Muyanga . . . they rode the horses that were stabled at the back of the farm and, occasionally, her father's truck. Their wives were shy, dark-skinned women who smiled at her distractedly when she came upon them washing clothes in large tin basins. They were pleased to hear her speak oshiWambo, but they would no more have talked to her than they'd have talked to Mama. Their children were different. Bold, and cheekily confident, they teased her about her hair, her clothes, her milky white skin, her blue eyes and her pink mouth and tongue. To them she was just another kid. Mwane, who was the chief herdsman's son, was her best friend. He was a year older than her and, on Mama's insistence, had begun taking lessons with Hannelore – reading, writing, spelling. He was bright, Mama noticed, possessed of an instinctive curiosity that surprised and pleased her. His German was already flawless, just like Hannelore's. The schoolteacher, Herr Brandt, came three times a week and, after some initial hesitation, simply taught them together. The clouds of dust that his old car kicked up as he came stuttering up the hill hung in the air for hours after he'd gone.

There she was, five years old, chatelaîne and princess of a domain that stretched as far as the eye could see, but was as empty as she imagined the moon to be. Her companions were few. A handful of cheeky African children; a boy who was a year older than her and who was her only friend; a mother who cried herself to sleep at night and a father who mostly wasn't there. That was it, the sum total of the world around her. There was nothing more.

She slid down further in the cooling water, alternately disgusted and fascinated by the sight of her own pearly pink body under the water, so different in colour, texture, feel from almost everyone around her. Mwane's body was a smooth black sheath that gleamed sleekly in the sun. Her skin grew blotchy and red; she broke out in a sweat that produced a rash, which in turn produced blisters that bled and wept. Mwane *belonged* here. Everything about him merged seamlessly into his surroundings – his language, the food he ate, the clothes he wore, the way he walked and talked. She on the other hand did not. Everything about her was foreign, alien to the land. She submerged herself in the dirty water, delighting in its cool touch on her face. She'd always had a strange longing for water, the result, Mama always said, of living in this land where there was none. At the bottom of the hill, next to the bore-hole, there was a tiny seasonal river. After the yearly day or two of rain, it ran for a few hundred metres, then sogged into the ground and stopped. For the rest of the year it was a grey, cracked trough through which lizards darted. One of the paintings in the dining room was of a winter's scene on Schauinsland, one of the mountains near Lörrach. She used to stand in front of it, staring at the whitened landscape – frozen water, Mama told her. Snow-laden beech branches bowed under its weight. A frozen, silent land, buried under water-turned-to-ice. She mimed a shiver in front of it. Brrr.

2

SIX YEARS LATER
Bodenhausen, 1954

She was eleven now, and her world was coming to an abrupt end. She was about to be sent away. Herr Brandt could no longer provide her with the education she deserved, she overheard him telling Mama and Papa. They were sitting on the veranda in the white wicker chairs that Witbooi and Mwane had washed only the other day, hosing them down in preparation for spring. She crawled behind the huge water containers and slipped under the veranda, squatting in the still-cool shade underneath. Through the cracks in the wooden flooring she could see them. Her skin began to prickle in distress.

'But *where* should we send her?' Mama asked, her hands going out to the silver teapot, lifting it carefully and pouring, a thin, steady stream of fragranced tea that Hannelore could almost taste on the back of her tongue. 'There *are* no schools around here.'

'*Ja*, I know.' Herr Brandt sighed heavily. 'Well, either she goes to the German school in Swakopmund . . . we can find a family to take her in during the term-time, you know. Or you send her south, to South Africa. There *are* some excellent schools in the Cape area, as you know. Not German-speaking, but still . . . it's an option we must consider.'

'Cape Town? But it's so far away . . .' Mama's voice trailed off wistfully.

'Hildebrand, we have no choice. What do you want? Must she grow up half-witted?' Papa was impatient.

'Herr von Riedesal,' Herr Brandt began hesitantly, 'if I might suggest—'

'It's a *lovely* school,' Mama said the following morning, spooning more cinnamon-flavoured porridge into her bowl. She dusted it lightly with icing sugar, Hannelore's favourite. 'Herr Brandt has seen it, you know.'

Hannelore stared at her bowl and the nausea rose in her throat. She would never eat porridge again. 'But I don't *want* to go,' she said, her voice trembling. She fought to keep the vomit and her distress down.

'You must go, *mein Schatz*. We have no choice. Now eat your oats. Getrude put raisins in it specially for you this morning.'

'I . . . I can't.' Hannelore's hands were trembling. 'I *can't*.'

'Hannelore! Stop this childish nonsense at once! It's a very good school and you'll have a lovely time there. You'll make lots and lots of new friends.' Mama's voice was unnaturally loud and her eyes were bright. For a second, mother and daughter stared at each other, then Mama turned away. She didn't want Hannelore to go any more than Hannelore did. Hannelore could tell. She saw for the first time and with something approaching fascination that adults too can lie. She pushed the bowl away from her and slid down from her chair. 'Hannelore! Just where do you think you're going?' Her mother turned in surprise. 'Hannelore!'

But she'd had enough. Out of the corner of her eye she could see Getrude and Ella exchange glances. It was part of her newly discovered power. Her mother had been caught out. She knew it. Hannelore knew it. Another lesson; subtle but profound.

'So what will you do when you get there?' Mwane asked. 'Will you have a new uniform? And new books?'

Hannelore nodded, though in truth she had no idea. 'And . . . and a bed in a room that's called a dormitory.'

'Dormitory.' Mwane pronounced the word slowly and carefully. 'Dor-mi-tory.'

They were squatting in the red dirt, poking at a long, thin string of ants with the broken end of a stick, directing and redirecting their busy, purposeful path from the cracked concrete *stoep* where she and Mwane were sitting, to the roots of the tree under which they'd made their home. The door to the storeroom was open; the familiar smells wafted out – paraffin, sacking, maize meal . . . there were grains of sugar and rice which had spilled out of the tins and sacks and gritted beneath her feet. Little yellow sun-birds darted in and out of the gnarled fig tree whose twisted, hollow roots were big enough to lie in; the wild pigeons cooed in the early morning sun. Down there in the valley the mist still hung over the watering hole, the grasses moved slowly, lightly touched by the wind. It was all happening so fast. In a fortnight's time her trunk would be packed, new clothes ordered and fitted, new shoes, ribbons for her hair and a whole raft of garments she'd never heard of – chemises, slips, blouses, stockings, pinafores. She and Mama had gone through the terrifyingly long list of things she ought to have, bring, wear. 'What's a pinafore?' she'd asked. The shapeless garment that was produced looked more like something Getrude would wear than an eleven-year-old child with very particular tastes.

'*Werde ich dir fehlen?*' she asked Mwane suddenly, looking at him very straight. 'Will you miss me?'

'*Ondeku lyuulukwa.*' His voice was also suddenly solemn. *I will miss you.*

3

St Anne's College for Young Ladies, Constantia,
Cape Town, South Africa, 1954

'And this', the dark-haired lady who'd introduced herself as Mrs Carmichael said, looking down the long length of her nose at

Hannelore, 'is your bed.' She indicated to Hannelore that she ought to place her small overnight case on it. Behind them, sweating slightly with the effort, two porters carried her trunks. She'd been at the school all of one hour and she'd already made a mistake. '*One* trunk only, Hannelore,' Mrs Carmichael said disapprovingly as soon as she'd stepped off the train. 'Those are the rules. When we get to the school, you'll go through them both, please, take out *only* what you need and we'll see to it that the second trunk is returned.' She'd turned and swept off without so much as a 'welcome to Cape Town' or a 'how are you?' Now she stood with Hannelore in the doorway of the dormitory that was to be her home for the next year. Hannelore's eyes were like saucers. The dormitory was long and narrow and the beds were grouped in threes. 'You'll be sharing with Petronella Doncaster and Mary-Ann Jellicoe. They're both at games at the moment. *Very* nice girls. Tea is at four p.m. *promptly* in the dining hall. Please don't be late.' And with that Mrs Carmichael barked out a final set of instructions to the porters and turned on her heel.

The room was suddenly quiet. Her click-clack footsteps died away down the long corridor. The porters lined up Hannelore's trunks in silence. 'Th-thank you,' Hannelore said, risking a hesitant, timid smile, longing for a little human warmth. It had been two days since anyone had addressed her other than the ticket inspector on the train down from Windhoek. More than that, since her arrival in Cape Town that morning, she hadn't seen anyone smile. Mama had taught her to be polite to everyone, including and especially the servants. But these two didn't smile back. They eyed her coldly. There was a hardness in their faces and eyes that frightened her. One of them muttered something to the other in their own language and they left the room.

She sat down gingerly on the bed Mrs Carmichael had indicated would be hers, feeling even more miserable than she had the night before when the train pulled out of the station and she saw Mama and Papa waving, their figures becoming more and more blurred until she couldn't see them any longer. She wasn't crying now but the ache in her heart hadn't lessened and the trembling in the pit of her stomach certainly hadn't stopped. She looked at her brand-new wristwatch, a present from Papa, her fingers running over its smooth, convex dome. He'd given it to her the night before she left in a solemn ceremony that seemed to have more to do with what *wasn't* being said. It wasn't actually new, at least not in the strictest sense of the word – quite the opposite, in fact. It was a family heirloom, brought with them from Lörrach, or so Papa said. She was to look after it, always. *Jaeger-LeCoultre*. She traced the delicate, spidery lettering with her finger over the thick, domed glass. A worn leather strap, slightly too big for her wrist, a solid winding-up mechanism that stood proud of the steel. There was something in the quick, almost furtive looks flashing between her parents that made her understand it had been intended for someone else. Him. The *brother-to-be-that-never-was*. It made the gift doubly special. Wearing it next to her skin brought her closer to the ghost of the brother she'd spent almost a year preparing to love but had never seen.

Suddenly the door burst open and two almost identical, red-faced girls in pigtails appeared. 'Are you the new girl?' one of them asked, looking her quickly up and down, assessing her for something Hannelore couldn't quite grasp.

Hannelore nodded eagerly. 'I . . . I just got here,' she said shyly, risking another quick smile. It wasn't returned.

'What's your name?' one of them demanded imperiously.

'H-Hannelore. Hannelore von Riedesal zu Lörrach,' she said nervously, remembering what her father had told her. Full name, always.

The two girls looked at each other then burst into peals of derisive laughter. 'Hannah *what*?' one of them snorted. The other let loose with a stream of unintelligible words that ended, unmistakably, with the words '*Heil Hitler*'. They giggled again, looking at each other before turning back to her. There was silence in the room. Hannelore's cheeks were on fire. She was only dimly aware of who Hitler was – she'd overheard enough furiously whispered conversations between her mother and father and Herr Brandt to know that it was because of Herr Hitler that her father had been absent from the farm in 1944, though no one had ever told her *why* he'd had to leave, or where he'd gone. The following year, Germany lost the war, though again, no one ever said why. She'd heard whispered accounts of something called a *Konzentrationslager* and once, she and Mwane, crouched underneath the veranda trying to catch a rare, large-winged butterfly, had overheard the most terrible argument between her father and two of their neighbours, Detmar von Schaffheusen, a German, and Aloysius Reinert, an Afrikaner. Awful, mysterious things were said that she and Mwane discussed intensely for days. What was a *Konzentrationslager*? And why had the Jews been sent there? Herr Brandt was unable to answer when they asked him; he simply went brick-red, turned away from them and the case was closed.

Now, standing in front of her with their arms closed were two girls whose faces carried the same expression as Aloysius Reinert's – a mixture of contempt and anger – but there was also a strange, unfathomable fear. She could see it in their eyes and the way they stood, arms folded, as if against a threat. It was Mwane who'd taught her how to read the signs. 'Look at their feet,' he'd always told her. 'Pointing outwards means they're afraid.' It was almost always true. He was clever like that, Mwane. He could read people better than anyone she knew. He was the one who'd shown her how to wrap the rest of the household around her little finger. She wished desperately he were here now. She missed him more than she could say.

Supper that evening was a dismal affair. No one spoke to her, certainly not her two new room-mates. Aside from the unforgivable fact of being German, she'd also arrived at St Anne's three weeks late. The friendships around her had been formed weeks, months, even years before her arrival. She sat at the end of one long, wooden table, her posture upright as she'd been taught, blinking back the tears that lay like a thin film behind her eyes. There were perhaps two hundred girls at St Anne's, ranging from the very young ones of six or seven, perhaps, to the impossibly grown-up, poised young ladies who sat at a table on a raised dais at the end of the room, surveying everyone else down the imperious lengths of their noses. From the snippets of whispered conversation around her, she understood that the tall, red-haired, stern-faced girl sitting at one end was the head girl, whatever that was, and that the girls sitting to her left and right were all prefects, to be feared, respected and sucked up to in equal amounts.

She stared down miserably at her plate. She'd never had to fear or suck up to anyone in her life. She didn't even know how. She soon found out. At Bodenhausen she'd been the surrogate lord and master of all she surveyed; the authority of her parents' coursed through her own veins in the same way it did their veins. Mama had taught her to exercise her power discreetly, and with charm – insofar as an eleven year old understood the lesson – but the truth of the matter was that back there, at home, everyone deferred to her, always, in all situations at all times. Even Ella's muttered threats to report her to her mother, her exhortations to her to brush her hair, take a bath, eat her supper, were delivered in the knowledge that it was Hannelore who wielded control over Ella, not the other way round. Age held no sway; the relationship was held together by mysterious, unspoken chords of race and class and trust. At St Anne's, that world did not exist. To begin with, there were no Africans. There were porters and gardeners – she could see them in the grounds that sloped away from the dormitory towards the out-of-bounds ravine at the bottom of the hill – but no one, least of all the girls, took any notice of them. They wore green overalls; sometimes in the late afternoon when the sun was beginning to go down, they lay on the grass, practically indistinguishable save for their dark, neat heads and the dusty yellow soles of their bare feet.

In the kitchen, beyond the swing and pull of the large double doors, there were the cooks and maids that belonged to every household she'd ever known, including the school's. But they did not come to the table; they didn't venture beyond the doors. At every mealtime, the solemn-faced prefects took charge of supervising the distribution of platters and tureens and linen-covered baskets of bread. The rest of the school was kept outside the dining hall, waiting in lines under the watchful eyes of another group of girls – line monitors, they were called – and then, when the last of the bowls had been placed and the servants dispatched back to the kitchen, the great doors were opened and everyone streamed in. There was certainly a hierarchy here but not one she could recognise or take part in. Nothing she'd ever encountered before could have prepared her for this strange new world of privilege and position, neither of which she possessed.

She saved up the details – the odd rituals, the strange looks, the muttered, offhand comments that were loud enough for her to hear but not the teachers – to write in her letters to Mama and Mwane, but there, too, something mysterious held her back. Mwane would know what she meant, what the *real* message was, hidden between her lines and words. Mama wouldn't; she couldn't. It was another of those instances where she felt herself to be in possession of a strange kind of knowledge that was entirely separate from what Herr Brandt had taught them. She could somehow sense that Mama's health depended almost entirely on the maintenance of a fiction that had everything to do with how she would like things to be, and nothing to do with how they really were. Her letters home ran on two parallel but not-touching tracks. *Liebe Mama, es geht mir sehr gut. Dear Mama, I am very well.* She wasn't, of course, but only Mwane could see that.

4

She fingered the pages of the magazine reverentially, making sure she neither creased nor stained a single one. She was sitting cross-legged on her bed with a satisfyingly large stack of them waiting to be paged through, pored over, their every detail studied and committed to memory. Miss Weston, her art teacher and – family aside of course – her favourite person in the whole world, had given them to her. *McCall Style News. Buttericks.* And, the best and most glamorous of them all, *Vogue.* She had two, one British *Vogue*, featuring Jean Patchett on the cover, the other an American edition, with the model Lisa Fonssagrives. She devoured the images hungrily. Jean (she was on first-name terms with them) was wearing a black-and-white suit with a beautifully detailed net across her face and a wide, broad-brimmed hat. Lisa was in a chalk-green dress that complemented her hair and make-up perfectly. Hannelore reached under her bed and pulled out her sketchbook, opening it to a crisp, clean, white page. She picked up her favourite pencil – a 2B – and began to sketch.

Half an hour later, she held up the page, looking critically at what she'd done. She was nearly twelve. Miss Weston said her drawings were better than anyone's she'd ever seen. She'd shown her how to shade, highlight, etch, how to capture the way light fell on a fabric, how to draw folds and creases, pleats and tucks, how to make wool look heavy or light, the best way to illustrate floating, soft materials. She'd shown Hannelore that she was good at something, that she had something to be proud of. When she first arrived, she'd struggled with her lessons, unable to grasp even the simplest things. Back home, she'd been a good pupil under the careful eye of Herr Brandt but she quickly saw that it meant nothing here. Back there, she'd had only Mwane for company and competition, and despite his obvious talents, what Herr Brandt had taught them was so far behind her new companions that she couldn't see how she would ever catch up. She'd cried herself to sleep every night for the first term, not just because she missed home and everything in it, but also because she'd never before been the object of ridicule – *real* ridicule, not the teasing, playful scorn of the farm children who, for all their jeers, secretly admired and fussed over her. St Anne's was different. The girls were vicious, their judgements swift and cruel. She'd never experienced anything like it. Nothing was off-limits – her accent, her name, her hair, her legs, her non-existent breasts . . . the list was endless.

But halfway through her second term, things changed. It started with Alison Henning-Prescott, three years above her but in the same boarding house, who asked her as offhandedly as she could if she could help her with drawing some flowers for a biology project. 'I hear you're quite good at art.' Hardly a compliment but the look of pleasure on Alison's face when she gave her back her copybook said it all. 'Oh. You really *are* quite good,' Alison said, visibly impressed. Two more requests came in from Alison's classmates – a complicated plant and a skeleton – and it wasn't long before she was regularly being asked to draw things that others couldn't. Within weeks she'd gone from being an object of derision to someone other girls actually pointed to in awe. Being good at something – *anything*, it didn't matter what – was the missing currency, the secret ingredient that made all the difference between fitting in and being frozen out. Strong girls quickly figured it out; the more timid ones didn't. After her first horrible six months where she was barely talked to, let alone befriended, she was determined not to spend the next six years in the same way.

By the time she made the long, lonely journey back to Okahau at the end of the year, she was no longer the girl everyone laughed at or scorned.

5

'A *fashion* designer?' Mama put her hand to her throat. Hannelore might as well have said 'prostitute'. Hildebrand looked quickly at her husband.

'What's wrong with being a fashion designer?' Hannelore asked, puzzled.

'Sewing clothes for other people?' Her father looked up from his newspaper. 'Over my dead body. No daughter of mine is going to sew for other women.' He rustled the sheets of the paper in irritation and then went back to reading again.

'No, not *sewing*,' Hannelore hastened to explain. 'Although, I suppose you *do* have to know how to make things but—'

'Hanne, *liebchen*, don't be ridiculous. You're not at school to learn how to knit and sew.'

'It's not knitting and sewing,' Hannelore protested angrily. 'It's about art and history and fabrics and—'

'Did you not hear what I just said?' Her father rustled the pages again, angrily this time.

'But—'

'But *nothing*!' His voice was an angry roar. Hannelore looked from one to the other in bewilderment. Her mother got up and went to the piano. She lifted the lid, settled herself down and began to play. After a few minutes, Hannelore got up and left the room. She simply didn't understand it. She'd been away from the farm for nearly three years and in that time everything had been turned upside down. Ella and Getrude were no longer there; they'd been dismissed whilst Hannelore was at school. 'They . . . they had to leave,' was her mother's hastily worded reply when questioned. With her keen ear for whatever was not being said, Hannelore pushed her further.

'Why?'

'Because . . . because they were getting old.' Her mother refused to meet her eyes.

'They're not *old*,' Hannelore said scornfully. It was true. Ella was in her mid-twenties, if that. 'Ella's hardly older than me!'

'Too old to do this sort of work,' her mother snapped suddenly and turned away. It was on the tip of Hannelore's tongue to say something about the cook who'd replaced Getrude – a woman in her fifties, with a shock of curly white hair – but something in the stiffness of her mother's back made her close her mouth again. Something had happened, she was sure of it, but the limits of her fifteen-year-old imagination made her stop.

Mwane wasn't much help. He held out his hands in front of his stomach in a parody of pregnancy that had them both helpless with laughter in seconds. 'But where's her husband?' Hannelore said, wiping the tears from her eyes.

'She hasn't got one. Ella neither. They both going to have a baby.'

Hannelore's eyes grew wide. 'So . . . so how did they get pregnant?'

Mwane's eyes were almond-shaped, the clear bright white coming out of the smooth blackness of his face like a diamond mined from the earth's depths. He had a way of drawing back from a question that he didn't like, or to which he had no answer – a fold of skin at the corners of his eyes flattening taut. He said nothing, and that in itself was an answer of some sort.

She took in a quick, shallow breath, her imagination skimming dangerously over the facts. Then she jumped up and ran all the way through the blonde, swaying elephant grasses, her skirts flying behind her and her hair whipping around her face. As she passed the living-room window, running past it in a blur, the echoes of Handel's 'Messiah' came to her on the breeze. *Part III, No. 53. Amen.* She recognised it from afar. Her mother's fingers roved wildly across the keys. Hannelore could feel her heart thundering in her chest and the furious pumping of her blood in her veins. She ran on. Mwane caught up with her easily. At nearly seventeen, a year and a half older than her, he was three times as fast. His arm went out to cuff her round the neck, as they'd always done. She was crying, she realised, as she tasted the salt of her tears on her tongue. He wrestled her to the ground, trying to provoke her into a fight. That way she'd be forced to bring the sadness and the anger out from inside her, forcing it into the open. He was the one who'd told her never to keep things inside, bottled up where light and sound and the touch of another's hand couldn't reach them. Where his insights into the human condition came from she had no idea. Mwane could see into the very heart of you, tell you what you were feeling before you felt it yourself. The grass was a soft mattress beneath her legs. The sky was a dazzling blue, fading to a delicate pinkish white over the hills at the edge of the land. She lay on her back, winded, struggling with her tears. Mwane's arm was flung across her chest. 'Don't cry, Nogiti,' he said, using her oshiWambo name, the name he'd had for her since childhood. 'Don't cry.'

'I'm not crying,' she mumbled, reaching up a hand to fiercely brush the tears away. She opened her eyes. His face was above hers. She saw it again, that folding back of the eyelids that laid his almond-shaped eyes almost bare. She began to see something else in him . . . she put up her hand and touched the springy black hair that had fascinated her as a child and that now, for some years, she'd been shy to touch. She was fascinatedly aware of her distinction from the others at school who would sooner have *died* than touch Mwane, or any of his kind. *I am not like them*, she sang softly under her breath as they arranged themselves more comfortably in the grasses, their limbs touching and entwining in a way that seemed simply an extension of the conversation held when they were both standing upright. His arm fell naturally across her chest and she rolled towards him, her face seeking some reassurance in the warm cup of his neck, the only place in the world where she felt she belonged.

She returned to school at the end of the summer holidays. She looked out of the train window across the yellowing sea of the veld and caught the scent of a decaying, imploding world on the back of her throat. It was 1958. That summer, boundaries were crossed, borders broken through, new alliances were formed, old ones destroyed. Everything had rolled over in the fathomless, bottomless barrel of her world and steadied itself again, but differently this time. Something – some way of life or under-standing of it – was drawing to a close, but that in itself wasn't the end. Not yet. The end, she thought to herself with a clarity of vision that would later astonish her, that was yet to come.

6

NEARLY TWO YEARS LATER
Windhoek, South-West Africa, 1959

She was seventeen. She had matriculated from St Anne's and her schooldays were over. In a white cotton dress that she'd made herself – a high-waisted, A-line dress with a shallow neckline that showed off the pretty, freckled skin of her shoul-ders and the beginnings of her (very) slight cleavage – with a wide straw-brimmed hat and white peep-toed shoes, she sat in the Windhoek garden of one of her mother's friends and sipped slowly from a glass of freshly made lemonade. Tante Bärbel was a few years younger than Mama, with dyed-red hair, a red slash of a mouth and something of a 'reputation'. She was an artist – the first 'proper' one Hannelore had ever met – and lived in a modern, sprawling bungalow on Uhlandstrasse, in the shadow of the Klein Windhoek hills. As a seventeenth birthday treat, she was being allowed to spend the week in the capital city with her aunt and uncle before continuing her journey northwards to Bodenhausen. It was to be a fun-filled week of shopping and outings and parties, befitting a seventeen year old who had just finished her exams. Tante Bärbel had arranged tickets to a concert, an art exhibition, a choral performance at the

Tintenpalast and, best of all, a trip to the salon where she promised her 'any treatment you fancy, *mein Schatz*'. Tante Bärbel's husband, Onkel Fritz, was in Germany on business. He was the owner of Schaeffler's, the colony's largest automotive dealership on the outskirts of Windhoek, where Papa and every other farmer she knew bought their tractors. Tante Bärbel and Onkel Fritz had no children and although Hannelore privately thought Tante Bärbel the most interesting and beautiful person she'd ever met, she'd never quite been able to work out why she and Onkel Fritz had ever got married. They were as unlike as it was possible for two people to be. Tante Bärbel was a butterfly, a vivacious, flirtatious being whose dark, made-up eyes darted this way and that, her bejewelled hands following. Onkel Fritz was old, large, slow. He studied the world carefully through half-lowered lids, appearing almost asleep. They made the oddest couple.

'Suits you, white,' Tante Bärbel commented, plonking herself down in the chair next to Hannelore's, taking a sip of her own drink – a G&T, not lemonade, like Hannelore's. '*Lemonade*? No *ways*, darling!' she exclaimed, exaggeratedly derisive when Hannelore offered to pour her a glass. *Vays*. She retained the 'v' of her native tongue, though she spoke English to Hannelore and everyone else. Germany, she was fond of declaring, was dead. Bankrupt. *Over*. America was where it was at. She had been to New York twice. 'You can't *imagine* it, darling. So much fun!' No, Hannelore couldn't imagine it. Aside from boarding school, the occasional stopover in Windhoek and the towns around the farm – Ondekaremba, Oupembamewa, Okujo, Omunjeke – she'd never been anywhere at all. New York was about as likely a potential destination as Antarctica. 'Very elegant,' Tanta Bärbel said, looking at her more closely.

'I made it myself,' Hannelore said a touch self-consciously.

'Did you now?' Tante Bärbel murmured. '*Ja*, you're talented. I always told your mother. Such a pity.'

Hannelore said nothing, but the knot of resentment that had lodged itself in her chest ever since her father had forced her to turn down the place she'd been offered at the Royal College of Art in London tightened. She'd made the application secretly, at Miss Weston's urging. 'You can't let such a talent go to waste, Hannelore. Let's do the application together.' She'd done it, been offered a place and then told her parents. Her father's reaction was predictable. Out of the question. *'Da gibt's keine Diskussion.'* The matter was closed before it could even be opened. At supper that evening, her parents mapped out the rest of her life. She was to go overseas. To Europe. She would spend a summer in Munich with an elderly aunt of her father's, whereupon, it was hoped, a suitably connected young man would appear . . . and that, more or less, would be that. What, Hannelore wondered bitterly, had been the point of sending her away to school? She would easily have fulfilled what appeared to be her destiny without the benefit – or curse, as she was beginning to conceive of it – of an education.

'*Komm Schätzle*, stop with the long face.' Tante Bärbel looked at her sympathetically. 'Let's go into town. There's a new dress in the windows of Gütemann's that I saw yesterday. I'm *dying* to try it on.'

Twenty minutes later they were on their way down the hill towards Kaiserstrasse, the main thoroughfare in Windhoek. Tante Bärbel drove; her large, shiny American-looking convertible was a delight. Red leather seats with cream piping, an enormous, beautifully polished wooden wheel and everywhere the smell of cigarettes and perfume that seemed the epitome of glamour and sophistication, worldly and polished in a way Bodenhausen would never be. Just being inside it with Tante Bärbel at the wheel brought a smile to Hannelore's lips. She saw how people turned their heads as she sailed through the intersections, one after the other, not even slowing down. It was not, Tante Bärbel declared, giggling, a car to go slow in.

They parked opposite the Zoo Gardens where black men in overalls were weeding and pruning the grass and hedges, just as they'd done at school. Tante Bärbel tucked her arm in Hannelore's and together they walked across the road. Hannelore caught a glimpse of the two of them in the shop window as they passed – two stylish, striking women, less like aunt and niece than two friends, she in her white dress and Tante Bärbel dressed in dark green which clashed wonderfully with her hair.

The city was quiet. There was a slow, sparse stream of traffic rumbling along Kaiserstrasse, a few strolling couples, a harried-looking mother or two, infants and a nanny in tow. Tante Bärbel marched along with the pleasurably alert look of someone who is always expected somewhere and whom everyone knows. They were stopped half a dozen times; German housewives who spoke to Tante Bärbel in German and whom she answered, amusedly tolerant, in English; a couple of Afrikaans-speaking girls, farm girls with their hair in braids and the thin gold-hoop earrings that most of them wore. There was one woman, triumphantly ugly with a head of close-cropped silver-white hair and the same red slash of a mouth, who stopped and kissed Tante Bärbel on both cheeks, leaving a dab of lipstick behind. She was tall and slender and wore a pair of turned-up men's jeans with a pair of flat cream leather shoes. A man's cotton shirt hung loosely off her tall frame, caught on the small, shaking points of her breasts. Hannelore stared at her as she waved them merrily on their way.

'Who was that?' she asked curiously.

'Oh, that's Marjory, Countess di Savoranello. She's English, married to some Italian count who lives in Genoa. He's never here,' Tante Bärbel said as soon as they were out of earshot. 'He absolutely loathes it. Not that Marjory minds terribly, it has to be said. You can't *imagine* the parties she throws. Divine. Just *divine.*'

Yet again Hannelore's imagination failed her. Aside from the rather tame school parties she'd been to in her time at St Anne's, she'd yet to attend a proper 'party', with young men present and real wine for the tasting, let alone one hosted by an androgynous Englishwoman married to an Italian count. St Anne's was a whole world away from Bodenhausen but Tante Bärbel's world was further still. It was hard to believe that in just under a week's time she would be back on the farm, surrounded by silence and the soft tinkle of the piano of an evening. Afterwards, her mother would turn to her and the two of them would quietly discuss the following day's menu. There would be an exchange of complaints between her parents about the servants, the rising cost of fuel, the 'situation' down south, the Afrikaner government and the slow death of German-ness. At Bodenhausen, all was complaint. Little wonder; the world, as they knew it, was ending. Here, sitting in the little cafe in the passage between one shop and the next, a poor imitation of a Parisian arcade but still with the little round tables, each with a single rose, and the silver teapots with bone handles that the owner had brought back from Berlin, it was different. A different world. Things were just starting, opening up. She felt a sudden tremor of revulsion for the farm and the way of life she was shortly about to return to.

A woman passed them and stopped suddenly; a chair was hastily pulled out, another coffee called for. She was Griselda von Schleuttwein, the wife of the former mayor. Hannelore stared at her. Another masculine-looking, confident woman of the sort that Tante Bärbel seemed to attract. This one was a poet; her last collection of poems had been sold as far away as Munich, and Hamburg, she was delighted to report. She and Tante Bärbel talked about poets and artists, new galleries and openings and dealers, who was going up in the art world, who was going down, all of which they would have to wait another six months to see. Hannelore sat a little to one side, studying the scene in front of her, trying to commit it to memory. The murmuring talk of the two women about people and places she didn't know gently washed over her, exposing the limits of her understanding and interest. A wave of what appeared to her to be nostalgia flowed over her – a strange, bittersweet longing for something she'd only half-grasped, but how could it be? How could she be nostalgic for something she'd never seen, never experienced? She was stopped, momentarily, balanced precariously between two stages of her life, one of which was yet to come. On the one side was the path that had been so carefully selected for her. After the week-long 'treat' in Windhoek, she would go back to the farm, to long dreamy conversations with her mother about her 'future', preparing her for a journey that would lead her calmly from one kind of safety to another, from Bodenhausen to Lörrach, that other home to which she'd never belonged and never seen. Waiting for her at the end of the journey was marriage to someone as yet unknown. A final frontier – *the* final frontier – and a new beginning of a kind. And yet, on the other hand and in complete contrast, Tante Bärbel's world presented an image of another kind of life, one that she only partially recognised. It led her in some unspoken way to a strong sense of belonging to Mwane and Tante Bärbel and the woman in mannish clothes whom they'd just met, all of whom lived in a world that was unfamiliar to her, but intoxicating all the same. Books, art, places, people, the world of *ideas*.

She leaned back in her seat, overwhelmed by it all but content, at least for the time being, to observe the slow gathering pace of both lives around her, swirling, eddying, but inevitably set on some collision course from which she already knew she would not easily recover.

7

They were driving back up Kaiserstrasse about an hour later, on their way home, when the first of a long line of police vans overtook them, sirens blaring, clearly in a hurry. Tante Bärbel braked suddenly and pulled over to one side. A steady stream of black vans roared up the main street, followed by a handful of large white trucks with policemen sitting in the back. 'What d'you think's happening?' Hannelore asked, craning her neck to see where they were headed. 'Where d'you think they're going?'

Tante Bärbel hesitated for a second, then pulled out into the slipstream of the convoy. 'Only one way to find out,' she said. 'Let's follow them and see.' They roared up Kaiserstrasse, then Pietersen Street. The power station loomed into view, then was gone again. Suddenly the air was split for the second time by a loud hooter. It seemed to suck in the sleepy quiet of the Saturday afternoon and blow it out again in alarm. 'That's the emergency siren,' Tante Bärbel said. 'What the *hell* is going on?'

'Isn't this the way to the Location?' Hannelore asked, suddenly catching sight of a street sign.

'Yes, it is. Perhaps there's a riot, or something,' Tante Bärbel murmured.

A *riot*! The word conjured up a sense of excitement and wonder. 'What sort of riot?' Hannelore asked breathlessly.

Tante Bärbel hesitated for a second. 'There's talk of the authorities moving some of the natives from the Old Location to a new one, north of the city. I'd heard there was a bit of resistance,' she said slowly.

Hannelore's eyes widened. Riots, resistance, sirens . . . it was all so far removed from what she knew of the sleepy little capital with its cafes and teashops, the one cinema and the dance hall where the previous summer a succession of stiff, acne-scarred boys had asked her to dance. She felt again a slow, deep tug of excitement begin to burn inside her.

They rounded the corner and were suddenly on the crest of a small hill, overlooking a valley filled to capacity with small houses that looked as though a child had drawn them – a simple, single rectangle with a door and two windows on either side. Hannelore gazed down at the scene curiously. The vans had formed a protective cordon around the perimeter fence; inside were hundreds of policemen, spilling out of the ungainly white vans, rushing in and out of the makeshift houses, sticks raised. She drew in her breath apprehensively. There was a lot of dust and smoke, people running back and forth, an immense babble of sounds and shouts reaching them from below. There were dogs, too, still leashed but leaping ahead of the blue-uniformed police with their strange, peaked caps who walked up and down, shouting orders at a sullen, mutinous line of natives swathed in blankets, sitting obstinately on the ground. 'What's happening, Tante Bärbel?' she whispered, even though there was no need for a lowered tone. 'Why are they sitting on the ground?'

'They don't want to move. They call the new place Katutura, or something like that.' She wrinkled her lovely brow.

'Katutura. That means "the-place-we-do-not-want-to-go",' Hannelore spoke the words softly. 'How sad.'

Tante Bärbel looked at her in surprise. 'How d'you know that?'

'It's oshiHerero. I don't speak it as well as oshiWambo, but I can pick up most of it,' Hannelore said, surprised that she should ask.

'You speak a *native* language?'

'Yes, of course.'

'There's no "of course" about it,' Tante Bärbel said, surprise still in her voice. 'I don't know anyone who does. Anyone European, I mean, of course. And your mother? Does she speak it too?'

Hannelore shook her head. A sudden confusion broke over her. It seemed to her that something else was being said, but again, like before in the cafe, she couldn't quite catch hold of it. 'No,' she said slowly. 'But Papa does. A little.'

'Ah. Ludwig. Well, *he* would, wouldn't he?' Tante Bärbel murmured cryptically, starting the car. 'Come, that's enough. High time I took you home. Wouldn't want your father to think I'd been taking you to unsuitable places, hmm?' She swung the big shiny car around and they drove back slowly the way they'd come.

Hannelore sat beside her, her throat full of an emotion she didn't understand. She folded her hands in her lap and tried not to think about what she'd just seen. *The place we do not want to go.* She thought about her upcoming trip to Europe. That too was a place she didn't want to go but it wasn't the *place* that worried her, it was the thought of what awaited her. She had an appointment with a destiny she was determined not to keep.

'Let's have a glass of wine, hmm?' Tante Bärbel said gaily as they walked through the front door. 'A glass of wine before dinner. I think we both need one.' She rang the little brass bell that stood

36

on the console beside the fireplace. Seconds later, Anna, her maid of thirty years, appeared without making a sound. 'Two glasses of that lovely red wine Madame Marjory brought the other day, please, Anna, yes, the big glasses. The ones on the second shelf.' Anna padded away softly, silently. 'Come now,' Tante Bärbel said, touching Hannelore's forearm, pulling her away. 'We can have it on the terrace. It's not too cold.'

'I'll just get a shawl. I'm a little cold,' Hannelore said and slipped quickly down the corridor. She opened the door to her room and blinked in pleasure. Tante Bärbel's house never failed to impress her. In contrast to the old-fashioned elegance of Bodenhausen, it was modern, clean, unfussy. There were exposed brick walls, whitewashed, but with the dense brickwork pattern still clear. Bookshelves ran horizontally across one wall, from floor to ceiling, densely packed with more books than she'd ever seen, more even than in the library at school, it seemed to her. Windows were simple enormous panes of glass through which carefully edited views of the garden could be seen. The furniture too was simple and beautiful, mostly of pale wood with low, clean horizontal lines. Nothing was fussy, as it was on the farm. Here there were no heavily framed pictures of German landscapes, no clusters of teapots and ornate vases or those porcelain figurines that her mother so loved. In Tante Bärbel's house everything was sharp-edged and modern. She loved it, instinctively.

She walked towards the low chest of drawers and slid open the top one. She pulled out a pale green cashmere scarf. She'd found it in one of her mother's trunks, had cut off the patterned border on either side and painstakingly hemmed it herself so that the cut didn't show. She wound it carefully around her neck in front of the mirror. She turned her head to one side, admiring the way the early evening light made her blonde hair almost translucent, a pretty contrast to the ethereal green of the scarf. She slowly became aware of someone else in the mirror and turned her head. Tante Bärbel was standing in the doorway.

'Suits you, that colour,' she said, smiling at her. She was

holding a glass of dark red wine, her fingers curled protectively around its domed bowl. She moved forward into the room and came to stand behind her. The fading light in the room made a shifting rainbow of colours in the mirror; the pale, white-blonde of her own hair, Tante Bärbel's hennaed tresses, the burgundy of the wine and the pale, chiffon green of the scarf. Tante Bärbel's quick, flashing green eyes caught the light like jewels. They stood in silence for a second, both caught by the image. 'Come,' Tante Bärbel said, putting a hand on her shoulder. She left it there for a fraction longer than was necessary, the tips of her fingers touching her bare skin lightly. Yet again Hannelore felt the mysterious pull of some other command being given, something else being said. But then Tante Bärbel's hand slipped away and the feeling was gone.

Hannelore followed her out of the bedroom, a little dizzy with the effort of trying to understand what she instinctively grasped could not be said.

PART TWO

8

LINDI JOHANSSEN
EIGHTEEN YEARS LATER
Oslo, Norway, 1977

Three teenagers with linked arms and bulky backpacks that protruded behind them like the hump-backed shells of strange woodland creatures kicked and scuffed the autumn leaves as they walked slowly back from school. Two were tall and blonde, with long hair that fell to their waists, almost mirror images of each other. The third, sandwiched between them, was much shorter, a petite girl with mocha-coloured skin and long, curly black hair pulled into an untidy ponytail from which half a dozen unruly tendrils escaped. Her face was suffused with a sunniness that seemed to come from within, making her stand out even more. Their voices were high and excitable as they told and retold some incident that had happened in school that day and about which the entire class was still talking. Arms still linked they sauntered up the path, failing to notice the line of cars parked outside the house or the car with the blacked-out windows on the other side of the road, or the two young men standing watchfully at the kerb, arms folded over their jackets in a way that was wholly out of place in the beautiful old suburb in which Lindi Johanssen, the dark-skinned girl in the middle, lived.

She pushed open the front door to find her mother standing waiting anxiously on the other side.

'*Elskling*,' her mother said, smiling at the two girls standing on either side of her daughter. She put a finger to her lips and lowered her voice. 'We've got guests,' she said, pointing towards the sitting-room door.

'Who?' Lindi shrugged off her school backpack and let it fall to the floor with a thud.

'I'm so sorry, girls,' her mother said, ignoring her for a moment and turning to her friends. 'We'd love you to stay but another time, all right? For security reasons, you understand. But there's a son, he's a bit younger than you . . . they'll be arriving any minute. Perhaps you can all take him out after supper?'

'Sure,' both girls chorused, unfazed. They'd been friends with Lindi Johanssen since kindergarten and were used to the comings and goings of important figures in the Johanssens' lives. 'OK, call us later. Bye!' They wriggled fingers at Lindi and her mother and let themselves out the kitchen door. 'Wonder who it is this time?' Lindi heard Toril whisper to Klara as they walked down the steps.

'Who's here?' she asked her mother again.

Siv hesitated, waiting until the girls were safely out of earshot. Not that the name would have meant much to them. 'It's Nujoma,' she said finally, her voice lowered. 'They arrived this afternoon from Moscow. Please don't say anything, *vennen min*. Not even to Toril and Klara.'

Lindi's eyes widened. *Nujoma*? Samuel Shafiishuna Nujoma was the leader of the banned liberation movement, SWAPO, who counted the Johanssens amongst their most important foreign sympathisers. They were amongst the few people outside the organisation who'd actually seen the man who'd spent most of the past decade underground, a word that had terrified her until Siv explained it to her. 'No, he's not *really* underground, *vennen min*. It just means he's in hiding. No one except those very, very close to him can ever know where he is.' Lindi was ten years old when the movement's leadership-in-exile met secretly at their home on Oscarsgate, minutes from the palace and the Slottsparken. For almost a week the house had been full of men coming and going, meeting in the kitchen and the two living rooms, conducting whispered discussions and heated arguments behind closed doors. Going downstairs to the bathroom at dawn one morning, she'd come face to face with the great leader, himself on his way to the bathroom, wrapped in a splendid silk robe that Siv had bought him especially for the occasion. She'd seen him once or twice in the course of that week, his eyes drifting over her as he talked or argued with this one or that. He stopped in the passageway to smile at her fondly, distractedly. His voice was a deep, soft baritone.

'Lindiwe, *nè*? Lindiwe Odihambo.' He used her birth name. 'Your mother was an Ovambo, *nè*?' She'd nodded uncertainly. She had no memory of her birth mother, or her father, either. All she'd been told was that her mother had been a domestic worker for a German couple in Windhoek, and that she'd died shortly after giving birth. There was no mention of her father. It was clear from the infant's mixed-race complexion that he was white, but no one had ever said whether or not he was her mother's employer. She'd been placed in an orphanage shortly afterwards, but no one ever said by whom. She was six months old when a Norwegian couple visited the orphanage one day and Siv Johanssen refused to leave without her. Her husband, Erik, was the head of one of the larger aid agencies, and already in trouble with the authorities for his outspoken views. It took them several weeks to organise the adoption and they left the country with the baby girl days before a warrant was issued for his arrest. Meddling, they called it. Aiding and abetting SWAPO, a 'terrorist' organisation. They flew out one night via Addis Ababa on a tip-off from a contact somewhere deep inside the police force. They'd never been back. Norway was the only home Lindi had ever known.

Then, in the pre-dawn darkness, the man everyone knew affectionately but deceptively as the 'Old Man' looked at her and smiled again, slowly. 'You must come back to us, Lindiwe,' he said, smiling at her with the sweet, brilliant smile that was his particular trademark, concealing an iron-clad discipline and commitment to his cause. 'Soon,' he said, nodding slowly. 'Soon you will come home. When all this is over. It won't be long now, you know.' *You must come back to us*. Lindi told no one of their

43

accidental meeting, not even her mother. Nujoma's words became a private touchstone, something to whisper to herself, especially as she grew older and found herself struggling to make sense of who she really was – Norwegian or Namibian? She could remember nothing of Namibia; Norway was all she knew. A sassy, charming child, she'd been the centre of everyone's attention when they first returned. Pretty little dark-skinned girls who spoke such fluent Norwegian were a rarity in those days. Without knowing or understanding it, she was a symbol of hope in a time in desperate need of it. The anti-apartheid movement in Norway was one of Europe's strongest and most vocal. The Johanssens, with their cute, little adopted African child, became an unwitting poster-family for all. Lindi was the apple of everyone's eye, most especially Erik's.

Yet what had been so charmingly different in her at five was no longer quite so charming at fourteen. She came home from school one afternoon, having been pelted with stones by a group of aggrieved-looking skinheads in Slottsparken, so shaken by the names she'd been called that Siv forbade her to repeat the words they'd used. 'You mustn't even *think* those words in your head,' she said, putting a plaster over the worst cuts. 'They're just ignorant,' she said, tight-lipped with anger. 'Promise me you won't waste five seconds of your precious time thinking about them. *Promise* me, Lindi.' Siv's tone was one she'd never heard before. There was a ferocious insistence in it, but there was also fear. She'd looked at her mother, too bewildered to do anything other than nod. How *could* she forget? She'd tried pressing her hands against her ears but their jeers had followed her home. In the weeks and months that followed, she'd tried her best to heed Siv's advice but it was harder to brush off the humiliating experience of *not* being asked out, *not* being asked to dance, *not* being sought after by the boys in school like all the Klaras and Torils and Heidis in whose company she'd grown up. She became aware, perhaps even before the others did, of an array of defensive little spikes that had suddenly appeared in her, altering the sunniness that was both a hallmark of her skin and her truer nature.

With that in mind, the Old Man's innocently murmured words, *you must come back to us*, took on an even greater significance. They comforted her against something she couldn't yet grasp.

And now here he was, come amongst them again. 'He's here? In there?' she pointed to the living room, a wide, excited smile breaking out across her face.

Siv's answering smile was just as wide. 'Didn't you notice his bodyguards outside?'

'No.' Lindi's eyes grew round as saucers. She rushed to the window and looked across the short front lawn. Sure enough, there was a Mercedes with blacked-out windows, two silver BMWs and two young men standing falsely nonchalant against the hoods. She turned back to Siv. 'Is he staying for supper?'

Siv shook her head. 'No, they're leaving again in an hour or so. They've been holed up in there since morning. Someone else is coming, though. D'you remember the Herzes? Uncle Klaus and Auntie Sibongile?'

Lindi frowned, trying to remember. 'No, I don't think so. When did I meet them?'

'Oh, years ago. No, you're right, you were probably too young to remember. Well, they're at a meeting at the Palace. Dad's gone to fetch them. They're here with their son, Ree. He's a couple of years younger than you. I thought perhaps you girls might like to take him out with you after supper? You could go somewhere around here. What do you think? We haven't seen Klaus and Sibongile in ages. They've been in Zambia for the last couple of years,' Siv added with a half-envious smile. It was no secret that she and Erik would have given their right hands to return to Africa. There was little hope of that, however. After their hurried exit from Windhoek, Erik had been declared *persona non grata* in South Africa *and* all the surrounding countries for his blatant support of their various independence

45

movements. He'd even been temporarily banned from the United States as a result. Not that Erik gave a damn. He would miss the steaks at the Four Seasons, he often quipped, but not much else. 'So what do you think? You have supper with us, then the four of you go off somewhere on your own?'

Lindi nodded. She quickly ran over the possibilities in her mind. Although they were still only seventeen, they often managed to get into the pubs near the university. There was Smugget, a bar just off Rosenkrantzgate, near the water's edge, or the Irish Pub on Ramsgatan.

She picked up her school bag and ran upstairs to change. She couldn't remember ever meeting Ree Herz but it wasn't every evening that exiled leaders and the teenage sons of revolutionaries came to visit, after all.

'Ah, that's them now.' Siv sprang up from the couch and hurried to open the front door just as Erik's key turned in the lock. Lindi was aware of a pleasant knot of tension in her stomach. They so rarely had visitors from what she secretly called 'home' who were her own age. She was curious to see what Ree Herz looked like. She'd washed her hair and pulled it back from her face, tying it in a ponytail at the nape of her neck. Toril liked it better when it hung around her face in an untidy cloud of tight, black curls but the curls only lasted for the first thirty minutes. Within an hour, especially in the damp autumn air, the cloud would have become an Afro, clinging stubbornly to her scalp. *Not* a good look, both she and Klara agreed. 'Why can't it *stay* curly?' 'Why does it always go frizzy like that?' everyone asked. Neither Lindi nor Siv – nor anyone else, for that matter – could answer. 'That's just the way it is,' Lindi always said quickly, enviously eyeing their long, blonde, poker-straight hair that would never frizz, no matter the weather.

She quickly tucked a few loose strands behind her ear and looked at her hair anxiously in the mirror above the mantelpiece. No, no sign of frizz, thank God. She stood up and hastily surveyed her outfit. She'd changed into a long denim skirt and boots and a peasant-style flowered blouse with a cardigan thrown over it that showed off her long, slim waist and that made the most of her rather small breasts, or at least Klara swore that it did.

She could hear her mother chatting excitedly in much the same way she, Klara and Toril did. She smiled to herself half-enviously. Her mother had the gift of spontaneous, generous joy, unlike Lindi, who had long since understood the special satis-faction of tormenting herself with what she thought were hard truths about life. 'Come in, come in,' she heard Siv cry and heard the answering cry from a woman, a deep, rich voice, heavily accented in the familiar-yet-unfamiliar African way. 'Oh, you look so *nice*, Siv, really! You know how to take care of yourself, isn't it, Klaus? She doesn't look a day older! Not a day! How do you do it, Siv, eh?' She didn't hear Siv's reply. The living-room door opened suddenly, and they were all there, crowded in the doorway, her father's head above theirs, his face split in two by his wide smile. Some dim memory of Klaus Herz's face came to her as she was beckoned and pulled forward. She looked up. A high, deeply wrinkled forehead, greying hair. She turned her cheek up to be kissed, felt the hard, excited pressure of hands at her elbows before being pressed fiercely into his jacket. 'Oh, *mein Gott*! Lindi! I can't believe it! So beautiful! And so grown up!' She was thrust away from him again as the wife took her turn, pressing her to her soft chest, hooking her neck against her own. 'Look at her!' Klaus Herz roared. 'She was just a baby, *nè*? Remember, Sibi? Just a baby! Ree, where are you? Come, come, you remember Lindi, don't you?'

Lindi stood embarrassed in the fierce grasp of their embrace, conscious of her mother and father looking proudly on. Erik moved to make room for someone else and at the same time, the family dog came bounding up the stairs, barking loudly, full of wild pleasure at the unaccustomed noise. In the confusion that followed, with Sibongile leaping out of the way in alarm and Siv bending down to restrain him, Lindi missed the moment when the young man stepped into the doorway and instead found herself looking straight up into the darkest, most intense pair of eyes she'd ever seen. A charged bolt of excitement ripped straight through her. *This* was Ree Herz?

All through dinner, through the interminable chatter of the adults, she watched him. His unexpected presence had rendered her virtually dumb. She couldn't help herself. Not only was he the most handsome, most passionately beautiful person she'd ever seen, every time their eyes met it seemed to her there was a message contained within them that was for her understanding alone. The fact that he was nearly three years her junior made not the slightest bit of difference. At fifteen he was already a man. The most gorgeous young man she'd ever seen. She'd had crushes on boys before, of course. The disappointment of not finding herself quite as sought after as her best friends aside, she'd enjoyed her fair share of kisses and the fumbling, slightly awkward petting that went on at friends' parties and occasionally in the bars into which they sometimes blagged their way. But *this* . . . she had no words for it. She was filled with a sense of her own lightness as if some more awkward, heavier sense of herself had been put to sleep for ever. Everything seemed suddenly brighter; the candles glowed intensely, the wine was rich and sweet, the colours around her were tinged with gold. The evening shimmered and sparkled, even more so with the promise of the night ahead. It had all been arranged in hasty, whispered phone calls. She and Ree would pull on overcoats and scarves and walk down to Smugget to meet Klara and Toril. In a sudden spirit of generosity that flowed through and out of her, she'd urged them both to wear something nice. 'He's lovely,' she said, giggling into the receiver. 'Just lovely. You'll see.'

As soon as she judged it decent to do so, she pushed back her chair from the table and announced they were going out. She'd hardly been able to eat anything all evening and if she had to listen to one more story of how, when, where and with whom her parents and his had last met, she'd scream. Ree seemed to understand her urgency. Again his eyes signalled a message she was sure no one else present could read. *Let's get out of here*. She was only too happy to lead the way.

They muffled themselves against the cold and opened the front door. 'Not too late, hmm, Ree?' Aunt Sibongile called out just before the door banged shut behind them. 'Lindi, you have school tomorrow, *nè*?'

Lindi could feel the flush of embarrassment prickle through the layers of clothing. 'I don't *have* to go to school tomorrow,' she said airily, leading the way. 'I've got a free period in the morning anyway.' She had no idea what their plans were for the following day but she'd have gladly skipped school for the rest of the *month* if it meant hanging out with Ree Herz.

Ree said nothing but just looked down at her with that half-amused, half-tolerant expression on his face that already, in the space of just a few hours, she'd come to recognise as his. At fifteen he was already *so* grown up, she thought to herself in wonderment as they walked together down Oscarsgate. He seemed *so* much older. So self-possessed and confident. She found it impossible to grasp that it had only been a few hours since she, Klara and Toril had walked up the street in the opposite direction, heading home. It seemed a whole lifetime away. She resisted the temptation to keep up a running commentary on the roads, buildings and places of interest around them. There was something both restful and exciting in his quietness that brought out a deep sense of longing in her. As crazy as it sounded after only a few hours, she was content just to march alongside him, their elbows touching occasionally and sending sparks of quivering electricity running straight through her. She saw people looking at them as they waited to cross the road; she'd never before experienced such a surge of pride in her colour and her difference, in the way that she stood out. They stood out, together. He was *so* good-looking, and *so* stylish in his thick black overcoat, dark blue sweater and jeans . . . somehow it made *her* seem that bit more special. His beauty turned her into an object of some powerful, unspecified desire – she could see it in the eyes of those who watched them. If *he* wanted to be with her, surely they did too. It was heady stuff.

9

Two hours later, it had all changed. She sat nursing her drink in the most painful, humiliating silence. The hurt was so intense she actually thought she might faint. Across from her, her long, blonde hair falling over her face in that coquettish manner that Lindi knew only too well, Toril sipped her drink, raising her eyes shyly to meet his, playing with a long, silky strand, touching his forearm every now and then, smiling up at him. It was enough to make you sick, she thought to herself angrily. Worst of all was his response. He seemed to love it. She watched him clink his glass gently against Toril's and bend his head to whisper something in her ear. Toril laughed prettily. Lindi felt sick to her stomach. The room began to swim suddenly. She'd drunk far too much, downing the rum and Cokes that Klara kept on bringing to the table as if there were no tomorrow. She'd lost count of how many; it was the only way to cope. She stood up, swaying slightly. She felt terribly dizzy. Neither Ree nor Toril even noticed. It was Klara who came to her aid.

'Hey,' she said softly, so that the other two wouldn't hear. 'Come on, let's get you to the bathroom.'

'I'm OK,' she tried to brush off Klara's concern. 'I'm OK.' She was aware it came out louder than she'd intended. Across the table she saw Ree look up briefly, then bend his head back towards Toril.

'No, you're not,' Klara said urgently. 'Here, let's go. You need some fresh air.'

'I *don't.*' She could hear her voice in her own ears. 'G-get *off* me!'

'Hey, take it easy.' Ree's voice suddenly broke across her protests. She swayed slightly, and grabbed hold of the table to steady herself. She could see him bend towards Toril. In detached, but nonetheless horrible, detail she saw his hand come down gently on Toril's shoulder, squeezing it slightly. He bent his head close to that curtain of thick, glossy blonde hair and she felt her stomach turn over. She really was going to be sick. Klara was still hovering uncertainly by her side and now the bar – and everyone in it – was spinning out of control. She felt his hands grabbing her arm, but not in a kind way, not the way he'd touched Toril. Shame and disappointment flooded her senses and she could feel herself beginning to cry. She felt her coat being thrown around her shoulders and she was marched firmly to the door. She heard Ree saying goodbye to her friends, shaking his head as they offered to come. Dizzy and nauseous as she was, she was relieved. She wasn't sure she could bear to see him and Toril walking home together with her and Klara lagging behind. With his hand firmly on her upper arm, he quickly frog-marched her out of the bar. The cold air hit her like a slap, making her head spin even faster. She started to mumble something as he helped her along the pavement.

Cars zoomed by, mirroring the zooming in and out of sounds and images in her head. They reached the traffic lights by the park. She lifted her head to look at him, to apologise but the next thing she knew, she was falling, falling slowly and something bitter and hot was rising in her throat. She felt her stomach convulse and turn over. She clapped a hand to her mouth but it was too late. She leaned forward and vomited all over his legs. A car horn honked at them and someone shouted something in Norwegian, making her retch even harder. Tears and snot were running down her face as he hauled her roughly upwards. 'What the hell's the matter with you?' he yelled, looking down at his vomit-splattered jeans in amazed disgust. 'How much did you *drink*, for Christ's sake?'

'I-I'm so . . . so-sorry,' she gasped, the words tumbling out of her mouth. She tried to stand upright but without his support, she couldn't. 'I . . . I didn't mean . . . I didn't want . . . oh, God, I think . . . I love you.' She began to cry in earnest.

He stared down at her, amazement turning to incredulity,

then he began to laugh. But it wasn't the pleasant, light-filled laughter of an evening spent with friends. It was scornful, even derisive. She wanted the ground to open up and swallow her whole. Snivelling, trying to stop the world spinning in front of her and desperate not to vomit again, she was half-tugged, half-dragged helplessly along behind him.

It was a short walk home but it felt like the longest journey of her life. Ree's hand was still gripping her upper arm when they pushed open the gate. She could see her mother's face against the window turn to alarm as she saw them come up the path.

The front door was open before they reached it; all four adults stood incredulously in the doorway. 'What the—?' her father said in stunned disbelief. She'd never, in all her seventeen years, ever come home in anything close to the state she was presently in.

'What did you do to her?' Sibongile hissed as they half-dragged her in.

'Me? Nothing!' She could hear Ree's indignant yelp of protest. 'Absolutely nothing. *I* can't help it if she can't hold her drink!'

'Lindi, what happened? What on earth—?' In Siv's voice there was astonishment mixed with alarm. 'Help me, darling.' She turned to Erik, lapsing into Norwegian. 'I shouldn't have let her go. I knew she wasn't herself. Let's get her into bed. Now!'

She allowed herself to be led away upstairs, waves of shame and embarrassment crashing over her as she heard Ree's indignant account of the evening, echoing down the corridor. In her room, Siv closed the door and shooed Erik out. She helped Lindi out of her vomit-splattered clothes and ran a bath for her. She sat on the edge of the tub whilst Lindi cried into the hot water, shaking her head sorrowfully as she stroked her daughter's curly hair. 'What happened, *vennen min?*' she asked gently. 'Did something happen?'

Lindi could only shake her head through her tears. She was

almost sober now, having thrown up most of the alcohol she'd drunk, alongside the peanuts and crisps. 'He . . . he doesn't like me,' she sobbed, the humiliating sight of Toril's head bent close to his coming at her again. 'He . . . he likes Toril. I c-could tell.'

'Oh, *min lille Liefde*,' Siv whispered, gathering Lindi's head and cradling it against her stomach. 'I'm so sorry. So very sorry. You mustn't take it to heart. He's only fifteen, darling. There'll be lots of other young men for you, I promise.'

'N-not like hi-him,' Lindi sobbed uncontrollably. 'I w-want someone who l-looks l-like *me*,' she wept. 'I th-thought he liked *me*! T-toril can h-have a-anyone sh-she wants . . . *any*one. But n-none of the b-boys here want *me*.'

Siv was quiet. She simply held her until the torrent of weeping had passed, then helped her out of the bath. She wrapped her tenderly in one of the thick, terry-towelling robes that hung behind the door and led her, still sniffling, down the corridor to her room. Erik had thoughtfully and discreetly put out a glass of water and some aspirin. She passed the glass to Lindi, lifting it to her trembling lips and made sure she swallowed both pills, and drained the glass. She pulled back the covers and helped her into bed. 'Shhh,' she said, bending down to kiss her as she switched off the bedside light. 'Just go to sleep, *vennen min*. Things will look different in the morning.' She stayed for a few minutes, holding Lindi's hand until her grip slackened, her breathing deepened and she finally fell asleep.

She woke just before dawn, when the first sounds of the birds in the garden filtered through her dreams. She sat bolt upright in bed, wondering why she was wearing a bathrobe. Then the events of the previous night came rushing back. Her cheeks burned fiery spots of shame as it all came flooding back. The dinner, the wonderful, inescapable feeling of joy and then the hammer blow of disappointment, Toril's hair. Everything co-alesced shamefully in the image of Toril's golden hair. She was ashamed of her pathetically hopeless behaviour, of course, but deeper than that, and more troubling, was a sense that she had come upon some insurmountable weakness or defect in herself. Last night, for the first time in her life, she'd seen her two closest friends as different from her in a way that was more profound and unsettling than she could have imagined. They were on one side and she on the other. She would *never* be like Toril, or Klara. She would never have Toril's golden skin or long flaxen hair, or Klara's cornflower-blue eyes. Their beauty was not hers and never would be and the realisation of it made her ashamed, not just of the fact that it had taken her so long to fathom it, but of what she saw as her childish, stupid attempts to pretend it didn't matter. Of *course* it mattered. She hated this new understanding that put her at a distance from them, knowing too that the distance worked both ways. They could now see *her*, properly. All her life she'd thought of herself as their equal, no less. Now, in the short space of an evening, she understood how foolish she'd been.

The birds were singing properly now, their voices rising into the coming light. The way back to normality was to forget it had ever happened, just as her mother said. She had to completely erase *everything*, pretend it had never been. It was the only way she would get through the day ahead. She couldn't risk letting them know how deeply she'd been wounded, or how much the evening had hurt. And she *certainly* couldn't let Ree Herz know. She would have to brush it off, pretend it had been a bad reaction to the drink. Let him think whatever he wanted. Stupid, fifteen-year-old kid.

She rolled over onto her stomach, grateful that her head had stopped pounding and that her mouth no longer tasted of her own sweat. As she buried her nose in the pillow, inhaling the familiar, faintly perfumed scent of her hair, she had a premonition of another, more troubling kind. Erasing *everything* about the previous evening would also mean erasing the wondrous, heart-stopping joy she'd felt. In a way she couldn't quite make sense of, she understood that there had been a deeper price than mere humiliation, however painful it had been, to pay.

10

CALLAN DE SAINT PHALLE
Worcestershire, England, 1977

The chauffeur guided the big car gently off the motorway and onto one of the smaller country roads, bypassing the town. In the back seat, a woman and a ten-year-old girl sat together in silence. The girl, dressed in an uncomfortable-looking school uniform, was dozing on and off. She woke to the change in engine pitch at exactly the moment the landscape around her shifted from the hard, grey monotony of the motorway to a dense, patchwork pattern of thick, furry oak trees and smooth green fields. She struggled upright, eyes blurry with tears. She'd been crying in her sleep. She stole a quick sideways glance at her mother, sitting stiffly upright beside her, all her attention claimed by the thick stack of papers and reports balanced on her knee. A lone tear rolled down the surface of the girl's cheek and trickled wetly into her starched white collar.

'You must put on your cap, Callan,' her mother murmured without turning her head. 'We're nearly there.'

Callan didn't answer straight away. She'd been silent since they left London almost two hours earlier. In a sense of power she was only dimly aware she had, she stared down at her knees, richly sullen. Her mother's voice rang in her ears. *You muuust put on your cap.* Every now and then the faint trace of some other accent other than her mother's German-accented English could be heard. But she made no move to put her cap on and the silence between them deepened. She could almost feel her mother's mouth tighten in disapproval, even without daring to look. If there was one thing her mother couldn't stand, it was insolence. Talking back. Mutiny. All of which Callan was beginning to display in abundance, or so she said. 'It's all *your* fault,' Callan had said to her once, years earlier. 'It's my name. You shouldn't have chosen it.' Anneliese had been so surprised she'd burst out laughing. A rare event. Mother and daughter had looked at each other warily, Anneliese for once at a loss for words. Callan hated her name. It meant 'chatterbox' in old German. Apparently. Uncle Bruno had told her that once when she was very young. Bärbel, her middle name, was no better and as for her surname, Zander *de* Saint Phalle? Jesus. Callan Bärbel Zander de Saint Phalle. She felt sick with dread. At the boarding school to which they were now on their way, her new, terribly *English* schoolmates would display no mercy. Bärbel would become 'dumbbell', Zander would become 'wanker'. She dreaded to think what they'd make of the rest of it. She could feel her breakfast swirling around in her stomach and for one awful, trembling moment, she thought she might actually be sick. It was only the thought of the approbation that she'd receive if she vomited over her mother's cashmere coat that stopped her.

'Ooh! Mrs de Saint Phalle! How lovely to see you! Did you have a good journey up?' A mannish-looking woman with impressively square shoulders encased in tweed was standing in front of the grand, porticoed entrance. She was clearly excited to see them. 'Jolly good, jolly good!' she rushed on, without waiting for an answer. 'Oh, it's *so* nice to finally meet you! What a pleasure!' Callan could feel her mother recoil.

'*Miss* de Saint Phalle,' she corrected the woman in that calm, measured way of hers that sent sycophants packing. *Sycophants*. It was one of Callan's latest new words – in English, that was. She had a long list of favourite words in French, including *biche*, which was all the rage at the *École Française* in Kensington where she'd been a pupil for the past seven years. *Salût, ma biche.* They all loved the sound of it. It was dangerously close to 'bitch'. At the thought of her old school, her stomach tightened again and she actually had to put up a hand to her mouth. She concentrated on the back of her mother's legs as they followed Miss Molloy into the office of the school-that-looked-like-a-fortress. As she trailed behind, she caught the faint whiff of her mother's perfume on the back of her throat and her eyes suddenly filled with tears.

'Well, I'll see you at half-term,' her mother said briskly, after they'd been shown around the school and its enormous grounds. She'd never felt so utterly lost and alone in her life. There was an awkward pause as they looked at each other warily, then Anneliese bent down, hugged Callan briefly and straightened up immediately. Callan only just managed to resist the temptation to grab hold of her mother and pull her close again. A hug from Anneliese was a rare thing indeed. It wasn't that she didn't want to hug *her*, she just wasn't big on hugging full stop, Callan had to remind herself as she watched her mother get into the car. Or kissing, or cuddling or any of the other things that her friends' mothers did. She'd always looked on enviously when Céline's mother stroked Céline's hair, or Dominique's mother put her arm round her waist. Anneliese would *never* give in to those sorts of feelings. The chauffeur slid into his own seat and started the engine. The car swung silently away from the entrance towards the gates. Anneliese didn't look back. The last glimpse Callan had of her was of her profile, bent back down towards her reports.

'Come along then, my dear,' Miss Molloy said, placing a hand firmly on Callan's shoulder. 'Time to get you settled in.' Miss Molloy's voice was bright and authoritative, the sort adults use when talking to upset children. She was marched back through the arched doorway and down one depressingly dark corridor after another until they stopped outside a closed door. Miss Malloy pushed it open and they both stepped inside.

'Ah, you must be Callan.' An equally square-shouldered, large-bosomed woman turned from the window as they entered. 'Welcome to Mortimer's. I'm Miss Patchett, second-form housemistress. I'll be looking after you this year. Did you have a good journey up, my dear?'

Callan nodded, not trusting herself to speak. She'd sooner have *died* than let either woman know just how wobbly she felt and how much she was dreading the days and weeks ahead. 'Y-yes,' she mumbled, looking stonily at the ground.

'Jolly good. Well, I'll take her from here, Miss Molloy. I'm putting her in with Clarinda Palmer and Abigail Derwent-Hughes in Hyacinth. They'll look after her splendidly.'

Clarinda. Abigail. Callan's heart sank. She thought of her best friends in London – Céline, Amélie and Dominique – and felt lonelier than ever. She followed Miss Patchett down the corridor in silence, their heels echoing loudly against the cold stone walls.

11

TARA CONNOLLY
Kitwe, Zambia, 1977

Pale blue skies, delicate as eggshells, whitewashed almost to the point of nothingness at the edge of the horizon but a deep, inky cobalt directly overhead. Tara leaned out of the window, turning her face up, eyes closed, feeling the last of the heat on her cheeks. The great, wide African sky. The carefully composed seventeen year old was on her way to Lusaka Airport. In the front seats, their heads turning from one to the other, her parents continued their low murmuring. The journey was almost over. In a few hours' time, the last she would see of Africa would be the great, blazing bushfires as British Caledonian made its way north across the hot, dreamy landscapes of the continent until they emerged, blinking, into the cold, watery dawn of England. She looked down at her bare legs. The following morning they'd be encased in brown wool, as they always were at school. Today was the last day of many things – sunlight, bare legs, bare feet . . . the freedoms that being at home brought, those same freedoms that school took away.

'Looking forward to going back?' Her mother turned her head to look at her, smiling fondly.

Tara nodded. 'Mmm. Can't wait.' They both knew it was a lie. Necessary, perhaps, but a lie nonetheless. The sort of lie you told when you wanted to protect someone, shield them from hurt. She'd been doing it for over ten years, every holiday, year in, year out. Leaving was a way of life for people like them. Mike Connolly, Tara's father, was the Compound Manager at Kitwe Consolidated Mines, one of the largest mines on the Copper Belt, some two hundred miles north of Lusaka, the capital. Kitwe was a medium-sized mining town when Mike arrived in 1959 with Annabel, his wife of six months. Now, almost twenty years later, it was Zambia's second-largest city but it had always retained something of its provincial, outpost ways. It was one of those places that had sprung up simply because something lay beneath the surface of the earth that men would go to extra-ordinary lengths to extract. Copper was its *raison d'être* and copper was the reason Mike and Annabel Connolly had left England in order to fashion a new life for themselves six thou-sand miles from home. Despite only visiting sporadically, they still referred to England as home, as though they'd be returning one day, as though Africa were a mere interlude in a life that took place mostly back there, back 'home'. But Kitwe was the only home Tara had ever known. Her world for the first eight years had been perfectly contained by the low hills to the north of the town, the different townships and suburbs, Kawama, Nkana, Mindolo, Garneton, those areas where she could and couldn't go. The boxy, corrugated shape of the mine itself and the yellowed, sandy mine dumps surrounding it formed a natural protective barrier to the east and west.

Everyone she knew was held, precariously balanced, within the world of the mine, the club and the school that she and every other child whose father worked on the mine attended, where at midday, the sweat dripped from your fingers and ran down the length of your pencil and it was too hot to think. But the men who chipped away at the earth down there underneath it and whom she saw as they walked back and forth from the township where they lived – *those* men sent their children to another school, across the dusty fields on the other side of the mine where girls like Tara were not supposed to go. Chipo, who was their houseboy (though he was hardly a 'boy' – he was probably older than Mike), he sent *his* children to that other school. Tara and her friends went from the tiny kindergarten to the small privately run primary school and then, at the age of eight or nine (ten, if you were lucky) you were sent, along with the same girls and boys you'd been with all your life, overseas. Overseas. Home.

It was a concept that puzzled her enormously. As far as she could work out, the only home her parents had was Kitwe. There was nothing for them back in England. There were no grandparents, no aunts and uncles, no siblings, no house, nothing. Mike was from Doncaster, a place Tara had only ever seen on a map. He was from a large Catholic Irish family who'd refused to have anything to do with him when he married Annabel O'Riley, a young Protestant girl from Belfast. Annabel was an only child; cut adrift from their respective families, they'd left England on a cold, rainy day in November and docked in Mozambique three weeks later. There, in the sweltering heat, they'd reinvented themselves. Mike worked his way up the ladder, becoming the Mine Compound Manager at the age of forty-four, a position he'd never have attained 'back home'. The Connollys owed everything they had to the mine and the lifestyle it afforded them – the pleasant little bungalow, the servants, afternoons at the clubhouse and the big bag of golf clubs that stayed in the boot of the car. Tara's schooling was paid for by Consolidated Mines and when she was eight, alongside Fiona Garson, her best friend, and Gwendoline Owens, who most certainly wasn't, she was sent overseas to England to boarding school, also paid for by the mine. So why did they persist in calling England 'home'? 'Because it is,' was all her mother would say, firmly, when pressed. 'This isn't home. How can it be?' Tara had no idea how to respond. Of course it was home. She belonged there, just as Chipo did. As everyone around them did. It took her a few years to work out that not everyone felt the same way.

'Head girl, now.' Mike spoke up suddenly. He looked into the rear-view mirror for a second and their eyes met and held. There was such pride in his face that Tara was forced to look away. It was no secret that she'd made her parents prouder of her than any parent had the right to be. She'd overheard them say it on more than one occasion to their friends and colleagues on the mine and at the club and she knew it to be true. Both Annabel and Mike saw in her what no one had ever seen in either of them: a future that didn't require her to go halfway round the world to find or invent it. They were anxious for Tara to have everything that had been denied them: a good education, private, at that, *and* with all the extras that came with it – riding lessons, piano lessons, swimming lessons, even gymnastics and ballet until the teacher gently suggested lacrosse. Tara was more the athletic, not graceful, type, she said, letting them down gently. Tara grinned when her mother broke the news. She preferred kicking a ball with her feet to forcing them *en pointe*. They were not deterred. It was her mother's single-handed ambition to turn her daughter into something she would have liked to be – a well-educated, well-brought up *nice* girl from the Home Counties with a wardrobe, accent and ambitions to match.

Tara hadn't the heart to tell them they were wasting their time. Kitwe, Zambia was home. It was the only place she felt at home; the landscape was the only one she felt she belonged to, the sights, smells, sounds the only ones she truly felt she understood. Despite the ten years she'd spent at boarding school in England, it would always remain foreign. In Kitwe she was firmly at the centre of her own life. As a young child, cycling home alone in the hot afternoon from school, her satchel hanging off the handlebars and her tongue sticking wetly out from between parted lips as she panted with the effort, she would meet at least half a dozen people along the short route who knew her almost as well as she knew herself – a group of young mothers coming back from the club, hair still wet and in tendrils from their afternoon swim; Mary, the neighbour's maid who'd looked after Tara on Sundays, when their own maid, Charity, was off; the gardener from the house on the corner; someone's younger brother, calling out plaintively from behind a hedge, 'Ta-ra . . . where you *go*-ing?', the sound echoing hollowly along the empty street behind her. *That* was home. Those were the people she knew and loved. England was the opposite. She knew no one. No one knew or cared about her. Her first few days were spent in a bewildering, unhappy blur of tears and the constant nagging doubt that no matter how hard she tried, she would never quite be good enough, that she was lacking in some subtle but important way. Whatever she'd been taught at school back in Kitwe was clearly of no use or importance to her here. Her clothes were wrong, her manners atrocious, her accent impenetrable. Elocution took care of the last; it was up to her to attend to the rest.

It took her a few months to work out that the only way to survive would be to master the game and then beat everyone else at it. If she didn't or couldn't do that, she'd sink quicker than the stones that she and Chipo used to chuck into the disused well at the back of the house to see if there were snakes living in it. Fast, in other words. Well, she wasn't about to let *that* happen. She did what she had to. At the age of eight, instinctively and before she even knew how to articulate what was happening to her, she began the slow and painful process of splitting herself in two – English Tara and Kitwe Tara, to be trotted out as appropriate. Aside from the fact that they both looked the same, there was precious little else between them that was shared. They spoke differently, their accents adapting themselves smoothly to whatever situation they were in: clothes, hair, even their expressions. As the years went by, English Tara became all those things that Kitwe Tara wasn't – bookish, sober, responsible, calm. Kitwe Tara, during the long summer holidays which she lived for throughout the year, was sporty and funny and a brilliant mimic. She shimmied up trees, scratched her knees, got into fights with the local boys and usually won. If anyone who knew her at Mortimer's had seen her, racing back from the pool on her bicycle, chasing a football around a dusty patch of grass with Jeremiah, Chipo's eldest son, or screaming at the television during a rugby match with friends, they simply wouldn't have believed it. Tara Connolly? Shouting at a television to 'Come *on!* Come *on!*'? Impossible. Tara Connolly? Head girl and Oxbridge candidate? *No, you've got the wrong girl, surely?*

They hadn't. But only Tara knew that. As far as everyone else was concerned, including her beloved parents, Tara Connolly was a well-adjusted, confident, capable young woman on the cusp of doing great things. The outsider had become the consummate insider, English to the core. That, and the fact that she'd grown up in the way her mother understood and valued – slim, pretty, with long auburn tresses and green lash-fringed eyes – was a constant source of joy and pleasure to her parents who'd only ever wanted their daughter to have, and be, the best.

'Here we are, then,' Mike announced, swinging the car into the parking lot at the airport, his voice taking on the false chumminess that Tara associated with the end of summer. 'Nice and early.'

It took Tara a few seconds to compose her face and her emotions. The airport was always the most painful moment of separation. As soon as she'd hugged them goodbye and turned to troop across the linoleum floor towards the departure gate, all traces of the laughing, bubbly Tara who'd arrived eight weeks earlier would be gone. When she climbed the rickety metal steps to the aircraft, the face she presented to the smiling flight attendants would be one her parents would not recognise. Careful, a touch wary but exquisitely composed. The stewardesses would sometimes comment to each other as she passed down the aisle holding her small school satchel like a shield, 'Beautiful, isn't she? *Very* polished. Obviously wealthy, don't you think?'

'Well, that's class for you,' the other might note, nodding sagely. 'Money's one thing. Class is something else.'

Indeed. Little did they – or anyone else – know. Tara, sometimes overhearing the whispered comments, received them as if they were talking about someone else. In many ways, they were.

12

TARA/CALLAN
Worcestershire, England, 1977

The door to the library burst open and shut again with a loud bang. Tara looked up in surprise. No one ever banged the library door – ever. She frowned. It was *that* girl – the new girl with the ridiculous name in the fourth form who'd broken the school record for detentions – *and* she'd only been at the school a month! She stood in front of Tara with a mutinous look on her face, simply *inviting* approbation. Behind her Tara could hear the two girls she'd been supervising start whispering excitedly to each other. She turned round and swiftly silenced them with one of her famous 'looks'. They stopped as quickly as they'd begun. She turned back to the girl standing in front of her who was . . . she frowned. No, she couldn't be? Yes, she *was*! She was actually chewing gum! She blinked slowly, trying to conceal both her irritation and her astonishment. She'd been head girl for just over a month but it was already known throughout the school that Tara Connolly wasn't the sort of girl to be trifled with. She had the kind of face that could melt an iceberg, or so she'd heard someone say. One look from her and an unruly line fell miraculously and silently into shape. Her detention sessions were famous for being utterly silent. No talking, no whispering, no passing of notes, certainly no banging of doors and certainly no standing in front of her, chewing gum! The girl's arms were folded insolently across her chest and her dark eyes flashed out a warning that was only too clear – *stay the hell out of my way.* She was *way* out of line. To her great surprise, Tara felt the corners of her mouth tug suddenly upwards. She immediately stifled the urge to smile.

'And you are?' She spoke quietly, her voice authoritative but measured. Only one way to meet defiance like that – calmly.

The girl's head lifted ever so slightly. There was a moment's hesitation during which they stared at each other unflinchingly. 'Callan.' Her voice was tight, but her stance had shifted almost imperceptibly. Tara could see the breath rising and falling in her chest. Despite her outward defiance, she was scared. Somewhere, deep inside her belly, Tara felt the answering tug of sympathy. She too had been scared. She recognised the fear.

'Callan what?'

'Callan Zander de Saint Phalle.'

There was a muffled snigger behind Tara. She turned around and stared at the offender. 'I assume you find it funny because you can't pronounce it, Gillian Pinkerton?' she said icily. Gillian Pinkerton's smile faded abruptly and she bent her head, red-faced, back towards her detention book. Tara turned back to Callan. 'Well, take a seat over there by the window. Where I can see you. And be quiet about it. Where's your detention note?'

Callan handed it over silently.

Tara read it and raised one eyebrow. 'From Mr Collins?' she murmured. 'Wonder what on earth you could've done to upset *him*. He's practically deaf. Right. Over there where I can see you.'

The girl's eyes flickered upwards; she looked at Tara warily, as if trying to decide whether the comment was intended as a rebuke or a shared joke. They looked at each other again for a second, each sizing the other up. Tara's lips twitched. There was something about Callan Zander de Saint Phalle that she couldn't quite put her finger on – defiant, yes. Bold as brass, too. But there was something more. The moment passed; the younger girl dropped her gaze and turned around. Tara watched her walk over to the window and sit down, kicking the chair out from under the table noisily, but not before flashing Tara a quick, culpable glance. There was defiance in the gesture but there was also a wary kind of hope. She was desperate to be noticed. Tara's wrath was infinitely preferable to the dismissal with which her classmates probably treated her. Her mouth opened for a moment in unease and in that second, their glances met and held again. She looked at Tara out of the depths of a lonely, dark childhood, her own, and in Tara's answering gaze found something that spoke to her there. Tara's lips twitched again. She couldn't have said why but there was something about the small, tightly held younger girl that she liked. She clamped her lips firmly shut. She was the head girl, after all. Wouldn't do to be seen smiling at what was rapidly turning out to be the naughtiest girl in the school.

Inside, Callan was quaking, though she'd sooner have *died* than let the head girl see it. She'd been rude to Mr Collins, her geography teacher, for the second time that week and he'd clearly had enough. It was her sixth detention in less than a month and, if Miss Molloy was to be believed, one more and she'd be sent home. What none of them seemed to realise was that that was her *goal*. She *wanted* to go home. She didn't care what they all thought of her. *Callan, you are* quite *the naughtiest little girl we've ever had here!* She didn't *care* if she were sent home in disgrace. All she wanted was to be free of Mortimer's, of the rules she had no intention of keeping, the girls she had no intention of befriending – not that they cared. They'd made it clear to her from day one. She was the outsider, the girl-with-the-impossible-name; the girl-whose-mother-was-famous; the girl-with-a-trunk-full-of-clothes; the girl . . . the girl . . . *the girl. My name's Callan, not 'the girl'!* she longed to scream at them – and sometimes did. Although she'd learned pretty quickly that screaming at them would get her precisely nowhere. They just laughed at her.

That first night, after her mother left and Hatchett-Face Patchett (as she'd learned to call her – *and* to her face, once,

66

which had earned her the first of her six detentions) frog-marched her up to Hyacinth Dormitory which was to be her home alongside twelve other girls, *and* she'd stupidly unpacked her trunk in front of the others, she'd cried herself to sleep. Her skin practically crawled when she thought about how stupid she'd been. She'd flipped open the lid of the trunk whilst the other girls sat on their beds, cupping their chins in their hands, watching her. At the first rustle of tissue paper, she ought to have realised. *Put your clothes away when there's no one watching.* Someone gasped as she peeled back the first layer of cream A*d*SP-embossed paper and picked up a navy blue cashmere jumper. And then a grey one. And then a black one. Caroline, one of her mother's many assistants, had done the shopping. And the packing. Layer upon layer of tissue paper, pile upon pile of soft sweaters, cardigans, pleated skirts, woollen trousers . . . they'd been given a list but Caroline (and Anneliese presumably) had seen fit to interpret it in their own way, of course. It was only the first of many mistakes but a major one. She was seen as a show-off, lording her clothes over everyone else who had to obey the rules. By the time she'd finally shut the last drawer on her exquisite clothes, she'd also shut the door on the possibility of making any friends or allies amongst the goggle-eyed girls see-thing with envy sitting watching her.

For over a month now, she'd given herself up to the certainty that she would never find anyone remotely like her at this cold, awful place to which she'd been banished; she would never again giggle hotly over a secret the way she, Dominique and Céline did; there would be no whispered conversations in bed at night, the way the three of them did when they slept over at each other's homes. She was completely baffled by the way the girls at Mortimer's had turned their faces and backs against her, without her ever having uttered a word. It was as if they'd made up their minds to dislike her, no matter what she said or did . . . and they did. They appeared to hate her without even knowing her. It hurt her more than she was prepared to admit, even to herself. Her only defence, she reasoned with herself, alone in her bed at night, crying herself silently to sleep, was her defiance and her disdain. The more they taunted her, the less she appeared to care. She walked to and from the dining room alone; she walked to lessons alone and she walked up the long path from the games pitches alone. She held herself very still at all times but most especially when they were watching and the only time she gave in to the anger and frustration that had slowly but surely built up inside her was when she spoke back to her teachers – and earned herself a detention in the process.

But today was different. She walked over to the desk by the window as the head girl directed, aware of an unfamiliar pressure in her chest. There was something in the older girl's eyes – a look, a quick, fleeting glance of something that was almost a shared complicity, as if she understood what Callan was thinking. Her voice washed over her again. *Wonder what on earth you could've done to upset him? He's practically deaf.* It wasn't what she'd been expecting her to say. She couldn't remember the head girl's name. Tammy? Tabitha? No, Tara. That was it. Tara Connolly. She'd overheard someone say she was frightfully clever. She *looked* clever. Not like a swot, like Gemma Gibson, but more like . . . she pondered the similarity for a moment. She looked a bit like Anneliese. Not so much her features, but her expression. Anneliese always looked preoccupied, as though she were focusing on something or someone who wasn't in the room. Tara Connolly had the same look. She spoke slowly and carefully, like Anneliese. As if she'd thought about every word before it came out of her mouth. Not like Callan, whose words often preceded any rational thought. She was pretty, too. Callan rather liked the combination of reddish hair, green eyes and pale, pale skin – she was Callan's polar opposite. Just as Anneliese was.

She blushed suddenly, aware that she was staring at Tara and that the two other girls in the room were watching her. Her cheeks felt hot and she let her dark hair fall across her face. A memory suddenly floated up from the depths of her consciousness. Once, so long ago she could scarcely remember

68

where it had happened, Anneliese had come up to her in the middle of the day and kissed her, as if in recognition of something that had happened between them or to her. She'd looked up expectantly, shocked by it – she remembered that – but Anneliese said nothing and moved away. She'd put her hand up to the place Anneliese's lips had touched her brow and felt it glowing for a long time afterward, just as she felt the shy warmth of Tara Connolly's gaze. Now, as then, she put a hand up to her cheek, the tips of her fingers brushing lightly over her burning skin.

PART THREE

13

CALLAN DE SAINT PHALLE
TWENTY YEARS LATER
Manhattan, New York, 1997

'Honey . . . will you *pick up* the phone? Line five . . . it's your mom. It's the *third* time she's called today and I'm runnin' outta excuses!'

Callan covered the mouthpiece with her hand and motioned frantically to her assistant. 'I'll call her back,' she mouthed.

Deanna, her gum-snapping, too-busy-to-take-your-crap, wisecracking PA shook her head firmly. 'No way, José. Pick *up*. I'm tired of hearing her voice. I can't understand her accent. Where the hell's she *from*, anyway?'

Callan shook her head in exasperation. 'I'd better go,' she said to the person on the other line. 'I'll call you right back.' She cut the line and stared at the blinking red light for a second. She could see Deanna glowering at her through the window that separated them. She drew in a deep breath and picked up the call. 'Hi, Maman. Sorry, it's just been a really busy day.'

'And yesterday? And the day before that?' Anneliese's voice was crisp and sharp. 'Anyhow, I didn't call to argue with you. I want you to come back.'

'Come back? Come back where?'

'Back to London, of course. As soon as possible. I can't stand it that you're so far away.'

Callan almost dropped the phone. *Can't stand it?* Since when could Anneliese not stand *anything*, never mind the fact that her only daughter lived six thousand kilometres away? 'Maman?'

she asked, not bothering to hide the incredulity in her voice. 'Are you all right?'

'Of course I'm all right. I'm just saying – it's enough. You've been away for nearly seven years. It's enough. It's time to come home. It'll be Christmas in a couple of weeks.'

'Maman, I'm *at* home. I live here. *This* is my home.'

'Callan, you're being tiresome. There are some things I'd like to discuss with you and I need you to be here.'

Callan was speechless. It was so bloody typical of Anneliese! Seven years ago when Callan, her heart in her mouth, announced her decision to take a job in New York, Anneliese's only visible reaction had been the tightening of her mouth and a faintly beating pulse at her temple. She'd looked at her in that maddeningly calm way of hers, up/down, once/twice, then shrugged. 'New York? I see.'

And that, pretty much, was it, the sum total of the discussion. Did she leave with Anneliese's blessing or her dismay? Callan never found out. Much to her irritation, Anneliese had gone ahead and set up things ahead of Callan's arrival – a bank account, an apartment (which Callan had stayed in for a total of three weeks before moving out and finding something she liked); a monthly allowance (which Callan tried not to touch) and recommendations and contacts at half a dozen investment firms, all of which Callan declined to use. Armed with her degree from Cambridge and her own list of people to see, she'd tried to do things her way. There was simply no way to even bring the subject up. *Maman, I want to do this on my own.* Anneliese would have just looked at her, declined to comment and, like every other time there'd been even a *hint* of disagreement, Callan would have been left to swallow whatever resentment or irritation she felt and deal with it in her own way. *That* was Anneliese's way. No arguments, no discussions, no outbursts . . . nothing. Calm disapproval when things didn't go exactly the way she planned, a faint smile when they did. Tara once said it was the hallmark of very successful people. They very quickly figured out where their energies would be best spent and rarely deviated from The Plan. Callan wasn't so sure. Yes, Anneliese was successful – spectacularly so – and yes, aside from Uncle Bruno, Anneliese's best (and only) friend and business partner, she'd done it all on her own, no help from anyone, *thank you very much*, and yes, she'd *definitely* figured out that her energy and passion were best spent in the design studios that she'd built next door to the house she and Callan shared in St John's Wood . . . but aside from all of that, there was something else in Anneliese that just couldn't be got at, no matter how hard you tried. She was an enigma to everyone, but most especially to her own daughter. And yet, for all her sternness and self-control, Anneliese was capable of acts of such kindness that it left you almost breathless with admiration and longing. Just look at what she'd done for Tara – who else would have come forward in the way Anneliese had, as soon as the news reached her?

'So, when are you coming?' Anneliese's voice broke into her thoughts.

Callan sighed. She knew her mother well enough to know there was little point arguing – for now, at any rate. If Anneliese thought she was simply going to give up her life in New York and trot meekly back to London, she had another think coming. But arguing with her over the phone wouldn't work. And in spite of her irritation, there was something in Anneliese's voice that niggled at her. What was it? Buried underneath the usual crispness there was something else . . . but what? 'All right,' she said, conceding quicker than she'd have liked. 'Fine. I'll come back next weekend. But just for the weekend. I'm not staying for Christmas.'

'I'll have Justine send you a ticket.' Anneliese's voice was calm.

'Thanks.' Callan hesitated. 'Maman,' she asked suddenly. 'Is . . . are you . . . is everything all right?'

There was a faint hesitation before she replied that sent a quick tremor of fear running through Callan. 'Of course I'm all right,' Anneliese said abruptly. And then the line went dead. She'd hung up. Callan remained at her desk for a few minutes, staring at the phone. Then she got up, avoiding Deanna's piercing, questioning gaze and walked quickly down the corridor to the toilets. The tears that were lodged in her throat were already flowing before she shut the door. She sat down on the edge of the toilet and put her face in her hands. She knew what was coming next. A weekend? Who was she kidding? Anneliese wanted her back and if there was one thing in this world she was certain of, it was that Anneliese always got what she wanted. Damn Anneliese. Damn her!

14

The wig was short and blonde, curling inwards at her nape with a short, straight fringe. She looked at herself in the mirror and made the last few, final adjustments. A pin here to secure it more firmly, a last dab of mascara and a quick squirt of perfume. She turned her head carefully one way, then another. The image staring back at her looked nothing like her, though wasn't that the point? How long had it been since she'd last visited the club? A year, maybe even longer? It was hard to believe. There was a time when she'd been there almost every weekend.

She picked up her keys, switched off the lights and locked the door behind her. She walked quickly to the lift, hoping she wouldn't bump into any of her neighbours. She shut the heavy metal grille doors behind her. The lift creaked and groaned as it dropped the six floors, landing with its customary thump. Tucking her hair into her collar, she pushed open the industrial-sized front door and stepped out into the biting wind. It was December in Manhattan – two weeks before Christmas and the streets were already full of late evening shoppers. She headed west on W 13th towards Hudson, then cut across Hudson to W 14th. In the seven years that she'd lived here, the neighbourhood had changed, almost beyond recognition. Where there had once been butchers and the odd abattoir, Korean all-night corner stores and 7/11s, there were now art galleries galore, trendy little coffee shops and a plethora of boutiques. Diane von Furstenberg had recently opened on the corner and Hugo Boss was already across the road. Anneliese had turned her nose up at the district Callan had chosen to live in, but if those other designers were anything to go by, they'd obviously seen something Anneliese hadn't. Not that Anneliese would care. She wasn't the sort that followed the herd or even paid it any attention. She charted her own course, listened to her own counsel and instincts (and, occasionally, Bruno's) and rarely, if ever, took advice. It was a formula that appeared to work; in the thirty-odd years A*d*SP had been in business, Callan couldn't remember a single year when they *hadn't* made a profit. Some years were better than others, of course, but Anneliese had somehow weathered the storms that had sunk other, even bigger and more prestigious, houses *and* emerged relatively unscathed.

She walked quickly, hands thrust deep into the pockets of her black coat. It was long, reaching almost to the ground, with a row of covered buttons that ran up the entire length. Her high-heeled boots tapped out a staccato rhythm on the uneven surface of the street – tip/tap; tip/tap. She looked up at the first-floor windows along W 14th. Abe & Arthur's, DDC Lab, Boca, La Perla . . . and there it was. No 655, sandwiched in between La Perla and the offices of GRM, whatever they were. She stopped for a second, looking up at the building. Yes, it had been more than a year since she'd last visited 655 W 14th Street but the façade looked exactly the same, the discreet blue light in the corner of the first-floor window a sign to those in the know. As she was.

She fished her mobile out of her pocket and quickly flicked through her contacts. *Giovanna, Gordon, Graeme. Graeme Schultz.* She dialled the number, her heart beginning to thump in anticipation.

'Graeme? It's me, Callan.'

'Callan? Callan, *baby*! Wow . . . it's been an *age*. How are you?' Graeme's voice was just as she remembered it. Smooth, buttery, warm. He sounded delighted to hear from her. As he should be. She'd been one of his most frequent visitors. She couldn't even bring herself to think about how much money she'd spent in his establishment.

'I'm . . . I'm fine. I was just wondering . . . are you open tonight?'

'Honey, we're open *every* night. Where are you?'

'Downstairs. In front.'

'Come on up, baby. You know the drill.'

Nothing's changed. Rooms are the same; there's the red room, with the thick velvet drapes; the blue room with the gigantic mirrored light in the centre; the dark candlelit passageways that seem to go on for ever. Same clusters of people, some masked, some not . . . semi-naked girls with trays of drinks held aloft, smooth, gleaming skin; men in suits with ties yanked impatiently aside, smoking cigars, cigarettes, joints . . . the air thick with the acrid smell of marijuana and nicotine, all of it mingling with the cloying jasmine-scented candles and the unmistakable scent of sweat. All the same. It's all exactly the same. Nothing's changed. I'm still the same.

'Callan.' Graeme came up to her almost as soon as she walked into the hallway. He took her by the shoulders, holding her a little away from him, appraising her. 'Where've you *been*?' he asked, half-petulantly, his beautiful mouth turning downwards in a pout. 'We haven't seen you in, like, *years*.'

'Not true,' Callan laughed, her nervousness slowly beginning to dissipate. It was all flooding back. The warmth, the friends, the openness. At the club, no one cared who she was, how she made her money, whether she was married, straight or gay. It was its own special island. At the club she was both somebody and nobody. It was what had kept her coming back, at first. 'I was here last Christmas, remember?'

He gave a theatrical wave of the hand. 'Like I said, *years*. How *are* you, baby?'

'I'm fine.'

'You look *great*, by the way. I *love* the hair. Come, I want you to meet some people. *New* people. You'll love them. You still into . . . ?' He cocked an eyebrow at her. *Anything. Everything*.

Callan nodded quickly. 'Uh, yeah. Sure. Whatever you've got.'

'Good girl. Let's get you started. Gimme your coat.' He laid it carefully across one arm and snapped his fingers. 'Suzy! Something for our guest!' A young girl with long auburn hair appeared at her side, smiling widely and holding up a tray on which four perfectly straight white lines were neatly laid out, alongside a colourful assortment of pills and several flutes of champagne. Callan hesitated for a split second, then picked out her selection – a white pill, a yellow pill and a glass of champagne. She tilted her head, threw back the pills and swallowed. She left the cocaine for someone else. It had never been her drug of choice. Too addictive by half. It would take a few minutes for the drugs to hit and when they did, she would not be the same. The tablets changed everything, including her. She could feel the slow, charged build-up of excitement and anticipation burning its way up through her body – legs, thighs, groin, stomach, breasts, right up into her neck and her face, spreading across her skin like a flush, a deep stain. She could feel the music coming from one of the rooms, and then the heat. She put out a hand; on either side of her Graeme and the red-head grabbed hold of her and pulled her forwards into the crowd.

It's the touching that I like. The touch and feel of another's hands on my skin. The slip, stop, slip, slide. Skin against skin. The caresses, someone stroking my hair, my cheek. That's what I come for. Not the other stuff. Anyone can have the other stuff, and for free, too. You don't have to come to a place like this, leave your credit card at the door, be introduced by friends of friends of friends . . . put on a wig or a mask or change your name. Not that I changed mine. I couldn't. You see, everyone comes here to be someone else. I don't. I come here to be more like me, the person I think I am. Most of all, I come here to get away from her.

79

15

ANNELIESE ZANDER DE SAINT PHALLE
Croombe d'Abitot, England, February 1998

The gardens sloped away from the house in a sweep of dark, manicured green. From the large windows of the formal living room which was also her boardroom, Anneliese could see the long line of oaks, now bare, that fringed the lawns. In summer, the meadows beyond were hidden; now, with the trees stripped of their foliage, she could see right across the small valley to the farms beyond. When the weather was better, she sometimes wandered out after supper, walking barefoot across the beautifully cropped grass. Occasionally she bent down and pulled up a weed, more for the pleasure of feeling its roots give way and for the crumbling, earthy scent that was released than out of any secret sense of husbandry. Not that she had one. The gardens were amply looked after; no need for her to pretend otherwise. She'd never quite understood the English obsession with gardens – she preferred her nature raw and wild, unprocessed in the way European landscapes can never be.

She brought her attention sharply back to the room. In the far corner were the men in suits, helping themselves to more coffee and pastries as they waited for Callan to arrive. She glanced at her watch. It was almost two p.m. and the light was beginning to fade. Callan was late, as usual. Anneliese felt her lips tighten. She disliked tardiness – a trace of the German in her that would never be erased. She herself was *never* late. Never late and always prepared. Two lessons she'd learned early in life. She looked at her watch again. Still no sign of her car. Her lips tightened further.

Fifteen minutes later, the silver BMW swept into the forecourt, scattering stones. Almost before it had stopped, the back door opened and Callan jumped out. She was flustered, Anneliese noted, looking up from her notes. Even at that distance, Anneliese could tell the colour was up in her face. She grabbed her briefcase and ran across the gravel, taking the stone steps two at a time. There was a second's pause between the slam of the heavy front door and the sound of footsteps outside the lounge. The door opened and there she was, all flashing dark eyes, wild dark hair, flushed dusky cheeks. Her knee-length olive skirt (A*d*SP, A/W 1998, Anneliese noted with a touch of amusement) was creased; she'd forgotten to smooth it out. For a moment Anneliese saw her not as a mother might, but as a woman, looking another woman over in the way that women do. She was beautiful, extraordinarily so, made more so in Anneliese's eyes by the fact that they were so different, so *un*alike. In thirty years no one had ever made the assumption unless otherwise told that they were mother and daughter. Callan's was a wild dark beauty, nothing like Anneliese's cool Nordic looks. Small and compact, all curves and sleek toned muscle, she was at least a foot and a half shorter than Anneliese, and several shades darker.

When she was younger and hadn't yet learned *not* to press Anneliese on the subject or expect an answer, the question of who her father might have been was almost an obsession. Where did she get her looks and colouring from? Was he Italian? Spanish? North African? Native American? The suppositions became more outlandish as her teenage years approached. Why didn't Anneliese just *tell* her? Anneliese's response was always the same: silence. In thirty-something years she'd never once uttered his name. She never would. She looked at Callan again and her lips relaxed. She felt strangely calmed now that her daughter was here.

'Sorry I'm late,' Callan said, hurrying forward into the room. The four men standing at one end turned, surprise marked on their faces. With the exception of Bruno, none of the others had met Callan or had any idea who she was. She could also see their confusion. She'd told them that A*d*SP's new managing director would be joining them – so who was this young woman? She cleared her throat. 'Gentlemen. Allow me to make the introductions. Callan de Saint Phalle. Our new managing director.' There was an almost audible intake of breath from the men standing staring at Callan. Anneliese knew exactly what they were thinking. How could someone so young possibly be the managing director of the company they believed they'd come to save? Anneliese had to turn her head to one side lest she show her irritation. Thank God Callan would do the talking.

She couldn't bear the thought of what lay ahead. Days of negotiating for control of what had always been hers. She was still shocked by the speed at which things seemed to have unravelled, and was quite frankly baffled by the pessimism of their bankers and accountants, not to mention Bruno himself. How many recessions, near bankruptcies and sudden dips in fortune had they gone through since 1967 she asked as they argued back and forth about what to do. Hadn't they always weathered the storms, come out on top, usually even stronger than before? What was so damned different about this latest one she shouted at him. She was fed up to the teeth of the pressure they were putting her under. All this nonsense about branching out into perfumes and wallets and God-knows-what. She was a *fashion* designer, not a bloody storekeeper! Bruno, maddeningly, wouldn't rise to the bait. 'We've got to do *some-thing*,' he said, his unease masked by a calm passivity that unnerved her. 'We can't go on. We simply can't. We'll lose everything if we don't. Everything, Anneliese. Everything.' She'd looked at him then, and for the first time a ripple of real fear ran through her. It seemed inconceivable to her that the company she'd spent the better part of her life building could be in danger. Inconceivable. And then Callan arrived and suddenly it was all too real.

'Callan.' Bruno came forward immediately, his arms outstretched. Anneliese watched as they embraced, her throat suddenly full of an emotion that she normally suppressed. Dear Bruno. As much as they argued and bickered, as much as they shouted at one another, there was no one like him. He'd been her best friend, business partner and confidant for over forty years. Still handsome, now balding, with the same black-rimmed spectacles he'd worn on the first day they met at university in Berlin all those years ago. In the beginning, everyone had speculated wildly as to the *real* nature of their relationship, much to their mutual amusement. They needn't have bothered. Bruno's interest in women was confined to their dressed form, preferably in A*d*SP. Jasper, his long-time companion, had been at his side for over ten years. It was an open secret that Jasper and Anneliese did not get along but both were careful not to show it. They all knew their roles and played them impeccably. Bruno's career owed everything to Anneliese, though the reverse could easily have been said. Jasper's lifestyle – the homes, private jets, chauffeur-driven cars and the holidays whenever and wherever he wanted – was similarly indebted. It was therefore in Jasper's best interests to keep his animosity hidden and Anneliese, somewhat to everyone's surprise, agreed to do the same. Why not? If it made Bruno happy . . . ? It was an arrangement that suited everyone.

'*Ach*, still so glamorous, *hein*?' Bruno held Callan away from him, inspecting her outfit. 'This I like.' He touched the silver chain that she wore at her neck. It wasn't something Anneliese herself would have worn – far too bold, even a little crude, for her tastes – but she had to admit Callan sometimes surprised her with what was a rather good eye. Funny, wasn't it? Throughout Callan's childhood and early adulthood she'd shown absolutely no interest whatsoever in fashion. None at all. She'd turned her back on it as soon as she could. When she went off to university, it wasn't to do anything even remotely concerned with the world her mother inhabited. An English degree? Anneliese was baffled. Three years, even if it was at Cambridge, to study something she already spoke? That she appeared good at it was neither here nor there. Of course she was clever. She was her mother's daughter, no? Anneliese was baffled as to why anyone would be surprised. But the *coup de grace* and the blow from which Anneliese had never quite recovered happened afterwards. Throughout Callan's difficult years at Mortimer's where it seemed as though every other week she was on the verge of being sent home for one irritatingly minor infraction or another, Anneliese had done her level best to remain calm, supportive. She'd gone off on that ridiculously named 'gap' year (a gap between what?), travelling to the sorts of places Anneliese would sooner have *died* than visit. Papua New Guinea? *Borneo*? Whatever for? But she'd let her go and although Callan would never, ever know it, she'd sat by the telephone for six months, frozen with fear, waiting until she came home safely. That year had been A*d*SP's worst. She'd been unable to design a single thing. Not a thing! Bruno understood the source of her distress and said nothing. Callan was her only child, after all. She was *allowed*.

Callan did come back, more deeply bronzed than ever, a faded cloth bracelet on either wrist and peeling skin on her arms and legs. She'd shown them pictures of things Anneliese would rather not have seen but she'd been so grateful for her safe return that she bit her tongue. Anneliese had just got used to having her back home again, seeing her clothes being ironed and folded in the laundry room next to the kitchen, her favourite bottle of white wine in the refrigerator and the sound of her and Tara's chatter, late into the night, and then Callan dropped another bombshell. She wanted to leave again. This time to New York. This time it would be permanent. There was no arguing with her; no changing her mind. Callan was adamant. She wanted to go. So Anneliese had done the only thing she knew how: she'd tried to minimise the risks. The thought of Callan traipsing the streets, looking for a job, cap in hand, had almost finished her. She'd pulled out every contact she'd ever made and presented them to her – and Callan hadn't used them. Not one. Not once. She'd made some stupidly immature comment about wanting to do things *her* way – what way would that be? She was twenty-three! What twenty-three year old had a way of doing *anything* other than torment her only parent? Again, it was Bruno who'd stepped in. 'Let her go. She'll be back, you'll see. It might take a while, *mein Schatz*, but she'll be back.' She wasn't. She was gone for seven whole, long, lonely years until the day Bruno told her that A*d*SP was in trouble – *really* in trouble – and that even he, with his indefatigable optimism and his stoic calm, wasn't sure they'd survive.

So she'd picked up the phone and again did the only thing she knew how. She told her daughter to come home.

Now, seated opposite her, looking at the calm, capable way she settled herself, clearing her throat and preparing herself for the tough negotiations ahead, she felt a sneaky sense of pride. Callan glanced at her quickly, opened her briefcase and extracted several clear plastic folders, one for each person present. She slid them down the table and waited until everyone was settled. Her perfectly modulated voice, so thoroughly English in a way Anneliese's would never be, broke the silence. 'Thank you for coming, gentlemen,' she said, smiling briefly at them in turn. 'And my apologies for keeping you waiting. I'm glad you were all able to make it here today. Some tough choices to make, as I'm sure you'll appreciate, but I'm confident we'll come to an agreement that will be of mutual benefit to us all. Now, if you'll turn to the first page of the report in front of you.' She deftly led them straight into the discussions they'd come from Milan to have, the same discussions Anneliese had been putting off for almost two months and the reason behind her Christmas invitation. Callan would never know what it had cost her to make the phone call – and the request – though she was aware Callan wouldn't think of it as such. *A request? Since when do you make requests, Maman?* She could hear the note of incredulity in Callan's voice.

She studied Callan discreetly whilst she spoke, watching in amusement the way none of the men, not even Bruno, could keep their eyes off her as she talked. The reports lay exactly where they'd placed them, practically untouched in front of them. It was hard to focus on a sheet of paper with Callan in front of them. It was true that she and Callan bore almost no physical resemblance to each other, Anneliese mused, but in other ways the link between them was clear. She had Anneliese's no-nonsense manner of speaking, the same cool, confident delivery, the same carefully modulated tone. She was easily twenty years younger than anyone in the room yet you'd never have known it. Anneliese felt again a sharp tug of pride as Callan calmly ran through the list of demands that Anneliese had drawn up before negotiations could even begin. She watched as Giancarlo Matuzzi ran a finger under the collar of his shirt, loosening it. A small, almost insignificant gesture that hinted at his own nervousness. She'd made him uncomfortable. Anneliese was childishly pleased. If they thought that they were going to walk in, grab the lion's share of *her* company and waltz back to Milan, they were very much mistaken. No, she wanted full – and she meant *full* – creative control. No matter what Bruno and all the nervous accountants said. Any less and she'd chuck it all in. Walk away. She'd do it, too. After all, AdSP wouldn't be the only thing she'd walked away from in fifty years.

16

TARA CONNOLLY
Islington, London

Tara slowly replaced the receiver but remained where she was at the window for a few moments, arms folded across her chest, looking down at the street below. In the background the TV was on, putting out a dull, fuzzy light that flickered desultorily in the windowpanes. The traffic slowed as cars negotiated the hump in the road that the council had seen fit to erect, right outside her flat. Until its appearance, she'd never given more than a passing thought to the traffic that streamed up and down the road outside. Now it was all she heard, all day long. The squeal of brakes, sometimes the thump of an undercarriage and then the sound of the engine revving up again as drivers picked up speed. She'd thought of complaining to the council but what good would *that* do? They'd simply move it a couple of yards down the road and she'd still be able to hear it.

She turned away from the window and walked back to the sofa. The pile of first-year essays that she had to get through was sitting exactly where she'd left it. She sat down and picked up the first one, skimming over the words, but her mind wasn't on it. She kept thinking about the phone call she'd just received from Callan. She and Anneliese had gone down to Croombe d'Abitot for the weekend – a weekend of endless meetings and angry negotiations, Callan said, her voice dropping an octave. A*d*SP was in financial trouble. Big trouble. 'Turn on the TV,' Callan said drily. 'It'll be on the news at six.' Tara did as she was told and had been stunned to see Anneliese's face, then Callan's. 'In a move that is widely seen within the industry as an attempt to calm investors' fears, Ms de Saint Phalle's daughter, Callan de Saint Phalle, has been appointed the company's managing director. With a background in finance and international relations, the younger Ms de Saint Phalle is well placed . . .' Tara watched the newscaster, her mouth agape. 'Negotiations are under way', the nasal-sounding voice droned on, 'to secure a buyer for the thirty-year-old clothing line who've found themselves in trouble after the global economic downturn which has seen the closure of nearly thirty stores worldwide.' She watched the news with the phone wedged to her ear, stunned. For one thing, she'd always assumed Anneliese's empire to be practically immune to the vagaries of economies worldwide, and for another, why hadn't anyone told her?

'But you never said a word!' she protested, going back to their conversation and turning down the sound. 'Why didn't you tell me things were so bad?'

'Because they're not,' Callan said calmly. 'That's just hyperbole. You know what journalists are like, specially where Anneliese is concerned. They can't bear it that she doesn't play ball. *You* know that. Anyhow, that's not why I called.'

'A*d*SP's going down the tubes and you're calling me about something *else*?' Tara was genuinely upset.

'No, we're not about to go down the tubes, I promise you. It's *way* too valuable a brand, trust me. We've got some liquidity problems but nothing that the right investors won't be able to solve. No, I want you to do something else for me.' Tara marvelled at Callan. Tara was a historian. There were no pressing issues in the world of history. No lawsuits, no insolvencies, no buyouts or corporate bailouts. No negotiations, no brinkmanship. The world of high finance – Callan's world – was Greek to her.

'Me? What can *I* do?'

'Have you ever heard of the Palmyra Group?' Callan asked.

Tara shook her head. 'No. Should I?'

'*I* hadn't. They're owned by the Matuzzi family; they're the ones who've come down from Milan. They're interested in buying a stake – fifty-one per cent – in A*d*SP, but they're insisting on retaining what they call "creative direction" and Anneliese won't agree to it, of course. D'you know what she said to Matuzzi senior this morning?'

Tara grimaced. 'No, but I can guess.'

' "I could *eat* you for breakfast, gentlemen. For breakfast. And I'd *still* be hungry." You should have seen Bruno's face.'

'Happy I didn't,' Tara said drily. 'But I still don't see what I can do to help.'

'I want you to find me something on the Matuzzis,' Callan said firmly. 'Some dirt. Scandal. Something that I can use.'

'Dirt?'

'Yes, dirt.' Callan sounded momentarily impatient. 'I want to know if they've ever had tax evasion issues, if they've been accused of bribery, paid off a judge or a developer . . . you know. Run-of-the-mill stuff.'

'How on earth am I going to do *that*?'

'You're the historian, darling, not me.'

'Jesus. When d'you need it by?'

'Yesterday.' She heard Callan's chuckle and then the line went dead.

She walked over to the couch, sinking down into it as though sinking into water. She couldn't quite grasp the conversation. A*d*SP in financial difficulties? The threat of bankruptcy? A takeover? None of it made sense. For as long as she'd known Callan and Anneliese they'd been nothing short of spectacularly wealthy. The sort of wealth that was both limitless *and* effortless, a bottomless cup. Anneliese had everything money could buy, and more. A string of beautiful homes around the world, chauffeur-driven cars, holidays when and where she pleased, the sort of clothes that other women bankrupted their husbands to buy. Choices, in other words. Anneliese and Callan had *choices*. Not that Anneliese hadn't earned it – she was quite simply the most driven person Tara had ever encountered. What Anneliese termed 'holiday' was simply work in another location. Anneliese's whole *life* was work and nothing but. The very idea that she was about to lose what she'd worked her entire life to build was unthinkable.

Tara pulled her lower lip into her mouth, biting it softly in agitation. Of course she would help; she owed it to both Anneliese and Callan to do whatever she could. But where on earth would she start? *You're the historian, darling, not me.* A typical Callan comment. There were times when the six-and-a-half-year age difference between them seemed reversed. She'd never forgotten the first time she and Callan Zander de Saint Phalle had set eyes on each other. Detention – Callan's, of course. She'd slammed the library door, practically daring Tara to punish her further. She hadn't. She'd seen something in the defiant eleven year old that touched her greatly, and to everyone's astonishment, they'd become friends.

A more unlikely pairing had probably never existed at Mortimer's. The head girl, the most serious, studious girl in school, and the naughtiest. No one could quite believe it. Tall, calm, poised Tara Connolly and that wild, wilfully spoilt brat Callan de Saint Phalle? *Impossible.* Not so. Over the course of the next term, while impulsive, passionate Callan chattered away, Tara, quiet and attentive, listened with half an ear, planning an essay in her head and reading beneath the lines. She understood Callan more than either let on. And in her own, precociously intuitive way, Callan understood Tara. They complemented each other in ways that no one else could see. Tara was the older sister and confidante that Callan had never had; Callan, for her part, was the wilder, more impulsive side of Tara that she repressed. Each saw in the other some missing part of herself. By Christmas, the friendship had taken hold and people no longer commented or stared. At Easter, seeing that Tara had nowhere to go but to the farmhouse in Wales that the school kept for those girls whose parents lived overseas, Callan brought her friend to St John's Wood and introduced her to a surprised but quietly pleased Anneliese. To Callan's delight, and almost in spite of Anneliese's abruptness and cool manner, a warmth sprang up between her mother and her odd best friend that neither of them could explain. And then when the unthinkable happened a few months later, it was Anneliese who stepped forward, no questions asked.

She stood up abruptly, sending the pile of unmarked essays tumbling to the floor. She swallowed rapidly, as she always did whenever her mind skirted too close to the past. She put up a hand to her eyes, pressing them gently shut. It took her a few minutes to swallow the lump in her throat; mother, father . . . nothing but loss. Slowly, carefully, she pressed down on the surge of sorrow that always left her drained. She couldn't afford to give into it, not tonight, not now. She'd known Callan and Anneliese for twenty years and tonight was the first time she'd ever heard Callan ask for help.

17

CALLAN
Croombe d'Abitot

Cigarette smoke hung slackly in a bluish haze in the room. It was mid-morning; empty coffee cups lay about the table.

Anneliese had departed the night before, leaving everyone in a state of mild tension, which, to everyone's surprise except Callan's, had all but disappeared over dinner. Callan stubbed her cigarette out, catching Bruno's eye. A quick look of guilty, shared complicity flashed between them. Anneliese would never have allowed it. *Cigarettes?* In *her* home? She looked down the polished length of the table. The four Italians were arguing excitably amongst themselves whilst she and Bruno looked on. The atmosphere was strangely relaxed now that Anneliese was gone. No, she wasn't surprised that they were all getting along now that the principal source of tension was gone. If there was one thing her time in New York had taught her – other than the bits she'd rather not remember, of course – it was that deal-making was *all* about compromise, all about the give-and-take. Fortunately or otherwise, 'compromise' wasn't a word in Anneliese's vocabulary. She would argue something to *death* on point of principle. Not so Callan. She enjoyed it; no, be honest, she cautioned herself sternly, she *loved* it. She loved the game. She loved the flirtations, the teasing out of truths, the withholding of information and the release, the bluff. Brinkmanship wasn't Anneliese's way but it was hers – and Bruno's too. He understood perfectly well what she was doing. She was playing with them, using her extraordinary charm to bring them round, especially old Giancarlo Matuzzi. She'd seen immediately that there was something about Anneliese that offended his Latin sensibilities and that whatever her mother lacked, in his eyes, she more than made up for. Somewhat stiff and formal at first, he opened up under her flirtatious manner like a flower, although it was clear to her that it was his as-yet-unseen son who wielded the real power. Until he arrived, no deal would be made. So she buttered him up in the meantime, charming all three men so that the confrontation with the son who was due to arrive any minute would be done with at least the majority on her side.

Bruno watched it all with that very slight, almost sardonic smile on his face that let her know she was doing fine, that she had things under control. His subtle show of approval made everything safe, made sure she never lost control. It had always been that way between the two of them. Bruno held himself steady, and in doing so gave Callan free rein to roam. She hadn't told him yet about the phone call to Tara. She didn't need to. When the time was right and she had something to offer, she would.

She turned her head away from the group and looked out over the gardens instead. There was an early morning mist that had stubbornly refused to clear; it hung low and heavy over the flat lawn and the stone balustrades that flanked the lawns leading all the way down to the folly at the edge of the property. Of Anneliese's six homes, Croombe d'Abitot was her least favourite, perhaps because it reminded her of Mortimer's. Something about the high-ceilinged rooms with their polished wooden floors and the heavy oil paintings that the interior designers had chosen brought the draughty dining room at Mortimer's to mind. Tara disagreed. Mortimer's, she said, was cold and forbidding. Croombe d'Abitot wasn't. There were Persian rugs on the floors, radiators everywhere you looked and fresh flowers from the gardens on almost every surface. At Mortimer's, she'd reminded Callan primly, there hadn't been a fresh flower in sight.

Suddenly the droning, whirring noise that she'd been peripherally aware of for a few minutes began to grow louder. Giancarlo Matuzzi looked up. 'Ah. At last.' He smiled at everyone. 'My son.'

She looked out of the window just as the black dot on the horizon took shape. It was a helicopter – black, sleek, its blades completely transparent, it bobbed its way gracefully across the lawns. Their conversation was completely drowned out as it settled itself on the gravel driveway, sending up a flurry of small stones and leaves as it came to a halt. She gaped as someone – the pilot, it seemed – jumped out and slid open one of the back doors. In all the years they'd been coming to Croombe, she was pretty certain no one had ever arrived by helicopter. A tall, fit-looking young man clambered down and began walking towards the front door, bending his frame against the wind. There were two other men who clambered down and ran after him. As they disappeared from view, it dawned on her that they were probably his bodyguards.

She looked back down the table. Giancarlo Matuzzi was already on his feet as his son and his bodyguards entered the room. She looked up and felt the blood draining slowly from her face.

18

ANNELIESE
St John's Wood, London

Anneliese stifled a small yawn of relief as the car pulled up outside the two glossy grey doors of numbers 8 and 10 Bridgeman Street, St John's Wood. Home. At last. Jonathan, her chauffeur, leapt out and walked smartly around to her side. 'Ma'am?' He held the door open for her. She murmured her thanks, picked up her handbag and the dark grey pashmina she'd spread across her knees and got out. She walked slowly up the steps, stopping to pick a dead leaf out of the terracotta pot outside the two front doors, one leading to her home, the other to the studios where all of her designing was done. She'd bought the handsome Regency townhouses in the late sixties, just after Callan was born. A few years ago, after nearly a decade's worth of fighting with the council, she'd completely gutted the pair of them, leaving only the ornate, classical façades. The interiors were beautifully minimalist, pared back to a luxurious, clinical nothingness. A little like the woman herself, one journalist had commented, after securing an almost unheard-of interview with her. It was the last time she'd allowed a journalist inside her home.

The door swung silently inwards as she reached the top step. It was Mrs Betts, an expectant smile on her face. The housekeeper at Croombe must have telephoned ahead. 'Thank you,' she said, handing over her bag.

'Everything all right?' Mrs Betts wasn't in the least bit put off by Anneliese's formal ways.

Anneliese smiled slightly. 'I've left Callan in charge. She'll probably do a better job than I will.'

'Probably.' There was nothing in Mrs Betts's expression to suggest she knew any more about what was going on than Anneliese had told her – which was very little – but Anneliese wasn't fooled. In the way of most house help, there was very little she *didn't* know. Not that Sue Betts would *ever* let on.

'How *is* Callan?' she asked half an hour later, as she brought Anneliese her customary evening glass of white wine and a plate of sliced apple and cheese.

'She loves this sort of thing. You know what she's like.'

'Aye. That I do,' Mrs Betts said, smiling.

Better than I do, Anneliese thought to herself, then quickly quashed the uncharitable thought. 'Did a package arrive for me today?'

'In the dining room. Delivered just after you left.' Mrs Betts set the tray down. 'Anything else you need?'

Anneliese shook her head. 'No, thank you, Mrs Betts. That'll be all for tonight.' Mrs Betts withdrew, leaving Anneliese alone. She picked up the glass of wine, took a slice of apple and walked through the hallway to the dining room. The package was indeed sitting on the table. It was impressively large, too. She picked it up – light as a feather. She tore open the plastic wrapping eagerly and pulled apart the cardboard envelope. The fabric samples slid out easily. She gasped in pleasure, plunging her hand into the mixture of texture and colour – squares of cashmere as light as gauze; squares of exquisitely fine, grey silk tulle; rich velvets in strong, soaked colours – a burgundy so dark it bordered on black; iridescent, midnight blue and a deep, dark green that brought the forest to mind. She emptied the packet and took a deep, satisfied sigh. Sweeping up the material samples, she carried them off into her study like a prize. Or a distraction, she thought to herself wryly as she settled herself down in her black leather Eames office chair and spread the samples out before her.

Unlike most, she sourced her fabrics almost exclusively in Japan. Yuchiko Misimata, the textile engineer she'd worked with for almost three decades, was nothing short of a genius. She loved the shimmering, almost-liquid quality of the silk and cashmere blend she'd come up with. The smooth, long lines and generous folds of the fabric were perfect for her upcoming S/S collection – the material would practically design itself. She paused for a moment. Would there even *be* an upcoming S/S collection? She felt the sharp, never-quite-buried needle of fear slowly assert itself. She'd grown accustomed to its shadowy presence, a pin-prick reminder if she ever needed one that *this* – her life and everything she'd worked for in it – was not hers for the taking, but for the earning. She was owed nothing, not even luck. Those who claimed to know her attributed her formidable work ethic and steely self-discipline to Germany, to the culture they believed her to be part of, despite having spent most of her adult life away from it. She alone knew it had *nothing* to do with being German – nothing whatsoever. Her Puritan, highly attuned work ethic came from another source altogether and one that would have surprised those who considered themselves her friends. Guilt. No one, not even Bruno, would have guessed it. What on earth did she have to be guilty about? She who worked so hard for everything? She remembered a dinner party some years back – one of those glamorous, black-tie events that she'd been forced to attend. Someone at the table was talking about a mutual friend who had recently had an affair but had chosen to stay with his wife out of guilt. 'Guilt? How ridiculous,' Anneliese had murmured, unable to stop herself. 'Guilt is a waste of time. Pointless. A pointless emotion.' She no longer remembered exactly what people's reactions had been – after all, it was precisely the sort of comment the Ice Queen would make. But she did remember the sharp stab in her chest as she said it. *Liar.*

She, more than anyone present that night, ought to know. Guilt was *not* a pointless emotion. After all, it guided pretty much everything she did.

19

CALLAN

His skin was the colour of honey, even in those places where the sun hadn't reached. She remembered that about him, even if she'd known very little else. Certainly not his surname. At the club, as far as she could remember, he was simply Marco. Nothing else was needed. She wasn't sure she'd ever addressed him anyway. He was just one of many men whose bodies she'd known during the course of an evening, or a weekend. She looked at his chest underneath the light blue shirt that she'd unbuttoned, but only halfway down. Brown, honeyed skin, just like her own. Fine, silky brown hair, broadening out in a powerful 'T' across his chest, tapering smoothly below his navel and disappearing into the waistband of his trousers. He still had his trousers on, though she'd unzipped him. 'Callán,' he whispered hoarsely, accent on the wrong syllable. 'Now,' he said urgently. '*Now.*'

She shook her head slowly from side to side. 'No.' She slid her hand through the opening of his trousers, teasing him. 'Patience, Marco, patience. Don't you remember?' She was smiling.

He was unable to answer. She stroked him to an almost unbearable hardness before bending her head and taking his penis into the soft warmth of her mouth. He would have grabbed her head, she thought to herself wickedly, if his arms had been free. But they weren't. They were cuffed to the radiator with his own belt. It was part of the game. They were in the small living room on the second floor: his father, the two accountants and the company lawyer – and Bruno – were fast asleep in their rooms just down the corridor. The door was wide open. If any of them had stumbled down the corridor – for whatever reason, to go downstairs for a glass of water, a moonlit walk in the gardens, whatever – they were in full, splendid view. The lights were off but a single scented candle burned in one corner of the room. She was naked, on her knees in front of him; he was dressed. Just the way he liked it. She remembered that about him.

He thrust himself into her mouth suddenly, desperately seeking release. It had been over an hour of the most exquisite torture and he was losing the battle to hold himself in. She pulled back for a second, leaving him with a gentle 'plop'. His eyes were tightly closed. She got up slowly and then lowered herself on him, inch by exquisite inch. His eyes were screwed tightly shut as he began to race towards release. She paused, lifted her bottom a fraction and held herself above him. The groan of frustration sounded loudly in her ears. She put a finger across his mouth and bent her head towards his. '*She* gets creative control,' she whispered. '*Total* creative control.' He nodded frantically. 'You get fifty-one per cent of the holding company.' He nodded again, his whole body thrusting upwards, trying to meet hers. 'No change in management and *all* the stores stay open. No closures.' She bore down hard on him once more. He began thrusting again and again she held herself back. 'Say it, Marco. I want to *hear* you say you agree.'

'Fuck, Callán . . . yes, yes . . . what*ever*! *Yes!*'

She grinned, and bore down on him, covering his mouth with hers. He exploded at exactly the same moment the flashes went off.

They were both quiet, although Marco was still breathing heavily. It took him a few minutes to climb down. She had pulled a cigarette out of the packet lying on the table beside them and had lit it by the time his eyes were seeing again and the flush was beginning to recede from his face. She was smiling. He was not. She made no move to cover herself but lay beside him, drawing the smoke down deep into her lungs.

'Callán.' His arms were still bound by his thin leather belt. His blue shirt had come out of his trousers. He had the dishevelled, half-wanton look of a woman; there was a softness about Marco Matuzzi that she quite liked. But she wasn't here to dwell on his qualities, she reminded herself. She was here to do business, in a manner of speaking. And she had. He jerked his head upwards, indicating his bound arms. She finished her cigarette and stubbed it out. She leaned across him, her breasts raking his chest as she unbuckled him slowly and was gratified to feel him hardening again. That too, she remembered. But she had no desire to start again. She'd got what she wanted. Photographs and all.

'There you go,' she said lightly, reaching over and freeing him.

He rubbed his wrists where the belt had been tightest. 'Callán,' he said again, frowning. 'Why that?' He nodded at the camera. 'Was it really necessary? You have my word.'

'I know, darling. But it's nothing, just a little memento. You know . . . a little something just in case you forget.'

He shook his head slowly from side to side, still looking intently at her. Then at last he smiled. 'You *are* a little bitch.'

'Don't sound so surprised, Marco. I haven't changed. And you know what? Neither have you.' She got up from the floor, picked up her own clothing and the camera and then turned to look down at him. She was still completely naked. She wiggled her fingers, blew out the candle and calmly walked out of the room.

20

ANNELIESE

'What do you mean, they just gave in?' Anneliese asked incredulously.

'I don't know. All I know is that in the morning we had a deal. You keep forty-nine per cent, as we discussed, they get fifty-one, *but* you get to keep total creative control *and* they make sure there are no further store closures. Exactly as you wanted. It was the son who signed. I don't know how she did it. She beat them down. On everything.' *Everysing*. Bruno's voice would never be rid of its German inflection.

'*Complete* creative control?' Anneliese reiterated suspiciously. 'One hundred per cent?'

'*Ja*. Complete. I'm sending the documents over to you now. I'm telling you, after that first breakfast meeting she figured out *he* was the one she needed to talk to, not the others. The others are really just employees; they do whatever the old man wants and the old man listens to everything the son says. She was right. It's done, Anneliese. We're back in business. We got exactly what we wanted.'

Anneliese was silent. There was a part of her that was almost afraid to believe it. She really shouldn't be surprised. Callan was a tough negotiator. She of all people should have known that. Just look at what she'd been like as a teenager. She'd been more worried than she cared to admit about what others might think, including Bruno, of course. But Bruno had every faith in Callan. Whom better to hand things over to than her, he'd mused over their usual Friday evening meal the week before Callan was due to arrive. 'After all, what's the point of all this –' he waved his hand at their general surroundings – 'if there's no one to leave it to.' Anneliese said nothing but had read in his voice the sadness that surfaced occasionally. She could do nothing about it. Bruno had no one. Yes, there was Jasper, but it wasn't the same.

'So, what happens next?' Anneliese asked, coming back to the moment.

'We're coming back tonight. Marco Matuzzi's giving us a lift in his helicopter. I've got the originals of the agreement with me. I'll drop them off at yours tonight. It's all done, *mein Schatz*. You just get back to doing what you do best. We've got a show in May – that's less than three months away. You've got a collection to design.'

'The samples arrived from Japan last night, by the way. Stunning.'

'Good. That's good. Anneliese?' He seemed about to say something, then changed his mind. 'No, nothing.'

'What?'

'I . . . I just—'

'*What?*' Anneliese tried to keep the impatience out of her voice. It wasn't like Bruno to be hesitant.

'Well, I was just wondering. Does Callan know the Matuzzi family? Does she know the son?'

Anneliese shook her head. 'No, I don't think so. Why?'

'*Ach*, it's nothing.'

Anneliese was aware of a very faint tremor of unease slipping through her. 'She would have said something, I'm sure.'

'*Ja*. Well, it makes no difference. She got us what we wanted. See you later, *Schatz*.'

Anneliese didn't reply. She put down the receiver and stared at her hand. It was shaking very slightly. There were things about her daughter she realised she didn't want to know, or guess at. Bruno was right. It made no difference. They'd got what they wanted; who cared how they'd accomplished it?

As she turned away from the phone and walked back through the living room to the kitchen, a phrase from the past suddenly leapt out at her, without warning. Something someone had once said. About *her*. A high-veld winter's day. Walking down Kaiserstrasse with Tante Bärbel, stopping to look in the shops. Two women walked past and noticing them, paused briefly. Their voices were loud and clear. *Wie der Vater, so der Sohn.*

Like father, like son. She'd turned slowly, wondering what they were referring to. Tante Bärbel's hand was on her arm in a flash, forcing her back towards the window. She remembered the women's laughter and the rejoinder. *Wie die Tochter, meinst du, Marianne. Es gab keinen Sohn.* 'Like the *daughter*, you mean, Marianne. He didn't have a son.' Another burst of laughter and then they slipped out of earshot. Tante Bärbel said nothing but the tightening of her jaw led her to understand that she'd heard them – and that she'd understood.

Anneliese walked briskly from the room, the memory settling unpleasantly over her, like light, stinging rain.

21

CALLAN

Callan stood for a moment in the doorway of her new flat, breathing in the scent of the roses that had been delivered whilst she was away. She eased off her shoes, not wanting to mark the brand-new, pale ivory carpet and tossed her briefcase onto the dining-room table. She walked into the living room and looked around. Despite her headache, she gave a small sigh of pleasure. It *was* lovely. Anneliese had outdone herself. It was all part of the charm offensive to get her back to London, of course, but there was no denying the care she'd taken to make sure Callan would feel immediately at home. It was nothing like her New York loft – no exposed brickwork and there wasn't a polished concrete floor in sight – but Anneliese had made sure her favourite art hung on the walls and there were calla lilies, her favourite flowers, in every room. The furniture was that mixture of plush, comfortable classics and cutting-edge modernism that she knew Callan liked. She sank down gratefully into one of the impossibly plump sofas.

She couldn't believe how quickly everything had happened. There she was, the week before Christmas, happily ensconced in her New York life, dashing from her office to the gym to her loft, dinner with friends, the theatre, coffee at her usual stand on W 14th Street, business as usual. A single phone call later and her world was turned upside down. She shook her head, still not quite ready to believe that that part of her life was over. She picked up one of the grey silk cushions and pressed it against her cheek. She felt utterly drained. She couldn't believe she'd run into Marco, of all people. He'd been one of the regulars at the club when she first started going there, soon after she arrived in New York. Just another one of the impossibly rich, impossibly handsome men in town who sought something a little different. It was Karel who'd first taken her there. Karel and Lance. Lance was her first lover in New York. A systems analyst who worked for the same company. Karel was his best friend. Callan's cheeks burned as she recalled how they'd fought for her attention and how she'd played them off against each other. One night, deep in the middle of winter, she'd left Lance's apartment at midnight, naked save for a floor-length mink coat from one of Anneliese's winter collections and met Karel in the bar across the road. He'd looked at her curiously for a moment, bought her a drink, then took her gloved hand in his. 'I want to show you something,' he'd said in that husky, *mittel* European voice of his. 'Something I think you'll like.' He was right. She *did* like it. She liked it almost every weekend for the next five years until something inside her snapped and she stopped liking it and was ashamed of it — and of herself — instead.

She fished around for the remote control and switched on the television. She would rather watch the news than think about Karel and Lance and New York and the Club on W 14th Street. She would rather not think about that at all.

22

TARA

The microfiche sent out a watery greenish light; in the deep silence of the library, she sifted through the pages of old newspaper reports, press cuttings, articles, court reports . . . there was certainly plenty on the Palmyra Group and the Matuzzi family but none of it particularly useful. Their parent holding company, CDS, seemed to have fingers in just about every pie on offer. It made Tara's head spin just following the list. Newspapers, magazines, books, radio, a television station, new digital and satellite technology companies . . . the list just went on and on. And quite why a media company had decided to take a major stake in a high-end fashion business was a mystery to her.

She smiled wryly to herself as she scrolled on through the pages. Most things were a complete mystery to her, with the exception of history, of course. She'd always liked it. At school, it was her favourite subject, even after the accident. There was something so reassuring about the careful dissection of the past in order to throw light on the present that she'd always been drawn to. She loved the research, the careful sifting around for the facts from which to spin a convincing narrative, the objectivity and the fact that it was always written in the third person, never first. History *happened*. Wars were fought and lost, empires rose and fell, dates did not shift. It wasn't made, bent, distorted, fabricated. History was one of the last knowable disciplines and she loved its resolute certainty. Compared to the cut-and-thrust world of finance that Callan occupied, hers was a haven of tranquil texts, polite discussion, subtle disagreement. Whenever she'd visited Callan in New York, as much as she enjoyed the hectic pace and the galleries and dinner parties at which Callan and her friends shouted each other down and drank each other under the table, it was always with a sense of relief that she returned to London and her quiet Primrose Hill flat where her books and papers and computer screen quietly anchored her in a way that nothing else could, especially not since the death of her parents.

She turned reluctantly back to the screen. *The group was restructured and taken over a number of times, most particularly in the 1980s, when two of its senior executives were embroiled in the collapse of Banco Ambrosiano. Following the death of Roberto Calvi, the group applied for bankruptcy protection and downsized accordingly.* Her eye was caught by the sentence. *Roberto Calvi. Banco Ambrosiano.* Ah, here was something! Wasn't that the same Roberto Calvi who'd been found hanging from Blackfriars Bridge? She quickly scrolled to the top of the page. Perhaps she'd be of some use to Callan after all? Her heart began to beat a little faster. It was the first time Callan had asked for help and despite her misgivings, it thrilled her to be able to deliver.

Her euphoria was short-lived. 'I should've phoned you earlier,' Callan said, sounding inordinately cheerful. 'And saved you a whole load of work. Sorry. I just got a bit caught up. No, it's fine. I don't need anything any more. It's done. We got what we wanted.'

'How?' Tara was stunned by the speed at which things seemed to be moving. One minute A*d*SP seemed in danger of complete collapse, the next minute everything was fine. She felt absurdly deflated.

There was the faintest hesitation before Callan's voice came back down the line. 'Oh, we just beat them down.'

'Oh.' Tara had no idea what to say.

'But thanks anyway, darling,' Callan went on quickly, before Tara could say anything more. 'I've got to run. What're you doing on Friday, by the way?'

'Friday? I've got a book launch in the evening. Someone in the Art History department. Why?'

'Let's have dinner afterwards. I'll meet you outside your building. And don't bring your bike. I'll get Jonathan to drive us home.' And before Tara could protest, Callan had hung up again. She slowly put down the receiver, even more puzzled than before. She looked at the stack of cuttings she'd brought back from the library. Clearly Callan had found something else to bargain with. What? she wondered as she went into the kitchen. What had she found? She plugged the kettle in, and picked a tea cup off the rack, but her mind had already started to wander. Callan had a new sure-footedness about her that Tara marvelled at, and envied, too, if she were honest. For most of their long friendship, it had been the opposite. Callan was the tempestuous one, forever spinning off on one tangent or another. Tara had always remained steadfast, knowing exactly what she wanted to do with her life and accomplishing it with the minimum of fuss and drama. In nearly twenty years, there'd only been that one time when their roles were reversed. She paused in the act of making tea, not wanting to remember but unable to stop.

'Um, Tara?' One of the fifth years whom she vaguely recognised was standing in front of her. She'd been so deeply buried in her book she hadn't noticed her come in.

'What is it?' She placed a paperclip at the paragraph she'd been reading.

'Miss Molloy wants to see you. She said it was urgent.' The girl had the air of having been given something important to say.

Tara sighed inwardly. What now? She nodded and closed her book. 'I'll be there in a minute,' she said, picking up her bags.

'She said to come straight away.'

'I'll be right there.' The girl hesitated for a second, torn between curiosity and obedience but one further look from the head girl and she fled.

She walked down the corridor towards the headmistress's office, wondering what the urgency was. It was a Saturday morning and most of the school were at games, or in their dorm rooms. The absence of their voices was like a presence in the passageways that led to the staff offices.

She lifted a hand and knocked on the door. It was opened almost immediately. Mrs Simmonds, the deputy headmistress, and Mr

Friedland, the chemistry teacher, were standing by the window. Miss Molloy's back was to her. A faint scent of something — some inexplicable tension — hung in the air. She felt her calves prickle as they always did when she was nervous. Miss Molloy turned to face her.

'Tara.' She was unable to hold her gaze. It slid from Tara's face to the floor. There was a stifled sob from someone in the room. Tara turned her head slowly. Mrs Bailey, the head of Raglan House, was weeping. 'Oh, Tara—' She stopped suddenly, her voice catching. Miss Molloy came towards her. There was a second's wait and then her mouth opened and some words came out. Something terrible has happened. On the road last night. It was instant, my dear Tara. Absolutely instant. They didn't feel a thing, apparently. Tara stared at her. The words were spinning like a thread, a spider's web of loss that slowly thickened, tightening itself around her. What was she saying?

It took almost half an hour to put the pieces together. The accident had happened almost two days earlier. It had taken almost a day for the news to reach the mine, and from there for it to reach Mortimer's. The details were patchy. Her parents were returning from Lusaka on the long road back to Kitwe that she knew so well. She could just picture it — her father at the wheel, smoking, one arm bent out of the window; her mother, gazing out at the fleeting countryside, occasionally murmuring something to her father as they passed. Tara knew the route by heart — she knew all the towns and villages along the way — Kapira, Kamilonga, Mlimba, Kabwe, Mubanga. They'd turned off the highway at Chamankondi to avoid going through Ndola, the closest town to Kitwe. The accident happened just before they rejoined the highway at Fisenge. A mammy-lorry, one of the huge, ancient Bedfords that lumbered along the route between Kitwe and Ndola, laden to the rafters. It overturned, taking the Connollys' Ford Fiesta with it. It was instant, Miss Molloy kept repeating. Instant. We're told there was no suffering. None whatsoever.

'Fisengé,' Tara said suddenly, abruptly. 'Not Fisénge. You're not pronouncing it right.' Everyone looked at her uncertainly. She looked at the ground. Why was it suddenly so important to get the pronunciation right? She was used to everyone constantly mis-pronouncing the place where she'd spent most of her life. Half the girls at Mortimer had no idea where Zambia was, let alone Kitwe. Where? Kitwi? No, Kitwe. Where's that, then? Africa. There would invariably be a snort of laughter. Don't be ridiculous . . . how can you be from Africa? You're not even black. You're Irish! Tara Connolly. You're not African!

'Do . . . do you have anyone else in this country?' Mrs Bailey asked, blowing her nose. 'A grandparent? Or an aunt, perhaps?'

Tara shook her head. She swallowed. There was no one. Her parents' marriage had cut them off entirely from their families. Where her other friends had countless photographs of relatives back 'home', wherever that happened to be, the Connollys did not. Not that Tara or her parents had seemed to mind. Their whole world was constructed around each other; for eighteen years it had been enough. Not having a birthday card from some grandparent somewhere whom she might only see every other year like some of her friends didn't bother her. Mike and Annabel and Chipo were her home. There had never been anything or anyone else. 'N-no, Mrs Bailey,' she said slowly, her voice barely audible. 'There's no one.'

'Oh, dear. Well, there'll be all sorts of formalities to go through,' Mr Hardcastle, the school registrar, spoke up suddenly. 'I expect they'll have left a will and all that. But don't let any of that worry you now,' he added, glancing quickly at the others.

'Mr Hardcastle, please.' Miss Molloy gave him a withering stare. She turned to Tara. 'If there was someone . . . it'd be best for you to have a few days away from school, Tara.'

'There's no one,' Tara repeated quietly. She looked at the floor, a cold numbness seeping through her. 'Can I go now?'

'Of course, Tara. I'm so very sorry.' The adults looked at her, strangely helpless. She opened the door and walked out.

*

She lay on her bed, watching the duvet cover rise and fall with each breath. She drew it in and out, shallowly, hesitantly, as though taking it down into the depth of her body might release something – some awful, dreadful emotion – that she was working hard to suppress. Her absorption in the task deepened, like the different stages of sleep. The door to the room burst open suddenly. Callan stood in the doorway. Her olive-toned face was as white as a sheet, drained of colour. Tara felt the horrible thickening of tears in her throat that she'd managed up until then to keep down.

'Tara?' Callan's voice was barely a whisper. 'Miss Molloy came to fetch me. She said—' Callan stopped, her eleven-year-old voice beginning to break with dread.

Fear burst all over Tara in a turmoil of emotion, a physical feeling like a blush, that she'd never experienced before. Everything began to run together – the diagonal stripes on her mother's favourite dress, the one she wore to the club whenever there was a function on; the faint sheen of powder on her face where her brush hadn't reached; the white, carefully protected skin on the back of her hand. She thought of her father and the thin brown tie he always wore and the scent of cigar smoke that he left in every room he passed through. She looked across the room to where Callan stood, still clutching her hockey stick, her little face crumpling in an expression of hurt and shock that, if anything, seemed greater than her own. That was Callan for you. Whatever you felt, she felt it more. She looked at Tara with some-thing – love? – something deeper than compassion, or sympathy. She knew. Suddenly, she was beside Tara, her face pressed against hers on the pillow.

'Don't worry about anything,' Callan said forcefully. 'You're not to worry about anything. You're going to be with us now. Maman will take care of everything. We'll look after you.'

And Anneliese did. Not a formal adoption – Tara was already too old for that. She'd simply assumed responsibility for Tara in the same way she assumed responsibility for Callan, her only child. 'This is Tara. Callan's older sister.' It was about as close an explanation as Anneliese would ever give. It was enough.

23

CALLAN

The bar they sat in was all light and shade, the distant sound of others coming to them lightly in waves of tinkling laughter. A plate of half-eaten sushi lay between them. Callan fingered the stem of her wine glass uncomfortably. Tara's unnervingly candid gaze was upon her.

'What d'you mean you "sort of" know him? Where'd you meet him?'

Callan could feel the blush steal over her neck and throat. She took an extra large gulp of wine. 'I . . . I just met him a couple of times in New York, that's all.'

Tara's eyes narrowed slightly, as they did when Callan said something she didn't believe. She said nothing, but as Callan was acutely aware, she didn't need to. The expression on her face said it all. *I don't believe you.* There was silence for a few seconds. Callan's fingers gripped the smooth cold stem tightly. A minute ticked by in silence. Then Tara picked up her own glass and smiled slightly, wryly, signalling defeat.

Callan breathed out a silent sigh of relief, picking half-heartedly at a piece of sashimi. Her appetite was gone. Lying to Anneliese was one thing; lying to Tara was another. But what could she do? She could hardly divulge the truth of what had actually happened in the study at Coombe d'Abitot to Tara. How would she even begin to explain it?

'Callan . . . are you all right?'

She nodded quickly. 'I'm fine. It's . . . it's been a long week. Anyway, enough about me. What about you? How's work?'

Tara shrugged. 'Fine, I suppose. I'm halfway through my thesis . . . I'm hoping to finish it by the end of this year.'

'Ah.' Callan tried not to let her surprise show. Tara had been halfway through her thesis for the past three years . . . how much longer would it take? Her world was a mystery to Callan.

In the business world, things were so much clearer. Profit or loss. Black or white. Sink or swim. What, she often wondered, was the point of spending a decade studying medieval German art? Or whatever it was Tara had chosen. 'So, are you coming to Scheherazade for Easter?' she asked, changing the subject again. 'Maman asked me if you were coming.' There was a sudden flash of warmth between them. They smiled at each other, Callan half-guiltily. There'd been a time when she couldn't have imagined keeping *anything* from Tara. But that was then. She suddenly longed for the simplicity of the past.

TARA

Something was definitely wrong, Tara thought to herself as she watched the car disappear with Callan ensconced in the back seat. She'd declined a lift with Jonathan; her bicycle was waiting patiently for her, chained to the railings outside the department in its usual spot. She unlocked it, lost in thought. There was a worried look in Callan's dark, clear eyes that bothered her. Perhaps Anneliese would know? She hadn't spoken to her in over a week. It was time for her to call. It was another, peculiar feature of their relationship – she was always the one to call, not Anneliese. If she didn't, and more than a couple of weeks passed, there would be a brief, terse message on her answering machine – never her mobile. 'Are you well? Here is Anneliese.' It was Tara's cue to call back. Yet despite her abruptness, a warmth existed between the two of them that neither could explain. Callan's relationship with Anneliese was different. It was harder somehow. There were times back then in school, when Tara, listening to Callan's long list of complaints about her mother, very nearly blurted out what she *really* thought of Anneliese. Yes, she was cool and distant and always, always reserved. And no, she didn't rush up for every school play, every holiday, every recital. But she was *there*. Her mark and presence were everywhere, *all the time*. Anneliese would never forget to send the chauffeur to pick both girls up at one o'clock on the dot, just as it said in the circular sent to parents. She would *never* forget to pay the school fees, or ensure Callan's tuck box was full. Her love and care were evident in the beautifully packed trunks that Callan began each term with, in the crisp white stationery and those thick, creamy envelopes in which something small – a book token, or, when she was older, a delicate necklace or a pair of earrings – was always tucked. No, Callan had it wrong. Anneliese *did* love her, even if Callan couldn't see it. They were like two people who spoke different dialects of the same language, each somehow and narrowly missing exactly what it was the other said, or wanted to hear.

She unlocked her bicycle and hopped on, albeit rather awkwardly. She'd had two glasses of wine, after all . . . large ones, too. She cycled down Torrington Place, winding her way past the late-night curry shops and the pubs that were just about to close. It was an unusually warm April evening. Instead of the persistent drizzle of the past fortnight, she'd stepped out of her flat that morning to find an unexpected balminess in the air. It wouldn't last; by the weekend the rain would have returned but the warmth had momentarily stopped her in her tracks. She felt the peculiar, strange-but-familiar tug of her own estrangement coming at her, just the way it had all those years ago when she'd first arrived. Zambia came back to her suddenly, immediately – the scented, wood-smoke mornings, the fat yellow-and-green birds who chirruped all day long in the flamboyant hibiscus bushes at the bottom of the driveway. Kitwe. Home. She hadn't been back in over twenty years. She cycled slowly across the park, her mind suspended somewhere between past and present, taking in the budding trees as they floated past, yet seeing at the same time the tremendous, knobbly fig tree that stood halfway between the bungalow on the compound and the club.

Ten minutes later, slightly out of breath from the climb up Pentonville Road, she turned left into Barnsbury Road. She could have cycled the route in her sleep – down Copenhagen

Road, skirting along the edge of the park, right into Richmond Avenue, then a sharp left into Stonefield Street. Once round the small, communal gardens at Lonsdale Square and then straight down Barnsbury Street. It was a winding, slightly roundabout way to get home but she loved it. She loved the patchwork of London street names that connected the city to its past. It was one of the first things she'd noticed about it – history in London was everywhere. People talked about it as though it were in the past. For Tara, it was the opposite. History was here, present everywhere, all the time. She only had to cycle home from work to understand that. The pretty little one-bedroom flat on Napier Terrace was Anneliese's graduation present to her. She'd smiled when Tara told her earnestly why it was even more special. It was named after David Napier, a Victorian-era engineer who was descended from the Scottish branch of the Napier family. 'One of the Scottish Napiers, Sir John, was the founder of algorithms, did you know that?' Anneliese's eyebrow went up a fraction. She shook her head. 'But there's more,' Tara said excitedly.

'What?' Anneliese was tolerantly amused.

'Well, they don't actually know where the name itself came from, but there's one theory that I like. Did you know that the word for a napkin in Old French is "nappe"?'

Anneliese shook her head. 'No, I didn't. Go on.'

'So, the word "napery" also means the place where royal linen is stored. In medieval times, a "naper" was someone who had custody of the linen in a royal household. Because people didn't use forks back then, they used their fingers instead, and there were two people who were really important at the dining table – the "ewer", the person who brought bowls of water to the guests, and the "naper", the person who handed over the napkin or the cloth. So, Napier Terrace has this history of textiles and engineering . . . and that's what you studied, isn't it? Didn't you tell me once that you'd studied textile engineering and that's why—' She stopped suddenly, mid-sentence. Anneliese had got up. 'Anneliese?' Tara said uncertainly. 'Did I—? Is something wrong?' Anneliese shook her head and quickly left the room. Tara was left alone in the dining room, wondering what on earth she'd said or done.

Presently Anneliese came back. Her face was perfectly composed but there was a faint shininess around the nose. She was followed immediately by Mrs Betts, bearing a silver tray with a bottle of champagne and three delicately fluted glasses. Anneliese poured all of them a glass. Nothing further was said. In the way she'd somehow divined about Anneliese, Tara realised there were moments when it was better not to ask. She, Mrs Betts and Anneliese all drank to Tara's new flat. It was left to Tara to wonder what she'd said that had touched Anneliese so deeply, and why.

She pushed open the front door, slipped the lock on her bike and propped it against the radiator, then made her way up to her own front door. She'd been in the flat for nearly seven years now, longer than she'd lived anywhere except Kitwe, and it was very firmly home. Anneliese, typically, had offered the services of her interior designer but though Tara loved the classic, elegant simplicity of Anneliese's homes, she wanted something warmer and cosier for herself. Something that would, in some as-yet-unspecified way, remind her of Zambia. She had no talent for it; she couldn't tell one end of a curtain from the other. But somehow, with Callan's help, they'd managed to choose the right colours, fabrics and furniture so that the flat looked comfortable, if not exactly stylish. The kitchen was a warm, deep yellow; there were sky-blue curtains in the sitting room and an assortment of cushions covered in colourful, multi-hued and multi-patterned fabrics from West Africa. She'd bought a few African masks and stools; her hundreds of books were lined up on shelves that stretched across one wall . . . yes, it was home.

She eased off her boots, hung up her coat and plopped herself down on the sofa with a faint but deep sigh. She reached for the remote, pulled her legs under her and tried to switch off her thoughts. They made an odd trio, herself, Callan and Anneliese. There were ties between them that ran deeper than anything else

she'd ever experienced and yet there was so much that was left
unsaid. Perhaps it was always that way in families? She didn't
know; couldn't say. She was acutely aware of having nothing
now to compare it with.

24

LINDI
21 Laura Gundersensgate, Oslo, 1989

The speed with which they left was equalled only by the speed of
pursuit. On a winter's day when the temperature outside had
dropped so far below the snow-point that everything – air,
clouds, water – seemed to hang in frozen suspension, waiting
for some change in the atmosphere that would trigger a release,
Lindi lay in the still-warm fug of tangled blankets, feather
pillows and her own clothing and watched Lars Tøve, one of
her law professors, hastily gather up his own clothes. He who
had once declared he could – and would – stare at her beautiful
face for ever . . . now couldn't look at her. She let out a small,
inaudible sigh and rolled away from him, not so much as to spare
him the embarrassment of having to look anywhere but at her as
he collected his socks, buttoned his shirt and tucked it into his
jeans, but to spare herself the sight of yet another middle-aged
man beating a hasty and terribly undignified retreat. Outside
was pitch dark; *9:37 p.m.* The clock on the dressing table at the
far end of the room sent out a faint, iridescent glow. Her breath
rose and fell evenly. She could hear him patting about in the
semi-darkness, looking for his keys.

'On the dressing table. By the door.'

'Oh, yes . . . thanks. Um, well . . . I'd . . . I'd better get
going.'

'See you, Lars.' Her voice was muffled by the pillow. She
didn't turn round. There was a moment's awkwardness and then
her bedroom door opened and closed quietly and she was alone

again. The faint rumble of the tram going up Louisasgate floated up from the street, as much vibration as noise. In the flat below, she could hear the television coming through the walls. All around her were the signs of people going about their evening routine. Cooking, talking, listening to the news, watching yet another quiz show. There was a sharp burst of laughter from people walking slowly along the frozen street and the blast of a car horn as someone stepped off the kerb. Then all was quiet again. *9:54 p.m.* She ought to get up, take a bath, get ready for bed. But she was already *in* bed. She could still feel the damp trail of his semen on her thighs, the faint stickiness on her arms and breasts where he'd kissed her, mumbling inarticulate, desperate endearments he didn't mean, making promises he had no power to keep. She pushed aside the sheets impatiently and stood up. The room still smelled of him, of sex. She pulled on a dressing gown, irritated with him, with herself. She walked over to the window, pushing it open with difficulty and stepping back from the blast of freezing air for a few seconds before shutting it firmly again. All gone. The cold had a smell all of its own.

She walked into the bathroom and turned on the taps. Her hair, which she usually kept in a tight, controlled knot on top of her head, was loose and wild, standing away from her head like the caricatures of Africans she'd seen in comic books as a child. Once, when she was very small – or so Siv told her – she'd been taken to a bookshop somewhere in Oslo to choose herself a new book. An African man had wandered into the children's section, probably by mistake. He was tall and very dark, much darker than her. She'd stared at him; he was probably the first black man she'd seen – she had no recollection of the incident. The story, like so many others, was simply part of family myth. 'Ma,' she'd asked, in a voice that was both loud and innocent in the way only children's can be. 'Look. Is his hair like that or has he just had a fright?' Even now, twenty-five years after the incident, Siv went bright red when telling it. They had no way of knowing whether the young African with the enormous Afro could understand Norwegian. There were loud guffaws from customers around them; Siv picked up the bundle of brightly coloured clothing that was her child and rushed out of the section. She looked at herself in the mirror – her hair was standing up on end. Now she was the one who'd had the fright.

The bathroom was rapidly filling up with steam. She shrugged off her dressing gown and lowered herself into the hot, scented water. Her skin was very dark against the gleaming white of the tub. She submerged herself slowly, right down to her cloudy hair. Underwater, her ears attuned themselves quickly to the difference in pitch. Lars Tøve. Johan Gunarsson. Stefan Kleist. Patrick Berg. She ran lightly down the list, remembering. Justin Cartwright, the visiting professor from New York University who'd taught her the basics of tort in first year . . . it made no difference who they were or where they were from; whether they were married or single, lawyers, doctors, even Steve O'Hara, the bloody taxi driver she'd met on holiday in London. The story was always the same. A first, giddy rush of enthusiastic chase, a few, heady weeks of drinks and dinners and films or even the theatre . . . then a rapid cooling-off period which lasted anything from a day to a week, followed by a quick, complete exit. She was twenty-nine years old and had never had a relationship that had lasted longer than a month.

Toril and Klara were happy in their long-term relationships and for the majority of her friends the situation was the same. Some lasted longer than others, of course, but everyone's lasted longer than hers. Boyfriends and lovers came and went but few within the space of six weeks. It was only her. There was clearly a problem. She had no trouble *attracting* men; she just couldn't keep one. When she left high school and enrolled at university, the sudden, unexpected interest from the opposite sex had almost overwhelmed her. In high school, where everybody knew everybody and everyone certainly knew Lindi Johanssen, the adopted daughter of Erik and Siv Johanssen, she'd been the oddity, the one who stood out, not always for the most flattering of reasons. At university, in contrast, and for the first time in her life, she was suddenly exotic. Beautiful. Rare. Someone to be pursued, won over. And then jettisoned at precisely that moment when her guarded, hesitant reserve had just begun to thaw. She spent hours analysing where she might have gone wrong, what she'd failed to say or do, what the mistakes might have been, but came up empty-handed. Oddly enough, their withdrawal seemed to have little to do with her – it was simply what happened. There was a boundary in them that she was unable to cross, or perhaps vice versa, and so they simply bailed. In that respect, Lars Tøve was no different. Married, yes. Her professor, yes . . . but no different. For a month he'd told her she was the brightest, most beautiful, most precious thing he'd ever seen, taught, loved. For a few days now, she'd sensed his withdrawal, his preparing to leave. Tonight's brief encounter would be their last. When he saw her next in class, his eyes would hood over as if they'd never met. Of that she was one hundred per cent sure.

She leaned her head against the side of the bath and closed her eyes. In the steam it wasn't possible to distinguish between beads of sweat and tears.

25

ANNELIESE
Rue Chauveau Lagarde, Paris, 1998

There wasn't a city in the world quite like Paris, even in November when the evenings were short and the nights long and dark, and the sky seemed saggy under the weight of rain. Anneliese walked across the herringbone oak flooring of the hallway, her heels marking out a neat, precise beat, and pushed open the intricate pair of off-white, carved doors that led into the living room. She paused for a moment in the doorway, savouring the long view of the apartment. For once she was glad she'd left Stéphane, the interior designer someone had recommended, alone. The colours he'd chosen complemented the particular quality of Parisian light perfectly. 'What time of the year are you most often here?' he'd asked her. She'd been surprised by the question at the time but now she understood why.

'March and November, mostly. For the shows.'

Stéphane nodded, making small, neat notes. March/November. Spring/autumn. He'd chosen the palette with those two seasons in mind. Each of the apartment's six rooms had been decorated in a palette of colours that ranged from creamy off-white, to gold, bronze and almost metallic ochres. The first time she'd seen it, she'd cried out in delight. *Most* unlike her. They'd stripped, bleached and relaid the flooring, stripped the walls and the decorative plasterwork of colour, replacing it with shades that ranged from sandy and beige to yellow gold. Now, from her vantage point on the threshold between the hallway and the large yet comfortable formal living room, she could see the beautifully aged marble of the fireplace with its slate surround; the ornate ceiling roses and cornices, now painted a delicate shade of buttery cream; the brushed gold velvet of the four-seater couch that turned from khaki to bronze, depending on the light. There was a set of double doors at the end of the room which opened onto the dining table, a magnificent slab of dark mahogany with twelve high-backed chairs, upholstered in stiff dark-brown twill. The early winter light bounced off the surfaces, throwing textures into sharp relief. It was, in all senses of the word, a feast for the eyes. Even the underside of the large, half-moon lamps that hung above the dining table had an unexpected twist: matt, smooth black on the outside, burnished gold underneath. They cast a beautifully soft, rosy light on the table and on her guests.

Ah, her guests – she quickly came back to the task at hand. She was having a dinner party that evening, after the last of the shows. She made a quick mental note to call her assistant. One more to add to the list. Lagerfeld. The undisputed king of couture. His own assistant had rung earlier in the week to say M'sieur Lagerfeld would be in Paris during that week after all. For all that the press enjoyed the rivalry between them, the truth was they were closer than most people guessed. Both German, for one thing, though they spoke French to one another, for reasons she'd never quite understood. And for another, Karl understood her obsession with fabric and cut like no one else. They appealed to a very different market – AdSP's clothes were hardly ever seen on the sort of celebrity women who bought Chanel – but they understood and respected one another. She wouldn't dream of coming to Paris to show her new collection, hosting a dinner party for twelve of her closest friends and colleagues and *not* inviting Karl. Friends. She pondered the word for a moment. Was Karl a real friend? Or Caroline of Monaco? Or Galliano, the young English upstart who'd taken over the house of YSL? Colleagues, certainly . . . she kept abreast of what they were doing, season after season, the way they surely kept abreast of her. She saw them at the shows and at those dreadful 'events' that the fashion industry kept dreaming up which Bruno insisted they attend.

He'd practically kidnapped her the other week, forcing her onto a plane to Japan for that awful party hosted by LMVH. Standing to one side in the giant tent they'd erected in the grounds of some hotel or the other, watching her contemporaries gyrate on the dance floor, she'd wondered – not for the first time in her life – whether any of this was worth it. *Dance? You must be joking.* And certainly not to that dreadful music. She'd sipped her champagne, nibbled distractedly on a canapé and then, well before midnight and after yet another troupe of coked-out models and aspiring actresses arrived to 'freshen things up', she escaped to her hotel room and the luxury of sleep. Bruno and Jasper were still there on the floor, bumping and grinding into one another and anyone else who happened to come close. Ridiculous. At *our* age? She'd looked at him disapprovingly but she had to smile. It was a touchy subject. Bruno *was* her age; Jasper was not. For all his sanguinity and cool-headedness, she knew just how terrified Bruno was that Jasper would one day leave him for someone younger, more handsome, more full of life. It was a taunt Jasper liked to throw at him in his spoilt-child moods. At moments like those, Anneliese longed for nothing more than to slap him soundly. A spoilt child indeed. Didn't he *know* how lucky he was? She herself had only the vaguest outline of what he'd been and where he was from before Bruno had picked him out of the crowd in a nightclub. They'd practically had to teach him how to hold a knife and fork! His luck – *and* his life – had changed from the moment they met. It *infuriated* her to see him playing the spoilt ingénue, just as it infuriated her to see Bruno succumb. Still, she mused, we all have our weaknesses.

She turned away from the subject of her friendships and opened the giant, bevelled shutters at the far end of the dining room. She looked out over the gardens below. It was almost five o'clock and the pearly Paris light was fading. In another thirty minutes or so, it would extinguish altogether and darkness would close in. The butler would come in shortly and begin switching on the lamps, lighting the scented candles, making sure everything was ready for the moment her guests would arrive. From the kitchen at the other end of the apartment came the soft, occasional sound of a pan being washed or someone's voice being raised a fraction. Madame Boulicaut, her chef and housekeeper, would have everything under control. Bruno had once asked her what was the point of keeping a full-time housekeeper in every one of her residences, some of which she only visited once a year. 'There's every point,' she'd murmured. 'They're my homes. I couldn't function without them.' It was true.

She'd long understood that her work was a combination of seeing and being seen. She engaged with the world in order to draw inspiration from it but she had to retreat from it, too. Her various homes were places she could withdraw to in safety, assured that whatever she found in one would be found in the other. The world, for all its beauty and complexity, was wild and unpredictable, impossible to grasp or contain. One's home (or in her case, her homes) provided exactly the necessary security from which to view it, marvel at it, indulge. She could still remember the day she'd discovered that there was more to the world than the singular image her parents provided. It was through Mwane. The two of them had been wading through the waist-high grass that grew along the side of the river-bed, waiting for those few days of rain once a year when everything around them would spring into life. Mwane had stopped suddenly, pointing to the tips of the grass. She held her breath and bent her head, excited by his air of discovery.

'There . . . see?' He brought a perfectly still finger to within an inch of the tip.

She narrowed her eyes the better to focus, and then suddenly drew in her breath. It was the most magical moment of her life thus far. Thousands of tiny, metallic green insects, half the size of her fingernail, were clinging to the tips of the stalks around them. The whole field around them glittered iridescent in the sunlight. She'd never noticed them before. How could she not have seen them? She felt as though she'd only ever seen the world through a single pair of eyes, her own, and now, seeing it through Mwane's, she'd somehow clumsily grasped that there was always more. A never-ending, limitless string of possibilities, provoked and encouraged by the insights of others but always retaining some aspect that was hers alone. From then on, she told herself, the important thing was to be alert and ready for that moment of discovery when someone else opened a door or a portal through which another view of the world might emerge. Later, much later, when she'd had to steel herself against those very same doorways, shut down that part of herself that remained open, and trusting, and ready to embrace another's perspective, she realised that her homes provided what no one else could – her own safety.

One home was not enough. There were too many landscapes, too many memories, too many tongues within her to find resolution in one. So she had several, each different but corresponding in some elemental way to the different places she'd known. In Paris it was the light; in Mustique the sun. In London it was work, and the calm of knowing at all hours of the day and night that her studio was there, next door to her, and that come morning, it would be filled with the buzz and activity of the people who'd worked for her for so long. In Hamburg, in the villa on the shores of the lake, there was something else at play . . . the sound of German all around her, the Christmas rituals, the smell of burning logs and the snowy landscape that never failed to bring another quasi-imaginary landscape to mind. Her schedule every year was the same. November in Paris, the shows and the dinner parties and the yearly catch-up with her friends and colleagues, then it was back to London for a couple of weeks, wrapping up the spring orders that had been placed since the shows. Halfway through December, barring a trip to the Far East to see Yuchiko, she would decamp to Hamburg where Christmas was always spent with Callan and Bruno – Jasper, too, and Tara, of course . . . and then it was off in the other direction, to Scheherazade, to celebrate the New Year in the sun. This year, of course, there was even more reason to celebrate. AdSP's continued survival. She felt a sudden rush of warmth for Callan, and Bruno, and everything they'd done to make it happen. She brought her hands up to her cheeks which were suddenly warm. There was a sudden tap at the door. She looked up from her private reverie. '*Oui?*'

'*Madame?*' It was Madame Boulicaut, come to make last-minute enquiries about the menu and the place settings. She ushered her in. Just as well, she thought to herself, fishing her spectacles out of her bag and settling herself down beside her at the dining table.

'*Alors . . . nous sommes où?*' she asked, studying the sketched layout that Madame Boulicaut placed in front of them.

'*Je vais placer Monsieur Lagerfeld là,*' Madame Boulicaut began, efficiently rearranging the table so that all the guests would feel they'd been perfectly seated according to proximity and rank. Heaven knew there was nothing more disastrous than a dinner party where someone felt miffed. She'd been at one too many of those; not in *her* house, thank you very much.

They went down the list together, Anneliese nodding to

herself, making the odd suggestion about flowers, fruit, food. She and Madame Boulicaut had done this a dozen times at least. There would be no unpleasant surprises, no disasters, no last-minute change of plans. The evening would go off perfectly, as ever. In the morning there'd be huge bunches of white lilies and roses from the guests who'd attended. *Merci, chère Anneliese. Merci pour tout.* Everyone would have had a good time; the wines would be outstanding, the conversation even better. That was another reason she so liked having Karl's presence at her rare soirées, and why she always chose her guests with such care. In sharp contrast to the popular image of fashion designers, the small coterie around her were anything but frivolous and vacuous. Karl, Miuccia, Hubért . . . they were all formidable intellects, capable of discussing practically anything but with the right amount of charm and grace. When Callan and Tara were younger and still sufficiently mesmerised by the sight of Princess Caroline or Jean Paul Gaultier at her table, she'd often brought them along. Conversation was an *art* form, she was fond of telling them. It requires patience and practice. Neither had quite got it right; Callan was often too impatient and Tara too tongue-tied, but she was glad she'd done it just the same. Oh, all the tiny, taken-for-granted lessons she'd been so careful to teach them . . . funny, really. No one had taught *her*. On the contrary, those lessons she'd somehow gleaned from childhood had done nothing to prepare her for the world she'd entered, or even the one she'd left behind.

The dinner party was going exceptionally well. Everyone was having a good time. Under the benign influence of excellent wines and Madame Boulicaut's cooking, everyone had begun to unwind. Anneliese sat at one end of the beautifully decorated table, looking down its length with pleasure. Her guests were all engaged in animated discussion, a sure sign that she'd chosen well. She caught Karl's eye. He smiled, that lovely, private smile she'd come to enjoy, and raised his glass to her. Earlier that evening he'd said something to her, meant for her ears alone.

'You and me, *Schatz*. There's only a handful of us left. The rest are rag-makers.' She'd actually blushed with pleasure. I'm getting old, she thought to herself in amusement. But a compliment from him was all the more meaningful because it was rare, and genuine. Karl was someone who only spoke the truth.

'*Excusez-moi, madame* . . . there's a phone call for you. It's urgent, apparently. I wouldn't have disturbed you otherwise.' Madame Boulicaut was suddenly at her elbow. Her voice was apologetic.

'I'm sorry. Do excuse me.' Anneliese stood up, carefully folding away her napkin. She smiled briefly at her guests and walked into the hallway, following the round, ample behind of her housekeeper. '*Merci*, Madame Boulicaut,' she murmured, accepting the phone. 'Here is Anneliese,' she said briskly.

'Anneliese?' A woman's voice.

She felt the cool hand of delicious surprise slide up and down her spine, followed swiftly by irritation. She waited until the door had closed behind Madame Boulicaut then she gripped the receiver. 'How did you get this number?' she asked.

'I'm sorry.' The woman on the other end of the line was contrite. 'I got it from the studio. I . . . I wanted to see you. I'm in Paris.'

'In Paris?' Anneliese gripped the receiver even more tightly. 'What are you doing in Paris?'

'I wanted to see you. I heard the news.'

'Don't. Don't call me at this number again.'

'I won't. I promise. But can I see you?'

Anneliese hesitated. The surprise and irritation that had washed over her as soon as she heard the voice on the other end was swiftly replaced by something else. 'All right,' she said finally. 'But not here. Don't even think about coming here.'

'Where then?'

Anneliese thought quickly. 'Hotel de Chambourd-Clémency. It's on Boulevard—'

'I know where it is. What time?'

'Late. I've got friends here. After midnight.'

'I'll be waiting. Congratulations, by the way. I heard it was close.'

She put down the phone. Aside from the irritation, something else was coursing through her veins. Her mouth was suddenly dry. Desire. It had been a while. She put up her hands to her face. It was hot and damp. She drew in a deep breath and tried to steady herself. It was nearly ten p.m. Another few hours. She touched the silver pendant she wore around her neck, closed her eyes briefly and then headed back to the dining room. 'Nothing, nothing . . .' she assured her guests as she slid into her seat. 'Just a bit of housekeeping.'

'Well, *ma chère* Anneliese . . . if you *will* insist on having twenty homes,' Hubért joked, lifting his glass.

'No, not twenty,' Anneliese murmured, taking the compliment as it was intended. 'A couple, *c'est tout.*'

'*Quand mème,*' Hubért fluttered his eyelids. '*Quand mème.*'

There was a murmur of acquiescent laughter from the others. She caught Bruno's eyes as she lifted her glass and drained her wine in a single gulp. He had no idea who had just called her. Just as well. He would never understand.

'So, I heard you'd struck a deal.' The woman lying next to her reached across for her cigarettes.

'Haven't you stopped smoking yet?' Anneliese looked at her and frowned.

The woman was unperturbed. She lit a cigarette and carefully blew the smoke out of the side of her mouth, away from Anneliese. 'I tried.'

'It's bad for you.' Anneliese got up from the bed and looked for the dressing gown that the hotel so thoughtfully provided. She was sounding prim, she knew it, and disliked it in herself.

The woman yawned, stretching languorously. 'So you keep telling me, *chérie.*'

'Doesn't Robert mind?'

The woman laughed. 'Robert doesn't even notice. You've cut

your hair again. It's too short. I like it when it's a bit longer. Makes you look softer, more approachable.' She laughed again.

Anneliese put up a hand to her hair self-consciously. 'I like it short.'

'I know you do. That's the last thing you want, isn't it? To seem softer.' She stubbed out her cigarette and slid out of bed. 'I'm only teasing,' she said, walking round the bed to join her. She pushed her body against Anneliese's back, wrapping her arms round her waist. 'Thank you,' she said quietly, her lips moving against the silk of the dressing gown. 'Thank you for the money. And I'm sorry I called you at home. I wanted to see you and say it in person. You're too good to me, you know?'

Anneliese closed her eyes. What Jeanne didn't know – and would never know – was how much the opposite was true. She passed a hand over Jeanne's freckled forearm, gripping it tightly. They stayed there like that for a few moments, both women lost in thought. Then Anneliese disengaged herself gently, belted her dressing gown and moved on, in more senses than one.

26

LINDI
Oslo, 1990

It took Lindi a few minutes to find her voice. Somewhere deep inside the house, the grandfather clock that Siv's grandfather had passed on to his son, Siv's father, who had in turn passed it on to her along with the other beautifully polished and burnished antiques amongst which Lindi had grown up, solemnly ticked out the minutes of the hour. Nine o'clock in the evening. A Wednesday evening in the middle of March when the first signs of spring were pushing their way through the hard crust of ice that covered the city. Siv and Erik had been busy planning their annual Easter pilgrimage to the log cabin in the woods north of Oslo – another of the gifts her family had left them –

when Lindi wandered in, banging the front door behind her. They both looked up from the table in surprise and pleasure. It was quite usual for her to come home during the week, put a load of dirty laundry in the huge American-sized machines that were Siv's pride and joy and then stay to supper, nibbling on a carrot stick or slices of carefully cut apple as Siv prepared their evening meal. It was a particular feature of their lives together that Lindi's friends envied. In the Johanssen family, there was nothing that couldn't be discussed. Her friends loved it. Their conversations dipped and turned, ebbed and flowed, beginning in some event in the day or another and ending where no one could have predicted. There were many nights during her first few years at university when she'd come home like that, unannounced, and wound up sleeping back in her old room, curled up amongst the soft toys and posters of her teenage years.

But not tonight. Tonight was different. Tonight she'd come home with her laundry and the excuse of a decent meal – but that was all it was – an excuse. There was another reason behind the visit, of the sort she'd never exercised before. It was the first time in her life she'd hidden something from them, not out of fear, but out of a desire not to hurt them. It had taken her almost six months to prepare the speech she'd come to deliver and now that the moment had arrived, she felt herself both fearful of it but also strangely exhilarated. She drew in a deep breath, letting it out slowly, preparing herself.

'What is it, *vennen min*?' Siv's clear blue eyes were upon her, disarmingly frank, worried.

'Ma,' Lindi said hesitantly, her fingers lacing themselves together automatically. 'There's something I want to talk to you about. You too, Pa.'

'What is it?'

'I . . . I've been thinking . . . I know it's going to seem as though it's just come out of the blue, but there was this advert I saw,' Lindi began hesitantly. 'On the departmental noticeboard. It's for a job – a posting – back home.' The word slipped out unintentionally. 'I mean, in Windhoek.'

Her parents looked at each other fleetingly. 'What d'you mean, "back home"?' Siv asked, her normally composed face crumpling in concern. 'Namibia? But *this* is . . . this is home, surely? You feel at home here, don't you? Of course you do!'

'Yes, yes, I do!' Lindi said hurriedly, rushing to assure her. The hurt and surprise were etched on Siv's features as though she'd uttered her pain aloud. 'Of course it's home. It's not that.'

'Then . . . what is it?' Siv asked. Lindi saw some memory of an earlier conversation between them surfacing in her face in alarm.

'It's just . . . well, I just think it's the right thing to do. *Now*, I mean, at this point in my life. I know I've never been there and I've no idea what the place is really like, but I was *born* there, wasn't I? It's still part of me.'

'Of course it is.' Erik's voice was gentle. 'You've obviously been thinking about this for a long time, darling. You don't make a decision like that out of the blue. Why didn't you talk to us about it?'

Lindi looked down at her interlaced hands. She didn't know what to say. It was the only time in her life she'd kept something from them. Her father was right; you didn't come to a decision like this overnight. She didn't know how to answer him. Although it wouldn't be one hundred per cent true to say it *wasn't* because of Lars or Gunnar or any of the others, neither was it true to say it was solely because of them. And how would she phrase it, anyway? *I'm tired of being dumped? I'm tired of being the girl they all leave?* Siv had stopped asking her why she never brought a boyfriend home, probably for fear of opening up the conversation they'd had all those years ago and not being able to give Lindi the answers she sought or needed. After all, how many times could Siv utter the same meaningless assurances? *I'm tired of being different.* That was it, in a nutshell. That was the problem – but how to phrase it? She had never felt any different from *them*. To her, Siv and Erik were her parents, as simple as that. Their faces were dearer and more familiar to her than anyone else's. Their large, beautiful house on Oscarsgate was the only home she'd ever known. The feeling when she walked through the front door was that she'd returned in some deep, mysterious way, to *herself*. She couldn't imagine feeling that way anywhere else, and especially not in a place she'd never seen.

She had no memory of Namibia. The photographs she'd seen provoked a deep curiosity but it was a curiosity once removed. The landscapes, people and places they spoke of bore almost no relation to her life; they were strange to her and she'd listened to her parents' stories with polite, distracted attention. But two things had happened whilst she was still a teenager that were so deeply ingrained in her as to have been physical, like the tribal markings she saw on the faces of Africans in the large photographic books that lay on the coffee table in the formal lounge: Nujoma's visit when she was ten and her encounter with Ree Herz. Both were bound up, in some as-yet-inexplicable way, with her sudden longing to leave. Although both incidents had arisen as a result of wildly differing circumstances, they'd opened up a wound inside her that had never fully healed. *Who am I? What am I?* In her first year at university with her newly discovered charms at the full height of their power, she fell under the spell of one of her professors who freely admitted a teenage-like infatuation with her. It was heady stuff. 'You're special,' he said to her over a drink one night, two or three weeks after he'd seduced her. 'Special because you're like us and yet you're not. It's a powerful combination, Lindi. Use it wisely.' She'd looked at him uncertainly, unsure of what he was trying to say. It was a compliment, surely? Or was it? When he broke it off a week later, she understood it differently. Now, with the gift of bitter experience, she understood exactly what he'd been trying to say. She didn't belong and she never would. She *almost* belonged, but not quite. Almost didn't count. When she saw the advert on the noticeboard, it was as if her life had just declared itself to her.

'It's a posting at the Ministry of Trade and Industry,' she said slowly, finally. 'For three years. They're looking for a lawyer who speaks English, Norwegian and French. There's a section within the ministry that deals with fishing and the Norwegian govern-ment, our government, is helping them draft the concession agreements.'

'That's why they need a Norwegian speaker. Under Hamu-tenya, I take it?' Erik spoke up suddenly. He ignored Siv's astonished look. 'I saw it in *The Economist*. Never thought you'd apply,' he added reflectively.

'Y-yes,' Lindi stammered. She looked at her father uncer-tainly, but with relief. Siv was still staring at him, open-mouthed.

'Well, Hamutenya's a good man. We knew him pretty well, didn't we, darling?' He turned to include Siv. He got up from his chair to refill his pipe. The room slowly filled with the particular sweet scent of her childhood. He'd done it deliber-ately, she reflected later that evening, going over the con-versation in her mind. Under its release, she was freed of the awkwardness of her decision and the pain it had no doubt caused them. She looked at him in gratitude. His gentle, deft steering of the conversation away from her decision to the more practical matters of what to do once she got there defused the awkwardness and pain of the moment. Somehow, as always, he'd managed to acknowledge the bonds that tied them but at the same time gave way to her with a grace that allowed her to slip free.

PART FOUR

27

REE HERZ
Shoreditch, London, 2000

He took the steps two at a time, his left knee twingeing in faint protest. He hadn't been to the gym in almost a week, he reminded himself. The ages-old rugby injury that niggled at him occasionally suddenly asserted itself. Nothing much, just another one of those little reminders that his body threw at him every now and then; he was no longer eighteen and therefore immune to practically everything that life cared to throw at him. He winced, slowed down his steps and pushed open the door to his studios. Once inside, he felt immediately calmer. Large, untidy and unruly, the place looked exactly as he'd left it the night before – chaotic. He liked that. There were still scraps of model-making equipment lying on the floor, bits of cardboard and torn-out pages from magazines, discarded coffee cups and the remnants of someone's pizza that the near-blind cleaners had failed to see. He encouraged his young staff to work as messily and chaotically as they dared. The offices of *Riarua Herz Associates* were most emphatically *not* the smooth, pristine, all-white spaces of many of his contemporaries.

'Morning,' he said cheerfully as he walked past. Terri, his secretary, was standing in the reception area, talking to the girl who answered the telephones and made the coffee. Unfortunately, as he'd found out only the week before, her skills extended no further. He'd come out of his office one morning, looking impatiently for Terri and found himself face to face with her, the girl whose name he couldn't remember ever having known.

'Could you photocopy these?' he'd asked her, handing over a stack of papers. She'd looked at him blankly.

'I don't do photocopying.'

He looked at her, nonplussed. He thought at first she was referring to her job description. 'Well, you do now,' he said shortly.

'No, I mean, I don't know *how*.'

'What d'you mean? You just press the button.'

'I . . . I don't know where it is.'

'The photocopier? It's right behind you.'

'Please don't make me,' she whined.

He'd stared at her incredulously. Her face was beet red. He wondered how old she was but before his temper really got the better of him, Terri appeared. She took the sheets from him, made some suitable excuse and popped them under the glass cover herself. He'd had to return to his office, bewildered. 'Where the hell did we get her from?' he asked Terri when she appeared a few minutes later.

'Work placement,' she said blithely. 'From one of the local schools. She's only here for a month, Ree.'

He shook his head, baffled. Why didn't they just hire a proper receptionist, he wanted to ask her, but didn't. He had other, more important things on his mind – two competitions, a potential large commission from an important art collector and a proposal for the City Hall – and if he didn't oversee each of them, right down to the last detail, he'd a feeling he could kiss each one goodbye. They were in a delicate situation. He'd had enough press coverage in the last twelve months to guarantee that people would certainly come knocking, but not enough cash to hire the right kinds of staff to make sure they got the jobs. He was thirty-eight years old and the firm had been going for over a decade. In the past year he'd won more competitions than any other architect in the UK but there were still those who complained he'd won not on the basis of his skills, *per se*, but because of the colour of his skin. It was so fucking irritating it didn't bear thinking about – except, of course, he couldn't help himself.

He shut the door behind him and surveyed the bomb site that was his desk. His office – in reality little more than a box carved out of the cavernous space of the larger office – was now the only place he could truly be alone. It was impossible to find the time or the space to himself at home, the large sprawling loft in Shoreditch that he and Hayley shared with the kids. He'd bought it when he first started working, years back, for next to nothing. No one wanted to live in Shoreditch back then. Huge, dirty, abandoned, the building which had once been a London Transport depot was located directly opposite the sort of pub that no one, except the die-hard locals, wanted to drink in. He'd fallen in love with it on the spot. He'd convinced his bank manager to give him a modest loan and he'd set about transforming the space himself, clawing precious time in the evenings and at weekends from the practice where he worked. The bank manager was rewarded with a copy of *Elle Decoration* in which his client's home was featured. Alongside the captions was one that hit the spot. *Major thanks are due to my bank manager, David Clarke, for believing in this project when no one else would.* The framed page was still prominently displayed on David Clarke's wall.

Shortly afterwards, he won a commission from an artist who'd recently moved into the area in search of more space and authenticity than Kensington presumably could provide. That job had led to another, and another . . . and a year after that first article appeared, he had just enough work to quit his job and branch out on his own. That was eleven years ago. He'd spent five happy bachelor years in it and had lost count of the number of girls whom he now met at dinners and shows who'd spent the night in it somewhere along the way. When he met Hayley, they were both in the full flush of their respective careers. She was a successful model with shows and assignments all over the world. He was nurturing his fledgling practice, hunting down clients, entering competitions, doing whatever it took. Neither of them was ever properly 'there'. The loft suited them perfectly. They came in off flights from New York, Tokyo, Berlin, the Bahamas, tossed their bags on the floor, made love in the middle of the day in the various corners of the single-space room and jetted off again. The perfect space for the sort of couple they'd been, back then at least.

But then, for reasons neither could quite fathom, the exotic overseas jobs suddenly dried up for both of them and Hayley fell pregnant. Nine months later, Zoë was born. The oversized room in which they'd done everything was invaded by a screaming, colicky child. He'd reluctantly partitioned off a room to one side and for a couple of years they'd somehow managed. But it was the arrival of Ottie, their second child, that really put the nail in the coffin, so to speak. The circumstances of Ottie's birth had changed more than just the space around them. She was born six weeks early, by emergency Caesarean. They'd been so lucky with Zoë. He understood that the night they waited by the tiny in-cubator, too frightened to speak to one another. But she'd survived the night, somehow, and the one after that and then, the doctors assured them, she was out of the woods. They took her home to the loft that now held two screaming children, not one, and a mother who seemed unable to do anything other than weep. Ree was at his wits' end. Hayley seemed to think her baby would die the minute she put her down, and her neglect of Zoë was nothing short of criminal. Everyone called it post-natal depression, and seemed convinced she'd come out of it. Ree wasn't so sure. It seemed to him that there'd been a fundamental split between their life before Ottie arrived and their life after it. Nothing would ever be the same again, and certainly not be-tween them.

Hayley seemed to think it was all *his* fault. He worked too hard. He was too selfish. *His* career came before hers, before everything else, including their children. If he hadn't left her alone as much, none of this would have happened. If, if, if. The list of 'ifs' went on and on and he was always, somehow, implicated. Part of it, he reasoned with himself, night after night as he held Zoë and tried to get her to sleep whilst Hayley slept in their big double bed with Ottie at her side, was true. He *did* work hard. But he'd worked just as hard before Zoë arrived, and certainly before Ottie. In fact, it was one of the things in the beginning that Hayley claimed had drawn her to him. 'You *work*. I mean, you *really* work. You *live* to work.' It was true. He was puzzled as to why it attracted her so. 'You don't know the sort of men I get to meet,' she'd said drily. That, too, was true. After a year together, he'd understood what she meant. Her world – models, actors, fashion people – was different. There was a part of him that found it fascinating and, yes, *fun*. *Her* crowd worried about nothing, planned for little other than the next party and the one after that and where and with whom they might spend the holidays and the vast amounts of money they seemed to make. It was fun and frivolous and, for a while at least, a welcome respite from the rather morbid seriousness of the world he inhabited from nine to five. Or six to eight, as Hayley was only too quick to remind him.

But it soon began to grate on him. He was quickly bored of the vacuous conversations and the discussions that led nowhere. He wasn't bored of *her*, at least not yet, but the signs were there. But by that time she'd moved in, they were *together*, an *item*, as often in the press as they were out of it. Having Hayley on his arm seemed to generate a disproportionate amount of coverage until it got to the point where he wasn't sure whom they were after. It didn't seem to hurt his work – on the contrary. The commissions kept coming in, small ones to begin with – a shop front here, an interior there, an extension to someone's home. He discovered that the rich and famous liked having models and actresses and wannabe models and actresses around, but at the same time, they liked having beautiful homes and bars and hotels. The fact that Hayley Summers was going out with an architect who could not only provide them with the sort of glamorous homes and interiors that they craved but who brought a certain amount of cachet to their gatherings himself . . . well, so much the better.

He was young, good-looking (or so the magazines said), black *and* talented. The small jobs kept coming in, and in that first year, they were the only jobs, too. There was a part of him that worried about the nature of the work. After all, who *cared* whether Mr X had a larger, more luxurious pad than Mr Y? How many new bars and clubs could he reasonably be expected to churn out? But everyone said those jobs would soon be a stepping stone to the more serious sort of work he craved – public buildings, a bigger scale, something he could really get his teeth and his practice into. So he waited, designed and built one stunning house after another and then Zoë and Ottie appeared and all of a sudden, it was a whole new ball game and everything changed.

'Ree?' Terri breezed into his office without knocking. 'This just came in. Thought you'd want to see it.' She handed him a fax.

'Don't you ever knock?' he asked mildly, knowing full well what the answer would be. He took the piece of paper from her. It was from the mayor's office. He read through it quickly, his pulse beginning to race. They'd won a new commission. Finally! A new centre for contemporary photography in East London. 'When did this come in?' he asked, trying not to show how pleased he was.

'On Friday, apparently. Katie wasn't sure what to do with it.'

He rolled his eyes. 'Before we go any further, send her back to wherever she came from. Let's get a proper receptionist.'

'You said we couldn't afford one,' she began hesitantly.

'I've changed my mind. Get someone with a few functioning brain cells, won't you? And will you send a quick note back to them,' he indicated the fax. 'Apologise for the delay in getting back to them and just say how delighted we are to accept, et cetera. You know the score. Something short and sweet.'

'Will do. Coffee?'

'Mmm.' He swivelled around in his chair and faced his computer screen. His mind was already six steps ahead. A new job and potentially a new direction for the firm. A *public* building, not some coked-up music producer's new bedroom, and an important one at that. At long fucking last.

It was raining by the time he left the studio. The day, which had started out with blue skies and blazing sunshine, had turned. Autumn was definitely on its way. He pulled up the collar of his coat and hurried down Rivington Street. He'd spent the better part of the day holed up in his office, flicking through books on photography, film, video art . . . exactly the sort of day he loved but rarely had. Terri took all his calls; the four young architects who worked with him handled everything else – even Katie, the hapless receptionist, had been shown how to photocopy. Everything ran like clockwork, smoothly, no dramas. He glanced at his watch again. It was eight thirty. He really ought to go home. Hayley would be waiting for him. He hadn't seen the girls since the night before . . . yeah, he *ought* to go home. He got halfway down the street, stopped, hesitated, then fished his mobile out of his pocket.

'Cheers.' They clinked glasses. He took his first, pleasurable sip of whisky. Warm and silky, just the way he liked it. He felt some of the day's tension begin to slip away, leaving the still-pleasant afterglow of the morning's news behind.

'New job, eh?' Geoff looked just as pleased as he did. 'Saw it online this afternoon.'

Ree nodded. 'Yeah, long time coming, I can tell you. We were down to our last two projects. I've been wondering if we'd make it past Christmas. Doesn't get any easier, does it?'

Geoff shook his head, though the stress of running a firm wasn't one he'd ever known. They'd studied together, although Geoff had done what he thought at the time was the 'sensible' thing and had gone to work for a large firm. Fifteen years and countless working nights and weekends later he was a senior partner. The work was largely commercial and boring and there was a part of him that missed the adrenalin that came with the smaller, more experimental firms, like Ree's, but he had a wife and three kids . . . he wasn't sure he could stand the uncertainty of it all. 'Well, that's the trade-off, mate,' he said, although not without a touch of envy. Geoff's name would never come up in lights, regular salary or no.

'Yeah, so they say.' Ree smiled. 'I keep thinking, *now* it's going to get easier. *Now*. After this one, or the next. *Then* I'll be able to relax. It never does, though.'

'You're doing all right, though, aren't you? You're in the papers all the bloody time,' Geoff said, frowning.

Ree gave a short, semi-bitter laugh. 'That's the other thing I've learned,' he said, taking another sip of his drink. 'Having your name in the papers hardly ever translates to a job, or if it does, they're the sort of two-bit jobs that barely keep us in tracing paper. I keep telling Hayley—' He stopped suddenly, brought up short by his own conscience. It wasn't Hayley's fault. She couldn't help her job or her looks or the interest she generated. It wasn't her fault everyone she knew seemed to want her husband to design them a new kitchen. 'Anyway, this new job's a welcome change. I spent the morning looking at Muybridge, would you believe it?'

'Takes you back, doesn't it?' Geoff mused. 'Staying up all night to work, the intensity of it all. I miss it sometimes, don't you?'

Ree nodded, smiling wryly. 'Are you kidding? I'm *still* up all night. Anyhow, this'll put us on a different kind of map. I'm sick of doing house extensions.'

'At least they're million-pound house extensions. Try building office blocks.' They both grinned. It was a long-running joke. Ree looked at his watch. It was nearly nine thirty. Hayley would be fuming. He pulled his phone out of his pocket and glanced at it. Three missed calls. He slid it quickly back in. They would all be from her. He took a last swallow of his drink. 'I'd better run,' he said reluctantly. 'Hayley'll have my head on a block.'

'Yeah, me too. I haven't seen the kids since Sunday.'

They paid and pulled on their coats. Outside, they gave each other the quick, slightly embarrassed hug of men who've known each other too long for a handshake but are uncomfortable with a kiss on the cheek, and walked off in opposite directions, Geoff to catch a train to leafy Richmond, Ree to their loft just up the road. Lately Hayley had started dropping comments – more commands than comments, really – about moving to a bigger place 'in the country'. He could no more imagine living in the country than he could on the moon. London was in his blood. It was there, from the crowded, cosmopolitan streets around Shoreditch, Hoxton and Hackney that he drew his inspiration. Not from the glamorous bars and residences that had somehow become his trademark, but from the other stuff. As he walked to and from his home to his office, in his mind's eye he saw the libraries he wanted to design, the community centres, art galleries, public spaces . . . the stuff that *really* made his heart beat. To move to one of those suburban houses in Surrey, or a converted barn in Norfolk, would kill off whatever chance he had of establishing himself as an architect who *counted*. He didn't *want* to be known as an architect to and for film stars. That morning, before coming into the office and after the breakfast argument he'd had with Hayley, he'd again started doubting the choices he'd made. But the confirmation of the photography centre had changed his mood. He felt momentarily giddy with delight, the sort of feeling he hadn't had in a long while, he thought to himself as he put his key in the lock and opened his front door.

The loft was quiet, stretching out in front of him in a long, satisfying sweep of polished concrete flooring and exposed brick-work, little furniture, the odd rug or two. In the far corner of the room, the TV was on, though Hayley wasn't sprawled out in front of it. He absolutely loved his home. He remembered the conversation he'd had with his parents the day he'd decided to buy it, years ago.

'You're staying, then?' Sibongile said, disappointment evident in her tone.

He'd suppressed a grin. Staying? Of course he was staying. 'Yeah. Where else would I go?'

There was a moment's hesitation. 'I just thought . . . well, *we* just thought perhaps you'd like to come home?'

'I *am* home, Mum.'

'No, I meant here, to Windhoek.'

'Ma, what on earth would I do in *Windhoek*?' He sighed, thankful she wasn't there to see his face. It was a decades-old argument. Since the country's independence, his parents had begun to drop subtle (and then increasingly not-so-subtle) hints about coming 'home' to help build the country they'd spent the better part of their life fighting to free. He refused to take the bait. *His* home was London, England at a push. They were the ones who'd sent him there at the tender age of seven when Sibongile decided their itinerant life was no life for a child. They were constantly on the move, not just out of a real fear of assassination or incarceration – after all, hadn't it happened to more colleagues than they cared to remember? – but because she and Klaus were more useful to the cause outside the country than in it. In the seventies and eighties alliances were constantly shifting. One minute they were in Cuba, petitioning Castro, the next they were sent to Moscow. For some time they were based in Geneva, which was the only city Ree could reasonably claim to remember, but soon word came from the leadership in exile – Zambia, please. They arrived in Lusaka late in the evening after an exhausting journey that had taken them from Geneva to southern Africa via Libya and Lagos. Sibongile took one look at the accommodation that had been arranged for them and put her foot down. It was one thing for her and Klaus to suffer the deprivations of exile, quite another for their only son. They both had their contacts to call upon.

He was sent to prep school just outside Brighton. In the half-terms and holidays he went to an exiled South African family in Hampstead whilst his parents criss-crossed the globe, seeking support for the cause. From there, at the age of ten, he was sent to boarding school in Hampshire. Now his holidays were spent in Oslo, Dar-es-Salaam, Leningrad. He saw his parents intermittently, though it did not occur to him to be resentful.

Namibia's struggle was simply part of a wider struggle to rid the continent of its colonial masters. From Ghana in the 1950s to South Africa – it was all part of the same goal to which Klaus and Sibongile had dedicated their lives. As the eighties gave way to the nineties and, for the first time, independence in both Namibia and South Africa became a real, viable possibility, the family found themselves at the centre of international attention, almost as much for what they'd come to represent as for the strength of their political convictions. It was Ree's first lesson in media expediency.

His first trip to Namibia coincided with the independence celebrations and the swearing-in of his father into the new government. He was interested in the proceedings – who wouldn't be? – but it was with the semi-curious outsider's interest that he watched it all. He didn't speak the local language – neither Sibongile's, nor German, his father's. He'd never been to Katutura, the township his mother had grown up in, nor to Klein Windhoek, where his father was born and raised. Both sets of grandparents on both sides were dead; a handful of Sibongile's relatives still lived in tin shacks in the reserve to the east of the country where they'd been forcibly removed. They spent an uncomfortable weekend amongst them, Ree unable to do much more than smile, Sibongile clearly embarrassed by her failure to teach him anything other than '*shikê*' in her language. *Hello*. He watched the ritual slaughtering of a goat in his honour with interest, not emotion. For Sibongile and Klaus it was an emotional homecoming, but not for him. It bothered *them*; it did not bother him. Home was London. Shoreditch. His job and his circle of friends. Namibia was a politely interesting distraction, one that he observed through the detached lens of an outsider, in all senses of the word.

So, Sibongile's perennial pleas for him to come 'home' to Windhoek were a source of mild amusement, tinged with irritation on his part and increasing agitation on theirs. They adored their two grandchildren, whom Sibongile lamented bitterly were strangers to them, just as her own child had been. It didn't help matters that the lawyer daughter of his parents' best friends, that dreadful girl Lindi Johanssen, who had vomited over his trousers years ago, had actually moved back, going so far as to take up a position in one of the ministries. Sibongile talked of little else these days. Lindi this, Lindi that. He could barely remember much about her, other than the fact of the vomit. Quite how she had wound up one of the rising stars of the new government (if Sibongile was to be believed) was beyond him.

In any case, he was suspicious of his mother's motives in mentioning Lindi Johanssen in almost every breath she took. Sibongile positively *loathed* Hayley, though her feelings had softened somewhat with the arrival of her grandchildren. Hayley and Sibongile had absolutely nothing in common. Hayley baffled Sibongile entirely and, Ree suspected, the reverse was true. In the beginning he'd made a few half-hearted attempts to bring both of them round but quickly saw it was pointless. When he announced his decision to marry her, Sibongile, for once in her life, was lost for words. 'Wh-why?' she'd spluttered finally, her voice crackling down the international line. He could just picture her in the living room of the house they'd bought in Hochland Park, a new suburb of Windhoek that, ironically, had been built on the razed grounds of the township where she'd lived for the first five years of her life. The new black township, Katutura, where she'd grown up, meant 'the place we do not want to go'. He found it poignantly poetic. Sibongile, predictably, did not. Poetry was not in her nature.

'It's what people *do*, Ma,' he said, aware of his own temper beginning to rise.

'Don't you get fresh with me, young man,' Sibongile snapped. 'She's a *model*, for God's sake.'

'So?'

'What do *you* want with a model?'

He sighed. 'She's a good person, Ma. You just don't give her a chance.'

There was silence for a few minutes, then his father came on the line. Sibongile had apparently declared herself unable to talk.

'If you're sure, son?' His deep, heavily accented baritone voice expressed what Sibongile could not. They'd expected something else from him – something less frivolous. In a way that had never openly been expressed between them, it was acknowledged that their decision to send him away had its consequences – this, then, was one of them. They had no rights where his life and the direction it took was concerned. They'd given those up a long, long time ago, along with the bedtime stories and the easy childhood confidences. He'd bought the loft against their better judgement; he'd established his own firm when they'd advised him not to and now he was marrying Hayley. Klaus understood his decisions as a rebuttal of their guarded attempts to present alternatives for his life, and was forced to respect it as such.

But when the grandchildren arrived, a kind of truce was established, especially after the drama of Ottie's birth. Sibongile was beside herself. She flew to London, was at Ottie's side within hours and refused to leave until Ottie was able to breathe on her own. She stayed in London – at Claridge's, of course – until she was satisfied the danger was over. It did little to bring her and Hayley closer together but it did humble Ree. In a way, he saw, with a perceptiveness that surprised him, she was able to express what she'd never been able to previously – her love for her grandchildren and, indirectly, for him. It didn't stop the hints completely, but it did lessen their impact.

He pushed open the door to the girls' room. They were both fast asleep in their bunk beds, Zoë on top, as always, lying on her side, a thumb in her mouth, and Ottie flat on her back, below. He stood in the doorway for a moment, watching them. It was still a miracle to him how he and Hayley had managed to produce two such angelic, yet different, little creatures. Zoë was tall for her age, a slender, slightly darker-skinned version of Hayley. She had dark brown eyes, Hayley's dark brown hair and a light smattering of freckles across her nose which baffled both of them; no one in either family had freckles. But they were as characteristic of her as her laugh was, which she'd inherited, almost undiluted, from Klaus. Ottie was small and pleasingly plump. She had Hayley's hazel eyes and the most astonishing mass of tight, curly blonde hair. Both girls, though very different from their parents, were beauties in their own way. He hoped, for Hayley's sake, if not for theirs, that it would stay that way. She was forever examining them for flaws. She despaired over Ottie's thighs, incredible as it sounded. 'Ottie's *four*, Hayley,' he'd said in astonishment as she removed a second helping of carrots from Ottie's plate.

'Yes, but that's where it starts,' she muttered darkly. He'd turned away, out of his depth.

He frowned. Where *was* Hayley? He shut the door quietly and looked around. It was one advantage of a loft – there were no other rooms. The kitchen was as empty as the dining area. There was no curled-up figure in the far end where the bookshelves made a small alcove. The place was empty. Just then he heard the slam of the front door downstairs and the sound of footsteps on the stairwell. A second later, she rushed in, no coat, with just a scarf trailing behind her. 'Where've you been?' he asked. 'Don't tell me you left the girls alone?'

'I just popped down to the corner shop. We're out of, er, milk,' she said breathlessly, unwinding the scarf from her neck. 'I've only been gone for a couple of minutes, Ree. Don't panic. Where the hell were you, anyway? I've been calling you all bloody evening.'

'I had a drink with Geoff,' he said, still frowning. 'Where's the milk? Didn't you get any?' he looked at her empty hands.

'Oh, they're sold out.' She ruffled her hair with her hands. 'Make me a coffee, will you, darling?' She hurried towards the bathroom.

'I thought you said we're out of milk?'

'Black, then.' She disappeared into the bathroom and closed the door.

He stood uncertainly in front of the refrigerator for a second, unsure whether to be annoyed or relieved. He opened the door.

There were two cartons of skimmed milk sitting on the top shelf. He stared at them. Had she simply not seen them? He sighed and set about making a pot of coffee. He decided against bringing the subject of milk up. She was so damned unpredictable these days. Anything could set her off. The 'darling' she'd casually tossed out could mean one of several things: a thaw after an evening of missed calls; a general thaw after their arguments of the past week or so; a call from her agent, always guaranteed to put her in a good mood . . . or even – he stopped to consider the possibility – sex? He almost laughed out loud. He couldn't remember the last time they'd had sex . . . a month? Two? He'd been so busy of late. A trip to New York to view a potential competition site; another trip to Berlin for a meeting with a group of developers that had come, as usual, to nought. Then she was gone for a week to the south of France to see her mother. And then, of course, there'd been that spectacular argument over her going back to work. Yes, in all likelihood, it had been well over a month.

Funny, he thought to himself as he measured out the coffee grounds. In the beginning they'd hardly been able to keep their hands off one another. *This*, he'd thought to himself when it first started, is what all the fuss is about. It wasn't just that Hayley was the most beautiful woman he'd ever set eyes on. She was a model, the face of a major cosmetics company; he couldn't remember which, now. Lancôme? Lanvin? He tried to recall the cartons of products she kept on her dressing table in that tiny flat she lived in, just off Old Compton Street. She was tall, nearly six foot in her bare feet, with bleached blonde hair, cut close to her scalp. She was half French, half English and had that marvellously careless look of wealth and class that marked her out as special, even before she'd opened her mouth. She was fluent in both languages, equally. It was one of the qualities that he'd so admired. Being with her was like being with two women, simultaneously. She slid from faultless, upper-crust English to the French equivalent without drawing breath. Her mannerisms were quintessentially English, and yet they were not. She had the additional charm of confusing her gestures sometimes – a Gallic lift of the shoulders accompanied by a rolling of the eyes that was bored, spoilt Londoner, nothing but. She *enchanted* him, yes, that was the right word. And he her, or so she claimed. She jetted in from her assignments, her skin, although carefully protected, always with a light dusting of gold that brought the summer to mind. Funny that her name was Hayley Summers. 'Aylee, as her French mother called her. He was the first person she called or texted in the morning, and the last person she made contact with at night. 'I want mine to be the first voice you hear,' she said, over and over again. She would assiduously set her watch or phone or whatever device was to hand in the five-star hotels she stayed in, making sure that she knew precisely when it was 5.45 a.m. in London or wherever he happened to be.

Funny how things change. Although it had been over a year since her last modelling assignment, he couldn't imagine her setting her alarm clock in order to ring him, irrespective of why. These days their phone conversations had a military kind of logic to them. 'When will you be back? Who's picking Zoë up? Did you remember to get eggs?' *Yeah, Roger that. Over and out.* It was something he half-joked about with one or two of his closer friends, blokes like Geoff and Keith who'd some-how wound up in similar circumstances, in relationships with these serious, harassed-looking women they'd long since ceased to recognise as the passionate, carefree, *interesting* girls they'd once known. He stopped himself again. He was being unfair. Hayley was still passionate. Just not with him.

28

HAYLEY SUMMERS

She left Ree still making the coffee and opened the bathroom door. She shut it behind her and sat down on the toilet. Her movements felt jerky, as though she'd had too much coffee. She was breathing fast, partly with the effort of running all the way down Charlotte Road to meet Dixie, but also out of fear. It was the same general, unspecified fear that flowed over her almost every waking moment. If you'd asked her, she probably wouldn't have been able to say what it was she was afraid of. Accidents. Illnesses. Flying. Death. Other things, too, though, that were somehow less acceptable and therefore harder to describe. Take tonight, for example. She'd come home after meeting up with Erin and Natascha consumed with fear. They both looked fantastic; they were on top form. They both had every reason to be. Erin had just come back from Milan where she'd opened the show for Armani and Natascha had just heard from her agent that Lagerfeld had requested her specifically for his Paris show in a couple of weeks' time. Erin and Natascha, whom she'd met when they first all started out together, were both five years younger than Hayley, and it showed. Not so much in her face or body, both still as sleek and perfect as ever, but in her choices. She had two small children; they did not. She had a husband; they did not. She had a home to run; they did not. They, like the sort of girl she *had* been, were free to pick up, pack up and jet off at any given moment, permanently on call. A shoot in New York on Friday? No problem. Tokyo the following Wednesday? *Daiyubu desu.* No problem. She smiled weakly, remembering the odd word of Japanese she'd picked up over the years of her visits. No problem? No, everything these days was a bloody problem; *that* was the problem. Her husband, her children, her *life.*

She could hear Ree opening and shutting the cupboard doors quietly, not wanting to wake the girls. She stuck a hand in her coat pocket and pulled out the little plastic bag she'd picked up from Dixie. Two grams of grade A, pure Colombian coke. Enough to last her the weekend, cut her appetite and give her a reason to get up in the mornings. She picked up one of the magazines that lay in a tasteful wicker basket beside the toilet bowl, pulled a credit card out of her wallet and expertly fashioned herself a line. She flushed the toilet at the same time as she bent her face to the cover, her snort of inhalation drowned out by the rush of water. She waited for a few seconds for the all-too-familiar dizzy rush of blood and drugs to her head . . . then carefully put the magazine aside, brushing off the last few crumbs of coke and rubbing them quickly on her gums. It was good stuff; she was already beginning to feel better. More alive. Sparklier. Funnier, too, if she could be bothered to talk.

Ree, she'd noticed, was in a rather good mood. She'd seen it as soon as she came through the doorway. It was in his eyes. Everything was in his eyes. More than anything else, it was his eyes that had drawn her back then. Not his height, or his build or the breadth of his shoulders. It was all in his eyes. Dark brown, but with the faintest trace of hazel that gave them a striking depth, especially when viewed in a particular light. She'd never met anyone of such depth or intensity. His gaze was always focused. She liked that about him. He was serious, committed, a *proper* person. He had an energy and purpose about him that made every gesture, every decision, seem considered. Unlike the others, he wasn't frivolous, even though he knew well enough how to have a good time. She knew herself to be frivolous, but in a light, playful way – a charming way, or so she'd always been told. He didn't seem to mind it, at first. He loved the fact that she and her circle of friends were light, easy. They were exceptionally good company, fun and interesting in an undemanding, self-sufficient kind of way. He was tired of *heavy* women, he said. She'd met a few of the girls in his circle of friends. Heavy was the right word though it had nothing to do with weight. Serious women – some of them beautiful – but weighed down with all sorts of worries, from the Gulf War to the price of oil to the budget deficit of countries she'd never heard of. Hayley and her crowd couldn't have cared less about the price of oil but it didn't mean they were stupid – far from it. They were savvy and cosmopolitan, well-travelled, well-brought-up girls who simply embraced life and all its messiness without wanting to *fix* it. He liked that. Or so he said. She wondered when he'd stopped liking it and began to want something else instead.

She stood up, feeling momentarily dizzy. She put out a hand to steady herself and looked at her image reflected in the mirror. She looked well. She was beautiful, still. She'd stopped dyeing her hair blonde years ago, though she'd barely changed the cut. It was dark brown, very short and feathered and it suited her. For all her teenage years she'd had long, thick wavy hair, falling almost to the small of her back. She'd cut it off on her first modelling assignment, aged seventeen, and had never looked back. Her eyes were deep and slightly hooded, giving her the sultry, half-bored expression she'd been so famous for. Tight, high cheekbones; you could cut coke on them, as one photographer had kindly said. She'd never quite got used to the sight of her face staring back at her from some giant billboard in various capitals around the world. She remembered getting off a flight to Buenos Aires to do a campaign for someone – Rolex? Cartier? – she couldn't remember. Hers was the first face she saw – staring back at her from a height of ten metres, almost a hundred times its size. She saw it, gaped at it in astonishment and stopped dead in her tracks. *That* was when she knew she'd made it. She was twenty-two and she'd practically conquered the world.

'Hayley?' Ree's voice interrupted her.

Shit, shit, shit. 'Coming,' she mumbled hastily, rubbing her gums one last time and rinsing her hands. She swept a quick look around the toilet – it was clean. No tell-tale tiny crystals lying on the floor or the toilet seat . . . the credit card was back in her wallet and the plastic bag with the other gram safely tucked up in her coat. 'What's up?' she asked, opening the door. 'There's another loo in the bedroom.'

'I know. You've been in there for ages . . . you all right? Your coffee's cold.' He frowned at her, as though trying to work her out.

'Doesn't matter. I'll drink it anyway.' She could hear her own voice in her ears. Too bright. She tried to tone it down. 'So . . .

how was your day?' she asked in as sweet a voice as she could muster.

He looked a little confused, as though it wasn't the question he'd been expecting. 'Um, good. Pretty good. Got a new job.'

'Oh, yeah? Was it that music producer? Phil what's-his-name? The one we met last—'

'No, not him. It's a public building. A new photography centre.'

'A photography centre? For the *public*? Whatever for?' She could feel herself getting shrill and exasperated. 'Why don't you want to do Phil's house? He's got tons of money, more money than he knows what to do with. Julian Morpeth told me—'

'I'm sick of doing other people's houses.'

'Then why don't you do ours?'

He looked around. 'What's there to do? It's done. It was done long before you moved in.'

'No, not *this* one,' she snapped, more brusquely than she'd intended. She could see him beginning to bristle. 'Why don't we buy that place we saw near Horsham . . . you know, the one with the big garden and—'

'Hayley, we've been over this a hundred times. I'm not moving to Sussex or wherever the hell it is you want to move to. If *you* want to move, fine. Take the kids, find whatever pipe-dream of a house it is you're looking for and raise your fucking chickens. I'm *not* coming. Get that through your head.'

She could feel the conversation beginning to slide away from her. She tried to grab on to it, to bring it back under her control but she no longer knew what it was she was trying to hold on to. She was married to a man who had absolutely no interest in her, or her dreams, or her life and the things she held dear. What *did* she hold dear? Her children, of course. And that dream of a house in the country somewhere, though she had no clear idea why or when she'd first begun to want one. All the other girls had a country pile – Natalia, Liz, even Kate . . . they'd all kept a small London pad, of course, but there was something about the fresh air and the space and the lawns . . . she too longed for some fresh air and some space. As big as their loft was, she was fed up to the teeth of always tripping over some cardboard model or another, a set of drawings and, God forbid one of the girls stood on one, Ree's damn scalpels that he always left lying around. She'd no idea what he used them for – he was an architect, not a bloody surgeon!

She turned away from him suddenly, unwilling to share the bewilderment that she was sure was reflected in her eyes. She longed for another room, somewhere to run to that was away from him and the children and the never-ending noises of their lives – the TV, the fridge, the radio, the various alarm clocks. She'd had enough of the huge loft with the windows that let in too much light and the hard, polished concrete floor that bounced back too much sound. She wanted something quiet and cosy where they all weren't living on top of one another. They all said he was brilliant at planning spaces, that there was no one quite like him when it came to designing a home. Bullshit, all bullshit. He could do it for others; just not for *them*. Their own home was rapidly becoming a disaster.

She heard the sound of running water in the bathroom behind her and let out a small sigh of relief. He was taking a bath. She was angry; she was upset; she was afraid. As usual, once she'd had a hit, she couldn't decide which. She walked over to the TV. The silently flickering screen was just about all she could handle right now.

29

LINDI
Sossusvlei, Namibia, 2000

The desert rolled like a heaving sea around them, giant, reclining waves of sand; slurring, shape-shifting mounds of soft matter. The tallest sand dunes in the world moved imperceptibly under her feet, constantly forming and reforming, both sides stacked up to the thin, fluid edge that marked the summit. Walking was not easy; they staggered up the dune in the zigzag, half-embarrassed pattern of people trying, and failing, to grasp solid ground. With arms outstretched, occasionally clutching at each other for support, they made their way unsteadily towards the top. The sky was a spectacular peacock blue, suffused with light so that the whole earth around them seemed bathed in it, not just golden, almost fluorescent too. It was dry and hot and the sand beneath their soles was burning. It was one of those early autumn days when nightfall seemed a remote, almost shocking possibility. Turning back to look at the path they'd cut across the dunes, Lindi felt a strange melancholy come over her. She brought up a hand to shield her eyes from the blinding sunlight. All around her, the caramel dunes gazed silently back at them. Nothing of their presence remained. The shifting sand covered their tracks; they might never have been.

She fell a little way behind the others as they continued their slow, staggering, swaying path to the ridge. The men carried the backpacks of wine and snacks; the women clutched at each other, giggling, holding down their hats with their free hands. They were a pleasant enough group – Dieter, the filmmaker; his best friend Karl; Karl's sister, Birgitte and two of her friends who'd 'come out' to Namibia to escape the European winter. Young, well educated, well travelled, well heeled – the sort of crowd she'd known in Oslo and hadn't expected to find so easily in Windhoek, but she had. In many ways, sitting at the table at a dinner party in someone's home in Klein Windhoek, it was hard to tell where she was – here or there. She could have been in anyone's flat in Bislett or Aker Brygge – or London or Paris or New York, for that matter. The food, wine and conversations were the same.

Leaving Norway and everything she knew to come to a country that had been little more than a romantic, fanciful dream all of her life had been the biggest, most important step she'd ever taken. She'd overcome the smaller differences – weather, language, landscape – but it was slowly beginning to dawn on her that the huge, dramatic change that she'd anticipated might not come after all. The 'return', as she'd constructed it, not only to herself, but to her friends and parents, was less of a return than a plain old 'arrival'. No one at Windhoek International Airport knew or cared who she was. To the baggage handlers, eyes flicking over her in casual disinterest, she was simply another visitor to the country that had seen thousands of foreigners stream in since independence, come to save Africa from herself. The continent was awash with people trying to help, save, rebuild, restructure, develop. Sometimes she wondered how on earth 900 million people had managed before the arrival of the NGO brigade but it wasn't a line of questioning she was keen to pursue. After all, was she any different? In ten years she hadn't managed to wrap her tongue around any of the local languages – oshiHerero, oshiWambo, Nama – other than to say 'hello'. Out of some curious, half-buried sense of respect for Siv, she hadn't made any attempt to find people who were either related to her biological mother, or who might have known her. She hadn't even visited the grave, even though Siv had told her she was buried in the Old Location Cemetery, less than half a mile from the house where Lindi now lived. In so many ways her life hadn't changed at all – and it was that fact that saddened her sometimes, like now. Without being fully conscious of it, she longed for a way *in* to this new, closed society that would somehow validate the choice she'd made. She lifted her head to catch the faint, cool breeze that occasionally rolled up the side of the dunes, bringing with it the fresher promise of evening.

'Time for a drink!' Karl yelled out to the others, collapsing into the soft sand a few yards up ahead. He shrugged off his backpack, prompting Dieter and Philippe to do the same. One by one the girls reached the little group; soon they were all sitting cross-legged on the blankets that they'd carried up the dunes. They passed around the plastic cups of wine, a sense of pleasurable tiredness settling over them as they fell silent, watching the light slowly beginning to leach out of the sky. In another hour or so, dusk would have fallen.

'You OK?' Dieter had moved towards her, sensing her mood.

'Yeah,' she said, smiling at him. 'Just thinking.'

'When are you off?'

'Next month.' She looked down at her feet. 'I can't quite believe I'm going back.'

'But only to Geneva, no? Not back to Oslo?'

She nodded. 'Yeah. Two years in Geneva . . . but it's almost the same thing. I haven't been back since . . . well, since I came here. I've forgotten what it's like over there.'

'Oh, you'll remember soon enough. Rain, crowded buses, grey skies.' Dieter laughed suddenly. 'You'll see. You'll miss this place like hell when you first go back but after a week you'll have forgotten you ever left.'

Lindi shook her head. 'I guess that's just how it is,' she said slowly, tracing the outline of her foot in the sand. 'We're part of both worlds, aren't we? There's always something about the place you've just left that you long for.'

'Yeah, you're right.' He looked away from her and she followed his gaze across the dazzling desert landscape. The breeze wafted over them again, bringing some relief from the heat. She looked out across the silent, immovable mounds and felt as though she were waiting for something, for some sign . . . something that she could attach herself to and follow. Some*one*, perhaps? Was *that* the problem? she wondered. No man? She shook herself briskly. Ridiculous thought. She wasn't waiting for anyone, least of all a *man*. Like most of the women in her small group of friends, she'd had more than her fair share of offers, mostly from men she couldn't imagine spending an evening with, let alone a weekend. Windhoek was full of married men whose wives lived overseas, back wherever they came from – Belgium, Holland, Spain. The arrangement seemed to work for everyone – the men lived alone, as bachelors, and the women took care of the children, preferring to remain at home where the water was safe and the trains ran on time. There were enough young women walking around the small city to satisfy the curiosity and needs of the pseudo-bachelors, as Lindi called them – she certainly didn't want to add to their number. Most of the men were baffled by her, in any case, unable to reconcile the smooth, American-inflected English and the lawyer's demeanour with her dark skin and wild, curly hair. They weren't sure how to treat or approach her and as a result, mostly got it wrong. She offended the fragile sensibilities of Namibian men, who, by and large, preferred their wives and girlfriends docile – simply impossible in her case. All that remained, therefore, were the few young men like Dieter, who was gay, or the odd returned exile, like herself, who invariably came with a partner. She knew she cut an odd, rather lonely figure in town. Still, as she said cheerfully to her closest girlfriend, Norah, herself an exiled Namibian who had returned a few years earlier, she would rather be happy and on her own than in a relationship and desperately *un*happy – and there were plenty of *those* sorts of women in town.

She looked out over the dunes again. It was autumn in the southern hemisphere, spring in Europe. The air was dry and cool, tinged with mauve as the sun began its final quick slip towards dusk. Here, almost at the foot of Africa, night fell swiftly. She'd never get used to it, she thought to herself, taking a slow mouthful of wine, feeling the bittersweet taste flood her mouth. She'd missed those long, Scandinavian summer nights when night was always an hour or two away until it was suddenly morning again and winter seemed to belong to another era. The light was smudgy now, the dunes already beginning to lose their crisp, clean outline, turning mauvish-pink. In another hour or so all would be plunged into darkness. She felt a sweet, almost painful tug of nostalgia. Spring in Europe. She was aware of a quick lightening of her mood, deep inside her, as though she'd only just now been made aware of what it was she'd missed.

30

CALLAN
St John's Wood, London, 2000

'Callan? Um, Mr Herz is here.' One of Anneliese's assistants stuck her head nervously around Callan's door. Callan looked up from her computer screen with a barely controlled 'tsk' of impatience. She'd been going through the latest spreadsheets showing losses in the three new stores they'd opened – New York, Tokyo and Dubai. Things weren't going according to plan. The desperately needed injection of cash from their Italian investors hadn't managed to staunch the losses. Of their twenty-two stores worldwide, only New York was showing a profit. In a week's time she'd be on a plane to Milan to meet with their new shareholders and her mind was already tripping over itself to work out what she needed to look for, analyse, change, improve. Times were slowly changing. The women who'd previously thought nothing of spending three or four thousand pounds on a new winter coat were having a rethink – with disastrous results. 'Who?' She looked questioningly at the girl. 'Who's here?'

'Um . . . Mr Herz?' She pronounced the name hesitantly, looking at Callan for confirmation. There was no answering sign of recognition. 'The, um, architect?' she ventured further.

'The architect?' Callan's mind had drawn a blank. 'What architect?'

'Um . . . he's got an appointment with Anneliese . . . ?' The girl, who was incapable of ending a sentence on anything other than a question mark, trailed off, shrugging charmingly, if helplessly. She lifted her shoulders again. 'I . . . I don't know. I just thought . . . well, I thought *you'd* know?'

'Why would *I* know?' Callan muttered. 'No one tells me anything.' She was irritated now. As if she didn't have enough on her plate. She tried to remember what Anneliese had said to her the previous day, before leaving for Hamburg – *check on the new stores, make sure the delivery to the new women's clothing floor at Selfridges had come in, speak to Bruno, Marco Matuzzi, organise a meeting with the accountants to look at taxation issues in Japan* . . . she couldn't remember her saying anything about a bloody architect. 'Who is he?'

'I . . . um . . . Richard . . . Richard Herz? He's waiting outside.'

'Christ, that's all I need. All right, I'll be there in a minute.' She pushed her chair away from her desk. The assistant practically ran from the room before she could be asked anything further. The name 'Richard Herz' didn't mean a thing to Callan. She pulled her hair back into a rough ponytail, pulled on her jacket and opened her door.

He was standing with his back to her, arms folded, looking down into the small courtyard at the rear of the townhouse, absorbed in something she couldn't see. She had the vague impression of someone of great height and breadth, legs standing very slightly apart, solidly planted in the manner of a man who stood on the ground as if he owned it. He was wearing a dark blue suit of exquisite cut – Armani, Callan thought to herself as she studied him. Her eyes ran down the considerable length of his body. He wore black, rubber-soled shoes and just above his collar she caught a glimpse of a crisp white shirt. His hair was very short and very dark, and as he turned, hearing or sensing her presence in the hallway, she saw, to her great surprise, that he was black. A tall, imposing-looking, impeccably dressed black man. No, not black, she corrected herself, her eyes widening before she could stop herself. His skin was the colour of deep, dark coffee, the colour of dark, velvety syrup, burnished from within. She'd never seen anything like it. She put up a hand to her neck, touching herself lightly as if in reassurance, though against what she couldn't say.

'I'm here to see Anneliese de Saint Phalle?' His voice broke over the strange silence that had come over her. A wonderfully resonant sound that reverberated deep in his chest. 'She's not here, I take it?'

She found her voice. 'No, I'm Callan. Her daughter.' She held out a hand, hoping it wouldn't shake.

'Ree Herz.' His grasp was firm and cool.

Ree. Ree Herz. Not Richard Herz. She had to stop herself jerking her hand away, as though she'd burned it. 'Anneliese isn't here, I'm afraid,' she said, as coolly as she could. 'She's in Hamburg at the moment. She's back tomorrow, though. Can *I* help with anything? Won't you come in?' She gestured towards her office. What could he have come to see Anneliese about? she wondered, racking her brains.

He was quick, she noticed. He'd sensed her confusion immediately. 'Your new store on Bond Street,' he said, following her into her office and answering the question she hadn't dared ask. 'We're supposed to go over the sketches I gave her together.'

'Oh. *Shit.*' It came back to her in an embarrassed rush. 'Oh, of *course*! She did ask me to look over them. I've just been too busy.' She hurriedly sat down. 'Would you . . . would you like some coffee?' she said, picking up the phone. She had to do *something* with her hands.

'No, thanks. You mean you haven't seen them?'

'No. I'll . . . I'll have a look now if you like?'

'No point. I'd prefer to go over them with Anneliese,' he said curtly.

His tone brought a flush to her cheeks. 'Well, she's not here. Look, we can either go over them together now,' Callan said, more sharply than she intended, 'or you can wait until she's back. Whatever you prefer.' He'd unsettled her. She felt as though he'd caught her out, no matter that she had other, far more pressing things to deal with.

He hesitated for a moment, then bent down and reached into the leather bag at his feet. He withdrew a slim, black folder and placed it in front of her. 'OK. Tell you what,' he said, his tone suddenly mild, catching her off-guard, 'I've made some revisions to the stuff I left her. Why don't you look through these and get back to my office if you've got any questions.' He straightened up. Again, his size and presence were overwhelming. She hurriedly scrambled to her feet but even in her five-inch heels, she barely reached his chest.

'Th-that's fine. I'll do that. Um, thanks for coming, Mr Herz,' she stammered. 'I'll certainly look through them and . . . and I'll . . . we'll get back to you shortly.'

He nodded curtly, turned around and then almost as abruptly as he'd arrived, he disappeared. Callan was left standing behind her desk, staring at the door. She opened her mouth and then closed it again. His folder lay on her desk. *Riarua Herz Associates*. An East End address. *Riarua Herz*. What an unusual name. He sounded utterly English but, like her, there was something deeper, more foreign about him that she couldn't place. She wondered where he was from. She put out a finger, touching the cover cautiously, as though it might bite. *Ridiculous!* She caught sight of her flushed, apprehensive face in the mirror opposite. *Just ridiculous.*

Half an hour later, she turned over the last page and realised she'd been holding her breath. She wasn't sure *what* to call the folder of drawings he'd left her to look over – 'sketches' seemed a paltry misnomer. Anneliese would *love* them, she thought to herself, with a pang of something that was dangerously akin to jealousy. Flicking through them had stirred up what she'd hoped were long-buried feelings of inadequacy. As a teenager, she'd been acutely aware of the enormous gap between her mother's abilities and talent and her own. In a flash, she was six years old again, standing behind her mother in the studio, in mute, speechless awe, watching her work. Anneliese's hand would fly across the paper, turning lines into complete outfits, shading something so that it appeared real, floating, soft to the touch. On those rare occasions when Anneliese allowed her inside the studio, or simply forgot that she was there, she would stand next to her, watching, utterly rapt, as her mother spun out her beautiful creations. She thought of Anneliese as a magician and was devastated to find that none of the alchemy had rubbed off onto her. Callan had no such ability to see beyond the surface of things, bring inanimate objects to life or draw forth an idea in the way Anneliese could, literally drawing a piece of fabric into life. Ree Herz's talent was the same; raw, explosive and utterly magical. She closed the folder slowly, reverentially. Ree Herz was the same sort of alchemist, but with space, not cloth.

Her mood darkened suddenly, as it always did when she was faced with some version of herself that did not meet the expectations placed upon her. 'Callan is a hard worker. Not talented, granted. But she works hard. There's a lot to be said for that, you know.' The memory flew at her savagely. One of Anneliese's rare visits to Mortimer's. For some reason, she'd been waiting in Miss Molloy's study when Anneliese and Miss Molloy walked into the next door office. The door was open, but neither woman realised Callan was waiting there. They were discussing her, of course. She flushed as she recalled Anneliese's dismissive response. 'Hard work is not enough. Anyone can work hard.' She'd remained where she was, her legs growing numb underneath her, her skin crawling in shame. She wasn't talented. Not like Anneliese. Or Ree Herz, for that matter. The old, unhappy feelings of inadequacy that were never far from the surface in her, rose suddenly. She reached for the phone. There was only one person who would understand. Tara.

'Herz? Yeah, I've heard of him. He's black, isn't he?' Tara said curiously.

'Well, yes, I suppose so.'

'You *suppose* he's black?'

'No. I mean, yes. Yes, he *is* black.'

'Good-looking, too, if I remember rightly.'

'I suppose so.'

'You're doing an awful lot of "supposing",' Tara said drily. 'You just met him. Either he's good-looking or he's not.'

'OK. Yes, yes, he is. He, er, brought some sketches for Anneliese to look at. He's very talented.'

'And very married. To some model or other.'

'Oh.'

'Why d'you say it like that?'

'Like what?' Her heart sank. This wasn't quite the direction she'd planned to take.

'Come on. When was the last time you asked me about a man? Never. That's when. So what's he like?'

'Who? Ree Herz?' Callan winced as she said it. Her non-chalance wouldn't fool Tara.

'Is that why you rang me? To talk about some good-looking, married architect?' Tara sounded amused.

'No, no, not at all. I was just looking at his stuff and it made me think of Anneliese, that's all.'

'What about her?'

'D'you remember when we used to sneak into the showroom the night before the show and I used to try on all the clothes?' The memory suddenly surfaced.

Tara laughed. 'Of course. Remember the time she caught you?'

Callan chuckled. 'Christ. I thought she was going to strangle me.'

'You? It was *me* she was angry with,' Tara protested.

'No, it wasn't. She *never* got angry with *you*. It was always me. "I'm *so* disappointed in you, Callan. *So* disappointed." Don't you remember?'

'Well, you're her daughter. I'm not.'

'Don't say that.'

'Why not? It's true,' Tara said mildly. 'Of course she had higher expectations of you.'

'Don't say that,' Callan repeated. 'You are her daughter too.'

'Well, it's nice of you to say so,' Tara laughed. 'Even if it's not quite true. Anyhow, when's she back?'

'On Sunday. Are you coming to lunch?'

'Of course.' Tara hesitated, as if she were about to say something more. 'Callan,' she said slowly, then stopped, hesitating again.

'What?'

163

'She thinks the world of you. You do know that, don't you?'

Callan swallowed. She wanted to say something but there was a lump in her throat that blocked her speech. She choked out a hasty goodbye and put down the phone before Tara could ask or say anything further. She looked at her desk, slowly becoming blurry with tears. She despised herself for it, some buried weakness in her that surfaced every now and then, like a glass shard, piercing the hold over which she held her nerve. *Anneliese thinks the world of you.* It wasn't true, no matter how Tara saw it. No one thought the world of her. No one thought very much about her at all. She knew it was her own fault. There was *something* – some fatal, deadly hidden flaw somewhere in her that caused those around her to turn away. How else to explain it? She who'd been given everything had almost nothing. Those first few lonely weeks and months at Mortimer's, with only Tara for company and even then, only sporadically, were the worst of her young life. Tara was six years older and the head girl to boot. Her time was limited and in the strange, semi-mystical world of school rules, there were many occasions when it just wasn't done to be seen with the new girl, no matter who she was. She'd long since buried the shameful memories of crying herself to sleep, night after night, sobbing into her pillow quietly, almost suffocating herself in the desperate attempt not to be overheard.

A ripple of shame made her shoulders hunch. At the age of eleven, for reasons she couldn't fathom, Anneliese had suddenly ripped the carpet from underneath her feet and sent her spinning into a world she could barely make sense of, let alone enjoy. In London, despite being permanently ignored, she'd somehow managed to find herself at the centre of *some*thing – school, her friends, life at home with Mrs Betts. It worked. She remembered herself as *happy*. The hardest thing to bear was the realisation that that was the last time she could remember being happy, content, untroubled. Her arrival at Mortimer's signalled another, deeper kind of loss – she seemed to know, without it ever being said, that she would never again face the world with her feet planted on anything other than shaky, unstable ground.

The defiance and the sullenness she quickly adopted as her weapons were nothing but the mask she wore to stop anyone else from seeing inside. There was something about her that was incomplete. She wasn't quite whole, finished, in the way other girls were. She didn't even know who her father was. Anneliese had never said a word – *not a single word!* – on the subject. When the other girls asked, which they did, she hadn't known what to say. 'There's only me and my mother.' 'Yes, but what *happened* to him?' She'd looked at them blankly, not knowing what to say.

At school in London, there'd been many girls without one parent or another but the difference was that they *knew* each other. Dominique and Céline were as often in her home as she was in theirs. It wouldn't have occurred to either of them to ask who Callan's father was, at least not in the spiteful way that the girls at Mortimer's did. Everyone knew someone whose parents were divorced. In London, there were more odd-ball, patched-together families than there were traditional ones. Céline had three half-brothers, two step-brothers and a string of 'uncles', some of whom became 'daddy' for a while. Dominique's world was momentarily turned upside down with the discovery of a baby brother whose mother worked in her father's office. No matter; things shifted, broke apart, came back together again. It wasn't anyone's fault. At Mortimer's, Callan was made to feel like a freak. Fatherless. Meaningless. 'You don't even *know* who your father was? That's *weird*.' The phrase rang in her ears for months.

For a while, as a teenager, she'd carried photographs of this movie star or that in her wallet, taking them out every once in a while to stare at them, searching their features for some clue that might unlock the mystery of her own life. It was Tara who'd stopped her. 'It doesn't matter,' she said, on one of her frequent visits back to Mortimer's whilst everyone waited for Callan to grow up and move on. 'What matters is who you are *now*. You never knew him; you can't miss what you've never had.' Her normally clear green eyes had clouded over suddenly. Tara had had what Callan hadn't – one of those picture-perfect loving families, a mother *and* father who'd clearly doted on her, were proud of her, followed her every move. She'd never argued with them; her mother was her best friend. Callan couldn't even imagine a situation where she'd describe Anneliese as a friend, let alone her best friend. It made Tara's loss that much harder to bear. Tara *knew*; she'd experienced that awful, gut-wrenching pain herself. Callan's hurt wasn't of that order – hers was more the bubbling, quivering unease that sat beneath her skin like a second network of capillaries and arteries, requiring only the slightest prod to deliver their payload of pain.

She pushed the folder away from her impatiently and stood up, pressing the backs of her hands against her eyelids. Any second now the door would open and one or other of Anneliese's assistants would walk in. She couldn't remember the last time she'd cried in front of anyone, let alone an employee. She stood still for a moment, breathing deeply. Her brief encounter with the enigmatic Ree Herz had disturbed her. She'd caught a note of some strange, powerful vibrancy in his voice or in his eyes that had stirred something in her, leaving her feeling unaccustomedly out of sorts.

31

REE

He walked quickly and purposefully down the street, wanting inexplicably to be alone with his thoughts. Callan de Saint Phalle. She'd surprised him. He'd been expecting something – someone else. Someone more in the mould of Anneliese. Tall, statuesque, blonde. He'd been expecting a similar coolness to Anneliese but Callan de Saint Phalle was anything but cool. Dark, compact, intense. Beautiful, too. She'd come out of her office with a frown on her face and he'd been completely taken aback. He'd had to forcibly resist the temptation to reach out and stroke the frown away. Crazy. Mad. Beautiful. His confusion had made him brusque, not that he wasn't habitually brusque, he had to admit. Hayley was always nagging him to be a little kinder, nicer . . . more approachable. But Callan de Saint Phalle certainly didn't require charm or kindness. She'd simply taken the folder from him and placed it carefully on her desk. Watching her he realised he liked it. The way she'd squared it up, placing it neatly amongst her other things. Her movements were quick and precise. He'd barely said two words to her but already he could tell she was someone who appreciated order. She hadn't even looked inside it, the way some people would have. She'd simply put it down, said something about how busy she'd been . . . no apology, nothing. In the blast of confusion that came over him for the second time, he'd been even more abrupt than normal. She'd offered him something – coffee? – but he'd declined. It had been years since he'd been unnerved by a woman. He waited at the lights to cross the road and his breath rose and fell in short, sharp bursts. Something was bothering him; *she* bothered him. He shook his head in disbelief. What on earth was wrong with him? He couldn't remember the last time he'd felt this way about anyone, let alone a woman he'd only just met. He shook his head again, this time more firmly. Forget it; forget her. There were many more important things to con-centrate on, like getting the job. He'd only met Anneliese Zander de Saint Phalle twice before but he could already tell there was a synergy between them that happened only rarely between client and architect. He'd forgotten who made the introduction – it was at some gallery opening or the other. She'd turned, in that slow, cool way he'd come to recognise as hers, her face guarded yet curious, as the introductions were made. 'An architect?' she murmured. 'Yes, I'm in need of one. Why don't you drop by my studios?' He'd given her a card; she'd given him hers. A week later they met and again, he found himself drawn in by her quiet, precise confidence. Her studios were a little too exquisitely formal for his taste – too many calla lilies and glass tables – but in her clothes he recognised an edginess and inventiveness that quickened his pulse. The renovation of her new store certainly wouldn't be the biggest commission he'd ever had – it was tiny! – but it might well turn out to be one of the most creative. In their second meeting, the talk between them was different. This time they spoke of art, philosophy, politics . . . he was astounded at her grasp. Halfway through, she got up and brought him a piece of fabric. From the way she described its properties, he understood two things. She was a woman of considerable intellect and she expected the same of him. It was again rare. A client who pushed him beyond his own limitations? It was generally the other way round. Their collaboration might turn out to be better than either expected. *That* was why he had to put any and all improper thoughts about her daughter firmly out of his head.

32

ANNELIESE
THREE MONTHS LATER

A few minutes of sustained hammering, followed by a loud crash, signalled the collapse of the last interior wall. At the far end of the space, a cloud of chalky white dust spiralled lazily upwards. There was an exaggerated sigh of relief from the foreman who stood in the doorway with her, watching his men clear away the last of the rubble.

'That's it, then. All done.' He pulled out a none-too-clean handkerchief and mopped his brow. 'That's the last one. Thank God for that. Hard as stone, them walls.'

Anneliese declined to comment but was secretly pleased. Aside from the constant banging and drilling, it was the first time since the work had begun the previous week that she'd fully grasped what it was Ree Herz was suggesting. He certainly knew what he was doing, she thought to herself, looking down the full length of the space and out to the street beyond. What had once been a poky, corridor-like leftover squeezed in between two shops was now a long, slender hallway full of light and air. He'd pushed through to the floor above so that the space had dramatically opened up. Yes, no question about it – he knew his stuff. Theirs was an almost perfect pairing, she mused, leaving the foreman and walking the length of the room to better understand the proportions. She'd sensed it the minute she laid eyes on his drawings. He'd proposed leaving it almost empty, but with what he called a 'rainbow wall' at one end, akin to an art installation that would flood the room with filtered light prisms. He'd shown her the computer-generated images and she'd actually gasped in pleasure. The wooden parquet flooring was being pulled up and then they would pour a floor of liquid, glossy white concrete, designed to reflect the spectrum of colour streaming through the glass wall. It was beautiful, rich and simple – exactly what she wanted before she'd even guessed it.

She walked to the back of the room and opened the door that led out into the tiny courtyard. It was cool outside, and quiet. She put a hand into her coat pocket, half-smiling to herself, and pulled out a packet of cigarillos. She lit one, enjoying the sharp, acrid rush of smoke as she drew it down into her lungs. She almost laughed out loud. Callan would scarcely believe it. Her mother – *smoking*? Bruno knew she enjoyed the occasional cigar but her displeasure over Callan's habit meant she could hardly light up in front of her. She followed her own signature of smoke as it trailed upwards into the air. There was the faint, already dissipating spittle of an aircraft overhead; the skies were deep, iridescent blue.

She thought about Ree Herz again. Over the past three months, they'd met only a few times. More often than not, either she was too busy, or he. One or other of his many young assistants would bring the latest drawing or sketch over to show her – there would be an exchange of emails or phone calls and a decision was quickly reached. He understood her in a way few people ever did. He showed her his ideas, waited for her to digest them and then they moved together, as one, on to the next stage and then the one after that. She'd spent enough time with architects and interior designers over the years and most of those relationships ended in tears – usually theirs. She was no longer on speaking terms with the two young architects who'd designed her house and studios. A clash of egos, everyone called it. Anneliese was stubborn and strong-willed and knew *exactly* what she liked and what she didn't. Herz's genius seemed to be that *he* knew what she liked before she did. He forced her to question *why* she liked something, and, more often than not, come up with something better. It had taken them barely three months of conversation and now here they were, on site. The project would be finished on time, and on budget. It was one of the first things he'd promised her – and she believed him.

She stubbed out her cigarillo, grinding it underfoot. It was almost four p.m. Callan was meeting the accountants in just under an hour but there was no need for Anneliese to join them. Callan could – and would, of course – handle everything. She could tell from the worried expression on Callan's face that things weren't going quite the way they'd planned but she refused to lose sleep over the fact. They'd survived countless downturns before – no reason to believe this one would be any different. She belted her coat and pushed open the door.

'Anneliese.' She looked up in surprise. Herz was suddenly in front of her, his hand still gripping the door handle.

'Oh! I didn't expect to see you here,' she said, oddly flustered. She was tall, but he was taller. She wasn't used to looking up at anyone.

'I just popped in to see how they're getting on. I had a meeting down the road that ended early.'

'It seems to be going well,' she said carefully, nodding at the men who were still clearing up rubble. 'Not that I can tell . . . just clouds of dust at the moment.'

'Are you on your way somewhere?' he asked, glancing at his watch.

She hesitated, then shook her head. 'No. I was just on my way home.'

'D'you have time for a quick coffee? I'll come back later and have a look round.'

She hesitated. It wasn't in her plan. 'Why not? Yes. Why not? Better yet . . . how about a drink?' she heard herself say. 'My club's just around the corner.'

'After you.' There was the sound of a smile in his voice.

Oddly pleased, she belted her coat a little more firmly and they walked out together. She led the way down Bloomfield Place, slightly dazed. She couldn't remember the last time she'd made a spur-of-the-moment decision to go off and have a drink in what was still the middle of her working day!

'Mrs de Saint Phalle . . . how nice to see you. We haven't seen you for a while.' The manager at Bruton's, the discreet club where she'd been a member for nearly twenty years, greeted them warmly. If he seemed surprised to see her with a good-looking young black man, he was far too seasoned to show it. 'Table for two?'

She nodded briskly. 'Near the window, Simon, please.'

'Certainly. Can I take your coat?' He made a great show of settling them in, flourishing the extensive wine and cocktails menu, then withdrew discreetly.

'What'll you have?' she asked Ree, looking at the list almost guiltily.

'Wine?' he asked, and the note of amusement was still there in his voice.

She nodded. 'Red or white?'

'You choose.'

She could feel the corner of her mouth tugging upwards in a smile. Was he *flirting* with her? The idea was so absurd she nearly laughed out loud. She was old enough to be his mother! No, it wasn't flirtation, though there was certainly a pull of some sort of attraction between them. She ran a finger down the list, pondering the unfamiliar question. What was it about him?

'Well,' she said, a few minutes later, raising her bowl-shaped glass of rich red wine. 'Cheers. This is a bit of a surprise. For me, anyway. I can't remember the last time I had a drink before sundown.'

'Cheers.' He brought his own to his nose, swirling it around appreciatively. 'Good choice.'

'Can I ask you something?' she said suddenly. 'Where are you from? Your name, I mean. Ree. And Herz, too. It's German.'

He smiled. 'It *is* German. Well, almost.'

'What d'you mean? You have German ancestry?' She looked at him disbelievingly.

'Not exactly ancestry.' He laughed. 'No, my parents are Namibian. Your old ex-colony, I believe. My father's the German one. From Swakopmund. It's a tiny little town on the coast, quite quaint, really. Like a little piece of Germany transplanted to Africa. My mother's Herero, though she grew up in the north, near a place called Omaruru. That's where my name comes from. Riarua, actually, though no one calls me that except my mother, and even then only when she's cross with me. I'm named after one of the Herero chiefs, actually. Samuel Maherero's son. I don't know much about the history – that's my mother's department.'

Riarua. Samuel Maherero. She felt the cool wash of disbelief ripple through her, like water sluicing through a trough. The closeness and familiarity of the words collapsed the distance between them, the vast expanse of time and space contracted and ballooned out again. She could hear his voice but it came to her only distantly. The muted background chatter of the salon behind and around them roared in her ears.

She saw herself get to her feet, saw the look of surprise, then alarm, on Ree's face as she stumbled away from the chair, from the table. She could see herself shaking her head at him, at the manager, saw the faces of others turn towards her as she backed away from the room. Her coat was a soft shapeless object in her arms and the cool evening air slipped under the sleeves of her shirt. She stepped into the path of a taxi, hailed it down frantically and yanked open the door with a force she didn't know she possessed. She could see herself talking to the driver, giving him directions, but she wasn't aware of what had come out of her mouth. There was a great trembling darkness inside her. The moment was intolerable; she drew in great shuddering breaths, trying to get at the next minute, and the one after that, waiting to carry her through.

REE

He ought to go after her, was his first reaction. He half-rose from the table as she backed away from it but there was a panic in her eyes that stilled him. She fled from the room and whatever it was he'd said before he could properly react. He was aware of the other diners looking curiously at them – at her, as she stumbled towards the exit. He heard the front door open, the anxious exchange of words with the manager and then she was gone. He saw her flag down a taxi and clamber inside, her customary coolness completely gone from her. He hesitated; should he call her office? Speak to her daughter? What the hell had just come over her?

'Everything all right, sir?' The obsequious manager appeared silently.

Ree nodded curtly. He stood up. 'I . . . perhaps she wasn't feeling well,' he offered, not wanting to be drawn on the subject of what might have come over her. He was only too aware that they made a strange couple – the tall, blonde woman in her mid- to late-fifties, he guessed, and himself . . . young enough to be her son, in some ways, improbable though it seemed. 'Let me just settle this.' He indicated the two practically untouched glasses of wine.

'That won't be necessary, sir.' The latent accusation in the man's voice lay between them. It would have been easy to pick it up, explain. *I'm her architect*. He remained silent and walked quickly from the room.

33

ANNELIESE

She drew the white wooden shutters against the glow of the
sodium-yellow street lights and turned slowly to face the empty
room. Her bed, a smooth expanse of crisp white linen and
plump, perfectly upright pillows, stood in the centre, its serene
blankness an affront to the churning mess of emotion going on
inside her, not just in the depths of her stomach but in her heart,
her head. She crossed the floor in her bare feet and sat down on
the edge of it, feeling its softness give way underneath her. She
sat very still, as if holding her breath. She spread her hands
outwards on either side of her, staring at her fingers as if she'd
never seen them before. Large hands . . . long, capable-looking
fingers, the nails short and buffed, never polished. On the
middle finger of her left hand was a ring she'd worn for nearly
forty years. Silver, squared-off, heavy-looking. She lifted her
right hand and touched it hesitantly, feeling underneath her
fingertips its familiar, worn, faintly pocked surface. She sat for a
long time, the faint sounds of the household two floors below
her coming through the cracks in the door, the walls, even the
floorboards. Callan was still there; she'd brushed past her when
the taxi dropped her off. 'Why didn't you call and let me send
the chauffeur?' she'd asked as Anneliese climbed the stairs.
She'd mumbled something offhand and incoherent in response
and escaped before Callan could question her further.

Namibia. Swakopmund. Omaruru. *You've probably never
heard of them. Few people have.* She drew her long legs up onto
the wooden edge of the platform surrounding her bed and
wrapped her arms around her knees. Few people indeed. What
Ree Herz couldn't possibly know was that she had heard of
them. She, of all people. She *knew*.

PART FIVE

34

HANNELORE
FORTY YEARS EARLIER
Swakopmund, South-West Africa, 1961

Gulls shrieked overhead, swooping about, making long slow
circuits out of the air, circling in a leisurely, dreamy fashion,
then darting sharply away only to reappear minutes later with
their strident childish cry. Hannelore stood on the upper deck,
watching the land rising gradually towards the blue mountains
that were a pale, soft colour now but would turn lilac, then
purple later in the day. The shore, with its waving mass of people
who'd come to see the latest batch of passengers off, was a
distant, thin line, moving steadily away from them, but at an
angle, like something seen through a camera lens. All around
them the waves lifted themselves in a slow, glossy roll, pausing
for a moment then rolling oilily and evenly towards the last
remnants of land. It was hard to measure their progress; one
minute the companionway that bridged the gap between the
ship and the shore could still be distinguished, next minute it
was gone. An hour or so ago, sitting in the gaily decorated ship's
bar with everyone, she'd felt her eyes slowly fill with tears, a
brimming she couldn't control. Across from her, Tante Bärbel
noticed and made some comment about her hair having escaped
her scarf. Hannelore was wearing a new dress – lemon yellow,
with a swirling pattern of orange and white – a gay summer
dress, despite the cold into which she was about to sail. She felt
Tante Bärbel's hand slide under the silk scarf to tuck the offending strands back in. She put up her own hand in a mixture

of embarrassment and confusion and for a long, trembling moment, their fingers touched and held.

'There, that's better,' Tante Bärbel said at last, leaning back and blowing out her cigarette smoke in lazy overlapping rings. Behind her, moving discreetly through the crowd of well-wishers, friends and relatives who'd come on board to wish the passengers one last farewell, the ship's officer indicated to the staff that they should stop serving drinks now. It was time for the ship to leave. They sat smoking in silence together as the minutes to Hannelore's departure ticked by. Presently, a bell clanged, sending the seagulls swooping upwards in protest. *All non-passengers are requested to leave the ship. Will all non-passengers kindly leave the ship.* The words were very carefully enunciated. There was a great sighing and scraping back of chairs as the groups around them began to break up and disintegrate. The ship's band broke into a song; gulls shrieked again and again and the bell sounded once, twice. Tante Bärbel's face was pulled together tightly; Hannelore found she couldn't speak. They got up and clumsily embraced, Tante Bärbel holding her tight by the elbows. A great feeling of loss came over her. Her world had turned itself upside down; from now on, nothing would be the same. She was released suddenly, and thought for a second she might even fall.

She watched Tante Bärbel walk down the companionway with everyone else, noticeable not only because of the red wide-skirted dress she wore and her neat black pillbox hat, but because of her straight-backed, beautifully upright posture. She was wearing gloves; it was Hannelore's last image of her, slowly pulling one long white glove, then the next, over her smooth, pale arms. She turned and gave a half-wave, her hands slowly slipping back down until she was hugging herself, white gloves against her red dress, a dancer's elegant pose.

The hooter sounded again, solemnly marking the moment of parting and Hannelore had to turn away. The ship broke away from the land, no longer part of it and the water rose around them. When she was sufficiently composed to look back, the shore had become a line; the crowd had melted together as one and the red dress was nowhere to be found.

Their progress out towards the vast greyness that was the open sea was slow. The gulls began to drop away, prepared to circle only so far from the safety of land. The slow, steady rolling of the ground beneath her – the ship's deck – was something she would have to contend with for the next three weeks until they finally docked in Brindisi. She and Tante Bärbel had traced the ship's path in much the same way she'd traced her mother's journey back from Europe, all those years ago. Swakopmund. Walvis Bay. Round Cape Town, then up the great sweep of the coast to Durban. Lourenço Marques. Mombasa. Then through the narrow Gulf of Aden, and the even narrower Gulf of Suez. Onkel Fritz had business interests in it, she gathered. Now she would sail through that very same canal and into Europe. And a new life.

She turned away from the deck and, holding tightly onto the handrail, descended to her cabin. Tante Bärbel had booked her in first class. 'Of *course* you'll go first class, *mein Schatz*. What a question!' The compact room with its neat little bunk, the washbasin and, in one corner, a small toilet with a tiny, incongruously pink bath. Everything was miniature, perfectly made and neat, like a doll's house of the sort she'd played with back on the farm. She sat down heavily on the bunk bed. The lull and roll of the ship, the distant but distinct throb of the engines somewhere far below, even the muted sounds of the conversation in the berths around her . . . all these came to her now as a sudden change in pitch, like those odd moments when the frequency inside her ears shifted slightly, making her newly aware of sounds that had previously lain unheard. She looked at her hands. The ring – a parting gift from Tante Bärbel – had slipped to one side. It was fractionally too big for her finger.

She sat very still and began to trace its surface with the fingers of her other hand, the way a blind man might feel his way over the surface of a letter written in Braille. Her mind had gone completely and utterly blank; there were no words to contain what she felt. Her whole being had suddenly turned over, like one of those large rocks that dotted the landscape around the farm and that someone – or something – had upended. The underside that was revealed might never have seen the sun, or light. Underneath, in the damp, dark, yeasty earth, a different kind of life was teeming. She remembered how, as a child, squatting there with the others, they would look upon those translucent creatures with wonderment and awe and disgust. Pale ants, their bodies slick with clear fluids; termites, so light and clear they seemed almost invisible; grey, plump maggots, thick and fat, their squirming shapes ringed with light orange-coloured stripes . . . Mwane had names for them all. Once they'd found a long fat slug curled tightly into a ball, like a caterpillar or a centipede gone into its protective curl. When they came back later that afternoon, it was still there, but had turned dark, almost black. It was the sun, Mwane explained. That's what happens to those creatures that live without light. She shuddered and took in a deep, careful breath and the finger tracing out the pattern of the ring stopped, grew still.

35

Mombasa was the first stop where they were actually allowed off the ship, a week later. They anchored just after midnight and in the silence that followed the shutting down of the ship's engines, Hannelore woke up. She lay for a few minutes, then slid quietly out of bed. She opened the round, porthole window and leaned out into a warm, tropical night that had the softness of childhood. The stars were huge and heavy and she could just make out the activity on the quayside as the companionways were creaked and hauled into position, waiting for dawn. There were soft lights up and down the quay and in the near distance palm trees stood silhouetted against the glow. She knelt at the window for a while, nostrils widening imperceptibly against the unfamiliar smells of spice and heat, even at night. She could hear shouts and the sharp, guttural commands of men in charge of others that are the same all over the world, even if she couldn't understand the language in which they were spoken. She listened drowsily. It wasn't just the language around them that had changed; all week they'd been steaming steadily northwards, towards the tropics and the equator . . . now they'd finally crossed it and it was as though another dimension had been reached. For the first time she was truly hot. Her cotton nightdress was clinging uncomfortably to her. There was a great clanking and swaying as the anchors were dropped and the ship docked properly at last. She climbed back into her bunk, pushing the covers away from her. In the morning she would wake up to a whole new world.

'I say, are you going ashore on your own?'

She looked up from fastening her sandals to see a young man with a round, pleasant face looking down at her in some concern. 'Yes,' she said slowly, wondering why he'd asked.

'Well, in that case, might I accompany you?'

She hesitated. She'd seen him each day since Cape Town in the dining room or on one of the decks, usually with a book in hand. He was English. He too seemed to be travelling alone but ate dinner together with a loud group of English and Italians who'd boarded at the same time. 'That's kind of you to offer, but it's not necessary,' she said at last.

'Oh, I can see *that*,' he said quickly, his concern replaced almost immediately with a smile. 'You look quite capable of handling yourself. No, I just thought it might be pleasant, that's all. You know, a day away from the rest of the crowd.' He waved a hand in the vague direction of the small group of diners to whom she'd assumed he belonged. She could see one or two of the women looking over curiously at them. They reminded her of the girls at boarding school; she disliked their high, girlish English voices as soon as she heard them.

'You're not spending it with them?' she asked, looking over in their direction.

'God, no. Dinner every night is quite enough, thank you.' He lowered his voice conspiratorially. 'There's a certain kind of Englishness—' He stopped suddenly, laughing at himself. 'Listen to me. How priggish. I'm as English as they are!' He stuck out a hand suddenly. 'I'm Toby, by the way. Toby Parnell.'

Hannelore hesitated. Other than the captain and the ship's registrar, neither of whom had spoken to her since she boarded at Swakopmund, no one on board knew that the nineteen-year-old young woman in first class, cabin 187 was Hannelore von Riedesal, the only child of Ludwig von Riedesal zu Lörrach and his wife, Hildebrand. No one knew where Bodenhausen was, or what had happened there. No one knew who she was or what she'd done. Aside from Tante Bärbel, not a single person in the world knew where she was going. She'd been cut loose, pushed out and rejected, but for the first time in her life she was free. Free to be whomever she pleased. She opened her mouth. 'Anneliese. I'm Anneliese Zander de Saint Phalle.' The names slipped out easily, comfortably. Anneliese after Tante Bärbel's great friend, Anneliese von Niekerk, the stylish wife of the mayor of Windhoek. Zander was her mother's maiden name. Hildebrand Zander. And de Saint Phalle in homage to the young French artist, Niki de Saint Phalle, whose works she'd studied at school in Cape Town. *Anneliese Zander de Saint Phalle.* It suddenly seemed perfect. Standing there on the upper deck overlooking the tepid, turquoise calm with the odd young Englishman who'd singled her out, she felt the last jagged crystals of the person she'd been for the first nineteen years of her life melt in the enormous heat.

'Gosh, that's a bit of a mouthful. I like Anneliese,' Toby said cheerfully. 'It's awfully pretty. Can't say I can pronounce the rest of it but I dare say I'll learn.' His inoffensive, rather clumsy English charm was wasted on her, but the ease with which he accepted the lie was both a balm and a surprise. But why shouldn't he believe her? What on earth could there be in his innocent, fresh-faced past that would prepare him for what she'd done? Her whole body gave one of those violent shudders that wracked her periodically when the effort of burying her memories momentarily failed her. She turned away from him, praying he wouldn't notice. There were still nights when her dreams were so soaked with her own pain and guilt that she woke into the stunned awareness of morning with no sound other than her own ragged breathing, unsure as to whether she'd cried out or not. 'They'll never forgive you, you know,' Tante Bärbel told her the night she took her away. 'Never. They'll forget you, but they'll never forgive you.'

'And me?' She'd been afraid to voice the words. 'Will *I* forget?'

'You must, *mein Schatz*. You *must*. If you don't, you'll die.'

'Well, Miss Anneliese?' Toby Parnell was looking down at her. His voice, in all its innocent cheerfulness, cut across the shroud of her grief like a knife. 'Shall we?' He offered her his arm. She took it wordlessly and together they walked towards the metal gangplank. 'Let's take a taxi into town,' he said, moving purposefully and confidently through the crowd. 'Have you been to Mombasa before?'

'No, never.' She shook her head, absurdly grateful to have someone in charge.

'Lunch, I think, first . . . and then perhaps a swim? We could take a taxi to Nyali Beach. It's beautiful and it'll probably be the last bit of heat for a while – we're heading into winter when we get to Europe. When do you come back?'

'Come back?'

'Here. To Africa.'

She stopped suddenly, forcing him too to come to a halt. All around them the crowd of hagglers, tourists, fellow passengers and traders moved and flowed, taking no more notice of the two of them standing still in its midst than the flies that buzzed noisily from one pile of rotting vegetables and discarded banana skins underfoot to the next. 'No,' she said slowly, shaking her head. 'No. I won't *ever* come back.'

Toby looked at her in some surprise. 'Oh, I say . . . I didn't mean to upset you.'

'You didn't.' She adjusted the shoulder strap of her handbag and moved on again, this time taking the lead. There was a small cluster of taxis waiting under the shade of the nearby palm trees. She walked towards one, the heat of late morning finally melting the last remnants of Hannelore von Riedesal away.

36

Toby Parnell was right about one thing; it *was* winter in Europe. By the time they docked in Brindisi a fortnight later, the heat and dust and the blinding sunlight of the Red Sea as they steamed towards the canal were forgotten as if they'd never been. The harbour was come upon through a curtain of light grey rain. A quick storm had come up as they moved through the Mediterranean, changing everything, including the light. By the time they began the slow, laborious process of disembarking, it was clear they had entered a new and different world. She came down the gangplank with the porter behind her, carefully putting out one foot after the other. For a moment she panicked, as though the ground beneath her had suddenly given way, then she realised it was the unfamiliar sensation of being on dry land. As the last of her bags was stowed carefully in the trunk of the taxi that had been summoned to take her to the train station, she turned to look at the ship one last time. She'd already said goodbye to Toby, who seemed genuinely sorry to see her go. She felt nothing. As pleasant a companion as he'd been, she'd lost the ability to feel anything, let alone pleasure in another's company. The second- and third-class passengers were still streaming down the gangplank.

She looked down at her hand which was on the door handle, ready to pull it open. It was trembling faintly, as if it recognised the importance of the moment before her brain could. The huge, white ship behind her was her last tie to Africa, to what had once been home. From Brindisi, she would take the train north through the Italian countryside, all the way to Milan. From there, she would board another train for Berlin. For nineteen years, the talk in her home had been of Lörrach, of the Schauinsland and of Munich, perhaps. No one had ever spoken about Berlin. But Berlin was Tante Bärbel's idea. Berlin was exactly the sort of city she could lose herself in safely. There was a hotel she'd suggested in one of the older, more beautiful parts of the city that hadn't been completely destroyed in the war. In the peace and anonymity of Berlin she could rest and 'recuperate', as Tante Bärbel delicately put it, and decide what she wanted to do with the rest of her life. *The rest of her life.* When spoken about like that, it seemed so far off, so remote from anything that might happen in the present, now.

But if there was one thing she'd understood after the events of the past year, it was that everything had a consequence. Absolutely everything. Just as nothing happened without a reason, everything that happened produced a result. Actions and consequences, events and results, just part of the huge and hugely unfathomable order of things. The events of the past year could never be erased. In time, perhaps, the pain might lessen, perhaps even dull. But it would never go away, not fully. And for that reason alone, she couldn't afford to make another mistake. From now on, every single decision had to be taken with great, tender care. She couldn't afford *not* to. From now on, everything had to be perfect. For her at least, it was the only way. As had happened so many times in the previous few months, she felt herself rising towards the surface of her own life. She pulled on the door handle and climbed inside.

37

The Hotel Adlon was a graceful, imposing building on Mar-athonallee, a tree-lined street in Westend close to the Heer-strasse cemetery and the Olympiastadion. She paid the taxi driver and got out a little uncertainly, clasping her hat to her head. It was nearly five in the evening and it was bitterly cold. The ground was hard and frosty, though there was no snow. 'No snow yet,' the driver said cheerfully, 'but there soon will be. You'll see. You haven't had a winter until you've had one here. You're not from Berlin, are you? You don't sound it.' She shook her head and turned away before he could ask her anything further. A bellhop appeared and she gratefully gave up the charge of her suitcases and followed him in.

The hotel must have once been a family home, she thought to herself as they entered. The entrance hall was low and fairly small, although there was a magnificent curved staircase that led away from the hallway, winding its way above her head. The décor was old-fashioned in a way she recognised from houses in Windhoek – the same heavy wooden panelling, oriental rugs and heavy furniture with ornate curlicue arms and legs. A makeshift reception bar had been erected in the shadow of the staircase. She moved towards it, wanting only to get a room and be left alone. The receptionist was a young uniformed girl with the long lank hair and sallow complexion of people who spend most of their lives indoors. Her eyes widened as Anneliese withdrew a thick brick of notes from the mannish-looking satchel that served as her handbag.

'How long will you be staying?' she asked eagerly.

'I'm not sure.' The less she said about her plans the better. It covered the confusion of not yet knowing what they were.

'Very good, Fraülein.' The girl quickly recovered her manners. Her expression indicated that she'd recognised Anneliese as a young woman of some considerable means. 'Would you like to keep your money in here?' she asked hesitantly, looking at

Anneliese's bag. 'Or in a bank, perhaps? It's not . . . well, it's not usual to carry such a lot of cash. Not now.' She looked around her and lowered her voice. 'Especially not now. We have a lot of . . . foreigners here now.'

Like me, Anneliese thought to herself. 'I'll take care of it tomorrow,' she said firmly. She had no idea where to go or what bank to take the money to, but it could all wait until the following day. She was tired and hungry and there was a throbbing behind her left temple that was threatening to deepen. 'Is it possible to get something to eat?' she asked.

'Yes, certainly. The dining room's just through there. We don't have many guests at the moment but the kitchen's usually open.'

'Thank you.' Anneliese took the heavy key and turned to go upstairs. The thought of food was making her mouth water. She'd had nothing to eat since changing trains in Milan, some twelve hours earlier. With the bellhop following, she went upstairs to the room that would be home for the next few months.

It was a pleasant room, high-ceilinged, with a small en suite bathroom that reminded her a little of the ship. There was a wide, low bed pushed against the wall, facing the large windows. The carpet was a little threadbare but there were two or three thick, colourful rugs and the heavy velvet curtains looked new. She tipped the bellhop, noted his look of surprise at the folded note and his swift grin, and quickly closed the door behind him. She walked to the window and pulled back the curtain. Night had already fallen on the cold, hard city and the ground was bristling with frost. The moon was full and high, casting an eerie white light across the lawn to the rear of the hotel, picking out the silver birch trees that skirted the fringes of the garden. There was a greenhouse of some sort at the bottom of the garden and next to it, an upturned wheelbarrow. She stood for a moment, taking it all in. This wasn't the Germany of frozen lakes and snow-covered hills that she'd grown up hearing about; it wasn't

Neuschwanstein, the fairytale castle whose image hung on a painting above the piano in the drawing room on the farm. Berlin was different. Hard and cold, even brutal. Although she'd only been in the city for a few hours, she knew instinctively that this was a different Germany from the one her parents had known and left behind.

It was November 1961 and the whole world was in flux, perhaps nowhere more so than Germany, which was once again at the centre of things, straddling the communist East and the capitalist West. Although she'd once declared Europe dead and buried, as soon as it became clear that it was the only option, Tante Bärbel, typically, grew excited. She spoke of the cafes and bars along the Kurfürstendamm, where all of fashionable Berlin came to sit in summer; she described Berlin's different districts, where to buy the best furs and whose *café crème* was worth drinking and whose not. Now a wall was being built to close the border between the Russian-controlled parts of the city, East Berlin, as they called it, and the rest. West Berlin would become a little enclave, an outpost in the middle of East Germany. 'But we're used to that, *ně*?' Tante Bärbel said, a little wistfully.

It was hard to imagine the conversation, now that the moment of arrival had come. She closed the curtains and picked up one of the suitcases, lugging it over to the bed. She opened it and for a moment, as the familiar smell of her own clothes and that of home, of Africa, was released into the room, the tendons on her neck swelled and the room began to blur. She sat down hard on the edge of the bed and pressed her knees together. It had been a few days since the hammering fists of anguish had set upon her with such ferocity. Once or twice on the long journey towards Europe she'd lain on her bed almost unable to breathe for the sorrow. It came upon her now. Her knees were so tightly pressed together that the skin shone white through her dark stockings, as though she were lit from within. She made no sound. Her breath came and went, blindly, stupidly, mechanical, for which she was grateful. Minutes passed in silence, then slowly, the evidence of life around her began to reassert itself.

Overhead, a floorboard creaked intermittently as someone walked back and forth. A door slammed down the corridor; an engine revved somewhere across the street and there was the whoosh of an unfamiliar bird outside her window. Her hand went out to clutch at the bed sheet, steadying her against the hurricane that had blown up so suddenly inside her. Her fingers moved over the knobbly weave, feeling out its pattern. Slowly, agonisingly slowly, the turmoil inside her began to lessen as she touched and felt her way back towards calm. That shape there a rose, another a leaf, a petal here . . . a dense pattern of flowers. It took her a few minutes to bring her breath under control until at last, finally, she was able to stand up. She tucked her hair behind her ears and placed the trembling heel of her hand against her stomach. The great shuddering had given way to deep, regular breaths.

She began to unpack her things, carefully stowing her clothes away in the cavernous wardrobe and the matching chest of drawers. Putting her belongings in order brought about some semblance of normality. Out came the cashmere sweaters that she and Tante Bärbel had gone to Hartmann's to buy together. Three black, three grey. A white angora cardigan and the long, thick, dark blue coat that she said would keep her warm, no matter the temperature. She hung the two woollen dresses she'd chosen and neatly lined up her shoes. Her undergarments and stockings went into a separate drawer and she laid out her small store of cosmetics in the bathroom. At last it was done. It was time to take a bath. She turned on the taps and the small bathroom quickly filled with steam. She took off the clothes she'd been travelling in, hanging her long skirt on the hook behind the door. She unhooked her brassiere and was about to hang it up when she suddenly caught sight of herself in the mirror. She stopped. Her back was a ghostly map of thin silver scars that ran from the nape of her neck to her buttocks. Those she could touch with her fingers she already knew by heart. There was the long thin one that ran diagonally from one shoulder blade to the other. She turned slightly, still staring at herself in the mirror. There was another that ran across her clavicles, ending in a small nick just above her breast. There were others too that were deeper, satiny, puckered strips that gave up their meaning easily. She turned back to face the mirror again, her hands going automatically to her stomach. Here there were no scars. She touched the skin gently, tracing a line from the navel to her pubic bone. Then she stopped. The long memory of the body. She wanted no reminder of what it had done. She stepped into the hot water, submerging herself almost immediately, blocking out all sound.

The dining room was deserted when she finally came down but the receptionist came through the double doors at one end, tying a frilled white apron around her waist and took her order. An omelette, *mit Schinken und Käse*, and two slices of buttered rye toast. The food came quickly and was good. She ate hungrily, pausing only to wipe her plate with the last piece of bread. Then she pushed the plate away from her and leaned back in her chair.

'Can I get you anything else?' The receptionist suddenly appeared again. She'd probably been watching her curiously from behind the bar.

'An espresso, please,' Anneliese said, taking the pack of cigarettes she'd bought at the station out of her pocket. 'Single.' She tapped one out on the table top. An *espresso*? It was nearly ten p.m. but she knew sleep would not come easily. She held the little demi-tasse in one hand and her cigarette in the other, and sat quietly smoking until the last dregs of coffee were gone and the cigarette had burned down to its filter. She saw the elderly waiter behind the bar in one corner of the room look at her with interest. She met his gaze evenly and he was forced to turn his eyes elsewhere. She looked down at her camel-coloured slacks and the mannish tan brogues . . . underneath her trousers she had on a pair of thin silk stockings which Tante Bärbel had told her to wear at all times. 'Silk, not nylon. Nylon won't keep you warm.' The contrast in texture between the wool of her trousers, her cream-coloured silk blouse and the pale pearly stockings pleased her for some reason. She examined the fine weave of her trousers, wondering how it was she'd never noticed the faint spidery orange thread that lifted the colour, turning what might have otherwise been a rather dull fabric into something that had both texture and light.

She allowed her mind to drift for a moment. There were so many things that needed sorting out – a bank account, for one thing. She couldn't keep the stack of Deutschmarks that Tante Bärbel had given her in a plastic bag at the bottom of her suitcase for much longer. And then there was the question of what she was going to *do* – not just in her immediate future, but with the rest of her life. *Find yourself something to do as soon as you get there*, was Tante Bärbel's advice. *Don't waste any time*. Money wasn't a problem. She easily had enough to last a year or more, and there would be more if she needed it. No, it was about having a purpose, a structure to her life that would not only take her mind off what had happened but would also give her something to live for. All through the long journey northwards she'd thought about it and there was really only one answer. Fashion. She would be what she'd always wanted to be – a fashion designer. It was the only thing that interested her and the only thing she'd ever been any good at. She would make enquiries at the local universities, she thought to herself, collecting her things and making her way back to her room. First, a bank account, then a career. She had to hold on to that thought or she'd be finished before she'd even begun.

38

Even she couldn't have predicted how easily the decision was made. She walked down one long, polished corridor after another, hearing her own footsteps dying away behind her, scrutinising the signs on the doors. She stood in front of noticeboards outside the different faculties, reading course descriptions and notices of upcoming lectures. She looked at the preoccupied faces of students, men and women, streaming past her, carrying piles of books and walking with purposeful, determined strides. Her eyes ran down the list of available courses and finally came to rest on one. *Textile Engineering.* She looked at it for a moment, then shouldered her bag. She walked straight to the enquiry office.

An hour later, it was done. She joined the throng of students streaming in and out of the great doors of the Technische Universtät Berlin. She was a whole semester behind; no matter. Herr Doktor Professor Maximilian Tröstler, head of the department, filled in the necessary forms, dispatched his secretary to make this enquiry or that whilst he sat behind his enormous, paper-covered desk and explained she would be the only girl in an engineering class of thirty men.

'Unusual choice for a girl, I'd say,' he said, leaning back in his chair and bringing his fingers up to a 'V' in front of his face. He was a short, rather plump man with a jet-black goatee and deeply hooded dark eyes behind wireless glasses. 'But your application form is interesting,' he continued, pointing to the form that lay on his desk between them. '*Ja,* interesting. And I like the fact that you can already draw. And you'll be able to post us your school results in due course, you say?'

'Yes, sir,' Anneliese murmured, not wanting to divulge more than she thought was necessary. She couldn't believe how easy everything had been. She'd filled out the application form, given the hotel address as her own and Tante Bärbel as a reference. She would worry about how to obtain high-school references and an *Abitur* certificate in the name of *Anneliese Zander de Saint Phalle* later.

'You grew up in Windhoek, you say? Interesting, interesting. We've never had a student from the colonies, so to speak. At least not in this department. And an orphan, too. Tragic, to lose your parents at such a young age. Just tragic.'

'Yes, sir,' Anneliese murmured again. Tante Bärbel would understand. *Forget about everything here. Start again.*

'Well, you'd better come to class tomorrow, first thing. I'll introduce you to the rest of your fellow students. They'll be able to help orientate you to the department, show you where the lectures take place, that sort of thing. It'll be quite novel for them, having you in their midst. I'd watch out for some of them, if I were you!' He gave a small, self-satisfied chuckle, as if it had been his initiative and undertaking that had brought her here, to his office, his department.

Anneliese said nothing. The less she said, the better. He looked up at her questioningly, and she understood the interview, such as it was, was over. She was a student now. Her life, which had been taken up so abruptly, had been set down again on a different course and for the second or third time utterly changed. As she rose, she recognised the welcome in his face that was the sign she'd unwittingly been waiting for.

She walked out of the great doors of the engineering faculty and buttoned up her coat. She pulled out her gloves from her satchel and put them on. She ought to buy one of those fur-trimmed hats she'd seen people – mostly men – wearing. It had started snowing in the hour or so she'd been in Professor Tröstler's office. She turned her face up to the sky in delight. She'd never seen snow before. Tiny, swirling, feather-light flakes fell past her face, touching her lightly before melting into the thick wool of her coat. She walked towards the Franklin-strasse gate which led to the river. Streams of people moved past her, students and shoppers, housewives, children muffled in clothing that doubled their size. She walked past a confectioner's shop where women in fur coats and suede boots sat at the counter, eating and ordering pastries. On impulse, she pushed open the door and met the blast of warm air. She took a seat at the rear of the fug-warm cafe amidst the society ladies and the housewives with their morning purchases strewn around them. Ordering a *café crème* and a slice of lemony sponge cake with a dollop of cream, she ate it slowly with a long-handled spoon. There was a young couple sitting next to her who said little to each other, concentrating instead on finishing the slice of chocolate cake which they shared, turn and turn about, all the while murmuring dreamily, '*Gut?*' '*Oh, ja, ganz gut,*' to one another. She lit a cigarette and smoked it as the cafe slowly emptied, leaving only her and the dreamy couple next to her, the clock on the wall behind her ticking away the silence until they too got up and left. She was the last to leave. The snow had ceased but the skies were still fat and heavy, trembling with the next unshed load. She walked across the bridge and stopped halfway across it, looking down at the slick, slow-moving Spree flowing underneath. The river; the cafe; the university; the hotel . . . the scenes of the morning flowed with it, merging into the current and disappearing upstream.

39

As Professor Tröstler had predicted, her arrival the following morning in the lecture hall caused quite a stir. She'd chosen her outfit with care – a white shirt with a stiff collar, high-waisted dark blue gabardine trousers cinched at the waist with a thin leather belt and the same flat, tan brogues she'd worn every day since her arrival in Germany. She pulled her long blonde hair away from her face and tied it into a knot at the back of her head. No make-up, other than a light dusting of powder across the nose, and no jewellery. She looked at herself in the mirror before pulling on her overcoat – a touch severe, perhaps, but she was only too conscious of her status as the only woman in the department; there was no need to add to the general impression of her as inept by appearing even more girlish or feminine. She picked up her satchel, switched off the light and made her way downstairs to the dining room.

Two cups of coffee and a piece of toast later, she was ready. She finished her cigarette and folded away the map she'd been consulting. It was eight a.m. Her first class would begin at nine thirty. She would take the U-Bahn for the first time, negotiating the confusing corridors and the even more confusing map and get there in plenty of time. She said goodbye to the receptionist, whose name she'd learned was Ulrike, and stepped into the cold, frosty morning, feeling slightly light-headed with anticipation and nerves.

The U-Bahn was less tricky than she'd feared. She changed lines once, and less than half an hour after leaving Hotel Adlon she emerged at Hansaplatz, just across the river from the university. She walked up Levetzowstrasse and crossed the river, marvelling at the solidity of the buildings, their air of impenetrability. The streets in the centre of the city were long and wide and full of cars and busy, purposeful people. Here everyone walked in the same direction; those going towards the university walked on the left, those walking away from it on the right. No one broke rank or moved out of turn. Their faces wore the tight, carefully controlled expressions of neutrality that she'd come to recognise as uniquely European, so different from the faces of people back home. She stumbled over the word, correcting herself sternly. No, that was no longer home. *This* was now her home. She hurried with the rest of them, moving in the right direction, trying to compose her own features so that she wouldn't stand out. She passed under the portico of the great hall, took in the alabaster plaster statues of Goethe and Hegel and God-knows-who-else staring loftily down upon her. She made her way down one long corridor after another, as she'd done the day before, until she finally found the hall where she'd been told the first lecture of the day would take place.

She pushed open the double doors cautiously. The hall, with its tiered rows of seating sloping sharply upwards towards the back of the room, was exactly as she'd pictured it. It was also completely empty. At the front, a few yards from where she stood, there was a small raised podium, a lectern and a screen which covered the blackboard entirely. There were clerestory windows high above the rows of seating which let in a weak, diffuse winter light. The lights were still off; she had no idea where to switch them on and even less idea if she should. She took a seat in the row closest to her, pulling her notebook and pen out, laying them neatly on the ledge in front of her. She looked at her wristwatch. It was just past nine a.m. She had another half-hour to wait but what else was there to do? She folded her arms, closed her eyes and tried to concentrate on what was to come.

The noisy burst of the swing doors brought her sharply back to her senses. She'd been hovering back there on the edge of a dream but kept snatching herself back into wakefulness, afraid of what she might find. There was a sudden lull in the conversations as the students filed into the lecture hall and caught sight of her sitting there, pen and paper at the ready, legs crossed elegantly at the knee. She met their curious gazes head-on; not defiantly, but not shy either. They were a rather mixed lot; some younger-looking men amongst them, faint wisps of beards and moustaches, the pock-marks of adolescence still visible on their faces. Then there were a couple of older men, perhaps in their late twenties and thirties, distinguishable not only by their beards and their more solid, less boyish frames, but by the air of bored nonchalance with which they took their seats. There was one who was even older, grey hair standing out in sharp contrast to the blacks and chestnut browns around him. Someone slid into the row in front and moved along until he was almost level with her.

'What department are you looking for?' he asked, not unpleasantly, but with the clear assumption that she was in the wrong place and ought to be redirected.

'This one.' She was equally clear.

'This is the engineering department.'

'As I said.'

'You're a *student*?' Now there was disbelief in his voice. 'An *engineering* student?'

'Are you?' She looked at him. He flushed immediately.

'You're a new student? That's pretty cool.' Someone else spoke to her, from the row behind. She turned round to look at him, wondering if she was going to be answering questions all day long. He was a little older, with curly dark brown hair and a dark, almost Mediterranean complexion, the beautiful lines and planes of his face appearing as if they'd been finely etched and scored. 'As you can see, hardly any women in here,' he said with an almost apologetic smile.

'None, actually. What's your name?' The first young man spoke again, determined not to be outdone.

'Anneliese,' she said quietly. She had no desire to draw any further attention to herself.

'I'm Klaus.' He held out a hand.

'And I'm Bruno.' The beautiful man behind her also stuck out a hand. She looked at both outstretched arms and began to laugh. But before they could join in, the doors opened again and a hush fell over the room. The lecturer had arrived. So too had the beginning of the rest of her life.

40

ANNELIESE
FIVE YEARS LATER

'What are the five stages of cotton processing?' Bruno lay on the end of her bed, one hand holding open the textbook they'd both been studying for the past few hours, the other held loosely, possessively, on her bare calf.

'Cultivating and harvesting, preparation, spinning, weaving and finishing.' She looked up from her own book and threw him a withering glance. 'Ask me something harder.'

'OK. Give me the Latin name for Indian cotton.'

'*Gossypium arboretum*. Harder.'

'Christ, Anneliese. Is there *anything* you don't know?'

'Plenty. But give me something more obscure. You know what Tröstler's like. The exam'll be full of horrid questions that only he knows the answer to.'

'No, it'll be full of questions that only *you* know the answer to.

OK, here's another one. When did the patent on Crompton's Spinning Mule expire?'

'Um . . . 1781? No, 1783?'

'Correct, goddamit! OK, now you ask me something.'

'Date of the first artificial fibre?' Anneliese asked slyly.

'1699?'

'Only out by a hundred years. It's 1799.'

Bruno groaned and held his head in his hands. 'Fuck, I'm gonna fail, you know that, don't you? Five years of my life down the drain. I don't know what my parents are going to say. You're doubly lucky, Anneliese.'

'How so?'

'*You're* not going to fail and even if you did, at least you don't have parents to worry about. I know there aren't *many* advantages to being an orphan, but that's got to be one of 'em.'

Anneliese only just managed not to throw her book at him. 'There's still my aunt,' she said mildly. 'And besides, you're not going to fail.'

'Wish I had your confidence. Is your aunt really coming over for your graduation?'

Anneliese nodded. 'That's what she said.'

'I can't wait to meet her. She sounds so . . . so . . . *glamorous*. Not like an aunt at all.'

'She isn't. Not really, anyway.'

'But she's all you have left, isn't she? Apart from your uncle, but you never talk about him. Why's that?'

Anneliese gaped at him. Even after five years of the closest friendship she'd known since leaving Bodenhausen, Bruno's appetite for the details of her life astounded her. He was fascinated by the little snippets she couldn't help but let fall. His life, he declared miserably, was boring in the extreme. He was from Eich, a small town near Frankfurt. Both his parents were from Eich. Both sets of *grandparents* were from Eich. It was Eich and nothing but stretching back to infinity. She, on the other hand, had the sort of background that he dreamed of. Exotic, distant, free. It was the freedom that attracted him, she came to understand. She was free. Despite the changes sweeping through Europe that had begun properly in France in the early sixties and were now laying waste to so many of the old conventions, Berlin had resisted the strident calls for change. She was wrapped up in her own internal drama between East and West. With the building of the wall and the deaths that had occurred – and were still occurring – as people desperately tried to break through to the West, the desires of a young, twenty-something-year-old man to 'come out', as he put it, and live openly as gay seemed puerile, even childish. Anneliese sometimes wondered if the reason why she and Bruno got along so well – and had done, right from the start – was because they'd both recognised in each other the capacity for evasion. They were both liars, in their own way, reconstructing their histories and selves to suit the circumstances around them.

'He wasn't around that much,' she said lamely, finally. 'I'm much closer to her.'

'Well, I can't wait to meet her.' Bruno rolled off the bed and stood up. He walked to the open windows. 'It's summer,' he said, peering out across the park. 'And here we are, stuck inside. God, I can't wait for these exams to be over.'

'They soon will be. And then what?'

'What d'you mean?' Bruno turned from the window to look at her.

Anneliese sat up, smoothing the bedspread around her, a sure sign that she'd been thinking deeply about something which she'd yet to put into words. 'Well, what d'you want to do afterwards?'

'What do *you* want to do? Come on, spit it out. What've you been thinking about?'

'London.'

'London?' They looked at each other. Anneliese's heart was beating fast. For almost six months it was all she'd been dreaming of. London was the Beatles and Mary Quant and mini-skirts and the centre of everything that was happening in the world, and Anneliese desperately wanted to be there. Berlin, with its student politics and the wall and memories of the war that refused to die, wasn't for her. Berlin was all about the past – London was the future and she desperately wanted to be part of it. For the past year, alongside her studies, she'd quietly been designing her own collection, using the extraordinary knowledge of fabrics she'd gained to put together a small range of outfits – 'capsule wardrobe', as the Americans called it. She was drawn to the buzz and energy surrounding London but the women she had in mind weren't the mini-skirted, Beatles-crazy teenagers who thronged Carnaby Street or any of the other places she read about. She was interested in a different kind of woman. The talk was all of freedom, of sex, drugs and rock 'n' roll, of emancipation and contraception and the rights of women everywhere. It interested Anneliese, but only in a peripheral way. She couldn't have said why, but she saw further than most. Having been in the engineering faculty for the past five years, she'd seen more and more women entering the male-dominated professions. She had acquaintances who'd studied medicine, law, accountancy. In a few years' time, those same women would be in their thirties. Not only would they need wardrobes that were commensurate with their professional positions, they'd be able to afford them too.

She was interested in women like her. Serious. Smart. Career-minded. She studied the magazines coming out of Paris and London and New York and made up her mind. She would be the first to cater for such a woman. A woman who required clothes that were beautiful and feminine, but not girlish or overtly sexy. Such women would take their clothes as seriously as they did their own careers. She realised she knew only two kinds of women: *girls* such as could be found in the university bars and in the departments of languages and modern history, and *women*, like Tante Bärbel, who, although stylish, still relied on their husbands to live lives that they referred to as 'free', but in reality were anything but. A new kind of woman was emerging and Anneliese wanted to be the first off the mark. Bruno, she felt, wanted the same.

'You want to go to London?' Bruno asked her, and his voice was suddenly quiet, as though he'd realised the real importance of the moment.

She nodded. 'Not just *go* to London. I want to *live* in London. I want us to open a boutique together. You and me.'

'A boutique?' Bruno turned away from the window and came to sit beside her on the bed.

She nodded again. 'I've been doing this collection,' she began hesitantly.

'I know.'

Her eyes widened. 'Have you been snooping on me?' she asked, though there was no irritation in her voice.

He shook his head. 'No, not snooping. But you sometimes leave things out . . . and I've seen you in class, scribbling away when you're supposed to be taking notes. Will you show me?'

She reached down under the bed and pulled out the slim black portfolio whose pages were filled with the sketches and photographs she'd spent the last year working on. There was absolute silence in the small bedroom as Bruno reverentially opened the first page. Her heart was beating so fast and hard that it hurt. As she watched his face anxiously for the signs of approval or disapproval – expressions in him that she knew as intimately as she did in herself – it came to her slowly that she *would* go to London, that she and Bruno *would* open their own store and that they would remain committed to it, and to each other, for the rest of their lives. She had the curious, covert certainty that everything that had gone before had been leading her up to this moment – *this*, sitting on the narrow bed in the small flat that had been home to her for the past four years, next to the one person whose opinion counted above all others, taking in the beginnings of what would be her life's work. There would be nothing else for her. When he came to the end of the portfolio and raised his eyes to meet hers, she saw that it was the sign she'd been waiting and watching for, not knowing what it would be until it came.

41

'Oh, Anneliese . . . there you are. Professor Tröstler wants to see you. Right away, if you don't mind.'

Anneliese paused outside the departmental secretary's door. The door to the professor's office was partially open; he would have heard her voice. Her heart sank. She knew what he wanted to see her about. There were only three days to the start of final exams and for almost six months now, she'd had weekly reminders that her high-school certificates still hadn't been submitted to the university and that she would not be allowed to sit the exam until they'd been produced. In the Byzantine way of university administration, she'd managed to avoid the issue for four years – now, with the final examination upon them, she'd run out of time, and excuses. 'Right away?' she asked, her mind already racing ahead.

'Right away,' the woman confirmed, her mouth pursing itself into the thin line that all the students in the faculty knew and feared.

Anneliese shifted the weight of her shoulder bag and reluctantly stepped inside the office. She tapped on the door under the woman's watchful, already suspicious eyes. She'd never made a secret of the fact that she couldn't understand *why* a beautiful young woman like Anneliese Zander de Saint Phalle would want to spend five years in the department of engineering, or, more to the point perhaps, why the girl in question was such a stuck-up, snooty bitch.

'Come in.' Professor Tröstler's smooth, slightly nasal voice commanded her to enter.

'Er, good afternoon, Herr Doktor Tröstler,' Anneliese said as pleasantly as she could. 'I understand you're looking for me?'

Professor Tröstler looked up at her from his dark, deeply hooded eyes which remained half-shuttered, as always. She met his gaze warily. She didn't know what it was about him that unnerved her so, but there it was. He'd been a rather shadowy figure at the margins of her academic life for nearly five years. He rarely, if ever, taught himself – the lectures and seminars were done by a stream of younger men in badly fitting pullovers who never failed to show their surprise when she proved herself to be every bit as good, if not better, than the rest of her fellow students. In contrast, Maximilian Tröstler was a neat, dapper man, despite his plumpness and his old-fashioned manners that brought another era to mind. His skin held a fine, mauvish shadow beneath the fat and his hair was brilliantly black, as if it had been polished. There were rumours amongst the students that he was Jewish, or Romanian, or had gypsy blood . . . whatever it was, there was an aloof strangeness about him that she both recognised and shrank from. He made no secret of the fact that he found her presence interesting but there was something else in his liquid, watercoloured gaze that she instinctively shrank from, but she couldn't have said why. On the rare occasions she'd talked to him over the years, she'd found herself trying to ingratiate herself, smiling when she wouldn't normally have, or laughing with him, a trait she detested, both in herself and in others, but it seemed to come out of a compulsion to align herself with whatever frightened her. 'Ah. Anneliese. So . . . if you won't answer letters, what will you answer to, hmm?'

'Oh, is it about my school certificates, sir?' She could hear the false girlishness in her voice but couldn't prevent it.

'Well, what else would it be about?'

She looked upon the steely blackness of his hair, the way his dark brown tweed jacket strained slightly at the shoulders, a few millimetres too narrow to contain the plump, milky skin that lay beneath the layers of fine cut and cloth. She felt a peculiar sinking feeling in the bottom of her stomach, as though something she'd tried to suppress were struggling to rise. Her mouth suddenly went dry. She'd run out of plausible excuses. 'Yes, sir. I know.'

There was a second's worth of carefully balanced silence into which the sound of the ticking clock on the mantelpiece behind him began to fall. Tick/tock. Tick/tock. 'I don't make the rules,

Anneliese,' Professor Tröstler said finally, his hands coming up into what she'd come to recognise as his habitual position, hovering just below his chin. 'And there we have it. You require your academic transcripts in order to matriculate. You must matriculate before you graduate and you must sit, and pass, your final exams in order to graduate. A simple but logical progression.'

'I know, sir.'

'So what are we to do about it, hmm?'

The silence deepened, again measured out by the clock she couldn't see. 'I . . . I don't know, sir.' It seemed pointless to invent another excuse which she knew he would immediately understand was a lie. She had the distinct sensation of having successfully run away from something, only to find it standing behind her, waiting to pounce.

'Why don't you come back later this afternoon, after classes? I'll have a think about it. It seems such a shame to let five years of quite brilliant study go to waste, hmm?'

'Y-yes, sir.' She had no idea what he might mean. She turned to go and was surprised to find her legs shaking. Some quiet threat had been made, so subtle she wasn't sure she'd understood it, but its shadow was upon her, that much was clear. She walked out under the secretary's silent frown.

There *was* no threat. Only a quiet, passive acceptance of what was to follow. She was astonished at herself, not just at the way she offered no resistance whatsoever but at the way she understood the entire scene, as it unfolded, as the way things would be, even *should* be. From the minute she knocked hesitantly on his closed door just after five p.m. when the suspicious secretary had long departed, to the way he opened it, solicitously ushering her in as though it were a social visit, not the final act in a play of power over which she had little control. 'Something to drink, perhaps? Come sit down. Have a comfortable seat—? Yes, that's it. Perhaps a small sherry? Yes?'

She took the drink he offered, sat in the seat he proposed and when his hand moved from his own thigh to hers, she simply looked at it as if she'd always expected to see it there. Her mind refused to make the connection between the short, stubby and almost hairless fingers with the thick gold signet ring on one hand and the thin marital band on the other, and the smooth, freckled whiteness of her own thigh. He kept up a murmuring, patterned commentary, more to himself than to her, as he divested her of her clothing, folding each piece neatly before laying it carefully to one side. She remained seated; it seemed more appropriate, somehow. She was at least a head taller than he; standing, the faint air of ridiculousness would have over-whelmed them both. It was only at the last minute, when she was almost supine in the comfortable chair, that he took hold of both her hands and pulled her down to join him on the richly patterned rug in front of his desk. She found herself staring up at the ceiling, past his brilliantly black hair and the slow rise and fall of his head.

Although much of the university was modern, the engineer-ing faculty had remained housed in a splendidly baroque build-ing and the intricate plasterwork above her head absorbed her attention completely. The centre-point of the room from which a suspended, rather dusty chandelier hung, was a large arrange-ment of fruits. She began tracing out the individual pieces – grapes, of course, and the usual assortment of pears, peaches, apples . . . incongruously, arranged in a kind of triangle of form, were three pineapples, pierced in their centre by the striped cord which held the light. She was following it with her eyes when she felt the man moving on top of her stiffen, releasing himself in a shuddering rush of fluid and mumbled, incoherent words. She lay in absolute silence, her gaze shifting from fruit to the line of his jowl, his thick, uneven skin with its waxy pallor and open pores, like the sweat-sheen on a piece of cheese. Her body was held away from his, despite their proximity and her hand which he had covered with his own was stiffly formal. He softened as he withdrew from her; there were the embarrassing sounds of release – a plop, the sliding off of damp skin one from the other, the rustle of his clothing. He hadn't even taken off his trousers.

Now that it was over he was in a hurry to get her out of the room. He handed her her clothing, piece quickly following piece. She dressed quickly, averting her eyes. She bent down to lace up her shoes and when she rose, she saw him standing in front of her, his arms dangling rather helplessly before him, as though something had fallen from them. She picked up her satchel and walked steadily towards the door. The large silver key was still in the lock. She turned it round, unlocked the door and opened it.

'Anneliese—' He started to say something but she didn't reply. She shut the door gently behind her and continued on her way.

The following week, along with the thirty-odd other students in her year, she sat her final exams. Nothing more was ever said about her Abitur results, or her failure to produce the necessary records. In due course, the examination results were posted. Anneliese Zander de Saint Phalle had graduated top of her class of thirty-four students, the only female. Bruno Schroers, her closest friend and the only fellow student who could reasonably claim to know the statuesque, icy-cool blonde, came third. She was seen once, after the results were posted, with an older woman, tall, like Anneliese, but with short red hair and matching lipstick, walking down the corridors of the faculty, pointing out the lecture halls and rooms where she'd spent the last five years. Another student, Detmar von Gunstieger, claimed he'd seen the two of them at dinner one evening shortly afterwards, in the beautifully appointed dining rooms of the Kampinski Hotel, overlooking the Tiergarten, a stone's throw from the river. She didn't see him, Detmar told the others, or else she pretended not to. There was something odd about the way the two women were sitting, he reported, though he couldn't exactly say what it was. He'd heard she had an aunt in town but the woman whose hand loosely stroked hers didn't seem like an aunt to him. Yeah, she *was* a strange one, he mused. She'd been in the department for five years but not *of* it. Aside from Bruno Schroers – and God knows *he* was strange enough! – no one knew a damn thing about her. She'd come first, though, they had to give her that. Strange and aloof, stuck-up, some said . . . but brilliant nonetheless. It had to be said.

42

ANNELIESE
London, England

A*d*SP. She looked at the lettering in the centre of the window for the umpteenth time that morning. Was it large enough? Too large? Too bold? Or too subtle, perhaps? Alongside the bright colours of the rest of the street, her austere white shopfront with its single pane of glass and the lettering dead centre, obscuring the clear view all the way to the back, seemed dull, even boring. 'No, not boring,' Bruno said, coming up to stand beside her. 'Classy, yes, but not boring, *mein Schatz.*'

'Are you sure?' She looked at his face anxiously.

'Of course I'm sure. It looks great. I can't believe it, can you? We're really here. We're really doing it.'

Anneliese was quiet. In some ways she wasn't surprised. She'd always known she could do it. The logistics aside – and those were taken care of by Tante Bärbel, as always – the question wasn't whether or not they would manage to get to London, or find a suitable premises, or find the team she needed to turn her sketches into garments . . . the question was whether anyone would buy them. *That* was the larger issue and the only one over which she had no control. After five years in Europe, during which time she had no one else to consider other than herself, she'd grasped what she already knew would be a truth she would never forget. As she looked at the window and the sign that meant so much more to her than just a collection of four small letters, she saw again that the world – insofar as she understood it – was really divided in two: things she could do something about, and things she couldn't. Getting her and Bruno to London, persuading Tante Bärbel that this latest investment would prove to be as good a bet as her education had been; finding a premises they liked and producing their first collection . . . all those were logistical problems, more or less surmountable. Her energies would be best spent on those. Would the collection be deemed any good? Would women actually want to *wear* her clothes? Would the magazine editors write about them and would there be enough interest to produce a second collection, or a third? Those were things over which she held absolutely no sway. No point in even thinking about them.

She turned her attention back. '*Ja*, you're right,' she said briskly. 'Classy, not boring.' They looked at each other at the same moment, a quick, half-shy glance, and then away again, as if they'd been caught out. As sometimes happened, a moment of such deep intimacy and understanding passed between them that was so strong and powerful they both had to pull back, a little afraid of one another, and of it. She turned away from him; there was a tightness in her throat and lungs that stopped her from saying anything further. The doorway was open; she walked into the shop, out of the daylight. It was cool and dark inside, a welcome relief from the unusually warm October afternoon. It had been a long, hot summer, first in Berlin, then in London. They'd arrived together at the end of August when the city was still in the grip of a heatwave. Friends of Bruno's had found them a flat in Primrose Hill, close to Regent's Park. Anneliese's first memories of London were of the park where people sat on brightly coloured blankets, bare toes wriggling shyly in the sun and grass. They'd immediately set about looking for a suitable shop and had found a small space sandwiched between a chemist's and a jewellers on Blandford Street, just north of Mayfair. It wasn't quite what she'd pictured – too small and narrow, for one thing, but they'd had to strike a balance between the location and their budget. For now, this was what they could afford – and they had to make it work.

Tante Bärbel had come with them to look for it. After all, she was one of the shareholders in A*d*SP Holdings, the company they'd formed at Onkel Fritz's insistence. They had a lawyer, recommended by his German attorney, an accountant and a bank manager. Anneliese enjoyed the formality of it all; somehow, the more seriously Onkel Fritz and Tante Bärbel took the enterprise, the more certain she felt of its success. She approved of the little shop on Blandford Street; a week after they'd viewed it for the second time, they signed the lease. A*d*SP was officially now in business.

She looked around the small interior. It had been a bookseller's before the owner had decided to sell up and retire. They'd done little more than take down the shelves, sand the floorboards and paint the walls an off-white, chalky colour. It was in her second year at university that she'd first heard of the Bauhaus, the famous school of design in Dessau that the Nazis had closed down before the war. She was inspired by their philosophy of bringing all the arts together under one roof, but even more by their spare and minimal approach to everything – furnishings, textiles, architecture, graphic design. Almost unwittingly, she'd adopted the same – her store was no different from her clothes, and vice versa. Unadorned, deceptively simple clean lines and clever detailing. There was a single long bleached-wood shelf that ran the length of the shop. With no visible fixings, it appeared to float on the chalky surface of the wall.

She'd found a cordonnier in Paris whose shoes she particularly liked and had placed an order for six of his women's styles. A sample of each sat on the shelf at evenly spaced intervals. Below it, at the same vertical distance, was a single chrome rail that followed the shelf. Her designs hung in neat, ordered rows along it. Four pairs of trousers, beautifully and simply tailored to fit the slender, boyish frame that she so admired; white and off-white shirts with invisible seams, no pockets and a flat seam down the front that hid the buttons; two long A-line skirts of a combination of cashmere and wool that flared around the ankles and four jackets of the same. *AdSP A/W 66*. Even her labels had been sourced from a specialist embroiderer. 'God', as her favourite architect, Mies van der Rohe, famously said, 'is in the detail.' Well, he certainly was in hers.

She'd found a pair of Italian seamstresses, sisters, who'd worked for Dior in a tiny atelier in the Marais district in Paris. They'd accepted her first order with exclamations of surprise. Such detailing! Such fabrics! Such quality! Everything by hand, she'd insisted. No machines. Their professional curiosity and pride had immediately been aroused – who on earth was this tall, cool German young woman with the business acumen and manner of someone decades older. How old was she? Twenty-three? Twenty-four? And already with such a knowledge of fabrics? It was a pleasure to talk to her, they both acknowledged after she and Tante Bärbel had left. She knew as much as they did about the fabrics she brought to them. She knew all the different wool types – cashmere, mohair, angora, chenille, flannel, worsted, the linens, cottons, silks and all the new, man-made fabrics, and she knew how to blend them, too, to create new materials that suited the exquisite sketches she showed them. After the first samples were done and sent to her for approval, she'd written back with such detailed instructions on what to alter and what to keep that they'd both looked at one another, mouths agape. Working with Mademoiselle de Saint Phalle, they both agreed, would be a challenge but one they were eager to embrace. She came to Paris with her business partner, the equally young but charming Bruno, and the contracts were signed. Chalk and cheese, those two, they commented to one another afterwards. Bruno was all fire and charm, whereas Anneliese was cool. But they complemented each other perfectly. Giovanna, the elder of the two, recognised immediately that this was a professional relationship that would last. Although she wouldn't have admitted it at the time, it was something Anneliese hoped for, too. That was another lesson she'd grasped. Loyalty. It was more important to her than she cared to admit. She didn't dare examine why.

She stopped by one of the shirts, fingering it gently. Suddenly she became aware of a taste in her mouth that made her stop, and stand very still, as if trying to catch the scent of something previously forgotten. A sour, metallic taste. What had she eaten for lunch, she thought to herself, frowning. And then, just as suddenly as it had come upon her, it vanished. She parted her lips a fraction, drawing down a breath of fresh air. Bruno had entered the shop and came to stand next to her. 'Are you all right?' he asked. 'You've suddenly gone pale.'

She shook her head. 'I'm fine. It's the paint, I think. I can still smell it.'

'It'll be gone by tomorrow.' He looked at her closely. 'Come on, let's go and choose the flowers for the opening. You wanted lilies, no?'

She allowed him to lead her out of the shop. For the time being, they had no assistants: just her and Bruno. In a month's time, they'd both agreed, they would see where things stood. They walked up Marylebone High Street in companionable silence, each preoccupied in their own way with Monday's opening. At the florist's on the corner, they stopped and placed an order for a dozen white lilies. Their pungent, aromatic scent filled the small shop. She felt her mouth fill with water suddenly, and her stomach begin to heave. She clasped a hand to her mouth; the sour, metallic taste of vomit rose in her throat. She rushed outside, fighting to keep down whatever was threatening to burst out. Bruno ran after her, grabbing her by the arm and pulling her round to face him. 'What's the—?'

'I'm going to be—' And she was. She couldn't stop herself. To her shame and horror, she was practically forced to her knees. She threw up all over Bruno, her own coat, the pavement . . . everywhere. A woman jumped out of the way in alarm; a small dog, sensing something was wrong, began barking wildly. Bruno ran back into the florist's and came out with a roll of tissue paper. She did her best to clean the mess she'd made but he stopped her, pulling her away from the edge of the road.

'Come on, let's get you to a toilet,' he said gently. 'There's a pub just up the road. I'll get you cleaned up.'

She followed him, her stomach still trembling but there was a greater, deeper fear that threatened to overspill. She'd had that same taste in her mouth before, had the same, uncontrollable urge to vomit, not only in the mornings, as Tante Bärbel had warned her, but all day long, at any time, any moment, without warning. The dread of what she knew to be happening inside her was greater than anything she'd ever known. She pushed open the door to the Ladies', shaking her head at Bruno's offer of assistance and went into one of the stalls. She sat down on the toilet and put her face in her hands. It couldn't be, she kept whispering to herself. No. Not again. The fear hit her then like a force that was greater than the urge to throw up, or to scream. She started to cry out but no sound emerged. The terror was hammered right back into her throat, where it had started, and she gasped, fearing she might choke. Not again. Please, God . . . not again.

43

ANNELIESE
London, 1967

Bruno held her hand, refused to leave her side, even under the disapproving eyes of the midwife and the junior doctor who assisted her at the birth. Her waters broke around midnight but it was hours before the contractions began in earnest. In the small flat off Portland Square where they'd been living and working together for the past six months, he helped her into her coat and called a taxi, darting this way and that, making sure the overnight bag she'd packed was ready and that there was nothing she'd missed. In complete contrast to her own subdued mood, he could not have been more excited. It was almost as if he were the father. He asked her nothing about the circumstances of the pregnancy and she didn't offer. She steadfastly refused to allow the pregnancy to interrupt their plans, or the work they put into the shop on Blandford Street, but Bruno could think of nothing else. He'd even decorated the little box room next to the living room that had initially been earmarked for a study and turned it into a tiny nursery instead. As six months became seven, and seven merged into eight, Bruno danced around beside her all day long, bringing her small cartons of apple juice that she liked and snacks that she didn't. He refused to allow her own terrible indifference to the child to infect his own mood. She couldn't bring herself to tell him why. She looked upon the moment of birth with a dread that flowed right through her; she could feel it seeping through her, night after night.

One such night when Bruno had long fallen asleep and the flat was quiet in that terrible, dark silence just before dawn, she lay in bed pushing her fists into her mouth, trying to control her sobs. She felt as though she'd been overtaken by some awful, impersonal force that rippled through her, weeping *for* her, and she was startled by the harshness of her own breath. She was afraid of the birth and of what it would unlock. She stared down the awful length of the long, terrifying days and nights ahead, wondering how on earth she would get through it.

But when it actually happened and she felt again the stirrings within her that signalled the beginnings of birth, another fear rose unexpectedly in her throat. What if it went wrong? Suddenly her fears switched tack. Now, as they wheeled her down the corridor towards the delivery room under the harsh neon glare of the strip lights, the dread that something might happen to this one overtook her. Her heart was racing; she could see the doctor look down at her and frown. Her blood was thundering in her ears and neck as they pushed her through the double doors and hoisted her from the gurney to a bed. She tried to speak but there was a choking hold on her throat. She heard the doctor bark out a command to one of the nurses, heard them shout something about her blood pressure and a monitor and God knows what else. Bruno's face hovered somewhere in the background, white and terrified. Someone lifted up an arm, pricked the surface of her skin and something else was hurriedly strapped to her other arm. She could hear the beeps and blips of machines all around her and in her panic, tried to sit up. She was pushed back down again and this time, it wasn't just the force of the doctor's hand that kept her down.

'She'll be fine,' she heard someone say. 'Her blood pressure's a little high but she's panicking. We've given her something to calm her down. She'll be fine.'

Her head felt thick and woolly. It was Bruno they were speaking to. She could see his chestnut-brown head nodding up and down vigorously. One of the nurses said something she couldn't catch. Something cold travelled the length of her arm, up towards her chest and as it went, she could practically feel herself begin to slow down. A slow, thick calmness descended on her. 'There you go, love,' she heard someone say. 'That's the ticket.'

'Will she be all right?' That was Bruno again. A terrible drowsiness was beginning to steal over her.

'She'll be fine. It's not her first, is it?' The nurse who'd been examining her straightened up. 'Dunno why she's panicking so, to be honest. How many d'you have?'

She tried to open her mouth. She heard Bruno say something but before she could properly make it out, a heavy curtain seemed to come down over her eyes, shutting out the light. The voices in the background faded away and she was left with only a faint ringing in her ears as the anaesthetic did its work. There was a momentary fuzziness, the ringing sound intensified and then slowly disappeared. At last all was still. The world around her faded to black.

Fine black hair, plastered to the crown. A red, screwed-up face. Marbled white skin, blotchy patches of red, folds of fat. And the noise. The first one hadn't been like this. Screams that went on and on, dying down for a second whilst the baby drew breath, all the better to belt another yelp out, and another. Everyone around her looked pleased, even delighted. Through half-lowered lids she watched the child being passed from one pair of hands to another. A pause in the screaming, then it started again. It was only when they finally brought the child round to her, tightly swaddled in some sort of prickly cotton blanket, that it stopped. As soon as she opened her arms to receive it – he? she? – the screaming ceased abruptly.

'See? Mummy's girl, already.' A nurse spoke. Anneliese looked up into a dark-skinned, smiling face. 'Lovely girl you have there, ma'am. Just a little scrap of a thing, isn't she?' She turned to Bruno, still hovering by her bedside, for confirmation. Bruno could only nod; he couldn't yet speak.

A girl. Longing and relief mingled in her. She gathered the bundle of dark hair and pink, plump skin to her and drew aside the fabric of her nightdress. The forgotten sensations were physical: the first touch of damp skin, the tiny hands that clutched at anything and everything within reach; the guiding hands and greedy, nuzzling mouth . . . and the first few moments of pain as the child latched on. She had to close her eyes. Everything came flooding back as though it were yesterday.

'Look, she's a natural,' she heard another nurse say. 'Will you look at that? It takes some of 'em a week to learn how to do it!' A lilting, Irish voice. A laugh from someone else. Bruno's shaky laugh of relief. Her eyes were still tightly shut. She felt as though she were floating, carried off on a tide of emotion and instinct. Her hands that were holding the small bundle tightened; she could not let go. This one she would never let go of. *Never.*

PART SIX

44

ANNELIESE
St John's Wood, London, 2001

She carried the thimble-sized cup of bitter espresso into the studio and pulled out her chair. The pile of photographs that Bruno had left out for her the previous night were sitting waiting for her. She took a sip, her tongue curling pleasurably around the piping-hot, thick liquid, put on her glasses and picked them up. She sighed in exasperation almost immediately. One dull, uniformly pretty blonde after another, this one with blue eyes, that one with green. A handful of sultry-looking Mediterranean types of the sort she'd seen on the catwalk for decades; waifs aplenty, discovered on the streets of Vilnius, Moscow, St Petersburg . . . she yawned indiscreetly, forgetting to cover her mouth. But she was alone; there was no one to see her. It was a Saturday afternoon and her studio was completely empty. She took the last mouthful and set the little demi-tasse carefully to one side. She looked at the photographs again. A vague dissatisfaction trembled at the edge of her consciousness, not just with the spread in front of her and the open sketchbook that was lying on the glossy white desk beside her – and had been there, untouched, for several days – but with everything. It had been months since her conversation with Ree Herz and ever since, her customary balance had deserted her. She'd always been able to find solace in her work – not now, not any more.

She pushed the photographs away from her impatiently and got up. It was a bright, sunny afternoon in May and the air held the vague but welcome promise of summer. She had a sudden longing to be outside. She carried the empty espresso cup through to the small kitchen at the rear and washed it, her mind running ahead. She would walk through Regent's Park towards Bond Street and check on the new shop. It was almost finished. She hadn't seen Ree Herz since that awful day six months ago, but he'd kept her up to date with progress. The opening was less than a fortnight away. Callan was handling it – the press and the inevitable opening-night party. She suppressed a small sound of annoyance. When had it all become so complicated? Twenty years ago things were much more simple.

She could remember when they opened three or four stores simultaneously, in different parts of the world – Milan, Tokyo, San Francisco – with none of the fuss that Callan claimed was not only inevitable, but crucial too. She'd tried to explain it to her. The 'evolution of sales', she called it. Suddenly it wasn't enough to just design beautiful clothes. No, they had to advertise, market, brand . . . they had to have the right models, the right photographers, the right make-up artists and the right campaigns. Utter nonsense. Now the talk was of 'lifestyle'. The Matuzzis – father and sons – bandied the words about at every opportunity. At one particularly annoying meeting Anneliese simply walked out. *Lifestyle?* What the hell did that mean? The smug, ridiculously good-looking one, Marco, had looked up from his notepad with that special look of bored tolerance that he seemed to use only when dealing with her and murmured something about having to move with the times. 'Everyone does it now, *cara* Anneliese. Everyone. Armani, Missoni, even Valentino. Now they sell everything. Accessories, handbags, perfume. We have to keep up.'

'Oh, don't tell me. Next we'll be making sunblock,' Anneliese snapped on her way out the door, ignoring Callan's look of exasperation. The man *infuriated* her. How dare he call her '*cara*'? She was at least three decades his senior! Odious little creep. She put up a hand to her temple. Thinking about Marco Matuzzi had brought on an almost instant headache.

She opened the cupboard door beside the front door and pulled out her coat. She wrapped herself in the wonderfully thick, soft blend of cashmere, angora and wool and immediately felt calmed. It had a lovely wide belt and fell almost to her ankles. She looked down at her feet. Black boots with a small, unusually curved heel, very simple, no stitching, just the polished sweep of buffed black leather. Her pale cream trousers from last year's winter collection swung out over the boots, peeking beneath the hem of her coat when she moved. She checked her reflection in the mirror. Her hair was practically silver now, she noted with interest. It had been white-blonde for so long that the grey and silver streaks had gone almost unnoticed. She rather liked it. She'd never been vain, thank God. Her passing concerns over the years about her figure and her face had more to do with her formidable control than any insecurities about her looks. One advantage, she supposed, of being alone. '*Du, du bist in einer nachdenklichen Stimmung*, Anneliese,' she murmured to herself in German as she locked the front door behind her. She pulled a quick, surprised face. German? She rarely spoke it, much less to herself. Another sign that things were off-kilter. She belted her coat and walked out, turning her face up to the unaccustomed sunlight.

The park was crowded with scores of teenagers in T-shirts, throwing and catching balls, shrieking with laughter. She cut across the grass, avoiding the clusters of families sitting on blankets with squalling infants and whining children. She had never understood the British enthusiasm for picnics. She personally couldn't think of anything worse than an afternoon spent sitting on the grass eating soggy sandwiches, swatting away wasps. By the time she reached Great Portland Street, her earlier dark mood was beginning to lift. She continued down Portland Place, cutting her way through the smaller backstreets until she emerged on Oxford Street, a few minutes away from the shop. She cut through the crowds shuffling dispiritedly up and down Oxford Street and walked down New Bond Street. Her pulse quickened as she approached the shop. She fished the keys from her handbag and walked up to the front door. To her surprise, it was partially open. She hadn't expected to find workmen in on a Saturday afternoon. She nudged it fully open and stepped inside. There was someone standing in the shadows, hands in pockets, clearly deep in thought. Her heart missed a beat. It was Ree Herz. He turned as she entered and they looked at one another for a moment without speaking. She saw that the memory of their last meeting was there in his eyes and face. He said nothing as she approached and did not save her with an interruption or a greeting of some kind that would ease the moment. She was aware of a blush of embarrassment underneath the layers of her clothing, staining her neck, travelling upwards through her face. 'Ree,' she said slowly, holding out a hand. 'I didn't expect to find anyone here on a Saturday.'

'Best time to come,' he said, taking it. 'It's the only time I can get a feel for the place without all the distraction.'

They stood looking at each other in the rainbow-coloured light. She felt again the heat coming up into her cheeks, staining outwards to the tips of her ears. Suddenly there was intimacy between them, but of a kind she'd never known – it was not sexual, nor was it familial, such as she sometimes had with Callan, even Tara. It was of an entirely different order. They approached each other as equals, nothing less. Not yet as friends – though that possibility was there, between them – but as collaborators, two people on a journey of some sort, together, but without knowing precisely where it would end. It was the strangest thing, she thought to herself, as they turned and looked at the various details he pointed out – the shadow gap at the junction of the ceiling and the walls, and again, at floor level, where the skirting board had once been; the mottled grey marble of the counter-top – did she like it? The tension that had existed between them and in her mind for almost six months was gone. In its place was an understanding that something profound had passed between them, easing whatever awkwardness there might have been. As they walked through the space together, commenting quietly to one another, they seemed to have stepped into a place of extraordinary calm. Again it came to her that the root of their intimacy was not sexual in any way. They had moved towards that moment and passed over it, leaving it far behind. He pointed to a thin, spidery crack in the ceiling that he told her they would plaster over first thing on Monday morning. She smiled; she recognised in him an obsession with perfection that was equal to her own.

Suddenly a noise behind them made them both turn. Someone had walked into the space. 'They only had filter, Ree— Oh, sorry! I didn't realise anyone else would be here.' A tall, very slender young woman walked towards them, two Styrofoam coffee cups balanced in either hand.

'No, thanks. I'm fine,' Anneliese said automatically, staring at the woman. She was extraordinarily beautiful, especially in the soft, half-light of the interior. She'd seen her face before, somewhere, she was sure of it. She frowned, trying to place her.

'Anneliese,' Ree was gravely formal. 'Can I introduce you? This is Hayley, my wife.'

The woman smiled, and set down one of the cups on the floor. 'It's so nice to finally meet you,' she said, taking Anneliese's outstretched hand. 'I'm a huge fan. I think my agency tried to book me for a couple of your shows once. Christy got the job instead, I think. I sulked for days. But that was *ages* ago,' she added with a charming little shrug of her shoulders.

'You're a model.' It was a statement, not a question. Anneliese nodded to herself. Of course. She'd seen the woman before. She really was exquisite. Short, feathered dark brown hair, cut close to the scalp; almond-shaped hazel-green eyes under arched, tapering brows. A thin, very sculpted nose with an indentation at the tip that was mirrored in the finely chiselled line above her lips. Lovely high cheekbones and a long elegant neck that disappeared into the large cowl neck of her woollen poncho. She was whippet-thin, long legs encased in dark jeans, made even longer by the high-heeled suede boots she wore.

'I used to be,' she said, blushing slightly. 'Years ago.' She glanced quickly at Ree as she said it. Anneliese could feel an uncomfortable tension between them – anger? Irritation? She couldn't tell. The subtle and often not-so-subtle workings of couples were often beyond her and she was less interested in what might go on behind the scenes in their marriage than she was in the face in front of her. As she studied the woman – Hayley? – she was aware of a quickening in her own blood. *This* was the face she'd been looking for, without ever having been aware of it. She looked from Hayley to Ree in a kind of stunned disbelief. She wasn't the type to believe in fate – the concept was too vague to be trusted. Life, insofar as she understood it, was simply a series of incidents. Every once in a while, something might happen that would bring an earlier moment to light, or cast it in a different light entirely. This, she thought to herself as she followed them around the shop, was one such moment. Her meeting with Ree Herz, however much it had disturbed her, was simply part of a larger picture, unfathomable in the present moment, but whose meaning was beginning slowly, piece by piece, to become clear.

A few hours later, she and Bruno stood at the light table in her studio, poring over the photographs her stylist had just sent over.

'*Ja, nicht schlecht.* How old is she?' Bruno straightened up, nodding.

'Thirty-five.'

'Hmm. A little on the old side.'

'Rubbish. She's perfect.' Anneliese frowned at him.

'She's still represented by Rain?'

Anneliese nodded. 'They sent them over. Look.' She pointed to the pile of photographs that she'd pushed to one side on her desk. 'Hundreds of them. I've been through them all. I've had every agency in town looking . . . and nothing. For six bloody months they've been sending me the same rubbish. I don't *want* some sixteen year old. I design clothes for *women*, Bruno, not children. And Hayley Summers is a woman.'

'Fine. There's no point in arguing with you, *mein Schatz*. Your mind's already made up, I can tell. Let's book her and see.

I'll organise the photographer. Who d'you want? Patrick? Mario?'

'No. Let's get one of the younger guys for now. I'm not even sure she'll agree to it. We haven't spoken yet.'

'Well, speak to her then and let me know. Let's get this show on the road. You've got three months and I'm worried, Anneliese. All this traipsing around a building site. You're just procrastinating, darling.'

'It's not a building site,' Anneliese started to protest, then stopped herself. '*Ja*, OK, you're right. But, I'm excited. She's got *some*thing, you know. It's . . . it's inspiring.' She shook her head bemusedly. 'It's strange . . . I've never worked this way before.'

'It's not strange. You've found a muse, that's all. They've all got them . . . Karl, Yves, Giorgio. Well, if she inspires you, I'm all for it.'

'Let's see if she wants the job first,' Anneliese said cautiously. 'She said herself it's been years since she's worked.'

'Of course she'll want the job. Who in their right mind wouldn't?'

45

HAYLEY

'Me? She wants *me*?' Hayley almost dropped the phone. She grabbed hold of the receiver just before it fell from her clutch. 'You're joking. You're joking, aren't you?'

'No, I'm not. She rang up this morning and asked us to bike over your book. I didn't want to say anything, just in case she changed her mind.'

Hayley was speechless. 'I can't believe it,' she said finally. 'I can't fucking believe it. How long's it been?'

'Three years, darling.' Davinia gave a low, knowing chuckle. 'She's in a hurry. We've booked you in for a session with her photographer on Thursday. You OK with that?'

Hayley's heart was beating so loudly she was sure Davinia could hear it. 'Yes, yes, of course,' she stammered. Her mind was racing ahead. Thursday was three days away. She would eat nothing between now and then, book herself in for every single beauty treatment going, eyebrows, a facial, a couple of sunbed sessions wouldn't hurt either. Everything. She would do whatever it took. AdSP? *Anneliese de Saint Phalle?* She clutched the phone so tightly her knuckles hurt. 'Thursday's fine.'

'Lovely, darling.' Davinia blew a couple of kisses down the line. 'It's *fabulous* news, it really is. We've *missed* you! Welcome back!'

Hayley put down the phone slowly. She wasn't taken in, not for a moment, but hell, it felt good. She knew the score. She could remember those years when *everyone* was calling. Not any more. She stood in the middle of the living room still too stunned to think. Anneliese de Saint Phalle wanted her. *Somebody* wanted her. At long fucking last.

Ree's reaction wasn't quite what she'd been expecting. He put down his knife and fork and stared at her. '*You?*' he said finally, incredulously. 'What are you talking about?'

She could feel the resentment rising up in her throat. She ignored him and concentrated instead on cutting Zoë's chicken. 'There you go, darling. All cut up.'

Zoë looked at her uncertainly. She wasn't used to her mother cutting up her food for her. That was Chantal, the au pair's job, and when Chantal wasn't around, it was Daddy's. Mummy hardly ever ate with them. 'No, not like that,' she said, frowning. 'I don't like it like that.'

'Oh, for goodness' sake, Zoë!' Hayley couldn't help snapping at her. 'What does it matter what the pieces look like?' Zoë looked immediately crestfallen. Ottie started crying. She couldn't stand the slightest bit of tension in the air. Ree sighed. One of his long, drawn-out sighs that expressed everything he rarely said these days. She knew exactly what it meant. She ignored Ottie's crying and Zoë's looks of reproach. And Ree's sigh. She tried to concentrate on her own good mood. There was no way she was going to let him – or anyone – spoil it. 'She rang up Davinia and made a booking. That's how it's done. You *know* that's how it's done.'

Ree was quiet, concentrating on his food. Ottie and Zoë exchanged glances of tearfully complicit solidarity. Hayley took a sip of sparkling water and smiled brightly at everyone. It had been a while since they'd all eaten dinner together. Chantal had bought flowers from the Columbia Road market that morning – sweet peas, Hayley noted. Their scent lightly perfumed the air. She'd also placed a couple of new tea-lights in the small glass holders that Hayley had pushed to one end of the dining table. She pulled out her lighter and lit the candles. The small, flickering lights sent wavering, rosy beams across the table. Across from her, she saw her family exchange wary looks of disbelief. She didn't care. Nothing could dampen the sudden radiance inside her. After three years of doing the odd job here and there, being forced to listen to one rejection message after another, putting up with the resigned, slightly impatient tone in Davinia's voice every time she rang up, to be greeted with the news that someone had actually requested her – and not just *someone*, Anneliese Zander de Saint Phalle – was enough to put a smile on anyone's face, let alone hers! She took another sip of water. She'd eaten nothing all day and her already flat stomach was almost concave. Two more days and her cheekbones would be even more finely etched. She loved her body for its immediate responses to anything and everything she did to it, good and bad. 'Just like a racehorse,' her mother had said to her once, uncharacteristically generous. 'A thoroughbred. You got that from me.' She'd never forgotten the compliment or the way it made her feel.

She got up suddenly, ignoring Ree's questioning glance and went into the bedroom area. She opened the chest of drawers quietly and fished around for the little plastic bag she'd put in there only the other day. Her fingers found it underneath a pile of underwear and she drew it out almost reverentially. She slipped into the bathroom and closed the door behind her. It took a couple of seconds to prepare three short, neat lines, her fingers moving quickly over the surface of the mirror that lent itself so bloody well to the preparation of her drug of choice. One quiet, discreet snort later, then another and another and she tipped her head back, waiting for the rush. It was glorious, made all the sweeter by the warmth of her good mood. She dropped her head back down and looked at herself in the mirror above the sink. Gorgeous, fucking gorgeous. At thirty-five, she still had *it*, that magical, mysterious *some*thing that was so hard to define and yet when you saw it, you knew. Anneliese Zander de Saint Phalle had taken one look at her and seen *it*.

She felt the delicious glow of confidence seeping through her pores. It had been so long, *so* fucking long since she'd felt this good. Living with a superstar wasn't easy, especially since it had once been the two of them, not just Ree. In the beginning they'd been talked about in one breath, Ree-and-Hayley. Summers-and-Herz. Magazine editors couldn't wait to get pictures of the two of them, together, she with that million-dollar smile of hers that could light up an entire concert hall, as someone had once said. Ree rarely smiled but his face was the sort that drew the eye. They'd looked so good together. No gallery opening, art show, dinner party or reception was complete without them. She'd picked up a whole new vocabulary when she met him, and he introduced her to what she and her friends called The Serious Set – the architects and artists and collectors and gallery owners who were his friends. She went from knowing next to nothing about contemporary art to knowing who Damien was and how much his last piece had auctioned for. She hung out with Tracey and air-kissed Jake and Dino when they met. She knew who was on their way up, who was sinking and who was practically on the floor. She learned how to stand in front of a nearly blank canvas and tilt her head thoughtfully to one side. She could tell a Barcelona chair from an Eames and she'd even learned to like glass and steel. She was quick and eager to learn. She picked up a couple of books about Namibia, that odd little country of his that he hardly knew and where his bloody parents now lived and could talk reasonably comfortably about its long struggle for independence and how pleased she was that she and Ree could now visit without fear of arrest.

'Can you *imagine?*' she'd say to whomever she happened to be talking to, a wary eye on whatever blank canvas they were staring thoughtfully at, another on her companion's face. 'Ten years ago we'd have been thrown in jail. Makes you think, doesn't it?'

The gallery owner or art dealer or journalist (even better) standing opposite her, glass in hand, would nod meaningfully. 'She's really bright,' she overheard someone say once, after one such encounter. 'Don't believe all that bullshit about models being stupid. She's frightfully clever.' *Frightfully clever.* The glow that that description had lit in her was similar to the one she was experiencing right now. More than anything she longed to be taken seriously. Standing around, half-dressed, as Valentino prodded your breasts disinterestedly or Galliano fussed about with your hair did wonders for your bank balance but not much for one's self-esteem. There, she was a piece of meat – beautiful, granted, and every girl knew just how hard it was to achieve *that*, but anyone with good genes and a good haircut could manage it. What Ree had – talent – was of an altogether different order. He had it; she didn't. Simple as that. Being beautiful didn't count. So when Anneliese de Saint Phalle, who had as much talent as Ree and, if anything, commanded even more respect, came along, asking for *her* . . . well, it put a whole new spin on things.

Ree could be mercilessly scathing about her world, even if he didn't mean to be. He had no idea how much it hurt to be thought of as stupid and inconsequential. No one had ever thought that of him. And Hayley knew just how much he respected Anneliese. Not only was she a great fashion designer but she was a *thinker* – no higher praise in his book. He talked about her often. She had an amazing art collection, a wonderful 'eye', she read widely, could talk about practically anything and the walls of her design studio were covered in bookshelves that held, equally, political memoirs and books on African fabrics. A real person, in other words. Not a *chimera*, as she'd once over-heard him say at a dinner party, describing someone they all knew. Beautiful, but with nothing really 'there'. She'd known then, even if he hadn't, that he was referring to her. He was wrong. She was no chimera, whatever the fuck that was. Anne-liese clearly didn't think so and—

'Hayley?' His voice made her jump. *Shit*. She turned on the tap, hurriedly wiping the traces of coke off the mirror. 'You OK?'

'Yes, I'm fine. I'll be right out.' She squeezed out a dab of toothpaste and quickly freshened up her mouth. She took one last look at herself in the mirror. Her eyes were clear and steady. It was one reason she preferred coke to dope. Smoking grass, although it calmed her, made her lethargic and unfocused. Coke sharpened everything. A lover had told her once, a long time ago, that she shone when she drank; her beauty came to the surface – it didn't disintegrate the way some women's did. She'd loved the compliment, even if she hadn't quite understood it. Now she did. Coke was like that. It brought the sheen under-neath her skin to the surface, not in a shiny, sweaty way, but glossily. 'Coming,' she called out again, more gaily now. She checked her watch. It was eight o'clock. Time to put the kids to bed. She might even persuade Ree to open a bottle of wine. She wouldn't have any. Nothing to eat or drink except water until Thursday. But perhaps with a glass of wine he'd thaw a little, show her a little warmth. She wrapped her arms around her waist, rubbing the skin on her upper arms. Warmth. He used to be so warm. Especially with her. There was a sharp knock at the door again. She checked herself one last time and opened it. He was standing there, frowning at her, and it wasn't warmth she saw reflected in his eyes – anything but. They narrowed suspi-ciously. 'What are you doing in there?' he asked, keeping his voice low. 'Are you . . . ?'

She shook her head vehemently. 'Don't be silly. I haven't

done anything like that in years, you know that. I . . . I just wasn't feeling very well. Something I ate, maybe.'

'You haven't eaten much, Hayley,' he frowned, clearly unconvinced.

She felt a momentary flash of elation. He'd *noticed*? But her elation was followed swiftly by irritation. 'Who are you now? My jailer?' she asked angrily, pushing past him. She felt, rather than saw, his attention slide past her to the interior of the small bathroom. Too late. She whirled back round but it was too late. The mirror on which she'd cut her lines was still lying in the sink. She'd washed the evidence away but had forgotten the blade. Their eyes met and held. She could feel the embarrassment rising in her, like a tidal wave. He said nothing, just looked at her, then turned and walked away. She had the impression it was more than just her presence he was trying to escape.

46

ANNELIESE

She studied the photographs through the monocle Bruno had handed her, bending close to the prints so as not to miss anything. The woman moved in front of the camera with the graceful, practised ease that comes after a long career in front of the lens. None of the coltish coquetry of most of the girls these days. The photographer had clearly been in awe of her — you could practically sense his hesitation through the lens. She seemed, if anything, more in control than he was. Yes, she'd made the right decision. In the hands of a Patrick Demarchelier or a Mario Testino, Hayley Summers would simply come alive. She straightened up. Bruno was looking expectantly at her. She nodded firmly. 'She's *it*. Let's see if we can get Patrick on the line. I've got a few ideas I'd like to share with him.'

Bruno looked relieved. 'Good, good. I'll try him now. Now,

will you get into the studio, Anneliese. We've got two months to go and I'm nervous as hell.'

'Don't be.' Anneliese felt giddy with relief. Bruno was right, of course. Two months was hardly any time at all but she was bursting with ideas. For the first time in a long while, she had started to think about a new collection not in terms of fabrics and cut and detailing, but in terms of a *story*. That was the magical, unknowable ingredient Hayley Summers had brought to the photos. She looked like a woman with a story to tell. A woman with a past. Her face hinted at things – past lovers, great times, days of sun and wine and roses and the sort of limitless capacity for happiness that only the young and beautiful seem to have. But there was also something else in her face that spoke of passion and disappointment, sorrow and pain. She looked like someone who'd *lived*. Anneliese's mind was already beginning to fill up with places, settings, circumstances, secrets, lies, trysts and missed opportunities, as well as those taken. The clothes and the fabrics would soon follow suit.

She gathered up the photographs and carried them off to her office like a prize. Out of the corner of her eye she could see Bruno exchange a quick, excited glance with the others. A week ago, things had seemed very different. She'd fled from Ree Herz that day in fear of what his presence in her life might unlock. Well, it had certainly unlocked something but it was not what she'd feared. The panic that had blown up inside her had transformed itself, emerging as the energy of another set of passions and what remained was a burning desire to produce, to draw, to sketch, to create. For the second time in as many days the word 'fate' popped into her head. She'd never believed in it, never. You made your own luck, fate, fortune . . . whatever people wanted to call it. But the coincidences of the past couple of months couldn't be explained away by chance. Ree Herz had stepped into her life, unexpectedly enriching it. Now his wife too was present; she was acutely aware of having only grasped the edges of something, not its whole.

She picked up her pencil, smoothed out a piece of crisp, yellow drafting paper of the sort she'd always worked on, ever since Berlin, and began to draw. She bent her head, narrowed her eyes, slowly and purposefully entering that other, mysterious world of the imagination where anything could happen, things were not always what they seemed and the only communication and connection with the present was the sound of her own breathing and the steady, confident movement of her hand.

47

REE

His phone was flashing but he made no move to answer it. He glanced at the screen. *Hayley Mobile.* He'd been expecting her to call. Either she'd got the job with Anneliese, or she hadn't. Either way, the result would be the same: a quick trip to her dealer. He wondered who it was now. For a while it'd been a greasy-looking bloke who sat as if rooted to the spot inside the doorway of the Cat and Fiddle, the slightly seedy pub halfway down their street. He disappeared after a while, only to be replaced by the sort of slick, quasi-stylish man you met at parties and wondered why he was on the phone the whole night. Whoever it was, she was either on her way to meet him, or on her way back. If he were lucky, she would remember to leave instructions on what to do with the girls with Chantal. Ever since he'd seen the tell-tale signs in the bathroom, he could have kicked himself. Why hadn't he seen it coming? He should've guessed. Not just the lack of appetite or the unexplained absences late at night, but the mood swings, the highs and lows. One minute she was on cloud nine, all smiles and radiant energy, the next she was lethargic and weepy, especially after talking to her so-called best friends, those vacuous girls with whom she'd once flown halfway across the world on assignments. He found it hard to believe he'd ever thought of them as fun. He couldn't even remember what they looked like, let alone their names. They all seemed to be named after flowers – Rose, Petal, Jacaranda. Or months of the year – June, May, January. Or days of the week. What the hell was that redhead called? Monday? Tuesday? Tuesday, that was it. She'd come up to him in the kitchen one night, a bottle in one hand and a joint in the other. He'd had to push her away, astounded at her audacity. Hayley, her 'best' friend, was only on the other side of the partition!

'Ree?' Terri tapped on the door and stuck her head round without waiting for an answer, as was her wont. 'I've got the final invoice ready for the A*d*SP shop project. D'you want to see it before I send it out?'

He looked up and paused. 'No, just print it out and I'll take it over there myself.'

Terri looked surprised. '*You* don't need to do that. I can take it over if you'd rather we delivered it to her personally.'

He shook his head. 'No, I'll do it. I feel like getting out of the office for a bit. Just give me a shout when it's done.'

'Sure. It'll only take a minute. And don't forget you've got a meeting with Arup at six. Their offices.'

'I won't.' He looked at his watch. It was nearly two – plenty of time. He had no idea if Anneliese would actually be there, but taking the invoice over in person was the sort of gesture he thought she'd appreciate. He'd missed the night of the shop's unveiling – he'd been in a meeting in New York that weekend – and although he'd made sure others from the office had gone along, he'd have liked to have been there himself. Hayley had been invited, although the new campaign in which she featured hadn't yet hit the stands. She'd said very little about it, which made him uneasy. He couldn't think of anything he'd less like to hear than his wife making a fool of herself in front of Anneliese Zander de Saint Phalle. Or anyone else, for that matter. He grabbed his jacket, picked up the envelope from Terri and left the offices before anyone had the chance to stop him.

*

Half an hour later, the invoice and a large bunch of semi-open, beautiful white lilies under his arm, he ran up the steps of Anneliese's studio and rang the bell. The door was opened by a young woman in an exquisitely tailored suit, and an even more exquisitely tailored haircut. Ms de Saint Phalle's new assistant, she explained. She shook her head apologetically. No, Ms de Saint Phalle wasn't in, but she'd be only too happy to take the lilies for her. Was there a note perhaps? Ah, an invoice. Yes, she'd make sure Ms de Saint Phalle got both. He was just about to turn round when he heard someone come through the connecting passage that joined the two townhouses. A woman in high heels, he thought to himself immediately. There wasn't a sound like it in the world.

'Gosh, those are beautiful.' A strange ripple of anticipation crept up his neck. It was Callan, Anneliese's daughter. He hadn't seen her since the day they met, six months earlier.

'Yes, the architect brought them round for Ms de Saint Phalle.'

'The architect?' Callan's clear, precise voice echoed in the small hallway.

He was halfway down the steps. The door opened fully and suddenly there she was. He turned and looked up at her, feeling inexplicably as though he'd been caught off-guard.

'Oh, hello,' she said, her face partially hidden by the enormous, just-opening flowers. 'Are these for Anneliese? They're lovely.' She smiled down at him. The corners of her lovely mouth flicked upwards, softening the sultry perfection of her face. He could feel the heat rising up his neck.

'Yes. No. I mean, yes. They're for her. Well, for both of you. I'm sorry I missed the opening.' He was astonished at his own confusion.

'D'you want to come in and wait for her? Is she expecting you?'

'No, no. I . . . I was just passing and thought I'd drop them off. With the invoice,' he added quickly. 'Just took a chance she'd be in.'

'Oh. Well, I was just about to have a coffee. D'you have time? Would you like one?'

The words were out before he could even think. 'Yes, I'd love to,' he heard himself say. 'If you're sure? I'm not interrupting anything, am I?'

'Absolutely not. Come in.' She stood back, watching him walk back up the steps. 'Come through. I'll just pop these in some water. Let's go into the boardroom. It's nice and quiet in there. Would you get us two coffees?' she asked the assistant, then smiled up at him. 'Go straight through. I'll be right there.' There was that marvellous sound again of her heels clicking their way across the floor. He only just managed to stop himself turning round to look. He walked into the boardroom, a long, spacious room at the rear of the studios, painted white, with a long white marble slab of a table and twelve pale oak chairs. With the exception of a large, ornate chandelier, a low sleek sideboard and a huge photograph hanging over the fireplace, there was nothing else in the room. He looked at the photograph with interest. It was nearly two metres wide. In the foreground, a man was looking down on a city, some fifteen or twenty floors below him. Despite his face being out of focus, the level of detail in the foreground was extraordinary. The photographer had captured an astonishing array of minute, almost inconsequential details – the dark, pimpled skin on his face, his frown, the tentative parting of the lips to reveal his teeth; the yellowish whites of his eyes, startling in his pitch-black skin. He was wearing a worn leather jacket. The soft sheen across his shoulders revealed myriad cracks. He looked more closely at the city. Modern buildings, spread across a neat grid. Not a European city, then. He wondered where it had been taken.

'It's Johannesburg.' Callan came into the room. 'They came as a pair. The other one's in my office.'

'Johannesburg?' He was surprised.

'Mmm. Braamfontein. Ah, here's the coffee. How d'you take it?'

A woman came bustling in with a silver tray laden with coffee,

236

milk, sugar, cakes, biscuits, scones. She set the tray down and closed the door behind her. He laughed suddenly.

Callan looked at him, a corresponding smile beginning to show around the corners of her lovely mouth. 'What's so funny?' she asked, pulling out one of the chairs.

He sat down opposite her. 'Look, I admit I don't know Anneliese very well,' he said, shaking his head, still smiling. 'But the thought of her sitting down every afternoon to scones with jam and cream just makes me laugh. She doesn't seem the, er, type.'

Callan smiled. 'You're absolutely right,' she said, pouring him a cup. 'I don't think I've ever seen Anneliese eat anything sweet. Ever.'

'No, not sweets.'

'None.' Callan agreed, still smiling. 'Sugar?'

'Er, no.' He couldn't get over how nervous she made him feel. She got up suddenly and walked across to the sideboard. She turned, with that sideways movement of the hips that a woman makes when moving between pieces of furniture, and pulled open a drawer. The sudden blast of desire that broke over him caused him to choke. He coughed, furiously. 'So . . . so how is Anneliese?' he asked hurriedly, embarrassed beyond belief.

'Oh, she's in her element.' Callan came back to the table with a small packet of sweetener. She tipped the contents into her cup, stirring it gently. 'She's signed up a face for the new campaign, apparently. I just heard from Bruno. Hayley some-body-or-other – what was her last name? Summers. That's it. Hayley Summers. She was there at the opening but I didn't get the chance to meet— oh, are you all right?'

Ree nodded vigorously. He was choking again. 'Just . . . just went down the wrong way,' he stammered. He could have kicked himself. Now his confusion intensified.

'Shall I get you some water?'

'No, no . . . I'm absolutely fine, thanks.' He got up suddenly. 'I . . . I just remembered something. I . . . I forgot. I've got a meeting . . . completely forgot. I'd better dash.'

Callan looked up at him quizzically. Their two almost full coffee cups were on the table in front of them, as was his scone with a bite missing out of one side, in the manner of a cartoon. Wave after wave of confusion broke over him. 'I'll . . . I'd better run,' he said, grabbing his jacket before she could say anything further. His last impression was of her dark eyes watching him with a mixture of amusement and disbelief as he practically fled from the room – and from her.

Idiot. Idiot. *Idiot!* He jogged down the short flight of stairs, two at a time, his pulse racing absurdly. He hadn't behaved this stupidly since his teenage days – and even then, he doubted he'd ever made such a fool of himself. He hailed a cab almost immediately and climbed in. He had no meeting to go to and no desire to return to the office. *Why didn't you just say, "Hayley's my wife"? Why didn't you just say it? She's going to find out sooner or later and then you're going to look like a prize idiot, or worse. What explanation could you possibly have?*

He was still berating himself when he pushed open his own front door an hour later. The loft was still and empty. He threw his coat and bag on the chair beside the door and went straight to the fridge. He tossed a couple of ice cubes in a tumbler and poured himself a small measure of whisky, tipping it back in one gulp. He stood at the sink for a moment, looking down onto the street. He'd never experienced such confusion, and certainly not over a woman. His relationships with women had always been easy, smooth, even when they were brief. He had Sibongile to thank for that, he supposed. Despite the distance, she'd always made him understand women were to be respected, cherished. She was strong; he thought *all* women were strong. Barring Hayley, whose strengths (if you could call them that) lay in the opposite direction from Sibongile's, he'd only ever really known strong women, lovers and friends included. And Callan de Saint Phalle was certainly strong – and bold, and beautiful and so thoroughly enigmatic that he found it difficult to put her out of his mind. He picked up the empty glass, chinking the ice cubes slowly around, lost in thought. He knew nothing about her. Was she married? With someone? Children? He had no idea. She ran the business side of Anneliese's affairs, that much he knew, and from the odd snippet he picked up from Terri, she wasn't one to suffer fools. Much like her mother, then. He'd met her twice and both times had had to run from the confusion she provoked in him.

He frowned, trying to grasp why she'd unsettled him so. It was her expression, he decided, closing his eyes to recall it more precisely. The way she looked at him. Both bold and wary, knowing and yet curious. He felt the heat come up in his face again. He couldn't remember the last time a woman had looked at him that way. As if she wanted something other from him, something deeper than the usual bored banter that strangers exchange. It was both sexual and not, flirtatious and yet profound. He shook his head. He shuddered to think what Hayley would do if she found out he'd even had so much as a passing attraction towards another woman. She'd told him once, not long after Ottie was born and she'd suspected him of flirting with someone – he couldn't even remember whom. 'If you ever, *ever* cheat on me,' she'd warned him, 'you'll never see your kids again. That much I can promise you.' It was no idle threat. Hayley was easily capable of that – and much worse. At times like those, she was very, very French.

He rinsed the glass slowly, and put it away. He wanted no reminder of the trouble he'd suddenly found himself in.

48

CALLAN

For a long while after Ree Herz practically ran from the room, Callan remained there, deep in thought. To say his behaviour was odd was an understatement. What on earth had she said to make him flee like that? She looked at his still-full cup, his half-eaten scone . . . he'd literally taken one bite before he bolted.

Her hand went out automatically to the scone. She picked it up, brought it to her lips and carefully bit off a piece, just where his lips had touched it. She gave an embarrassed little laugh, swallowing it quickly. Now it was her turn to feel foolish. There she was, sitting in the boardroom, eating the leftover piece of scone that some man had abandoned, just because it was a way to get closer to him? Absurdly, tears pricked at her eyelids with a strange, tender pleasure. It had been months since she'd felt even the stirrings of curiosity about a man, let alone desire. Like Ree Herz had just done, she too had fled from something she felt she couldn't possibly bear. She'd run away from New York and only understood it as such when she landed in London. That was why she'd stayed away for so long. She'd been afraid to admit to the desperation of the life that had somehow become hers, there. It was only when she was back in London, amidst the familiar, beautiful surroundings of her mother's home that she realised it was the one thing she'd failed to do – make her own home. New York had started out as an escape and in the end, she'd escaped *it*. But wasn't that what she always did? Escape, run, flee, hide – she was always in motion, either running furiously towards something or beating a hasty retreat. Suddenly she pushed the plate of scones and biscuits away from her impatiently and stood up. Damn that man! She hadn't had a moment of such horrible introspection in *months*! She walked quickly out of the room.

'Who brought the flowers?' Anneliese asked, sticking her head round Callan's door.

'Ree Herz. He stopped by earlier. Said he was just passing by. He dropped them off with the final invoice.' Callan didn't look up. She could already feel the blush creeping over her face.

'That was kind of him,' Anneliese murmured appreciatively. 'I should have him round for dinner. I'll ask Melissa to organise it. You're here for a couple of weeks, aren't you? When do you go to Dubai?'

'On the twenty-third. Yeah, I'm here. And no, I won't be

bringing a date, if that's what you're about to ask,' Callan said quickly.

Anneliese raised her eyebrows fractionally. 'No, I wasn't,' she said mildly. 'Although he'd be very welcome.'

'Why d'you always assume it'll be a "he"?' Callan asked, picking up the letters that Anneliese had signed. Anneliese stared at her, a hand going to her throat. For once, she seemed at a loss for words. 'Just joking, Maman,' Callan said hurriedly. 'Er, what d'you want me to do with these?' She pointed to a couple of unsigned memos.

'Those?' Anneliese seemed miles away. 'Oh, those. Um, you can just leave those. I still need to check a few things.'

'All right. Well, I'm meeting Tara for dinner so I'm going to head home.' Callan picked up her jacket from the back of her chair and collected her things. 'I *was* just joking, Maman,' she added as she moved towards the door, seeing Anneliese's still rather dazed expression. 'Don't worry. I'll show up with Mr Right one day. Maybe not next week, but one day soon, I promise.'

'Yes, yes . . . of course. Well, I . . . I'll just get on with these, shall I?' Anneliese said faintly, pointing to the unsigned letters.

'Night, Maman.' Callan stopped suddenly, and kissed her on the cheek. Vulnerable certainly wasn't a word she'd ever used in connection with Anneliese but a sudden wave of tenderness came over her.

For once, Anneliese didn't pull away. She put up a hand to her cheek, just at the spot Callan had touched. 'Goodnight, darling,' she said softly, her hand still touching her face.

Callan hesitated. 'Darling' wasn't a word she heard Anneliese use very often, and certainly never to her. She opened her mouth to say something, then thought better of it. 'Night, Maman,' she said again, and then quickly left the room.

The television screen flickered silently in the background. Sitting with her feet curled under her, Callan absentmindedly stroked the crooked little toe that had resisted all Anneliese's efforts to straighten it for the first five or six years of Callan's life. She rather liked the tiny malformation. In sandals, it sometimes peeked out. As a teenager, she'd been rather proud of it. A fault in her that Anneliese couldn't control. Such a strange day, made all the stranger by Ree Herz's unexpected visit. She replayed their conversation for the umpteenth time. His face at the door, the grace with which he moved towards her, passed through into the offices and the scent of his aftershave which she didn't recognise but which lingered faintly after he was gone. Just what was it about him that drew her in? She frowned, trying to work it out. It wasn't just his looks – Christ, she'd had more than her fair share of handsome men – or his charm. She'd had enough of blank, blandly charming men. His build? Not just tall, but graceful. Athletic – that sexy combination of size and strength, tempered by grace. His appeal was both physical and intellectual.

She smiled to herself, half-embarrassed. Friday night and there she was, alone at home, sitting on her beautiful lemon-yellow tweed couch, stroking her deformed toe and fantasising about a man she'd met all of twice! What the hell had happened to her? Callan de Saint Phalle, one of the most sought-after girls on the party circuit in Manhattan without whom, or so it was said, no party, no soirée, no after-dinner party was complete. She used to turn down invitations, not seek them out. She'd been one of the first girls in her circle of friends to own a cell phone – it was a constant joke amongst those she'd known that without it she'd collapse. It rang constantly. She looked down at it now. She couldn't remember the last time she'd taken a call from someone she actually wanted to hear from. 'I'm happy,' she suddenly whispered to herself. 'Aren't I?' Her fingers stopped their rhythmic pattern. *Was* she happy? On the surface, certainly. She had everything. A beautiful flat, a career, holidays when and where she wanted, a wardrobe to die for, more shoes and bags and coats than she could reasonably ever wear and more money than she could reasonably spend. She had Anneliese, and Bruno, and Tara. She had it all. No boyfriend or husband, but she wasn't looking, was she? She couldn't remember exactly when it had slowly dawned on her that the things other women sought – stability, a partner, a family – were not the things she longed for, but it had been that way for so long she couldn't remember a time when she *didn't* want what she already had: her freedom.

She got up from the couch and walked to the kitchen. There was a half-bottle of wine that Anneliese had insisted she take from the previous Saturday night's dinner. She opened the doors of the antique dresser that Tara had bought her as a house-warming gift and took out one of the lovely, bulbous Riedl glasses that Anneliese had given her as the same. She poured herself a generous measure, admiring the way light filtered through the deep ruby colour of the wine. She looked at the bottle – Bachelard Moutrechon '78. Anneliese knew how to pick her wines. She knew how to pick everything, Callan thought to herself with a wry smile. No one she knew had better taste. It was evident in everything she did, everything she made, everything she designed or chose. Growing up, Callan had always felt a poor copy, always second best to her mother's impeccable touch. She remembered one particularly mortifying incident, her face reddening even now. She'd lined up all her childhood toys along the window sill – the woollen bunny rabbits, the dolls, teddy bears, felt stuffed animals and trinkets that she'd either collected or bought somewhere along the worn path of child-hood. She'd spent hours arranging them, this one next to that, this one carefully dressed, this one with the holes in its innards hidden . . . it took her hours to get them exactly right. At last it was done. She'd gone to sleep that night – must've been a holiday, back from school? – with a lovely warmth that lasted until morning. Her toys were watching over her, watching her as she slept. The feeling was short-lived. When she came home at lunchtime from riding school, everything was gone. 'Where are my toys?' she asked Mrs Betts, half-fearfully.

'Oh, your mother cleared them out. Said they looked silly, all lined up like that. I think she threw them out. Now, what d'you want for lunch?'

It had never quite left her, she realised suddenly, standing by the kitchen window, looking down on the garden below. That feeling of desolation and utter despair. She must have been eleven – yes, it was the Easter holidays with only the summer term of her first year there to go. At Mortimer's there was a strict rule: one teddy bear, or a doll. At home, she'd lined them up like sentinels and Anneliese had thrown them away. She wasn't able to put it into words, not back then and certainly not to Mrs Betts who looked at her face, already crumpling in tears, in puzzlement. 'They were *old*, lovey,' Mrs Betts said, already busy with the task of dishing out whatever it was she'd cooked. 'Time to get new ones.'

'But they . . . they were my *friends*,' Callan blurted out, trying desperately not to cry.

'No, they weren't, you silly thing. Your friends are all at school. How can you say a thing like that? They're *toys*, Callan. They're not real.'

She'd known even then that it was pointless trying to explain. Anneliese, Bruno, Mrs Betts – they all thought the same thing. That she enjoyed Mortimer's. That she *liked* being at school. That she had friends, was popular, didn't miss home or anything about it. She'd have sooner died than tell them the truth. Tara Connolly was the only friend she had – and in just over a term, she too would be gone.

She took another sip of wine and carried the glass back through to the living room. The television was still on but she regarded it blankly. She set the glass carefully down on the carpet, and drew her legs under her again. She rested her chin on her knees, a hand going behind her head to release her thick brown hair from its ponytail. As her hair cascaded over her face and shoulders, she fancied she could still detect Ree Herz's scent. She brought a strand across her face and inhaled deeply. The blast of longing that swept over her left her suddenly weak. Absurd as it seemed after such a short time, what she'd been drawn to in Ree Herz, she realised, was his strength. The way he stood on the ground as though he owned it; the way he spoke; the gestures and the quick change of expression that was so subtle you had to look hard, you had to concentrate. That afternoon, brief as their conversation had been, she'd found herself looking at him more intently than she'd ever looked at anyone, she realised, not wanting to miss a single thing, a single beat. As though there might be some tiny, insignificant clue in the way he moved his hands, or glanced at her, or an expression flitting across his face that would allow her *in*, past the mask of calm, careful control. He was strong, properly so. He had somehow managed to turn the flaws he sought to conceal into strengths. She had not. Her weaknesses remained on the surface of her skin, visible to anyone who cared to look. Not Ree. He was in control. *That* was what she sensed in him and that was what drew her in. Whether he would allow it was another thing. A question of a different order.

49

HAYLEY

The dress, a knee-length, perfectly tailored shift of raspberry merino wool with a wide, T-shaped neck and hidden side pockets, fitted her like a glove. Was it bad taste to wear something from the hostess's own collection? No, don't be silly, Hayley, she admonished herself silently. Anneliese would be flattered, wouldn't she? It had been one of the leftover dresses from the photo shoot of the previous week. She'd forgotten all about those little details. The leftover dresses and shoes and make-up and all the things that others worked five days a week, fifty-odd weeks a year, to be able to afford. Not only were models paid ridiculous sums of money, they practically had free access to the very things they sold. She turned and admired her rear. As pert and shapely as it had ever been. She wasn't wearing tights. She'd been on the sunbed twice that week and besides, her olive-toned skin never went that marbled, translucent shade of pearly white she so feared when she saw it in others. She slipped on a pair of high-heeled, tan slingbacks (Blahniks) and picked up a tan leather bag (Mulberry) and stood back to admire the effect. Raspberry, olive and tan. Perfect. As she herself tried to be. She flashed herself a quick, congratulatory smile in the mirror and closed the door behind her.

Things could scarcely get any better. The photo shoot with Patrick had gone exceedingly well. He'd recognised her, of course, and seemed genuinely delighted to see her 'back', as he put it. '*Je préfère les vieux*,' he'd teased her, lapsing into their native French. He liked the old girls. Cindy, Naomi, Linda, Hayley. They were *professionals*. They knew what to do, when to do it, how to move, talk, stand, pose. They didn't require translators for every fucking command, didn't burst into tears on the fifteenth take and didn't sneak off to nibble cake. The young ones – those half-starved teenagers with names that held too many consonants – Patrick shook his head. *Ridiculous*. There were days he felt like a grandfather, never mind a father. Hayley laughed with him, delighted by his delight in her. She didn't mind being called 'old', not by Patrick Demarchelier. They were due to fly to the Caribbean in a week's time to shoot the A*d*SP campaign. She was excited – it was good to be back at work, amongst people with ideas, people who appreciated and valued her. Christ, she'd missed it.

'You ready?' Ree came out of the bathroom, adjusting his cufflinks.

She looked at him uncertainly. He still had the power to make her catch her breath, she thought to herself, looking him over. He was wearing a dark, blue-black Hugo Boss suit, a pale blue shirt, no tie and a pair of rubber-soled black shoes that gave an edginess to the rather formal outfit. His hair was still wet; a few beads of water still clung to his scalp. She felt suddenly weak at the knees. 'Yep,' she said, as lightly as she could manage. After the tension of the previous few weeks, she didn't know how to admit to the sudden longing that had come over her. 'What d'you think?' She struck a pose, presenting herself to him, palms turned outwards for inspection.

He looked her over quickly and nodded, pulling a small, half-culpable face, as though he guessed what she was thinking. 'You look good. Is it one of hers?'

'Mmm. From the winter collection. It was a leftover from the shoot.'

'Here, there's something . . . just here, on your shoulder.' He brushed a small piece of lint off the dress. The gesture, so commonplace and so familiar, brought a sudden, unexpected rush of tears to her eyes. She couldn't remember the last time they'd been standing this close, inspecting each other's outfits, getting ready to go out. Behind the partition she could hear Zoë laughing. Chantal was reading them a bedside story and they'd been promised a mug of hot chocolate before she turned the lights out. Just another ordinary family night of the sort they hadn't had in months. She turned away. Ree must have sensed her sudden sensitivity. He came up behind her, put both hands on her shoulders and squeezed lightly, just as he used to. She turned gratefully, leaning into his embrace. It had been months since they'd stood together that way. She pushed her face into the heat of his neck. His aftershave, once so familiar to her and yet now so strange, tickled lightly at her nostrils. She felt the strong, unexpected tug of desire, deep inside her, signalling a warmth that began in her thighs, spreading up through her groin and belly. 'Ree,' she whispered. 'Ree.' But he moved away. She was left standing in the middle of the room, rigid with embarrassment, desire rapidly cooling, her face suddenly blotchy with shame. She stood very still, trying to compose herself. At that moment, she'd have given *anything* for a quick line, something to pick her back up. But there was no time. She took a deep breath, steadying herself. It was time to kiss the girls goodnight, get into the cab, prepare herself for the evening ahead. She had to calm herself down.

'Mummy looks nice, doesn't she, Daddy?' Ottie said as soon as she appeared.

'She smells nice, too,' Zoë interjected swiftly, not to be outdone by her sister. Their fierce, innocent possessiveness brought a lump to her throat. Drugs did that to her. They always made her that much more sensitive to everything – criticism, praise, love, compliments, *everything*. When she was high, she was like a walking, talking live-wire, every nerve-ending alive and alert and when she was down, like now, she felt nothing but despair.

'She does indeed,' Ree said gravely. "Night, girls.' He winked at them and held open the door for her.

If only he meant it, Hayley thought to herself despondently as she passed in front of him. If only.

Half an hour later, feeling, if anything, worse, she followed Ree up the steps to Anneliese's front door. They'd said practically nothing to each other during the taxi ride over. Ree seemed lost in thought and she certainly wasn't about to risk another rejection by trying to talk.

The door was opened immediately by a uniformed maid who took their coats and ushered them into what appeared to be the formal living room. Hayley looked around her with interest. Just as she'd imagined, the room was stunning. The walls were painted a soft, pale grey and the wooden floors were chalky, off-white, polished to a faint sheen. Furniture was minimal – a deep, rich aubergine-coloured sofa in front of the bay windows at one end of the room, flanked by two chocolate-brown leather chairs and one of those glass and wood coffee tables that she recognised but couldn't name. A long, low concrete shelf ran down the entire length of one wall – a few books, beautifully chosen objects, simple white orchids in silver pots and, above the fireplace, a huge, expressive painting in colours that perfectly complemented the room. A door opened and Anneliese walked in. She wore a long silver-and-white dress of some unidentifiably sheer and soft material that swirled around her ankles and a long silver cardigan in a slightly darker shade that went well with her hair. She looked beautiful.

'Ree, Hayley,' she said, coming towards them, as formal as ever. 'Lovely to see you. Thank you both for coming.' She held out a hand. Clearly not a woman to kiss.

Hayley only just managed to resist the temptation to curtsey. 'Thank you for inviting us.' Being in her presence was a bit like being in front of royalty. Hayley had never quite forgotten the day the Princess Royal came to her boarding school, deep in the Cotswolds. Having been brought up in France, where they'd chopped off the heads of *their* royalty, as her mother was fond of saying, she hadn't known to curtsey in front of her as she passed down the line. She'd been so dumbstruck by the dashing Captain Mark Phillips, who walked a few paces behind his wife, that she'd failed to notice the other girls bobbing up and down like mad, and she'd stuck out her hand instead. It had earned her a quick slap from the matron afterwards and two nights' detention – *and* a lifelong urge to bend her knees whenever someone important approached. Like Anneliese. She quickly straightened up. 'What a lovely home you have,' she mumbled hastily.

'Thank you. Ah . . . here they are.' All three of them turned as the door opened and two young women walked in, followed by Bruno. 'My daughters.'

Hayley looked at them with interest. She realised she knew very little about Anneliese's private life. They couldn't have been more different from one another, or from Anneliese. The voluptuously petite one, with the thick, dark brown hair and dark, dark eyes, was absolutely beautiful. Her sister, who was fair-skinned with short, strawberry-blonde hair and pale, freckled skin, was at least a foot taller, and almost as slender as Hayley. They made a rather striking trio – the tall, cool blonde; the petite, dark-haired beauty and the slender, boyish-looking redhead. 'Hello,' Hayley said, holding out a hand. 'I'm Hayley. Ree's wife,' she added, glancing quickly at him. The dark-haired girl looked confused, looking first at her mother, then at Ree. A tremor of unease rippled lightly up and down Hayley's spine. Why was she frowning?

'Oh.' She sounded surprised. 'You're his *wife*?' She turned to look at Ree in a way that Hayley didn't like. Did they know each other?

'Indeed I am. Six years this summer,' she said firmly, staking an immediate claim. 'I didn't catch your name, I'm sorry.'

'Callan.' The young woman recovered herself quickly. 'Gosh, I'd no idea. Well, it's nice to finally meet you. The new photos are stunning. Bruno showed me some of them.'

'Thank you.'

A maid appeared with drinks and silver trays of canapés, distracting everyone. Hayley gratefully took a glass of champagne, but declined any food. The photo shoot was less than a fortnight away and she was no longer eighteen, she reminded herself sternly, seeing that Anneliese had also noted her abstinence. Discipline, above all else. Anneliese herself looked as though she knew a thing or two about discipline, self-control. But not her daughter, not the dark-haired one. Excess was her game. Hayley recognised the look in her eyes immediately. She stole another glance at her. She was standing next to her sister – she'd never seen two sisters who were so unalike – but her eyes were all over the place, especially on Ree. She felt another tremor of panic ripple through her. Why was she watching Ree? She looked across the room to where he was standing, chatting to Anneliese. The tall girl, Tara, was partly in the way. She tilted her head to one side, watching him intently. He was unaware of her, she saw, his mind elsewhere. The tremors of fear were coming thick and fast now. She swallowed the rest of her champagne in one gulp, feeling the cold, sharp bubbles slide down her throat. Ree lifted his head and looked across the room, but not at her. He was looking at Callan and the look in his face was like thirst.

TARA

It was perhaps the strangest dinner she'd been to at Anneliese's, Tara thought to herself, reaching for her glass. The tension in the air was palpable, tangible. She looked around the table. Callan was on edge, as was Ree – you'd have to be blind not to notice the attraction between them – but that wasn't the source of it, or at least not the only source. Bruno and Jasper had clearly been arguing; Anneliese was irritable. Haylcy, Ree's wife, looked panicked, as though she couldn't decide where to place her fears. One minute her attention was on Anneliese, whom she was desperately trying to please, the next her gaze had slid back to her husband, who was patently and deliberately ignoring her. She'd eaten next to nothing – just kept refusing the food that was presented to her – but she'd drunk her body weight in wine. Three flutes of champagne, two glasses of white and now she'd started on the red. Who am I to count? Tara cautioned herself sternly, taking a sip herself. She'd already had two glasses. There was something unsettling about the evening, and it wasn't just to do with the company. She'd arrived in a bad mood, unnerved by the simple task of getting ready and dressed. Callan's simple question earlier had started it: 'What are you wearing?'

She'd wedged the receiver between her chin and shoulder as she pulled open her wardrobe doors. 'What d'you mean?'

'What are you wearing?' Callan repeated it patiently, as if to a child.

'Clothes. Why? Is it a special dinner?' She felt suddenly panicked.

'Not especially. Er, Ree Herz is coming.'

'So?' She was aware she was sounding belligerent but she couldn't help it. She hated those formal dinner parties at Anneliese's with all those fashionable fashion-people – she always felt spectacularly out of place. It had been ages since she'd been invited to one of them anyway. Anneliese knew exactly how she felt about them.

'Nothing.' Callan backed down immediately, which made Tara feel worse. She could tell from Callan's voice that there was more to be said – and probably on the subject of Ree Herz – but Tara was already in a bad mood and she had just under an hour to decide what to wear . . . and it wasn't looking good.

'I'll call you back.' She hung up before Callan could say anything further. She surveyed the contents of her wardrobe with dismay. She was a university lecturer, not a bloody fashion plate! She had twenty pairs of jeans, roughly the same number of shirts and sweaters, a couple of jackets and two skirts . . . and that was pretty much it. Anneliese had given her various outfits over the years, tried in her own, somewhat unsubtle way to suggest she wear something – *anything* – other than her standard uniform of jeans/shirt/jacket, but even Anneliese had had to admit defeat. She just wasn't interested. She would never admit it – least of all to Anneliese, or even to Callan – but part of her distaste for the world the two of them occupied (and controlled) had very little to do with fashion, and even less to do with them. Fashion. It was almost the last conversation she'd had with her mother and there were still times when thinking about it made her weak with longing, and with rage. She stood in front of the wardrobe, her eyes going mechanically over the rails but her memory taking her elsewhere.

It was a Saturday afternoon. A lunch was being held at the club. Someone had been promoted; someone had died. Someone's daughter was getting married; someone's first grandchild – Tara couldn't re-member. Her mother was sitting in front of her dressing table, slowly and dreamily powdering her nose. Tara hovered somewhere in the background, watching her with feigned disinterest. She loved watch-ing her mother get dressed. The ritual was always the same. At the same hour, every time, her mother would emerge from the steamy bathroom wearing her white terry-towelling robe, belted tightly around her waist. Her hair would be pulled back into a tight turban on top of her head, only the occasional strawberry-blonde strand peeking out from under its scraped-back edges. She would sit down at the dressing table, arranging her little pots of cream and scented lotion, little black boxes of eye-shadow and sharpened pencils with which she drew a new, brighter and bolder face than the one she habitually wore. Tara, who at eighteen had never even owned a tube of lipstick, let alone plucked her eyebrows or applied a dab of perfume to her wrists, was enthralled. She would sit at the edge of the bed, picking at the lace coverlet, an open book beside her and for the next hour as her mother 'worked' on her own image, would recount stories from school, tell her mother about this friend or that, pick up whatever book it was she'd been reading and read a passage or two aloud, her mother's attention only peripherally on her as she readied herself for whatever function she was just about to attend. It was a deeply feminine ritual; her father never came into the bedroom during those afternoon hours, even if he'd been at home, which he rarely was. 'You girls.' He'd shake his head at them affectionately from the sofa or the easy chair by the window. 'You girls.' Just one of those ordinary, unremarkable rituals that bound her so tightly to the place she called home and in which she could no longer claim she lived.

That afternoon, she remembered, her mother was wearing the red-and-white striped cotton dress with thin shoulder straps that she loved. The stripes were diagonal, not horizontal, making a V-shape down the seam in front. 'Don't wear horizontal stripes, darling,' she said, taking the pins, one by one, out of her mouth and using them to hold up the chignon she'd fashioned at the nape of her neck. 'They make you look fat.' It was one of their last moments of intimacy. A few days later, she was on her way back to school. A few months later, they were dead. She was eighteen at the time; now she was forty-one. Twenty-three years had passed since their death. She'd been alive longer than her parents had been dead.

She yanked a plain black dress off the hanger from the back of the wardrobe. Her eyes were blurry with trembling, unshed tears. She pulled off her jeans and sweater impatiently and walked into the bathroom. The evening was ruined and it hadn't even begun.

*

'Tara. You're rather pensive tonight, *mein Schatz*. Something wrong?' Bruno's voice in her ear suddenly brought her back to herself.

She gave a startled, embarrassed half-laugh. 'Oh, don't mind me. I was just thinking.'

'Clearly. I can see that. What about, if it isn't too personal?'

She flushed. 'Nothing much. I . . . just . . . I was just thinking about how well Ree and Anneliese seem to get on. I . . . I've never seen her like that before,' she said, desperately casting round the table for something else to say.

Bruno smiled, following her gaze. 'Yes, they do seem to get along well, don't they? He's a likeable chap.'

'Yes, but it's more than that. They seem to understand each other on a different level from the rest of us. Oh, I didn't mean . . . I don't mean *you*, of course. You're like brother and sister, really.'

Bruno smiled again. '*Ja*, we are. But it's different with Ree. You're right.'

'D'you know, I don't think I've ever asked you. Where did you meet Anneliese?' Tara asked, suddenly curious. As long as she'd known Anneliese and Callan, she'd rarely spent much time alone with Bruno. She looked at him as if seeing him properly for the first time.

'Oh, at university.' He pulled a funny, self-deprecating face. 'A long, long time ago. On her first day, as a matter of fact. We were both outsiders. Both running away, I suppose.'

'How d'you mean?'

'Well, I was brought up in a small town just outside Frankfurt. Eich. Do you know it?'

Tara shook her head. 'But why were you running away?' she asked again.

He gave her a quick, sideways glance. 'Well, you can imagine what those little towns are like. Let's just say it was difficult for someone of my, er, *orientation*, as it were.'

'Oh. Of course. I'm being dense. But what was Anneliese running from?'

Bruno shrugged. 'I've never asked her.'

Tara turned to stare at him. 'Why ever not? I thought you two were best friends.'

'We are.' Bruno lifted his wine glass to his lips. 'And sometimes that's what best friends do. When she's ready to tell me, she will.'

'But.' Tara turned her head to look at Anneliese again. 'But aren't you in the least bit curious?'

'Sometimes. Of course. But I've also learned that there are some things you can't speak about. Even to those closest to you. It's a form of survival. When she's ready, Anneliese will tell me what she thinks I need to know.'

Tara fell silent. It was the deepest and most profound conversation she'd ever had with Bruno. She looked across the table at Callan. Callan too had secrets. She'd known the minute she came back from New York that something had happened. What she couldn't have guessed at was that Callan wouldn't – or couldn't – say. For the first time in their long friendship, something had come between them. There was a wariness in Callan that hadn't previously existed. Every once in a while, particularly in those first few months, she would catch sight of Callan's face when she thought no one was looking and be shocked by the loneliness and desperation she found there. At first she'd tried to find out. 'What's the matter? What are you thinking about? Is there something wrong?' Each time, Callan came back to herself with a start, forcing a smile to her face, deflecting the questions and slipping deftly from Tara's grasp. *Nothing. Oh, nothing. No, absolutely nothing.* The answers-that-were-not-answers flew easily out of her mouth. She didn't fool Tara. Callan was holding something back, holding something in – and there wasn't a thing Tara could do to help. She could do nothing but stand by helplessly as Callan worked whatever it was she tried to conceal out for herself.

As the months went by, Tara was aware of a different emotion that surfaced in her when she thought of Callan. Resentment. It was a new experience for her. An only child, she was free of the murderous rages that sometimes blow up between siblings, life-long competitors for their parents' attention and love. She'd had it all; there'd been no one to wrestle with. When all of that was taken from her and she'd moved from the orbit of her parents' care to Anneliese's, her outsider status in the de Saint Phalle household meant that there could be no competition. Besides, it wasn't in Callan's nature to compete. That was what was so wonderful about her – she was all openness, all generosity and love. When she returned from New York she was a different person. And it brought out a hidden, secret anxiety in Tara that she struggled desperately to suppress. If Callan could change, seemingly overnight, so could anyone. Including Anneliese. Including herself.

REE

Dinner was a song played in two keys, simultaneously. One, taking place at the level of conscious thought, was a light and easy *aria*, circling lazily around the conversation between him and Anneliese. She was both more and less formal than he'd imagined. Beneath the frosty, cool exterior was a surprising warmth and a sense of humour that was very much like his own. But he saw too that if he pushed for a familiarity beyond the point which she was prepared to concede, there was an immediate, practised withdrawal. He had to turn his head so that she wouldn't see him smile. He understood her better than she thought.

The other key, a deeper, darker tune, had to do with Callan and the slow, sombre understanding that there was a hidden language between them that had not, as yet, been spoken. The air between them was heavy with the weight of what couldn't possibly be said. Every time their eyes met – and he tried to avoid it, painfully aware of Hayley's pinprick attention on him throughout – a small, sharp charge flowed through him, the way electricity flows through pylons across space and time – merging

into a heightened awareness of her that unsettled him, profoundly and throughout. She was seated next to Hayley and
the contrast between the two women couldn't have been more
pronounced. Fire and ice. Cool and warmth. One you gazed at,
the other you longed to touch. Once, as she got up from the
table and excused herself momentarily, he had to sit on his hand
to stop himself reaching out to touch the thick curtain of shiny,
wavy hair that fell down her back as she passed.

The food came and went; his hand went automatically from
his glass to his lips. Anneliese murmured something to him; he
replied. He was on autopilot, skirting carelessly back and forth
between safety and danger, numbness and desire. He'd never felt
such desire, he thought to himself as he watched Callan move
across the room, settling herself back into her seat. His whole
body was swollen with it; not since his teenage days had he felt
such desire. He saw Callan say something to Hayley and was
transfixed by the way her mouth moved, by the small, delicate
upward flick of her lips at their edges, the neat, beautifully
scrolled mouth now painted a soft, shiny red. Her hands moved
through the air as she described something. She was fire and
heat and warmth – everything Hayley wasn't. He had to drag his
eyes away.

His gaze fell on Tara, Callan's sister-who-wasn't-a-sister, and
he suddenly stopped dead, as if he'd been slapped. His eyes
narrowed. Tara hadn't noticed him and in the momentary lapse
whilst everyone's attention seemed to be claimed elsewhere, a
shadow had fallen across her face. She was staring at Callan, who
had moved to the sideboard to fetch another bottle of wine. Her
expression was that of his children, that same look of unbridled
jealousy that he caught on them when they fought each other for
his attention. He blinked, startled. On an adult, and one who'd
seemed so placidly quiet, the expression was ridiculous, obscene.
As he watched her, she suddenly became aware of his glance.
In a flash, the expression was gone. He blinked slowly. He'd
imagined it, surely? Hayley's hand was suddenly on his arm. He
stared at it; pale, lightly freckled skin; long, tapering fingers with

their painted nails and the too-fussy diamond ring that she'd insisted he buy. All of a sudden he was overcome with a weary irritation and a desire to be elsewhere, anywhere but there, sitting at the table with a group of people whose language he was trying – and failing – to speak. He looked around him and caught Anneliese's faintly enquiring glance. There it was again – the barely discernible sensation that there was something more between him and Anneliese than either was able to say. He hesitated for a moment, then placed his own hand on top of Hayley's, sealing the gesture and receiving from her a pleased tightening of her own grip that meant she'd noticed his lapses of attention – and that she'd also noticed the source.

50

CALLAN

Alone at last. The exquisite torture of the dinner party was over. At long fucking last. She slammed her bedroom door behind her, kicked off her high-heeled pumps and pulled off her clothes, piece after piece, tossing them onto the ottoman at the foot of her bed. Naked, except for her jewellery, she walked into her dressing room. She stood for a second looking down its length. Wardrobes on one side, shoe racks on the other. Everything was ordered, tidy, her racks of sombre-coloured clothing, most of which had come directly from the showroom, were spaced almost to the millimetre on the pale grey ash hangers that Anneliese had once spent a whole month in Italy sourcing. A*d*SP. Each hanger was branded. Nothing was out of place. Twice a week the cleaner came in and dusted everything, making sure her shoes and boots were polished, that the clothes were spotlessly clean, that things that had been sent to the dry-cleaners had been returned, slipped free from their plastic skin and hung exactly where they ought to be. En masse, the effect of so much careful order was hypnotic. She picked a dressing gown from the back of the door and switched off the light.

She was tipsy, her head swimming pleasurably, caught on the cusp of drunkenness, but not unpleasantly so. She sat down on the edge of her bed and picked at a stray black thread that had somehow settled upon the starched white bedspread. She stopped herself suddenly; it was exactly the same sort of putting-the-world-to-rights gesture Anneliese had never been able to stop herself making. As a child, Callan could never simply walk into the room without Anneliese's hand going out to brush her skirt, tidy her hair, pick at imaginary threads or pieces of lint that disturbed the otherwise perfect image her daughter presented. It was Anneliese all over. Nothing could possibly be right until Anneliese's hand had been laid upon it. It had taken Callan years to rid herself of the urge to have Anneliese check her over before leaving the house.

She got up suddenly from the bed and walked into the bathroom. She had the sudden urge to wallow in a deep, perfume-scented bath. The dinner had unsettled her. No, be honest, she muttered crossly to herself as she turned on the taps. It was the news that Hayley was Ree's wife that had unsettled her. She still couldn't get over it. Hayley Summers. A*d*SP's new face. Of *all* the fucking people! She was beautiful, of course, and of course she knew who she was, or had been. Time seemed only to have sharpened her stunning features so that the woman sitting next to her, her gaze going protectively to her husband every time she sensed Callan's glance, appeared like some other-worldly goddess, whippet-thin and icily controlled, contributing almost nothing to the conversation. But what did he *see* in her? she wondered. She was disappointed, she realised, in him. Hayley Summers was exactly the sort of woman men like Thierry and Karel and Charles – and practically all the men she'd ever known, or slept with (which amounted to pretty much the same thing, she realised, her cheeks reddening) – wanted. A model. Face and body, not much else. A trophy. Something to be paraded, on occasion, something that made you feel good, not because you wanted it, but because everyone else did. She'd thought Ree Herz different, capable of more.

The foam was almost spilling out of the bath tub. She turned off the taps, let the robe fall to the floor and stepped in. The hot, scented water made her gasp. She slid down into it, wallowing in its hot, possessive embrace. She lifted a leg out, inspecting it carefully. There was a small bruise, right there on the inside calf muscle. Where had she got it? she wondered. She could feel the heat coming up swiftly in her face. There'd been a time when every bath, every shower, was occasion to find something new – some mark or blemish that had been inflicted upon her without her even knowing. Sometimes, standing naked in front of the long mirror that she'd propped against the bookshelves in the apartment on Brewster Street, she'd slowly and anxiously turn round, stretching her neck to view herself from as many angles as she could. A small bruise here, another there, on her buttock, the faint yet clear outline of a man's fingertips. She shivered, suddenly cold. She hated the way her mind worked sometimes, creeping up on her completely unawares. Memories were like that; you couldn't control them, no matter how hard you tried.

She thought of Ree's face. The way he looked at her, and the way his eyes flitted immediately away, as though he'd been burned. There were moments during the evening when she didn't have to look at him to confirm his gaze. His attention was like sunlight. She felt herself instantly bathed. She reached forward and turned on the hot tap again, feeling the current of warmth stir another warmth in her that came from between her thighs. It spread upwards through her body, nipples suddenly erect and tingling, her mouth parting as though her own breath were too hot to bear. His name was a silent, secret whisper as her fingers moved automatically to that small spot of pleasure that was hers alone. For someone as carefree as she had been with her body – care*less*, Karel had admonished her once – she had never, ever experienced anything like the pleasure she could give herself, with another. No man had ever brought her to orgasm. Not once, not ever. The way she was with them – all performance, all daring, all bravado – had nothing to do with pleasure and everything to do with pain. Her own, unspoken, unarticulated pain. Suddenly, for the first time in her entire life, she'd come across someone who promised something else. Something more. Fingers parting flesh; the soft, knowing touch, an easy caress. Ree. The exquisite crash when it came was all the sweeter for saying his name.

HAYLEY

She just couldn't help it, no matter how hard she tried. All through the dinner, she'd been aware of Ree's attention slipping away from her and landing on that fucking woman, Anneliese's daughter. Callan. No, she corrected herself sternly. Ree's attention hadn't *slipped*. It simply took off the minute the girl entered the room and that was that. For the next three hours, he hadn't returned to her, not once. She knew him well enough to know that the small gestures she'd forced him to make – his hand on hers, his dark, always unreadable eyes turning towards her but seeing past and beyond her – meant nothing. She was aware of the tense knot of panic that usually sat just below her ribcage threatening to rise every time she caught him looking at Callan, or vice versa. The bitch tried hard not to appear anything more than professionally interested in whatever he was saying but it was pointless. They fooled no one, least of all Hayley. The very air between the two of them crackled, regardless of what wasn't said. In the car on the way home he'd been quiet – not that Ree ever spoke much, and certainly not these days – but whatever warmth had been generated before they got to the dinner party, it was well and truly over.

She jumped out of the car almost before he'd brought it to a halt. She ignored his questioning 'Hey?' and slammed the door shut behind her. She fumbled with the lock and ran up the stairs to the front door. She couldn't wait to be in the safety of the toilet with the door closed and a line of coke in front of her to calm her down. Sleep would be hard. It was funny, she thought to herself bitterly as she threw her jacket across the bed and kicked off her shoes. She'd spent the past few years in a state of what could only be described as heightened anxiety, waiting for the moment Ree walked in the door and announced 'it's over'. She'd thought about it, dreamed about it, *agonised* over it for so long that the fear of it had, she realised suddenly, become her reality. How many mornings had she woken from some unspecified nightmare redolent with loss to find herself lying next to him, having to put out a hand to touch him to convince herself that it really had been a dream. That he *wasn't* on his way out of the door and her life? That the home they'd built and the two children they had were the very assurances she needed against his leaving?

She heard the door downstairs close and the sound of his footsteps as he came up the stairs. She quickly locked herself in the toilet. Facing him now with guilt and fear written all over her face was the last thing she wanted to do. She pulled her make-up bag from behind the sink and fished around inside until her fingers touched on the small plastic pouch. Silently, and with quick, neat precision, she cut herself four short lines.

A few discreet snorts later, the sounds drowned by the running tap, she lifted her head and leaned her forehead gratefully against the mirror. It would take a few seconds for the hit to reach her. She could hear the soft murmur of Ree's and Ottie's voices. She closed her eyes. Just another of the many differences between them and a mark of how low she'd sunk. No matter where he'd been or how long he'd been away, Ree's first instinct was to check on the girls – always. It was never hers. Yes, another of those differences between them, and unfortunately, one that would always count.

51

ANNELIESE
Malcolm's Beach, Providenciales, Turks and Caicos Islands

'You've got to hand it to her, she's a real trooper,' Bruno murmured to Anneliese as they watched Hayley crouch down in the shallow waters, preparing to jump skywards at the photographer's command. It was perhaps the fifteenth take. *Trooper.* The word sat awkwardly on Bruno's tongue. It was the sort of old-fashioned English expression that he occasionally picked up, God knows where. Anneliese looked across the shimmering, turquoise sea to where the rocky outline of one or other of the small islands that dotted the bay emerged out of its own blueness, breaking the horizon.

'One more time, *chérie*,' Patrick called out. '*Pour la dernière fois, je te jure.*' He coaxed her into action.

Anneliese watched in silence as Hayley jumped. A flash of bronzed limbs, that perfect smile, small crumbs of sand dusting her firm, perfectly toned thighs. Even from a distance, Anneliese knew the photos would be good. Hayley's sun-kissed body, the smell of coconut oil, dark green palm trees and white sand, the sort of pictures that made women long to escape. It wasn't their usual sort of location. Anneliese had always favoured edgier, mostly urban settings for her seasonal catalogues and campaigns but she'd been persuaded by Lars, her new creative director, and Bruno to try something different. And for once, she was forced to admit they were right. Hayley brought another dimension to the photos that was a million miles away from the sun-and-sand images she'd first conjured up when Bruno suggested it. There was no other way to say it – the woman *reeked* of class. Of the good life, of good taste and the finer things in life. What was more – and of greater importance to Anneliese – she looked as though she'd earned it. Herself. She could have been anything – the CEO of a giant multinational, a high-powered lawyer, a scientist, a film-maker. Hayley's intelligent, powerful beauty was far from the cookie-cutter plasticity of the current crop of models, who looked in desperate need of a good meal, never mind a decent pay cheque. She had the self-possessed, self-confident look of a woman staying at one of the world's most luxurious resorts, not because some man had paid for it, but because she could. She belonged there. She provoked other powerful intelligent women into thinking the same. The Amanyara resort – though it too was a million miles away from the word 'resort' – was another piece of inspired casting. They'd rented one of the beach pavilions, a splendid piece of contemporary, minimalist design located on the edge of one of the prettiest beaches she'd ever seen. Best of all, it was entirely private. There was no threat of squabbling, squalling children or curious onlookers to disturb them. They worked in complete peace and quiet as they set up the various shots that would carry the campaign.

'OK, *chérie*. That's it!' Patrick yelled out at last, straightening up. '*Fantastique*. Come, *ma belle*. Take a look.' He beckoned Hayley over. One of the assistants immediately rushed forward with a kaftan of sheer cotton and helped Hayley slide it over her head. It was four o'clock in the afternoon and although the shadows were long and deep, there was still enough kick in the sun to burn. They had another two days' worth of shooting left and the last thing anyone wanted was an angry strip of reddened skin anywhere on their prized model.

Anneliese watched as Hayley peered intently into the back of Patrick's large and impressive digital camera. She nodded, gave a small, tight smile of satisfaction and walked back towards them. Yes, Bruno was right, she thought to herself as Hayley approached. She *was* a trooper. They'd been there for four long, hard days and she hadn't heard her complain once. It made a refreshing change. She'd stopped accompanying Bruno when they went on location after one memorable occasion where the models had inflicted so much damage on a hotel room they'd practically had to rebuild it. Not so Hayley. She showed up every morning, on time, full of enthusiasm for the resort, the photographs, the weather, even the food. She ate well and sensibly, Anneliese noticed. A good breakfast, a salad or some protein for lunch and very little at dinner. She wasn't a big drinker, either, unlike *some* of the models she'd worked with who'd forgo all food during the day in order to down a bottle of wine at night. All in all, she was rather more delightful to work with than she'd anticipated. She felt a sudden surge of warmth for the woman. She stopped. It was *most* unlike her.

'I'm going up to the villa,' she announced abruptly. 'I'm going to lie down.'

'Are you all right, *Schatz*?' Bruno's attention was immediately solicitous.

'Fine, fine. Just a little tired, that's all.' She turned and walked back up the sandy path to the villa before he could ask anything further.

Her bedroom, vast, open, all warm tropical woods and carefully chosen fabrics, was the perfect place to spend an hour or so before drinks on the terrace overlooking the ocean. She put her basket down, kicked off her sandals and walked into the enormous bathroom. A quick shower to refresh her, then a cooling drink of lime and tonic water. She had a few phone calls to make, including one to Callan who was just about to depart for Dubai. She felt a faint tremor of unease. She was flying out to oversee construction of the latest and newest AdSP store in the just-finished Dubai Mall, said to be the world's largest. Anneliese wasn't happy. Malls were not her favourite or natural habitat and malls in Dubai even less so. She'd paid the whole project scant attention, leaving everything to Callan, which *wasn't* the way she normally liked to do things – far too controlled for that. But she simply couldn't bring herself to be more involved. She knew it irked Callan, and Bruno, come to that.

Things were far from rosy. The much-needed injection of cash from the Italians had brought AdSP some relief but the truth – as both Callan and Bruno were fond of repeating – was that the world had changed, and that they had to change with it. The pool of American and European women who had always been her customers was changing. It wasn't that they *didn't* have disposable income or that they no longer had money to spend. On the contrary. As Anneliese herself knew only too well, the truly rich are always protected from the dips and swings of the market. No, the issue had to do with choice. Simply put, there were too many designers 'out there', offering too much. Wealthy women now had a bewildering and ever-increasing array of designers to choose from – Valentino, Armani, Jil Sander, Max Mara, De Meulemeester . . . the list just went on and on. In Anneliese's opinion, of course, none offered quite what she did – but it was a rare customer who didn't get side-tracked and distracted . . . and as a result, she now shared wardrobe space with all kinds of designers, and her profits too. For a few months now, Callan had been muttering something about a cheaper range. Anneliese simply put her hands over her ears lest the word 'cheap' sneak in.

She came out of the shower wrapped in a soft, terry-towelling robe, damp tendrils of hair still sticking to her cheeks and ears. The evening breeze was lovely and cool. Her waiter had discreetly left a tray with her drink and a portion of small, freshly baked snacks and fruits. She picked up the phone and carried it out onto the terrace, settling herself comfortably into one of the enormous chairs. She bit into one of the savoury snacks, took a sip of her drink and dialled Callan's mobile. It was a pity she'd met Ree Herz *after* the plans for her Dubai store had been drawn up, she thought to herself as she waited for Callan to answer. He would have done something quite spectacular.

'Callan? Here is Maman.'

'Oh, hi, Maman.' Callan sounded breathless, as though she'd been running. 'How're you?'

'Just checking that everything's OK.'

'Yes, everything's fine. I'm just going over a couple of last-minute things to do with the lease. Barry's here, and the Matuzzis are coming round this afternoon.'

Anneliese's lips tightened. 'Good, good,' she said, as neutrally as she could manage. 'I was just thinking . . . it's such a pity Ree Herz isn't doing this one for us. I'd feel much happier if he were in charge of the design. Isn't there another mall opening up soon?'

'The Mall of the Emirates. Let's get this one up and running, first, Maman.' Callan gave a short laugh. 'I thought you weren't interested in the Middle East?'

'I'm not. But I *am* interested in his work,' Anneliese said crisply. 'Anyway, we can talk about it later.'

'How's the photo shoot coming along?' Callan asked, quickly changing the subject.

'Fine. She's very good, you know.'

'Well, that makes two of them, doesn't it? A real *über*-couple,' Callan said with more than a hint of sarcasm in her voice. 'Anyhow, I'd better run. I'll call you from the lounge tomorrow night, all right?'

'All right.' She rang off quickly. Anneliese replaced the receiver slowly. It was clear Callan didn't like Hayley. Anneliese had sensed it as soon as Callan walked into the room at dinner the other night. She wondered why. But then again, Callan had always been the sort of woman other women disliked. Aside from Tara, Callan had few close female friends. In that way, she mused, she and Callan were alike. Not that *she* had many friends, male *or* female, she reminded herself crisply. There was really only Bruno. Better to have fewer, closer friends than a whole *smorgasbord* of people, most of whom one couldn't stand anyway. There was only one person she'd met in the past twenty, thirty years whom she could imagine befriending, strange as it seemed. Ree Herz. No, that wasn't quite true. There *was* someone. There *had* been someone, once. But she couldn't allow herself to think about that. She stood up more abruptly than she intended and sent the phone crashing to the ground.

52

REE
London/Dubai

Leaving the girls behind was always hard, but it was doubly so when Hayley was away. Ottie's little face pressed tight against the huge windowpanes of the living room as they waved goodbye burned on his retina for most of the cab ride towards Paddington. Zoë never cried; it was always Ottie who sobbed uncontrollably, as though there would never be another meeting or another hug or goodnight kiss. He wondered often where she got it from. Neither he nor Hayley were particularly demonstrative; neither was Zoë. All three were experts in the art of buttoning up their emotions, but not Ottie. He sighed. They'd only be alone with Chantal for a day. Hayley was due back the following morning from her jaunt. No, not a jaunt, a *job*, he reminded himself quickly. Her job was every bit as important as his, though the pictures she'd sent them the other night seemed to make a mockery of the statement. Blue skies, blue water, white sand, tanned bodies everywhere you looked. There'd even been a shot of Anneliese, standing at the water's edge, watching the action with the same wry, slightly tolerant smile that he'd come to recognise as hers. Clearly, Hayley was having the time of her life. He'd no idea what happened to models over a certain age but it certainly seemed as though his wife had done something few of them managed to achieve – a comeback. He'd picked up a copy of *Metro* on the way to work the other day. To his great surprise he'd seen Hayley's face on the second or third page. *The new face of luxury clothing brand AdSP. Not bad for an old broad.* Or something along those lines. He was more worried by his own dispassionate lack of response than he was by the tag. An old broad. He wondered what Hayley would make of *that*.

'Here we are, sir.' The cab driver interrupted his thoughts.

They were already at Paddington. 'Need any help with your bags?'.

'Nope. Just got the one.' Ree picked it up, shoved a twenty-pound note through the window. 'Keep the change.' He got out and sprinted across the road.

Ten minutes later, his laptop open and his mobile phone clamped to his ear, he was on board the Heathrow Express, hurtling towards the airport. He pulled out his tickets impatiently, checking his flight times. First-class tickets. He pulled a surprised face. In his line of work, a rarity. He listened with half an ear to his never-ending stream of messages – there was nothing Terri or any of the other architects in the office couldn't handle in his absence. And nothing from Hayley. Idly he realised it had been a couple of days since he'd heard her voice. He ought to miss her. Curiously, sadly, he didn't.

On impulse, and perhaps to atone for his uncharitable earlier thoughts, he found himself half an hour later, his mobile still wedged between his chin and his ear, wandering through the perfume section of the duty free shop in Terminal Five, picking up one bottle after another, wondering which she'd like. Chanel? YSL? Dior? He had no idea what sort of scent Hayley wore these days. Her dressing table at home was covered in a bewildering array of bottles of all shapes and sizes, none of which he recognised. His mother had only ever worn Chanel No. 5. Hayley's scents came with names like 'So Pretty' and 'Dangerous' and 'Flowers'. Bewildering. He picked up a bottle of something he vaguely recognised and pulled off the cap.

'Can I help you, sir?' The sales assistant was on him in a flash. 'Is it a present?'

He nodded reluctantly. 'Yes, I was just looking for—'

'Something for the wife? Or girlfriend, perhaps?' She didn't even let him finish. He noticed the quick, automatic way her eyes fell to his left hand. He'd never worn his wedding band. Not out of any statement or intent, mind you, he just didn't like jewellery. It had annoyed the hell out of Hayley at first; she wore hers like a trophy she'd just won.

'Er, yes. Something for my wife.'

'How about this one, sir?' He let himself be distracted by her sales patter as he followed her from one identical-looking stand to the next. On what basis would he make a choice? He had no idea, and neither, clearly, did she. Ten minutes later he was back in front of the same counter.

'I'll . . . I'll just take this,' he said finally, picking up a bottle of something called Chance. At least it was by someone he recognised. Chanel.

'Fifty or a hundred millilitres?' There was disappointment in her voice.

'A hundred.'

She brightened and turned to pluck the larger of the two sizes from the shelf behind her.

'Ree?' A woman's voice addressed him suddenly. He turned round. His skin prickled pleasurably, even before he managed to open his mouth. He stared at her in a mixture of confusion, embarrassment and joy.

'Callan?'

She laughed. 'I was just walking past . . . on my way to the lounges and I thought, no, it can't be – of course it's not – but yes, it *is* you.'

'It is me.' He was aware he sounded foolish. 'What are you—?'

'Are you—?' They both spoke at once. 'Are you on your way somewhere?' he asked, feeling even more foolish. What else was there to do in Terminal Five?

'Yes, Dubai. I've got a meeting there tomorrow morning. How about you?'

He was aware of a great build-up of pressure just behind his eyes and of a tightening in his chest. Dubai? Both of them? And on the same flight? 'The same,' he said weakly, happiness flowing through him, unchecked. He cleared his throat. 'This is just unbelievable. I've got two days of meetings. A new project . . .

well, it hasn't been decided yet . . .' He stopped. She was staring at him. There was a flush of colour under the collar of her shirt. He was aware of the salesgirl looking at them both curiously. He felt dazed; the old, long-forgotten sensation of having got his head caught in a rugby scrum at school came to him suddenly. 'Thanks,' he mumbled, taking the perfume from her.

'Ah. Present for the wife?' Callan asked, and there was a teasing note in her voice. 'I gather she's delivering the goods,' she added. 'I spoke to Anneliese this afternoon.'

'How . . . how is she? Anneliese, I mean?' He thrust the bottle in his bag and stuffed the receipt in his pocket. They turned naturally to walk out of the shop together. He was deliciously and unbearably aware of her perfume and the scent of her hair as it swung in a glossy arc from side to side. 'You've cut your hair,' he said, looking down at her.

She put up a hand self-consciously. 'It gets a little long,' she said quickly. 'I . . . I was just going up to the lounge,' she said, uncharacteristically hesitant.

'Me too.' He recognised the hesitation. He touched his jacket pocket and smiled. 'First-class tickets, courtesy of my client. Doesn't often happen. To architects, I mean.'

She smiled and blushed. 'Anneliese won't fly any other way. Look, at least she doesn't have her own jet,' she added gracefully.

'At least.' Ree found it suddenly easy to match her tone. As with Anneliese, there was an initial awkwardness that gave way to something deeper and, curiously, easier. They'd reached the entrance to the BA lounges; the girl behind the desk either recognised Callan or didn't feel the need to check their boarding cards. They were ushered deferentially through.

'Well, I think this calls for a drink, don't you?' Callan said as they put their bags down. 'What'll you have?'

'Something dry. Vermouth.'

She raised her eyebrows. 'Good choice. I'll join you.' She turned and walked towards the bar. He was aware of several pairs of eyes following her. He was used to it; wherever he went with

Hayley, especially in the beginning, he'd grown used to seeing people's eyes light up whenever she walked past, especially women's. It was a peculiar feature of women that he'd never been able to fathom. Women brought far more scrutiny to bear upon each other than any man in his right mind ever would. They noticed everything, every tiny, insignificant little flaw. Men noticed general things – hair, smile, a woman's overall shape, but not much else. He'd lost count of the number of times a woman had walked past Hayley and she'd dissected her to pieces – bra size, shoe size, whether or not her skirt was correctly lined – before the poor woman was even out of earshot. Callan was different. Hayley was made to be gazed at from afar. Callan, on the other hand, was made to *touch*. He checked himself immediately.

She returned quickly and set the glasses down carefully between them. 'So, what's the project?' she asked, taking a seat opposite him. In a manner that brought his wife to mind, he took in every single detail: her cashmere coat, which she took off and folded carefully across the arm of the chair, her knee-length patent black boots, the silky, encased sheen of her knees in sheer tights beneath the cream wool skirt; a pale, off-white blouse; discreet diamond studs in her ears.

He became aware she was looking expectantly at him. She took a sip of her own drink and set the glass back down. He stared at it. Her lipstick had left a faint but clear imprint on the glass. He stopped himself from thinking any further. 'The project?' he repeated. 'Oh, right, yes. The project.'

'Aren't you going to tell me what it is?' she asked, her tone light and teasing again. 'Or is it some kind of state secret?'

'God, no,' he laughed. 'Not at all. It's an office building, that's all. A rather large one.' He gave another laugh. 'In fact, by the time they're finished, it may well wind up being one of the largest in the world.'

'Is that why you're doing it?'

He smiled and shook his head. 'No, not that sort of architect, I'm afraid.'

'Size doesn't matter?' She raised a quizzical eyebrow.

He found himself laughing again. 'In this instance, no.'

'So why're you doing it? You don't strike me as an office block type of architect.'

She was perceptive. 'So how do I strike you?' he asked, enjoying the sensation of scrutiny.

'Professionally, you mean?'

He nodded and took a long, slow sip of his vermouth. He hadn't enjoyed a conversation this much in months. 'Well, yes. For now.'

She took her time, choosing her words carefully. 'You're very talented, but you don't need me to tell you that. A bit arrogant, like most gifted people. But there's an anxiety there, you know. You've got things to prove. You don't want anyone to think you haven't *earned* it, you know?' She stopped suddenly, colouring. 'Listen to me. Is there anything worse than an armchair shrink? Don't pay any attention to anything I say.'

'*Au contraire.* You're very perceptive. And *you*?'

'What about me?'

'It's not so different for you, either. You don't want people thinking the only reason you are where you are is because you're Anneliese's daughter. Am I right?'

There was a moment's silence between them. Behind him, he could hear flights being announced, luggage being fetched, the low aggravated murmur between passengers waiting to board a plane. *You've got the tickets. I gave them to you, remember? No, I don't have them.* He studied her discreetly. The unsung song was there between them again. All of a sudden, his face felt stiff with loneliness. It had been months since he'd had anything like as deep a conversation with anyone, let alone Hayley. In fact, the last time he'd talked properly, intimately, had been with Anneliese, that afternoon, at her club. And it had ended so abruptly, leaving him with the longing for it, even as he accepted it couldn't be had again. He felt the rush of words as a rush of saliva in his mouth; it was all he wanted to do – talk.

*

'Shall I see if I can seat you together, sir?' The smiling BA ground staff took their boarding cards from them. They looked at one another. Why not? Ree shrugged. They'd been talking intently for almost an hour. There seemed to be no reason to stop. The faint nagging at the back of his brain which told him there was *every* reason to stop was silenced, at least for now. He'd done nothing wrong, nothing untoward. What harm was there in talking to her? None at all. 'There you go, sir. Ms de Saint Phalle's got the window seat. Enjoy the flight.'

Callan took her new boarding card with a quick nod. She was clearly accustomed to people going out of their way to please her. 'Thank you,' she murmured. Like Anneliese, she had a way of shielding herself from the curious glances and interest of others. In her face was that strange, peripheral awareness that the well known or rich and famous carry with them, wherever they go. Again, he recognised it but where Hayley positively sought out the admiring stares and glances of others, Callan deflected their attention. He liked that about her. That and many other things.

They walked down the escalators towards the gate, following the other passengers automatically. At the entrance to the plane, they were ushered deferentially towards the front. Once or twice as they were fussed over and shown to their seats, his arm brushed hers and he jerked back, as though the touch were painful. If she noticed, she said nothing. She took her seat next to the window, folding her blanket neatly across her knees. As they taxied out to the runway and the captain busied himself with the usual announcements prior to departure, it came to him slowly, and not without embarrassment, that in the short hour and a half that he'd been talking to Callan de Saint Phalle, not once had he thought about Hayley, neither had he thought about his children, or even his upcoming project. He'd sur- reptitiously turned his phone off on the way to the lounge. For the first time in years, he'd no desire to answer it. He felt strangely hollow, as though she'd emptied him of himself. If he could have seen himself as she saw him now, he wondered, how would he look? Guilty? Eager? He watched as she smoothed

down the soft fabric of her skirt in a gesture that, absurd as it
seemed, was now familiar to him. Her hands, like Anneliese's,
were strong and capable-looking, the tanned, polished skin
stretched taut over the tendons. Blunt, squared-off fingers with
short, unpolished nails. He found himself wanting to know
more about her than was either healthy or wise. As the plane
began its lumbering journey down the runway, gathering speed,
the thought that he would have to spend the next few days
holding himself in settled over him uncomfortably, digging in.

53

HAYLEY
Malcolm's Beach, Providenciales, Turks and Caicos Islands

Out there, just below the thin line where the sea and the sky
came together as one, there was a school of dolphins, or por-
poises, perhaps. What was the difference? she wondered. They
broke the surface of the water, one after the other, plunging in
and out of her line of vision. Hayley watched them in fascinated,
silent absorption. It was their last night on location. The four of
them – her, Anneliese, Bruno and Patrick – were having a drink
on the terrace. The younger members of the crew had gone into
Provo, the only town on the island, to party. A few years back
she'd have been leading the way, Hayley thought to herself wryly
as she brought the glass of ice-cold Chardonnay to her lips. Not
any more. The thought of spending an evening jammed up
against some sweaty local with a beer in either hand whilst the
models took it in turns to do lines had suddenly lost its appeal.
Speaking of which. She gave herself a small, self-satisfied smirk.
She'd been away from home for almost a week and she hadn't
had a single line or drag. Not one. Not once. Taking a couple of
grams on board would have been madness enough, even if she
hadn't had Anneliese to contend with, but, much to her great
surprise, not once on the island had she felt the urge.

It was Anneliese. It wasn't the first time she'd been on a location shoot with a designer but the week she'd spent in Anneliese's presence was unlike any she'd experienced before. On the first day, rising just before dawn, she'd walked out onto the terrace of her bedroom to see her walking along the sand, her kaftan billowing behind her as she staked out what she thought were the best angles, the best view of the sea and the gently rolling dunes. No other designer she'd ever worked with went to such lengths. Patrick, as formidably professional as he was, took his cues from her, not the other way round. She got used to seeing his dark, curly head bent in deference as Anneliese looked through the viewfinder of his camera, judging his shots. They worked quietly, calmly, with none of the high emotion and drama she was used to. At eight every morning, the entire crew broke for breakfast which they had together, on Anneliese's private terrace with the last of the morning's cool breezes wafting over them. From then until three in the afternoon, they were free to do whatever they wanted. Anneliese worked, of course. Sometimes, as Hayley passed her on her way down to the beach, she would see her sitting outside on the veranda, a roll of the buff-coloured tracing paper that she used spread out before her, pencil in hand. She had a small Leica camera that she carried everywhere. In the mornings, she often saw her bending down to photograph something that had caught her eye. It occurred to her to ask but somehow the moment never seemed right, or came.

'What a spot,' Patrick murmured lazily, as the waiter carefully placed another platter of prawns before them. 'Have you been before, Anneliese?'

She shook her head. 'No, it was Jessie's idea. She saw it in a magazine and showed it to Lars.'

'Lovely, *ja*, but not as nice as Scheherazade,' Bruno remarked lazily. 'Nowhere near as nice.'

'*Ach*, they're all special. In their own way,' Anneliese said quietly.

'What's Scheherazade?' Hayley asked.

'It's Anneliese's private island,' Bruno turned to her with a smile. 'Her own private paradise. She can't stand the crowds, can you, *mein Schatz*?'

Anneliese looked momentarily annoyed. 'It's not my private island.'

'Practically. How many homeowners are there? Six? Seven?'

'Ten,' Anneliese said crisply. 'And it's a tiny island. More wine, anyone?'

'Why don't you shoot the campaign there?' Hayley asked curiously.

'That's my home,' Anneliese said, a note of surprise in her voice as if the suggestion baffled her. 'I would never do that.'

'Count yourself lucky.' Bruno leaned across and touched Hayley lightly on the arm. 'She's only known you a couple of months and you've already had an invitation to dinner at St John's Wood. Some people wait for years.'

'Rubbish,' Anneliese said quickly. 'Absolute rubbish.'

There was a playful, teasing tension between them, Hayley noticed, that spoke of a long friendship. She wondered how they had come to know each other. They were both German, but she'd never heard them speak German to each other, aside from the odd endearment which Bruno meted out to everyone, German or not. In fact, she knew very little about Anneliese at all.

'Have you heard from Callan?' Bruno suddenly murmured to Anneliese. 'Did she say how it's going?'

'Only that it's hot and dusty and that the hotel's quite nice, but that was last night.' She glanced at her watch. 'They'll have finished the first round of meetings by now. She'll call to-morrow.'

'Where is she?' Hayley asked curiously.

'Dubai,' Bruno said. 'We're opening up a new store in one of the malls. You'll be seeing your face up there soon. What's the matter?'

It took Hayley a few seconds to bring her voice under control. 'N-nothing,' she stammered, reaching for her glass. 'D-Dubai?'

'Mmm. Rather her than me, I have to say.' Bruno's tone was disparaging. 'All that air-conditioning and those *shoppers* . . . thousands of them. I find it exhausting. Are you sure you're all right? You've gone quite pale.'

Hayley was suddenly unable to answer. She got up abruptly, alarm coursing through her veins. There was a noise in her ears that until then had been the pleasantly distant thrum of the sea. Now it was the thumping sound of her own fear. 'I . . . I just need to make a phone call,' she said quickly, almost knocking over her glass. 'I just . . . I just forgot something . . . the girls.'

She was gone before anyone could speak.

He answered on the fourth ring. Panic and anger surged through her. 'Where are you?' she hissed.

'Hayley?' His voice was groggy. 'It's four in the morning . . . what's the matter? Is something wrong? Is it the girls?'

'Where is she?'

'Who? Who the hell are you talking about?' He sounded genuinely confused.

She took a deep breath. 'She's there. She's there with you, isn't she?'

'If you're talking about Callan, no, she's not with me.'

'Swear it. Swear on the girls.'

'Hayley.' His voice had lost its tint of surprise and confusion. He was angry now. 'Have you lost your mind?'

'Don't you dare—' Her own anger and confusion were mounting. It was always this way.

'Go to sleep, Hayley,' he interrupted her. 'I've got a meeting in a couple of hours. We can talk when we both get home.'

'I want to talk *now*!' She could hear herself beginning to whine, and hated herself for it.

'There's nothing to talk about. Callan's here on business, that's all. I didn't know she was coming. Neither did she.'

'So you've seen her?'

There was a moment's hesitation. 'We were on the same flight. We bumped into one another at Heathrow.'

Panic was bubbling in her throat, along with the threat of tears. 'But—' She started a sentence without any clear idea of what it was she wanted to say. 'How d'you mean you just "bumped" into her? You must have *known* she'd be on the same flight. You must have— Ree? Ree?'

There was a long silence and then it dawned on her that he'd hung up the phone. She clutched the receiver to her chest, as though pressing it against her would bring him back. She sat there for a few minutes, paralysed by the liquid fear that was steadily rising through her stomach, chest, neck and face. She felt hot and cold simultaneously. Outside the small group carried on without her. She could hear Patrick's low, lazy drawl and Bruno's answering laugh. Anneliese said something; the two men chuckled. The world was going on as normal. Inside, in the air-conditioned chill of her room, she was beginning to fall apart. Callan. Ree. In Dubai *together*. Her palms were sweating profusely. She had no idea what to do next. Should she call him back? No, he wouldn't pick up the phone and then she'd feel worse than ever. She was being silly. Ree was right – it was a coincidence, nothing more. She looked down at her bare knees; they were shaking. She slipped her hands underneath her thighs. A coincidence. A coincidence. She mouthed the words quietly to herself, like a mantra. Ree wouldn't leave her. He wouldn't dare. There was too much history between them, too many ties. Not just the children, either – the home they'd built together, his practice, their life.

She suddenly had the urge to talk to someone, anyone . . . but who? She could hardly call her mother. Ghislaine du Plessis wasn't the sort of woman you could easily confide in. Even before the divorce from George Summers, Hayley's father and Ghislaine's third husband, she'd hardly been the type to go to for advice. After it, she'd been consumed with such bitterness that Hayley had been afraid to go near her. Hayley was six when her parents divorced. By the time she was eight, Ghislaine had found another husband. Now, in addition to the two half-sisters from Ghislaine's first and second marriages, she had a baby brother and three step-siblings, two of whom were half-Spanish. It was bewildering. She'd learned to field the questions that invariably arose about how the children were all related and why Hayley's surname was different and why her brother and sister spoke Spanish and why Hayley spent her summer holidays with her paternal grandparents in Devon and why her mother never came to visit. 'Where's Devon?' the other children in her class at school in France asked her. She didn't bother explaining. She learned very early on how to split herself in two so that there wasn't a trace of French in her when she arrived at Dover, or later, at Heathrow, to be picked up by her grandparents and only ever occasionally by her father (who had taken a job in Brazil and, she overheard the maid in the house say once, now had another family). What did that mean, 'another' family? Did he mean to get rid of the present one? Her included? Equally, a few days before her return to France, she began to erase everything that was English about her so that there'd be nothing left by the time she went back to the elite Parisian lycée where she'd been enrolled practically before birth. She was *Hayley* for three months of the year, *Aylee* for the rest.

Ghislaine seemed satisfied by the arrangement. Ghislaine almost never spoke of George Summers, except when she was drunk, and then only disparagingly. It was all over now, all the marriages and the children and step-children and the settlements and lawyers. Her fifth – and final – husband had left her. She'd retired to a small villa in the lavender-covered hills above Nice. The old bitterness towards men – all men – had returned. Ghislaine's looks had faded. Occasionally, sitting opposite her after a shower, her face pulled firm by the towel turban she'd wrapped around her now thinning hair, the lost, useless beauty emerged. In those moments, Hayley was filled with dread. Was that how it would be for her, too? Living alone, surrounded not by her children and those she'd loved but by servants and stray dogs and cats?

No, speaking to her mother would bring her no solace whatsoever. She sat alone in the deepening gloom, the sound of the others outside rising gently around her, trying to hold on to the ridiculous, bubbling fear that kept threatening to overspill in her, holding it, along with her breath, all in.

54

CALLAN
Burj-al-Arab, Dubai

A steady, practised hand – outward brush of mascara, flicking away from the corner of the eyes so that the lashes at the corner were dramatically lengthened. She stopped, considered the effect, and added a little more. She pulled her head back, examining herself critically. Behind her the late afternoon sunlight danced around the room, reflecting off every surface – the polished marble floors, the mirrors and their gilt frames, the gleaming expanse of her desk, even the glossy, highly lacquered legs of the chairs that were dotted around the suite. She came back to the task at hand. In just under an hour, she was due to meet Ree downstairs in one of the hotel's many sumptuous lobbies. She tried to keep her mind on the job she'd flown out to Dubai to do, not on Ree Herz. It was her third visit and although she privately wondered how A*d*SP's muted, understated brand of elegance could possibly thrive in the atmosphere of heady exuberance that seemed to epitomise Dubai, Marco and the other shareholders who'd come to the meeting had no such doubts. This, Marco declared a touch pompously, was where the future lay. Dubai, Mumbai, Shanghai. Why did they all end in 'ai'? she wondered to herself. The bold new retail frontiers, all east of Europe now, and with their own particular way of doing business that Anneliese found so hard to understand. She'd been forced to make some design concessions, including introducing colour and texture – bling, if she were honest – into the new, 330-square-metre store. She'd slipped the computer-rendered images into her briefcase without a word. Anneliese would have a fit. She'd studied them with a sinking heart. They were about as far away from Ree's cool, intelligent handling of their Regent Street store as it was possible to be. Marco and his father were adamant; anything less and they'd be overlooked. The shoppers who thronged the Dubai Mall had more choice than shoppers anywhere in the world. 'You must *grab* their attention, Callan. Grab it and hold it.'

'That's not how A*d*SP works,' Callan shot back, already irritated.

'It is now.' There was no arguing with him.

She sighed and plucked a lipstick from her bag. She was wearing a light, seashell pink sheer top with white, tailored trousers and a white jacket that she'd thrown over the arm of the chair. Despite it being nearly fifty degrees outside, the entire city was sealed and air-conditioned to almost freezing. On the few occasions she'd actually stepped from a car to the hotel door, she'd been half-stunned by the ferocity of the heat – blinding, instantly drying – before finding herself, seconds later, enveloped once more in the cool. What on earth had they done before air-conditioning? she wondered, as she picked up her bag and jacket and slipped her feet into a pair of flat Ferragamo sandals that she'd bought a few days before leaving London. She couldn't wear *only* A*d*SP, after all.

Ree was already seated near the window as she came down the last flight of stairs into the salon on the twentieth floor, looking out over the Arabian Gulf to the mirage of skyscrapers that was Dubai across the causeway from the hotel. He was reading a newspaper, completely engrossed, and didn't look up as she approached. It gave her the chance to study him in a way she hadn't felt bold enough to do before. He was wearing a fawn-coloured linen suit and a light blue shirt, open at the neck, no tie. Against the light colours, his skin appeared much darker, absorbing the light, rather than reflecting it. His whole posture was of someone utterly at ease with himself, one leg lifted casually across the other, his trouser leg riding slightly to reveal a strong, finely turned ankle. He wore reading glasses which he adjusted as he turned the pages of his newspaper.

'Anything new?' she asked lightly, plopping herself down into the plush sofa opposite.

He looked up, his face breaking into an immediate smile. 'Not unless you count trade wars, suicide bombings and currency collapses as "new", no. Nothing new.'

She grinned. His ease made things easy between them, at least for now. 'How about a cup of tea?' she asked.

'Tea?' he said, and there was a teasing note in his voice as if he'd seen precisely why she'd chosen it.

'Tea,' she echoed faintly. 'Yes, tea.' The polite and uniformed waiter was immediately by her side. What sort of tea would madam like? And cakes? Sandwiches? Biscuits?

Five minutes later they looked at each other then at the table in front of them, slightly bewildered by the sheer quantity of food laid out. 'Reminds me of school,' Ree said, helping himself to a perfectly trimmed cucumber sandwich on a dainty porcelain plate.

'Not *my* school,' Callan snorted. 'They always left the crusts on.'

'Where did you go to school?' he asked, biting into it.

She had to look away. Watching him eat was rather more disconcerting than she'd imagined. 'Oh, some dreary place near Wales. Anneliese's choice. She was desperate for me to have an English education; don't ask me why.'

He smiled slightly. 'Same here. The desperate bit, I mean. My mother particularly. She wasn't keen on dragging me across Africa with them.'

'Where are your parents?' Callan asked, eyeing a scone. She had to have something to do with her hands.

'Namibia. Back home. That's all they've ever wanted – to be back home.'

'Funny, I can't quite think of you as Namibian,' Callan said, pronouncing the word carefully. 'I'm not sure I even know where it is.'

'South-West Africa. Former German colony. I'm surprised. You *should* know it.'

'Why? I'm not German.'

'Aren't you?' He raised his eyebrows questioningly.

Callan shook her head. 'I mean, yes, technically. But apart from the odd trip to Hamburg or Berlin, I've never been there.'

'But you speak German, don't you?'

'Sort of. But that's from school, not from Anneliese. We've only ever spoken English together.'

'You call her "Maman", I noticed.'

Callan smiled. 'That's my affectation. I went to the *Lycée Française* in Kensington until she shipped me off to boarding school. Anyway, enough about me.'

'Why? I rather enjoy hearing about you.' Ree grinned at her.

'Your wife's French, isn't she?'

There was a second's hesitation. He looked at her, his sandwich caught in mid-air as he narrowed his eyes very slightly, very faintly, as if letting her know he understood the question exactly as she'd intended it – as a warning, though whether to herself or to him, even she wasn't clear. He nodded slowly. 'Yes, yes, she is. Half French.'

'Where did you two meet?' she asked, suddenly hungry for details.

He gave her another one of his slow, considered looks that had her turning the other way. Her whole face was on fire by the time she heard him call her name. 'Callan.' She turned back to him slowly. 'I don't want to talk about Hayley,' he said, shaking his head. 'It's complicated.'

'Then we won't. We'll talk about everything *but* Hayley. Or your family,' she added with a slight, wry smile. 'But only if you promise to talk to me about everything else.'

'Deal.' There was an answering smile playing around the corners of his lovely, lovely mouth. She looked down at her hands and when she raised her eyes again, the tension her question had generated was gone. For now. She breathed out a slow, quiet sigh of relief.

55

ANNELIESE

'Who on earth chose *this* colour?' Anneliese held up the offending image of the interior of the shop and grimaced. It was every bit as bad as she feared. Worse, in fact. Silver? Gilt? *Velvet?*

Callan leaned across the desk and shrugged. 'Marco, I guess—'

'You *guess?* You were supposed to go out there and make sure—'

'Maman, I tried,' Callan interrupted her. 'But there's no way we could stick to the same colours that we use here. They'd just get swallowed up.'

'I don't *care* if they get swallowed up. The only people who come to the store are people who know what we do. We've never relied on passing trade, least of all passing trade in the *Dubai Mall!*'

'I know, I know . . . but the thing is, everything around us is so . . . so *bright.* We've got Dolce & Gabbana on one side and Versace on the other. We've got to do something to stand out. Ree said that—'

'You spoke to Ree about this? When?' Anneliese looked at her sharply. She wasn't aware Callan had been in touch with him of her own accord.

Callan blushed. 'Well, actually . . . I . . . I bumped into him . . .'

'Where?' Anneliese stared at her. Why had she gone so red?

'In Dubai, actually. We, er, ran into each other at Heathrow. I . . . I showed him these.' She pointed to the images. 'Just to get his opinion, that's all.'

'I see. Well, what did he say?'

Callan's face was the colour of one of the cherry tomatoes Anneliese had had for lunch. 'He said to take just one of the colours – bronze or gold, whichever – and then work around it . . . have as many different shades of one of the colours as possible, instead of ten different colours.'

Anneliese was silent, considering. It wasn't a bad suggestion. 'Fine,' she said eventually. 'Choose one and do as he says. I'll have a word with him later.' She pulled the images into a tidy stack and quickly left the room. She had no desire to let Lars or Bruno – or even Callan – know just how flustered the whole exchange had left her.

She walked into her office and closed the door carefully behind her. She sat down at her desk, swivelling her large leather chair away from it towards the window. It was early spring in London and the garden at the rear was just beginning to come into bloom. The two stately oak trees that flanked the edge of the garden were still bare but in a few months' time, their thick, lush foliage would completely screen off the back of her neighbour's house and the privacy she craved at all times would be practically complete. As it was she could see over the stone wall right into their garden. A child's tricycle lay overturned in the sand pit; there were a few discarded buckets and spades. She sometimes saw the children, usually supervised by a string of nannies, playing outside. Today the garden was empty and quiet.

She sat still for a few moments, the fingers of one hand going automatically to her ring. A trick of light showed her face reflected not only in the windowpane in front of her, but in the mirror that stood behind her, on the mantelpiece. She gazed at it for a few seconds. Aside from the routine glance each morning as she got dressed for the day, she rarely looked at herself. Sometimes a whole day went by without her catching sight of her own reflection. In that unguarded moment before she recognised herself and pulled her features into the neutral, calm expression that she always wore, a look had come out into the open that she might not otherwise have caught. There was worry there, and something else she would ordinarily not like to name: jealousy. Ree was *her* prize, her find. She was drawn to him, not in the way one might think, no – at her age, ridiculous! – but in another, much deeper way that even she didn't care to examine. If she'd been pressed she would have found it almost impossible to explain. All she could admit to now was anxiety. Anxiety that Callan too was drawn to him. It wasn't something one liked to admit about one's own children, she thought to herself uncomfortably, but Callan would stop at nothing to get what she wanted. There was a ruthlessness in her that had angered her as Callan was growing up, a wilful stubbornness that made her bold in the face of reprobation and fearless, too. Good qualities in business, clearly, but nowhere else. As she'd grown older, and less prone to childish outbursts, Anneliese had dared allow herself to think that the wilfulness had been stamped out of her. She, after all, more than anyone around her, knew what sort of trouble it could bring. Twice in her own life she'd— She stopped herself just in time. She took a deep breath and let it out slowly, forcing herself to calm down. When in doubt, *do nothing*. It was a philosophy she'd learned to trust and so far, at least, it had served her well.

PART SEVEN

56

TARA
Islington, London

Her first thought after she'd read through the email for the third or fourth time (just to make sure there'd been no mistake; yes, it *was* addressed to her) was exactly the sort of thing Callan would say. *What the hell' m I going to wear?* She printed off the email and carried the pages through to the sitting room, balancing her cup of coffee awkwardly in one hand as she read it yet again: *Dear Professor Connolly, I write with pleasure to invite you to give a paper at our forthcoming conference, Merchants and Marvels: Commerce and Art in Early Modern Germany, to be held at the Department of History, New York University, New York, on the 6th and 7th of March, 2001. Further details to follow, following your acceptance, and a brief abstract of your proposed paper.* She took a cautious sip of coffee. Then another. And then she read it again.

'Well, what *are* you going to *wear?*' Callan sounded distracted. Tara's skin prickled with discomfort. It was unlikely Callan would ever know – or even care – just what it had cost Tara to pick up the phone.

'Wear?' she repeated woodenly, her fingers itching to hang up. It was different for Callan. She flew halfway round the world at the drop of a hat. Christ, in the past month alone she'd been to more countries than Tara had visited in the last twenty-three years. And the question of what to wear would simply never come up. She could feel the stirrings of jealousy – an emotion she tried to keep firmly in check. She had so much to be grateful for, she reminded herself sternly. Without Callan there would be no invitation to a conference. Without Callan and Anneliese she wasn't sure where she'd have wound up, or what she would have become. But there were days when it was hard to be grateful. Like today. An invitation to a conference in New York was just about the most exciting thing that had ever happened to her – and Callan sounded as though she couldn't wait to get off the phone.

'Yes, wear. What do people wear to conferences?' Now she was beginning to sound impatient.

'I . . . I'm not sure,' Tara said hesitantly. 'A suit?' She tried to cast her mind back to the two or three conferences she'd attended, but drew a blank. She'd been far too focused on what was being said to notice what the speaker might have been wearing.

'Yes, but what sort of suit? Conservative? Modern? Cutting edge?'

'Christ, I don't know. A . . . a *normal* suit?'

'No such thing. Look, come into the shop on Saturday morning. I'll get Marisa to pull out some stuff. I'll meet you there.'

Tara hesitated, guilt breaking all over the surface of her skin. 'Are you sure?'

'Course I'm sure. It's your first conference. I'm not letting you go across the Atlantic without being properly dressed. Consider it an advance birthday present. Or Christmas present, whichever. And I won't take "no" for an answer.'

'But—'

'No "buts", either. See you Saturday. And well done, by the way!' She hung up before Tara could make any further protest. Tara slowly replaced the receiver. Her fingers were shaking and there was a lump in her throat that was difficult to ignore. It was so typically Callan. One minute Tara wanted to slap her, the next she was almost prostrate with guilt. Their relationship, which had once been easy, was never free of conflict and drama, a battle of wills, though Callan would have been shocked to hear Tara say it. Since that morning when Callan had burst into Tara's room at Mortimer's, her little face pinched tight with

Tara's pain, there'd been a slow reversal of the roles that had first set them upon the long, easy course of their friendship. Overnight everything changed for Tara, and there were few who could ever have guessed at the conflict those changes had wrought. She'd gone from being a figure of authority to a figure of charity. And although there had never, *ever* been even the faintest hint of it in Callan's and Anneliese's dealings with her, Tara was often tormented by the knowledge that she owed them more than she could ever bring herself to say. Pride, her mother used to caution her, will always end in a fall. Well, there'd been a fall all right . . . a complete fall from grace. *Tara Connolly. Head girl. Orphan. Charity case.* Stop it, she cautioned herself, getting to her feet. Her heart was racing and her hands were clammy. Stop right there.

The clock in the hallway chimed suddenly, marking out another quarter of an hour. There were many nights she'd lain in bed, unable to sleep, dependent on its slow, reassuring chime marking out the quarter-hours until dawn. The night Jeb left, she'd counted not only the quarters, but the minutes as well. If you lay very still in the big double bed they'd shared for five blissful years, you could hear the metallic 'click' as the hands turned over, pushing you from one moment to the next. That night, which in her memory was almost as bad as the first night after Miss Molloy had called her into the office, she'd grasped through her tears that time also dealt in finalities. That the clock's steady, measured pace counted out not only the abstract seconds, minutes and hours of time, but that it also closed off whatever had gone before. Like her parents. Like Jeb.

She forced herself to look down at the email once more. Her day had begun well. She tried to catch hold of the easy, hopeful lightness of those earlier moments. That usually did the trick. For the first few months after her parents died, she'd focused on one thing. She thought about Chipo and those moments when she spotted him coming up the road to fetch her from school with his swinging, loping gait. In the beginning, when she was still light enough, he'd carried her on his shoulders, her school satchel dangling from his arm, the faint whistle of some pop song or other coming up to her from the warm, sonorous depths of his chest. In those days, love was warmth. The warmth of the sun, of Chipo's arms, the warm, soft grass, her mother's bed . . . even the warm, acrid smoke of her father's cigar, curling itself lazily upwards, spiralling towards the ceiling before dissolving in the light.

Zambia was warm; England was cold. Love and hate. The two existences jostled along inside her, each in its own clear and fixed place. When the world turned upside down and finally righted itself, she was unable to reconcile the new order of things with what they'd once been. Callan was warm; Anneliese was not. Yet between them, it was Anneliese she trusted. There was something in Callan that reminded her of all those other warmths – Chipo, her parents, Kitwe, Jeb. They all left. From one day to the next. One minute you were there, basking in it . . . the next they'd disappeared, leaving only a chill that never seemed to dissipate. She'd read somewhere that memories generated their own heat. That you'd eventually be able to look back and remember and that all you'd feel was warmth. Whoever it was who'd said it had lied. When she looked back she found nothing but the cold, hard chill of loss.

She pulled on a coat and hurriedly wound a scarf round her neck. She had to get out of the flat. There was coldness creeping in under her skirt and up through the slim frame of her body that had nothing to do with the outside temperature. In fact, she was colder than anything autumn could throw at her. A distraction was the only thing that could warm her up. She pushed open the front door, wheeling her bike out in front of her. At moments like these, the only way back to some kind of normality was through habit: a cup of coffee, a croissant, nibbling on something sweet, the sound of other people around her. The sounds of other people's lives.

'That one. What d'you think?' Callan turned to Marisa, the Bond Street shop manager. Beneath their gaze, Tara squirmed.

As ever, she was torn between the desperate longing to be the centre of someone's – anyone's – attention and the desire to disappear beneath the sleek, polished concrete floor.

Marisa, cool, stunningly elegant, nodded, looking Tara over with a careful, practised gaze. 'Yes, definitely. You'll need to do something about her hair, though.'

'My hair? What's wrong with my hair?' Tara put up a hand in alarm.

Marisa ignored her. 'You can't wear a two-thousand-pound suit with that kind of haircut. Is it actually a haircut?' she asked, and her voice was simply curious.

'I'll take her next door,' Callan said quickly. 'No, we won't do anything drastic. Just . . . just tidy it up a little, that's all. When was the last time you had it cut?'

Tara shrugged. She knew better than to argue with Callan, or the formidable Marisa of whom she was already terrified. 'Dunno,' she muttered. 'A few months ago. I did it myself.'

'Shows.' Marisa's voice, like her own haircut, nails and suit, was clipped and precise. 'So, let's see. You're taking the black suit, the two grey wool dresses, the herringbone jacket and three pairs of shoes. Anything else?'

'Throw in some sweaters,' Callan said firmly. 'Cashmere and merino. And that white shirt. You know, the one with the asymmetrical collar.'

Tara closed her eyes briefly. Without looking at the price tags, the bill for the hour they'd spent in the shop would come to half her annual salary. 'I don't *need* so many things,' she protested faintly.

'Need's got nothing to do with it,' Callan said with a smile. 'Besides, you do. This is only the first of *many* conferences, my darling. You'll need a different set of outfits for each. Trust me.'

Tara didn't know what to say and so she said nothing. In the first place, how did Callan *know* she'd ever be invited to another conference, and in the second, even if she was, she would never again allow Callan to spend that sort of money on clothes that she'd only wear once, if that. She couldn't *imagine* the looks on the faces of her colleagues if she showed up to lecture first-year students in a £2,000 A*d*SP suit. Or a white shirt with an *asymmetrical* collar. Julia would have a *fit*, she of the brown-cardigan-and-black-shoes brigade. She looked down at the growing pile of cream-and-black bags, each with their discreet A*d*SP logo embossed on the side. Despite herself and her innate reluctance, she had to admit to a little tremor of excitement. She'd never really paid fashion much attention. Unlike Callan and Anneliese, she had little interest in it beyond amusement at the amount of time, energy and effort it took to stay abreast of the trends and a horrified fascination at the sheer amount of wealth such interest could generate. But even she had to admit there was something oddly pleasurable about standing in front of a long mirror looking at her own image suddenly transformed.

'Not a bad figure, all things considered,' was Marisa's only comment. Tara was too afraid to ask what else might possibly be considered. Callan took her by the shoulders and turned her around to face herself. She opened her mouth in surprise. She looked totally different, but in a subtle, discreetly powerful way. She looked older, a woman to whom others ought to listen, pay respect. She looked – she hesitated over the word – *poised*. She would never have Callan's sultry glamour, or even Anneliese's icy cool, but she looked as different from the Tara Connolly in her perpetual jeans-and-sweater combination as they did.

Callan, quick as ever, nodded with satisfaction. 'That's the beauty of her clothes,' she murmured. 'They bring out what's already beautiful in you.'

Tara felt the prick of tears behind her eyes. The memory of standing next to her mother's mirror, watching her powder her face, burned before her. Was that why she paid so little attention to her own appearance? There was something about mirrors and the dreamy self-absorption that only women can ever bring to the study of their own faces that frightened her. She turned abruptly away, not wanting anyone, least of all Miss Eagle-Eyes Marisa, to see just how moved she'd been, and how difficult it was to accept their praise.

57

LINDI
Geneva, Switzerland

She brushed her eyelashes with a steady hand, first one eye, then the other, and sat back, pressing her lips together to blot her lipstick, just the way Siv had taught her so many years ago. She looked at her face this way and that, then pulled a few curly tendrils from around her ears. The tightly scraped-back knot into which she usually tied her hair was a bit too severe for the occasion. Wetting a finger, she curled the strands tightly, and then released them, watching them spring around her cheeks. They softened her face, made her look less like a schoolteacher. She grinned at herself. All done. She stood up, slipped on her black high heels and turned round slowly in front of the mirror. Her black, floor-length dress, like most of her clothes, was simple, almost plain. *No, not plain, severe.* It was a word many used to describe her. *Lindi? Lindi Johanssen? Nice, but a bit severe.* She liked its connotations. Tough. Stark. Strong. But fair, too. Good qualities in a lawyer. She flashed herself another quick grin, took one last look at herself in the mirror, picked up her pashmina and opened her front door.

A young man in a grey pin-striped suit with a bright pink carnation peeping rather incongruously out of one pocket stopped her at the entrance. He had the self-righteous, pompous air of a schoolchild having been given an important task.

'And you are—?' He licked his forefinger self-importantly and began thumbing through the list of names held in one hand.

'Lindi Johanssen,' she said laconically. She was used to his type.

'Yo-hanson.' His eyes scanned the list of names in front of him. 'Yo-hanson.' She saw that he had gone to the last page.

'With a "J",' Lindi supplied drily. 'Not a "Y".'

He was flustered, and annoyed. 'Yes, yes. With a "J", I know, I know. OK, there it is. You can go in.' He waved her through imperiously, his nostrils widening perceptibly in displeasure as she passed by.

She'd done it again, she thought to herself as she advanced into the hallway and stood in line to dispose of her coat and scarf. There was something about her that annoyed her fellow countrymen. *Especially* the men. Particularly the younger ones, those now scrambling for toe-holds on the lower rungs of the ladder of power. In some ways, it was entirely predictable, as her father kept pointing out. The Old Man, in whose honour they were gathered at the ambassador's home, was ailing. His successor hadn't yet been named and if there was one thing she'd learned in the eleven years since she'd moved to Namibia, it was that there was nothing quite so dangerous as the inevitable vacuum created by the transition of power. There were several contenders jostling to be picked. Tonight's dinner was simply one of the many set pieces in a game that would culminate in someone, somehow, rising to the top.

'You must be careful,' her father had warned her when they had dinner together in Paris the month before. He was en route to Nairobi. They met at his favourite restaurant on the Île de la Cité, a few metres away from the Seine. She was conscious of the waiters' eyes on them as they threaded their way through the tables. She was used to it. A dark-skinned younger woman and an older, white-haired man. She often wondered what people thought. It was probably safer not to, she had to remind herself. 'It's an uncertain time.' He was gently enquiring about things as they ate and drank. It had been a few months since she'd last seen her parents, though they spoke every week. There was an awareness that lay unspoken between them that in choosing to live in Namibia, she had also moved away from them, in more senses of the word than they could comfortably admit. His way of accommodating the change had been to guide her in the way he knew best – politically. *Watch out for this one, pay attention to that.* She listened, aware that something more was always being

298

said. 'And Hamutenya?' he asked, reaching for the bottle of wine, pouring her a little more. 'How is he?'

Lindi shrugged. 'Creepy,' she smiled. 'He hates me.'

Erik smiled at her indulgently. 'How could *anyone* hate you, darling?' he asked, the corners of his mouth tugging downwards in disbelief.

Lindi grinned. 'Oh, easily. He hates the way I talk, the way I dress, the things I say. He hates just about everything about me but I think he *especially* hates the fact that I'm not married. A good husband would've slapped some sense into me.' She giggled suddenly. She knew she'd been sent overseas partly to get her out of his hair. It was no secret in the ministry that Lindiwe Johanssen wasn't quite what he'd bargained for.

Erik was suddenly serious. 'Be careful, darling, won't you?' He looked at her over the rim of his glass. 'The next few months are going to be tough. Harambe's the West's choice and Hamutenya knows it. He'll stop at nothing, that one.'

'Oh, no one cares about me, Pa. I'm just a lowly civil servant.' Lindi tried to make light of his tone.

'Don't underestimate yourself. You're one of the brightest people they've got.'

Lindi could feel the heat steal into her cheeks. 'No, I'm not,' she mumbled in the way she always did when someone paid her a compliment.

Erik laughed. 'I'm not going to argue. Not with a lawyer. But you *must* be careful. I know it's your way – *our* way – to say things openly, say what's on your mind. But things are different there. You know how it is. Watch your back.'

'Pa.' Lindi laughed. 'You make it sound so dramatic. I'm just a lowly lawyer. I'm not even a proper lawyer. I've never even *seen* the inside of a courtroom. You know that. I'm no threat to anyone, really.'

Erik took a mouthful of wine, letting it swirl around in his mouth in the manner she knew so well, his Adam's apple more pronounced now than she'd ever seen it. He was ageing, she realised suddenly, with a catch in her throat that made her draw breath. 'I'm just saying . . . be careful, that's all. Don't make unnecessary enemies.'

'Choose your battles, right?' She smiled at him, masking her sudden concern with tenderness.

'*Absolut.*'

'I will, Pa. I promise.'

Well, she'd obviously not paid close enough attention, she thought to herself as she wandered across the thickly carpeted living-room floor to stand in line and pay her respects to the ambassador. The queue was long and fawningly obsequious, a depressing combination if there ever was one. She stood behind a couple she didn't recognise – the woman was several inches taller than her husband and almost twice as wide. Her headdress, a brilliantly and intricately wrapped swathe of patterned and textured cloth, was wound tightly around her coiled ropes of braided hair, darting in stiff, peaked folds this way and that. She found herself studying its convoluted geometry as they shuffled forward, one by one.

Suddenly there was a stir at one end of the long room; people's voices rose. Lindi turned along with everyone else. The double doors that led to the garden were flung open. There was a great scurrying to and fro as bodyguards and security personnel walked up and down, securing doors and barking instructions into their walkie-talkies, and then, finally, there was the low sort of murmur that accompanies someone of importance. All of a sudden, he was there, in front of them all. The Old Man himself. Walking slowly to his seat, aided by a man whom she vaguely recognised as his eldest son. She heard the slow but quickening swell of applause as his son guided him from dignitary to minister to guest and back. The chest was still wide and fleshy, moving with deep breaths. The white trademark beard was still there, as was the surprisingly sweet smile. It had always been a distinctive feature of his, the disarming Hollywood smile.

When she was reluctantly nudged forwards to offer her own congratulations, she saw, however, that the smile did not quite reach his eyes. He was as alert and wary as ever. Someone murmured her name as she moved forwards. There was a momentary flickering of the eyelids. If he had kept somewhere the image of the young girl he had met once, long ago, just before dawn, both on their way to the bathroom they temporarily shared, she in her pyjamas, he in the dressing gown Siv had bought for the occasion, there was no sign of it in his face. He inclined his head graciously, accepting her murmured words. Just as quickly, she found herself passed on, passed along. She took a glass of champagne from a liveried flunky in a white jacket and a brilliant blue cummerbund. There was no one to talk to. The only women present were wives and partners of the men in the room; as usual, she stood out.

'Lindi! You're here!' Someone spoke to her. She turned. It was Klaus Herz. One of the last exiles to return, he'd recently been appointed to the Ministry of Agriculture. In his long, flowing West African robes with his thick, bushy white beard and those dark eyebrows that framed his face in the way of an elaborate painting, he was easily one of the government's most recognisable – and popular – figures. 'Who cares about the Ministry of Agriculture,' he was often heard to joke. 'What threat can a bunch of farmers possibly be?' Unlike many of the other ministries, Agriculture tended to attract those who actually knew something about it. There was something to be said for keeping one's head below the parapet, Lindi often thought. Out of sight was also out of danger.

'Uncle Klaus.' Lindi delightedly offered up her cheek.

'Oh, for goodness' sake! Don't you "uncle" me now!' Klaus Herz said, hugging her warmly.

'Old habits die hard, I guess,' she laughed.

'You look lovely, by the way.' He held her slightly away from him in swift appraisal, as he'd always done. '*Ach*, when are you going to come to your senses and marry my son?'

'When he comes to his,' Lindi said lightly. She'd long ago buried her embarrassment about Ree Herz. When she saw his picture now – and he was always in the press these days – she found it hard to connect his face with the face she'd gone to sleep sobbing over, for months afterwards.

'Hmm. That may take a while,' Klaus said drily. 'But, we're always hopeful.'

Lindi laughed again. She'd read he'd married a model, or an actress, something along those lines. 'Well, don't hold your breath.'

'And what are you doing here, my dear? You didn't come just for the birthday party, I take it?'

She shook her head. 'No, I'm working for UNCTAD now. Been here just over a year, and I've got another eight months to go. We're in the middle of drafting the new trade and development agreements. Someone back at the ministry thought it would be a good idea for me to be here,' she said, as diplomatically as she could.

'Ah. Hamutenya, probably. How's old Harambe?' They slipped into the easy, insider gossip of people working in the same circles, although at opposite ends. She could feel several pairs of eyes on her as she stood to one side with him, sipping champagne and listening to his droll accounts of the comings and goings of life at the top. Across the room, someone was watching her carefully – Sipho Kgomane, whom she'd rubbed up the wrong way on more than one occasion. She could feel his eyes boring into the back of her skull. His expression, when their eyes met fleetingly, was one of unbridled anger. She turned her head and stared him down. He was the one to turn aside but not before she'd seen the flaring of his nostrils and the tight, compressed line of his mouth. He was a couple of years older than her and like most of the young, upcoming politicos, he'd been raised in exile – Germany, then Finland, Russia for a while. He'd returned just after independence to take up the sort of junior position she now occupied and had swiftly clambered up the ranks. She couldn't remember all the various ministries he'd worked in or the positions he'd held, but now, in his mid-forties, he was on the Executive of the National Planning Commission. Rumour had it that he was tipped for a ministerial post. She couldn't work out why the sight of her seemed to enrage him so. Still, it was his problem, not hers, or so she tried to tell herself. Her father's warning came back to her again. *Don't make unnecessary enemies.* She ought to set about disarming Sipho and a few of the other men whom she appeared to have unwittingly irritated – but how? She wasn't the type to flirt, and even if she was, Sipho was hardly the type she'd flirt with. Too short, for one thing, and he was certainly no oil painting. She turned her back on him and tried to concentrate instead on what Klaus was saying.

'And you? Not married yet?' he asked, gently teasing.

She shook her head. 'Me? Not a chance,' she said cheerfully. 'I seem to scare the hell out of most men; I've no idea why.'

'*Ach*, all in its own good time,' Klaus Herz said indulgently, smiling at her. 'And in the meantime, I hear only good things about you.'

Lindi laughed. 'Now, we both know that isn't true,' she said, still grinning.

'Well, *mostly* good things,' he laughed, having the grace to acknowledge his stretching of the truth. 'Be careful, though, Lindi. Change is in the air. These are rather uncertain times.'

She nodded, holding up her wine glass, bringing it to rest against her cheek. 'No one cares about me, Uncle Klaus,' she said, repeating what she'd told her father the other month. 'I'm just a lowly civil servant. What threat can I possibly be?'

Klaus Herz's response was the same as her father's. 'Don't underestimate yourself.'

'I don't. I won't. Besides, I'm stuck all the way out here now. I haven't been back in months. I go to work, I come home, I write reports – that's it. I'm going to New York next month to visit some old friends and that'll be the highlight of my year.'

'Well, I'm sure you'll have a lovely time.' Klaus Herz patted her arm affectionately. 'Now, I'd better run along and press the flesh. You know how it is.'

'I do,' Lindi laughed, reaching up to kiss his cheek. 'Believe me, I do.' She watched him thread his way across the floor, stopping to chat to this one, shaking hands with that. He did it all with an air of such unhurried, unflappable ease that Lindi could only marvel at him. She didn't know how they did it, these politicians who'd learned to hide their real emotions and differences under their expensive three-piece suits, their feelings buried beneath layers of wool, linen and fat. She couldn't. When her passions were roused, they appeared directly on the surface of her skin.

58

TARA
New York

She'd never experienced cold like it. From the moment she stepped outside the terminal building at JFK, her whole body shrank inside itself, turning away from the biting wind and air. Her eyes were thin slits through which she could only just make out a line of yellow taxis. She'd been promised a pick-up directly from the airport but she'd emerged bleary-eyed into the arrivals hall to find no one waiting with a sign held to his chest which read Professor Connolly, as she'd been promised. She waited for almost an hour but no one appeared. Her mobile didn't work and it hadn't occurred to her to jot down a telephone number of anyone at the university. Still, she had the departmental address. She knew where to go, more or less. She hoisted her laptop bag onto her shoulder, grabbed her small suitcase and made her way outside.

'Thanks—'

'Are you—?' They both reached for the door handle at the same time as the taxi moved towards them. Caught by surprise, Tara turned sideways, caught her ankle on the edge of the kerb and with a startled yelp, fell backwards, letting go of her laptop case and her suitcase at the same time. There was a deadly sounding crunch as the taxi rolled over her laptop and then the squealing of brakes, followed immediately by a squeal from the woman standing next to her, her arm still outstretched towards the cab. It had all happened so quickly.

'Jesus!' The cab driver was out of the cab in a flash. 'You okay, lady?' he yelled down at her, surveying the flattened case in dismay.

Tara swallowed hard. Her arm was throbbing, as was her ankle. She struggled into an upright position, wincing as her arm bore her weight.

'Don't!' The woman crouched down next to her. 'Don't put your weight on it. Oh, God . . . maybe it's *broken*?'

'No, it's not.' Tara shook her head. She knew that much at least. 'No, I . . .'

'Here, lean on me.' The taxi driver crouched down on the other side of her. 'Put your hand on my arm, that's it.' Slowly, between the three of them, they managed to get Tara to her feet.

'Oh, shit.'

'Your laptop.' The woman looked even more distressed than Tara. 'I'm so sorry. I was waiting in the line . . . I just didn't see you. You stepped out of nowhere.'

'No, it's my fault,' Tara said hastily. 'I didn't realise there was a queue.'

'Listen . . . you think you can walk over there?' The cab driver interrupted them, pointing to where a man in uniform was looking at them. 'You'll need to make a statement to the controller. Unless . . . ?' He trailed off hopefully.

Tara and the woman looked at each other. 'Are you hurt?' the woman asked.

Tara shook her head. 'No, a bit bruised, that's all. Just my arm.'

'Let me take a look.' They carefully peeled away Tara's coat. There was a small tear at the sleeve, but there was no blood. 'Skin's not broken,' the woman said, nodding. 'Hell of a bruise, though.'

'I'll live.' Tara looked at the ground. 'Laptop's dead, though.'

'I know. I am so, so sorry.'

'It's not your fault. I should've looked where I was going.' Tara turned to the driver. 'No, it's fine. I don't need to make a statement. I'll . . . I'll get in the line and take another cab.'

'Absolutely not. I'm taking you wherever you need to go. It's just as much my fault, you know. Where are you headed? We can ride in together and I'll make sure you get to wherever you're going.'

Tara looked at her. She was about the same age, dark-skinned with thick black hair pulled into a knot on the top of her head. Her eyes were dark, liquid pools and her smile, though tentative, was wide and generous. She was very pretty, even beautiful, but more than that, she looked kind. Concerned. She bent down and picked up the battered and flattened laptop. 'It's shattered,' she said mournfully. 'I can feel it. Oh, God . . . I just hope you've got back-ups. And insurance.'

Tara nodded faintly. Her ankle was throbbing, and the beginnings of a headache threatened. She allowed the woman, who'd introduced herself as Lindi, to help her into the back seat. She gave the equally solicitous cab driver the address of the history department and leaned back against the seats. 'I'm fine,' she murmured, as Lindi fussed around her with a blanket. 'Honestly.'

'You don't look it. You're awfully pale. D'you work there or something?'

Tara shook her head. 'No, I'm giving a lecture tomorrow evening. They're putting me up in a hotel.'

Lindi looked even more concerned. 'Look, why don't you stay with me tonight? I'm staying at a friend's place, just off Washington Square. It's not far from the university. I've got the keys and my friends aren't back until the weekend. I'd much rather someone kept an eye on you tonight. Don't worry, it's perfectly safe. I'm a lawyer,' she added with a smile.

Tara swallowed. She felt ridiculously close to tears and the thought of spending a night alone in a strange hotel room in a strange city was almost too much to bear. 'Are . . . are you sure?' she asked hesitantly.

'Of course I'm sure. Give me the department's number. Someone must be expecting you. I'll just ring and let them know what's happened. Don't worry, honestly. I'll make sure you're as right as rain by tomorrow.'

Tara nodded gratefully. She leaned back against the seats as the cab sped over the bridge and swept into town. It felt good to let someone else take charge. For once.

The flat Lindi brought her to was on the thirty-fifth floor of a high-rise building overlooking Washington Square. To say it was lovely was an understatement. She limped in, her head pounding by now, her gaze falling on an enormous mahogany mask. 'Senufo,' she said, eyebrows rising in appreciation. 'From Cameroon.'

'Top marks,' Lindi said, wheeling her case in behind her. 'How did you know? Are you a collector?'

Tara shook her head, smiling faintly. 'No, my . . . er, aunt is a collector.' She was never sure how to describe Anneliese.

'She's got good taste. Now, I think you probably need an aspirin or two, and maybe a cup of tea?'

'Tea would be lovely.' Tara sat down on the couch, sinking into the silk cushions, and looked around her with interest. 'What a lovely flat. What do your friends do?'

'Manthia's a film-maker and his wife's a curator. I met Manthia on an exchange programme at university . . . oh, it must be ten years ago. Just one of those people you meet for a fortnight and then wind up being friends with for life.' She smiled at Tara. 'Odd, isn't it? Half the people I grew up with I've no desire to see again and then you meet someone out of the blue . . . funny how it works.'

Tara nodded slowly. She liked Lindi immediately. It had been a very long time since she'd met anyone with as much warmth. It had been a very strange day – the flight, the cold, her arrival and the small accident. She closed her eyes briefly. It was almost four in the afternoon in New York, but nearly midnight in London. She was tired. She yawned widely, covering her mouth in embarrassment. 'Sorry,' she mumbled. 'It's been a long day. I didn't even ask you . . . where have you just come from?'

'Geneva.' Lindi walked into the small kitchen. 'But I'm going to try and stay awake until this evening. You take a nap, though. I'll just go and make sure the bed's made up. Now, what sort of tea would you like?' She rattled off half a dozen varieties but by the time she was finished, Tara's eyes were firmly shut. The next thing she knew, she was faintly aware of Lindi's perfume and her hands, helping her stand up. She allowed herself to be led into the bedroom, still yawning. Lindi quickly closed the curtains and the room was plunged into shadow. She was tired. She sank back into the soft down comforter and closed her eyes. 'Just take this,' Lindi instructed, 'before you go to sleep. I'll wake you up at dinner time.' And then she was gone. Tara swallowed the bitter painkiller, set down the glass and was asleep almost before her head touched the pillow.

59

LINDI

Tara was still fast asleep when she knocked on the door. She pushed it open cautiously. She lay curled up under the comforter, almost entirely covered except for her short, reddish-gold hair now sticking almost straight up. Lindi put a hand to her mouth to hide her smile almost at the same instant Tara's eyes opened.

'I didn't mean to wake you,' Lindi whispered.

Tara's eyes opened more fully. 'You didn't. Well, OK, yes, you did. What time is it?'

'Nearly nine. You slept for about four hours straight. How're you feeling? How's the head?'

Tara sat up cautiously. She was still fully clothed – her shirt was creased and rumpled and there was a welt across her cheek where her jacket sleeve had pressed into it as she slept. She did look better, though, Lindi noticed. 'Much better,' Tara said, rubbing her cheek. 'Four hours? It feels as though I only just closed my eyes.'

'And the ankle? And your arm?'

Tara touched her arm. 'Better, too,' she said, smiling in relief. 'Much better. What're you cooking?'

'An omelette. Are you hungry?'

Tara nodded. 'Starving, actually.'

'Good. Let's have a glass of wine. The bathroom's in there. Come through when you're ready.'

Tara swung her legs out of bed and stood up. Her ankle was a little stiff but nowhere near as painful as it had been earlier. 'Yes, much better.' She smiled. 'God, that smells good.'

'Wait until you taste it.' Lindi grinned. 'Omelettes are about the only thing I can cook, sadly.'

Tara pulled a face. 'I doubt that,' she said drily. 'Cheers.' She lifted up the glass Lindi handed her. 'I've got to say, I wasn't expecting my first night in New York to be quite like this.'

'Me neither.' Lindi smiled. 'And the spectacular loss of your laptop aside, I'm rather glad it happened. And your ankle. And your wrist.' She quickly served up the omelette. It had been years since she'd made the sort of spontaneous, unexpected acquaintance with someone that seemed to happen only every other day in your teens and early twenties, she thought to herself, taking a sip of her wine. She cut two pieces of toast in neat quarters and arranged them on the plates, just as Siv might have done. Nowadays everyone was a little too cynical, a little too suspicious. She'd been in Geneva all of fourteen months and she'd yet to make a proper friend. She couldn't have said why but there was something about Tara that she both liked and trusted. Tara Connolly. *Professor* Tara Connolly, she corrected herself, although in truth, Tara looked nothing like the professors she had known. 'So tell me a bit about yourself,' Lindi said curiously. 'You look awfully young to be a professor, if you don't mind me saying.'

Tara smiled and shook her head. 'I'm not exactly a professor, more a junior lecturer, actually. I think it's only in America that everyone's automatically a professor. Even the teaching assistants.'

'Ah. So what are you lecturing about tomorrow?'

Tara took the plate from her. 'D'you really want to know?' she asked, smiling.

'Absolutely. I might even come along and listen.' Lindi walked over to the window with her own plate and sat down. 'I've got three days here on my own until Manthia and Lydie arrive . . . why not? I'm sure it'll be interesting.'

'I hope so,' Tara said fervently. 'It's my first big conference.'

'Then all the more reason for me to come along.'

'Where are you from?' Tara asked suddenly. 'It's your accent. It's hard to place.'

Lindi smiled. 'Namibia. Large, rather empty country next to South Africa. South of Angola.'

'I know where Namibia is,' Tara said quickly. 'I'm from Zambia.'

'You're *Zambian*?' Lindi couldn't keep the surprise from her voice. She stared at the red hair and freckles. 'You don't look very Zambian.'

Tara blushed. 'Well, I grew up there,' she admitted. 'Lots of people think that doesn't count.'

'Oh, don't I know it. I grew up in Norway. It's the same thing.'

'In Norway?' Now it was Tara's turn to be surprised.

'Mmm. I was adopted. As a baby. Don't remember Namibia at all. Not that it was Namibia back then, of course.'

'That's funny, you're the second Namibian I've met recently,' Tara said, warming to Lindi.

'Really? There's only about a million of us so I'll probably know who you're talking about. Who?'

'He's an architect. He works for my adopted mother. Well, she's not exactly my *adopted* mother. It's a bit of a long story,' she said apologetically.

'Ree Herz?' Lindi asked with a smile.

310

Tara stared at her. 'How did you guess?'

'Well, like I said, there's only about a million of us in total. And he's pretty famous. So, you're adopted too?'

Tara blushed. 'Well, not exactly—'

'So, you're not exactly Zambian and you're not exactly adopted and you're not exactly a professor. Hmm. So what exactly *are* you, Tara Connolly?' Lindi's smile was wide and deep.

Tara had to laugh. 'Like I said, it's a long story.'

'Are you in a rush? More wine?'

'Yes.' Tara was surprised at her sudden rush of enthusiasm. 'Yes, please.' She polished off the last piece of omelette and settled herself into the sofa. She hadn't felt the urge to talk to anyone other than Callan in so long she'd almost forgotten how. The warmth that Lindi generated spread itself easily and comfortably over her. She tucked her feet under her, her hand settling itself over her ankle, touching it lightly, shyly pleased.

60

ANNELIESE
St John's Wood, London

The door closed with a sharp bang that ended the tense exchange between her and Callan and she was alone. The awful descent of dismay came over her and she had to sit down. There was a half-eaten apple on the plate beside her; she looked at it with distaste. She'd been in the middle of cutting it methodically, popping one crisp slice into her mouth after another when Callan knocked on the door. She hadn't been prepared for it – the sales figures, the spreadsheets with their neat coloured columns showing profit or loss, mostly loss. Her first reaction had been hostile – a mistake, of course – and then the conversation had rapidly disintegrated into something deeper, more personal and more hurtful, of course. Callan accused her of being too proud, too inflexible, a snob. She'd stared at her, an angry prickling bursting out across her skin. 'A *snob*?' she'd repeated indignantly.

'Yes, a bloody snob.' Oh, Callan gave as good as she got. She stood her ground. 'We're sinking, Maman. We're haemorrhaging cash, d'you hear me? We have got to do something otherwise we go under. This isn't 1975, Maman. This is 2001 and women have choices. We either get with the programme or we close up shop.'

Get with the programme. Close up shop. Callan would never know just how those phrases irritated her. It was the same sort of management-speak against which she shut her ears when she heard it from the mouths of those dreadful Italians. Even in their language it sounded no better. 'Fine. Then we close up shop. No, even better, let's close up *all* the shops. Then there'll be nothing for you to complain about.' She was being childish and she knew it – but she couldn't stop herself.

Callan stamped her foot. Yes, she actually *stamped* her foot. 'You're being ridiculous, Maman. This isn't about me!'

'No? When has it *not* been about you, Callan? Tell me that, hmm? You don't fool me, *meine Kleine*. You don't fool me for a second.'

There'd been a moment's horrible pause. Callan flushed, a dark, angry stain that spread across her face and neck. 'Why would I need to fool you, Maman?' she asked, her voice suddenly quiet.

She ought to have stopped it there. She couldn't. She didn't. 'Because that's what you do, Callan. You fool everyone. Don't think I don't see the way he looks at you.'

'Who are you talking about?'

'Marco Matuzzi. D'you take me for a fool, as well? I don't know what you did to broker the deal, Callan, but *I* certainly didn't ask you to prostitute—' She stopped herself. The word dropped like a stone between them. Callan's face hardened suddenly into a coldness that she'd never seen. With a rising sense of panic, she realised she'd gone too far. 'No, that's not—

I didn't mean—' She stumbled over the words. 'What I meant was—' She fumbled to make amends. But it was too late. Callan turned on her heel and walked out without saying a word. There was only the angry shutting of the door and then the terrible sound of silence. She put up a hand to her face and discovered to her horror that her cheeks were wet. She wiped them away angrily. She couldn't remember the last time she'd cried.

61

CALLAN
Rue Chauveau Lagarde, Paris

It was nearly seven in the evening. The light was fading fast and the garden below was already deep in shadow. In half an hour, she would take a shower, get dressed and go downstairs in the old-fashioned elevator to meet Marc. She stood at the window, looking down four storeys below her into the courtyard and the small garden beyond. The olive trees that stood sentinel had their first, tentative buds. It was March but Paris still felt wintry. She looked down at her bare feet. She'd kicked off her boots as soon as she entered the apartment. She still had the faint residue of the tan she'd acquired in Dubai. The memory of the time she'd spent with him came back to her immediately. After bumping into him at Heathrow, she wasn't sure what to expect – would he call her once they'd both settled in? Would they have dinner together? She had no idea. At the hotel, with the vague promise of getting together for a drink, they both went their separate ways. She had a dinner meeting that evening anyway – when she got back to her room, to her disappointment, there was no message from him. The following afternoon, she finished her meetings early. It was three thirty and it was still baking hot. She'd gone to her room, changed into a simple black halter-top bikini and grabbed a sarong and a beach bag. She made her way down to the lobby and walked out of the hotel towards the small, private beach. An hour or so in the sun, perhaps even a cocktail . . . then she'd finish reading through her notes, make her reports and have a shower and then go downstairs for dinner. Who knows – she might even bump into Ree? A cheerful young waiter led her to a spot near the water's edge and quickly and expertly adjusted her umbrella to just the right amount of shade. He took her drink order, smoothed out the towel with the flat of his hand and silently disappeared.

The beach was quite empty; it was a Thursday afternoon and since most of the hotel's guests were either business people or members of the various Gulf royal families who had their own private beaches, there were few people about. She took off the sarong, pinned up her hair and stretched out on the supremely comfortable lounger. The sea was a splendid expanse of hazy blue, punctured on one side by the shimmering steel-and-glass towers of the city and on the other by clusters of dark palm trees, all exactly of the same height and shape, giving the place an even more unreal air than it already had. The perfectly pale, perfectly shaped crescent of sand disappeared around the corner – she had the odd but distinct impression of being on a film set somewhere, waiting for a cast who might never appear. The sound of the sea was a quiet murmur; at Scheherazade it roared. She picked up her magazine and brought it up to her face, shielding her eyes from the sun. Her drink silently appeared beside her. All was still, hazily hot. She looked away from the print towards the dazzling surface of the sea. She closed her eyes, dozing like a cat in the sun.

'You'll burn if you're not careful.'

Her eyes flew open. His face and body were very black against the sun. She woke from her dream of intoxicating softness and sat up. 'Wh . . . what time is it?' she asked weakly.

He grinned. 'Nearly four. I finished early and stopped by the hotel. The concierge said I'd find you here.'

'W-would you like a drink?' she stammered, aware that her face had turned a deep shade of red.

'Why not? What're you drinking?'

She turned her head to look at her already-melted piña colada. She'd fallen asleep before taking the first sip. 'Well, it *was* a piña colada,' she said, smiling ruefully. 'It's just slush now. I must've been more tired than I thought.'

'It's exhausting. All this bizarre perfection.' Ree waved a hand in the direction of the hotel and the city beyond. 'It's my third or fourth time here and I still struggle to get my head round it.'

Callan didn't know what to say. That was the thing about Ree. He said things that were often just a provocation to a deeper conversation, as if what went on in your head was of far greater interest to him than your legs, or the shape of your bottom in a pair of jeans. It wasn't that she'd never met a man who found her interesting, or even stimulating . . . it was just that with him, it seemed to be *the* most important thing, not an additional, unexpected bonus. 'How did your meeting go?' she asked, trying to retrieve her sarong from the foot of the lounger without having to get up.

He picked it up and handed it to her. 'Pretty well. It's a big project, more urban planning than building, to be honest. I suppose that's what's interesting about it – the chance to do stuff on a completely different scale.'

'You love what you do, don't you?' Callan asked suddenly.

He seemed surprised by the question. 'Of course I do. Don't you?'

She was silent for a moment. 'No, not really,' she said finally, shaking her head. 'I mean, not in the way my mother loves her job, or you. I don't *hate* it,' she added quickly. 'It's just not what I thought . . . well, it's not what I dreamed of doing, as a kid.'

'What did you dream of doing?' Ree was sitting on the edge of the lounger opposite. He cupped his chin in his hand, idly tracing out a pattern in the sand with a finger. His manner was relaxed, even offhand, but it didn't fool her. She knew he was listening intently.

She smiled self-consciously. 'I don't really know. I suppose that's part of the problem. I did economics and political science

315

at university, not merchandising.' She glanced at him, then looked away again. 'I shouldn't complain, I know. Compared to most people I've got an absolute dream job. All this travel, the clothes, the shoes . . . most women I know would die for this.'

'But you're not most women,' Ree murmured, his attention still focused on the sand.

She blushed, a deep, violent warmth that spread from the centre of her stomach up through her chest and neck. She wasn't sure how to respond. 'No,' she said uncertainly. 'I . . . I suppose not.'

'You'll figure it out,' Ree said, finally looking up. Now he looked down the length of her body. 'Brown legs, red toes . . . sexy,' he said and smiled faintly.

The warmth intensified, along with a sensual swelling of her body. She was quiet, savouring the moment. Her toes tingled, as if he'd touched them. She fought hard to resist rubbing the instep of one foot against the other, in the way she'd have liked his hand to do. 'Did you order a drink?' she asked, breaking the silence.

He shook his head. 'No.' He stood up suddenly. 'It's nearly five,' he said, looking at his watch. 'I've got some phone calls to make. I'll just pop back to the hotel and freshen up. How does seven sound?'

'That's fine,' Callan said faintly. Seven? That was two whole hours away!

'Great. See you then,' he said, brushing the loose, fine grains of sand from his trousers as he stood up. He looked down at her again. 'Yes, sexy.' He grinned, confirming his earlier opinion and then turned and walked off. Callan had to close her eyes. It did nothing for the heat her own body had produced.

Now, standing at the window in Paris, looking into the bare, wintery garden, her bare feet hovering at the edge of her vision, she was overcome with a blast of longing so strong that she felt as though she might fall. It had been almost a month since she'd seen or talked to him and in that time so much had happened.

She longed to talk to him – about Anneliese, their argument, her flight to Paris . . . everything. She missed him with a ferocity that stunned her. Ree. Ree. She mouthed the words – his name – to the frosty windowpane. He would understand. Without it ever having been said, she knew he would understand.

She turned reluctantly away from the window and walked through the apartment. She pushed open the heavy carved doors that separated the living room from the dining room and sank down into the gold velvet sofa. She'd always liked their Paris home, especially after Anneliese had allowed the interior designers to just get on with their job. It was richer and more sensual than any of her other homes, which tended to blur into each other – all whites, greys, neutral shades. No patterns, no texture, no colour. Paris was different. Gold, bronze, chocolate brown – a rich, textured palette that stirred the senses.

She walked through to the hallway. The door to Anneliese's room was closed. She hesitated for a moment, then pushed it open. It was quite a masculine space – acres of pale oak wardrobes, splendidly severe without even a handle to disturb the flat, matt surfaces; a large, wide bed with a deep, dark brown leather headboard and a black leather Mies van der Rohe day bed at its foot. The sheets were a dusky brown, with a thin black piping detail around the edges. An ornate gold and glass Murano chandelier hung above the bed and on either side a pair of chrome, wall-mounted, office-type suspension lamps gave a tougher edge to the whole room. She walked over to the bed and sat down gingerly. It had been years since she and Anneliese had been in the apartment together. The place was mostly empty. Madame Boulicaut, who'd been the housekeeper for as long as Callan could remember, came in on a daily basis, cleaning, polishing, watering the plants . . . keeping everything in immaculate, pristine order should her employer decide on the spur of the moment to visit.

She lay back on the freshly washed and starched sheets and looked up at the ornate plasterwork ceiling. She turned her head, pressing it into the luxurious softness of the pillow. Four pillows;

two firm, two soft. Another one of Anneliese's rules that hadn't changed in thirty years. Her mind drifted back to Anneliese and their argument. Her whole body still burned with shame; the word Anneliese had spat at her still rang in her ears. Revulsion crept up through her stomach, emanating from somewhere deep within. How did she know? How could she have known?

The first time. That very first time. How old was she? Fifteen? She didn't even remember his name. It was after one of those interminable school dances at Mortimer's. The boys had been brought in en masse from the college further down the hill. After the dance was over, she'd slipped out of the hall without one or other of the teachers seeing her and made her way across the forecourt. She had a packet of cigarettes in one hand and she held up the crumpled folds of her dress in the other. She remembered the dress. It had arrived in a pale cream box with the embossed lettering AdSP across the front. It was floor length and of a stiff, sheer fabric that no one could name. It fitted her perfectly, of course. Had there ever been anything sent to her from the AdSP studios that didn't? She didn't even remember telling Anneliese there was a dance. Perhaps Tara had told her? She felt a momentary tug of pain, though whether it was the longing that Tara provoked in her now that she was no longer at Mortimer's, or whether it was a slight stab of jealousy at the thought of Tara and Anneliese together in London without her, she didn't know. She didn't like to dwell on it either. At fifteen she was astute enough to realise that her feelings towards them both were complicated, at best. She'd been so determined to make it work. There was Tara, her best friend in the whole wide world, alone, without a single person to rely on. It was unthinkable that she and Anneliese wouldn't step in. Anneliese had said very little about it, other than a simple 'yes, of course'. That Tara was grateful to her – and to Anneliese – was beyond question. What she hadn't counted on, she realised, was how they would feel about each other. From the outset, there was something about Tara's quiet reserve that Anneliese responded to. She liked Tara. After that first summer, Callan realised that Anneliese liked Tara more than she liked her. With Bruno in the picture,

Callan had always felt herself to come a poor second in Anneliese's eyes. Now, with Tara's arrival, she was third. At first it hurt like hell. Tara was so much more serious, more grown-up, quieter, more thoughtful . . . everything, in other words, that Callan was not. Nothing was ever said, of course, and Tara was always so appreciative of everything she and Anneliese did for her. But it was difficult to remain angry with Tara. She loved Tara, almost as much as she loved Anneliese and, in truth, Tara was a hell of a lot easier to love. After that first summer when they sent her away again and she was at Mortimer's alone, her enforced solitude was made even more difficult by the knowledge that back in London, Anneliese and Tara had each other, whilst she had no one.

So when a sixth-former whose name she couldn't recall called out to her softly as she crossed the forecourt on her way back to her room, 'Hey . . . hey you. Callan, isn't it? You're the one with the funny French name, aren't you?', it took her only a second to stop, turn and start walking in his direction. He was smoking. The tip of his cigarette glowed orange in the dark.

'Yeah. That's me.' She stood very close to him so that she could feel his excitement. And his fear. He was afraid of her, she realised, and in that realisation, for the first time, there was awareness and power. It made her strong. Suddenly she wasn't the one consumed with longing. He was.

'Wh-where are you going?' He pulled fiercely on his cigarette.

'Follow me.' She had no idea where she would take him but one look at his face told her he would have followed her anywhere.

It was uncomfortable back there amidst the leftover props and piles of costumes but she remembered seeing an old mattress somewhere . . . she felt her way carefully in the dark, holding him by his arm, tugging him forward. They bumped into it at the same time so that they both fell, giggling, into its dusty softness. At first it was all smell, her nose seeking out the warm space between his chin and neck, breathing in the unfamiliar maleness, taking the scent deep down into her lungs and expelling it slowly, like smoke. She'd never been this close to a man before. Bruno, for all his familiarity, kept a physical distance that she had never crossed. No father, no uncles, no *grandfather, godfather. No one. She pushed her hands impatiently under his school blazer and under his shirt. His skin contracted in a tense shiver of pleasure and his breath quickened. He would have made the next, practised moves if she'd allowed him but she didn't. For the first time in her life, she was properly in control. From where had the knowledge of what to do come? She had no idea. She let her hands and mouth lead her and he simply, blindly followed. She watched the change come over him with a sense of detached amazement. His whole body was snatched up in a mad, desperate frenzy which responded only to her touch. She had never had this much power over anyone. She teased, withheld, turned away . . . and he followed, blindly. She wasn't even aware of her own release. Her body arched under his of its own unseeing accord but her mind, always, was elsewhere. She could feel the onslaught of his passionate release but she herself felt little. He reminded her of a bird she'd seen once, trapped, beating itself again and again against the net in a desperate rush towards its own death.* Le petit mort. *The French phrase came back to her; it was strangely appropriate.*

The boy — why couldn't she remember his name? — was the first of many, some more skilled than others, especially later, but none ever touched her, not on the inside, where it mattered. None.

She rolled onto her side, her face falling between the gap in the pillows. Something caught her eye; she brought up a hand and pushed it under the pillow. Her fingers touched something hard. She pulled it out. It was an earring, a long, dangling earring. She sat up, holding it in her hand. It was gold — a thin gold chain with what looked like a cluster of tourmalines and rubies at the end. She looked at it closely, frowning. It was so unlike anything Anneliese would ever wear. She'd worn the same pair of diamond studs for as long as Callan could remember. She wondered who it belonged to. One or other of Anneliese's guests who'd ignored her cast-iron rule: no guests in her private bedroom, ever. Even Callan felt uncomfortable being there.

She got up off the bed, carefully smoothed down the counterpane and plumped up the pillows. Madame Boulicaut would change the sheets long before Anneliese's next visit but she didn't relish the thought of even Madame Boulicaut knowing she'd been in there. She left the room, closing the door quietly behind her, then glanced at her watch and nearly yelped. She had exactly ten minutes to shower, get dressed and get to the restaurant on time.

Marc was waiting for her at a table by the window. She hurried over, unwinding her scarf from her neck as she sat down. He stood up and they bumped cheeks a little awkwardly. 'Callan,' he said, holding her by the elbows, looking her over for a second, before releasing her. She caught a whiff of his aftershave. The scent catapulted her immediately back. Instead of the crowded Parisian restaurant, they were both back in New York. Instead of the gentle murmur of other diners, there was the soft, slippery sounds of their bodies.

'Marc,' she murmured. 'Still the same scent.'

'*Mais oui*. Force of habit. And you still look the same. How long has it been? And how long are you here for?' he asked, picking up the wine list and pretending not to be interested in her answer.

'Too short for whatever it is you have in mind,' Callan said with a wry smile. 'You always try it on, don't you, *chéri*?'

'And you always resist, *n'est ce pas*?'

'Well, yes. So, what are we drinking?'

'I thought a bottle of the Bâtard-Montrachet?'

'You're buying, I hope,' Callan quipped, raising an eyebrow.

'But of course.' He summoned a waiter.

Callan leaned back in her seat, studying him. It had been almost three years since she'd last seen Marc, and almost ten since they'd first met. A good-looking, charming man, he was probably in his late forties now. Still handsome. His dark brown hair was greying but he had the same piercing blue eyes and the same slow, mischievous smile. It was his smile that had first got her attention. She'd walked into the boardroom on her second or third day at Morgan's, half an hour late. Her boss had flashed her a look of withering impatience which she'd responded to with a charming smile, confusing the hell out of him. Marc smiled and winked at her as she took her seat and had asked her out for a drink afterwards. The journey from an after-work drink to dinner to a weekend in bed was shorter than he'd anticipated but rather than diminish his respect for her (she was a colleague, after all), it had curiously increased it. She was, hands-down, the most uncomplicated woman he'd ever met, he told her on their third date. She knew what she wanted, when and how and saw absolutely no reason to pretend otherwise. In many ways she was more like a man, he mused. Not just in her wonderfully uncomplicated attitude towards sex, but more importantly, in her expectations of what came with it. She expected nothing. She was the first woman he'd ever known who genuinely didn't want 'more', an expression that at first puzzled her. 'What d'you mean "more"?' she asked curiously. They were lying in his bed in the one-bedroom apartment on the fifty-fifth floor of a luxury tower building on Pearl Street, a couple of blocks away from their offices on Water Street, not far from where the Twin Towers had once stood.

'Exactly that. You want this.' He placed her hand on his thigh, then on his still-erect penis. 'And this. But not this.' He moved it upwards and placed it on his chest.

'Your chest?'

'No,' he laughed. 'Heart. My heart. But you don't want my heart.'

'Don't be ridiculous. You're married. Of course I don't want it.'

He looked at her. 'That doesn't stop most women.' He smiled, looking for a cigarette.

'I'm not most women,' Callan said with a smile. 'Here, give me one.'

Now, sitting opposite him in the small, elegant restaurant he'd chosen knowing she would approve, she felt an unbearable sadness wash over her. It was partly the fight with Anneliese but there was something else that she was unable to put into words. Something had changed – or was about to change – and she was having difficulty grasping the moment, or its importance, or both.

'Whatever's the matter?' he asked, quick as ever to pick up on her moods.

To her horror, she felt her eyes suddenly flood with tears. She shook her head, blinking quickly in an attempt to brush them away. 'Oh, nothing,' she said, trying to make light of it.

'Callan . . . *qu'est ce qu'il y a?*'

His voice was so full of genuine concern that the tears simply began falling. 'No . . . nothing,' she stammered, furiously trying to wipe them away.

'Something's the matter . . . hmm? What is it? Your mother?'

She shook her head. 'No, no, of course not. When have you ever seen me cry over Anneliese?'

'*Jamais*. So what is it? No, don't tell me . . . a man? You're crying over a man? *You?*' His eyebrows rose almost comically.

'Don't sound so surprised, Marc,' Callan sniffed, trying to raise a smile.

'I am surprised. You're the last person I expected to see crying over some *man*.'

'He's not just "some" man,' Callan protested, but at the same time, a wave of relief and release flowed over her. She could tell Marc. He of all people would understand. 'It's complicated,' she said hesitantly.

'So . . . who is he?' Marc leaned back in his seat. He held up his hands. 'No, don't tell me. He's married, of course. There's a wife. But since when was that a problem?'

Callan stubbed out her cigarette, took a deep breath and then hastily lit another. Her fingers were actually trembling. It wasn't just that she'd never talked about Ree to anyone, it was also that she was hardly able to make sense of her own feelings, even to herself. She'd never felt this strongly about anyone, ever. That much was immediately clear. The more she got to know Ree, the more she longed to know him. At times the longing was like a physical ache. Was it love? Was that what love reduced you to? A violent, unbearable longing that nothing else could assuage? She had no idea. All she knew was that she could no more stop thinking about him than she could stop breathing, and that mixed in with it all was her unbearable shame. Ree liked her; she could tell. But he didn't *know* her, not yet. And when he did, his feelings towards her would change. How could they not? She wasn't worth *anyone's* love, least of all his.

She talked for nearly thirty minutes without drawing breath. Finally, when the tears had dried on her cheeks, she stopped and looked at him nervously. There was silence for a few moments. 'Wh . . . what do you think?' she asked after a minute or two when it was clear he wasn't about to comment.

'About?' Marc drew on his own cigarette and carefully blew the smoke out through his nostrils.

Callan's heart fell. She knew him well enough to know what the deliberately obtuse response meant. 'Don't be like that,' she said, touching his arm.

He gave a small, short laugh. 'Like what? All right, all right. Yeah, I'm pissed off. I mean, here we are. It's been what, two, three years? You breeze into town, we have dinner, drinks, maybe a peck on the cheek—'

'Marc,' Callan said quietly. 'Come on. You're married.'

He gave another short laugh. 'So's he.'

'You know what I mean.'

'No, I don't. Callan . . . ever since I've known you, you've been with married men. It's what you do. It's who you are. It's never made the slightest bit of difference. You've never wanted anything more. It's what I – we, I guess – always liked about you. No strings, no drama, no headache. You're the perfect mistress, you know that? That's what Olivier always used to say about you—'

'You discussed me with *Olivier*?' Callan's eyes widened incredulously.

'Of course I did. What did you think? I was your boss, he was *my* boss . . . hell, the fact that you were screwing both of us was kind of funny—'

'Funny?' Callan almost shouted the word.

He looked at her indignantly. 'What are you getting so worked up about? Of course we talked about you. Everybody talked about you.'

Callan's eyes filled with easy tears. 'You know what, Marc?' she said, getting to her feet. She grabbed her bag off the back of the chair. 'You can be such a . . . a prick,' she said hotly, ignoring the alarmed look the waiter who had hurried forwards threw at him. 'Such a *prick*,' she repeated, thrusting her arms awkwardly into her coat. 'I never discussed you with *anyone*.'

Marc threw his hands up in despair. 'Why would you? It's not like I was screwing *your* best friend, *chérie*. No, that's your department.'

'You arsehole!' Callan hissed, staring down at him from her momentary advantage of height. 'You absolute arsehole!'

Marc laughed. He too was angry. She could see it in his face. 'Christ, if I wanted to be an arsehole, Callan, there's a lot more I could have said, you know.'

The fear that was dancing lightly all over her skin ceased suddenly, replaced by the hot flush of shame. An image of herself came to her. The interior of the club, the music, the thick pall of smoke, the oily, cloying scent of drugs. And the bodies, slick with sweat. She could feel her eyes fill with cold, heavy tears. What desperate lengths she'd gone to, she thought to herself miserably, to escape. She blinked, once, very slowly and then she picked up her coat and left.

62

LINDI

Despite her height, she was only a scrap of a thing, really, Lindi thought to herself as Tara walked onto the stage. She was so slight and with that boyish haircut that made her look even younger, she looked as though the wind might blow her away. There was a smattering of applause but it was clear she was neither the star speaker nor a particularly important one. Lindi felt a pang of sympathy as she fumbled with the microphone, trying to adjust it to her height. Finally it was done. She shuffled her papers and Lindi could see that her hands were shaking. But when she opened her mouth, her voice suddenly took on an authority that her posture didn't yet have and as she went on, her shoulders straightened, she lifted her head and looked people straight in the eye. She was utterly transformed. *The civilising mission was one of the very few aspects of the nineteenth- and twentieth-century colonial tradition that Hitler rejected, and in this regard, art played an important role.* Lindi stole a sideways look at the woman sitting next to her; she was listening intently. Tara spoke for just over half an hour and when she finished, there were more hands raised than Lindi had seen in any of the sessions all weekend.

'Well done!' Lindi was one of the first to greet her as she came off the podium. 'That was brilliant!'

'Really?' Tara looked at her suspiciously.

'Really,' Lindi said firmly. 'Didn't you notice how many questions people had? Everyone loved your talk. *Everyone.*'

Tara looked as though she might faint. All the confidence she'd displayed up there had evaporated. 'I was just praying they wouldn't get bored,' she whispered as she allowed Lindi to lead her away from the assembled group, many of whom looked as if they'd like to ask her further questions still.

'God, for someone so bright, you're absolutely clueless,' Lindi murmured, pushing her purposefully towards the door. 'Come on, it's nearly five. We've got time for a quick drink before I have to meet Manthia. There's a bar across the road. I have a feeling you'll be swamped as soon as you get back.'

*

'So,' Tara said after taking her first sip of wine. The colour had returned to her cheeks, Lindi noticed. 'Was it all right, d'you think?'

'More than all right,' Lindi said, raising her own glass. 'You're bloody good. You should come out to Namibia and visit, you know. Give a talk to the university. You already know a heck of a lot more about the place than most people, including those of us who live there.'

'Oh, that's just academic stuff. No one's that interested. But yes, I'd love to,' she added, almost shyly. 'Anneliese would probably enjoy it. From some of the images I saw when I was doing the research, I think it'd appeal to her . . . the colours, the landscape, that sort of thing.'

'Well, you must ask her. I'd love to have you visit. And her daughter? What's her name again?'

'Callan. Yeah, *she'd* love it.' There was an odd note in Tara's voice.

Lindi looked at her sharply but decided against saying anything. 'How long did you say you'd be in New York for?' she asked instead.

'Until Sunday.' Tara held up her wine glass to the light. 'I fly back on Sunday night. I'm glad this bit's over, though.'

'Why don't you come round and have lunch with us on Sunday? We can easily drive you to the airport.'

Tara looked shyly pleased. 'Are you sure?'

'Course I'm sure. Why d'you keep asking?' Lindi laughed. 'I wouldn't have invited you if I wasn't sure. So you'll come?'

Tara nodded. 'Yes, I'd love to.'

'Good. I'll come and fetch you from the hotel. Cheers. Here's to your talk. Well done.'

'Cheers.' Tara touched her glass lightly. 'And you must come to London. Anneliese and Callan would love to meet you, I'm sure.'

'I'll drink to that.'

63

ANNELIESE

For a long time after the door closed behind Callan, Anneliese continued to sit at her desk, occasionally bringing up a hand to her cheek, smoothing away the evidence of her distress until it was gone. The evening light deepened, darkened, until she sat in almost complete blackness. Then she roused herself, switched on her desk lamp and got up to close the curtains. The folder with all the financial information that Callan had come in to talk to her about was still lying on the glass desktop. She looked at it for a moment, then opened it. She drew out the pages carefully and set them in order. Then she fished her glasses out of the drawer, sat down in her swivel leather chair and began to read.

It took her almost an hour to go through everything, a task that would have taken Callan five minutes, she thought to herself wryly as she turned over the last page. She let out a deep sigh. Callan was right. They *were* in trouble. She took off her glasses and stroked the spot between her eyebrows in an unconscious gesture that hovered somewhere between despair and concentration. As she replaced them, an image of her father suddenly floated into view. It was a gesture she'd seen him make a thousand times before. She gave a little shudder. How many years had it been since *he'd* popped into her head? She hurriedly put her glasses back on and pulled out one of her ruled notepads. She began to write quickly, then furiously, pausing every now and then to chew absently at the side of a fingernail as she thought something through, and then bent her head back down again.

It was well after midnight when she finally stopped, laying her pencil to one side and leaning back in her chair. She'd been in her study since mid-afternoon and, aside from a single cup of tea that Mrs Betts had brought her earlier in the evening, she'd had nothing to eat or drink. She switched off the lights, pushed her chair in neatly against her desk and closed the door. She wandered into the kitchen, yawning, and pulled open the fridge. There was a half-bottle of wine on one of the shelves and a small piece of Parmesan cheese. She poured herself a glass, nibbling at the cheese and sat down at the kitchen table. It was so quiet, only the faint hum of the refrigerator audible above the occasional creak of the house as it settled into sleep. At the top of the stairs was the door to Mrs Betts's private apartment, a pretty, three-roomed home that had been carved out of the attic space and in which she'd lived for almost twenty years. Callan would be in her flat a few streets away, or so she assumed. And Tara was in New York, at some conference or another. She'd been so excited to receive the invitation, though she'd done her best not to show it.

Anneliese smiled faintly to herself. She and Tara were so alike; they understood one another on a level that both found hard to explain. At times, when she was in the middle of explaining something to Tara or listening to her talk, she had the distinct impression she was talking to herself. Did she love Tara? She shook her head. She *liked* her and would have done almost anything *for* her, but the emotions Tara brought out in her were nothing like those that Callan generated. She felt suddenly faint. Her love for Callan, which she acknowledged she had never, ever been able to show, was all-consuming, all-powerful, capable of bringing her to her knees. When she was born and she'd looked at the small, perfectly formed dark head and those intense dark eyes, she'd had to stuff her fist in her mouth to stop herself crying out. *That* was a love so strong it could bring her straight out of the deepest sleep at the merest whimper from the cot beside her and catapult her into a place of such fear at the thought of never seeing her bright little face again that she was afraid to close her eyes lest they remain that way. *That* love knocked her down, turned her sideways, made a fool of her – and in front of her own child. *That* love was too powerful to contain or explain. *That* love threatened to undo her.

So she suppressed it instead. And now, thirty years after she'd first felt it, despite her best efforts to lock and chain it, it had broken loose again. Only this time there was an added element of pain. Thirty years ago Callan's only instinct had been to reach out, greedily grasping towards Anneliese and the source of the warmth she sought. Now she had turned away from her and Anneliese knew she'd left it too late.

She got up from the kitchen table and rinsed out her glass. In moments like these she knew of only one thing that would help her manage the pain. Work. It was all she knew to do.

64

REE

'It's the perfect fit. Look, I know it's probably not the sort of work you're looking for. I mean, designing a few clothes shops is hardly going to win you prizes, but there's something about taking all of this –' Anneliese waved her hand behind her, gathering up her exquisitely designed surroundings – 'to the mass market. Why *shouldn't* good design be affordable?'

Ree caught his lower lip between his teeth, studying the pale buff sheets spread between them on Anneliese's desk. She was right. Designing clothes shops wasn't exactly what he'd been seeking for the past few years but he rather liked the way she phrased it. Design for the masses; *good* design. A collaboration between the high-street retailer Moda, and A*d*SP. It was a bold gesture. Then again, in the relatively short time that he'd known Anneliese, she'd never been anything but bold. 'So what's in it for you? Apart from more work, of course,' he asked her thoughtfully.

Anneliese got up from her chair and walked towards the window. 'It's not just about more work,' she said slowly. 'Although we could certainly use it. I've rather buried my head in the sand over the past couple of years and we're in more trouble

330

than I think I ever realised. Or wanted to realise. But this is not just about saving the company. It's about a challenge, a new direction. It'll give me more clout with the textile manufacturers. I'll be able to buy and demand fabrics in much greater quantities and that makes me much more interesting from their point of view. More volume means more influence with them; it's that simple.'

'But that's not the only reason, is it?'

Anneliese smiled. 'No, you're right. I like the idea of taking what we've learned over the last thirty years to a different market. Don't get me wrong – I'll always appreciate the kind of client who spends two thousand pounds on a jacket but I like the challenge of producing a jacket for twenty pounds that's equally well made.'

'Me too.' Ree nodded in agreement. 'I suppose it's exactly what the Modern Movement was all about – bringing good design to the masses. Just as you said. So where do I come in?'

'Well, here's the thing. I spoke to Dirk Theunissen this morning in Stockholm. He's the new chief executive officer of Moda. Now, his idea is just to have a section of their existing stores where the designs are sold but I want to do something different.'

'Like what?'

Anneliese walked back to the table. 'I want the collaboration to be something special in its own right; I want it to be *different*. I don't just want to stick a few cheaper clothes onto some shelf somewhere in an existing Moda store. I want to create something new.'

Ree nodded thoughtfully. He was beginning to enjoy the conversation. 'You're talking about creating a new brand, not just a spin-off . . . you're talking about making a new store.'

'Yes, a brand that's about more than just a T-shirt or a new pair of jeans. It's a way of *thinking* about design, about quality and creativity, collaboration . . . all the reasons why I went into fashion in the first place.' Anneliese's voice had taken on an unexpected warmth. 'Look, I'm a textile engineer, not really a fashion designer. I couldn't care less about the latest "look" or the newest must-have bag. I design clothes for a particular type of woman and now I want to see if I can extend my own range without compromising it.'

Ree nodded again. 'So you're talking about a new store, a new *kind* of store, yes?'

'*Exactly*.' Anneliese's expression was triumphant. 'That's exactly it.'

'How much time do we have?'

'As little or as much as we need. It's more important to me to get it right than it is to start selling ten-pound T-shirts.'

'What does Callan think of it all?' Ree was aware of the slight quickening of his pulse.

'I haven't told her yet. I haven't told anyone. I wanted to discuss it with you, first. She'll be furious, of course, but—' Anneliese shrugged. 'I need to be sure it's the right thing to do.'

Ree nodded. 'What's the next step?'

'We need to come up with a design. *You* need to come up with a design. That's if you want the job, of course,' she added.

Ree grinned. 'Of course I want the job. But you knew that all along.' They looked at each other and grinned. There was still an easy distance between them that they both enjoyed but they were both aware that this next move would signal a new closeness that hadn't existed before. A new relationship was developing and for the moment neither knew quite where it would lead. Yes, there was the matter of the new stores to be designed and the professional, rational side of his brain took stock of it, and was pleased. But, as always, there was another, more subtle thrill to be had at the thought of working with Anneliese, building something with her, rather than for her . . . and yes, he had to admit it, he thought to himself as he put away his pencil and notebook and followed her out of the boardroom, there was the secret, suppressed thrill that came from knowing himself to be bound ever more tightly to Callan. He was on dangerous, unstable ground but he couldn't help it. He'd done everything he could since Dubai to push the very thought of her as far away from his consciousness as he could – but it was no use. She surfaced when he least expected it and there didn't seem to be a damned thing he could do about it. She was there, always.

'Come down to Croombe,' Anneliese said to him as the maid fetched his coat. 'Come for the weekend. Bring the family. Let's lock ourselves away and thrash some ideas out. Let me know when you're free and I'll organise it.'

Ree nodded, slipping on his coat. 'I'm in Zurich this weekend – maybe the one after?'

'I'll set everything up. Give my best to Hayley. The campaign posters are nearly ready, by the way. She looks great.'

Ree said nothing. Thankfully, his dark skin prevented a blush from staining his cheeks. He shook hands with Anneliese and turned to go. There was something unsettling about hearing Hayley's name in Anneliese's mouth. It was just another little reminder of the web of relationships that were being spun around him, between them. He shoved his hands in his pockets and walked quickly towards the park. It was cold but he needed something to clear his head. It was full. Of things he would rather not think about.

65

CALLAN

It was a peace offering and Callan recognised it as such. But the invitation to come down to Croombe d'Abitot for a whole weekend took her by surprise. 'For the whole weekend?' she asked, hoping the sudden panic she felt wasn't evident in her voice.

'Why not?' Anneliese sounded surprised.

'No, nothing. It's just . . . you hate having people to stay.'

'That's not true,' Anneliese said mildly. 'I often have people to stay.'

'But children? What's there for a child to do at Croombe?'

'Oh, children love it down there. Besides, Hayley'll be there. She'll find something to amuse them with.'

'Er, yes.' Callan had no desire to speak about Hayley. Her pulse had quickened. She wasn't sure which was worse – the thought of a weekend with Ree, or a weekend with Ree *and* his wife and kids. It had been almost a month since their trip to Dubai and, as if by some silent, tacit agreement, they hadn't spoken. Not once. But not speaking to or seeing him had done little to stop her thinking about him – if anything, it made things worse. She hadn't so much as touched him but he was under her skin in a way no one had ever been. It was disconcerting and yet she found herself constantly longing for more.

'There's something else,' Anneliese said suddenly. 'There's something I'd like to share with you and Ree Herz . . . just an idea I've had. Will you come?' her voice was softer than it had been in years.

'I'm sorry, Maman.' Callan was suddenly contrite. At the sound of Ree's name her heart contracted. 'Of course I'll come. Shall I ask Tara to come? She's been back almost a fortnight and I just haven't had the time to catch up yet. It'll be nice.'

'Yes, come together. Bruno and Jasper are coming as well. We'll have a lovely dinner together on Saturday night.'

'The whole family,' Callan added with a smile. 'I'd better go,' she said quickly before Anneliese said anything further about Ree. 'I'll see you next weekend.' She hung up the phone and put a calming hand on her chest.

66

HAYLEY
Croombe d'Abitot

Clusters of thick, furry oak trees, their branches still bare; low, stone walls, covered in yellowing clumps of moss; fields thick with the white, hoary skin of frost . . . the countryside slid by soundlessly. As Ree drove next to her, Hayley's mind continued on its usual merry-go-round; the mild squabbling of the girls in the back seat; the calm, measured voice of the broadcaster; the piped, soothing music. All contrasting nicely with the shrill, insistent clamouring in her own head. *He's having an affair. He's having an affair. He's having an affair.* At times she wondered if she'd ever *not* worried about the fact that Ree was going to leave her. The refrain had become so much a part of the inner landscape of her thoughts that when it actually happened – as she was sure it would – she wouldn't be surprised. Perhaps that was why she couldn't let go of the thought? She was indirectly protecting herself.

'No, it's *mine.*' Ottie's voice broke out from the back seat.

'No, it's not. It's *mine.* You *had* yours – Mum?'

'Cut it out, you two,' Ree spoke before she could. 'Any more whining and I'll stop the car and you can walk the rest of the way.'

'Ree!' Hayley turned her head to look at him in surprise. She was the one who usually lost her temper with the girls, not him.

'They've been at it since we left London. I'm not having the weekend ruined,' he said, not taking his eyes off the road.

'They won't. You won't fight, will you, girls?' She turned round to look at them.

Neither spoke. Zoë looked obstinately out of the window. Hayley recognised the defiant tilt of her chin; it was her own. She brought her gaze carefully back to the window. They came off the M50 and turned onto the A38. *Ripple. Uckinghall. Naunton. Hill Croombe. Earl's Croombe.* The signs came at them, swimming blurrily into view, then slipping quickly past. They drove through the tiny village of Kinnersley, then under the bulky motorway, and then suddenly, they were there. *Croombe d'Abitot.* 'Turn left, one hundred metres. Turn right.' The impossibly artificial voice of the satnav reached her ears. Ree did as he was directed.

'Well, I guess this is it,' he said, turning down a small, oak-lined lane. The hedges on either side made a sharp noise like a fingernail on a blackboard and then the road widened out. There was a small gatehouse and a sign, *Private Property. Keep Out.* He stopped the car at the gate and got out. Hayley watched him push it open and pick up a stone to keep it so. 'All right, you two?' he asked as he got back in the car, turning his head to look briefly at the girls.

'Yes, Dad,' they chorused, all smiles.

'Is this it?' Ottie asked, sitting up very straight.

'Looks like it, doesn't it?'

'Does Callan have a horse?' Zoë asked, the question slicing through Hayley like a knife.

'I think so.' Ree nodded as he negotiated the car through the gate.

In spite of the stab of jealousy tearing through her, Hayley had to gasp as the house floated into view. The drive was a long, slow circular route around an immaculate lawn. At one end, perhaps half a mile off, was a small red brick tower with a skin of dark green ivy clinging to its walls. The folly was directly on axis with the front door, a huge, polished oak affair, flanked on both sides by stone balustrades and a delicate, wrought-iron and glass loggia. The house itself was massive, with at least two wings leading off the main entrance in perfect symmetry. 'Bloody hell,' Hayley muttered as she opened her door. In the back, the girls were clamouring to be released. She opened the door and helped Ottie out of her seat belt. 'It's huge,' she murmured, half to herself.

'Can I ride Callan's horse, Mum?' Zoë begged as Ree opened her door.

'We'll see. Come on. We'll sort out the bags later.' Ree's voice was firm.

'Ree. Hayley.' Anneliese suddenly appeared at the top of the stairs. 'It's good to see you. And you, girls.'

All four of them trooped up the steps, still awed by the beauty of her country home.

'Nice place, Anneliese,' Ree said as they drew level. 'We'd have dressed up if we'd known.'

Anneliese smiled. 'Don't be silly. We're all very informal here.'

'I doubt that.' Ree smiled back at her. Hayley was again struck by the tone of teasing banter into which the two of them always lapsed. There was a familiarity between them that on the surface seemed almost absurd. Anneliese simply wasn't a person whom you could tease – and yet Ree teased her, *and* she seemed to enjoy it.

'Hayley, welcome. How nice of you to come.' Anneliese extended a hand.

'Th . . . thank you for the invitation,' Hayley stammered, blushing like a schoolgirl. Anneliese always inspired a mixture of awe and dread in her, as if she were little older than her own children. It was partly down to the fact that she was her employer, after all, and the one who'd single-handedly rescued her from ex-model obscurity and that awful, awful dinner party line, 'I used to be—'. She was no longer a *has-been*. The first of the Malcolm's Bay campaign pictures were now in the magazines. In a month's time, they'd be on billboards across the capital. Six months later, they'd be in stores around the world. The agency had already spoken to her about the next campaign. In other words, it was all going swimmingly. Whatever else might be going through her head this weekend, all she had to do was not fuck it up. Easier said than done.

She looked around her nervously. Unlike the London home and the apartment she'd visited very briefly in Paris, Anneliese's English country home looked exactly like an English country home should. It had none of the austere, minimalist look of her other homes and shops – Croome d'Abitot was old, tasteful, elegant and surprisingly warm. There were thick, richly patterned Persian rugs everywhere, dark, polished wood panelling, plush furnishings, a mixture of antiques and some contemporary pieces specially chosen to blend in. There were artworks everywhere but a refreshing absence of those dreadful *objets d'art* that country homes were perpetually stuffed with. Child-friendly, Hayley noted automatically. No priceless vases to knock over.

'Hello! You're here!'

Hayley turned. Callan was standing in the doorway. She felt her stomach give a sudden, unpleasant lurch. She'd been out riding. Her hair was tousled; the colour was up in her cheeks. She looked as though she'd been caught in the middle of some splendid, exhilarating activity. Next to her, despite her tan, Hayley felt dull and washed out. She felt her mouth stretch in an automatic smile; her eyes were fixed on Ree. If she'd expected him to give some sign – of what, she wondered fleetingly to herself – she was disappointed. He smiled politely, his hands on the shoulders of the two girls. There was nothing in his manner or voice to suggest *anything* . . . but what did she expect? That he'd announce it?

'Do come in,' Anneliese said, ushering them in. 'Bruno and Jasper are already here and Tara's on her way down. But watch out. Callan's already had her claws into Jasper. Poor man was up at dawn riding.'

'Dad, can *we* go riding? Please?' The excitement in Zoë's voice was almost painful to hear.

'Of course you can,' Callan answered before Hayley could even open her mouth.

'We'll talk about it later, girls,' Hayley said warningly, flashing Ree a look of annoyance. How dare the girl answer for her?

'There's a pony that'd be perfect for her, and the horses are really gentle,' Callan said, catching the look. 'D'you ride?' she asked Hayley.

'No,' Hayley said shortly.

'Mum's afraid of horses,' Zoë supplied helpfully.

'Yes, she got bitten when she was a little girl.' Ottie, loyal as ever, chimed in.

'They'll be perfectly safe with me,' Callan said, smiling at them. Zoë was captivated by her; Hayley could see it. Her stomach gave another, sour lurch.

'Dad can come, can't you, Dad? *He* can ride,' Zoë said eagerly. Hayley felt as though she might burst into tears. They'd only been in the place five minutes and already everything was ruined.

She caught Zoë's eye and only just managed to resist the urge to slap her. Some of the resentment she felt must have registered on her face; Zoë flinched involuntarily, turning instinctively towards Ree. A memory burst through the surface of Hayley's consciousness like a firework. She was eleven years old. Michel Feucht, Ghislaine's fourth husband, was sitting at the dinner table, eating. Hayley and her older half-sister, Sandrine, were on either side of Ghislaine. Michel was a charmer; the girls competed with one another to make him laugh. 'I'm thirsty,' he announced, halfway through the meal. All three – Hayley, Sandrine and Ghislaine – jumped up. Hayley reached the fridge first. Just as she closed her hand around the bottle of Evian, Ghislaine prised it out of her grasp. She flashed the two young girls a nastily triumphant smile and vanished back to the dining room, clutching the bottled water like a trophy. Sandrine and Hayley looked uncertainly at one another – what was the meaning of it? They were too young to understand. Hayley was left with the uncomfortable, gnawing suspicion that she'd either done something wrong, or lost. Years later the scene – and the look she'd been given – came back to haunt her. Was her mother trying to compete with her own children? Why? The look of incomprehension on Zoë's face brought her up suddenly short. What was she *thinking*? She moved forward quickly to give Zoë a hug but the child had already slipped out of reach.

67

CALLAN

There was a side of her that wanted to erupt into one of the temper tantrums she'd been so famous for as a three or four year old before Anneliese had ground such behaviour out of her. She listened to her mother outlining her plans for the coming year or two with a sense of outrage and stunned disbelief. A new line? A*d*SP for the *masses*? She could scarcely believe her ears. Since when had Anneliese ever been interested in the *masses*? It was only the sight of Ree sitting opposite her, his eyes flashing her a warning that she found oddly calming that stopped her. *Don't*, he seemed to be saying. *Hear her out. Hear us out.* That same side of her that wanted to scream was also struggling to contain the wave of jealousy that swept over her when it became clear that Anneliese *had* discussed her ideas with someone – just not her. She and Ree had clearly found time to talk it through – why had they both kept it a secret from her?

Still, as angry as she was, she couldn't help but be impressed by the way both he and Anneliese spoke. There was nothing triumphant in his approach. When it was his turn to speak, he laid out a number of ideas, carefully seeking her opinion, drawing her into the conversation in a way that Anneliese, with her legendary brusqueness, couldn't, or wouldn't. This market, Ree seemed to be saying, was the market that Callan, more than he or Anneliese, understood. What did she think?

'It's a good idea,' she said finally, hoping her voice was steady. 'But it's risky.'

'In what way?' Ree looked at her and smiled faintly. He'd brought her round, he could see that.

'Well, pairing up with someone's exactly what you *didn't* want to do when the Matuzzis stepped in. I thought you'd sooner cut off your right hand than allow them to take creative control . . . and now here you are, talking about merging with *Moda*? I mean, you couldn't have chosen anyone less . . . less . . .' She struggled to come up with an appropriate metaphor. She looked at Anneliese helplessly. To her surprise, Anneliese was smiling. She was actually enjoying this!

'But that's the whole point, Callan! The women who buy A*d*SP will go on buying A*d*SP for the rest of their lives – and their daughters' lives too. We've spent a quarter of a century building up a clientele who'll follow me to the grave—'

'Don't say that,' Callan broke in sharply. She was alarmed to feel a tiny tremor of fear rolling up her spine.

Anneliese looked surprised. 'Why not? It's true. I can't go on for ever. No one does. And I like the idea of a new challenge, especially now.'

'I think it's a great idea,' Ree said quietly, breaking in. 'Anneliese and I talked about it briefly and we both agree it's a return to the principles you started out with – great, affordable design. Yes, A*d*SP's done fantastically well . . . I mean, it's bought all of this—' He looked around the wonderfully comfortable living room where they sat. 'But beyond that, this is an opportunity and a challenge to see if it'll work at the other end of the scale. Personally, I can't think of anything more exciting that's happened in fashion in the last decade. Not', he added with a self-deprecating smile, 'that I follow what happens in the fashion world. But you know what I mean.'

Callan had to hand it to him. He spoke with such quiet, easy confidence that whomever he was speaking to was seduced. He sat opposite her, a pencil in his left hand – he was left-handed, she noticed suddenly – idly drawing out an idea, a word. It was exactly what Anneliese did. She felt a sudden rush of warmth. In spite of her reservations and the unexpected anger that had surfaced as soon as Anneliese announced her plans, an excitement was slowly taking hold. There was a deal to be made. Negotiations to be struck. The game was on. 'So how far along are you?' she asked Anneliese.

'Not very far. I had dinner with Dirk Theunissen on Thursday. You remember Dirk, don't you? He likes the idea, of course; who wouldn't? It's one of those – what do you call them?' She looked at Callan with amusement. 'A win-win situation, isn't that what you always say?'

Callan blinked slowly. 'Not yet. We don't know what their wish list is going to be, or what sort of control they'll want to retain. Like I said, I didn't think pairing up was exactly your style.'

'It's not. But pairing's not always about sharing, I've come to realise. I'm not *sharing* control – far from it. But I am keen to move beyond my comfort zone; isn't that something you're always lecturing me about?'

To say she was surprised was an understatement. Callan was shocked. She'd been in the room less than fifteen minutes and already Anneliese had said three or four things that Callan had never expected to come out of her mouth. A partnership. A downmarket partnership at that. An admission that sometimes Callan was right. No, make that *two* admissions . . . she stared at her mother incredulously, wondering what on earth had brought it all about. She caught Ree's eye; he seemed to be trying to tell her something. She frowned. His fingers made a swift, small sideways gesture. *Leave it alone. Don't push.* She nodded imperceptibly. She was astounded. He had her measure, as well as her mother's. Was there nothing he missed?

It took the three of them a further hour and a half to thrash out a set of mutually agreed-upon objectives and some idea of the way forward. Anneliese was right; there was everything to be gained from the partnership, but only if they handled it correctly. It was almost eleven thirty by the time they finished. Callan was tired but exhilarated. She got up, shoving her hands in her pockets. She touched something hard and cold, but silky at the same time. Her fingers skirted round it – it was the earring she'd found in the apartment in Paris.

'Oh . . . look! I found this,' she exclaimed, drawing it out. 'In the apartment in Paris. It was lying on the floor in your room,' she said, omitting the fact that she'd actually found it in Anneliese's bed. Her mother would not take kindly at all to the idea that she'd been lying on her bed, in her room, snooping around. 'Someone must have dropped it. Don't know why they'd have gone into your room, though, but here . . . it's pretty.'

Anneliese looked at it and suddenly the colour drained from her face. She held out her hand. 'H-how unusual,' she said as Callan let the ornate, oddly feminine piece of jewellery fall into her palm.

'That's what *I* thought. I knew it wasn't yours. I just popped in your room to make sure everything was okay.'

'It's fine. I . . . there were so many guests last month.' Her voice trailed off. She quickly slipped the earring into her jacket pocket and gathered up her things. 'I . . . I need to speak to Bruno.' She disappeared before either of them could say anything further. Callan watched her go, puzzled. There'd been the faintest whiff of something familiar emanating from her – what was it? She caught her lower lip between her teeth, frowning in concentration. An expression, a gesture, a sign, she realised suddenly, that she herself often made. Absurd as it sounded, it was almost as though Anneliese had been caught out. That oddly feminine lowering of the eyelids, a surprised kind of bashfulness. She shook her head. What on earth could Anneliese have to be bashful about?

'Fancy a walk?' Ree asked as the door closed behind Anneliese. 'She's probably on her way to talk to Bruno.'

Callan nodded slowly. She sensed there would be some soothing of ruffled feathers to be done. Bruno, until Ree's unexpected appearance, would have been the first person she turned to, not the last. But things had changed. For one thing, Ree was in no way beholden to Anneliese as Bruno was; that made a difference. Power, and the myriad, mysterious ways it worked between people had always been an endless source of fascination for Callan – in Ree and Anneliese's odd, new relationship a different power play was at work, one she hadn't quite worked out. Their relationship was unlike any other she'd ever seen. It both fascinated and frightened her simultaneously. 'Sounds good,' she murmured, wondering where Hayley was.

'I need to clear my head . . . and there's something I want to ask you,' Ree said quietly,

Callan nodded. 'I'll just get my coat,' she said, moving towards the kitchens and the huge room halfway down the stairs to the cellar which was where all their outdoor gear was stowed. She re-emerged a few minutes later in a dark green Barbour coat – she had no idea who it belonged to, but it seemed to fit! – a pair of shiny black wellington boots and a striped Paul Smith scarf which she wound tightly around her neck. It wasn't raining – for once – but it was cold outside and the ground was muddy.

'Ready?' he asked, smiling down at her. Without her customary four-inch heels she felt even smaller than usual. She barely came up to his shoulder. 'Where d'you suggest we go?'

'There's a copse down by the river, on the other side of the driveway. It's about an hour's walk, all in all. It's beautiful down there. We'll pass the neighbour's horses . . . come on, I'll show you.' She led him through the kitchens where the housekeeper and her two harried-looking assistants were already busy preparing the evening meal. They went out the back door. It wasn't yet noon but the sun was hidden behind a dull, grey sky that parted every now and then to reveal a flash of blue, then closed swiftly lest anyone be fooled. The light was pearly and washed out and there was a bluish frost on the gatepost as she swung it open. They tramped away from the house and its carefully tended lawns towards the open fields and the cluster of trees nestled in the valley between the two low hills of the neighbouring farms.

'Nothing quite like the English countryside,' Ree said quietly, standing back to let her go through the stile. 'Reminds me of boarding school.'

'I'd rather forget boarding school.'

'Why? Didn't you enjoy it?'

Callan shook her head. 'No, not really. And it was mostly my decision. Not to like it, I mean. Oh, it wasn't all bad. I met Tara.'

'What's her story?' Ree asked curiously.

'What d'you mean?'

He said nothing for a few minutes as they walked alongside the hedgerow wall that separated Croombe d'Abitot from the neighbouring farm. 'It must be hard for her,' he said after a moment. 'Being part of the family and yet not, if you see what I mean.'

'No, I don't. She *is* part of the family,' Callan said, a touch of defensiveness creeping into her voice.

Ree was quiet again. Suddenly he stopped. 'There's something I've been meaning to ask you,' he said, shoving his hands in his pockets. He looked down at her and, as ever, his expression was impossible to read.

'What?' Callan asked, aware of her quickening pulse.

'Don't you find it . . . I don't know . . . a bit odd?' he asked. He was frowning.

'Odd? What d'you mean, odd?'

He bit his lip, as if choosing his words with care. 'The way she never speaks about anything,' he said hesitantly. 'Anneliese, I mean. She's so guarded.'

'She's not *guarded*, she's just . . . it's just the way she is. Why does it matter?'

He looked away from her, over the hedge to where the horses in the next field stood, the air blowing white from their nostrils as they shrugged their glossy, light-rippled coats in the cold. She could almost feel their warmth. 'Where's she from?' he asked abruptly.

'What are you talking about?'

'Do you know anything about her?'

She felt an unaccustomed anger slowly begin to burn its way up through her limbs. 'What's there to know?' she asked, perhaps more sharply than she intended, for she saw him draw his head back quickly, as though he'd been pushed. 'She's my mother, that's all there is to it. I don't care about the rest.'

'Hey, I didn't mean to upset you—'

'You haven't,' Callan said tightly, shoving her own hands in her pocket. She began to walk away from him.

He caught up with her easily. Taking her arm, he pulled her gently to a halt. 'I'm sorry. It was rude of me. There's just something that doesn't quite . . . I don't know . . . add up, somehow. I'm just being nosy, that's all.'

She found herself inexplicably torn; on the one hand, the unexpected criticism of Anneliese had roused a protectiveness in her that she'd never thought herself capable of, and yet on the other, Ree had given voice to something that had so long been dormant in her she'd forgotten its presence. He was right. Of course he was right. There was something strange and often disconcerting in Anneliese's behaviour. The way she never spoke about her past; the way she'd scrupulously pushed all sentimentality aside, not because it wasn't in her nature, Callan was beginning to suspect, but because she couldn't afford it. But *why*? Ree's somewhat clumsy questioning had awoken the slumbering desire in her to know more – to know everything – and it frightened her because she knew that an answer would never come. She put up a hand to her cheek; it was warm, despite the cold. She could hear her own voice, shaking slightly, as she tried to brush it off. 'No, you're not being rude. It's just . . . she won't, you know. She won't ever say. I spent half my childhood wondering about things. All sorts of things.'

'Who your father was?' Ree asked quietly, his eyes searching her face.

Callan nodded. There was a hard, painful lump in her throat. 'She'd sooner die than say,' she said slowly. 'Oh, when I was younger . . . I must have driven her mad.'

'It's only natural,' Ree said gently. 'Of course you want to know.'

Callan couldn't speak for a moment. 'You're right,' she sighed. 'There's always been something strange about her, about all of us. Me, Bruno, Tara . . . the way she keeps us all so close and yet so far . . .' She put out a hand, as if trying to express the distance Anneliese kept between herself and everyone around her. 'You're right.'

'Is it because something happened, I wonder?' Ree asked, though it wasn't really a question.

Callan shook her head. 'Don't think I haven't asked myself the same thing,' she said, still looking at the horses opposite them. 'But I couldn't tell you. There's nothing I can tell you. She's a completely closed book. Always has been, always will be, I suppose.'

'And you?'

'Me?'

'Are you the same? I hardly know anything about you.'

Callan was aware of some new, shifting territory opening up between them. She didn't want to meet his eye. She looked away again, over the icy fields and the neat, meandering stone walls that ran up one side of the hill, disappearing beyond the line of vision that was the horizon, frowning as if she might find some answer there. 'There's nothing to know,' she said as lightly as she could. 'And no, I'm not like her.' A strong consciousness of herself flooded through her suddenly, like a drug. The sun came out briefly and the air around them was lit with a weak, lemony light that faded almost as quickly as it had appeared. She glanced up at him and the tender expression on his face made her want to turn and run. They stood together for a few minutes, not touching, not saying anything, both acutely aware of the other, a spark, like static electricity, running backwards and forwards between them. Her stomach churned; he had stirred up so much inside her that she usually tried to suppress.

When was the last time anyone had asked her anything about herself? *I hardly know anything about you.* No one wanted to know anything about her – at least not the bits that counted. She was Anneliese Zander de Saint Phalle's daughter; that detail was enough for most. It had always been that way. The first betrayal was at school; she returned that first summer from Mortimer's to find Céline and Amélie and Dominique had simply moved on, moved off. Another girl had taken her place in the quartet of best friends and that was it. She was surplus to requirements. At Mortimer's, if it hadn't been for Tara, she might never have made another friend. Everyone had an *opinion* about her, even – and especially – those who'd never met her. She's rich; stuck-up; spoilt; privileged; snooty . . . the same, tired list of adjectives had followed her around her entire life. People she'd never even met seemed to have something to say on the subject of who Callan de Saint Phalle was, what she was like.

Cambridge was no different. Even if no one ever dared say it aloud, there was always a hesitation over her name. What was she doing at Cambridge? And more damning, how did she get in? The only place she'd ever been free of Anneliese was in New York. That was why she'd gone. And that, too, was the reason behind the club and the friends she'd made and the fact that no one there gave a damn who she was, how much money her mother made, or where and how she lived. At the club *everyone* was rich and therefore no one was. Wealth simply wasn't mentioned and in that rarefied air, she found herself for the first time truly free. Of course much later she realised it wasn't so; she'd simply swapped one set of shackles for another, but she didn't know that then, in the beginning. In the beginning there was only the thrill of being unknown and unjudged with nothing to follow other than her own nose for pleasure, and sometimes pain. She trembled suddenly. Thinking about the club whilst standing next to Ree Herz in a field at the bottom of her mother's property brought on a wave of revulsion that she found almost impossible to swallow. The urge to vomit came upon her without warning; her mouth flooded with saliva and she had to turn away.

'Where're you going?' Ree called after her.

She shook her head, and unable to speak, began to run. The blood rushed to her head as she stumbled, half-falling down the slope towards the trees. Her wellingtons were slightly too large; her toes were being pushed up against the rubber edge as she ran, stumbling over the loose stones and uneven ground. She could feel her heart beating wildly underneath the layers of clothing. She had almost reached the first cluster of trees when she felt the ground thudding behind her. Ree caught her arm, tugging her by the sleeve and whirled her around to face him. 'Leave—' she protested weakly, horrified to hear her own voice catch on a sob.

'What on earth's the matter?' Ree asked, his own breath coming faster and faster. 'Where are you running to?'

'Just leave—' She tried to wrench her arm away but he held it fast.

'Callan? What's wrong? What did I say?'

'No-nothing.' She stumbled over the words. 'Ju-just leave me alone.'

348

'I'm not letting you go until you tell me what I've done.' Ree's voice was gentle but firm. 'And don't tell me it's nothing. You don't just take off like that unless something's wrong.'

He was quick. She saw from the swift glance she gave him that he had caught the panic behind her eyes. He had her by the arm and was slowly pulling her towards him. Closing the gap between them seemed to her to take an age, and then more still. His coat was unbuttoned to the third or fourth button; his sweater underneath was a dark olive green, flecked with yellow. She could feel it against her cheek. Scratchy, but with a warmth that burned through the wool. His hand moved from her arm to the nape of her neck. She closed her eyes. The sensation was so unfamiliar that at first she had difficulty understanding his touch. Was it comforting? Had anyone – a man – *ever* laid his hands on her right there, in that way? His fingers touched her bare skin underneath her scarf and her hair; a whisper of a caress that forced the sob stuck in her throat out into her mouth.

'What's the matter, Callan?' His voice was a soft murmur vibrating against her cheek.

She shook her head again. They were standing so close to one another. His hand was still there at the nape of her neck. There was hardly any pressure but she turned and pressed her face against his chest all the same. A deep sigh of something that felt suspiciously like relief passed between them, as if they'd both been waiting for the moment since they'd first set eyes on each other. Ree dropped his head and kissed her, delicately, but with great passion. She moved closer to that centre of heat that was his body, pushing her arms under the thick blanket of his coat. *I've waited for ever for this*, she kept saying to herself, sinking against his body, her mouth following his, taking the soft flesh of his lips between her teeth with a teasing ferocity that excited them both. *I've waited my whole life for this.*

Ree's head was buried in the deep heat of her neck underneath the tangle of her hair. His breath came out moist and damp against her skin. One hand was flung away from him but the other held her tightly; his eyes were closed but he was not asleep. They were in one of the spare rooms in the attic. No one, except the cleaners, ever came up to the attic and they were all safely on break downstairs. It was almost three o'clock. She felt his tongue, wet and warm, touch the salty dampness of her skin, leaving a trail that felt cool against his breath. She lay there, still stunned by the frenzy of the past half-hour and of everything that had happened. They'd stood under the trees for what seemed like an hour, kissing, teasing, not saying anything. It was she who'd broken the embrace and turned and walked away, knowing he would follow. They walked together in silence up the hill, still not speaking but not touching either. It was two o'clock. The children would be back from their ride any minute; there was no telling where Hayley was, or what she might be doing. At the back door she turned to him and said quietly, 'Meet me upstairs. The staircase at the end of the corridor. Third floor. Wait for about ten minutes.' She walked ahead of him, not waiting for his answer. There was no one in the kitchen, or the hallway, or in any of the rooms she passed alongside. The stairs creaked as she walked upstairs; she heard, somewhere down the corridor, the muffled slam of a door. It was madness, she thought to herself as she slowly made her way to the attic floor. Utter madness. Anyone could come upon them at any moment; down there in the copse, anyone could have seen them. But a fever had come over them both and she was simply incapable of thinking beyond the next few minutes, and the next.

There were three bedrooms in the attic space; she chose the one furthest from the stairs. She pushed open the door and stepped inside. The room was perfectly made up. A small, narrow bed with a simple floral bedspread, plump pillows, a stiff crease running down the centre where it had been pressed, and pressed again. There were two white bedside tables with a glass jar of sweets and a bar of lemon-scented soap in tissue paper which gave off a fresh, spring-like scent. The narrow sloping windows looked back over the fields over which they'd just come. She moved to one of them and looked out over the landscape. She could hear Ree's footsteps on the stairs. She could already recognise his tread. She shivered suddenly and wrapped her arms about her, going to the door.

'In here,' she called out softly as he climbed the last step and appeared in front of her. He was so tall; his head almost touched the low ceiling. He gave a nod and walked towards her. Everything seemed to come to a complete standstill, time and distance compressing narrowly into that moment when he would pull her towards him. She clenched and unclenched her fists. She'd never felt such desire before; as though she were drowning in it. At last he was there, in front of her. She pulled him into the room and closed the door soundlessly behind them. They looked at one another in the now fading light. He put a hand out and pulled away a strand of her hair that had fallen across her face. Slowly, exquisitely slowly so that she thought she would remember every single, precious second of it for the rest of her life, he bent his head and for the second time, kissed her. This time there was no turning away, or back. She pulled his head down towards her with a force that surprised them both. She almost tore his clothes in her haste to peel them away from him so that she could look upon him properly, claiming something she knew wasn't hers. The silence around them was a thick, dense blanket; no sound other than that of their bodies as they slid together, finding each other with a sureness of touch that neither could have foreseen or imagined and yet which filled them both with such sensual delight. 'Callan,' he whispered urgently, just once, seconds before his body raced away from him. She said nothing. Her eyes were closed tightly, her lips silently tracing out his name on her own arm as she tried desperately to muffle her own voice.

'Are you all right?' she whispered, sliding herself down in the narrow bed until they were level. He nodded, but kept his eyes closed. Callan looked at him through the narrowed slits of her own, taking in every detail, every nuance. His hair was dark and lay very close to the scalp. Here and there were small flecks of grey; she felt an odd clutch of fear at her insides. They weren't teenagers and with that realisation came everything that they'd successfully managed to block out for the past hour or so that they'd been locked in their passionate, forbidden world. Somewhere in the grounds of her mother's house were his children. The trembling fear solidified slowly. Was this it?

'You?' he said, turning suddenly, propping himself up on an elbow to look at her. 'You OK?'

She nodded slowly. The falling terror of having come to the end of something that hadn't even properly begun continued to beat against her as the winter outside slowly darkened the room. She wanted to ask that question that she'd never asked anyone before. What happens now? She bit down hard on the impulse instead, perhaps out of some latent, buried fear . . . she might not be able to live with what she heard.

'I don't know what happens next,' he said suddenly, drawing a line across her skin with his finger. Had she spoken aloud? Her hard, flat stomach trembled as he touched her, tracing out some unspoken sentiment. He gave a small, tight smile. 'I know what you're thinking, Callan.' She hadn't spoken, then. He'd guessed at her thoughts – accurately, too – yet again.

She closed her eyes and when she opened her mouth it was as if someone else had spoken. 'I can't manage if this is the end of it, you know,' she said slowly. 'If it's just this once. I won't be able to . . . manage.'

Ree was quiet but his hand continued its slow, steady caress. It seemed like an age before she heard his voice again. 'Is that what you think this is?'

She hesitated, then shook her head. 'No. At least, not for me. But I'm . . . it's easy for me. Well, not easy, but, *easier*? Oh, you know what I mean. I've only myself to think about. There's no one else.'

He nodded. His hand stopped. He pushed himself up until he was leaning against the headboard. 'Christ,' he gave a short, muffled laugh. 'I could really use a cigarette.'

'You smoke?' Callan was surprised.

He shook his head. 'I used to. Gave it up when Hayley—'
He stopped abruptly. 'It's been a while,' he said with a half-apologetic smile. 'But I could do with one right now.'

She nodded. 'Me too.'

He turned to look at her, resting his chin on one hand. 'This has complicated everything,' he said slowly. 'Everything.'

'What are we going to do?'

He sighed and leaned back against the narrow headboard. 'I've no idea. All I know is that I've wanted this since the minute I saw you. I've hardly been able to think about anything else.'

'Me too,' Callan said softly.

'But this is the easy bit. This is nothing.' He turned his head fractionally to look at her. He shook his head slightly, as though he were trying to clear it. 'There'll be hell to pay. But that's my problem . . . let me sort it out.'

'But—'

He put out a hand and touched her cheek lightly. 'Don't,' he said. 'Leave this to me. I'm the one with the . . . complications. Leave them to me to sort out.'

Callan was quiet. It wasn't her way. She was always the one in control, the one who made things happen, who moved things along according to her pace, no one else's. It was the only way she knew how. Anneliese had made sure of it. At the thought of her mother, her stomach actually trembled. What would Anneliese say? She closed her eyes. Ree was right; it *was* complicated. They were bound in more ways than she could count – Hayley, Anneliese, A*d*SP, his children, his job . . . the list went on and on. He'd said he would sort things out. She had to do the one thing that didn't come naturally to her: trust. She had to trust him, and in doing so let *him* work things out.

68

HAYLEY

The sound of the shower woke her up. She struggled upright in bed; her mouth was thick and sour and her head felt like wool. The room was almost dark. She groped for the bedside light and flicked it on, wincing painfully as light hit her eyes. Through the partially open bathroom door she could hear the shower being switched off and the sound of wet feet on the floor.

'Wh . . . what time is it?' she croaked, more to herself than to Ree who was anyway beyond hearing. She peered at her wrist; no watch. She must have taken it off when she took off her clothes and fell into bed. She'd taken two Temazepam tablets just before lunch when it was clear Ree wasn't coming out of the meeting with Anneliese and that little bitch Callan anytime soon. Thankfully one of the gardeners had been only too happy to take the girls riding. She was left alone in the living room listening with half an ear to Bruno bickering mildly with that dreadful boyfriend of his, Jasper – what on *earth* did he see in him? – and flicking desultorily through a stack of magazines. Sod this, she'd thought to herself with an unhappy laugh. She got up, excused herself from the company that didn't even notice her departure and went upstairs. She swallowed two tablets with half a glass of wine (silly, really), peeled off her clothes and climbed into the amazingly soft, comfortable bed. The next thing she knew, the sound of running water had woken her and here she was, patting about on the bedside table, trying to find her watch. Her fingers touched it and she lifted it up with relief. She stared at the face; it was nearly six o'clock! She'd slept for almost six hours straight. Groaning, she put it away from her and tried to sit up. She wouldn't be able to sleep tonight, that was for sure. What was it Bruno had said to her as she left the room? Dinner's at seven. *We dress up*. Well, so did she.

She swung her legs out of bed and stood up, holding onto

the headboard as the blood drained away from her head. She shouldn't have taken *two* tablets. One was enough to knock her out for half a day but two? Crazy, and with that slug of wine, too. She put up a hand to her aching head. A couple of Solpadine, some fizzy water to clear her mouth and a shower, quickly. She had an hour before dinner and she was damned if she was going to appear half-stoned and not looking her absolute best.

'Oh, you're up.' Ree was standing in the doorway, a towel wrapped around his waist. His skin was still wet with beads of water glistening in the light. She looked at him, then away again. There were still times when he made her catch her breath.

'Yeah, I was . . . tired.'

'Where are the girls?'

'I'm not sure. I think they went out riding with one of the gardeners.'

'You *think*?'

She flushed angrily. 'No, I mean they *did* go out with one of the gardeners. They're *fine*, Ree. They're probably downstairs or in the garden or something.'

'It's nearly supper time.' Ree was glaring at her.

'Where the hell were *you* all day anyway?' She decided to change tack. 'Don't tell me you've been in a meeting all day long?'

He didn't answer, as usual. Just looked at her with those dark unfathomable eyes that said everything his words didn't and walked past her. He dropped the towel and with his back to her, began to get dressed. She watched in silence for a few moments. His body had always been such a source of fascination for her, so different from her own. He pulled on a pair of black boxer shorts and picked up a white T-shirt from the neat pile of clothes that were his. His shoulder blades with their finely rounded covering of muscle moved under his smooth, brown skin. His back was still to her as he pulled on a pair of trousers, flexing slightly at the knees as he zipped himself up. She'd seen him dress a thousand times, probably more. There was a damp patch in the small of his back; his T-shirt quickly absorbed the few drops of water that had collected there. She gazed at him. How many times had she run her lips and hands down that beautifully firm, muscular back, stopping there just where the water had pooled, sliding her fingertips further down the swell of his buttocks. She stopped herself, picked up a towel and walked into the bathroom, shutting the door carefully behind her. There was so much sadness in the air; every time she drew breath she tasted it.

69

REE

You little shit. He chastised himself silently. He turned as Hayley closed the bathroom door and the carefully held mask of neutrality that had been his face ever since he stepped out of the shower broke. He put a hand up to his cheek; it was warm with a mixture of anger and shame. He could hear Zoë's voice as the two of them came down the corridor towards their parents' room. She was bossing Ottie around, as usual. He slipped on his jacket and walked to the door to meet them. The next few minutes were taken up with their account of the afternoon's riding activities and how Ottie longed for a pony of her own and how fast Zoë went and how nice Simon the gardener was and how wonderful the whole place was and no, it wasn't cold at all. One of the housekeepers – how many were there? – had bathed and dressed the girls; he tweaked the ribbon she'd threaded in Zoë's hair, not knowing, of course, that she'd take it out the minute the woman's back was turned. Zoë hated decoration of any sort. 'Pretty,' he murmured, looking down at her.

She scowled. 'No, it's not.' She'd obviously forgotten it was there. He helped her take it out. Ottie gazed on the two of them, puzzled as ever by Zoë's fierce rejection of anything even remotely feminine.

'Come on, you two. Mum's getting dressed. Let's go down-stairs and see if we can help Anneliese.'

'Where's Callan?' Zoë asked. 'Simon says she's the best rider in the county. What's a county, Dad?'

He couldn't answer. The sound of Callan's name in his daughter's mouth was enough to end all speech. He gripped both girls by the hand a little harder than he ought to, perhaps, and walked off down the corridor.

Just as it had been that night at Anneliese's London home, the conversation at the table flowed over and around him, passing him by. He heard the words and the laughter but he couldn't have said what anyone talked about, least of all him. This time Hayley sat opposite him and Callan was two seats down to his left. He dared not move his head. For the first hour his focus was on the girls, who were delighted to be the centre of attention; they recounted their afternoon over and over again until he motioned to Hayley that it was long past their bedtime and the housekeeper stepped in. They were led off amidst much laughter and the table settled itself around the adults once more. He listened with half an ear to Anneliese and Bruno. The potential collaboration was the topic of the evening with everyone weighing in, except him. His mind was elsewhere. An affair. He, of all people. The *fact* of it wasn't a surprise. In some ways, the real surprise was that it hadn't happened sooner. And God knows he'd had plenty of opportunities. But it wasn't in his character, somehow. He'd always thought an affair was like an admission of *failure*, some failing on his part to see how things would turn out. He had such a high regard for facing the truth and what he called the facts, however painful they might turn out to be. It was a particular characteristic of his that others had always remarked on, and not always pleasantly. *You're far too hard on yourself.* It was his mother's favourite refrain. Lighten up. As a teenager he'd viewed what he saw as their reluctance to face facts as a weakness.

Later, when he had one or two of his own disappointments to

contend with, he'd softened somewhat, but never where he himself was concerned. Others took the drive to be a sign of ambition but he alone knew the truth; it wasn't born out of ambition, but rather a fear of failure. Years of being the 'only one' – whether at prep school, boarding school, university – had instilled in him a dogged determination never to allow *anyone* the luxury of dismissing him as a fluke, or worse, a fake. At the prep school he'd gone to, he was the only African in a sea of scrubbed pink skins and blue eyes. He'd been an easy target, yet even then was astute enough to realise it wasn't personal. They'd have picked on anyone, regardless of their difference. Fat kids, spotty kids, swotty kids . . . and the black kid. He stood out, that was all. Boarding school was no different.

At prep school he'd been the joker, the funny one. It was his defence and his weapon. At boarding school there were too many other funny kids for him to shine. Another means had to be found – and quickly. Some of the other black kids, the Nigerians and Kenyans who'd also wound up at a boarding school on the Sussex Downs, fell easily into the routes that had been laid out for them – sports, girls, music. Not Ree. He didn't want to compete at *that* level. Anyone can run and grab a ball, he reckoned, or sneak a girl into their room. He wanted something more, something harder that he was strong enough to take hold of and mould in his own way, a standard that he alone could set for himself, and judge. It took him a while to find his niche but when he did no one could touch him. He made sure of that.

The first few years were heady, made more so by his early success. He'd had to work hard not to allow it to go to his head. He knew how fickle the world could be; he'd seen it over and over again. In his case, the upstart outsider who'd slipped in almost unannounced, it would be harder still. All the liberal goodwill in the world still couldn't hide the disbelief in some people's eyes. *Him? He's* the architect? You're trusting *him* with the job? Well, he'd proved them wrong . . . all those who'd done their best to keep him out of the cosy clubs and the networks and the lunches that went on for ever . . . now they begged him. It had taken him nearly fifteen years to beat them at their own game. What was the hardest part? Not the fight or the challenge or the drive to prove them wrong. It was the struggle *not* to let it go to his head. *Not* to get distracted, arrogant, or to take things for granted. He'd had to fight with himself to keep himself level and grounded and interested in things that mattered, not the fame.

Hayley, he saw now, had been a mistake. He'd been at the height of his popularity, fêted by everyone, courted by all. To have her on his arm had confirmed it; there wasn't a man in the room – any room – who didn't look at him enviously, wanting what he alone had. Idiot that he was. Hayley too liked the attention and the dubious distinction of having chosen not another model or actor, as most of her friends did, but an architect. A *serious* person. The joke was that he was no more serious than she was. In their own way, for their own reasons, they'd both been as shallow as each other. Two children later and they were both effectively trapped. He'd resisted the women who'd practically thrown themselves at him over the past decade, not because he didn't find them attractive, but because deep down he'd been afraid of what it might lead him to admit. Until Callan de Saint Phalle walked into the room he'd been able to withstand what at times felt like an assault. She was different. He was in trouble now, and there wasn't a person he could confide in or tell.

He looked up from his plate. Hayley was studying him. He already knew from the look on her face – considering, calculating, careful – that she knew something was up. From now on it was simply a matter of time.

70

ANNELIESE

How little we know each other, especially those we call our own.
She looked down the length of the table to where Callan sat.
Ree's children were led away, protesting faintly as children do,
and suddenly the room was quiet again. Bruno sat to her left in
childish, sulky silence. It had taken her a while to bring him
round, not to the *idea* of their new business venture – theirs was
a long, established partnership; she led, he followed – but to the
reality of his being the last to know. There'd been a subtle but
profound shift in the balance of power between them and as was
always the way with these sorts of changes, it would take a while
for all the players to settle themselves into the new con-
figurations without the stubborn, mutinous resentment that she
could read underneath the smooth, cared-for surface of his skin.
She caught Callan's eye for a fleeting second and then quickly
looked away. She was still unsettled by the earring Callan had
found. There'd been nothing in her voice or eyes to suggest she
had any idea where it had come from, or how it had wound up in
the apartment but she didn't trust her own expression, not just
yet. Once or twice in the past few years she'd been startled by
the sudden flash of recognition that passed between them as a
thought that had just emerged had to be roughly thrust back
down, pushed aside. She knew that expression, recognised and
understood it: because it was her own. She glanced away, across
the heads of her guests, breathing slowly, shallowly, until the
thoughts that had broken free of the ceiling she placed over
them subsided again. Only then could she turn her head back
and rejoin the conversation. Only then was she safe.
    Callan looked beautiful, as always, but something was troub-
ling her. She'd been uncharacteristically out of sorts for weeks –
nothing you could quite put your finger on, but a certain – she
searched for the word – *Zurückhaltung*. Reticence, yes, that was

it. She was oddly reticent, as if her mind were somewhere else half the time, which was most unlike her. Other than herself, Callan was the most focused person she'd ever known. Even their discussion that morning hadn't provoked the usual sort of astute analysis which she could usually count on. If she were to admit it, she'd actually been disappointed by the ease with which Callan had taken the news. She realised now that she'd been looking forward to the sort of tussle between them that she relied on to sharpen her own wits. *That* was the special talent Callan brought to the table – a scepticism that forced you to prove your own points, to yourself. It hadn't happened. Callan had just listened to Anneliese and Ree . . . then she'd capitulated, practically on the spot. *Most* unlike her.

The conversation waxed and waned around her. Her mind wandered again, but on safer ground this time. It was a pity Tara hadn't been able to come, after all. She'd been back from her trip to New York for almost a month and they'd yet to catch up properly. Tara was busy with the new term; Anneliese had been away in Milan for a few days, then a week in Japan, and another couple of days in Hamburg . . . few people realised just how much effort it took to stay on top of everything – every store, every item, every employee. Still, she wasn't complaining. Far better to have too much to do than too little. What was it her mother used to say? *Faule Hände erledigen keine Arbeit.* She gave herself a small shake. What on earth had prompted her to think of *her*? She made herself a mental note to call Tara on their return to London the following day. In a few days' time she'd be off again – New York, Toronto and San Francisco, to oversee their American operations. Bruno would accompany her; no need for Callan to make the trip. Perhaps she ought to send Callan to Stockholm to see Dirk Theunissen and the rest of his team in her place? She mulled over the idea for a moment. The more she thought about it, the more excited she got over the new direction that had suddenly presented itself. She hardly dared admit it to herself but she was bored. Yes, bored. There'd been a brief rush of excitement when she signed Hayley on as the new face of A*d*SP, but the truth was Hayley would be *so* much better in the role of spokesperson for the new venture. What, she wondered idly, her mind skirting over the possibilities, would they call it? She straightened up in her chair suddenly. A^2. A^+. She stood up abruptly. Everyone looked up.

'I . . . I've just thought of something,' she said quickly. 'Please excuse me.' And without a further word, she hurried from the dining room. There was work to be done. Too dangerous by far to sit idly in that room, her thoughts roving uncontrollably all over the place. She reached into her pocket; the earring was still there. She touched it lightly with her fingertips, just as she'd lightly touched the skin of its owner. She pushed open the door to her private sitting room on the first floor, overlooking the gardens. Night hung over the grounds like a thick, dense blanket. She stood by the window, still tracing the delicate strands of beaded gold hidden in her pocket, letting them slip between her fingers, drawing them up again. At the far end of the garden, breaking up the darkness with a thin shard of light, was the small cottage where the housekeeper lived. She thought for a moment of other landscapes, of those wild, unbroken miles of pitch blackness in which most of her childhood had been lived. The flat, unending ground rising up at some point in the distance to meet the inky, fluid mass of sky and the tumbling wreck of stars. She turned away from the window, and away from the past.

PART EIGHT

71

LINDI
Windhoek, Namibia, 2002

She was finally going home. After more than two years away from it, she was returning. Her contract had been extended twice, much to her irritation. She wanted to go home. She flew from Geneva to Frankfurt, then from Frankfurt to Windhoek. She dozed when she was able, some distant memory of a geography class coming back to her in her waking moments as they flew steadily south. The Sahara stretched out endlessly below them, mile upon mile of wrinkled yellow sand, scale distorted by the distance from which she gazed upon it. Nothing lasts for ever. She woke to hear the captain begin his instructions preparing them for descent. When they finally touched down upon the earth once more, there was a burst of spontaneous clapping from the rear of the plane. To her surprise, a driver was waiting for her as soon as she came through the double doors. She blinked; she hadn't been expecting anyone. She motioned to him: *yes, that's me.* He took her bags and introduced himself briefly. 'I'm Nathaniel. The department sent me.' She followed him, confused. Who in her department could possibly have authorised a driver for her? He led her briskly away from the terminal building towards a brand-new Toyota Land Cruiser. She was even more confused. A brand-new car? All for her? She slid in, inhaling the scent of fresh leather, a faint sense of unease rippling lightly up her spine.

They swung out of the parking lot and began the long drive back towards the city. The airport was some forty kilometres out of town; the straight, empty road led directly into the city. She settled back in the seat, waves of tiredness washing over her. The sun was a high, brilliant pinprick in a cloudless, shimmering expanse of blue. The hills all around them were come upon in a flash; the skin of low green bush and shrub that clung on for weeks, sometimes months after the year's only rains had shrivelled up. Only the acacia trees – flat-topped, prickly – remained. She had the curious sense of having come upon a landscape in a dream, at once familiar and strange.

'How long have you been driving for the, er, department?' she asked Nathaniel suddenly.

'About six months, madam.'

'Call me Lindi,' Lindi said automatically, though she ought to know by now how pointless it was. Deference was a way of life. 'Don't waste your time,' her friend Norah intoned wearily whenever she brought the subject up. 'Just don't go around calling your superiors by their first names, that's all. No quicker way to ensure a good stab in the back.' Norah was a journalist and had seen it all.

'But it's so . . . so *antiquated*. We all work for a living,' Lindi protested.

'God, you Scandinavians. When will you learn?' Norah simply rolled her eyes. 'This is Windhoek, not Stockholm.'

'I'm from Oslo,' Lindi pointed out mildly.

'Whatever. The point is, we do things differently down here.'

'But I *hate* it.'

'Live with it. Get over yourself.'

She smiled faintly as the conversation came back to her. 'Who asked you to pick me up?' she asked curiously.

Nathaniel shrugged. 'They just told me on Friday I must come to the airport to pick up somebody.'

Lindi leaned back, chewing her lip distractedly. If Nathaniel knew, he wasn't saying. She'd been away for nearly two years and if there was one thing she'd learned during her short time in government, it was that things changed fast, and not always for the better. Especially when you were out of the country.

Her unease began to deepen. She'd seen the way Sibo Kavuma, the deputy health minister, had been ousted a few years earlier. She'd gone to London for a conference; by the time she returned, her job was no longer hers. If Lindi's memory served her right, she'd also been picked up at the airport by a driver and a dispatch rider. She remembered people commenting in half-whispers on it in the corridors. She was hardly in the same league as Sibo Kavuma, but you didn't have to be a deputy minister to be deemed a threat. Was it that odious little prick, Muwanga?

Nathaniel pulled into the parking lot at the ministry; Lindi was out of the car almost before it had come to a halt. She hurried up the front steps, burst through the doors and ignored the lift. Her office was on the third floor. She opened the door and shut it behind her, leaning against it for a few seconds, breathing deeply. She looked around her. Everything was pretty much as she'd left it. Empty, a little forlorn-looking, but the same. Her desk was still in the same place; same chair; same poster on the wall. Nothing had changed. She was being silly and irrational. If her job was indeed in danger, she'd have known about it. Someone would have said something. Her father, Uncle Klaus . . . *someone*. She walked over to the windows and looked out over the Parliament Gardens, just in front of the Tintenpalast. The pale green lawns sloped gently down the hill towards Independence Avenue, their borders a riot of colour, the gorgeous mixture of flowers and plants for which the city's gardeners had been famous. The Traveller's Palms swayed gently in the breeze; further down the hill were the majestic Royal Palms. All was calm on the still, beautiful summer day. Her heart was the only thing beating faster than normal.

There was a sudden tap at the door. She turned round just as her boss pushed it open.

'Ah, Lindiwe,' he said, in the gravely formal tone he used with everyone, not just her. 'You're back.'

'Yes, Minister.' He'd stated the obvious, as he was wont to do. There was nothing for it but to wait for him to continue.

Sometimes he did, sometimes not. She'd learned to hold her tongue.

'Good, good,' he said absently, his fingers going to one of his elaborate cufflinks. He fiddled around with it for a second. Lindi's heart began its accelerated pace again. He cleared his throat. 'You had a good time over there?' he enquired, as though standing in the middle of the room, conducting small talk were the most natural thing for the two of them to do.

'Yes, thank you, Minister. Very, er, interesting. I learned a lot.'

'Good, good.' He turned, as if he were about to leave. 'Oh, by the way.' He paused, and turned back. 'We've made a few changes.'

Lindi's legs felt as though they might give way. 'Ch-changes?'

'Yes, yes. Whilst you were away. Actually, I wasn't really in favour of them myself. I kept saying to the prime minister that I think he's making a mistake, to be honest.' *Ahhctualleee.* He drew the word out like no one else did, or could. It was one of his favourite words.

'A . . . a mistake?'

'Yes. Well, what can we do? We are but servants of the people.' He spread both hands before him. 'It's their will. Actually, it's the prime minister's will.'

'Wh-what changes, Minister?' Lindi somehow found her voice.

'Well, I'm thinking that the prime minister is the best person to brief you, *nè*? He asked me to bring you to him the minute – yes, *the very minute*, that's what he said – you come back. So I think we should go. Are you ready?'

Lindi could only nod. 'Should I take my bag?' she asked, somewhat absurdly.

'No, no. You can leave those things here, *nè*? I mean, it'll take some time to clear out the office and so on. We don't know yet who they will bring in. Anyway, we can discuss all of that later.'

Lindi stared at him. *Clear out the office?* It was worse than she feared. There was nothing for it but to follow him. He stood back to let her pass through the doorway. She was shaking as she walked down the corridor. The prime minister's offices were located in another wing altogether. Apart from the odd few times she'd been asked to deputise at a departmental meeting, she'd spent little time in Ground Zero, as the wing was occasionally dubbed. In the lift she looked resolutely at the ground. The doors opened; she followed her boss out, her mind racing. Had someone complained about her?

'Good morning, Minister. Yes, he's expecting you. Good morning, Ms Johanssen.' One of the many receptionists who fielded calls and visitors from the prime minister's lair smiled sweetly at them. Lindi was too nervous to smile back. They passed through one office after another; everywhere people looked up, smiled, greeted the minister obsequiously and included Lindi in their benevolence. She couldn't have cared less. She was simply trying not to cry. Finally they reached the lion's den. The two personal assistants who stood guard jumped up, ushering them in. There was a private sitting room attached to the suite of offices. 'Do take a seat, Minister, and you, Ms Johanssen. The prime minister will be with you shortly. Coffee?' She smiled brightly at them.

'Actually, yes, I will have a coffee. Lindiwe?'

Lindi shook her head numbly. 'No, thanks.' If they were about to sack her, she wasn't sure she could keep a coffee down.

The door opened suddenly behind the beaming secretary and she felt her boss stiffen to attention. 'Prime Minister,' she heard him say obsequiously. 'Good morning.'

'Morning, morning,' the prime minister ushered them into the office. 'Do take a seat.' He walked around his desk, indicating the two stiffly upholstered chairs on the other side. Lindi could only stare at him. She'd never met him in person before; he was new to the job. His predecessor, Hage Kavivo, had been ousted in one of the many bloodless coups and reshuffles that went on in a parliament as young as their own. Iago Rukoro, the new man in the job, was something of an unknown. Lindi knew a little about him. His mother was Angolan, but his father had been one of Namibia's most revered guerrilla generals, killed by the South African army somewhere in the dusty scrub north of the Kunene. Afterwards, the family scattered. Maria, his mother, fearing for her life, fled back to Angola, leaving Iago and his younger sister in the care of relatives of her dead husband. It was a mistake. The children somehow wound up in a camp for orphans of the struggle, as they were called, somewhere in Botswana, then at Cassinga, just inside the border.

They would probably have remained there for the next two decades but Angola's independence came sooner than everyone thought. After her husband's murder and her subsequent flight back to Angola, Maria Rukoro da Silva had risen through the ranks of the *Movimento Popular de Libertação de Angola*, and was now a member of the new cabinet. As soon as she was sworn in, she set about securing their release. She had her own connections to call upon. From the dusty camp where they had lived for almost two years, Iago and his sister were flown overseas, first to Lisbon, then London, and then finally, America. When Namibia declared independence some fifteen years later, Iago was still completing his studies at Harvard. He stayed away for a further five years, then made the decision to return. His rise through the ranks of the party was as swift as his mother's. It took him just seven short years to go from junior minister to prime minister. Now, with the Old Man fading fast, the bets were on him to take over. He was forty-seven, divorced, with two small boys, but beyond that, Lindi, like most other people, knew little. He had one distinct advantage over all the other would-be successors to the ageing president – no one knew him, or at least not well enough. He hadn't been back long enough to build up either a power base, or a group of detractors, and the fact that his mother was still in government in the neighbouring country made him all the more unusual. He shunned the spotlight and was rarely seen outside the usual political functions he was presumably obliged to attend. She'd seen him on television, of course, and once or twice caught a glimpse of his disappearing back as he strode in or out of the building.

But nothing she'd glimpsed prepared her for the intensely physical, almost overwhelming presence of the man in front of her. He was much bigger than she remembered, one of those men whose solid muscularity exerts a powerful, almost tactile attraction over everyone around him. His face was wide and smooth, a deep, almost charcoal colour and his smile, like the Old Man's, was surprisingly sweet. He had a small, neat goatee beard, turning grey at the edges, and the high, almost Asiatic cheekbones that occasionally slipped out in the people here, hinting at a past that most would rather keep buried. His eyes were almond-shaped, dark, darting eyes that she sensed missed absolutely nothing.

'Have a seat, have a seat,' he urged them. 'Did she offer you coffee?' he asked, looking over their shoulders at the back of the departing secretary. His voice was deep and sonorous with a layering of accents, American being the last and probably most recent.

'Yes, thank you, Prime Minister,' her boss said, exaggeratedly grateful.

'*Ag*, man, Peter, how many times do I have to tell you? Stop with all this "Prime Minister" nonsense. If you won't call me Iago, call me Rukoro, at least.'

'Yes, Prime Minister.'

Rukoro glanced at her quickly. Despite her nerves and the cold dread in the pit of her stomach, she saw with incredulity the faint but discernible look of amused sympathy he'd just thrown her. She tried to compose herself. She was sitting in the prime minister's office with her own boss, about to be sacked from her job with absolutely no inkling of what she'd done, or failed to do. She was determined to be dignified, if nothing else. 'So what do you say, Ms Johanssen?' Rukoro asked her suddenly.

'Me?' Lindi looked at him uncertainly. What the hell was going on? 'What do I say about what?'

'About the job.'

'Which job?' Now she was really confused. Was it some kind of trick question?

'No, it's not a trick question.' Rukoro seemed able to read her mind. 'Are you up for it?'

Lindi frowned. 'I'm sorry, sir . . . I . . . I'm not sure what you're talking about. What job?'

Rukoro leaned back in his chair. A mild flicker of annoyance crossed his face which he quickly suppressed. 'You mean no one's briefed you?'

Lindi shook her head. 'Er, no, sir.'

Her boss began to shift uncomfortably in his chair. 'Er, Prime Minister, I thought that . . . the message was . . . you instructed that you would be the one to tell her?'

'No, the instructions were for you to brief her prior to the meeting. All I said was for the position to be offered formally in person, that's all.' He turned his attention away from the now-squirming minister. 'Apologies, Ms Johanssen. Let me get to the point.' He laced his fingers together and brought them up to his chin. 'We've created a new post in this department, that of a permanent secretary. Third in command under myself and the deputy prime minister, with a staff of three directly under you. We've managed to get a number of new initiatives through Parliament this year and I'm keen to expand and capitalise on the goodwill we've earned. I need a good team behind me.' He looked at her enquiringly.

'Me?' Lindi squeaked. 'You're asking *me* to be the permanent secretary?'

'Indeed. Why so surprised?'

'I thought you were about to *sack* me,' Lindi blurted out.

'Sack you? Whatever gave you that impression?' Rukoro looked equally surprised.

'I . . . I'm sorry, I just thought . . . no one said anything,' Lindi stammered. Her head was reeling. Permanent secretary? What did that mean?

'It's a new position,' Rukoro said, reading her mind again with uncanny accuracy. 'Not in the historical sense, but certainly in this department. Peter and I have been discussing it for weeks,' he said, nodding in her boss's direction. 'And as sad as I'm sure he will be to lose you, we both agree it's the right move.'

Lindi straightened up in her chair. She was conscious of both men watching her. The last thing she wanted to do was appear like a grateful, nervous schoolgirl. She cleared her throat and dropped her voice an octave – a small tip Norah had given her. *Don't squeak. Or squeal.* 'Thank you, Prime Minister,' she said, in what she hoped was a suitably sombre voice. 'I'm honoured.'

'Good. And start as we mean to go on. It's Iago. Rukoro, if you must. And may I call you Lindi?'

Lindi nodded faintly, trying not to show her surprise. Iago? Every single minister she'd met since the day she'd first started working in government had insisted upon the most formal of addresses – now here she was, sitting in front of the second-in-command, and he'd asked her to call him Iago? 'Yes, sir. Er, Rukoro, sir.' She couldn't quite bring herself to call him Iago, and certainly not in front of her boss. Her *ex*-boss, she reminded herself quickly. 'Er, when would I start?'

'Right away. One of the girls outside will help you settle in, show you your new office, where things are, and so on.' He looked at his watch. 'I've got a couple of short meetings this afternoon but why don't we pencil in some face-time later this afternoon. I'm off to Washington on Sunday but we need to thrash out between us exactly what your role's going to be and I'm interested to hear what *you* think it should be. I gather you gained valuable experience in Geneva – let's put it to good use. So, let's meet at four thirty and we carry on over dinner, if need be.' He stood up, towering over the pair of them.

Lindi scrambled to her feet, her boss following suit. 'Th . . . thank you, sir. Rukoro,' she corrected herself. 'I'll be here at four thirty.'

'Good. Don't be late. The girls'll tell you. One of my pet peeves. I don't know how I manage on this continent, really I don't. *Everyone's* late. *All* the time.' He gave a mock sigh of despair and grinned at them both.

'Er, yes.' Lindi didn't know what else to say. She glanced

quickly at her boss. It was fortunate for him that a blush wouldn't show up on his complexion; he'd otherwise have been bright red. Peter Katjavivo was *always* late. She followed him out of the office in silence, her mind still racing. What would her parents say?

Erik, predictably, was beside himself with delight. 'I *knew* something was up,' he kept repeating.

'How?'

'Oh, you get to hear things,' he said vaguely. 'I had lunch with Uncle Klaus in Dar last month.'

'So why didn't you say anything?'

'Well, one doesn't want to interfere, *vennen min*. And nothing was fixed. But it's wonderful news. Just *wonderful*. And you'll be working with Rukoro. Splendid fellow.'

'D'you know him?'

'Not well. We've met once or twice over the years. He was at Harvard, if I remember rightly. Very bright. But be careful, won't you?'

'Why?'

Erik chuckled. 'He's got a bit of a reputation.'

'What for?'

Erik chuckled again. 'Women, mostly. I know he's divorced, but there were always rumours during the marriage. He's a persuasive man. What can I say?'

'Not that, Dad.' Lindi had to laugh. 'Come on, it's *me* you're talking to. I'm the *last* person in the world you have to worry about on *that* score.'

'I know, I know. I'm just saying, that's all. Here's your mother. She's dying for a word.'

Ten minutes later, she closed her phone with a thoughtful snap. What wouldn't she give to walk arm in arm with Siv down Hausmannsgate and pop into Café Sara for a hot chocolate and a *bjørnebær*, her childhood favourite dessert. She swivelled in her chair and looked around at the office that had been hers for the past few years. In the manner of most government offices, there was almost nothing to indicate it had been hers for more than a couple of days. A framed picture of her parents and the family dog; her degrees; a postcard someone had sent her stuck into the corner of her computer screen . . . the blue-and-white striped cushion she sat on and the porcelain teacup and saucer she'd picked up on holiday in London once. Her files were all neatly stacked in the filing cabinet which sat in one corner of the room. All in all it would take her less than an afternoon to remove all traces of her presence and reinstall herself down the corridor. Ms Lindi Johanssen, permanent secretary. She felt a nervous thrill in her stomach. It wasn't yet clear what exactly the job entailed but it was a promotion and it would mean working with someone she already respected, as opposed to working with Katjavivo, who was pleasant enough but who barely had her attention. He was the proverbial dull-as-dishwater politician; his entire ambition had been used up ensuring he never said anything even *remotely* controversial, or true. From the little she knew about Iago Rukoro, the opposite was true. She gave herself a small, giddy squeeze. It was a good start to the year – a *very* good start. Wholly unexpected, too, which made it all the sweeter.

72

ANNELIESE
Hamburg, Germany

Odd that the letter was addressed to her *here*, she thought to herself, bending down to pick it up. Few people even knew she had a home in Germany. She turned it over curiously. A stamped gold-and-silver crest: *Department of Arts & Culture, Republic of South Africa*. She turned the envelope over again. *Mrs A Zander de Saint Phalle, 62 Elbuferweg, Hamburg*. She walked over to her bureau, picked up her silver letter-knife and slit it open. It was signed by the minister of culture, Dr Jacob Mashabane. She frowned, puzzled. Why would the South

African minister of culture write to *her*? Still in her dressing gown, she went into the kitchen. Around her, the villa was quiet. It wasn't yet eight. The housekeeper usually came in around eight thirty. Her eyes flickered over the page.

'Twenty-four deceased liberation struggle heroes; Steve Biko, Oliver Tambo, Helen Joseph; Fidel Castro, Toussaint L'Ouverture; an empowering heritage destination; better human understanding amongst nations and peoples.' The phrases leapt out at her. Her frown deepened. She read on. 'The name *//hapo* means "dream", drawn from the Khoi proverb, *//hapo ge //hapo tama / haohasib dis tamas ka i bo*, which means, "a dream is not a dream until it is shared by the whole community".' She turned over the pages quickly. Her heart began to accelerate. 'In the eighteen months since we began our search, your name has come up repeatedly. We have seven other potential jurists, some of whom will already be known to you. It would be our great pleasure to welcome you to join them in our task to select the best possible architect to deliver the best possible design. I look forward to hearing from you at your earliest convenience. Yours sincerely, Dr Jacob Mashabane.'

She put the letter down. A Museum of Freedom. On the slopes of Table Mountain in Cape Town, overlooking the bay. Mandela's legacy. A worldwide architectural competition. And they'd asked *her* to judge it. Why? Did they know? No, it was impossible. No one alive knew anything about her past, least of all where it had been spent. Was it a coincidence? But how could it be? Yes, she had an extensive art collection and there were one or two gallery owners in London and New York who would open their doors at midnight if she called, and her collaboration with Ree had brought about a modest amount of publicity. She stopped suddenly. Ree. This was *his* project. It was *made* for him. There was no other architect on the planet who would do it justice. She picked up the letter and hurriedly turned to the last page. She scanned the last paragraph intently. 'A shortlist of six invited architects will be sent to you on your acceptance of the terms and conditions of the jury panel.' So the shortlist had already been decided? Was he on it? She *had* to find out. If he *hadn't* been approached, it would be an enormous slap in the face, and if he *had*, how would he feel, knowing she was a judge?

She picked up the phone, her hand hovering over it. There was only one person she could ask. Callan. She bit her lip. Asking Callan would mean admitting that she knew. *She knew.*

73

CALLAN
London

It was just past seven in the morning when the phone rang, dragging her out of sleep. She flung out an arm, groping blindly for it, knocking a glass of water off the table by accident before managing to grab hold of it and put an end to its shrill, insistent voice. 'Hello?' she croaked.

'Callan. Here is your mother.'

'Maman? What time is it?'

'It's just after eight.'

'Not where I am it's not,' she said, trying to clear her throat at the same time.

'Must you make that awful noise, Callan? Listen, there's something I want to ask you.'

'Clearly. I've got a cold.' She coughed loudly, hoping it might draw some sympathy from Anneliese. It didn't. She'd never been sick, so far as Callan could remember and took a rather dim view of those who succumbed. 'So what is it?' she asked, when there was no comforting comment forthcoming.

'Has Ree been approached to do a competition in South Africa?' she asked without preamble.

There was a moment's hesitation. Callan's skin prickled. She knew her mother well enough to know it was neither a simple question nor the prelude to a longer conversation. Why had she rung her and not Ree? Or even Hayley? Her stomach gave another lurch. She knew. 'Yes, he has,' she said finally, keeping her voice as neutral as she possibly could.

There was another hesitation. 'Is it a museum?'

'Yes. Yes it is.'

'I see. Well, that's all I wanted to know.'

'Where are you?'

'Hamburg. I'll be back in London on Saturday.'

'All right. Well, I . . . I'll see you then, I suppose.'

Anneliese rang off without anything further, as she usually did. Callan slid the phone back onto its cradle. She pulled a pillow from the other side of the bed and slowly sank her face into it. She longed to talk to Ree. She rolled over onto her side, still hugging the soft pillow to her chest. There were days when she thought she was being punished for every single relationship she'd ever had where she'd been in control. It made her skin crawl with shame for every man she'd ever promised to ring and didn't; every time she'd laughed off a declaration of affection or love; for every single time she'd watched herself break someone's heart, somehow maintaining the distance that allowed her to walk away unscathed. Well, she'd had her comeuppance, no question. This was *hard*. Harder than anything she could ever have imagined.

It wasn't just the question of his wife and children, difficult as that was. She'd never had a relationship with someone who wasn't attached in some way to someone else. But that wasn't it. It was far deeper and much more complicated than that. For the first time in her life, she was in love. Properly. Unashamedly. Completely and utterly. When 'it' first started, she'd been gripped by fear – a fear of losing him, of losing herself, of losing her mind. She dreaded who she might become. The thought of sitting at home, waiting for the phone to ring, waiting for a text message, waiting for some sign – any sign – that he still cared was enough to drive her to despair. She needn't have worried. Ree wasn't the type to make her wait. It wasn't in his nature. He was the one with the 'complications', as he put it, but he would no sooner have held her hostage to the situation than he would have risked losing his children. He couldn't live without her, and she without him. That seemed to be a given, right from the start. In the beginning, it was easy. Callan was a natural mistress, not a wife. She made few demands on him that he couldn't fulfil. From the depth of her own experience, she understood the necessity in him to separate out the various functions of his life – husband, father, lover – in order to carry on, and she adjusted her own expectations accordingly. She was fiercely independent. Her life was full and busy and interesting before he entered it and she saw no reason to change.

The hardest part wasn't sharing him with someone else; conversely, it was *not* sharing him. She told no one. Not even Tara. But as time went on, she was beginning to discover, the same strict compartmentalising that went on in Ree's life was difficult for her. How many times lately had she suddenly been overcome with the desire to say, just once, 'Oh, Ree said this funny thing—?' Or, 'D'you know what Ree said?' Two years of intense, sometimes heated arguments and conversations with the brightest, most *alive* person she'd ever met had expanded her own horizons and interests and there was no one to share her new-found wonder at things with. When they could get away for a weekend or a few days together, she came back filled with images, ideas, things she'd have loved to talk to Anneliese or Tara or even Bruno about. But she couldn't. Ree took her to Istanbul and she pretended she'd gone to a spa. He took her to Moscow; she invented a friend in Zurich. They rode together to Petra; she hid her passport, unsure as to how she would explain a sudden visit to Jordan.

It wasn't all one way, either. He told her over and over again just what it was that she brought to his life – energy and passion and a directness that entranced him. He loved her cool confidence when handling the business side of things. She could out-talk, outmanoeuvre and out-smart anyone, and all with the utmost charm. She knew more about the murky, half-secretive worlds of banking and finance than anyone he knew. As his own business grew and he had to show more than just talent to stay ahead of things, it was Callan he turned to. Her mind was sharper than his, he said. He found himself testing out things by presenting them to her, waiting for her to knock holes in his plans. If she didn't, or couldn't, he could be assured that it was sound. They fought often; Callan was no pushover and neither was he. But there was such delight in the time they spent together, including the arguments – he did not have to tell her he couldn't live without her. It was in his eyes and words and in his body, just as it was in hers. She sometimes laughed at the old cliché that mistresses only got the 'good' bits – the flowers, the passionate sex, the exotic holidays – and the wives got all the rest: the fights, the dirty dishes, the scattered clothing. The truth wasn't quite as simple. Ree wasn't the type to walk in with a bunch of roses, nor was he the type to duck a fight. What they had between them defied most of the usual categories, and then most of the others as well. What she did know was that she loved him beyond anything she'd ever thought herself capable of – *that* was the fear. What was it someone had said to her once? *Love makes you vulnerable.* It was why she'd resisted it for so long.

She pushed the covers aside. She had a full day of meetings ahead of her. A^2 had done better than anyone had dared hope. The limited run they'd put out at the beginning of the season had sold out even before the merchandise hit the stores. They were just about to launch a second run and as usual the supply chain was hit with a hundred minor problems from deliveries to making sure the stock was in and on time. She sighed. She'd yet to buy a single piece from the collection. Hayley was now so thoroughly identified as the face – and body – of A^2 that Callan couldn't even look at the clothes, let alone wear them. She slipped on her dressing gown and walked into the shower. Heartache aside, it was time to start her day.

74

REE
London

There was no sound whatsoever in the room. The door was locked. His iPod stood silent in its dock; the radio was switched off. Nothing except the sound of his own breathing and the occasional soft noise of a pencil stroking swiftly across a piece of paper. It was his third day of complete and utter solitude. No one, not even Terri, dared enter. Of the things he did on a daily basis, drawing was his favourite – and the one he was least likely to do. As the practice had grown, the amount of time he spent locked up in his office as he had been for the past week, using his pencil to draw ideas forth, from the depths of his imagination to the clean white sheet in front of him, had diminished to the point he'd almost forgotten how to do it. The past three days had changed that. He was back. Drawing, sketching, testing. Back where he belonged. He stopped for a second and held up the piece of tracing paper against the light. It was a process that was both mysterious and commonplace; he'd been doing it for the better part of twenty years and yet it was always a surprise. He couldn't remember the last time he'd concentrated quite as hard or enjoyed it as much, though the enjoyment was tempered by the almost-forgotten nervousness that competitions always brought out in him. And he'd never done a competition with quite so much at stake. Simply put, this one he *had* to win.

He looked over the sketches for the hundredth time. He'd honed and edited and cut away and pruned until only the basics remained. It was important to get those right and, in his experience, the more he pared those back, the better the outcome. The final sketch – the one his team would take and begin to work up until a series of drawings were done – was almost ready. It depicted a series of cuts into the landscape, some of which were buildings, others gardens, walls, terraces, a densely woven play of inside elements and outside spaces that alluded to the story of how the land itself had been colonised, tamed and then freed. He was almost satisfied. From bitter experience he knew it was always better to have doubts than it was to assume that everything was under control. Fear kept you on the edge – a tired old cliché, perhaps, but it worked.

All around him was the wreckage of the creative frenzy he'd been in since the day the letter arrived inviting him to be one of the lucky six who'd been selected to enter. He'd worked on bigger, more commercial projects before but this was the first major international competition and the first he'd been pre-selected to enter. He was up against it, he knew. He was the youngest, the only African and the only one of the six who didn't already have a major, world-class cultural institution under his belt. He *had* to win. Just to have been selected ought to have been confirmation enough that he'd made it. To be in the same company as the Swiss duo, Matthier Oppener, who'd won MoMA and the new Tate, and Franklin McMahon, the California-based giant, was proof that he'd 'arrived', as the press put it. And all this at forty. It was enough to turn anyone's head – but not his. For him there would be no slacking off, no pat on the back and certainly no coasting. He'd already had a taste of what it was like to have the media turn against him. Hard as it had been at the start of his career, the lesson had served him well. Never take anything for granted, least of all your talent.

He'd never been one to believe in that old saying that being black he'd have to work twice as hard just to keep up – it was the sort of old wives' adage his mother was fond of repeating, just to make sure everything was kept in check, including his own ambition. In her eyes, there was nothing worse than arrogance and if she detected as much as a whiff of it in her son, she'd be down on him like the proverbial ton of bricks. She needn't have worried; that sort of lazy arrogance wasn't his style. *This* – the graft – was more like it. He shuffled the sheets into a more or less tidy pile and leaned back in his chair. There were a dozen or more books splayed open beside him – everything from

Hieronymus Bosch to Dali. Images of African wax print fabrics; Ashanti gold weights; masks from Benin and Mahoney; contemporary Haitian art; South African landscapes, flora and fauna; scientific drawings; books on philosophy and legal histories . . . he'd left no stone unturned. If he didn't win, it wouldn't be for lack of research or effort. He could take some comfort in that.

He slipped his hand in his pocket and pulled out his phone. He'd been alone for almost seventy-two hours, bar a goodnight kiss to the girls and a hurried breakfast conversation with Hayley which had almost – thankfully not quite – erupted into a fight. There was only one person in the world he wanted to talk to. The sudden fierce longing to share what he'd done with her was so intense he actually had to press his fingers to his eyelids to stop them burning. She was on the other side of town; she might as well have been on the moon. If there was anyone who'd understand what he'd done, it was Callan. He sat for a few seconds longer, trying to resist the urge. He couldn't. He grabbed the sheets and a notepad, and his coat, and was out of the door before Terri or anyone else could grab him. He had to see her. He ran down the steps and flagged down a cab. He was breathing fast, with fear as much as passion, yet he knew the minute he laid eyes on her, that special sense of safety that she brought out in him would settle over him, over them both. But as the cab pulled away a sudden, inexplicable sense of foreboding settled over him, causing his shoulders to hunch. He drew in a deep breath, holding it, waiting for the moment to pass.

'So what d'you think?' There was a worried frown on Callan's face as she leafed through the sheets of trace. He felt his stomach turn over. He'd been so sure she would understand what he'd done.

She lifted her eyes slowly and he could see the apprehension in them. 'They're great,' she said slowly. 'I don't understand all of it, but they look amazing.'

'So what is it?'

She hesitated. 'I don't know if this is the right moment,' she began carefully. 'The thing is—'

'Spit it out, Callan. What is it?' His whole body was tense. What on earth was she about to tell him?

'It's Anneliese.'

'What about her?'

'She's one of the judges.'

'For what?' He frowned, not understanding what she meant.

'This,' she said, pointing to the sheets he'd just handed her. '*This*. The competition.'

'The museum?' he echoed stupidly.

She nodded. 'She rang me yesterday. She asked if you'd been approached.'

He watched her expression intently. 'What did you say?'

She sighed. 'I had to tell her the truth,' she said slowly. 'I said "yes".' She got up from where she'd been kneeling on the floor and came towards him, still on her hands and knees. He was sitting on the low leather sofa in front of the coffee table. She nudged the table aside and sat in the opening made by his legs, resting her arms on his thighs. 'She knows. She didn't say anything but just the fact that she asked me . . . well, she knows.'

Her head was a silky helmet of dark brown hair that fell on either side of her face, curling slightly inwards towards her chin. She'd had it cut recently; the shorter length suited her. He put a hand under her chin and lifted it, looking down at her. Her dark eyes were a glistening mirror in which he saw only his own image, staring back intently at himself. Despite the anxiety he could sense in her voice, her expression was her habitual one of absolute honesty. He bent his head and kissed her, putting into it the words he couldn't say. *I love you.* By some unspoken, tacit agreement between them, it wasn't a sentiment that either indulged in expressing, ever. To Callan, it belonged to the fairytale that she'd understood from the very beginning would never be theirs. She shrugged her shoulders at it, releasing him at once from the obligation to say it. He lifted his head and looked at her. 'So what does that mean?' he asked carefully. 'What does it mean if she knows?'

'There's a conflict of interest. And that you stand a better chance than most.'

His hand did not stop its insistent caress. 'That's not what I'm asking. Forget about the competition. I either win it on merit or I don't. I'm not talking about that. I'm talking about us. What does it mean if she knows *about us*?' As he looked at her, the aspect of her face that he knew so well changed. He studied her shining, olive-skinned cheeks; her lovely mouth with the faint lines around the edges beginning to mark her most habitual expressions; the hollow made by her bare collarbones and the way the taut, always perfumed skin sloped down to meet the hollow indentation of her breasts. She held her breath, keeping her whole body very still. To his amazement, her eyes began to glitter with tears. 'What is it? What've I said?' he asked in alarm. Callan wasn't the sort of woman who cried easily. In all the time he'd been with her, it was usually only in anger that tears appeared. She shook her head slowly from side to side, her mouth working to express something that he didn't catch. 'What?' he asked again.

'I love you.' The glittering tears splashed onto her mouth. He bent his head and brushed the side of her lips with his own. The saltiness was now his.

'Ditto,' he said softly. 'Ditto.'

75

LINDI
Windhoek, Namibia

And whereas the government of the Republic of Namibia deems it desirable to allocate the said licences covering the area of those territories located south of the Penguin Islands, namely those situated at 22°57′22″S 14°30′29″E. Lindi quickly checked the map coordinates. Yes, all correct. She continued scanning the document on-screen, her eyes going occasionally to the printed pages in front of her.

'You're not still working, are you?'

She jumped and turned. It was Iago. He was standing in the doorway, his jacket folded over his arm, watching her.

She felt the blush steal up through her neck and face. 'Wh-what time is it?' she asked.

'Long past closing time,' he said, looking at his watch. 'It's ten o'clock. What're you still doing here?'

Her face was on fire. 'I'm just checking through these,' she gestured at the pile of documents on her desk. 'Just making sure you're ready for tomorrow.'

'Oh, I'll be ready all right,' Iago said with a faint smile. 'But you don't need to do this. Get one of the interns to do it.'

Lindi smiled and shook her head. 'No, I'd much rather do it myself.'

'But it's late. You've been here since morning. I know; I've been watching you.'

There wasn't an easy way to respond. She opened her mouth, then closed it again. Then stammered, gauchely, 'Oh, I haven't really got anything else— I mean, I'm free tonight and it just seemed like a—'

'Come on. Get your jacket.' He cut her off.

'My jacket?'

'Yeah. Grab your things. I'm taking you to dinner.'

'To dinner?'

'Why d'you keep on repeating everything I say?' He smiled at her. 'It's not a request. Come on, get your stuff. You eat meat, don't you?'

'Er, yes . . . yes, I do.' Lindi hurriedly switched off the computer.

'Good. Thought for a moment you'd be one of those Scandinavian types.'

'Scandinavian types?'

'Lindi . . . is something wrong?'

'No, sir. I mean, Rukoro.' She looked up at him with such an expression of alarm that he burst out laughing.

'Come on. I think the Kalahari Sands'll still be open. Come on before I change my mind.'

She grabbed her coat and bag and followed him, half-running to keep up with his stride.

A table was quickly found for them to the rear of the restaurant, away from the irritatingly cheerful piano player and the sounds of other diners. The Kalahari Sands was the only five-star restaurant in town and Iago Rukoro was clearly a frequent diner. Two out of the three managers on duty personally dropped by their table to enquire if everything was all right, if the wines were to their taste, the meat tender enough . . . Rukoro waved them away with a lazy right hand.

'One of the many downsides,' he murmured. 'I sometimes long for the anonymity of New York.'

'Is that where you studied?' Lindi ventured shyly. She found herself perpetually tongue-tied in Iago's presence.

'Mmm. After Harvard,' he nodded. 'D'you know New York?'

'Only a little. I have friends there. I've been over a couple of times in the past couple of years. It's . . . it's a great city.'

'One of the best. No place like it.'

'Do you miss it?'

He chuckled and lifted his glass. 'Like hell. There are days when I wake up in my nice house in Klein Windhoek and think, "Is this it?"'

'How did I get here?' Lindi smiled. 'I often think that.'

'So how *did* you get here? I mean, I know the basic facts but that doesn't tell me anything about why.'

Lindi was quiet for a few moments. It wasn't the first time she'd been in a social setting with her boss – they were often at lunches and cocktail parties together – but it was the first time they'd ever been properly alone. She drew in her breath sharply. There was no question he was an attractive man. Like many men whose physical presence remained an integral part of their charm, he seemed able to switch it off and on at will. She'd seen him in meetings, sleeves rolled up the powerful forearms, his expression drawn together in one of intense concentration, oblivious to the world around him. Someone would ask him a question; he would raise his head, blinking slowly, and as his focus reasserted itself the feeling of having been caught in the powerful sweep of his headlights would come over the speaker and she or he would retreat in a blast of confusion. Lindi had been on the receiving end of both his indifference and his extraordinary charm, and indifference was safer. He kept her – and most other women, she imagined – in a permanent state of nervous tension. If he liked you – and he wasn't shy about showing it – you had absolutely no idea why. He would laugh suddenly at something she'd said, or an expression on her face, but make no further reference so she was always left wondering – what was it she'd said? 'I don't know,' she said slowly, her fingers playing with the delicate stem of her glass.

He pulled a disbelieving face. 'I doubt that very much,' he said, cutting off a slice of steak. 'I can't imagine you not knowing anything.'

'Me?' Lindi said, surprised.

'Yes, you. You're supremely capable, you know. I don't think I've ever seen you flustered. Doesn't matter what I throw at you, you just pick it up and run with it.'

Lindi bent her head back down to her plate. Now she really *was* blushing. 'Just, er, doing the job,' she mumbled.

'No need to be modest,' Iago chuckled. 'Not with me.'

They chatted for a few minutes about the meeting the following morning, much to Lindi's relief. Much easier to talk about work, with him. She watched the smooth, sharp face come alive under the dimmed restaurant lighting as though some internal source that only he was aware of had been switched on, deep inside him. As they spoke, she had the impression that he was tuned in to something that he was listening for, watching for, behind their conversation, and that in some way she'd confirmed whatever it was he sought. Another bottle was ordered; a dessert? Would she like some cheese, perhaps? Or some fruit? He ate and drank with great appetite, one of those men for whom all bodily pleasures – food, wine, sex – were the same. She was surprised at herself; how had she recognised it in him? He laughed at something she said and his hand came out, covering hers in the pleasure of laughter. She looked at it; the American-style college ring embedded in the dark flesh of his little finger; that line where the salmon-pink palm met the smooth blackness of his skin. Desire rose in her like a blush. He must have sensed it; he passed the same ringed hand down the side of her cheek in a gesture of such intimacy that she actually felt her knees tremble.

'Enough?' He indicated the remains of the meal.

She nodded wordlessly. He signalled to the waiter and withdrew a wallet thick with bills. He peeled off several and tucked them neatly under one of the unused plates. Then he turned to her, an amused smile on his face, as if to say, 'Well, miss?' He offered her his arm; she took it, and stood up. In her heels, she was almost his height but beside his thick, fleshy presence, she felt herself almost dwarfed. They walked out of the restaurant together, she conscious of several pairs of eyes on them as they rode down in the escalator together. Her hand was still loosely on his arm when they moved through the double entrance doors together. They stood for a moment on the pavement, looking at each other but not saying anything. Lindi was conscious of a pulse beating at the side of her neck, a steady throbbing of the sort she hadn't felt in years. She'd been working for Iago Rukoro for almost six weeks. He was without doubt the most interesting, enigmatic and deeply attractive man she'd ever encountered. He was also the most powerful, although that wasn't what she sought. No, there was something else in him that brought out a deeper, more profound need in her that she recognised dimly. It was the same fascination she'd had with Ree Herz, all those years ago. Same, but different. Iago was both like her; and yet not. The circumstances of her life were different from his – there'd been no refugee camp for her! But beneath the facts she recognised the same wary ambition, the same way of entering a room, eyes darting from side to side, seeking out those present who would be allies and those who would not. Nothing could ever be taken for granted, taken as read. She belonged everywhere and yet nowhere – so too did he. You earned the right to be listened to, counted and heard, and the strength lay in never forgetting that, not for an instant. She recognised it in him, just as he seemed to recognise it in her.

'My car's over there.' He indicated the dark blue Mercedes that she recognised from the parking lot. His bodyguards, Blessed and Temba, were waiting in the unmarked car beside it. Blessed was an odd name for a bodyguard, she'd often mused, but she'd long since ceased to worry about oddities. In Africa, things often appeared the wrong way round: what was normal and commonplace in Europe suddenly seemed outlandish, out of place. When she least expected it, a new perspective on something – some situation or phrase or event – would suddenly open itself to her, like the change in pitch that sometimes happened when her inner ear adjusted itself and sound took on a new frequency, just as it had done over dinner. Iago Rukoro had presented himself to her in another light; now he was not just her boss and prime minister of the country she'd chosen to call her own, but potentially something deeper. Iago. She tried the name out on her tongue, silently. 'Well, miss?' He spoke the words aloud.

She turned to him, her eyes narrowing, as if trying to read beneath the smile. She nodded again. 'Your place or mine?' she laughed suddenly, as if the absurdity of the situation had only just occurred to her.

'Mine.' He tucked her hand more firmly in his grasp and led her across the road.

76

HAYLEY
London

He was late. The bastard was late. He'd *promised* he would be there. That very morning, in fact. It was the last thing she'd yelled out to him as he left the flat. 'Don't forget. Steven's throwing a party tonight. It's Yolanda's birthday and *everyone's* going to be there.' What did he say? Yeah, I'll be there. So where the *fuck* was he? She tipped the contents of her glass straight down her throat and signalled to the waiter for another. They were in Steven's apartment-cum-studio overlooking the Thames – a gigantic, glass-walled space flooded with light, pumping with music, stacked to the rafters with supermodels, semi-naked waiters carrying tray after tray of drinks . . . and in the bedrooms and bathrooms all the drugs a girl could want. Not that she'd had any. Yet. She could feel her mood shifting dangerously. Ree had been an absolute monster to live with over the past few weeks, ever since that fucking competition had landed on his desk, to be precise. It was all he seemed able to think about; even the girls had failed to penetrate the *so-called* creative daze, which he'd been walking around in for days on end. He'd practically bitten Zoë's head off the other evening when she'd asked if she could go to the cinema with two of her friends.

'It's a school night,' he'd said, not looking up from his desk.
'But—'
'Didn't you hear what I just said?'
'But—'
'Goddammit! I said "no"!'
The shout had made them all jump. Poor Zoë just sat there, her face reddening with the effort of trying not to cry. She'd glared at him and gone to her, but Zoë, as usual, got up before she reached her and slipped into her room.

She blew out her cheeks in irritation. She watched as Yasmin and Simon Le Bon entered the room, arm in arm, as always. Fuck, now that was something to watch. The way he absolutely doted on her . . . no bloody wonder. At thirty-eight she'd give women half her age a run for their money. She was gorgeous. As was he. A real golden couple. She lit another cigarette. *She* wanted to be the other half of a golden couple, the way it had been before. Back then, there hadn't been a party in town to which they hadn't received the first invitation. She used to love walking in with Ree, watching the way everyone automatically turned their heads to look at them. Star quality – they both had it, in spades. Thanks to Anneliese and her wildly successful *A²* line, she was now a *bona fide* star in her own right . . . and yet, here she was, alone. Being married meant she couldn't simply show up at every party and every opening with a different man on her arm. The tabloids would have had a field day. Printing nasty things about glamorous, famous people was their stock-in-trade – didn't seem to matter whether any of it was true. And models came in for particular abuse. It was as if the general public – damn them – wanted to *punish* women like her for having it all – looks, money, fame . . . even a husband and kids. How dare she have it all? She gave a short laugh. Little did they know. Her kids couldn't stand her and her husband hadn't been near her in months.

She stubbed out the cigarette before she'd even smoked it halfway. She ground it under her Louboutin heel and headed for one of the bedrooms. Yolanda and her sexy new boyfriend with the unpronounceable name had just gone in and shut the door. They were either having sex or snorting a line. Probably the latter, knowing Yolanda, and she could certainly do with a little pick-me-up. Damn Ree. Damn him and his fucking competition.

She pushed her way through the crowds of beautiful people, baring her teeth in an approximation of a smile whenever she encountered a face she knew, and knocked on the bedroom door. She could hear Yolanda's high-pitched giggle. 'Who is it?'

'It's only me. Let me in, will you?'

'It's open!'

She pushed it open. Lying sprawled out across the sateen covers were Yolanda and her Turkish/Armenian/Azerbaijani boyfriend . . . and a small handheld mirror with three lines of coke. Hayley breathed in deeply. She sank down onto the bed with them. She wasn't meant to . . . she shouldn't . . . she really oughtn't to . . . but she did. Head down, nostrils to the glass, once, twice . . . she sat bolt upright. The rush was instant.

'Good, isn't it?' Yolanda drawled appreciatively. 'Usman brought it.' She looked at her latest young catch, his head bent over the mirror as soon as Hayley had vacated it.

'You like?' Usman finished his own line and looked up at her. He really was extraordinarily good-looking. Hazel eyes, nut-brown skin, thick, glossy brown hair . . . lucky Yolanda.

'Mmm,' she said, running her tongue across her teeth. 'Yes, I do. *Very* much.' She stretched full length along the bed beside them, kicking off her heels. The three of them began to giggle. 'God, isn't this brilliant?' Hayley murmured, more to herself than anyone else. She'd managed to put her anger with Ree to one side and focus on enjoying herself instead. Usman's lean, jean-clad thigh was touching hers and he made no move to roll away.

'Here,' he said, opening his palm, stretching his arm out towards her. 'Try these.'

'What are they?' She looked at the little blue-and-white capsules curiously.

'Just try them,' Yolanda drawled. 'They're amazing.'

'Go on. They don't bite.' Usman smiled lazily at her.

Hayley took one and popped it in her mouth. It was slightly sweet; the rubbery capsule disintegrated almost immediately on her tongue. She waited for a few moments for something to happen, some reaction . . . but there was nothing. Usman's hand was now on her bare thigh. She glanced nervously at Yolanda but her eyes were closed. He began to caress the skin, his fingers moving in light, feathery circles. It felt good . . . better than

393

good. She too closed her eyes and then it suddenly hit her. A wave of molten pleasure that seemed to start in the very centre of her belly, spreading outwards through her limbs, travelling along the surface of her skin; her whole body felt as though it were on fire. 'Fuck,' she breathed, opening her eyes. Both Usman and Yolanda were looking at her, smiling.

'Fucking brilliant, isn't it?' Yolanda breathed.

Hayley couldn't speak. Her tongue felt as though it were glued to the roof of her mouth. All she could do was lie there, wallowing in the rills of the most intense pleasure she could ever recall feeling. It was mind-blowing. Not quite an orgasm, but something close to it. Every nerve in her body felt as though it were being touched, stroked, teased. What kind of drug had he given her?

'I've got to take a picture of you!' Usman jumped up suddenly, causing the bed to rock. 'You look so fucking good like that, doesn't she, baby?' he cried, fumbling in his pocket for his phone.

'Take one of me, darling,' Yolanda squealed, struggling upright and draping herself across Hayley's back. 'Take one of both of us!' The two of them started giggling again. Usman flipped open his phone and aimed it at them. They horsed around on the bed, striking pose after pose. It was the best evening she'd had in months, Hayley kept shouting, as they both popped another pill. Usman was busy preparing three beautifully straight lines . . . she bent her head to the mirror, again and again. Yolanda produced a bottle of vodka. There was the chink of glasses and the sudden, unbearably erotic feel of Usman's mouth brushing her own, then Yolanda's. She pulled back for a second . . . fuck it, it felt good. She was dimly aware of someone pulling the straps of her dress away from her shoulders and then a hand sliding down her chest to her breasts. This time it really was an orgasm; she came fast and hard. It was the last thing she remembered.

77

REE

Terri looked up nervously as he came through the door. 'What's wrong?' he asked, flinging his bag on the chair beside the reception desk and picking up his mail.

She cleared her throat. 'Um, was just wondering . . . er, have you . . . have you seen the papers?'

'No.' He shook his head. 'Why? What's news?'

She was holding a copy of the *Sun* in her hand. 'It's just . . . well, you'd better read it.'

'I don't read the *Sun*,' he said, puzzled. Her copy was rolled up tightly, as if she'd been holding on to it for hours.

'You'd better read this.' She handed it over reluctantly.

It took him a couple of seconds to work out what he was looking at. It was Hayley. His stomach lurched. *Exclusive: Hayley's Highs.* His scalp tightened. He scanned the first few lines. '*Supermodel Hayley Summers, the face of A², and a former* Vogue *cover-girl, was photographed on Saturday night snorting lines of cocaine and popping an assortment of Class A drugs at a debauched drugs-and-drink party at photographer Steven Bailey's penthouse flat in Chelsea. The thirty-eight-year-old model who is married to star architect Ree Herz with whom she has two young children . . .*' He swallowed and put the paper down. His heart was hammering. Terri was looking at him anxiously.

'I'm so sorry, Ree. I . . . I thought you'd better see it first. The press . . . well, there's someone from the *Daily Globe* here. I've tried to get him to leave but he's in the boardroom.'

'How did he get in?' The tightness in his chest was painful.

Terri shook her head. 'He was waiting when I got here. I hadn't seen the papers . . . I thought he was coming to interview you about your work.'

'Get Alison Barrett on the line, will you?' His brain went

automatically into overdrive. 'And send someone in to tell that fucking journo that I'm out of the country.'

'Too late.' A voice sounded behind them. 'Fucking journo spotted you coming in.'

Ree turned round. A scruffy, unshaven young man with a camera slung around his neck was standing in the doorway. It would almost have been comic if he'd been in any state to laugh. 'Look,' Ree began, holding up his hands. He had to resist the temptation to punch him. 'I know why you're here but I've got nothing to say. I need to talk to my wife first—'

'Did you know she was sleeping with Usman Bargudjian?' he asked, flicking open his phone.

Ree stared at him. Who? 'I've got nothing to say,' he said, pushing past him. 'Terri, get him out of here or I'll call the police.' He turned on his heel, ignoring the looks of utter astonishment on the faces of most of his employees as he walked down the corridor to his office.

'Did you even *know* your wife was bisexual?' the reporter yelled as he strode away.

He could hear the gasps as he walked past. He pushed open the door to his office and slammed it shut behind him. His head was throbbing and his mouth was suddenly dry. The girls. His guts tightened at the thought of either one of them seeing the headlines. Ottie was too young to understand but Zoë . . . he put his face in his hands. He took several deep breaths and then walked round behind his desk and sat down. He had to act – fast. He picked up the phone. It was answered on the first ring.

'Ree? Thank God. I was just about to ring you.'

'Alison. You've seen the papers, then.'

'Yeah. You OK?'

He nodded. 'Yeah. It's the girls I'm worried about.'

'Where are they?'

'At school. The au pair'll pick them up this afternoon.'

'Don't worry about them. Not now. You'll think of something to tell them when you get home. Let's worry about the other stuff.'

He listened gratefully as Alison went into what she called 'lock down damage control' – a PR strategy that he would never, not in a million years, have been able to cook up. It took her ten minutes to outline what his next steps should be, whom to contact, which journalists to speak to . . . she covered everything. 'Remember, it's not *you*, darling,' she said forcefully. 'It's your wife. She's having a few problems. It's a bit too late to call it post-partum depression but I'll think of something. And remember that photographs aren't considered evidence in a British court, thank God, so the chances of her being arrested are exceedingly slim. In the meantime, contact the people I mentioned and set up a couple of interviews. I'm on my way over. And don't panic. This isn't you. And it's not the worst thing that's ever happened. You'll see. These fucking models . . . they do it all the time.'

Ree shook his head silently. *Not the worst thing that's ever happened.* What the hell could be worse? 'Thanks,' he said quietly when finally there was a lapse in Alison's cool, practical soliloquy.

'Don't mention it. That's what you pay me for. Hang tight, darling. In a month's time it'll all be over.'

He put down the phone. A month. He didn't have a month for Hayley's problems to take centre stage. He had a competition to win. His mouth suddenly went dry. The competition. Anneliese. Hayley. Jesus fucking Christ. A tidal wave of cold, hard fear ripped through him. Anneliese was on the jury. The news that her spokeswoman and favourite model had been caught snorting several fat lines of cocaine whilst some random dealer had his hand up her skirt would mean a swift end to *their* relationship. Forget the competition. He'd lost a friend – a good friend. He stared at the phone, hearing again Alison's voice. *Don't worry. In a month's time it'll all be over.* She was right. Dead right. He picked up the phone again.

Ree Herz calling. Answer. Reject. Anneliese stared at her mobile and swiftly pushed the red button. *Reject.* She was so angry she was shaking. Next to her, spread out across the dining-room table, was an assortment of the day's papers. Hayley's drugged face was on the front cover of almost all the tabloids with one ridiculous headline or another, alluding to the same thing: the face of A*d*SP and *A²*, two of the fashion world's most respected brands, had been photographed in what looked like a spectacularly bad porn flick. It was Bruno who'd helpfully brought her the papers. She'd taken one look at the first headline and she'd had to ask him to leave.

She picked up the *Guardian*. Thankfully it hadn't made any of the front pages of the broadsheets but – she scanned it carefully – there it was, on page six. The tone was marginally less hysterical but the gist was the same. She picked up *The Times*. Just seeing her name in the same paragraph as the words 'cocaine', 'drugs' and 'drunk' was enough to make her feel nauseous. *Why* hadn't she seen it coming? She tried to remember the last time she'd actually seen Hayley . . . it had to have been almost a month ago, maybe more. She didn't *need* to see her on a daily basis. And after this fiasco she didn't need to see her at all. Her lips tightened. How could she? How utterly, utterly stupid! She would have to be dropped immediately. She would get her marketing manager to draft a statement, the sooner the better. And then she'd have to make some phone calls herself – Dirk, the team at Moda, those blasted shareholders . . . her stomach turned at the thought. She'd better phone Callan. She twisted the ring around on her finger in agitation. And then there was that other situation to consider . . . Callan and Ree. *Now* what would happen? Oh, damn and blast that stupid, stupid woman!

Callan's first reaction was one of disbelief. 'You're kidding.'

'Do I sound as though I'm kidding?' Anneliese said crisply. 'It's not the sort of thing I'd normally joke about.'

'No, of course not,' Callan said quickly. 'Which paper?'

'All of them. Take your pick.'

Callan jumped out of bed, stubbing her toe in the process. She let out a silent howl of pain. Still clutching the phone to her ear she looked around wildly for her watch. The curtains were still drawn and her bedroom was in semi-darkness. She found it on the floor next to her discarded jeans. She picked it up; it was almost ten a.m. She and Ree had argued the night before; he was supposed to join Hayley at some party or other that he didn't want to go to. 'So don't go,' she'd said, shrugging. 'She probably won't notice.'

'I said I'd go.'

'So what? Tell her you changed your mind.'

'I can't. I don't like doing that.'

'Then go.'

And that had started it. They'd wound up arguing until it really was too late for him to go. And then, completely un-characteristically, she'd started crying. And then he stayed. And stayed. It was nearly three by the time he finally let himself out.

She rubbed her eyes and pulled back the curtain, still listening to Anneliese. 'So what're you going to do?' she asked, her mind racing ahead. Ree would be absolutely furious, she thought to herself, trying hard to suppress a thrill of hope. Perhaps this would be enough to convince him that he had to leave her. She'd never dared allow herself the luxury of thinking that way. But now . . . ?

'What am *I* going to do? *We're* going to fire her, that's what *we're* going to do. What a question.'

The emphasis wasn't lost on Callan. 'Yes, of course. That's what I meant.' There was silence between them for a few seconds. 'Has . . . have you spoken to Ree?' Callan asked tentatively.

'No, I haven't. I don't want to, either.'

'Why not? She's his wife.'

'I'm aware of that.' Anneliese's voice was dangerously cold.

Callan's heart sank. It was perhaps Anneliese's most unpleas-ant trait. Like no one else she'd ever encountered, Anneliese could cut a person dead – stone-cold dead. As if they'd never been or meant anything to her. She'd seen her do it more than once; she shuddered at the thought. 'It's not his fault,' she ventured hesitantly.

'He should have warned me.'

'Maybe he didn't know . . . ?'

'Oh, come on. How can you live with someone twenty-four hours a day and not see the signs. Of course he knew.'

'Maman, I don't think you're being fair—'

'Callan, I'm not interested in what you think. This is *my* company and it's *my* decision.'

Callan felt a fierce, protective rage begin to stir inside her. 'It's not *your* company alone,' she said hotly, rashly. 'You're not the only one with a say here.'

'I don't wish to discuss this any further. Bruno will draft a statement this afternoon. In the meantime, I'd appreciate it if you keep your partisan thoughts to yourself.'

'What are you talking about?' Callan's mouth suddenly went dry.

'You know exactly what I'm talking about. Let me warn you – if you try to turn this . . . this *disgusting* episode into something that you can profit from – in *whatever* way – you can consider yourself terminated as well.' The phone went dead. Callan stared at it in disbelief. She began to shake. It was all going hopelessly, disastrously wrong. *This* wasn't the way she'd intended to win him round – or win him over. She needed a cigarette. Fast.

The phone hadn't stopped ringing all day. On Alison's advice, he'd taken the few calls she deemed important and left Terri and the young account manager Alison had sent over to handle the rest. Keep calm, she kept telling him. Just keep calm. He glanced at the blinking red lights. How on earth was he supposed to keep calm, let alone work? Terri's voice interrupted him. 'Ree? Line one. It's your mother.'

He stared at the blinking signal for a second. Of all the people in the world he regretted having to face, his mother topped the list. He closed his eyes briefly in pain. Then he picked up the receiver. He listened to the torrent of adjectives and invectives in silence. There wasn't a thing he could say, either in his own defence, or, God forbid he should even try, Hayley's.

'Send them to us. Now. Immediately.' Sibongile's concern was for the children.

'Ma . . . it's the middle of term-time. It'd be fine for Ottie but Zoë's—'

'Riarua. Listen to me. We were not around, your father and I, when *you* were growing up. God knows, we wanted to be and we live every day with the thought that we failed you. Yes, you have made a wonderful success of your life and we couldn't be prouder. But don't think we don't know how hard it was. It wasn't God's plan for us, you know that. But I'm *still* your mother and I'm *still* the person who will care for you *and your children* better than anyone on this planet. And I'm telling you, there is nowhere safer for them right now. I don't know what is going on with that . . . that *woman* of yours and I don't care. You two must sort things out. But if you think, for one second, that I'm going to let you expose those two little angels to *anything* that might harm them, then you don't know who I am. Send them to us. We'll look after them until this is all over.' Sibongile's voice was calm but she enunciated every single word.

Ree couldn't speak. It wasn't in either of their natures to speak so openly about matters of the heart, and certainly not about their feelings for one another. Sibongile was even more adept at masking what she really felt than he was. *I'm still your mother and I'm still the person who will care for you and your children better than anyone on this planet.* He was alarmed to find his throat was thick with tears. He swallowed quickly, pushing down on the bittersweet relief that was threatening to overflow in him. 'Yes, Ma,' he said quietly, in a voice that sounded broken even to his own ears.

'Thank you.' Sibongile was also quiet, as if the outburst had cost her more than she cared to admit.

'I'll ring you later with the details. If I can't bring them myself, they'll fly with Chantal.'

'We'll be here to meet them. Get them to me as quickly as you can. And Riarua?' There was a hesitation in her voice.

He gripped the phone. 'Yes?'

'*Her* failures aren't yours. Remember that.'

He put the phone down and then put his face in his hands. He hadn't wept since he was a child. As he sat there, struggling with his own emotions, he remembered something he hadn't thought about in thirty years. He was eight or nine, perhaps even ten. At prep school. He'd just had a letter from Sibongile to say that they wouldn't be coming to England that half-term after all. At the last minute, his father had been told to go to Lusaka and she would be joining him. They would see him at Christmas, if everything worked out. He'd stayed behind in the empty classroom, looking at the wafer-thin blue paper that was his only link to home. It was February. Christmas was a whole year away. He'd last seen his parents the previous summer, for a fortnight. Sibongile had promised him they would come the following half-term. It came and went and they didn't come. Then it was Christmas. It too came and went and they didn't come. He spent it with his housemaster, Mr Pickering. And now this. At least she hadn't said 'this summer'.

'Hello, Ree . . . what're you still doing in here?' He looked up. It was Mr Griggs, the maths teacher. Ree liked him. He was less formal than some of the other teachers. Tall and athletic, he often played rugby or cricket with the boys. He was funny, too.

He was aware of a trail of coolness on his cheeks. He put up a hand to wipe his face immediately. Mr Griggs would never cry. 'N-nothing, sir,' he stammered.

'Letter from home?' Mr Griggs's voice was sympathetic.

'Yes, sir.' Ree quickly folded away the letter.

'Bad news? I hope not.'

'No, sir. It's . . . it's just I was rather hoping—'

He stopped, wondering if he'd said too much. Mr Griggs didn't seem to think so. He lifted himself up onto the desk opposite, cupping his chin in his hand as if he wanted to have a chat, just like that. Just as though they were friends. 'Hoping for a visit, were you?'

Ree nodded. His cheeks felt warm. 'They . . . my dad's been sent somewhere.' Even at that age, he'd known never to say too much.

Mr Griggs was silent for a moment. Then he put a hand on Ree's shoulder. 'Look here, Ree. I know a little bit about you, you know. Not much. Just the basics. And I can tell you that there aren't many boys here who'd manage the way you do. I know it's hard. You've got a lot to live up to with parents like that. A lot. And you've got to put up with a lot. But you're doing a pretty good job, I don't mind telling you. A pretty damn good job of everything. They'd be proud of you. So don't let it bother you if it sometimes gets you down. You've earned it.' And with that, he hoisted himself off the stool and walked out. From then on, it was Mr Griggs to whom he turned for guidance, spoken or not. From him he picked up everything he thought of as essential to being a man. Sibongile recognised it when they next met; they'd lost him, in some essential, invisible way. But the miracle of it was that for all that, he hadn't lost *them*. He was bonded to Mr Griggs and then others that followed him, but he was bonded to them as well. Her speech just now which he knew had cost her some effort, and then some, was a reminder to him of the fact, that was all. He blew his nose – a horrible, tearing sound that embarrassed him, even though he was alone, and wiped his face. He blinked several times; the sharp tears were still trembling at the edges of his lashes, blurring his vision. He put his glasses back on, took a couple of breaths to steady himself and picked up the phone again. His fingers dialled Anneliese's number. This time there was no answer. It just rang and rang and rang.

78

ANNELIESE

The buzzer sounded: two short, sharp jabs. She looked up from the press release she'd been studying. It was nearly midnight. She frowned. Who on earth could be at her door at this time? She waited for a moment. It buzzed again, twice. She got up and went to the window. It was raining outside; thin wavering rivulets streamed down the window-pane, making everything, including the street light, dance. She pulled the curtain a little further back and then gave a little hiss of annoyance. It was Ree. And he'd seen her. She felt a hot stab of anger in her chest. What the hell was he doing outside her house at midnight? She stood back from the window, torn by anger on the one hand and a sneaky admiration on the other. He'd phoned six or seven times that day – the last call had come through at nine or so, then he'd stopped. She'd very nearly switched off her phone.

He pressed the buzzer again, longer this time. She blew out her cheeks. Why couldn't he just leave her alone? A fourth time . . . even longer. She walked across the floor and snatched up the intercom.

He spoke into the phone before she could. 'I'm not leaving, Anneliese. I'll stand here all night if I have to.'

She blew out her cheeks again but pressed the entrance button this time. She heard the door click open loudly, and then close again, quietly this time, behind him. She opened the living-room door and walked onto the landing. She looked down into the hallway. 'Do you know what time it is?' she called down, her voice echoing loudly in the empty space.

He looked up. His face was wet; he had no hat or umbrella. He nodded. 'I had to make sure you'd be home.'

She made a small sound of exasperation. 'You could have just called.'

'I did. You won't pick up,' he said drily.

'*Ach*, you'd better come up. Unless you want to stand in the hallway all night.'

He said nothing, but climbed the stairs towards her. As he drew level, she moved back to let him pass. She was struck, as always, by how tall he was. It was as if she had to be reminded of it each time, anew. He ducked very slightly as he passed under the frame and walked to the centre of the room. Bach was playing softly on the stereo in one corner and there were the dying embers of a fire in the grate.

'So why are you here?' Anneliese asked from the doorway. They were both standing.

He spread his hands in front of him in some sort of gesture of appeal. 'Why else? I came to apologise.'

His directness was disarming. She glared at him, then took off her glasses, folding her arms across her chest as if to protect herself. She pointed at him with the arm of her spectacles. 'Why do you feel the need to apologise?'

'May I sit down?'

She nodded. 'But don't think that means I accept your apology.'

'I don't. In fact, I'm not sure you'll ever accept it but that doesn't matter.'

'So why are you here? Because of the competition?'

He stared at her incredulously. 'The competition? You think I *care* about the competition?'

'You should.'

'Well, I don't. I'm not here about that.'

'So what *are* you here for?'

'I came to talk about Callan.'

She blinked. *Mein Gott*, she thought to herself quickly. You *had* to admire his nerve. 'Callan?'

He nodded. 'In many ways, this whole . . . business . . . with Hayley wouldn't have happened if it hadn't been for . . . well, let's just say if my mind hadn't been elsewhere for the past two years.'

'And where *has* your mind been?'

He met her gaze squarely. Now she felt the need to sit down. She walked over to the sofa and sat down, drawing her legs up under her. He waited for a minute or two before answering. 'On Callan,' he said simply. 'It's been that way ever since I saw her.'

'And does Hayley know?'

'You know she knows. You know exactly what's been going on. Look, Anneliese, I didn't come here to play games, or to try and pretend it's not happening. We both know I've been sleeping with your daughter for more than a year. That's not the point. I'm here because I should have come to you then, not now. Now it's too late.' He stopped for a moment, and looked at his hands. 'The whole day I've been listening to everyone saying, "Look, this is *her* problem, not yours. *She's* the one in the photographs, not you. It's *her* career that's over, not yours."' He paused again. 'The thing is, they're wrong. Yes, she's the one who got caught but I'm equally to blame. This is as much my problem as it is hers.'

Anneliese was silent. She felt some obscure, resentful tug at the limits of her own experience, at her grasp on the complexity of things. She felt she'd somehow been wrong. She'd been so sure of herself earlier that day, that morning when she spoke to Callan. She'd felt herself butting up against some distaste in herself at what she perceived to be Ree's weakness, his inability to come out with it and face things squarely. Like a man, she realised, with a strange sense of wonder. It wasn't a phrase that came easily to her; she had no experience of what it meant to *be a man*, or a woman, really. She had no inkling, none whatsoever. She behaved according to how she felt. Not how she *ought* to feel.

But Ree was talking, talking still. 'If you'd asked me two years ago if I'd be the kind of man who cheats on his wife – or his kids, for that matter – I'd have said no. And I'm not talking about a one-off, the kind of thing that happens when you're away from home, there's no chance of being found out . . . a one-night stand. I'm talking about *months* of lying, hiding, pretending. Of not being there for her or for the girls because I'm somewhere else. And you know the worst thing about it?' He lifted his gaze from his hands to look at her. She didn't move a muscle. 'It's that I cheated on them both. Both Hayley and Callan.' He gave a short laugh. 'I was in a cab the other night going home from Callan's, just round the corner. The radio was on . . . it was Abba. That song. "The Winner Takes It All".' He shook his head. 'Thing is, there *are* no winners. Just losers. And I'm the biggest loser of them all. It's a betrayal, Anneliese, not a "situation", or a "problem" or even an "affair". It's a betrayal. That's the right word. I've betrayed all of you. *That's* what I came to apologise for.'

She stood up suddenly. There was a terrible roar in her own head that she couldn't suppress. She saw him look at her, a worried frown between his brows as he saw the agitation take hold of her. She put her hands up to her ears. He was saying something . . . She turned around, away from him. She couldn't bear to see him look at her like that. She wanted to walk away, get away, run away . . . be anywhere but there, in the living room, listening to his voice and that . . . that word. The din in her head intensified. She thought she might fall over, hit herself. She clutched at the mantelpiece and suddenly he was there behind her, his arms going under hers, pulling her up, forcing her to stand. He was shouting her name. She could hear it, but as if from a long way off. He'd managed to twist her round; she saw the fabric of his shirt come towards her and then she was pressed into it, the soft, male scent of him flooding her nostrils, her mouth. Salty tears, silent screams, the feel of his arms holding her upright . . . *betrayal*. That word. The word he'd uttered. The thing that she had done.

PART NINE

79

HANNELORE
FORTY YEARS EARLIER
Okahau, South-West Africa, 1961

'*Nkim.*' He touched the tip of her nose lightly with his fore-finger. '*Nkim.* Say it.'

'*Inkim.*' She tried the unfamiliar pronunciation.

He laughed. 'No, not *in-kim. Nn. Nn.*' He pressed his tongue against his teeth. 'Like that.' He tilted his head back so she could see. 'You see where my tongue is?' She nodded. 'Now you try it.' He watched approvingly as she did as he bade.

'*Nnnnnkim.*'

'Better. *Mbah.*' He pulled at a strand of her hair.

'*Mbah.*' She sighed and rolled away from him suddenly. 'Mwane, why are you learning Kimbundu?'

He looked at her and then looked away again. 'It's . . . useful,' he said finally.

'But why? Who here speaks it?'

He waited a moment before answering. 'Have you heard of Ghana?' he asked, pushing his bare toe into the dust, swirling it around.

'Ghana? You mean the country that just got its independence a few years ago?' she answered.

He nodded. 'Sixth of March, 1957,' he said proudly. He had the air of someone repeating something he'd been taught. 'Dr Kwame Nkrumah. Have you heard his speeches?'

She looked at him, amazed. 'Now, where d'you think I'd hear *those*? At school we're not even allowed to call it Ghana.'

'Of course not. *You* call it the Gold Coast.'

'*I* don't,' she said quickly, stung by the accusation in his voice. 'Anyway, why does it matter? What's Ghana got to do with Kimbundu?'

'Do you know who Sam Nujoma is?'

She pushed against his knee with her own bare foot. 'Why d'you keep on asking *me* questions? I'm asking you!'

'Do you?' he persisted.

She sighed. 'Yes, of *course* I do. He's the leader of the Ovambo People's Organisation. See? I'm not *stupid*, you know!' She tossed her long blonde hair over her shoulder.

'It's not called that any more.' Mwane was uncharacteristically quiet.

'What's it called, then?'

He stood up suddenly. His long, thin dark legs blocked out the sun. He shoved his hands in the pockets of his shorts and began to walk away without answering. She scrambled to her feet and ran after him. 'Go away,' he said fiercely as she tried to grab his arm. He shook her off. 'Just go *away*.'

She stopped, stung by the rejection. 'Where are you going?' she called after him angrily. 'Mwane! Stop!'

He turned round and there was a look on his face she didn't recognise. 'Is that an order?' he asked, an undertone of anger in his voice.

She took an involuntary step backwards. 'Of course not! I'm just . . . I was just asking where you're going,' she said uncertainly.

'Good. Cos you're not my *baas*,' he said, spitting out the Afrikaans word distastefully.

Hannelore was baffled by the sudden and unexpected nastiness in his voice. 'What the hell's got into you?' she yelled as he turned and started walking away again. Her eyes were suddenly smarting with tears.

'Go to hell.' The phrase, in English, floated back on the wind to her. She stood where she was in astonishment. Mwane spoke *English*? Her mouth was still open a few minutes later when his tall, loping frame disappeared from view.

*

'Where did Mwane learn English?' Hannelore asked Ella as they sat together shelling peas.

Ella's head flew up in alarm. She quickly looked around her. There was no one else in the kitchen. 'Who told you he speaks English?' she asked in a fearful whisper.

Hannelore was even more confused. 'I . . . I heard him. This afternoon. He . . . he said something in English.'

There was a knot in Ella's throat that bobbed up and down when she was agitated. Hannelore watched as she swallowed, and swallowed again. 'You mustn't say anything,' she said, still whispering. 'Not to your mama, not to your papa. You understand?'

'But why? Surely it's a good thing—'

'Not a *word*!' Ella jerked the enamel basin away from Hannelore's hands. She got up clumsily, spilling a little of the water over them both. Normally she'd have bent down to mop it up, fussing over the fact that she'd got Hannelore's dress wet. But not today. She rushed out of the kitchen and was gone before Hannelore could even get to her feet. She stood up, brushing a few stray peas from her skirt. What on earth had got into everyone? She hadn't seen Mwane since he'd stalked off in an apparent huff earlier that day . . . now Ella too had disappeared . . . what was going on?

At dinner that evening, sitting in the usual, uncomfortable silence with her parents, the question popped into her head. 'Papa,' she asked, putting down her wine glass. 'What's the new name of the Ovambo People's Org—' She didn't even have time to finish the word. Suddenly the glasses on the table jumped. His fist had come down with a deafening bang.

'How *dare* you!' he roared at her.

'Ludwig . . .' her mother murmured. 'Please.'

'Shut up!' He turned his reddened, angry face towards her. 'Don't you have any respect?'

'But I—'

413

'Hannelore . . . leave the table, please.' Her mother interjected swiftly.

'But I haven't finished—'

'You're finished when I say you're finished!' her father practically screamed. 'Leave the table *at once*!' She took one look at his face and fled.

In her room, she sat down gingerly on the edge of her bed. Her knees were shaking. It had been a day of inexplicable happenings. First Mwane, then Ella . . . and now her father. OK, so perhaps asking him about the Ovambo People's Organisation wasn't the smartest thing to do . . . but still. It wasn't as if she'd asked him about Hitler, which was one sure way to raise his blood pressure. She looked at her knees. There was still a small black scab from where she'd cut herself the other day, following Mwane up the mopane tree near the dam. She picked at its edges, lifting it as much as she dared. With a small prick, it lifted clean off. She stared at the pearly pink skin beneath. A tiny bead of ruby-red blood blossomed and then ran into the cracks of her skin. She rubbed it off with a forefinger, quickly licking it as she'd done thousands of times as a child. She suddenly felt very young and silly. Something had changed on the farm. She knew it, and yet she didn't. Perhaps she didn't want to?

80

It was impossible to stay angry for ever. Especially with her. It took Mwane a couple of days to cool down from whatever tantrum had gripped him. They passed each other as she was walking to the dam and he was returning from it.

'Hi,' she said, eyeing him warily.

He stopped. His hands were in his pockets again. He drew one out and opened his palm. There was a small pile of sunflower seeds tucked carefully in it. He offered it to her. They stood in the fierce midday sun, splitting the seeds with their front teeth, munching contentedly. Somehow, without either saying anything, their customary balance was restored. 'So where are you going?' he asked, with the faint emphasis on 'you' that she understood as he intended it.

She shrugged. She had a book in her hand. 'Down to the dam. It's so hot.'

'What are you reading?'

She showed it to him, suddenly shy. 'It's just come out in England,' she said eagerly.

'*Lady Chatterley's Lover.*' He read the English words easily, fluently, without comment. 'What's it about?'

She looked away. 'When did you learn English, Mwane?' she asked after a moment, her voice suddenly quiet.

He looked at her for a moment, then turned so that they were both facing the same direction. He began to walk away. 'Come,' he said, not looking back.

She followed him, a few paces behind, past the servants' quarters where they'd both played as children, past the row of tiny brick houses where he now lived and where his father had died a few years earlier. His mother still took in the washing; aside from the usual greetings, it had been years since Hannelore had had a conversation with her. Quite what the old woman thought of her son's friendship with her was beyond asking. In silence they walked down the dusty reddish track that led to the dam, the enormous circular, corrugated iron tank that held the farm's water supply. When they were younger and Hannelore was less fastidious about such things, she and Mwane would strip off at the height of midday, wallowing in the sweet, luke-warm water as though it were a swimming pool. The bottom of the massive tank was green with algae, and worse. Mwane sometimes dived under water and came up with a handful of sludge in which things wriggled and writhed. He would torment her with them. Not any more. She, accustomed as she had been to the crystal-clear, azure water of the school swimming pool in Cape Town, no longer scrambled over the sides and flopped noisily in.

They passed the tank, still in silence. The book felt heavy in her hand. Occasionally their forearms bumped; his, as black as tar, hers turning slowly pink in the sun. Past the dried-up river-bed, through the tall, grassy reeds that hovered hopefully at its edges, perennially waiting for rain. They came upon the mopane trees, had a few minutes' relief in their cool, mossy shade, and then they began to climb the long, sloping hill on the other side of the river-bed. The grass was tougher and sparser on this side. Twice she caught and stubbed a toe on an exposed rock. They scrambled easily over the larger rocks, Mwane leaning back to give her an occasional hand. The land they had entered into was different now, and had a different aspect. In the local dialect they called it the 'land of the grandmothers' – something to do with the custom of bringing the elderly women out here to die. She'd never been afraid of it – Mwane had taught her to respect nature, not fear it, but still there was something eerie and rather ghostly about walking over the dry, barren earth, which could just as easily have housed bones as a colony of ants. There was a small, dilapidated hut about half a mile off. It had once been painted blue – by whom? No one seemed to know – but the ferocious sun had leached almost all colour out of it. Only here and there, under what was left of an awning, or around the door frame, could traces of the aquamarine paint still be seen, ghost-like, a little like the land itself. They walked steadily towards it. She could feel the thin trickle of sweat begin at the point where her shoulder blades met. In the dry, high-altitude air of the escarpment, perspiration was rare. She thought of the hot, humid days of high summer in Cape Town, by the sea. Cape Town seemed another dimension, an experience that was suspended awkwardly in time and space. She knew without anything ever having been said that she would never return.

There was no longer a door to enter into the hut. It had rotted or been carried away; only the dull brass hinges remained. She studied it as they passed through the frame. *J. Hencke & Sohne, Düsseldorf.* The German name and town jumped out at her,

416

incongruous with their surroundings. There was an old mattress lying half folded over in one corner of the room. It was cool inside. Mwane kicked the mattress to unfold it; a startled beetle scuttled out. He quickly checked around him; nothing. No snakes, nothing slithered silently into the deep, shadowy recesses. They sank down together onto the mattress, lying on their backs, again not touching but breathing together lightly, as one. A bird flew into the empty doorway suddenly, landing silently on the dusty ground. It was small and dark blue, with a red fringe and collar and a soft, sandy-coloured underbelly. It regarded the two of them with frank curiosity, shifting its weight from one foot to the other as if in indecision. Then with a short, sharp chirrup, it lifted off again, disappearing swiftly into the white expanse of sky.

'*Hirundu*,' Mwane said softly. 'Swallows. They come down from Angola this time of the year.'

She turned her head fractionally to look at him. Out here, away from the farm and the authority of her father that had stamped every bush, rock, tree, Mwane had a different status that preceded Bodenhausen and her father's efforts to make it his own, bend it to his will. Here, lying on the dusty mattress in a house that some mad German − her father, perhaps? − had built to keep out the elements, such as they were − sun, wind, rain once every two years or less − something was added to Mwane that had been taken away from him. He entered back into a part of himself that was deeply bound to the land and its history in a way her own kind had forgotten, or most likely never knew. For him it was a giant, unending terrain of coded messages that he had learned, over time, to read. Where she saw only dust and rocks and patches of ground that stubbornly resisted her mother's efforts to grow tomatoes or spinach or white roses, whatever plant or vegetable that had leapt out at her from the pages of the recipe books she hauled off the top shelf in the kitchen, he saw other things: hints, clues, traces that opened onto a different way of understanding the world and the mysteries it contained. She was suddenly both shy and in awe of it.

She was still clutching her book. She opened it, as if trying to remind herself of her own mastery of things.

They began to read together. She was quicker than he; when she got to the bottom of the page, he put out a hand to hold her back. Did he understand the English prose? She couldn't tell. She reread the passage slowly until she felt him catch up. His lips moved as he silently read the words aloud to himself. They reached the end of the paragraph at the same time. She brought up her hand to turn the page but he pushed the book to one side, not as a rejection, but as an invitation to something else. She turned her head so that they were facing each other, unencumbered by Lady Chatterley and her burgeoning sensuality.

His breath was warm and light; it tickled her nostrils. The edges of her lips were full of a sweet sensitivity that made her want to laugh. He traced the outline with his fingertips; she did the same. They'd seen each other naked before, many times. They'd even kissed, slow, semi-erotic embraces that seemed nothing more than the overflow of the affection that each held for the other, naturally. But this was different. She knew without saying anything that they were about to cross a line that had been drawn between them for all sorts of reasons; and that, once crossed, they would never be able to return. She wriggled out of her skirt, sitting up to allow him to tug her T-shirt over her head. Her hair fell across her breasts in waves. He lifted first one strand, then the other, his tongue moving lightly over her bare skin. She arched herself towards him, her hands busy on him. A quickening of the pulse, their movements more urgent . . . she took his rock-hard penis in her hand, studying it curiously before bending her head to take him in her mouth. It was her first; it wasn't his. She didn't ask where the knowledge he displayed of how to pleasure her had come from – like his mastery of the land, his mastery of her body seemed complete. He brought a small yelp of triumph from her not once, but twice, leaving her shaking with the pleasure of it all, a surfeit of emotions she hadn't felt before.

'It will be better for you next time,' Mwane said, his voice already drowsy with an exhaustion that she sensed had nothing to do with sleep. His arm was a dead weight against her flat, taut stomach.

She couldn't speak. She reached up a hand and touched his springy, soft hair, so different from her own. 'It was good, for me,' she whispered shyly.

'No, it's never good, the first time.' Mwane was quietly authoritative. 'You'll see.'

She turned so that they were lying face to face, eyeball to eyeball. In the distorted convex lens of her vision, his face was all surface; smooth, coal-black skin, the tiny, pinprick pimples and imperfections magnified. She traced the small, delicately scrolled edge of his nostrils with her gaze, travelling upwards over the small, almost button-nose to the almond-shaped, faintly yellow whites of his eyes, the tightly curled thick lashes and the eyebrows that were the same colour as his skin, only the texture of the hair marking out the frame. It was a face that was as familiar to her as her own. Yet just then, when he was on top of her, pushing into her with a mixture of tenderness and power, he'd seemed a stranger to her, caught in the grip of some unseeing, terrible agony. 'Just now,' she whispered again, her mouth very close to his ear. 'It seemed like you were in pain.'

He laughed. The sound reverberated in her ears. 'Well, it *is* a kind of pain. *You're* a kind of pain, Nogiti. When you're not with me, I feel it here.' He took her hand and placed it against his heart. 'And here.' His head. 'And here.' His penis, now soft and wetly flaccid against his thigh.

She giggled. 'Then we'll just have to stay here for ever,' she said, sighing contentedly. She sat up suddenly, clutching her T-shirt to her bare breasts. 'Mwane . . . why did you ask me the other day if I'd heard of Sam Nujoma?'

His hand, which had been idly lying on her thigh, drew back. There was silence for a few minutes. A cricket somewhere in the room had begun its incessant whirring. She looked at him; his eyes were closed. She was just about to open her mouth to ask him again when he spoke. ' "Do not give education to the natives because if you do so, it would be as if you were giving the white man a razor to cut his own throat."' He was reciting something. Her eyes widened. 'D'you know who said that?' She shook her head. 'Hermann Heinrich Vedder. D'you know who he is?' Again she shook her head. 'One of our leaders. A former missionary. Now he represents "our" interests in Parliament. The whites-only parliament.' He turned his head to look up at her. There was an expression in his eyes that she hadn't seen before, ever. A hardness in his face and a coldness in his voice that sent a corresponding cool wind sailing through her.

He began to talk. To talk about where he was going, why he'd been picked up by the Movement, what they were training him to do. As the words fell out of his mouth, the bottom fell out of her world. He was leaving Bodenhausen. She felt herself falling slowly downwards, like the yellow and gold leaves in the school yard in Cape Town when the winter winds began to blow through the city, turning everything to dust. He'd put her hand on his heart. He'd sworn to her. He would never leave her. Shit and lies. That was all it was. Shit and lies.

81

The headquarters of the CID Special Branch in Omaruru, the nearest town to Okahau, was a far more modest building than the name implied. She looked at the small bungalow dubiously. It looked more like a general store than an outpost of the government. She clutched her small purse tightly and crossed the road.

There was even a bell that jangled as she walked in, just like a shop. The interior was cool and dark, a welcome relief after the fierce blast of sunlight that greeted her as she stepped off the train. A few people looked curiously at her as she walked down the main road, stopping every now and then to consult a map. Omaruru was small; it took her less than ten minutes to locate the office on Blaauwstraat.

'Can I help you, madam?' A native policeman stood behind the counter. He spoke Afrikaans. Her palms began to sweat.

'Is . . . could I see Captain van der Merwe?' she asked, her heart beginning to thump.

He looked at her and frowned. 'Is he expecting you?'

'No.'

'Do you have any appointment?'

'No.'

'Can I ask what this is about?' He looked her up and down.

'No.' She lifted her chin. He was not the man she'd come to see.

He stared at her and seemed at a loss as to what to do next. A young white woman in a flowery summer dress with a pink purse in her hand and white gloves . . . what was he to do with her? He looked around him, as if seeking support from the framed pictures of his superiors, including the stern but avuncular face of Hendrik Verwoerd, president of the Republic, whose blue eyes twinkled from every government office in town. 'Wait here,' he said finally, lifting the flap that separated them. He closed it carefully behind him, locking it with a flourish, as though he suspected she might slip through and usurp him of whatever authority his uniform provided. She nodded and turned to look out of the window.

'Can I help you, Miss . . . ?' A small, portly man in a stiff khaki uniform with a brightly coloured row of badges on his tight, fat breast walked into the waiting room. She turned. He was looking at her with a mixture of impatience and curiosity.

'Von Riedesal,' she said, drawing herself very upright. 'Hannelore von Riedesal.'

'Old Ludwig's daughter? From out Okahau way?' He seemed to relax.

She nodded. 'Yes. Bodenhausen.'

'So what can I do for you, *meisie*?' he asked, a hand coming up to stroke his moustache. The black policeman in the corner who'd been on duty when she walked in regarded them suspiciously.

'Not here. I need to . . . I'd like to talk to you alone. If I may.'

'By all means. Come this way.' He led her back through the passageway through which he'd just come. 'No, not you, Andreas. Man the desk. As usual.'

'Very good, *baas*.' The policeman's face registered his disappointment. He crossed the floor, his shoes marking out a clipped efficiency as he walked.

'Come through, come through.' Captain van der Merwe was solicitous. 'Mind your step . . . there's a loose tile just here. I keep telling the cleaners to be careful, but you know how it is,' he said cheerfully, one white person to another. 'Here we are. Do have a seat.' She sat down carefully on one of the two chairs in front of his desk. His office was small and rather airless. He noticed her quick glance towards the window and got up again immediately. 'A bit stuffy in here, ay?' he said, wrestling with the catch. All at once a rush of air and voices tumbled in, breaking into her thoughts. There were workers outside in the yard. The white overseer shouted in a mixture of Afrikaans and German; the blacks sang and laughingly swore at him in their language, which he did not understand, but she did. 'On account of the noise,' Captain van der Merwe said, coming back to his desk. Again there was the flash of culpability between them; one white to another. 'What can you do, ay? That's how they are. Now, Miss von Riedesal. What can I do for you?' He leaned forward expectantly. His hands were clasped under the pale, double folds of his chin. His expression was one of benevolent tolerance. A nice young girl like her, come all the way to see him. Pretty, too. He was middle-aged with daughters her age, but he knew how to appreciate a woman with a fine figure like hers, lovely long blonde hair. She smelled nice. Fresh and nice. Good breeding . . . you could tell. Nothing like it. All this was expressed without a word but Hannelore understood him perfectly.

'It's about a friend of mine,' she began hesitantly.

'Go on. It is a boyfriend? A nice young man you've got somewhere, ay?'

She blushed. 'No, it's not like that.' She hesitated again. 'I . . . I think he's in trouble.'

'What sort of trouble.' His eyes narrowed slightly. He leaned forward. 'What sort of trouble, ay?' he repeated.

The words came out in a rush. 'He's being used; they're just using him, but he doesn't see it. They want him to risk his life, his family, his friends . . . everything. I've *told* him not to do it. He's very bright, you see. He speaks German better than I do and oshiWambo and oshiHerero and he's learning Kimbundu—'

'Just a minute here, *meisie*. What's he learning all those Kaffir languages for? Who is this young man? What's a nice white boy doing with all that nonsense?'

Hannelore looked at him uncertainly. 'Oh, no. He's not white. He's Ovambo.'

There was a sudden silence. 'An Ovambo?' Captain van der Merwe frowned as if the explanation made no sense. 'An *Ovambo* friend of yours?'

She nodded. 'Yes, his name's Mwane. Mwane Nangolo. He's the son of one of my father's workers. I've known him since I was born. He's my best friend,' she said earnestly, failing to understand the dark stain that was beginning to spread across Captain van der Merwe's ruddy complexion. 'He's incredibly clever and—'

'Why d'you say he's in danger?' The captain's voice had softened suddenly.

She was relieved. She'd won him round, somehow. She was eager to share her worry. 'They've asked him to guard someone. He . . . he won't tell me who, but I think I can guess. He's coming north this weekend. I think he's going to make for the Bechuanaland border and they want Mwane to be his bodyguard. But he's not like that. He's the gentlest person you could meet. They've brainwashed him. Sometimes when he speaks I don't recognise him.' She stopped. The captain's expression was so kind it made her want to cry.

'Oh, don't you worry your pretty little head any more about it,' he said, bringing a finger up to stroke his moustache. 'Don't you worry. We'll have a quick word with your Mr . . . what's his name? Mwane Nangolo.' He reached for a pad and scribbled something down. 'You're out by Okahau, isn't it? Just after the turning to the Dierks' homestead?'

She nodded. 'Yes, it's the big house on the hill.'

'Know it well. All right, Hannelore. You've done the right thing. These young men . . . they're easily bamboozled, you know. We've seen it all before. This weekend, you said? Coming north?'

She nodded again. 'I . . . I think so. He didn't . . . he wasn't specific about the details but I know someone's coming to fetch him on Friday. I'm just so scared I'll never see him again.'

Captain van der Merwe smiled. 'Oh, you'll see him again. Don't you worry.' He pushed himself up from his chair. 'You've got a driver waiting for you?'

She shook her head. 'No. I . . . I didn't think it was right . . . to involve my father. I don't think he'd . . . well, understand. I came by train.'

'Quite right too. Leave it to us, Hannelore. We're used to this sort of thing.' He walked around the desk and opened the door. 'And don't say a word to young Nangolo. Best keep the element of surprise. There's no telling what they'd do to him if they knew you'd been in to see us. Seen it all before. Animals, that lot. Animals.'

She nodded again and got to her feet. The interview – or chat – was over. She walked a little unsteadily to the door. As she passed through, she could have sworn she heard him hiss something at her but she didn't catch the words. She turned to look at him – he was a little shorter than she – but met only blankness in his face. 'Well, thank you, Captain,' she said, as she reached the front door. The other man, the duty officer, was leaning against the desk, watching them.

'It's our pleasure, Hannelore.' He folded his arms across his chest and watched her open the door.

She stepped out into the blinding sunlight and hurried across the road with its row of fringed umbrella trees shading the sidewalk with its ubiquitous sign, *Blankes Alleen. Whites Only*. Blacks walked on the other, unshaded side. Tiny beads of sweat had formed on her upper lip by the time she reached the train station but they seemed to have nothing to do with the heat. The train was standing patiently by the tracks, as though waiting for her. She boarded the short first-class section, avoiding the other passengers' curious gaze. She had forgotten to bring her book; not that she would have pulled it out on this train. Across from her sat a farmer of the sort she was used to seeing around here – huge and splendidly solid, his chest and belly less body than a retaining wall of flesh. He was wearing the sandy brown khaki shirt that was almost a uniform in these parts. His knees, twice the size of hers, were bare, covered in thick, reddish-brown hair. She thought of Mwane's smooth black skin and distaste for the man opposite her, for Captain van der Merwe, for the stationmaster who'd looked at her sideways, rose in her like a fever. She turned her face away from his enquiring glance and stared out of the window. The parched landscape flew by, low undulating hills with their sparse peppercorns of thorny bush covering their flanks, the acacia trees now blonde with the summer's heat . . . and all around that smudgy, mauvish haze that hung over the hills. She closed her eyes and leaned her head against the cool windowpane. She'd done the right thing. Of course she had. Mwane was in way over his head. Somebody had to make him see sense. Who better than her?

82

They came just before midnight. It was the horses that picked up the faint, rumbling tremors in the earth, long before the first headlights appeared. She woke to the sound of their whinnying, long-drawn-out sounds of distress. She sat bolt upright in bed, clutching the sheets to her chest. There was a commotion in the yard behind the house; a door slammed, someone shouted. The cars swept into the yard scattering gravel and stones, one after the other. More slamming doors and the sounds of barking dogs. Her whole body went cold with fear. She heard her father's voice and their door opening, just down the corridor. She jumped out of bed and ran to the window. The yard was full of cars, their headlights picking out tunnels of swirling dust. The ghostly shape of men holding onto snarling dogs flitted across her vision. She felt her knees give way.

'Hannelore?' She could hear her mother shouting for her in fear. 'Hannelore . . . where are you?'

She opened her mouth but no words would come. She stood by the window, clutching the sill.

Suddenly there was a loud banging at the front door. Her mother began to scream. She heard her father shouting, running down the corridor. The front door burst open and she heard the angry exchange of words in Afrikaans. She recognised a voice. It was Captain van der Merwe. She began to shake.

Her door burst open. It was her mother, still in her night-dress, struggling to tie her dressing gown around her. Her long, silvery plait of hair lay down her back and there were strands hanging around her face. She looked old, Hannelore thought suddenly, absurdly, and more afraid than she'd ever seen her. But it was an odd fear that seemed to have little to do with the screams and shouts and the yard full of running men. She stood in the doorway, looking at Hannelore with a strange, almost pitying expression on her face. 'You'd better come,' she said, her voice low and fearful. 'You'd better come. Put something on.'

'Mama,' Hannelore began, but her mother turned and walked out of the room.

They made her wait until they brought him back. Or what was left of him after the dogs had finished with him. She sat in the living room between the two men, her father on one side,

Captain van der Merwe on the other, hearing the conversation that ran back and forth between them – though it would be wrong to call it a conversation. Her father listened in stony silence as the captain outlined what he called 'an unfortunate turn of events'. His terrible, fearful rage emanated from him; she could almost smell it. '*Ag*, we'll get him,' Captain van der Merwe said, almost chummily. 'The dogs'll get him.' He turned his pale, washed-out eyes to Hannelore, sitting stiffly upright in the chair. 'But this one . . . this one's a problem, *Myneer*. You don't need me to tell you that. What she's done is, quite frankly, *incomprehensible*. If word ever got out . . .'

'I will deal with her.' Papa's voice was devoid of feeling. Suddenly a scream pierced the air. There was a great volley of barking, and the sound of running feet. A shiver ran up and down Hannelore's spine. It was Maazuu, Mwane's mother. She could hear Ella's voice, and the screams of the other women as the police crossed the yard, dragging something – or someone – behind them. They began the familiar lament that the women sounded around the dead. The hair on the back of her neck stood straight up.

'*Ja*, they got him.' Captain van der Merwe stood up. He walked to the window and pulled back the curtain. The yard was full of commotion. He beckoned to Hannelore. 'Come. Come see.'

Hannelore couldn't move. Her father got up and hauled her roughly to her feet. He dragged her to the window, his grip tightening with every step. She was thrust in front of him, her face almost pressed against the glass. The policemen were dragging a body behind them, tied by the hands. From the way the head lolled against the chest and the lifeless legs dragged along in the sand, she understood he was no longer alive. She closed her eyes. After that, she remembered little. When the men finally departed, her father picked up his whip. She had no idea how long it lasted. At some point, someone – her mother? Ella? – must have cut away the nightdress and washed her, taking care to wipe the blood away from the cuts and welts that covered her.

She was put to bed; she must have slept. She had no recollection of anything.

In the morning when it was light, Tante Bärbel was there. She heard her voice in the dining room. She came into Hannelore's room, took one look at her and began flinging clothes into a bag.

'Come, *Schatz*. Get up. The driver's waiting.'

'Where are we going?' The words fell like stones from her bruised mouth.

'Away from here. You must never come back.' Tante Bärbel looked at her steadily. 'Never. They will never forgive you, you understand? Neither side. This part of your life is finished.' She stood in front of Hannelore, looking down at her. She lifted a strand of hair away from her face. Hannelore didn't have to look up to imagine her expression. The whip had caught her across her left cheek; even now, some seven or eight hours after he'd finished with her, the cut still stung. 'Yes, you must forget about coming back here again. As far as they're concerned you're finished. Finished and *klar*. You're dead to them. Don't ever forget it.'

PART TEN

83

LINDI
Cape Town, South Africa

They drove out of the airport in a hired car under a name and driver's licence she didn't recognise. 'Jonas Shilonge,' she read, taking a peek, bursting into laughter. 'So if you're Jonas, who'm I?'

'*Mrs* Shilonge.' He was tolerantly amused. 'It's a fake. Just in case it's required.'

She smiled to herself. It was a typically cryptic statement, of the sort Iago frequently made. The freeway led them away from the airport, straight into the city. She'd been to Cape Town a few times; nothing was ever sufficient preparation for the sight of the mountain, looking majestically down over the port and the long sweep of the bay. 'Where are we going?' she asked, almost jumping up and down in the seat with childish excitement.

'You'll see. I wanted to show you something first, before we get there. D'you see that patch of land up there?' He pointed with his finger as they approached the slopes. 'Where it's all blackened?'

She followed his finger. 'Yeah . . . what's up there?'

'It's the site of a new project. The Museum of Freedom. Mandela and Mbeki have been working on it for almost a decade. We just got word that the city has finally given the land.'

'Fantastic location,' Lindi said, craning her neck to look behind them as he drove past. 'The Museum of Freedom . . . I like the sound of it.'

'So do we.'

'Who's "we"?' she asked curiously. It was the second time he'd used the word.

He was silent for a few seconds. 'Me and the Old Man.'

'What d'you mean?'

'It's the biggest arts and culture programme on the continent. Nothing's ever been done on this scale before. It's got the official backing of the UN, UNESCO, the World Bank, the IMF, everyone. It'll put South Africa on the map in a way that'll link all the major museums in Europe, South America and the US – the British Museum, the Musée d'Orsay in Paris, the Smithsonian in Washington, MoMA in New York. This is going to be *big*, Lindi. It's ambitious and it's got everyone excited. It's a once-in-a-lifetime opportunity for the government to get it right.' Despite his obvious enthusiasm, there was a note of barely suppressed anger in his voice.

'So what's the problem?' she asked slowly.

He glanced at her, as if judging how much he was prepared to say. 'It's simple. The South Africans want the story to be about *them*. They forget they're only part of the history of this place. And they forget how much they owe us. You can't separate out their struggle from ours, especially Namibia's. They're linked. It doesn't make sense for this to be a museum only about *their* freedom. If they're intending to honour people like Castro and Guevara, why should the Old Man be left out?'

Lindi looked straight ahead at the road disappearing in front of them. 'So why don't they want to?' she asked hesitantly, although she already knew the answer.

He shook his head. 'Greed. The usual story. Everyone who's anyone wants a piece of this for themselves. It's feeding time. You know what it's like.'

'But it doesn't make sense. Surely there's room for everyone?'

He gave a short laugh. 'If there's anything I've learned in politics it's that there's rarely room for everyone. He who shouts the loudest. Look, you know how it goes. Anyhow, we've done a little digging around. If they're not prepared to let us in through

432

the front door, we'll go round the back. And that's where I'm hoping you can help.'

'*Me?*' Lindi stared at his profile. 'What can I do?'

'I believe you know one of the architects on the shortlist. Riarua Herz.'

'Ree? Ree's designing it?'

Iago shook his head. 'Not quite. He's one of six firms who've been invited to compete for the job. If he gets it – and it's still a big "if" – he'll be sympathetic to our cause, of course. His father's assured me. He's our best hope of bringing international pressure to bear on the trust who'll run the museum.'

'But I still don't understand. I've got nothing to do with the competition or the process or anything. How can I help?'

'Ah, but you do.'

'What are you talking about?'

'That friend of yours . . . the one you met in New York. The historian.'

'Tara? Tara Connolly?' Her mouth dropped open. How did Iago even know she knew Tara?

'Yes. Her. She was adopted by that German fashion designer. Anneliese somebody-or-other.'

'Anneliese Zander de Saint Phalle, yes. Well, she wasn't really *adopted*—'

'She's on the jury.' Iago cut her off. 'We need two things. We need Riarua Herz to win. *And* we need a sister institution in Windhoek. A second museum. Part of the Freedom Trail. That's the legacy the Old Man wants to leave behind. That's the legacy *I* want to create. And that's what we need you to help us get.'

The hard, stony mountains emerged out of the mist as the car rounded one bend after another. Shrouds of white cloud clung to their bare sides; down here, about an hour and a half out of the city, it had been raining all day. Iago turned off the main road and the view suddenly unfolded in front of them. The sea was a heaving, white-tipped mass, turning a dark, midnight blue out there where the world slipped off its edge. The mountain ran straight down into it, as though plunging its fist into the choppy waters, claiming a stake. Buffels Road, William Avenue, Hang-klip Road, James Avenue, Edward Road. Lindi read the names silently to herself as he drove. He seemed to know where he was going. At the last road before the mountain rose vertically in front of them, he turned left. Her mouth dropped open. A lilac and cream hand-painted sign at the gate announced proudly *Jeanette's Guest House*. The house, a beautiful two-storey Victorian property with a pretty, latticed veranda running the length of the upstairs floor, stood in the shade of two massive blue gums. Iago pressed the discreet buzzer and the gate slid open. They'd arrived.

The car park was empty. Iago took their bags from the boot just as a uniformed servant came up to them, gesturing wildly that it was his job, *no, no* . . . he took the bags from Iago with a smile so wide it threatened to split his face in half. He led them up the pretty garden path to the front door. An immaculately dressed middle-aged woman was standing in the doorway, smiling widely in welcome.

'I'm Jeanette,' she said, smiling broadly. 'Welcome to Pringle Bay. Do come in . . . how was the drive?' She led them through a beautifully decorated and appointed living room – plump, plush sofas; rich, warm oriental rugs, paintings on the walls, a mixture of antique and Provence-style furniture . . . it was gorgeous. The smell of freshly baked pastries wafted through the air; Lindi's stomach immediately rumbled.

Iago stopped at the doorway to let her pass. He slid a hand playfully across her bottom as she followed Jeanette upstairs. The gesture startled her. On the way down from the city, something had been bothering her. If Iago knew she knew Tara, or Ree, for that matter, why hadn't he mentioned it before? The project had been in the planning for almost a decade . . . if it was so precious to him, surely he'd have brought it up?

'Everything OK?' Iago's voice interrupted her thoughts.

She jumped. 'Yes, of course . . . it's beautiful,' she said slowly, looking round the room. There was a four-poster bed with a profusion of pillows and a snowy embroidered counterpane; thick, sisal carpeting and the same wonderfully patterned oriental rugs everywhere. The bedroom looked out over the garden and onto the scrubby slope of the mountain directly behind the house. The living room, which was almost as big as her living room at home, looked straight out over the sea. 'There's no one else here,' she added. 'We're lucky.'

'I booked the whole place. No wonder Jeanette's smiling,' Iago said drily.

'The whole place? For the whole weekend?'

'Of course. Can't have other people overhearing us now, can we?' He smiled at her. 'Come here.' He sat down on the bed and patted the space beside him. 'I know what you're thinking,' he said quietly, lifting a strand of her curly hair and pushing it away from her face. 'And the answer's "no".'

'But—'

'No. The answer's still "no". D'you really think I'd go to those lengths?'

Lindi looked down at her hands. 'I . . . no, of course I don't. It's just . . .'

'Just a coincidence, that's all. I remembered you talking about your friend – what's her name? Tara? You've spoken about Ree often enough . . . you had a crush on him. You told me that yourself. Or have you forgotten?'

She shook her head. Relief was beginning to flow through her. She'd forgotten how perceptive he could be. 'No, you're right.'

''Course I'm right. I just put two and two together, that's all. That's another thing politics has taught me. You've got to make things happen. If you don't, someone else will. And this one's important, not just to me.'

'Why?' She looked up at him. He held her hand loosely in his; tracing the fine lines in her palm with his fingertip.

He shrugged. 'I'm not a natural at this, you know. It's still distasteful to me, all the jockeying for power. Power's useful for those who don't have it. I was an academic before all this happened and I dare say that's what I'll go back to. Even if I succeed the Old Man, I'll only have two terms at the most – that's if I want the job in the first place.' He was quiet for a moment. 'But this, on the other hand, this is different. This project is a chance to outlive all of that. It'll be around for decades after we're gone. *That's* a legacy. This—' He passed a weary hand over his face, stroking his short, neat goatee. 'This will pass.'

She was moved beyond words. She took his hand in a way that she rarely did, lacing her fingers through his strong, broad ones. He brought her into a marvellously full appreciation of what it was to be alive, to be full of promise . . . in some strange way, he brought her back to that moment when the Old Man, on his way to the bathroom downstairs, had come upon her hurrying to the same in her skimpy pyjamas and fluffy woollen slippers. *You'll come back to us. Soon. When this is all over. It won't be long now.* She put up a hand to touch her aching throat. He'd done it again; he'd managed to bring the two halves of her life together not in tension, as was usually the case, but in peace. He'd stretched back into one of the most painfully confused parts of her past, extracted something that was useful and valuable and presented it to her in a way that she could make use of *now*, in the present, at the moment in her life when the struggle to reconcile the different aspects of who she really was was at its most intense. She turned to look at him and suddenly, there it was. She saw very clearly what it was that Iago wanted of her. He wanted her to see beyond the façade of power and influence that cloaked his real nature. He wanted to see himself *as she saw him*; not naked in the conventional sense, though she'd seen him like that often enough. He wanted her own estimation of him, freed from his position of power, to be reflected back to him. Only then would he have the true, proper measure of himself.

She turned to him, ignoring his look of surprise and his half-hearted, murmured protest and pushed him back onto the

436

counterpane. Through his trousers she felt his hardness immediately. She didn't bother with her own clothes, or his. She pulled down the zip, her hands lightly touching his chest and the dark, tightly curled hair around the nipples, and slid on top of him with an intensity that brought an astonished roar from him almost immediately. She had never felt closer to him, or to anyone, in her life. She lay her head on his chest, feeling in her ears and throat the raw, rapid thump of his heartbeat, now fused with her own.

84

'I don't understand. How can it be an affair? He's not married.'

Lindi wedged the phone in between her chin and her ear as she unsuccessfully tried to paint her little toenail. 'But it *feels* like an affair . . . that's my point.'

'How?'

'Well, everything's done in secret. I mean, of course people know. Windhoek's a small town. You can't go anywhere without someone noticing and it doesn't take long for people to put two and two together. But we never appear in public together and as far as I know, he hasn't told anyone. Apart from you, no one else knows. It feels weird.'

'What does he say when you ask him?'

'I don't.'

'You never ask him where it's going, or what he feels about it?' Tara sounded disbelieving.

Lindi sighed. 'No, I don't.'

'That doesn't sound normal,' Tara said diplomatically. 'Or like you.'

'No, I suppose not. It's hard. I mean, aside from the fact that he's my boss, he's the bloody prime minister.'

'All the more reason,' Tara said crisply. 'Look, it's been six months, hasn't it? That's long enough to work out that it's not a one-night stand or a short-term fling. Six months is an awfully long time for things to still be so unclear.'

'You're right.' Lindi sighed again. She capped the bottle of nail polish and put it on the bedside table. 'You're absolutely right. I should just ask him. There's no harm in asking, right?'

'Right,' Tara said firmly. Her calm, forthright manner made Lindi feel a little bit better. 'Anyhow, I've got to run. I've got a departmental meeting in ten minutes and I haven't even looked at the agenda. Let me know how it goes, won't you?'

'I will,' Lindi promised and hung up the phone. She lifted up a leg, inspecting her toes. Funny, she thought to herself, rather liking the contrast between the light blue nail polish and her dark skin, if anyone had asked her a year or so earlier if she and Tara Connolly would have become such good friends, she'd have laughed out loud. After all, they'd met only once, and only for a few days at that. She could still see the look of surprise on Tara's face as she fell backwards, hitting the kerb and spraining her ankle and then that funny little yelp she'd given, as though afraid to make any real noise and let anyone know just how much it hurt. Then she'd gone along to listen to her present a paper and had been completely taken aback by just how smart and well informed and confident she was. A curious friendship had ensued, marked by distance, of course, but to her surprise, it worked. Partly because of the distance, she was able to tell Tara things that she couldn't have risked telling anyone else. Iago, for one thing. Without Tara's calm, rational advice, even over the phone, she wasn't sure she'd have coped over the past few months.

She rolled over onto her stomach. Iago. It too had started out on a rather unusual note. Desire. Attraction. Lust. There were many names for the suddenness with which it had begun. She'd crossed the road that night, her hand still held firmly within his, without knowing where it would lead, knowing only that she wanted it – him – badly. She wasn't afraid. Although she seldom, if ever, thought about it, that early teenage encounter with Ree Herz had protected her against the sort of fallout that worried Tara. Her defences were intact and in place. No one would ever get close enough again to inflict that kind of pain and in the years that followed, it seemed to work. But Iago was different. To begin with, they were two of a kind. He rarely spoke about his ex-wife, or his sons. She knew they lived in the United States and that she was American – that was all. He too was a master at keeping things at bay. The boys were in some fancy private school in New England. They took it in turns to have them during the holidays but the truth of the matter was that his ex-wife lived nearby, and he did not. From the little snippets of information she picked up from others, Lindi understood that the divorce had been messy, painful and protracted, and that he'd sworn never to marry again. Fine by her, she reasoned. She wasn't looking for *that*. But what *was* she looking for?

The phone rang again, shattering the silence. She picked it up. 'Hello?'

'Miss me?' It was Iago. He was in Johannesburg; he'd been gone for almost a week.

'Oh, it's you,' she said, her voice suddenly weak with longing.

'What's the matter?' He was quick as ever to pick up on her moods.

'N-nothing,' she said quickly. 'The phone just gave me a fright.'

'Ah. What're you doing?' he asked, chuckling. She could hear his mouth was full.

'Nothing. What're you eating?' she asked weakly, happily.

'A chocolate. You know, one of those ones they leave on your pillow.'

'Of course. I forgot. Five-star luxury and all that,' she said, falling back into their easy teasing of one another. Her eyes smarted. She wished he were there.

'So . . . what've you been doing?'

She hesitated. For the second time that evening, a sixth sense emerged from somewhere inside her, she had no idea where.

'Nothing much,' she said slowly. 'Just reading a pile of those reports you left for me.'

'Anything interesting?'

'No. The usual stuff.'

'Did you speak to that friend of yours?'

'No, not yet. But I'll offer her the job of director if she manages to get Anneliese on board.'

She heard him erupt into laughter. 'You,' he chuckled. 'Ah, but you're a quick learner. Where did you learn how to do that?'

'You,' she said simply. 'I've been watching you.'

'And is that the only thing I've taught you?' There was still laughter in his voice.

'No,' she said again, more slowly this time.

'So what else?'

'Ah, but for that you'd need to be here,' she said, a note of teasing creeping into her own.

She heard him take a deep breath, drawing it into his body and exhaling slowly. 'I miss you,' he said suddenly. 'I never expected to.' And then he rang off.

Lindi sat holding the receiver, confusion breaking over her in waves. He confused her, deliberately or otherwise? She didn't know, couldn't tell. All she knew now was that there was a thin membrane separating love from lust, desire from admiration, longing from fear. Iago had done the cleverest thing possible. He'd won her over, by stealth.

85

REE
Cape Town, South Africa

The earth opened up with the first cut; a warm, fecund smell emanated from the gash, which was like a wound. There was a brief smattering of applause, someone clapped him on the shoulder and a cheer went up from the workers who'd gathered in small, expectant knots around the digging machines. Under the taut white awning, the ageing leader was seated, bodyguards, ministers, family and invited dignitaries surrounding him in concentric and sometimes overlapping circles. He took one last look at the machines at the bottom of the slope, busy turning what had recently been simply marks and instructions on paper into gritty, grubby, muddy reality. It was a process he'd been through a thousand times before – but this one was different. Somewhere back there in the crowds gathered to witness the ground-breaking ceremony were his parents, Sibongile holding tightly onto the girls. Hayley was not present.

He turned and walked back up the hill towards the crowds. It was November, almost at the height of summer in the southern hemisphere and the air was warm. Far below them, sweeping from left to right in an almost-perfect crescent, the bay and the port shimmered in the late morning sunlight. Beyond the port, snaking out away from the continent in a long, hazy line, the mountains disappeared towards the horizon. The air was crisp and clear; involuntarily he drew a great lungful of it down into his body, expelling it slowly. The following morning, after this ceremony in Cape Town, they would all fly together to Windhoek, to repeat the performance at the site of the Namibian project, in the hills just to the east of the city, overlooking the township. It had been a long, hard road to get to this point. He'd emerged from the drawn-out and at times bitter competition process a tougher, harder man. There were days when he wasn't sure he could take much more of it.

He'd always had a healthy respect for the media; now, after two years, he had nothing but rage and contempt. It was mostly on account of the girls. It was one thing to have your parents' marriage break up – it was another thing altogether to have it splashed across the pages of every magazine and newspaper in town. Without his parents, he wasn't sure they'd have survived. Hayley had gone into denial at first, then rehab. She was still 'recovering', a long and equally tedious journey that never seemed to end. 'Are you well?' Her answer was always the same. 'I'm getting there.' 'Getting there' wasn't enough; he had to be sure he could leave the children safely with her – and he couldn't. So Sibongile and Klaus had taken them. They were at the International School in Windhoek. In ways he didn't discuss with his parents, they were receiving the kind of childhood he'd never had. They wouldn't grow up not knowing the country their grandparents had fought so hard to liberate.

At first, being away from them for such long periods of time had been a physical wrenching so strong he felt as though he'd been amputated. Those first few weeks of coming home to the empty loft were made even more poignant by its openness. It was like coming home to ghosts. He'd always been able to see them as soon as he walked in, to catch sight of their heads or hear their voices. Those first few nights when the place felt like a graveyard – of his marriage, his family, his life – were amongst the worst he'd ever had. He couldn't explain to Callan what it was like. He'd felt himself withdrawing from her and he hated himself for it. But he was consumed with guilt. He couldn't bring her back to the low, wide bed he'd shared with Hayley, in which Ottie had most likely been conceived, whilst his wife lay in a clinic somewhere in the depths of Surrey and his children were 10,000 miles away. It wasn't possible; not for him. He'd fully expected her to end things. After all, what was in it for her, other than heartbreak, and then more heartbreak?

But Callan wasn't like other women. He knew that. She did not take offence, neither did she push her way back into his affections. She did what few women could have done. She simply retreated. She waited. It was so unlike her and what he knew of her fiery, passionate nature that at first he couldn't believe it. She didn't call; she didn't come round, she didn't write, but she wasn't sulking, either. On the contrary, when he did ring her, her voice was warm. 'Take your time.' That was all she said. She went about her business as usual, flying here and there, attending to business, meetings in Japan one week, the US the next. She wasn't available; but neither was she *un*available. She didn't enquire after the children, or Hayley. She did and said nothing. It was unnerving. It took him nearly three months. One Sunday morning he simply woke up with the strong feeling that he wanted to see her again. She didn't make him wait, either, or try to punish him for the distance between them that he'd created. 'Come round,' she said simply when he rang. 'I was just about to have breakfast. I'll wait for you.'

And that was it. They were able to resume not quite where they'd left off – that would not be possible, ever – but in a new way, on a different level. If anything, deeper than before. He had no idea how she'd managed it, given the way they'd always been with one another, but somehow she had. She now had from him what no other woman had ever been able to extract: his respect.

'Ree. I want you to meet someone.' One of the board directors had come up to him, and was now gently guiding him by the hand. He allowed himself to be taken into the group of men who were standing in a clustered knot. Docile. Motsamai. Mkhabela. Vusi. Heroes of the struggle. The men and women whose stories would form part of the narrative of the museum. He already had a consultant historian – someone Tara Connolly had recommended – and although it wasn't strictly his job, he was looking forward to watching the process of how conflicting versions of history would somehow be fashioned into an exhibition and narrative that everyone, victors and victims alike, could follow.

He bent his head respectfully and listened to their low, murmured conversation. Zoë was hovering in his peripheral vision. They'd kept rushing up to him throughout the day to hug and touch him, claiming him for themselves, then hanging back shyly if there were dignitaries around. He turned his head fractionally, and winked at her. Her face was transformed by her smile, rather like Hayley, he thought to himself, giving her a quick 'I'll-be-right-there' nod. The same smile. He felt a stirring of pity inside him for Hayley. What would happen to them all? he wondered. What now?

There was the usual press crowd waiting for them at the hotel by the Waterfront when they returned from the ceremony.

Standing to one side of the president and ministers whose hands, hearts and departments were involved in one way or another in the project, he answered the questions as patiently as he could. He longed to be free of the circus of publicity to which he was forcibly attached.

He caught sight of Anneliese's face somewhere in the crowd. She had on a pair of large, black sunglasses that almost entirely shielded her face. With her tall, elegant frame, the glasses and her cap of cropped, silvery hair, she looked more like a film star than one of the museum's trustees. They'd offered her the permanent position immediately after the judging process. He wasn't surprised. Since the evening he'd gone round to her townhouse and found her in a state that seemed, if anything, worse than his own, they'd grown even closer. She'd said little about why he'd come upon her like that, other than gasping out that she'd done something once that was so terrible she couldn't bring herself to remember, let alone speak of it. He knew not to push her. He'd simply held her upright until the storm of weeping passed over her, leaving her weak and drained. They'd shared a glass of whisky; not much more was said.

He'd left that night knowing that whatever happened next, he'd repaired the tear in the fabric of their friendship. They were able to take it up again where they had left off. For the moment, the task of the competition preoccupied them both. Fortunately for him, in the months that followed, she'd had to do little persuading on the subject of the winner. The decision to award him the project was almost unanimous – there were no special favours to be repaid or recalled. He'd won on merit, nothing less. And now, after months of finessing, lobbying phone calls and hurried visits, they'd gone further than either dared hope – two, twinned institutions, one in Cape Town, one in Windhoek. One by one the obstacles and objections had been met and then slowly overcome. Much of the credit for raising the necessary funds had to go to Callan; she'd come up with ever-more inventive ways to extract the cash and promises out of people who'd never even heard of South-West Africa, let alone Namibia. She'd done everything from private fundraising dinners to preview collection runway shows with all proceeds going to the museum projects.

He wished Callan were there, beside him, sharing in it. There were times when his longing was so intense it was physically painful. But they'd both agreed on it. Today was a day for his parents and his children, not for her. Who knew if there would ever come a time when he could share the two halves of his life without fear of losing one to the other. For now, it was enough that Anneliese was there. He glanced away from the sea of reporters to that other sea, calm and immovable beyond which there was nothing . . . until Antarctica. There were clouds out there on the horizon, a puffy mass of watery greys and whites. He watched them for a moment, shape-shifting at the speed of light. One minute something recognisable, the next the shape had dissolved almost simultaneously into the absurd. Rain, he thought to himself distractedly. Rain was on its way.

86

ANNELIESE

How to get out of it, wriggle or slip away? Unseen and unheard. The sunglasses were as much a protection against her own thoughts as they were against anyone else. She wasn't sure she could control the expressions of recognition or surprise on her own face. Who was there among the crowds who might, on seeing the woman who held herself apart, have some distant recollection of someone else? There was no one present who would have known her in another life and time. Hannelore von Riedesal, once a pupil at a school not so far from where they now stood, had disappeared without a trace. There was nothing in the world to suggest that Anneliese Zander de Saint Phalle, world-renowned fashion designer and now, after the media attention the Freedom Museum had attracted, a cultural commentator in her own right, even knew of Hannelore's existence, never mind a connection of a deeper sort. The places were so familiar. The Mount Nelson. The Waterfront. *Buitenkant. Heerengracht.* The Company Gardens, where as a fourteen year old in the company of other teenage girls, already skilled in the art of insubordination, she'd learned to slip away from the teachers who sat under the shade of the huge jacaranda trees, one eye on their youngest charges, whilst the older girls took it in turns to smoke behind the *Whites Only* public toilets.

Whites Only. How the city had changed. Driving in convoy from the airport she'd been assailed by one memory after another, but obliquely, as though someone had changed the focus or tilted the frame. When she was last here, fifty-three years earlier, it had been a different country entirely. Back then, the city was white, not black. In the streets the scent of perfumed women was strong; the buildings were brand new and shiny; the shop windows showed mannequins imported from Europe. There was nothing to show that they were not in London or Paris or New York, except for the occasional worker dressed in overalls who bent, quick as a flash, to pick up some discarded cigarette before melting back into the municipal truck from where he'd come, watching the crowds of Saturday shoppers – whites only – with a jeer, safe amongst his own kind. There was nothing back then to suggest they were a city and population on the tip of Africa. Everything that could have been done to erase it, had been. Now it was different. Now it really *was* like London or Paris or New York with its vast crowds of people of every hue. What a parody of Europe they'd been.

She turned away from the window of her hotel room which looked out onto an artificial lagoon only metres from the sea. The hotel was the latest word in luxury, or so the brochures said. Everything the discerning traveller could possibly want. Spas, shops, salons, sporting facilities . . . everything. Some of the finest dining in the world, only a step away. Tourists were advised *not* to walk about the city; instead, everything had been brought near. If the mountain won't come to Mohammed . . .

she gave a little grimace and sat down on the bed. The little silver travelling clock she always carried with her was on the bedside table. It was nearly six o'clock. They were all going to dinner at one of the city's top fish restaurants together with all the board members. In her wardrobe, her white linen trouser suit was hanging up after the maid had carefully pressed it. She'd chosen an emerald-green silk shirt and a pair of yellow and green pointed slingback stilettos. Her jewellery was laid out on the marble slab of a dressing table in the en suite bathroom. Two diamond studs, a white gold and emerald bracelet and her Cartier tank. All she had to do was shower and get dressed.

It wouldn't be a late dinner; the following morning the whole entourage were due to depart for Windhoek at dawn. There would be a second ceremony in the hills outside Windhoek, a dinner with the ageing president and the man most likely to succeed him, whose brainchild the Namibian institution had been. She would be shown around the city, the Tintenpalast, the State Gardens, driven down what had once been Kaiser-strasse where she strolled arm in arm with Tante Bärbel, now renamed Independence Avenue. The whole city had been remapped, streets renamed. Now there were avenues named Mugabe, roundabouts called Nkrumah and boulevards by the name of Nyerere. Where there had once been Görings and Himmlers and von Kleists, now the new, pan-African names had taken hold. All changed; all was made new. Only it wasn't that simple.

She looked down at her hands. She hadn't intended to come. 'But you *must* come,' Ree had insisted, looking at her in surprise. 'What d'you mean you don't want to see the sites?'

'I . . . I don't really need to,' she'd faltered.

'Of course you do. Have you ever been to South Africa? Or Namibia?'

She shook her head. 'No.'

'Then you must. It's not like it was before, I promise you. They're both incredible places. You've got to come. It won't be the same without you there.' So she'd come. Against every instinct she possessed.

She got up suddenly. The room was beginning to blur. She opened the wardrobe and pulled out her suitcase. She began flinging her clothes into it, clearing the suite as fast as she could of her presence. Ten minutes later, it was done. She picked up the phone and rang her PA in London. 'Get me on tonight's flight. I don't care what it costs.'

Half an hour later she was safely in the back of a cab, heading for the airport. A thirty-dollar tip to the bellhop who came in to take her bags ensured Ree would be given two messages. One, to be delivered immediately, said she wouldn't be attending dinner; she had a migraine and had gone to sleep. The other, to be delivered the following morning – *Apologies. Emergency in London. Will be in touch shortly. Best regards, A* – would mean she'd have time to escape. She closed her eyes as the cab sped towards the airport, blocking out the view that was at once familiar and not. She was a fool. She'd thought she would be able to handle it, to slip back into the past and emerge unscathed. She couldn't. It was as simple as that. And if Cape Town had been painful, Namibia would be worse. Every fibre in her being was screaming for release.

87

LINDI
Windhoek, Namibia

'She's not coming?' Lindi rushed around her bedroom, the phone glued to her ear. 'What a shame. I was *so* looking forward to finally meeting her.'

'Some emergency, apparently,' Tara's disembodied voice came down the line, crackling faintly. 'Yes, a real shame. I really wanted you two to meet. Oh, well, some other time. I'll ring her later this evening. So tell me again, what're you wearing?'

'White shirt and that cream trouser suit you sent me.'

'Good. And don't forget the scarf, OK? You'll need a bit of colour to go with it. What shoes are you wearing? Those tan high-heeled ones you told me about?'

'Yes!' Lindi practically shouted the words. 'Yes! I've got to go,' she pleaded, looking frantically around her bedroom for her earrings. 'I'll call you later, I promise.'

'OK but I want the full description,' Tara laughed. 'I want to hear everything. What he said, what he was like . . . how you felt, everything, you hear me?'

'I hear you, I hear you,' Lindi promised, laughing. 'But I've got to run.' She hung up before Tara could quiz her any further. She looked at herself in the mirror, tying the knot on her tan and blue silk scarf and tugging it to one side. The trouser suit, which probably cost more than half her yearly salary, though Tara swore blind that she never, ever paid retail prices for anything from AdSP, was an inspired choice. It was chic and smart, yet casual enough that she'd stand out amongst the boring, too-new, too-shiny suits of most of her colleagues. She turned sideways, admiring the way the suit was nipped in at the waist, gently flaring out at the sides and avoiding the boxy look of so many jackets. The trousers were slim-fitting and narrow, with a sharp crease down the front. A pair of high-heeled tan slingbacks and a matching bag completed the look. Not bad for an old broad, she mouthed at her image, with a grin. She wished Iago were around. He was in Croatia that week, then on a two-day visit to the UK. It would be almost a fortnight before she saw him again. She hadn't told Tara the complete truth, she thought to herself as she picked up her bag. Whatever her relationship with Iago might be called, in reality it was worse than an affair. At the very least, in an affair you knew what you were up against. Iago's lack of commitment seemed to come from another source, one she could neither see nor understand.

A short, sharp horn blast announced her driver. She shook her head at herself, closed the bedroom door and hurried through the house. She locked the front door behind her, clattered down the steps and slid into the waiting car. The ceremony was due to begin at ten; she had just under half an hour to get to the site.

She waited with all the other dignitaries at the top of the hill overlooking the city, the site that the president had bequeathed the museum. The ground shimmered in the mid-morning heat. The jumble of buildings, some tall, some low and horizontal, spread across the valley in front of them, thinning out at the edges before the scrub asserted itself and nature took over. People assembled in knots, one breaking away from this crowd to join the other, journalists running between them as somebody particularly important made an appearance or slid from view. She waited alone, under the shade of one of the many umbrellas that had been erected specially for the occasion. Somewhere, down there where the cars were still assembling, waiting their turn to bring passengers up the narrow dirt track to the top of the hill, was Ree Herz. She'd seen a few recent photographs of him. She more or less knew what he looked like now. Especially with the publicity around the museum, there'd hardly been a day over the past six months when the project wasn't mentioned in one way or another. But it had been twenty-five years since she'd seen him in the flesh. She was aware of a slight knot of tension in her stomach as she watched the snaking vehicles. One or the other of them contained him.

He came up the hill just behind his mother and father. His father was holding two young children by the hand; Ree's children, she realised as they drew near. Striking girls, both of them. They chattered in high, excited voices as they approached. She looked past them to Ree himself. A stone or two heavier than he'd been as a teenager, perhaps, but still the same darkly handsome face, the hair shorter and, she saw as he approached, now greying slightly at the temples. He looked around uncertainly for a moment, then spotted her. He walked towards her, the grace-fully sexy swagger she remembered still there in every step.

'Lindi.' He stopped and looked down at her with an easy, warm smile. 'Well, well, well. I thought it was you. Dad said you'd be here. Lindi Johansson. Christ, it's been *years*. How the hell are you?' If he recalled anything embarrassing about the last time he'd seen her, he gave no sign. His warmth seemed genuine. Her nervousness slowly dissipated.

'I'm fine.' She smiled and nodded. 'H-how are *you*? Con-gratulations, by the way. Quite a feat.'

He smiled and looked around him. 'Yeah, quite a feat. But no small thanks to you, too,' he said, generously. 'I hear you campaigned harder than anyone to get it built here.'

She shrugged. 'We all did. It's a great project for us,' she said. 'And I'm just glad we managed to pull it off before . . . well, before it was too late.' She indicated with her head the Old Man, sitting a few yards away in the wheelchair that now accompanied him wherever he went. It had been a few years since she or anyone else had seen him standing upright, let alone walking. 'For him especially.'

He followed her eyes. 'He's getting on, isn't he? Hard to believe, in a way. He's still got it, though. I had a couple of meetings with him and the prime minister earlier this year in London. Razor-sharp, the pair of them. It was quite humbling.'

'You met Ia . . . Rukoro?' Lindi said, surprised. Iago hadn't mentioned it.

He nodded. 'Good man. I liked him. What's he like to work for?'

'Er, fine,' she mumbled. 'Don't see much of him, to be honest.' She hoped the blush didn't show on her face. For-tunately they were distracted.

'Have you met the girls?' Ree asked, as his father came up to them, holding the two by the hand. 'Girls, say hello to Auntie.'

'Hello, Auntie,' they both chorused. Everyone laughed.

'Proper little African girls,' Lindi said approvingly. 'It took me for ever to learn to say "auntie" and "uncle" to everyone. Well done.'

'Oh, that's Sibo's influence. You know what she's like.' Klaus laughed, hugging Lindi warmly. They chatted easily for a few minutes as the girls looked on curiously, then he led them away. He seemed delighted to be showing them off.

'They're beautiful,' Lindi said as they watched them being passed around. 'Where's their . . . er, mother?' she asked delicately.

Ree sighed. 'Back in the UK. I'm sure you know the story. There doesn't seem to be a person on the planet who doesn't.'

'I'm sorry,' Lindi said quietly. 'It can't be easy for you.'

'No, not for Hayley either. It's hard on everyone. But it's been good for the girls . . . to be here, I mean. Getting to know the place. We didn't have that chance,' he added suddenly, looking down at her. 'What's it like, being back?'

Lindi pulled a face. 'It's home now. It's different for me, though.'

'How?'

'Well, I grew up in Oslo but it was never really *home* for me, at least not in the way I imagine London was for you. Especially back then. The only foreigner for miles around – it was hard to fit in. There's lots about it that I miss, of course, but I don't miss *that*.'

'And here? You don't feel like a foreigner here?'

'Yeah, sometimes,' she admitted, smiling slightly. 'I don't speak any of the languages well enough. I'll always be too European for most people's tastes, especially the men. You know how it is. But no one questions my right to *be* here, if you know what I mean. And there's other things that tie you to the place. My mother's buried here. My biological mother. Somewhere in the Old Location Cemetery.' She made a small grimace. 'I've never been to visit the grave. I *should* go, I know—' She stopped herself, embarrassed. Why on earth was she telling Ree all this?

'Let's go together.'

Taken aback, she looked up at him in surprise. 'What?'

'Let's go together. Tomorrow? I'll come with you.'

'Wh . . . why would you do that?' She was almost too surprised to speak.

'Why not? It's important and if you don't want to go alone, I'll go with you. We've known each other a long time, Lindi – we're practically family. If it were me, I'd want you to come with me.'

Now she really *was* too surprised to speak. She turned her head quickly to one side. She didn't want him to see the sudden rush of hot tears that had filled her eyes. She kept her head turned away from him, blinking rapidly, until the threat had passed. Again if he'd sensed it, he made no sign. They chatted for a few seconds more and then he left, brushing her lightly on the arm as he went. She stayed where she was, too touched to speak.

88

LINDI

It was nearly midday but thankfully the sun wasn't yet at furnace pitch when they set off down the path towards the graves. The velvety grass heads were very long and yellow, scratching at their bare legs as they pushed their way along one unkempt path after another. After the neatly clipped hedges and rows of flowers that bordered the more cared-for sections of the Old Location Cemetery, this, clearly for the poor, came as something of a shock. All around them the vibrancy of light shimmered like a mirage. They were both silent as they walked. Ree stopped every now and then to consult the crudely drawn map the guard had given them at the entrance. 'Yes, turn left . . . and then the first right,' he murmured, putting up a hand to shield his eyes against the blinding light. Lindi simply followed, unable to focus on anything other than her own feet, moving blindly after him.

It took them almost half an hour to find her. A dusty, barely there mound, surrounded by weeds. The grave obviously hadn't been tended in years. *Shekupe Mathilda Odihambo. B. 1942, d. 1960.* Lindi bent down and began tugging at the weeds choking the tiny cross that stood as headstone.

'Do you know much about her?' Ree asked, kneeling beside her. His strong, thin hands made quick work of the grasses that brushed back and forth. 'Who was she?'

Lindi shook her head. 'I don't know. I don't know much about her, other than the fact that she was a domestic worker and that my father was probably the master of the house. Usual story, I suppose. I . . . I just hope there was some sort of . . . well, relationship, you know? I'd hate to think . . .' She stopped. Ree was the first person to whom she'd ever confided or voiced her fears.

He didn't reply but smoothed away the reddish dirt from the gravestone. He was the one who'd thought to bring along a small plant. He busied himself digging a hole big enough to fit, carefully removing the plastic wrapping and damping down the soil until it was flat. He had a small bottle of Evian which he poured over the freshly dug soil. 'Twenty bucks to the old man at the gate'll keep it watered for the rest of the year,' he said with a faint, sad smile, jerking his head in the direction of the warders. 'It'll grow nicely here.'

Lindi said nothing but placed the back of her hand on the earth he'd just patted down, touching it lightly, respectfully. Ree got to his feet and held out a hand to her, pulling her up beside him. They stood and turned together, as one, to look out over the dusty cemetery to the town spread out below and the ring of hills that delineated the horizon. Seen from up there, the blonde line of the dust road that ran along the edge of the wasteland where the natives buried their dead was a neat, clear marker. There had been no rain for months. Everything around them was glazed, parched and cracked with thirst. A small swarm of minute birds burst into the air above them, momentarily clouding the sky.

454

Somewhere much higher up, at an altitude that could only be grasped from space perhaps, a jet plane drifted, the strange distortion of distance making it appear slower than the flock of travelling birds. A thin, trailing-off roar drifted down to them; the plane slowly dissolved into the light.

'Thanks for coming with me,' Lindi said softly. She touched him lightly on the arm. 'I'd never have come on my own. I . . . I wouldn't have been able to manage being here alone with her.'

'Of course you would,' Ree said, placing his own hand momentarily over hers. 'You're about the most capable person I know.'

'Me?' Lindi said, shaking her head. 'How can you say that? You hardly know me.'

'Ah, that's what you think. I *do* know you. I grew up hearing all about you. It was always Lindi Johansson this, Lindi Johansson that. *Have you heard what Lindi's doing? Lindi's doing law.* And then the one I dreaded. *Lindi's going back home. She's not afraid to discover her roots.* It was endless. I couldn't stand it. I hated you, you know.'

Lindi's mouth fell open. 'You've got to be joking,' she spluttered, staring at him. 'I hated *you*.'

'Me? Why on earth would you hate *me*?'

'Don't you remember?' She looked warily at his expression. He seemed genuinely puzzled. 'You don't remember what happened?' she asked incredulously.

'When? You mean when I came to Oslo?'

'That's the only time I can remember ever actually meeting you. You were absolutely horrible to me.'

'Me? *You* were the one who left me with those idiotic friends of yours! I can't even remember their names. One of them just wouldn't leave me alone! I didn't want to be rude but you completely ignored me.'

Lindi couldn't help herself; she began to laugh. 'No, that's not how I remember it.' She put up a hand to her mouth to stop giggling. 'All I can remember is vomiting all over you on the way home.'

'Yeah, I remember that bit. You threw up all over my new jeans and shouted, "I *hate* you!"'

'I did not!'

'Yes you did. I was *crushed*, I tell you. Absolutely gutted. I'd been hearing all about you for fifteen bloody years and when I finally met you, all you did was throw up over my new jeans and tell me how much you hated me.'

'Complete nonsense! I didn't say "I hate you". I said "I love you".' Lindi's face was ablaze. 'You spent the whole evening just gazing at Toril. And when I told you I . . . er, *liked* you, you just stomped off.'

Ree stopped to look down at her. He too began to laugh. 'I don't know how you can even remember *what* you said – you were blind drunk, remember?'

'Not so drunk that I don't remember those bits. You just looked at me as though I'd crawled out from under a bush. I cried myself to sleep for months afterwards.'

'Now you're talking absolute nonsense,' Ree said, still smiling. 'I can't imagine you crying over *any*thing let alone me.'

'You'd be surprised,' Lindi said tartly. 'You know what it's like when you're a teenager. You think the world's come to an end.'

Ree kept shaking his head, but he was still smiling. Again, without saying anything to each other, they both turned at the same time and began to walk back down the path towards the entrance. The dried grasses crunched underfoot; there was only the sound of their breathing as they walked. At the small office where they'd stopped to ask directions, the old man who acted both as guard and keeper was dozing on one of those worn-out schoolroom wooden chairs that she remembered from childhood. His eyes flew open; he fixed them with a rheumy, half-hopeful, half-despairing glance. Ree fished into his pocket and peeled off a couple of notes. There was much smiling and nodding, the universal language of a deal being struck. They exchanged a few words in a mixture of English and Afrikaans when he realised neither spoke the local language, then they shook hands. The deal was sealed. 'He'll make sure it's kept free of weeds and watered for the rest of the year,' he said, leading the way to the car. 'Until you come again.'

'Thank you,' Lindi whispered again, putting a hand on his arm. 'Really. I can't thank you enough. You've been so kind.'

'Not at all.'

They'd reached the car yet they both hesitated, somehow unwilling to part just yet. Lindi suddenly felt close to Ree in a way that was completely unfamiliar to her – not an attraction – something deeper than that. It was the sort of closeness she'd longed for in a best friend as a child – someone who understood her at a level that went beyond words, beyond shared experiences, beyond friendship, even.

Ree must have felt it too. 'Drink?' he asked, unlocking the doors. 'There's a good bar on the tenth floor of the Kalahari Sands. I discovered it last night.'

'I know it well,' Lindi said, smiling, weakly relieved. 'Lead the way. But I can't stay up too late, I warn you. I've got an eight a.m. meeting tomorrow morning.'

'One drink. I'm taking the kids down to Swakopmund tomorrow then it's back to London on Friday.' He opened the door for her and they both got in. 'I'd love to take them back with me but . . . well, they're enjoying it here. And Hayley's not "there" yet, wherever that is.' He paused for a moment, sliding the key in the ignition and starting the car. 'You never think it's going to end up this way, do you?'

Lindi was quiet as he pulled out of the driveway, gravel scrunching beneath the tyres. She wasn't sure how to answer him. She was beginning to understand her own mistakes. She'd made up her mind about certain things on the basis of one drunken evening in her teens and it now appeared as though she'd misread the entire evening. She'd been so sure . . . but of what? A couple of hours that he remembered entirely differently. 'I don't know,' she said after a moment, her voice suddenly small. 'I thought you could protect yourself from all of that . . . that *heartache*. I'm beginning to think I was wrong.'

'Heartache? Christ, if there's one thing I've learned over the past few years, it's that heartache's the one thing you can't do anything about. It'll find you no matter what. Like death and taxes.' He smiled ruefully and turned to face her. 'One drink, eh? I feel a nice, long philosophical chat coming on.'

Lindi smiled. 'Yeah. I'm a bit out of practice, though. You'll have to bear with me whilst I catch up.'

'You? You've got to be kidding. I've got to sprint just to keep up.'

She smiled again and shook her head. She was also beginning to understand just how much she'd misjudged him. And how much she'd missed out on.

The bar on the tenth floor was almost empty. They found a booth right by the window, overlooking Independence Avenue. It was nearly seven p.m. and there were few cars on the street below. 'It's so quiet. So different from London,' Ree said as he brought their drinks over. 'But I suppose you're used to it.'

'Mmm. Three cars at a stop sign and it's a traffic jam. I don't know London very well at all,' she said, taking a sip of her red wine.

'I couldn't live anywhere else,' Ree said simply. 'No offence.'

'None taken.'

'Thought I'd better say that,' he added, with a sly, sideways smile. 'I never know with you.'

Lindi laughed. 'Don't,' she said, blushing. 'Don't remind me. I can't believe I got the whole thing so wrong.' It was hard to believe they'd only met properly the day before. In less than twenty-four hours an ease had been established between them that she'd never had with anyone, not even her parents. In ways she was only just beginning to grasp, he was the brother she'd never had. They understood one another on a level that had completely taken her by surprise. She'd spent most of her adult life resenting him and it now came as a shock to realise not only had her resentment been misplaced but it seemed to belong to another character altogether. He was warm and funny and kind.

Generous too. She would never lose hold of the image of him on his knees, digging a hole with his bare hands in order to plant a flower for her mother.

'Well, maybe *I* got it wrong,' Ree said, grabbing a handful of peanuts. 'Who's to say it was you?'

Lindi took a sip of her drink. 'D'you know, I think we both got it wrong, somehow. It's just a . . . well, it's a shame. I think we both lost out.'

'You're probably right. But –' he raised his glass, saluting her – 'here's to getting it right from now on.'

'I'll drink to that.' They clinked glasses, both smiling. 'So how long d'you think the project'll actually take?' Lindi asked, grabbing a handful of nuts herself. She hadn't eaten anything since lunch.

'Well, we'd *like* to get it done in time for the World Cup,' Ree said. 'That gives us six years, which is usually plenty long enough for something of this scale. The design work's almost done but that's the easy bit, to be honest. The fun bit. It's the construction that's going to be more problematic. Especially from afar. I'm opening up a satellite office here but I can't be here all the time.'

'Why didn't Anneliese come?' Lindi asked curiously.

Ree shrugged. 'I'm not sure. She disappeared the night of the dinner. Said she'd had to go back to London. I spoke to her dau— um, I rang her office and they said she was fine. Dunno, really. She can be a bit odd sometimes.'

'Tara seems to adore her. She seems very close to Anneliese. And her daughter. What's her name again? Callan. Pretty name.'

Ree coughed suddenly. 'Yeah, Anneliese is great. I get along with her just fine. But she's very private. It's hard to tell what she really thinks most of the time. Outside of design,' he added with a smile. 'Then she's only too happy to tell you what she thinks. I like that, though. She's good to work with. But let me ask *you* something instead. How come *you* never married? Or did you? I don't know much about you either.'

Lindi picked up her glass and brought it up to her face, hiding it. 'No, never got married. It . . . it just didn't happen,' she said carefully, aware of a sudden warmth in her cheeks. 'I was in too much of a hurry.'

'To do what?'

She shrugged. 'To do other things. To study, have a career, travel, do things that *I* wanted to do, not what someone else wanted. And when I came here . . . well, let's just say that the number of men who might've been prepared to put up with that—' She made a telling gesture between her thumb and forefinger. 'Zero. But I *like* my life, I'm not complaining. I'm . . . happy. Yes, I'm happy.'

'You look it.' He said it genuinely. 'I envy you.'

'Me?' She was surprised. 'Now, why on earth would *you*, a world-famous architect, married man, father of those two adorable girls, envy *me*?'

He smiled. 'I hear things, you know. Your life's not as uncomplicated as you make out. Some people say *you're* the one who's headed for the top, not your boss.'

'Who?' she asked, frowning, surprised.

It was his turn to shrug. 'People. Journalists. People who make it their business to know.'

'Absolute rubbish.'

'Perhaps,' he said mildly. 'But that's what I hear. They say your boss had better watch out. Actually, he says it too.'

Lindi suddenly stood up. 'I'd better go.'

Ree looked up at her, perplexed. 'Did I say something?' he asked, concern in his face. 'I didn't mean to upset you.'

'No, no, you didn't. I-I'm just rather tired. It's been a long day. No, you don't have to drive me home. I live just on the other side of the park. No, please,' she added hastily as he made to get up as well. 'I'm fine. A quick walk'll do me good. Let's speak when you get back from Swakop.'

'At least let me see you to the other side of the road,' Ree said, shrugging on his jacket. 'And I won't take "no" for an answer. You're not the only stubborn one round here.'

Lindi's head was spinning. What did he mean, 'your boss thinks so too'? Why hadn't he said anything to her? The thought of anyone – let alone Iago – thinking she might be after his job made her feel quite sick.

REE

He watched her hurry up Independence Avenue and cross over the road at the lights. She turned and gave him a quick wave, then disappeared into the inkily liquid darkness. He shoved his hands in his pockets and walked back down the street towards the car. She had turned out to be the real surprise of the trip. How could it be that they'd walked off with such contrasting views of each other all those years ago? He'd thought her stuck-up and sulky; *she* thought he'd run off with her best friend. He gave a short, almost bitter laugh. He hadn't been joking when he told her he'd been gutted by what he thought was her reaction to him. His overriding memory of Oslo had been one of crushing disappointment. Disappointment that she hadn't found him as interesting as everyone else seemed to; disappointment that she hadn't simply fallen in line with his easy charm. He'd arrived at their house with the sound of her name, Lindi Johansson, ringing in his ears and left with his pride almost fatally injured. She'd evoked some niggling, worrisome worm of doubt in his own abilities that he wasn't sure he'd ever entirely got rid of. Over the years that strange, shocking sense of disappointment in himself melted into other passions and emerged as the ambition that drove his work. By then Lindi Johanssen was no longer a source of worry. He'd buried her, if not the lingering doubt that she'd provoked, and he'd more or less forgotten her.

But coming here, seeing her settled into a world that was as unfamiliar and foreign to him as Oslo had been all those years ago, had stirred up that old, half-buried fear that only she seemed able to see. Who *was* he, really? Lindi had found a way to come 'home', to be amongst people she called her own. He admired her for it; no, he *envied* her. She had a sure-footedness that he longed for, even if he didn't admit it to himself. In a

461

world that seemed to be constantly shifting, she'd found some sort of solid ground. She'd found a way to *be* here that didn't cancel out everything that had gone before, but that also didn't seem to place too much faith in it. There were many things about the choices he'd made – sometimes without really understanding them to be choices at all – that he found hard to understand. His marriage, for one. What had he seen in Hayley, other than the obvious? What did he think he'd seen? Yes, they'd produced – if that was the right word – two beautiful children. His girls. Yet he barely saw them. Without ever planning to, he'd somehow abandoned them in the same way he'd been left to his own devices, parentless, though for reasons that were hard to argue with back then. He and Hayley didn't even have that luxury. They'd fucked up, that was all. The girls were safe with his parents and probably all the happier for it. It had given Klaus and Sibongile a chance to right what had once been so wrong. Perhaps Zoë and Ottie would find what Lindi seemed to have secured for herself – a sense of belonging somewhere that *wasn't* contingent on circumstances, the way his had been. Kneeling in the dirt earlier that afternoon, tugging away at weeds covering a grave, he'd been struck by a sense of how utterly arbitrary it all was and yet, for all that, how deep and profound. Roots *mattered*. He, more than anyone, should understand that. He'd chosen a profession that absolutely underscored it. Digging into the earth as they'd done over the past two days, marking the land in ways that would become indelible, carving and scoring the history of a place into its soil . . . what else was the Freedom Project about, if not that?

He looked up into the night sky. Here the stars were hard and bright, clustered together in fat, dense constellations that seemed close enough to touch. There was little light pollution in a city with few inhabitants and even fewer street lights. Liquid, nightly infinity. There wasn't anything like it. Once he'd found a lump of obsidian, black volcanic glass, on a hiking trip in Oregon, just after finishing university. It had sat on his desk at the office for the longest time, most often used as a paperweight.

He'd picked it up the other day, just before leaving for Cape Town, and made the decision to make the entrance wall of both museums out of cut obsidian blocks – it occurred naturally in both places anyway, but there was something both mysterious and beautifully powerful about the deep, smooth black glass that moved him. Liquid, nightly infinity. It was the medium that bound him to this place, this rugged, dry, empty patch of the earth's surface in which his ancestors were scattered somewhere and buried, just like Lindi's mother.

He'd been moved that afternoon, just as he was now, by the sharp, uncomfortable contrast between the fluid lives they all led – London today, Cape Town tomorrow, Moscow next week – and the need to *connect*, at some level, with things that lay buried and unseen. Perhaps that's why we bury our dead, he thought to himself, reaching the car and unlocking it. Ashes to ashes, dust to dust . . . there was more to it than the mumbled comfort at the graveside or the threat of disease. Perhaps it was an unconscious return to that state of liquid invisibility inside the womb where it all begins, in secret, in silence and completely unseen. He gave a short, almost embarrassed laugh. Now where had all *that* come from? he wondered, as he started the engine and swung the car around. It was seeing Lindi, that was what had done it. He felt again the quiet tug of admiration for the feisty, self-assured woman who'd managed to do what he could never quite bring himself to – reconciliation. The moving line from Akhmatova that he'd first read as a student came to him as he drove away. *The guest from the future*, after her meeting with Isaiah Berlin. Was that how Lindi appeared to him? he wondered. As a guest from his own future?

As he drove towards Klein Windhoek where his parents lived, he was aware, not for the first time in the past few years, of a series of overlapping parallels, magnetic in their pull, that seemed to gravitate towards the vortex of emotions and coincidences that was Anneliese. Himself, Callan, Hayley, Tara and now Lindi . . . they were all, in one way or another, connected through Anneliese. What was even stranger, though it had only just occurred to him, was that the relationship seemed to function in a way he couldn't yet put his finger on, in the reverse. She was connected to *them*. Walking around Cape Town with her for three days prior to her sudden departure, he'd been struck by something odd about her. She seemed to know the place in a way that others in the group did not. It wasn't that she'd said anything. On the contrary, she was mostly silent. It was more oblique than that . . . harder to grasp. He struggled for the words. *Déjà vu*. That was it. She seemed to be experiencing a slow, recurring déja vu as they moved around the city, as if the sights that most first-time visitors experience were already known to her, familiar enough, yet not recently. He'd been to South Africa with visitors from Europe many times before and he'd always secretly enjoyed the strangely familiar aspect that the place seemed to hold for them – it was both like Europe and not. But Anneliese evinced no such surprise. Perhaps that was just her nature. But there was one thing he'd noticed that struck him at the time as odd, though he'd just filed it away. On their second day, one of the maids who cleaned the rooms in the hotel had run down the corridor after them. 'Ma'am,' she'd called out, not too loud so as to alarm them. They'd both turned round. 'You dropped this,' she said, holding out her hand. Nestled in the salmon-pink palm was one of Anneliese's diamond earrings. 'Just there, by the floor.' She turned and pointed with the other hand.

'Oh, thank you,' Anneliese said, putting out her hand to take it. And then it happened. A silly, insignificant gesture perhaps, but one that increasingly struck him as odd. The maid righted her hand, making to drop the earring in Anneliese's palm. Anneliese quickly turned her hand round so that it faced palm up instead. She stretched her left arm out towards the maid, her right hand going to the underside of her own elbow in the respectful gesture of supplication that is specific to southern Africa. He'd never seen it anywhere else. The maid clearly recognised the gesture, murmuring respectfully, '*Nkosi*, Mama,' before melting away. Anneliese slipped the earring into the pocket of her trouser suit and she and Ree continued on their way. Yes, it was an odd gesture in one who'd never been here before. Perhaps she had, during the dark days of apartheid, even, and out of some tender sensitivity towards him, didn't want to say? It didn't seem like Anneliese, though. She'd never struck him as one to duck any kind of truth, no matter how hard. Still, he had to admit, every now and then he was brought up against something in all of them – Anneliese, Callan, Tara – that didn't *quite* make sense. He was reminded again of that first evening he'd had dinner with them all in St John's Wood. Amidst the laughter and the music and good conversation brought about by good wine, he'd been very faintly aware of a different tune being sung, music in another, deeper key.

89

ANNELIESE
Milan, Italy

The enormous, cavernous hall, once the storage depot of the Milano Centro railway station, was so quiet you could almost hear a pin drop. It was an unusual feat for the gathered crowd of some three hundred journalists, magazine editors, fashionistas, celebrities, their friends and hangers-on . . . and the designers, of course. Anneliese parted the curtains a fraction and looked out. Everyone was waiting expectantly. She could see Lagerfeld in the front row, fidgeting with his iPod, and next to him, Galliano, holding up his phone to the light, taking pictures, no doubt. And there was Anna, of course, looking serene behind those giant sunglasses that gave nothing – and yet everything – away. She gave a wry smile. There were young designers who could write a thesis on the meaning of every turn of Anna's immaculately coiffed head. At a hundred paces they could tell if a skirt met with her approval or disdain on the strength of the merest of movements. Not that Anna's opinion made much difference to her clothes, or her sales. She admired the woman enormously, not just for her iron self-discipline which was evident in every gesture, but for her self-sufficiency in the face of such need. *Everyone* wanted a slice of her, at all times. Unlike Anneliese, or most designers for that matter, the person in charge of a multi-billion-dollar juggernaut like *Vogue* couldn't simply shut the door or disappear. She had to be "on", almost perpetually.

Her choreographer, who was standing to one side of the stage, looked up with an enquiring glance. Ready? She nodded. He gave her a thumbs-up and the music began. Ryuichi Sakamoto's track, 'A Thousand Knives', filled the air. Two minutes of music, then the first of the models. They'd been through the routine too many times to count. She looked over the line of girls standing nervously to attention, like fillies before a race. Irina and Ivanka, two wafer-thin Czech identical twins, were opening for her. Irina was white-blonde; Ivanka's hair had been dyed jet-black. They were a striking duo. They were both wearing her favourite outfit in the new collection – a slim, tailored trouser suit, one in dark, chocolate-brown tweed with the faintest sheen to it, the other in icy, very faintly metallic grey. The stitching was absolutely exquisite, not a stray thread or exposed seam to be seen anywhere. She offered up a silent prayer to Mrs Martinez, her head seamstress, whose ability to stitch into reality Anneliese's often complex, whimsical sketches, was unparalleled. She brushed a loose strand of hair away from Ivanka's collar, nodded and then watched as the curtain pulled back and the twins stepped out in unison. There was a few seconds' pause, as though the audience was holding its breath, then she heard the cameras begin to furiously click and whirr. Slowly, she let out her own.

'So, are you telling me she's better? One hundred per cent better?' Domenico Terme looked at her quizzically.

Anneliese nodded. 'So they say. Look, I know it's a bit of a risk—'

'A *bit* of a risk?' Domenico echoed her words incredulously, interrupting her. 'That's an understatement. I'm *so* tired of these fucking beautiful girls with their messed-up heads and their fragile egos . . . give me someone else, Anneliese, I beg you. The woman's a liability. Even when she's *sober*.'

Anneliese sighed. 'I know, I know . . . but surely everyone deserves a second chance? She's been in rehab, she's clean, she's determined to give it her best shot. Surely we owe it to her to try her out, at least.'

It was Domenico's turn to sigh. 'You're the last person I expected to say that,' he said, raising his eyebrows in defeat. 'OK, OK, let's give her a shot at it. But I'm telling you . . . the first sign of *any*thing, and she's out of there; I don't care what you say about second chances.'

'Thanks, Domenico,' Anneliese said briskly, getting up. 'I appreciate it. I'll let the agency know. Her booker can set everything up. When do you go?'

'Monday. I think all the visas are ready. Just a few last-minute details to sort out and we're good to go.' He picked up the portfolio he'd brought along to show her. Istanbul. Past and present. East and West. Old and Young. The shoot had been commissioned by *Tatler* – and unusually for them, they'd allowed Lars and Bruno a say in the way the story unfolded. It was Lars who'd come up with the idea of using Istanbul and its famously intricate architecture and landscapes to act as the perfect backdrop for Anneliese's new summer collection of spare, elegant outfits and clean, crisp colours. The plan was to spend a couple of days photographing inside the magnificent Dolmabahçe Palace on the banks of the Bosporus, for which, miraculously, they'd managed to secure permissions, then sail out to the Princes' Islands in the Sea of Marmara. 'I understand, Aní,' Domenico said suddenly, his voice uncharacteristically soft. 'She's *your* face. She's part of the brand. I get it. But sometimes . . .' He shrugged. 'Sometimes you have to know when to give up, let go.' He seemed on the verge of saying something more, but stopped. 'Look, we've got back-up, in any case. I'm putting those two stunning sisters out there on stand-by. If Hayley screws up, they step in. Don' worry,' he added to Bruno and Lars who were looking increasingly agitated. 'We'll get it done, one way or another.' And with that, in a sea of cameras and assistants, he swept out.

'If she lets us down,' Bruno said darkly, getting to his feet. 'I'll have her head on a platter.'

'She won't,' Anneliese said. 'I'm sure of it.' She wasn't, but there was no need to let Bruno see that. She picked up her cup of coffee, selected a small biscuit from the tray and quickly left the office. The shoot they'd been arguing over was an important one; unusually, *Tatler* had allowed her more rein than they'd give to most designers. On the one hand, it was a tactical decision. A^2 had done better than anyone expected, generating a whole slew of new, similar collaborations, but she'd been the first. She was now in control of two, almost diametrically opposed ends of the market. A*d*SP still retained its grip at the upper end whilst A^2 had cornered a whole new generation of savvy, clued-up shoppers who wanted quality and cut, but at a fraction of the price. Yes, the initial idea had been hers but she'd been surprised by how much she'd found herself listening to Callan, even Tara. In the three years since they'd launched it, it was Callan she'd turned to for design advice, something she'd never, ever have contemplated before.

Things had changed, she thought to herself as she waited for the lift. In her daughters – and she included Tara in the state-ment – she saw a different type of woman emerging. No, that was too dramatic. It wasn't that they were a different breed, rather that there were more options open to them in terms of how they might want to live. To love. To *be*. She supposed it was women like her who'd paved the way. Whatever success she'd had had been fought for – and won – entirely on her own. Yes, Bruno had helped in his own, precious way, but the truth was if it hadn't been for her, A*d*SP and everything it had given them simply wouldn't exist. But she'd paid the price for her own ambition and drive. Now she hoped that Callan wouldn't have to as well. This . . . *thing* . . . with Ree . . . much as she adored him, she hoped he wouldn't leave Hayley for her. She rarely admitted it, even to herself, but there was a side to Callan she feared. She'd always gone after what she couldn't have; as soon as she got it, she lost interest. She'd always been that way. She'd lost count of the number of little girls whose mothers had rung her, Anneliese – not knowing any better! – to enquire why Callan had stopped playing with their offspring or why she'd given poor Sophie or Dominique the cold shoulder. It was one of the reasons she'd sent her to boarding school. She couldn't continue having things entirely her own way – boarding school would soon put a stop to it. It hadn't. But then Tara had come along and for the first time she'd seen Callan put someone else's needs before her own. Now there was Ree. She didn't want to see him get hurt. That old phrase she'd overheard all those years ago came back to her. *Wie der Vater, so der Sohn.* Or, more accurately, 'like mother, like daughter.' Take your pick. Things connect, run in circles; lines are bound by blood.

90

HAYLEY
Istanbul, Turkey, 2005

They could hardly have been any more explicit. 'Fuck this one up, Hayley, and you're finished. *Finished.* D'you understand?' It was a sentence she'd heard so often in the past week it had almost lost its power to warn her. Almost. Anneliese hadn't quite used those words – she wouldn't say 'fuck', for example – but she'd made her point. 'I believe in second chances, Hayley. That's why I'm giving you one.'

It wasn't in Hayley's nature to fall to her knees but she'd had to stop herself from doing so. It was the first piece of good news she'd had in six months. 'Thanks, Anneliese,' she'd whispered. 'Thank you.' *Just don't fuck it up.*

So here she was, in her own suite at the recently refurbished Pera Palace in Istanbul, in a suite that was almost as big as the loft back home, overlooking the Golden Horn . . . she sat down on the edge of the enormous bed and put a hand to her mouth. The Inönü Suite was nothing short of magnificent. She looked around her – windows on almost all sides, covered in beautiful rose-coloured silk damask curtains; a four-poster bed; rich, intricate Persian carpets covering a pale blonde wooden floor . . . her own marble bathroom with a tub that could comfortably seat three . . . power shower, double sinks, her own private balconies. She could hardly take it all in. Her suitcases had been brought up by a butler who'd also left a discreet silver tray with two crystal champagne flutes full of pale gold champagne and a small plate of gorgeous-looking macaroons. Grace Donovan, *Tatler*'s art director, and Domenico Terme, the photographer, were in similar suites on the same floor; the rest of the team were in rooms scattered around the hotel. The whole trip had something of the air of a party about it – everyone was glad to be out of the doom and gloom of London in April – nothing but rain and grey skies.

She got up and walked to one set of French doors. She stepped outside. In London it was raining; in Istanbul, at seven p.m. on a late spring evening, the skies were slowly turning lilac and gold and there was warmth in the air. She could see the sea from her window, and the twinkling lights of the bridge. A scent of spices rose up from the street; her stomach rumbled suddenly. She felt like crying with relief. After a gruelling rehab, it was nothing short of a miracle to find pleasure in the most ordinary of things. Feeling hungry; feeling thirsty for something other than alcohol; missing her kids. At the thought of them, almost 10,000 miles away, her heart lifted. They were coming back to London at the end of term, just a few months away. She couldn't wait to see them again. It was something she'd learned in the four months of compulsory therapy that had accompanied rehab – focus on the future, not on the past. *Look forwards, not backwards.* Leave all the negativity and guilt and blame where it belongs – back there. It was time to concentrate on the things that mattered – her children, her career . . . and Ree, of course. At the thought of him, her stomach gave a lurch. Of all the things that had gone wrong, this would be the hardest to fix. She didn't want to even think about what might have gone on in her absence, especially with that little bitch Callan. But she had to tread carefully. She owed her tentative comeback to Anneliese; she couldn't afford to damage that relationship under any circumstances. But if she found out that something *had* happened . . . she would get her revenge, come what may. *No one* took what was hers; not even Callan de Saint Phalle. The bitch.

'Hayley? Are you there?' There was a tap at the door. It was Grace Donovan.

She practically jumped back through the doorway. 'Hi, yes . . . come in,' she said, hurrying to open the door. 'Hi.'

'Lovely, aren't they?' Grace swept in, followed by her mane of copper hair. She'd been a model in her day – a stunning, fiery redhead, still pencil thin and elegant in her late fifties and still able to capture a story like no one else. She'd been at *Tatler* for almost a quarter of a century and there was no one who even came close. She'd pounced on the Istanbul idea immediately. She was the one who'd thought of the Dolmabahçe Palace and its stunning gardens. 'Right, I want to run through the story-board with you, darling . . . just to make sure we're all on the same page. Marco'll go ahead of us tomorrow to do all the setting up but I want to go over some of the key ideas before we get there.'

'Absolutely.' Hayley was all ears.

'Let's sit here, shall we?' Grace sat down at the desk by the window. 'Pull up a chair.' She pulled a large portfolio out of her bag and spread the sheets across the desk. 'I'm thinking romance, darling, maybe even *forbidden* romance, affairs. We'll be shooting in the Ambassadors' Hall, as well as on the Crystal Staircase. Have you ever seen a chandelier this big?' She pulled out one photograph after another. 'Or walls this sumptuous? It's an art director's dream, I have to tell you. Domenico's in seventh heaven already. There's a whole wing . . . the Harem. I just love the sound of it.'

Hayley watched in fascination as Grace sketched out what amounted to a short, perfectly constructed film with all the elements that would turn a photo shoot into a fantasy world, full of glorious, theatrical detail – the perfect backdrop for Anneliese's minimal, sharp lines. 'It sounds wonderful,' she breathed, as Grace paused to draw her own breath. 'I can't wait.'

'Good. I'm excited. I think it's going to be one of our best location shoots ever.' Grace closed the portfolio with a snap. 'Champers, darling?' she looked across to where the two flutes were still standing.

Hayley shook her head. 'Thanks, but no,' she said firmly. 'I don't drink any more.'

Grace clapped a hand to her head. 'Of course. Silly me. Good for you. I don't envy you, mind. This mad world we live in.' She looked around the suite. 'Crazy, isn't it? I grew up in Cardiff . . . never thought I'd wind up here, like this. No wonder we're all bloody alcoholics!' She got to her feet. 'Anyhow, don't pay me any attention. Light supper tonight, no carbs. Early start tomorrow. You know the score, I'm sure.' She picked up her portfolio and the loose sheets and made for the door. 'I'm off to bed. I'm exhausted. See you tomorrow.'

'Goodnight,' Hayley said, suddenly shy. In the old days she'd have been at the bar already, flirting with the crew, drinking one cocktail after another. Not any more. She picked up the two still-full flutes, marched over to the window and tipped the contents over the railings. Somewhere down below, it was raining champagne. She grinned to herself and stepped back. She picked up the room service menu. A light salad, a bottle of sparkling water and a piece of fruit. She placed her order, lay back against the plump, crisply laundered cushions and sighed deeply. *Just don't fuck it up.* Not a chance.

91

'Turn a little towards me, yes . . . exactly. That's it. Just hold that for a moment.'

'Relax your hands. Do something else with them . . . yeah, that's good.'

'And a little more to my left . . . and now to the right.'

'Can someone fix that strand of hair?'

'What about the piano . . . shall we take a couple of shots over there? What about having her lean against it?'

'Don't move . . . that's it! Great. *Fantástico. Bella.*'

'And the chair? Shall I move it? Where d'you want me to put it?'

'Will *somebody* get me some fucking coffee!'

'Grace . . . there's someone from the museum here. He says we're not to move the furniture.'

'Oh, Christ. Will somebody please deal with them? Does anyone speak Turkish?'

'Um, I think he speaks English.'

'Yes, but it'd be easier to charm him in Turkish. Oh, fuck it, I'd better go. Just hold it for a moment, Domenico, I'll be right back.' Grace hurried off to the far corner of the room, trailing her hair and half a dozen assistants behind her.

'Here.' Domenico's assistant passed a small pastry to Hayley. 'You look a bit pale. Have one.'

'Oh, I don't think—'

'Come on, don't be silly. A bite's not going to make any difference. You look amazing. I'm André, by the way.' He held out a hand.

'Er, I'm Hayley,' she mumbled through the pastry.

'Yeah, I know *that*. I was on one of your shoots for A*d*SP, ages ago. I nearly got to go on the Turks and Caicos shoot but someone bumped me off at the last minute.' His smile was easy and light. He was young, perhaps in his late twenties, with a mop of curly brown hair and hazel eyes. Well built, nice broad chest, nice bulge of biceps under his T-shirt . . . jeans, long, lean legs . . . Hayley's mind took in the details automatically. Nice. He was *nice*. And kind.

'Shame you didn't make it,' she said as lightly as she could, taking another dainty bite. The sugar rush was instant. It was all she could do not to stuff the remaining piece down her throat whole. 'No, that's enough,' she said, refusing his offer of another one. 'Got to watch this,' she said, patting her absolutely flat stomach.

His eyes followed her hand. 'There are worse things to watch,' he said, raising an appraising eyebrow. 'You're perfect.'

She actually blushed. She could feel the heat staining her cheeks. She mumbled something inarticulate and gauche and slipped off the stool. She could feel his eyes following her as she made her way back to the centre of the room. Grace came back in, followed by the museum official who had been so thoroughly charmed that he even helped them move the furniture himself. It took another hour and a half to get the two shots that satisfied Domenico out of a possible two hundred. Yes, she was back in the thick of it, Hayley thought to herself as they took a short break for lunch. None for her, of course. She wouldn't eat until the day was over. She caught sight of André across the room. She could have sworn he winked at her. She picked up her bottled water and rummaged in her bag for her cigarettes. She could give up almost everything else – drink, drugs, food, even sex . . . but not her Marlboro Lights. Sex . . . she almost laughed aloud. She hadn't had sex since the night she'd been busted. Another pleasure that had gone the way of everything else. Would life ever return to normal? she wondered. Easy, she cautioned herself, repeating what her counsellor had told them only every other day. Baby steps. A day at a time.

They spent two exhausting days in the palace, from dawn to dusk. Hayley was pinched, teased, strapped and coiffed to within an inch of her life. The smell of hairspray was as familiar to her as cigarette smoke, or coffee. From Istanbul they would go by yacht to the island of Heybeliada, about an hour and a half off the coast and the second-largest of the charmingly named Princes' Islands. 'It's where they exiled Byzantine princes and Ottoman sultans,' André explained as the yacht slipped its moorings and began powering south. He was reading from a local tourist guide. Sunlight bounced off the waves in sharp bursts; the sky was clear and blue with gentle, wispy strokes of white. Portishead and Zero 7 on the small stereo that someone had brought along and plugged in. Grace was below deck; her porcelain skin and red hair meant she avoided the sun like the plague. She'd already instructed her assistants to lather sun cream on Hayley every half an hour. 'If you insist on exposing yourself, you'd better use this,' she said disparagingly, handing over a bottle of cream. 'Every thirty minutes,' she said sternly to one of the hovering girls. 'I don't want even a *hint* of pink on that gorgeous skin.'

'Yes, Ms Donovan,' they chorused, almost curtseying. They followed her orders too. But it was nice to give herself up to the forgotten pleasure of being pampered and looked after. She leaned back against the cushioned chaise, stretched her long legs in front of her and watched the Istanbul shoreline slip by. The sun dazzled casually on the water, flitting here and there as the boat made jerky progress out towards the open sea. She closed her eyes. André's voice was a warm, soft slur that mingled with the slap of water and the sudden cries of gulls. His knee was bent; every so often, in time with the tug of the boat slicing through the waves, it touched her foot. She sighed in contentment; the first such sigh in months.

The island was small and densely wooded. Red-roofed villas and homes snaked their way up the hill to the top, where an imposing military-looking structure stood, surveying the strip of blonde sand that was the crescent-shaped harbour. They glided in silently to where a group of horse-drawn carriages waited for them. 'No cars on the island,' André said cheerfully. 'Come on, jump in.' He held a hand out to her and she climbed into the rather rickety hansom cab. They clip-clopped their way away from the small jetty and down a cobbled street. Giant red and purple fronds of bougainvillea spilled over stone walls behind which enormous villas could just be glimpsed. The guest house where they would stay for the two days of the shoot was one such house; it had hosted George V and was perched right on the shore with its own private beach and swimming pool. The rooms were large and wonderfully airy, the gardens beautifully sculpted and planted; paths fringed with rose bushes led straight to the sea.

They met on the terrace for afternoon tea whilst Grace ran through the morning's schedule. Half of the shoot would be done at the villa, the other half on the yacht that had brought them over. 'Understated glamour,' she instructed the hair and make-up artists. They pored over photographs and Grace's mood boards, excitedly discussing the clothes. Hayley sat under the protective shade of a huge, yellow-and-white striped awning, drinking her black coffee and smoking, slowly drawing the smoke into her lungs like food. Far in the distance, only just visible, the shoreline of Istanbul shimmered. It was hard to imagine that in a couple of days' time, they'd be back in grey, wet London. She caught André's eye for the umpteenth time; he seemed to be watching her, but without menace. Just the flirtatiously interested glance of someone who was obviously taken by her . . . she was used to being stared at but there was something rather nice about the way she seemed to catch his attention and hold it. That hadn't happened in a while.

All afternoon she was pleasantly aware of herself, as if she were watching herself through someone else's eyes. She blossomed; Domenico was delighted. He stalked around the villa with his camera held in front of him like a weapon, testing the light, angles, views . . . and her, of course. He declared her 'absolutely beautiful, like a flower in bloom'. She flirted with the camera and with him, and everyone was pleased with her. *Don't fuck it up*. She hadn't and she wouldn't.

92

LINDI
Windhoek, Namibia

She locked the bedroom door behind her, making sure the door held fast. She gingerly held the thick, bound document that had just arrived by courier as if it was hot. She sat down on the edge of the bed, switched on the reading lamp and fished her glasses out of her bag. She put them on, opened the bound document and began to read.

Half an hour later, she put it down. There was no doubt that the pages she'd been sent were extracted from the large document she'd just finished reading. Her skin had puckered into goose bumps. The extracts she'd already seen belonged to a secret testimonial of two young women who'd been tortured at one of the liberation camps some fifteen years earlier, suspected of being spies. That such things could and did happen in the camps wasn't news to her, but if it ever got out, the blow to the reputation of the ruling party might prove fatal. Much of Namibia's inward investment depended on its squeaky-clean human rights record – the testimonial in her hand implicated at least half a dozen current ministers, perhaps more. She got up and moved to the window. She parted the curtain cautiously and peered out. In front of her, their soft, dark shape looming in the night silence, were the beginnings of the Klein Windhoek hills. She looked around; there was nothing but night-time quiet. She'd asked Tara to get hold of the documents not just because she was the historian, but because she was outside the country and therefore above suspicion. Until she found out who'd sent her the two sheets, it was far too dangerous for her to be seen asking questions. She wasn't *that* naive. She was a lawyer and knew there was a plethora of legal issues to be resolved before she even opened her mouth. Were the documents authentic?

Who'd written them? When? And how? Word of mouth testimonial or sworn?

She let the curtain drop into place again and walked over to the bed. Having the bound proof in the house was a little like having a gun – a smoking gun, she thought to herself nervously. She felt the urge to talk to Iago about it; after all, he'd know better than anyone if there was any truth to it, and perhaps more importantly, what should be done. She slid the document back into the padded envelope and pushed it to the back of her wardrobe. She picked up her phone, her fingers scrolling down to his number. But something made her hesitate. She sat there for a few minutes, biting her lip. Then she put the phone down again. She needed time to think.

93

HAYLEY
Heybeliada, Turkey

She pinned the giant silk rose carefully behind one ear and looked at the effect in the mirror. She was wearing one of the simple white shift dresses she'd worn on the shoot that afternoon. Asymmetrically cut off one shoulder, narrow and beautifully cut, it fell to just above her knees. The flower, made up of turquoise and midnight blues, brought out the honeyed tones in her skin and hair, and made those famous green eyes even lighter. She popped a quick pose at herself in the mirror – yep, she looked the part. Despite the lathering of sunblock she'd actually caught a few rays that afternoon and her nose and cheeks were prettily rosy. She picked up a pair of white, slingback kitten heels and her thick, chunky silver bracelet . . . she was ready.

She sat down on the bed, slipped on her shoes and picked up the phone. It was seven o'clock in the evening in Turkey, which meant it was eight o'clock in Windhoek. There was just enough time to talk to the girls before they went to bed. She dialled the number, hoping it would be Klaus who answered the phone, not Sibongile. There had never been much love lost between them; now, after the events of the past months, there was none.

'Hello?'

Her heart sank. It was Sibongile. 'Oh, er, hi, Sibongile. It's Hayley here. May I speak to the girls, please?'

'They're already asleep.'

'Asleep? But it's only seven o'clock! Here, I mean.'

'Well, it's nine o'clock here.'

Hayley bit her lip. Of course. Namibia was two hours ahead of Turkey, not one. She began to apologise nervously. 'Sorry, sorry. I'm in . . . in Turkey at the moment. I'm doing a shoot. It's my first . . .'

There was nothing but stony silence on the other end. 'Must I give them a message?' Sibongile asked finally.

'Um, yes . . . yes, if you could just tell them that I rang. And . . . and that I love them both very much and I . . . I miss them.' She stopped herself just in time. Her eyes were beginning to well up with tears. 'And that's it,' she whispered, swallowing hard.

'Goodnight.' The phone went dead.

She sat for a few minutes holding it loosely in her hand, composing herself, trying not to cry. She'd always been nervous of Sibongile; now she was downright terrified. She dabbed her eyes with her forefinger, taking care not to smudge her make-up. She took a couple of deep breaths and stood up. Her earlier buoyant mood had all but vanished and she desperately needed it back. She knew herself; it was in moments like these that the temptation to turn to something else to make her feel better was at its strongest. A drink, a line, a puff . . . anything to take the edge off. She smoothed down her dress, took another look at herself in the mirror. She looked great, gorgeous, stunning. She was beautiful, inside and out. She mouthed a couple of the phrases she'd been taught in rehab to herself, bolstering her faltering self-confidence. She picked up her small clutch purse, switched off the lights and made her way downstairs.

There was no one in the hotel restaurant on the ground floor. She walked across the parquet flooring, her heels echoing loudly as she went. She could hear voices on the patio outside, floating in through the French doors. She stopped for a second, just before going outside. She put up a hand to check the flower was still in place, and that her dress was positioned perfectly off one faintly golden shoulder.

'*You* seem to be getting along all right with the gorgeous Hayley,' she heard someone say. She stopped, her hand hovering over the door handle.

'Yeah . . .' That was André's voice, laconically amused.

'She *is* pretty fucking gorgeous,' someone else piped up. 'She's married, though, isn't she?'

Her heart was beating fast. *Listeners never hear good of themselves.* Wasn't that what her mother always used to say? But she couldn't move.

'Yeah, to that wanker architect, you know the one I mean. He's always in the papers. I don't think things are exactly rosy on that front, not after what happened last year. But d'you want to know what the best thing about her is?'

Someone laughed. 'Go on, then.'

Her heart had almost stopped beating. She heard the clink of glasses and the scrape of a chair as someone – André – moved closer. 'She's so fucking *grateful*. Women like that are starving dogs. Toss 'em a smile and they open their legs. It's practically automatic. Watch me. It won't take me long with her. She's desperate.'

She moved backwards, quietly, until she reached the door. Then she turned and fled. Her whole body felt hot with liquid, trembling shame.

94

CALLAN
Paris, France

Five, four, three, two, one. She took a third or fourth deep breath, put a hand on her stomach for a second, and yanked open the door. There he was. It took her a moment to take it in. It had been almost a month since they'd seen each other. Her eyes raked over him before her hands did. Everything there, everything as it had been, everything intact. The first touch; the first kiss. Ah, how she had waited for this! She caught his soft, full lower lip between her teeth and bit him playfully. 'I've missed you,' she said under her breath. 'I thought you'd never get here.'

'I've missed you.' His kiss left her lips almost bruised and in no doubt about the truth of his statement. He gripped her upper arms, lifting her clear off the floor. She gave a squeal of delight, wrapping her legs around him. It was just as it had been in the beginning, a kind of mad intoxication of everything – sight, smell, sound, taste, touch. They couldn't get enough of each other. They didn't even make it to the bedroom. He pushed aside her skirt impatiently, unbuckled himself and was inside her before she could even protest. Not that she would, or could have. They both came almost immediately, her fingernails raking his back whilst he mumbled her name, over and over again.

'I ought to go away more often,' he said, when they'd both recovered enough to speak.

'If you ever go away for a month again, I'll divorce you.' There was a second's stunned pause, then Ree gave a short, mirthless laugh.

'You shouldn't be talking about divorce,' he said, his hand still running up and down the length of her bare thigh. 'I should.'

Callan's heart gave a tight, painful lurch. She caught and held her breath. 'Wh . . . what d'you mean?' she asked carefully when there was nothing more from him.

He turned and propped himself up on an elbow. They were lying on the cream and rose Afshar rug that Anneliese had given her for her twenty-first birthday. She had a momentary twinge of guilt as she traced out a pattern of intertwined leaves and flowers with her forefinger. The rug was professionally cleaned each year; semen was probably not included in the list of routine stains. She smiled for a second. 'What's funny?' he asked, lifting his hand to push away her hair which had fallen over her face.

'Never mind,' she said, shaking her head. 'What were you saying about . . . divorce?'

He rolled away from her onto his back. It took him a few moments to speak. 'Anneliese rang me yesterday,' he said slowly. 'Seems Hayley had a bit of a relapse – yeah, I think that's the right term for it – on the shoot. I don't know what brought it on but they found her almost unconscious in her room the next morning. She'd downed a bottle of wine and two Nembutal. They had to throw her in the bath to wake her up.'

'I'm sorry, Ree,' Callan said after a moment. She meant it. She *was* sorry. As much as the word 'divorce' sent an electric jolt of hope and longing through her, she felt sorry for them all – the beautiful, wayward Hayley and her seeming inability to make anything stick; Ree, torn between wanting to 'do the right thing', as he put it, and what she instinctively felt he really wanted to do – be with her; and the kids, of course, those two beautiful little girls whose world had been turned upside down too many times to count. There was a side to them, especially prickly, self-sufficient Zoë, that Callan understood only too well but she'd deliberately – or instinctively – kept her distance. There were times when she amazed herself; she'd never been one to hold back or exercise more than the most rudimentary forms of patience but there was something about Ree's quiet, calm manner that brought out some finer, almost nobler, her. For almost the first time in her life, there were others whose needs were greater than hers. Both Tara and Anneliese were so scarily self-sufficient that the idea of having to consider anyone else whenever she had a decision to make was almost foreign to her. 'What're you going to do?' she asked quietly.

'Isn't it obvious? It's not going to get any better with Hayley. In fact, it's probably going to get a whole lot worse. I . . . I can't trust her. I can't trust her with the girls. But I can't risk a judge handing down a custody order in her favour – and if I don't want that to happen, I'm going to have to rake her through the mud. Either way, I don't want the girls to see it.'

'Let them stay where they are,' Callan said, turning to look at him. 'You said it yourself – they're happy there. Your parents adore them. It's the safest place for them.'

He sighed. 'Yeah, you're right. But it just doesn't seem right, somehow. I'm losing them, I can feel it. Every time I go down, they're just that bit more distant. We start off trying to make sure they don't go through what we did – or at least I did – and we wind up doing worse.'

'Don't say that,' Callan said, her throat suddenly thickening. 'You're doing the best you can. That's all you can do. *You* didn't make this happen. It just happened, that's all.'

'Yeah, but sometimes you just have to accept that your best's not good enough.'

Callan was quiet. She was out of her depth. She'd no idea what it was like to have a child, let alone two. She put a hand on his arm, trying to reassure him with her touch. 'You'll make the right decision,' she said finally. 'Whatever you decide. I know you will.' He would never know what it had cost her to say that.

He said nothing but simply covered her hand with his own. She could see her discarded clothing, her midnight-blue silk Lucille bra from Agent Provocateur, her upturned Jimmy Choo stilettos, and the cream angora jumper she'd bought only that morning . . . all lay in a discarded heap across the floor. She tried to quell the nagging voice at the back of her mind that said it wasn't going to be that simple, or easy. She'd seen Hayley's face one too many times when she felt threatened or thought there was something going on that she'd missed. She looked as though she were capable of anything. Anything at all.

95

LINDI
Windhoek, Namibia

The street lights ended; the car rolled slowly down the road, descending into the dark. Sitting in the back seat, squashed between two men to whom she'd briefly been introduced, Lindi glanced nervously through the window at the thin sliver of moon casting an eerie light on the gloom. They passed a wire fence that held a graveyard of broken-down vehicles; past bottle stores and small shops whose signs she couldn't read. *Mahatma Gandhi Street*. The car headlights picked out a street sign in a long, slow swoop as they advanced cautiously down the road. In the front seat, David Lawson, the British journalist friend of Norah's, and Sam Ntoma, a Namibian journalist, discussed directions.

'Mike said it was on the left . . . second turning on the left.'

'No, man. That's Marty's place. It's the one after.'

They turned into Kroon Street, past an open piece of ground, then right into Borgward. They followed the road around the bend, then Sam slapped the dashboard suddenly. 'That's it . . . back up one. *Ja*. This is the place.'

David threw the car into reverse and they bumped over the sidewalk and stopped. They opened the doors and got out. A stray dog with a stiff, upright tail regarded them suspiciously from across the road, then turned and trotted off. A furious, hysterical cackle from behind the fence erupted as several chickens started up.

'*Ja*, this's the one.' Sam nodded, confirming his choice. 'They're round the back. Let me just call Mike.' He fished his mobile out. He said something in oshiHerero, nodding as he spoke. 'OK, man. *Shiké*.' He closed the phone with a snap. 'She's round the back. Come on.'

Her heart thudding, Lindi followed the men down the narrow alleyway that separated the houses. Was she doing the right thing? She fervently hoped so. Norah had all sorts of ideas about involving the BBC and CNN and who knew who else, but Lindi was more cautious. 'First we've got to establish if it's true,' she said to Norah over a cup of coffee in her kitchen. 'We can't just call up the BBC without checking it out.'

'Fine. You check it out. You'll see. It's all true.'

'And even if it is true, what do *I* do about it? I work for the government, Norah. This could be . . . tricky.'

'Fine,' Norah repeated. 'So let *me* do the investigating.'

Lindi hesitated, stirring her coffee. 'But the extracts were sent to *me*. I've got to find out who sent them, and why.'

'You may never find that out.' Norah was older and more cynical. 'That's the way things work around here.'

'Even so. They were sent to me for a reason.'

'Sometimes it's better not to know.'

'I'll . . . I'll talk to her.' Lindi made up her mind. 'I'll talk to her and see.'

'Fine.'

So here she was, creeping down an alleyway in Khomasdal, in total darkness behind four men, none of whom she actually knew. They were on their way to interview Erika Tobias, a woman in her mid-forties whose story was contained in the pages of the document Tara had sent her.

'This is the one.' One of the men stopped in front of a door. A tiny, rheumy light hung above it, casting a square yellow beam across the entrance. He rapped softly, once, twice.

It was opened at once. A voice changed its tone on recognition of the speaker and it was swung wide to let them in. They trooped in, passing under the Fanta-coloured light and were led down a short corridor to the living room. It was warm inside: the cosy fug of a much-occupied room. There were plastic chairs of the sort that come out at funerals and weddings, and a sofa still partially wrapped in plastic with a series of carefully placed crocheted doilies on its back and arms. In one corner was a dining table with four chairs. An electric bulb with a plastic shade hung in the centre, throwing an eerie, green light over the ensemble. There were pictures on the walls, an incongruous mixture of cheap Coca-Cola calendars with a smiling girl holding up a can, and landscape watercolours, depicting scenes as far apart as Niagara Falls and the German Alps.

'You can have a seat.' One of the men turned to Lindi, pulling out a chair at the dining table. It made a high, squeaking noise that sounded very loud in the room. She pulled out a chair opposite and sat down. She wondered who the two men were – David Lawson hadn't said. Suddenly the door at the far end of the room opened and a woman walked in. She wasn't what Lindi had been expecting. She was of medium height and build, with a smooth, dark-skinned complexion and braids that hung in a bob to just below the chin. She was smoking; she stood just inside the room, looking at them. David Lawson was the first to speak.

'Hi, Erika. Thanks for agreeing to see us. Can I just . . . this is Sam Ntoma; he's from the *Windhoek Enquirer*. And this is Lindi Johanssen; she's with—'

'I know who she is.' Erika looked at Lindi, drawing deeply on her cigarette. Lindi had already risen to her feet. Erika dropped the lighted butt, grinding it out beneath her foot on the concrete floor, then bent down to pick it up. 'How d'you want to do this?' she asked David.

'I thought . . . well, if you don't mind, of course, that we ought to tape it. If that's OK with you?' David was quietly respectful.

'That's fine. You trust her?' She jerked her head in Lindi's direction.

'Yes. Absolutely. Norah put us in touch. I can vouch for her.'

Erika said nothing but walked over to the table, pulled out a chair and sat down. Her skin was smooth and clear, but on her left cheek and again on her forearm, Lindi noticed, there were small, round scars of puckered flesh, as though something had bitten her, causing the skin around the bite to contract and tighten. She caught Lindi's glance, putting up a finger almost unconsciously to touch the place and Lindi saw that she had no fingernails. Her stomach gave a sickening lurch.

'Right. Shall we get started?' David pulled out a small recorder. He and Sam took the remaining two chairs. The two men who'd accompanied them settled themselves on the sofa. They had the air of people who'd heard the story before; neither paid the four of them any attention. Again, Lindi wondered who they were. Erika had with her a small black file of papers which she placed on the table. There were photographs amongst the type-written sheets, some of which Lindi recognised. They were copies of the testimonials Tara had sent. There was also an official picture of the current cabinet, of the sort that hung in every government office, everywhere. Lindi saw herself, standing three rows behind the Old Man and those closest to him, including Iago. She dragged her eyes away from it and looked around the table. David was fidgeting, anxious to start.

'December fourteenth, it's eight o'clock in the evening and we're in Khomasdal. We're here with Erika Tobias, Lindi Johanssen, Sam Ntoma and myself.' David spoke rapidly into the microphone. There was a couple of seconds' wait as he replayed the recording; his disembodied, tinny voice filled the room. Then he pressed record and Erika began to speak. Her voice was low and quiet and there was absolute silence in the room.

She spoke for nearly two hours, chain-smoking, pausing only to light one cigarette after another. The room was thick with the white-blue pall of smoke by the time David finally switched off the recorder. They all avoided each other's eyes. Lindi fought down a wave of rising nausea as she tried to digest what she'd just heard. She had only one question and she knew, before she'd even finished asking, what the answer would be. 'Who signed the order?' she said, her voice breaking into the silence like shattered glass.

Erika paused, drawing on her umpteenth cigarette. 'He did,' she said, pointing to the spread photographs on the table. She

stabbed the official photograph with her misshapen forefinger.
'*He* did,' she said, clearly marking the spot. 'That's him.' She
looked at the image for a second, then lifted her eyes. She met
Lindi's gaze; for almost a full, agonising minute the two women
stared at each other. Lindi felt the blood drain from her face.
She knew. No one else present did. And that was why the
documents had been sent to *her*. It was Erika who'd sent them.
Fear began to spread in her, rising like fever.

96

They dropped her off just before one in the morning. She
pushed open the gate; they waited until she was safely inside,
then she locked and bolted the door, and in a futile gesture,
propped a chair against the handle. She went through to the
kitchen to make herself a cup of herbal tea. She put the kettle on,
but quietly, afraid someone would see or hear her. She closed the
blinds in the kitchen, even though her back wall looked out onto
nothing but the hill. With her arms folded tightly across her
chest, she waited nervously for the kettle to boil. She moved to
the phone on the wall and picked it up. She was just about to dial
Tara's number when the kettle began to scream, as if screaming
for her. She dropped the phone and ran to switch it off. No, it
was better not to call anyone, she thought to herself fearfully,
squeezing out the tea bag with shaking fingers. Not now. And
certainly not from her landline.

She made herself a cup, then turned and stood with her back
against the door, suddenly drained of the energy required to do
anything other than just stand there, her back slowly warming
the glass. It was deep night outside. She looked at her wristwatch. In London it was past midnight. She would phone Tara
from someone else's phone the following morning. She didn't
even dare ring Norah. Her heart was thudding slowly, but at the
merest hint of noise – the crackle of a twig or the call of a night
owl – it sprang into action, furiously pumping the blood through

her veins. She had never been so confused and scared in her life. Iago. Iago Rukoro. She felt as though she were being torn in two. She closed her eyes. It couldn't possibly be true. She slowly slid down the door until she was squatting on the ground, one hand wrapped tightly around the scalding mug without even noticing the heat. She thought of her parents and what they would say. She gave a soft hiccup, of the kind a child would make, and like a child she put her head on her knees and began to cry.

97

ANNELIESE
London, England

Enough. Enough already. Anneliese got up stiffly from her desk where she'd spent the past hour and a half fielding questions and complaints from a range of people – Bruno, Lars, the agents and handlers at Rain, Hayley's *ex*-agency. They'd dropped her for the third and final time. She was exhausted, tired of hearing the woman's name. After her silly little relapse in Turkey in October, she'd gone back into the clinic for a few more months to be dried out (or whatever it was they called it). She'd come out, been sober and drug-free for about a fortnight, then lapsed spectacularly again, this time at a party thrown by the boss of Top Shop. Needless to say, photographers were present. The images were on the front pages of the tabloids before the party finally wound up. This was the final straw for Rain. She was sacked with immediate effect. And this time, there would be no second – or in Hayley's case fourth or fifth – chance. She'd had no choice but to follow suit; Hayley Summers would no longer be the face of A*d*SP or A^2, or anyone else for that matter. She'd fled to the south of France where her mother lived, apparently. Thank God the children were still with Ree's parents. She heard, parenthetically, news of them from Callan, small drops of information that she couldn't resist letting slip. Anneliese had no comment to make. For the first time in her life, she was shy of Callan. There was so much to be said and asked – she had no idea how, or when.

She looked down into the garden at the rear of the house. In the windows of the house opposite, a Christmas tree flickered, on/off; on/off. She was filled with a sudden impatience with the muted, washed-out tones of London in mid-winter. It was time to leave; head for the sun. She brightened almost immediately. That was what was needed – a fortnight at Scheherazade. She would go ahead of Callan and Tara and spend Christmas on her own. All the villas at Pointe Milou were secluded, but none more so than hers. She would be in splendid, perfect isolation until a couple of days before New Year, when her friends and family would descend. She would invite Bruno and Jasper, of course, and Ree. Whatever else, the past few months had been hard on him. She wanted to talk to him about the museum project as well. She had an idea for a permanent collection that she wanted his opinion on. As she began the enjoyable task of planning the short holiday, her mood began to lift. Dinners, picnics on the beach, a barbecue or two beside the emerald pool . . . drinks at sunset watching the flaming colours of the sky as the red orb sank below the horizon and the hilly islands in the bay. She would take along her camera and her sketch books, of course . . . wander along the beach, pick shells with the local women. She loved the translucent, pearly pink interiors of the big conch shells that sometimes washed ashore. She would take a couple back to Japan on her next visit – Yuchiko loved the challenges she kept throwing at her. Make me a fabric exactly like that. She could just picture herself pointing to the shell, and Yuchiko's mock-exasperated face. They'd worked together for nearly twenty years . . . and not once had she failed.

She turned away from the window and walked back to her desk. She pulled open one of the drawers and took out a stack of her heavy, thick cards. 'Please join me at Scheherazade,' she began to write, in her trademark, precise, looping script. Callan,

Tara, Bruno, Jasper, Ree, Lars and Tone, his wife, and herself. And Karl and Princess Caroline. A nice, round number. The previous year she'd had Jean-Paul Gautier and his three friends, and the Bergstroms from San Francisco. Mark and Gillian stopped in as well. They lived in New York and California most of the year, coming to St Barts usually only at Christmas. Most of the residents in Pointe Milou were seasonal; if you could call a once-yearly visit 'seasonal'. Still, the islanders weren't complaining. Most of the year's economy centred around those few weeks when the world's rich and famous descended on the crystal-clear water and white-gold sands. This year it would just be family and a couple of close friends, she mused. And Ree was practically family now.

She finished the last invitation and stuck it in the pile for her PA to send in the morning. She got up, now yawning. It was nearly midnight. High time she turned in for the night. She climbed the stairs to her bedroom suite on the third floor, noticing as she went that her movements were slower than usual. She really was tired – a deep-seated weariness that seemed to go straight to her bones, like a chill. It had been an unusually busy week, topped off by the surprise visit from the new First Lady of the United States, Michelle Obama. Initially she hadn't been keen on the visit; after meeting her, she was thoroughly charmed. She'd selected a number of beautifully tailored outfits for her upcoming trip to Japan and left the showroom in a blaze of motorcycles and sirens which drew huge crowds and ensured that the salesgirls were rushed off their feet for at least a week after she'd gone. She couldn't have cared less about the sales – although the girls, who were on commission, as well as salary, were delighted – but spending an hour with Mrs Obama had been well worth the disruption. Delightful woman, no other word for it. A delight in every way.

She unbuckled her belt and took off her trousers, folding them neatly. Her shirt went into the dry-cleaning pile, everything else in the laundry basket. She slipped on the white bathrobe that was always hanging on the back of the door and walked into the enormous, walk-in closet that led off the bedroom. She opened one of the three-metre-high doors and stood for a moment, surveying the contents. Everything was in place; row upon row of colour-coordinated outfits, neatly hung in racks by the two young girls who came in once a month to clean out her closets, polish her shoes and make sure everything was exactly the way Ms Zander de Saint Phalle liked it. She spent a small fortune on her staff, whose mission it was to make sure everything was the way she liked it, wherever she was. *That* was the one thing money could buy – staff. Not much else, she thought to herself as she shut the doors. Certainly not happiness.

She walked into the bathroom, shrugged off her robe and stepped on the scales. 62 kgs. It had been her weight for most of her life. Age had brought with it other, more subtle signs – a thickening of the waistline, thinning hair and those dreadful liver spots at the backs of her hands – but all in all, she'd weathered the last few years remarkably well. Her hair was short and almost silver now, rather than blonde, but the change had been slow and barely noticed. She switched on the shower and braced herself. A few seconds' icy cold water to stimulate the circulation and tone the skin, and then the more gentle, relaxing warmth. Ten minutes later, her nightly rituals over, she was ready for bed.

She sank into the luxuriously cool sheets, stretching her legs as far as they could go. Her mind began to wander, as it usually did in those few minutes before sleep, a habit she'd learned to love and fear almost equally. It was the time of day – or night – when she was at her most creative. An idea would suddenly spring to mind, summoned out of nowhere. Sometimes she stretched out her hand and fumbled for the pencil and notepad that lay on the table next to her bed, jotting it down before it slipped away again, to be remembered the following morning in snatches, half-conscious musings that then seemed silly, leading nowhere. At other times, her mind veered dangerously off-track, like a racehorse she couldn't control. An image, a word, a scene. She would force herself awake, snapping back to the present with a jerk that bordered on the comic. Fortunately there was no one there to witness these forays into the past that disturbed her so. She was alone, always, for ever. There was no one there to witness any of it, joy or pain.

98

Pointe Milou, St Barts, French West Indies

Red-tiled roofs, furry green hills, thin slivers of land jutting out into an emerald sea . . . the tiny, four-seater plane swept along the coast, dipping below the clouds before coming in to land with a small bump. It was a journey she knew well. From London to Sint Maarten in one long stretch, and then a short, ten-minute flight in one of the small commuter planes that hopped from island to island. She loved the first glimpse of the blonde, fringed coastline and the way the water spun out in concentric rings of blue from the hump-backed islands – thousands of shades, each deeper and more translucent than the last.

'Merry Christmas, ma'am.' The good-looking young pilot whipped off his sunglasses as he turned round to make sure his two passengers had indeed taken all their luggage off his little plane. There were only four of them on the flight – two pilots, two passengers. She had no idea who the middle-aged man in dark shades who'd sat opposite her was and neither did she care to know. It was one reason she'd chosen St Barts above all the other jewel-like islands. The rich and famous had been coming here for years – no one paid them any attention, least of all each other. They came to St Barts to escape, not to stare at one another and compare property values. It was just as well. With her last renovation, which she'd done just before she met Ree Herz, she'd probably tripled the value of her own. Idly she wondered what Ree would make of it – all white walls, wooden parquet flooring and clean, sharp lines. He would probably approve, though she doubted he'd find it of much interest. His brand of design was cleverer – by far – than the minimal, tasteful blandness that the duo she'd hauled out from Miami had delivered. But tasteful minimalism was what the good residents of St Barts liked. She chuckled to think of what Ree might have given her.

She stepped off the last rickety step, breathing in deeply. The soft, balmy air lay like a caress against her cheek. There was nothing quite like the air of the tropics. The scent of the sea came to her slowly, saltiness mingling with the faint but pungent smell of flowers and oils. Even from here, across the thin strip of tarmac that separated the runway from the beach, coconut oil could be tasted on the back of one's tongue. It was Christmas Eve and the wealthy were already hard at play.

A smiling porter whose face she recognised saw her and waved. He hurried over, his dark skin making a sharp, brilliant contrast with his snow-white shorts and shirt. 'Morning, Miss Zander,' he said cheerfully, his face breaking apart to show a set of pearly white teeth, the likes of which she hadn't seen in a long, long time. She could feel her own mouth tugging upwards of its own accord. A cliché, perhaps, but true – the warmth of the islands could be felt in every glance, every smile. She followed him across the tarmac, already beginning to blister with the rising heat, and was whisked through the tiny customs area in no time. Godson, her guide, knew everyone; they waltzed from door to door with a lazy, friendly wave; fifteen minutes later, she was in the back of an air-conditioned Mercedes, pulling away from the little airport beach and beginning the slow climb towards Pointe Milou and the hidden gems that were the holiday homes of her tribe.

The wooden slatted concertina-style doors that led directly from the vast living room to the emerald pool had been drawn entirely back. As she walked in through the front door, her porter trailing behind her, she stopped, quickly suppressing the gasp of pleasure that always awaited her at Scheherazade. The view from the deck overlooked the bay that housed at one end Ile

494

Frégate, and at the other, the two smaller emerald humps of La Tortue. It was almost midday and the sun was a dazzling pinprick in the sky, directly overhead. Light bounced off the glassy surface of the pool, designed to lie perfectly still and flat against the pale travertine marble surround. The housekeeper had laid out the four mahogany sun-loungers with crisp, white linen cushions. There were towels stacked discreetly in a large wicker basket and from the kitchen she could hear the muted conversation that signalled the beginnings of lunch. She sighed deeply. The tension and irritation of the past few weeks had already begun to leave her. She looked around the living room. Whites, blues, greys with the occasional splash of blood-red or emerald silk. When the interior designers had first shown their sketches to her, she'd shuddered. 'But you *know* the colours I like,' she'd complained. 'White, off-white, grey, neutrals.'

Betsey, the brash, loud American one, shook her head. 'No, *those* aren't colours. Those are *non*-colours. *These* are colours.' She pointed to the silk samples – red, green, burgundy, wine and cerise. She'd shuddered, but she'd listened all the same. It had taken her nearly six months to come round but in the end, she was forced to admit, Betsey was right. The splashes of unexpected colour and texture were perfectly in tune with the lush vegetation that surrounded the house and brought the 'inside in', as Carola, Betsey's petite Italian sidekick, was keen to explain. Whatever the reason, it worked. She put her handbag down on the brilliant white floor and crossed the living room to the kitchens. Hélène, her cook and housekeeper of nearly twenty years, was standing with floury arms folded across her impressive bosom, supervising a young girl labouring over a tray of freshly folded croissants. '*Oui, oui . . . doucement, doucement,*' she could hear Hélène murmuring. '*Oui, comme ça . . .*'

'Hélène.' Anneliese stood in the doorway, unwilling to enter into what was effectively Hélène's domain.

'Ah, *madame*.' Hélène gave a small curtsey. Twenty years of employment had done little to relax the rules. She saw how the young cook-in-training swiftly did the same. '*Bienvenue*.'

495

'*Merci*,' Anneliese said, smiling at them both. 'It's good to be back. You're well?'

'*Oui, madame.*' Hélène's expression gave little away. It was strange, Anneliese thought to herself as they exchanged a few pleasantries. She and Hélène had known each other for twenty years but remained formal with one another at all times. It was similar in her other homes – in London, she knew little about Mrs Betts, or Madame Boulicaut in Paris, though she suspected they knew more about her than they would ever let on. Just as it had been on the farm . . . the servants knew everything, always did. She shook her head fractionally. There were some things no one knew – and never would. It was just as well.

'There's a tray on the patio, *madame*,' Hélène said briskly, probably wondering what Anneliese was doing lingering in her kitchen.

'Yes, yes,' Anneliese said vaguely. She wasn't hungry. 'I brought some things with me. For the dinner.'

'Of course. We will discuss the dinner *demain, plus tard*. First you must rest.' Hélène was firm. She was the second person in as many days who'd instructed her to rest, Anneliese thought to herself as she made her way across the living-room floor to the patio. Perhaps it really was as Bruno said – you wake up one morning and the old, tired face looking back at you in the mirror is, you realise with a start, *yours*. Bruno was terrified of ageing.

She took a small slice of Hélène's homemade rye bread with a thin sliver of salmon and an even thinner slice of cucumber and bit into it. Her mouth flooded pleasurably. She picked up the bottle of chilled Chablis and poured herself a glass, then walked to the edge of the terrace and stood, overlooking the steep drop to the beach. Far below the surf yawned gently in and out. She took a sip, savouring the crispness and looked out to sea. In a few days' time, the villa would be full of sound and life. For now, there was little to disturb her. She slipped off her sandals, enjoying the feel of the cool, polished travertine against her bare feet. The wind picked up a little, blowing a few stray strands of hair across her face. All was still and warm. The sounds from the beach were a muted, delicate murmur drifting up the hill. On impulse, she dipped a toe in the water and gave a tiny, childish squeal. She looked around her cautiously. It was so out of character that she laughed. She laughed again. There was absolutely no one around. She was completely alone. She hesitated for a second. The sun was high and hot. Swiftly, before she could change her mind, she pulled off her shirt and unbuckled her linen trousers, letting them fall to the ground. She remembered to take off her watch and with one last, almost furtive look around her, she slid straight into the cool, clear water. It closed over her like a silky, second skin. The sun was a blast of colour dancing across her eyelids as she submerged herself slowly, luxuriating in the feeling of weightlessness. She broke through the surface, putting up a hand to push her hair out of her face. She was free, of everything and everyone. She lay on her back and floated as the heat and light melted the last jagged crystals of the grey Europe she'd left behind out of her blood.

In the morning, she woke to the sound of Hélène walking into her room bearing a tray of glistening, freshly sliced fruits and a notepad. She opened the curtains to allow the light to rush in as Anneliese struggled upright. There was coffee on a silver tray, a porcelain cup and saucer and one of the croissants she presumed the young girl had stayed up all night practising how to make. She sank back into the pillows as Hélène poured her a cup.

'So, the dinner,' she murmured, taking a sip of the freshly ground brew. It was the highlight of Hélène's year – she spent eleven months preparing for it and although her strict instruction the night before had been for Anneliese to rest, she wasn't about to be cheated out of a single moment of the preparations.

'*Oui, madame.*' Hélène paused dramatically. '*Le dîner.*' There was a small table and chair by the window. As was their custom, Anneliese indicated that she should sit. Hélène sat down with a sigh of satisfaction and took the pen from behind her ear.

It took them the better part of an hour, but by the time the sun had slipped beyond the long, low eaves of the veranda and was slowly climbing its way to its midday zenith, the menu was done. Anneliese genuinely enjoyed the ritual; in all her other homes, dinner parties were invariably done with minimum input, from her at least. Here, with Hélène in charge, it was different. They discussed the various starters – so difficult to get good truffles in St Barts at this time of year! – the different types of crab and crayfish; where to get the best bread on the island and whether or not to bake their own. They decided on fish – spicy dorade stuffed with the beautifully fat and juicy prawns that were in season; vegetables from their own plot, new potatoes, asparagus flown in that morning from France . . . by the time they'd discussed whether or not to make a traditional Pavlova dessert or Bruno's favourite German *stollen*, Anneliese's stomach was rumbling. She watched as Hélène laboriously wrote out the last ingredients, her mouth working silently as she spelled out the words to herself. How old was Hélène now? Anneliese wondered to herself as she pushed aside the linen sheets and slid her legs out of bed. She'd come to Scheherazade as a woman in her mid-thirties . . . she'd be in her late fifties now, she mused. Her hair was as thick and curly as ever, but there were flecks of grey at the temples and the lines around her eyes were pronounced. For all that they'd spent every Christmas and New Year together for over twenty years, Anneliese knew very little about her. She had a son in Miami, she knew, and a daughter who'd long since left the island, following a husband or boyfriend to one of the bigger islands – Guadeloupe, perhaps? Martinique? She couldn't remember.

'It's not too much?' she asked Hélène suddenly, slipping on her robe.

Hélène looked up from her notepad, an expression of surprise on her face. 'Too much what? Food?' Her abruptness often hid what was essentially a shy nature.

Anneliese shook her head. 'No. I meant . . . it's not too much work? For you? You're not tired?'

Hélène smiled slightly. 'And you?' she asked simply. 'Are *you* not tired?'

The two women regarded each other, each more surprised than they could admit by the unexpected line of questioning. Anneliese sat down again suddenly. She was quiet for a moment, composing her thoughts. She shook her head. 'No, not tired. Just . . . things don't always turn out the way you think, do they?'

Hélène laughed faintly. She too shook her head. 'No, *madame*. Especially not with the children. You always think there's time, you know?'

Anneliese nodded. 'Except there isn't. It's funny, isn't it? You spend your whole life working, thinking you're doing it for them. Then you realise it doesn't matter. They'll do what they want.'

Hélène stood up. The exchange of confidences had unsettled her, Anneliese could tell. It was part of the unwritten rule between employers and employees, especially here on the island. The boundary between rich and poor, employers and employees was as carefully guarded as it had been on Boden-hausen. None crossed the line, certainly not at nine o'clock in the morning, as Anneliese had done, sitting in bed in her silk robe, planning a dinner party and suddenly asking about the direction of her life. It was rather too much for Hélène to bear. She beat a hasty retreat from the room, leaving Anneliese alone. She looked across the room to her dressing table where her mobile phone lay, flashing silently. She got up and picked it up. Two messages, both from Callan, *Hope you arrived safely, Maman.* And then the second one. *Just to let you know, Ree is coming. Merry Christmas.* She smiled faintly. She put down the phone and crossed the room to her wardrobe. A nice long walk on the beach, followed by a swim. It was Christmas Day. In exactly a week's time her extended family would be here and a new year would begin. She felt an unexpected surge of happiness. A new year, new possibili-ties, new chances just waiting to be taken. She slipped on a pale pink kaftan and picked a swimming costume from the drawer. A pair of white flip-flops, a sun hat and some sun cream . . . what better way to spend Christmas Day?

99

LINDI
Johannesburg, South Africa

'Are you sure?' Lindi gripped her phone tightly. She was sitting in the courtyard of the appropriately named Salvation Cafe in one of the trendy, up-and-coming parts of the city, sipping an expertly made cappuccino, struggling to reconcile the scene in front of her with her state of mind. She'd fled Windhoek the previous day without any clear idea of where she would go. She hadn't even dared ring her parents. She'd called in sick to the office the next morning, flung some clothes into a suitcase, together with the documents and her copy of the recording David Lawson had given her, and called a taxi. She got to the airport just before nine a.m. There was an Air Namibia flight to Johannesburg shortly afterwards. She bought a ticket, paid for it with cash and boarded. Once she got to Johannesburg, she thought to herself, she would figure out what to do.

She landed just after noon, took another taxi to the Holiday Inn in Milpark, close to the BBC offices and Wits University, where she'd stayed once before. After checking in, she walked across the road to the supermarket, bought a new SIM card and a cheap mobile phone and wandered across the road to the little complex of cafes and boutiques that she knew from her previous visit, although under very different circumstances. She took a table at the far end of the terrace, ordered a cappuccino and began making her calls. She rang Norah first; she'd be out of town for a couple of weeks, she told her, though she didn't say where. Norah asked no further questions, for which Lindi was grateful. It was impossible to know what Erika Tobias's allegations would mean for Norah. Next she rang her parents. She brushed off Erik and Siv's anxious questions – no, she was fine. Just taking a short break. She might come to Europe . . . she'd see. She would phone them in a couple of days' time, once she'd figured things out. In the meantime, would they just keep her whereabouts to themselves. 'Lindi . . . what's going on?' Erik wasn't fooled.

'I can't say right now, Pa,' Lindi said, her eyes burning with unshed tears. 'I . . . I've got to figure a few things out. But I'm fine. I'm absolutely fine. I'll call again in a couple of days.'

'Lindi?' It was Siv. 'What's the matter, darling? You're making me worried.'

'There's nothing to worry about, Ma, I promise. But *please* don't let anyone know I rang. No one, d'you understand?'

Both Siv and Erik were too accustomed to the kind of clandestine activity of the independence struggles they'd both lived through and, in their own way, fought for to argue. 'Phone us as soon as you can,' Erik said, taking the phone back from his wife. 'No more than two days.'

'I promise. There's nothing to worry about. I love you both.' Erik couldn't answer; Lindi knew why. She ended the call, blinking rapidly, trying not to cry. It was a beautiful summer morning in Johannesburg, in the last few days before Christmas. All around her people were shopping, drinking coffee, catching up with one another. The olive trees in the courtyard rustled gently in the breeze; the sky was that shade of light, luminous blue that only the high veld produces. A couple were arguing mildly next to her; the waiters rushed around purposefully, bringing out cappuccinos high and trembling with foam, plates of breakfast, pancakes dripping with maple syrup and glistening, freshly cut strawberries. All was well and beautiful in the world in a way that made the inside of Erika Tobias's small home and the long, narrative spool of her voice seem unreal, coming to her as if from another world. In a way it was; the hunger and horror and deprivations of the camps and the lonely years of exile had nothing to do with the glasses of freshly squeezed orange juice or the fluffy omelettes that kept coming out of the kitchen in front of her. And yet . . . for all that, it had *everything* to do with it. Erika's fight wasn't just about voting rights; in a roundabout, circuitous way it was also about the right to enjoy the spoils of freedom – including the pancakes and the mocha lattes, ridiculous as it seemed – in the same way the people sitting around her now were enjoying them. As she herself was. Twenty years ago, Lindi wouldn't have been allowed to sit up on the terrace, shaded from the sun by the pretty yellow awning, ordering a second coffee like everyone else. *Whites Only*. She wouldn't have been allowed to set foot in the cafe, let alone order something to eat. *That* was what Erika had fought against; that was what she and countless others had won for people like Lindi. What had happened to her then, and what was happening to her now, was a betrayal of the deepest, most painful kind. She finished her coffee and fished out her phone again. This time, it was Tara she rang.

'You're *sure* she won't mind?' she repeated, stirring her coffee slowly.

'Absolutely. It's the perfect place, Lindi. It's in the middle of nowhere. We're going for ten days. Anneliese is going ahead. Why don't you go to your parents for Christmas, then meet me at Heathrow on the thirtieth. We'll fly out together. I'll sort out the tickets and you can pay me back later. Say you'll come. Please.'

Lindi hesitated. It sounded almost too good to be true. A French West Indies island hideaway. A week in the sun. After what she'd heard the night before, it seemed almost sacrilegious. But Tara was right. She ought to go to her parents and tell them face to face what she'd learned. Erik would be full of advice and concern, but she had to figure out herself what she was going to do. She'd never had to face anything like this in her life; ten days away from everyone else would help her work it out. 'All right,' she said slowly. 'I'll come. Thanks, Tara. It's incredibly generous of you.'

'Don't be silly. You'd do the same. I'll send you the flight details and meet you in the lounge at Terminal Five.'

'Text them to me on this number. Don't email me,' Lindi said, her mind beginning to race ahead. 'And don't ring me at my parents'. I'll get another number when I get to Oslo.'

'It's serious, then?' Tara asked quietly.

'Very. I'll call you from Oslo.' Lindi put down the phone before anything further could be asked. She finished her coffee, peeled off a couple of notes and picked up her bag. She wouldn't even bother staying the night in Johannesburg. She would book a flight to Europe for that evening – London, Frankfurt, Paris . . . anywhere. From there she'd be able to catch a flight to Oslo quite easily. Home in time for Christmas. The thought of it made her want to cry. Again. Iago was on a state visit to Sao Paolo. He'd be back on Thursday, which was two days away. She would have to leave her Namibian number on; it was one of the earlier rules of their relationship. He called her; always. It was never the other way round. She'd baulked at it at first, but now she was grateful. It would buy her a couple of days and allay any suspicions he might have as to why she'd left without telling him.

She went straight up to her room, booked her flight, made sure everything she'd brought with her was safely stowed away in her bag. It was nearly lunchtime. She switched her phone off and lay down on the bed. She would grab a few hours' sleep, then head back to the airport. Her life was slowly being turned upside down. From past experience, she knew it was better to make crucial decisions whilst she was at least partially alert. She closed her eyes, willing herself to sleep.

100

CALLAN
Pointe Milou, St Barts, French West Indies

Contentment settled over her like a perfectly fitting glove. She looked out to sea where Ree was swimming, his powerful arms breaking through the water, a momentary flash of brown skin against the pale jade surface of the sea. The beach was quiet; on the other side of the thin sliver of sand and palms that brought complete privacy to the leeward side of the island, the faint roar of jet skis and motor boats could be heard. On the Pointe Milou beaches, silence reigned. It was why the residents paid more for their homes than practically anywhere else in the world. Four million dollars bought you a beachside view. Ten million bought you its silence. She had no idea what Scheherazade was worth. Priceless, would be Anneliese's dry comment. She valued silence more than she valued an artwork or a patch of land, even if it was on one of the world's most exclusive holiday spots. Well, she'd got it. On the other side of the hill, in Marigot, there was noise. Here there was none. Simple as that.

She looked down at the bare skin of her stomach, now turning a dusky shade of brown. Whoever her father had been, he'd blessed her with the kind of skin that bronzed easily, never burning. She rarely, if ever, used sunblock, much to Tara and Anneliese's horror. Tara was on her way, with Lindi. They'd arrive on the morning of the dinner party. Callan was surprised; she hadn't realised they were so close but Ree was pleased. He often said Lindi was like an older sister to him. It was funny how they'd all become so intertwined, she thought to herself, watching Ree as he ploughed his way back to the shore. From that first, miserable day at boarding school – to this. She and Ree, Tara and Lindi, Lindi and Ree . . . and above them all, tying them together in ways that were not always so apparent, there was Anneliese. Who would ever have thought things would turn out this way?

'You're burning,' Ree called out to her as he made his way up the sand.

'No I'm not. I never burn.'

'Says who? Your nose is going red.'

'Rosy, not red.' She squinted up at him. 'It's time to go up anyway. Mr Lagerfeld and the Princess Royal'll be here any minute.'

Ree smiled. 'If you'd asked me ten years ago if I'd be spending New Year's Eve on a private island in the French West Indies with a princess and two fashion designers I'd have said you were dreaming.'

'And what about me?' Callan asked in mock protest, getting to her feet. 'Am I a surprise?'

Ree stopped towelling his hair dry. 'Yes,' he said, suddenly serious. 'But not for the reasons you think.'

'What reasons, then?' She was being playfully coy – not her usual style – but she couldn't help it. It wasn't often that Ree admitted to his own feelings, let alone those that concerned her.

He began to dry his back. 'Hayley thought the reason I liked you was because of your looks. Which was odd, coming from her. It's not. I mean, you're beautiful, don't get me wrong. But that's not it.'

Callan was aware of the heat in her face. 'What, then?'

He shrugged. 'You're more *alive* than anyone I've ever met. You've got this appetite for things . . . people, places, *ideas*. I thought that when I first met you. I still do. I've never met anyone with more energy. Up here.' He tapped the side of his temple. 'That's what did it for me, I'm afraid.'

Callan had to turn away. It was the most precious thing anyone had ever said to her. 'Let's go,' she said, a little uncertainly. 'Anneliese'll be waiting.'

He caught her arm and pulled her close. 'And we mustn't keep your mother waiting,' he murmured, putting a hand under her chin.

She squirmed, half in embarrassment. 'She might be watching,' she said, casting a quick, nervous glance back up the hill.

'So?'

'So . . . it's embarrassing!'

'What is?' His hand began to slide down her back.

'Stop it.' Her protests sounded weak, even to her own ears.

'I'm not doing anything.'

He had somehow skilfully manoeuvred things so that they were almost lying on the sand again. It had been months since she'd seen him so relaxed. His words sent a warm, passive glow of sensuality running through her. *You're more alive than anyone*

I've ever met. She had a momentary glimpse of herself as she had been, all those years ago, at the clubs in New York with Marc and that whole mad, sad group of people whom she'd mistaken for friends. How things had changed. It was true – she'd been in such a hurry to experience everything away from Anneliese's control for the first time in her life that she hadn't stopped to think. How lucky she'd been. None of it had ever come back to haunt her. On the one occasion her past had caught up with her, fortunately for her, it had turned out well. It wasn't something she could afford to let happen again; Ree wouldn't understand. Her past was about as far from his as it was possible to be. It was about as far from anyone's as she could imagine. Tara, Ree, Anneliese . . . if they could have seen her *then*, would they recognise in the wild, reckless person she'd once been *anything* of the controlled, disciplined woman she'd turned out to be? She thought not.

And yet there were times, like right now, with Ree's mouth hungrily devouring her own, his hands running over her bare skin with a need that seemed to equal hers, when for one fleeting moment the desire in her to shock him with a trick or two out of her old repertoire almost got the better of her. Almost. She reined herself in as she knew she had to. Even now, with his hands pushing her whole body into the sand, his legs parting hers with an urgency that left her breathless . . . even now, she knew better than to let herself go. He'd changed everything, including that part of her that had longed to shock everyone, jolting them from what she thought was their estimation of her – safe, well brought up, almost chaste. Like Anneliese. Back then, she'd done everything to show those who cared to look that she was nothing like her mother. Now she wasn't so sure why she'd bothered. It was slowly beginning to dawn on her that she was more like Anneliese than she cared to admit. And that it wasn't such a bad thing either.

She gasped suddenly. Now was not the time to be thinking about Anneliese, or anyone else. She closed her eyes against the sight of Ree's smile as he looked down on her and the dazzling orb of the sun behind his head. Sea, sand, the softness of his hands, the taste of his skin in her mouth. There wasn't a better way to start the year. *Whatever* happened next. He paused for a moment in his thrusts, letting her catch her breath. When they both came together she could think of nothing else. He was hers, now and always. Hayley was a footnote belonging to the past.

REE

Happiness was a drug. He followed the shapely rounded form of Callan's bottom up the hill, only just managing not to reach out and fondle it as she wriggled and jiggled her way to the top. He'd never been anywhere quite as glamorous in his life. As they turned to look back at the beach from the small gate that marked the beginning of Anneliese's property, he could feel the strain of the past year sloughing off him, like the emerald water he'd swum in half an hour before. The sun was beginning its rapid slide towards the horizon over the fringed green islands that stood in its path. London seemed further away than he'd ever experienced. He'd come to St Barts for five blissful days, away from the drama that was his wife's life and the damage she'd left in her wake. Up at the house, with only a few hours to go before a dinner party like no other, preparations were at fever pitch.

The relationship between Anneliese and her housekeeper of over twenty years, Hélène, amused him greatly. They tiptoed around each other, each clearly respectful of the boundaries that their respective positions enforced, yet for all that, there was a warmth and affection between them that moved him. Hélène was tolerantly amused by Anneliese's efforts to supervise things. Her expression remained the same throughout the day – she needed no supervision whatsoever. She tolerated Anneliese's frequent stops in the kitchen and the pantry to 'see what was going on' but paid her no more attention than she'd have paid a wayward child. Everything, her expression implied, was completely and totally under control. Ever since he and Callan arrived, a series of delicious, mouth-watering smells arose from the rear of the house, making him permanently hungry.

Tara and Lindi were due to arrive shortly; Bruno and Jasper had landed a few hours earlier that afternoon. Lars and his wife were due any moment and the guests of honour, Karl Lagerfeld and his muse, Princess Caroline of Monaco, were due in sometime later. It promised to be an interesting gathering. Lagerfeld's knowledge of contemporary art was legendary and he'd heard from Callan that the princess was charm personified. His mother had only sniffed haughtily when he informed her he'd be spending New Year's Eve in their company. 'Oh, well . . . it's what you're used to,' she'd said tartly down the line. 'I suppose.' It wasn't, but there was no arguing with Sibongile, especially as she had the children. At the thought of them, his heart tightened momentarily. There was so much to be sorted, so many details to be thrashed out, lawyers to see. He stopped himself. He'd promised himself when he and Callan boarded the plane: no thinking about next year. For the moment, at least. Time off, that was what he'd promised himself – and Callan. They'd been at Scheherazade for nearly two days and he'd managed thus far.

'Drink?' Callan asked, turning to smile at him. 'Maman's on the patio with Bruno. Shall we join them?'

He was uncomfortably aware of the scent of Callan on his skin. He shook his head. 'Shower first. I'll join you later. Unless you want to join *me*?'

She grinned at him. 'No, you go ahead. I'll go and talk to Maman. She's probably feeling a little . . . er, peeved that I've monopolised you since we got here. You're *her* friend too, you know. Gosh, you're *everyone's* friend. Me, Lindi, Maman . . . popular man, you are.'

He shook his head again in mock despair. Women. He beat a quick retreat to the shower before he was dragged any further into it.

Half an hour later, he joined them on the patio overlooking the bay. Anneliese looked more relaxed than he'd ever seen her. A few strands of silver-blonde hair fell across her face, which was very lightly tanned from the extra few days she'd had in the sun before everyone descended. They were drinking Pimm's – a large jug stood on the glass-topped table, full of sliced lemons and oranges. Anneliese poured him a glass without asking. The sun was beginning to slide in the sky; it was nearly four o'clock. Tara and Lindi were expected any minute now. They drank in awed, companionable silence with the sound of the ocean floating up to them. He was aware of a pleasurable knot of anticipation in the pit of his stomach at the thought of seeing Lindi again. He glanced over at Callan; he was right. Her skin had turned a dusky shade of rose. She too had never looked more beautiful. The past few months were beginning to recede, like a bad dream. He took another long, cooling sip and listened with half an ear to the muted conversations around him. Bruno was fretting about work and the new collection they were just about to debut. He saw Jasper's attention wander, mostly in the direction of the young men who'd been hired to put the canopy together at the far end of the patio where they would eat dinner later that evening. He recognised the hungry, half-bored, half-watchful look on Jasper's face . . . the thrill of the unknown, coupled with a strange fear that something, somewhere, was being missed out on. It was the same face he'd seen for years on the faces of Hayley and her friends. He turned away from it, reluctant to face a reminder of what had been left behind.

'So who's this person Tara's bringing with her?' Bruno asked, changing the subject suddenly as Anneliese got up to check on things in the kitchen.

'It's that friend she met in America,' Callan said, helping herself to a handful of peanuts. 'She works for the government. Ree knows her.'

'Yes, Lindi Johanssen. She's great. I've known her since for ever. Well, since I was about fifteen.'

'Hmm. We'll be quite a gathering,' Bruno observed mildly. 'Fashion, architecture, politics. Should be fun.'

'And royalty,' Callan added. 'Don't forget.'

'Ooh, I can hardly wait!' Jasper's attention returned. He gave Bruno a playful slap on the knee. 'I *do* like having royalty to dinner, I must say.'

'Once a queen . . .' Bruno couldn't resist the quip, rolling his eyes. There was a burst of startled laughter that sent the birds nesting in the trees just below the deck flying upwards in protest.

Ree sipped his drink, content for the moment just to listen and observe. It had been months since he'd looked forward to an evening with anything other than a faint sense of dread at what it might bring. He savoured the moment.

101

LINDI
London, England

The patchwork of fields, neat rows of housing and the slow build-up of tower blocks drifted towards her through breaks in the cloud as the plane slowly lowered its bulk towards the earth once more. Lindi peered anxiously out of the window, her stomach churning with its now familiar mixture of fear and anxiety.

'Is your seat belt fastened?' A harried-looking flight attendant stopped briefly. 'Great, thanks.' She rushed on.

Lindi turned back to the window. The ground came up at them fast and hard. One bump, then another, and then the screech of brakes. It was almost seven in the morning and the thin, weak light of winter was only just spreading itself across the sky. In Oslo, where her parents were probably only now falling into a troubled sleep, it was still pitch black. In less than a day's time, she would be in the full glare of a tropical morning. She hadn't heard from Iago since fleeing Windhoek three days earlier, for which she was grateful. It wasn't unusual to go a week or more without hearing from him and she was certainly in no state to speak to him now. Erik had been utterly unmoved on the issue. 'Don't call him and don't say anything to anyone,' he'd instructed, his face grave with concern. 'No matter what. Go to St Barts and try to put this out of your mind for now. You haven't done anything, Lindi. Remember that.'

'But we don't know if he did it,' Lindi ventured cautiously. 'What if it wasn't him?'

'Let me be the judge of that.' Erik was firm. 'I still have friends to call upon, you know.'

'I *do* know, Pa. But . . . be careful, won't you?'

'Always. Now get some sleep. We'll take you to the airport tomorrow morning. I want you to put everything out of your head for the moment. You look exhausted.'

Lindi had been unable to do anything other than cry. In the morning, they took her to the airport and there was such warmth and strength in their tight embraces that for the first time since that terrible night in Khomasdal, she felt some of her old strength return.

But that was a few hours ago. Now, as the morning light broke over the capital, the doubts and fears returned. She hauled her bag from the overhead locker and made her way to the British Airways lounges where Tara had promised her she would be waiting. There was a three-hour wait for their flight to Sint Maarten. She went through immigration and customs, taking care to show only her Norwegian passport. Not for the first time in her life did she thank her lucky stars she had both.

'Lindi!' Tara was waiting, just as she'd promised. She came off the escalator and there she was, waiting just outside the lounges. At the sight of her familiar little face, now pale with anxiety, she very nearly burst into tears again. The smiling ground staff looked on discreetly as the two women embraced. 'Come on, let's have a coffee . . . or something stronger?' Tara held her at arm's length, inspecting her face anxiously. 'Are you OK?'

Lindi nodded, fighting back the urge to cry. 'I'm fine, honestly. No, coffee's fine. I don't think I could drink, even if I wanted to.'

The ground staff waved them on. 'I use Anneliese's card,' Tara whispered as they were ushered through to the first-class lounges. 'It gets you *everywhere*.'

Lindi looked around her. No expense had been spared to make tired travellers feel comfortable and at home. She was used to travelling business class on her government trips – not that she'd been on many – but this was a whole new level of luxury. Would they like a shower? Coffee? Breakfast? A polite young man brought them two steaming cappuccinos and then left them alone.

'So.' Tara turned to her once they were both seated. 'Tell me what you can. And I don't mind if you don't,' she added, her green-blue eyes regarding her frankly.

Lindi looked down at her cup. She twisted her hands nervously. So far, she'd told only Siv and Erik the full details of what she'd heard and learned, but Tara deserved to hear the truth. She bit her lip. Even talking about it made it seem a betrayal. But it was Tara who'd done most of the background research; of all the people involved, she deserved to hear the truth. She opened her mouth and began to speak. And then she found herself unable to stop.

TARA

Beside her, on the other side of the fan-like flap that separated the two seats, Lindi slept, finally unburdened of everything she'd been unable to tell anyone else. Tara, on the other hand, was fully awake. She couldn't get the story out of her head. Lindi's world was so far removed from hers as to make it practically unintelligible. She was no stranger to heartbreak, however, and it was the betrayal that set her teeth on edge, keeping her awake. How many years had it been since Jeb walked out on her? The pain was, if anything, just as intense as it had been that first afternoon she'd walked into the living room to find it empty, stripped of his presence, as though he'd never been. That and the silence that followed. For five glorious years she'd come home every day to some form of noise or another – his music, the sound of him on the telephone, things bubbling on the stove, the phone ringing. There'd been life and noise in the small flat in almost the way there'd been in Kitwe – Chipo whistling as he swept the floors; the birds outside; the gardener stopping to chat to the girl who came three times a week to do the laundry; her mother's voice as she made arrangements to go out. She loved the way things revolved around *her*. 'Has Tara had lunch?' she would hear her mother call out to the servants. 'Has the girl had her piano lesson?' 'What's Tara doing this afternoon?' She'd been at the centre of the small universe in a way that she had never, ever been at boarding school. There, she was just one in a crowd of many, most of whom were louder, prettier, cleverer than she could ever hope to be. At school it was almost impossible to stand out; in Kitwe, it was the opposite. *Tara, where you go-ing?* She could still hear little Stevie McIvor's voice, carried plaintively on the wind as she cycled away from the compound. She took another sip of her now-melted G&T. She didn't normally drink on long-haul flights but listening to Lindi recount the events of the past couple of weeks had profoundly unsettled her. What on earth must it feel like to be in love with someone who was capable of *that*?

LINDI

An enchanted isle. The line from some half-forgotten childhood storybook came back to her as soon as the door of the small plane that had brought her and Tara to the airport at Gustavia was opened. She knew next to nothing about St Barts. In her haste to get away from Windhoek she hadn't bothered to do more than glance at its location on a map. She gazed about her in barely disguised shock and pleasure at the green, thickly carpeted hills breaking through the emerald and turquoise water, the red-tiled roofs reminiscent of the south of France and the pretty, pastel-coloured buildings that seemed to serve as the airport terminal. Birds circled lazily overhead, the breeze coming off the ocean was warm but not hot, the sun shone . . . she felt as though she'd stepped onto the set of a glamorous film. All around her were little planes like the one she and Tara had just flown in. She'd never seen so many Louis Vuitton cases in her life. Everyone was hurrying to St Barts for New Year. Tall, broad-shouldered, ridiculously handsome young men ferried the cases off the planes and into the waiting cars. Beautiful people everywhere. She turned to Tara. 'You never said—' she trailed off, shaking her head in surprise.

'I know.' Tara grinned at her. 'The first time I came here I thought I was dreaming. I still do. It's magical, isn't it?'

'I haven't got a thing to wear!' Lindi wailed.

'Oh, don't worry about that. There's tons of leftover clothes. Callan's got a whole holiday wardrobe that she leaves behind. We'll find something, don't fret.'

'Jesus, Tara. You never said.' She gaped as two models sauntered by, exotic, stunning birds of paradise on the longest legs she'd ever clapped eyes on.

'Come on. It's nearly five. Anneliese will murder us if we're late. Don't turn round but I think Mr Lagerfeld and Princess Caroline are behind us. They'll make their own way up to Scheherazade later. He always stops off to say hello to friends on the way up.'

Lindi's eyes widened. '*Karl* Lagerfeld? Princess Caroline of *Monaco*?'

Tara nodded. 'Yup.'

'Oh, God,' was all Lindi could manage. 'Oh, *God*.'

'Don't worry about it. They're perfectly lovely. She's absolutely charming, you'll see. And you won't be able to follow anything he says. He's frightfully clever. Not that you're not,' she added hastily. 'But he's in a different league.'

Lindi couldn't answer. She followed Tara through the pink and pale yellow customs building, handed over her passport to an impossibly good-looking young man who waved them through, and wished desperately she'd thought to bring along a pair of sunglasses. She wanted to hide, for a different set of reasons than the ones that had sent her scurrying from Windhoek. The beauty and luxury and ease of everything and everyone around her was suddenly overwhelming. In the space of ten days, she'd gone from a tiny living room in Khomasdal, listening to the most horrific details of a woman's incarceration and torture to her childhood room in Oslo with its faded patches of Blu-tack on the walls where she'd stuck her favourite posters . . . and now, here she was, walking in the sunshine of a French West Indies island, rubbing shoulders with fashionistas and royalty. It was too much. She felt her throat thickening with tears. She climbed into the back of the waiting Jeep and turned her face away. It was hardly the time or place to cry but she couldn't help it. In spite of everything, there was still a part of her that ached to hear Iago's voice, to describe to him what she was seeing. She struggled to hold in her tears. Tara must have somehow sensed it; as they pulled away from the kerb and joined the stream of cars heading off towards the villas in the hills, she reached out, giving Lindi's arm a brief but firm squeeze. She said nothing, but her touch was comfort enough.

Scheherazade was almost at the top of a steep hill overlooking the entire bay. They drove along a narrow, single-lane road, with closely packed trees and bushes on either side, interrupted occasionally by splashes of vibrant, colour-soaked bougainvillea and plants she didn't recognise. The houses were shrouded in greenery. Tara pointed them out as they drove upwards, away from the clustered lower slopes. 'That's some Hollywood producer, can't remember his name. And Kate Moss stayed there last winter. And that's Uma Thurman's place . . .'

Lindi could only gape. They stopped at what was very nearly the summit of the hill. The driver leapt out, pressed a discreet buzzer hidden along a small stone wall. A few seconds later the slatted wooden gate slid back silently. They bumped down the short track, the trees opened out and suddenly, there it was.

White, low-roofed, ultra-modern, a series of cascading flat roofs that looked out towards the sea. Lindi's mouth fell open. It was stunning. She got out of the Jeep and slowly walked round to join Tara.

'Lovely, isn't it?' Tara said cheerfully. 'Come on. They'll all be on the patio. It's where we live when we're here.'

She stumbled after her, all thoughts of Erika Tobias, Iago, her parents . . . vanished. They walked across a small wooden bridge to the entrance, all white walls, buried glass lights and floor-to-ceiling windows – everything in the space focused on one thing: the sea. All around them, its blue, gently moving surface reflecting the dying sunlight. She tried to close her mouth, and failed.

'*There* you are! At long, bloody last! Thought you'd never get here!' A woman's voice called out to them from beyond the sliding doors.

'Callan!' Tara ran ahead of her, arms outstretched. A tanned, petite young woman with dark hair and a pretty, sun-kissed stripe of reddened skin across her forehead and nose jumped up to hug her. She was wearing a black string bikini with a rose-and-grey sarong tied loosely around her waist. She looked past them to where a group of people were sitting and saw Ree, her heart lifting immediately as she spotted a familiar face.

'Lindi!' He got up at once, coming towards her. She felt herself being pressed against his broad, warm chest and again felt her eyes flood with easy tears. He must have sensed her distress; his arms tightened around her. 'Everything OK?' he asked quietly, for her ears alone.

She nodded, swallowing hard. 'Not now,' she whispered, aware that Callan was probably looking at them. 'I'll tell you later.'

He released her, but kept hold of her arms, holding her lightly. 'You haven't met Callan, have you?' he asked, turning them both towards her.

She shook her head but saw, to her relief, that the petite,

dark-haired beauty was looking at them not in suspicion, but with warmth. 'No, not yet,' Lindi said, stretching out a hand.

Callan ignored her hand and came forward to kiss her. 'No, we haven't met,' she confirmed, kissing her on both cheeks. 'But I feel as though I know you already. Welcome to Scheherazade. I'm so pleased you're here.'

'Tara.' A woman's voice from behind them. She turned round. Standing in the opening made by the pulled-back concertina doors was a tall, extremely slender and elegant older woman. It was Anneliese Zander de Saint Phalle. 'You're here.' Her voice was deep and soft, with the faintest hint of an accent underneath its Englishness.

'Anneliese!' Tara went up to her and the two embraced, not in the exuberant warmth that was her daughter's style, but with a reserved yet affectionate air. 'We made it just in time,' Tara said, stepping back. 'I brought a friend with me. Did you get my message?'

'I did.' Anneliese nodded, then turned towards Lindi. 'And you must be Lindi,' she said, extending a hand.

Lindi moved forwards. There was a moment's strange hesitation as she looked up into the woman's eyes. She felt something ripple across her neck, the faint shiver of some odd, half-buried, half-suppressed recognition that she couldn't place. They looked at one another without saying anything. She was aware of Ree and Callan looking at them, frowning. She opened her mouth to say something but her mind suddenly went blank. She saw Anneliese's own eyes widen slightly, almost imperceptibly, and then a shutter came down, blanking everything out.

'What's the matter?' she heard a man ask. 'You've gone all pale.'

Anneliese seemed not to hear him. 'Lindi. Your name is Lindi?' The words came out in a whisper.

'Y-yes,' Lindi stammered. What was going on? 'Lindi Johanssen.'

'Lindi's the woman I was telling you about,' Tara broke in.

517

'We met in New York a couple of years ago. She's the politician, don't you remember?'

'Johanssen?' Anneliese seemed to be having difficulty getting the words out. 'Your surname is Johanssen?'

'Yes. I'm . . . I was adopted . . . I grew up in Norway.'

'Norwegians? Norwegians adopted you?'

'Anneliese . . . are you all right?' The man spoke again, moving to her side. Anneliese had indeed gone pale.

Suddenly a buzzer sounded loudly somewhere inside the house. A dog started barking somewhere and there was the sound of bare feet running across the tiles. 'Madame? It's M'sieur Lagerfeld.' A woman appeared in the doorway.

'I . . . I . . .' Anneliese put up a hand to her face.

'Anneliese?' Ree moved forwards. The man standing next to Anneliese suddenly put out his hand. Lindi watched in horror as the woman's eyes closed briefly, opened again and then, in slow motion, she crumpled straight to the ground.

102

ANNELIESE

Through eyes that were still half-closed, she could just make out her semi-familiar surroundings. She was lying in bed with a cashmere blanket thrown lightly around her legs. The air-conditioner was on; she could feel its low, throaty hum just below the level of consciousness. The windows were closed but a small breeze could be seen moving the muslin curtains at the end of the bedroom. She lay very still. Outside the room, she could hear them moving around, arguing in low, muted voices about what should be done. She heard the words 'hospital', 'doctor', 'fainted, poof!' 'Just like that.' Bruno and Ree were arguing over whether to take her to a hospital in Gustavia or call in a doctor. 'She's exhausted, that's all. She just needs some rest.' That was Callan. Even at that remove, she could hear the anxiety in her voice. The last thing she remembered before hitting the ground was Callan's anguished scream. She'd fainted only once in her life before, years ago. It was odd how the sensation was still so familiar to her. Everything slowing down, the freezing of time and place, waves of sound, advancing and receding until the sound disappeared altogether and there was only the awful, roaring silence inside her head. She moved her head a fraction. There was a painful bump near her left temple where she'd hit it, no doubt. Both Ree and Bruno had leapt forwards to stop her but she'd slipped free of their grasp, hitting the marble painfully with her forehead seconds before the world faded to black.

The door creaked open suddenly, spilling light into the darkened room. 'Maman?' she whispered. 'Are you awake?'

Anneliese couldn't answer. She gripped the sheets in either fist, swallowing hard. 'I . . .' she whispered, unable to do more than shake her head very slowly from side to side.

Callan advanced slowly towards the bed. She crouched down so that their faces were level. There was real fear in her eyes, Anneliese noticed. 'Ree has called the doctor,' she whispered. 'Are you all right, Maman?'

Anneliese shook her head fractionally. She brought up a heavy, slow hand to her forehead. 'It hurts,' she whispered.

'I know, I know,' Callan said soothingly. 'The doctor'll be here soon.'

'What about the others . . . ?'

'Don't worry about a thing. We got Karl and Princess Caroline in at Le Toily. I rang Catherine and she turfed out someone into one of the smaller villas. It's absolutely fine. And Lars and Tone are going somewhere else. Don't worry, Maman. Everyone's taken care of.'

'What about Tara?'

Callan was quiet for a moment. 'Tara's fine. They're on the patio. Was it something . . . did Lindi say something to you?'

Anneliese shook her head slowly. 'No. No, it's nothing to do with her,' she said haltingly.

'Then what was it? You took one look at her and just passed out. Do you . . . have you met before?'

Anneliese closed her eyes. She couldn't answer. She couldn't possibly answer. She knew. She'd have known that face anywhere. Anywhere in the world. Some things you could never forget. The face of one's own child was one of them.

103

HANNELORE
Windhoek, South-West Africa

She remembered little of the journey from Bodenhausen to Windhoek. They left without a word to anyone, driving down the yellowed, sandy road that led away from the farm until they joined the black sticky tarmac of the main road. Tante Bärbel sat with her in the back seat, holding her hand tightly as the big American car sped away. The images kept circling around in her brain. Mwane was dead; *she* had killed him. In her naive stupidity, she'd killed him. She'd wanted to keep him for herself and she'd wound up sending him to his death instead. Every now and then, the sound of her saliva in her own mouth as she swallowed rose up to engulf her. She couldn't even cry. In the boot of the car were her possessions, clothes and a few trinkets that Tante Bärbel had swept off the dressing table . . . nothing else. No photographs, no mementoes, no letters . . . nothing. Her letters to Mwane lay in the top drawer of the wooden chest of drawers. Papa would burn them, as he would burn everything else that belonged to her. She remembered him saying that. '*Ich werde alles verbrennen, verstehst du? Du bist tot, hörst du mich?*' I will burn everything. You are dead, d'you hear me? Dead. Then the whip came down on her once more and she remembered nothing else.

It took the driver two and a half hours to reach the city, driving at an almost breakneck speed. Tante Bärbel said nothing, just sat beside her, her face turned to the landscape, her hand pressing tightly against Hannelore's own. When they finally pulled up into the driveway of the house she'd spent so many holidays in, she turned to her. 'We will not speak of this again,' she said, her lips pressed tightly together. Hannelore looked at her and saw, with a growing sense of dread, that her aunt, if anything, was more afraid than she was. 'You must put it all behind you. It's not your fault, *mein Liebling*. You mustn't punish yourself. God knows you've been punished enough.'

Hannelore couldn't speak. She nodded dumbly and allowed Tante Bärbel to help her from the car. Her face and shoulders still ached from the beating she'd received but the pain was nothing compared to the leaden, searing pain inside her chest. She couldn't get the sound of the women's ululating lamentations out of her head, nor could she forget Maazuu's screams. Mwane was dead. She looked at her face in the mirror in the bathroom adjacent to the room she'd slept in so many times and it seemed to her as though the mark of a murderer was upon it. She would never be able to look upon that face again. She turned away, her mouth flooding with nauseous fluids, and lay down on the bed. Presently Tante Bärbel came into the room with a tray, but aside from a few sips of water, she was unable to eat a thing. Her throat was stopped with something she couldn't quite name. She lay with her face averted to one side, reliving the moment she heard the dogs barking and the policemen dragging Mwane behind them, her whole body crawling with shame. Guilt and shame. That night, lying stiffly awake whilst the rest of the house slept and the night sounds around her drifted just below her radar of conscious thought, she understood the difference between them. Even then she knew that the shame would eventually leave her but the guilt never would. She would leave South-West Africa as soon as she possibly could, and start again. Her betrayal, in her parents' eyes, of everything they stood for had conversely set her free. She was free now to do whatever she wanted. Tante Bärbel would help her in whatever way she wanted; she understood the power she'd always exerted over the older woman, though she'd been afraid to question it for fear of what she might find. Now things were different. She would leave this all behind even if she could never rid herself of the guilt.

In the morning she was somehow able to sit up when Tante Bärbel came in and eat something of the breakfast she'd brought her.

'*Mein Liebling*,' Tante Bärbel said, stroking her long blonde hair. 'My poor, poor *Liebling*. Eat a little more. You ate nothing yesterday. Nothing at all.'

'I want to cut it off,' Hannelore said, looking down at the hair cascading over her shoulders. 'I want it to be short, like yours.'

'Of course, *mein Schatz*. We'll go to the hairdresser first thing this morning. Finish your cocoa and let's get you dressed.' She traced the welt on Hannelore's cheek. 'And we'll have to get you some new clothes, too. I left almost everything behind.'

'Burn them,' Hannelore said, her voice trembling. 'Burn everything. I don't want anything from back there.'

'Of course, my darling. We'll get rid of everything. *Everything*. You'll be able to start afresh. You'll go to Europe, to Hamburg, or Berlin . . . wherever you want. You've got your whole life in front of you. Don't let this destroy you, *mein Schatz*.' Hannelore said nothing; there wasn't anything she could say. It had already destroyed her. From now on, nothing would be the same. Tante Bärbel took hold of her chin and turned her face towards hers. 'And in being with that poor young man, you've done nothing wrong,' she said, her voice suddenly low and urgent. 'Nothing that your father hasn't done himself, d'you understand?'

Hannelore swallowed. That was what Mwane had been trying to tell her. That was what the servants had sniggered about; it was what those sideways glances in Windhoek meant when she mentioned who she was. The knowledge of it made her feel sick. *He* had whipped her with the same stick he used to beat the servants and the animals on the farm and pronounced her dead to him because of something he feared and despised in himself? Tante Bärbel's fingers were still holding her chin. That was the morning she bent her head and kissed her, but in a way Hannelore didn't fully understand. That came later. For the moment, she allowed herself to be touched and stroked, somehow understanding too that she would never be with another man. That part of her had died with Mwane. It was as dead and buried to her as he was, and would always be.

104

LINDI
St Barts, French West Indies

They sat on the patio, sharing a second bottle of wine between them, not speaking much. It was nearly nine o'clock and the doctor had come and gone. 'Exhaustion,' he'd said, scribbling something on a prescription pad. 'I'll give her a couple of these.' He took a small vial of pills from his briefcase. 'Just to keep her going over the next couple of days. I shouldn't imagine there'll be a pharmacy open tomorrow. Let her take one tonight if she's having difficulty sleeping.'

'Will she be all right?' Callan's voice was tight with anxiety.

'She'll be fine. She's a little overwrought, that's all. Probably been working too hard.' The doctor, a young Frenchman, smiled cheerfully at them and left, in a hurry to get to his own New Year's Eve party, no doubt. Hélène and Ree showed him out; Tara, Bruno and Jasper were on the terrace, debating what to do with the mounds of food sitting in the kitchen, waiting to be served.

'Let's just put everything out,' Bruno said, sighing. 'There's no point in it going to waste. She's fine. She'll be up and about tomorrow, you'll see. The girls have been cooking all week. We can't *not* eat tonight.'

'I don't feel like a party,' Callan said miserably. 'I've never seen her like this.'

'No, not a party, *Schatz*. We'll just put everything on that table over there, let the girls go home . . . we'll serve ourselves, have a couple of bottles of wine. She's going to be fine, I promise you.' Bruno was gently persuasive. In the end, Hélène was dispatched to her quarters at the rear of the property and the three young girls who'd been pulled in to assist her were sent home.

'I'm just going to check on her,' Callan said suddenly, getting up.

'D'you want me to come?' Ree looked up.

Callan shook her head. 'No, I'll just peek in. She's probably asleep.' She hurried off before anyone could say a word.

'She's taking it hard, poor thing,' Bruno said, watching her go.

'She'll be all right, won't she?' Tara asked, the anxiety evident in her own voice too. Bruno was just about to reply when Callan suddenly appeared in the doorway.

'She wants you,' she said, looking at Lindi. There was a worried frown on her face.

'Me?' Lindi looked up in surprise. 'Why me?' She looked at the others in alarm. There was a strange look on Ree's face.

'I think you'd better go,' he said quietly.

'But . . .'

'She asked for you.' Callan's expression was hard to fathom.

Lindi looked from one to the other, then carefully set down her glass of wine. She got up, aware that the others were all watching her. Her heart was beating fast, as though she were moving towards something she couldn't quite grasp. She followed Callan through the house, Callan's flip-flops slapping out a soft beat across the terrazzo floor. Anneliese's room was right at the end of the long corridor that led away from the living and dining areas to the more private wings of the enormous villa. They stopped before the closed door. 'Go in,' Callan said, her voice low and urgent. 'Let me know if she needs anything, won't you?'

'Y-yes,' Lindi stammered. Her pulse was racing. She grasped the handle and pushed down. The door swung open silently and she entered, closing it behind her. The room was darkened; the only light came from a bedside lamp.

'Who is it?' Anneliese's low voice pierced the silence.

'It's me. Lindi.' She stopped halfway across the room.

'Come.' Anneliese's voice seemed to reach her from a great distance. The room was large with its own private patio overlooking the bay at one end, and an en suite bathroom and walk-in closet at the other. The bed was against one wall and there was a sofa and two comfortable chairs at the foot, angled towards the view. 'Pull up one of those chairs,' Anneliese commanded her, turning her head to look at her. 'And sit next to me.'

Lindi did as she was told, dragging one of the chairs over. She sat down and folded her hands in her lap, waiting for some sign from Anneliese as to why she'd been asked to see her.

For a few minutes, there was absolute silence in the darkened room. Anneliese's hands lay on top of the cover, the fingers of one hand going to the mannish, silver ring she wore on the third finger of her left hand. Over and over, her fingers stroked the smooth, polished metal. Her fingers were long and square, Lindi noticed. Pale skin, large knuckles and squared-off, unpolished nails. Like her own. She glanced down at her own hands. She frowned suddenly. Her heart started to accelerate. She lifted her eyes to Anneliese's. Blue where hers were brown but there was an expression in Anneliese's face that was so familiar to her she could have sworn she was looking into someone else's face: her own. 'Anneliese . . . ?' Lindi began but faltered.

Anneliese turned her head. Her eyes were clear but her expression was of the most intense pain Lindi had ever seen. 'Sunday. You were born on a Sunday. Did you know that?' she asked, her hands still gripping each other. She shook her head slowly, seeing Lindi's confused expression. 'No, I don't suppose

525

you would. Why would you? I never told anyone. Bärbel knew, though. *She* saw you. She was the only one.'

'Wh-what are you talking about?' Lindi whispered, her mouth suddenly dry.

It took Anneliese a few minutes to answer. 'I'd give anything to spare you this . . . but I can't. I'd better start at the beginning, I suppose. I'm not who you all think I am. Not even my name. I'm not Anneliese. My name isn't Anneliese Zander de Saint Phalle.'

Lindi swallowed. 'What is it?'

'I'm not who you all think I am,' she repeated.

'So who are you?' Lindi's head was beginning to swim.

There was a long, drawn-out sigh from the woman lying against the pillows, as if the effort of speaking was beyond her. A minute passed, and then another, and the only sound in the room was of the two women, breathing fast and in unison. Then Anneliese cleared her throat. Lindi knew what was coming before the words were out.

'Hannelore. Hannelore von Riedesal. I'm your mother.'

Epilogue

REE
St Barts, French West Indies

Something – some noise, a footstep? – woke him suddenly. He lay in the dark with the sharp blade of light coming through a crack in the shutters and the soft, heavy feel of Callan's hair against his forearm. A muffled, drawn-out creak, like a breath. He heard it again. Someone was walking past the door. He brought his wrist up to his face, squinting at his watch. 6.47 a.m. The numbers gave off a queasy, greenish glow. His tongue was heavy and he was thirsty. His head ached slightly; the recollection of the previous night came flooding back.

They'd all drunk too much whilst they waited for Lindi to come back. It was almost one o'clock by the time Anneliese's door finally opened and Lindi stepped out. Her face was a blank mask of complete and utter confusion. 'Lindi?' he'd said, getting up from his seat immediately. 'Are you all right?' Tara and Callan sprang up beside him.

Lindi swallowed. Her hand was still gripping the door knob. She swayed a little, as though she might fall. Her face was flushed, eyes glassy as though she had a fever. Ree was beside her in an instant. 'Lindi?' he asked again, grabbing hold of her forearm. 'You all right?'

Lindi nodded. 'I need to talk to you,' she whispered. Her voice was so low he thought at first he'd misheard her.

'Now?' He looked at Tara and Callan. They were both staring at Lindi.

'Don't you want us to stay with you?' Tara asked.

Lindi shook her head. 'No, I'm sorry. This . . . I need to talk to Ree first.'

Callan got to her feet. 'Come on,' she said to Tara briskly. 'Let's leave them to it.'

'But—' Tara got up reluctantly. Ree saw in her face again the same, swift expression that he'd seen at the dinner table years ago – the faintest hint of some old, buried resentment – but she quickly suppressed it.

Callan was firm. 'Come on. We'll come back when they're finished.' She gave Tara no room to protest further. The door closed almost soundlessly behind them.

'What happened?' he asked gently.

Her face was streaked with the traces of dried tears. 'I . . . I still can't quite believe it,' she said, and her voice was thick and heavy with emotion.

He leaned forward, aware of the tension rising in his own chest. 'Believe what?' he asked and it seemed to him that he knew the answer before it came.

He had to tell Callan. And then Tara. It was almost dawn before they finished talking. The news stunned them all; it would take time, he knew, for the tremors that Anneliese's revelations had thrust up to die down. And that would only be the beginning. The rest of it – the emotional upheavals, the tears and the questions – that would come later.

He'd gone out onto the terrace where the remains of the New Year's Eve meal still lay around, half-eaten plates of food, empty glasses and bottles of wine. No champagne, though. The bottles of Moët still languishing in the now-melted ice buckets. There'd been no toasts, no celebrations, just tears. He stood on the deck overlooking the bay, watching and listening to the sounds of other, far-away parties taking place, fireworks still exploding in showers of pink and green light over the water as they finally trooped indoors and went to bed.

*

It was light outside now. He got up, taking care not to wake Callan, sliding her limp arm from his and tucking the sheet around her. He still had on his boxer shorts; Callan's blue-and-green striped cotton *kikoi* was hanging on the edge of the bed. He wrapped it around him and opened the door. The house was completely silent. Soon the kitchen would fill up with staff; he'd overheard her telling Hélène the previous evening that breakfast should be served at nine, outside on the terrace. Was it really only less than twelve hours ago that everything had been normal? He walked through the living room and out again onto the terrace. Someone had indeed been up. The sliding doors were open and the gate at the far end of the pool was ajar. He'd made sure both were closed last night, before they all turned in.

He walked out to the edge of the terrace and looked down the hill. He saw her straight away. She was walking with her arms outstretched, as though she were balancing. Further down below, along the sandy shoreline, some of the local women were already in the water, hunting for shells. Anneliese's white kaftan billowed out behind her. She stumbled once or twice, then picked herself up. He watched her for a few seconds. There was something about the way she walked that bothered him. As if she were preparing for flight. She reached the water's edge and then it dawned on him. She really *was* preparing for flight. She walked straight out into the water without taking her clothes off. Without thinking or even hesitating for a second, he broke into a run.

The boat bobbed about gently on the early morning waves. On deck, a young blonde woman in the sort of red polka-dot bikini that had made Brigitte Bardot famous almost fifty years earlier suddenly sat bolt upright. 'Chris!' she shouted, pointing towards the horizon.

The tanned, good-looking man at the wheel turned to look at her. 'What?'

'Ohmi*god*! There's someone in the water! Look!' She scrambled to her feet. 'Look!'

'Where? I can't see what you're pointing at. Are you sure? Where?'

'Yes, I'm sure! Jesus . . . it's a woman! Ohmigod! It's a *woman*!'

'Where?' he shouted, pushing the throttle forwards and powering up the engine. 'Hold onto something . . . I'll get as close as I can!'

'Quick! Jesus Christ . . . there's someone else! *Ohmigod*!' The girl was screaming now, holding onto her bikini top with one hand. 'There's two of them . . . there's a man . . . he's swimming towards her! Hurry! He's trying to save her! Ohmigod!'

'Sue, I can't see—' Chris's voice was whipped away by the wind as he swung the boat around in the direction she was pointing.

It took him a few seconds to focus properly on the two figures, one bobbing helplessly on the surface of the water, the other swimming powerfully towards her. He could see the man was a strong swimmer but the current out there in the silky blue water was deceptively strong. He raced towards them, Sue still shrieking in his ear. It took a few seconds to get within twenty yards. He cut the engines, released the anchor and dived overboard.

He could actually feel the vibrating throb of the boat's engines in the water before he even heard the boat approaching. His arms were aching but there was only room for a single thought in his mind: he had to get to Anneliese before she went under for the last time. It had taken an agonising eternity to scramble down the hillside after her, slipping, falling, the *kikoi* abandoned halfway down the slope. He'd run with his heart in his mouth, flat out, in a way he hadn't sun since schooldays. He flung himself into the shallows, forgetting to take his bearings, wasting a few precious seconds working out where she was in front of him before striking out. He knew there were boats out there in the water but there'd been no time to even think about calling for help. *One, two, three . . . break for air; one, two, three . . . break.* His arms and legs fell into the automatic rhythm that propelled him forwards. He could still see her but she was rapidly being swept away from him. Her arms had come up once or twice, startlingly white against that shimmering blue expanse of water and sky and then disappearing below the dark, shadowy surface. He could feel the current tugging at him too. Better to go with it, he thought to himself, than fight against it. He'd only tire himself out and it wouldn't get him any closer to her. *One, two, three, four* . . . he changed rhythm, instinctively conserving his energy. He was gaining on her, his whole being charged with the most desperate surge of power he'd ever felt. *One, two, three, four . . . breathe.* On the last, he felt the vibrations in the water – a strange reverberation. He turned his head partially to one side and saw the white prow of the boat speeding towards them. Someone had seen them. He heard whoever it was cut the boat's engines and then there was the dull splash of someone diving headlong into the water.

'Where the *fuck*?' he heard a man's voice almost in his ear. One last stroke and then he grabbed her. She was face down in the water but it was impossible to tell how long she'd been like that. As he tugged her towards him, he felt her arms go up. The relief that flooded through him almost stopped his breath. He righted her swiftly, just as the person who'd come to the rescue reached them. 'She alive, man?' he yelled out, grabbing hold of her as well.

'Just,' Ree shouted.

'Here, I got her . . . follow me!' The man took Anneliese's limp body from him, kicking out powerfully towards the boat. He grabbed Anneliese under the arms and dragged her along, her kaftan floating up towards the surface, obscuring her face. She was naked underneath; Ree closed his eyes. He was right. She'd been preparing for something he couldn't bring himself to say.

The girl in the bikini stood on deck, her hand stuffed in her mouth as she watched the two men grab hold of the floating body. There were tears of shock in her eyes as she saw the woman's arms go up, weakly resistant. She was still alive! She watched Chris take hold of her as the man beside him followed, weakened by the effort of having swum so far.

'Is she . . . ?'

'Yes, she's alive!' Chris shouted up to her as he reached the short ladder. 'Give us a hand . . . here, grab her arm, that's it . . . yeah, and the other one.'

Together, and not without difficulty, the three of them hoisted Anneliese onto the deck, scrambling after her. She was coughing, her slender frame wracked by the effort. 'Call Joe,' Chris shouted to Sue, as he and Ree rolled her over onto one side and patted her back. The girl scrambled below deck for a mobile phone. 'He's our neighbour,' Chris said to Ree. 'He's a doctor. How long was she in the water?' he asked. Barely ten minutes had passed since Sue had spotted them. From experience, he knew every minute now would count.

'Ten, fifteen minutes,' Ree said, wrapping one end of the blanket around her. 'I saw her from the house, up on the hill. I just couldn't get down to the water fast enough.'

'Jesus, man . . . you're one hell of a swimmer.' Chris shook his head disbelievingly. 'I don't think I could've done it and I've been a lifeguard every summer since high school. Did she just get into difficulty?'

Ree shook his head slowly. 'I . . . I don't know. I could just see from up there that things weren't right.'

'She's gonna be fine. She'll make it. Did you get him?' He looked up. Sue came stumbling up the steps towards them, the phone still to her ear. 'Yeah,' she nodded quickly. 'He's calling an ambulance. There's a whole group of people on the beach, apparently . . . they came down from the house where y'all are staying.' She knelt down beside them, stroking Anneliese's arm gently. Her eyes were closed; the coughing had stopped. 'She's beautiful,' she murmured. 'She looks so peaceful.'

Chris got to his feet and staggered back to the prow. He powered up the engine again. 'Hang on there,' he shouted, but the rest of his voice was lost in the roar as he gunned the boat back towards the shore.

Anneliese stirred, moaning a little. Ree took hold of her hand. Her head moved slowly from side to side. 'L-Lindi?' she stammered, her eyes opening a fraction. 'Callan? Tara?'

Ree bent his head towards her. His grip on her hand tightened. 'They're fine. You're fine. You just hang in there, Anneliese . . . we'll have you back on shore in five minutes. Just lie back.'

'Who's Lindi?' Sue whispered to him as Anneliese's eyes closed again. 'What was the other name? Callan? And Tara?'

'Her daughters,' Ree said after a moment. 'They're probably on the beach waiting.'

'Pretty names.'

Ree said nothing, but Anneliese must have heard him. Her grip on his hand tightened. She held on.